KNIGHTS OF HELL

BOOKS 1 - 3

SHERILEE GRAY

INCLUDES: Knight's Redemption, Knight's Salvation & Demon's Temptation

ISBN 978-0-473-58147-3 (Epub)

ISBN 978-0-473-58148-0 (Kindle)

ISBN 978-0-473-58146-6 (Print)

KNIGHT'S REDEMPTION

Knights of Hell, Book One

PROLOGUE

Lazarus glanced up as Scarlet and Tobias walked into the control room.

"You flying or riding?"

Lazarus's retrievals went a whole hell of a lot smoother now that Scarlet partnered with him. She had a calming effect on people, an ability Lazarus lacked and then some.

She screwed her face up in the same way she'd been doing since she was young, since he found her alone and scared in an alley way. He couldn't help but smile.

"Man, I'd love to take my bike out, but I think I'd be cutting it fine," she said, looking disappointed.

Tobias tugged his mate into his side. "We'll take the bikes out when you get back."

Scarlet wrapped her arms around Tobias's waist. "Sounds perfect."

T leaned in…

"I don't need to see that," Lazarus said, more out of habit than anything else. He'd accepted his brother had mated and completely fallen for Scarlet a long time ago.

Tobias smirked at him. "Jesus, you're uptight. No wonder you're still unmated."

"I'm uptight? You're the one with a stick permanently lodged up your…"

"Okay," Scarlet said. "That's enough, you two."

"Tell him there's nothing lodged anywhere, baby," Tobias said, eyes dancing. He turned to Lazarus. "I mean, she'd know."

Scarlet groaned and rolled her eyes.

Lazarus flipped off Tobias. "It's like you want me to kick your ass again." He grinned at his brother's scowl then turned back to Scarlet. "Come on then, kid. We better make a move."

He strode out the double doors to the balcony, and Scarlet joined him a moment later, her eyes sparkling with humor, Tobias right behind her. "How old do I have to get before you stop calling me that?"

Lazarus shrugged.

"I'm far from a kid."

He dragged off his shirt and tucked it into the waistband of his jeans. "You'll always be my kid, doesn't matter how old you get." He glanced at T. "Or how long you're mated."

She smiled at him. It was teasing, but her eyes were brighter. "Love you too, Daaad."

Scarlet was teasing him, but he liked when she called him that. She knew it, too.

She turned to her mate and kissed him goodbye then started toward Lazarus, but T tugged her back. He buried his face in her hair at the crook of her neck and breathed her in before kissing her again. Something he always did.

"I'll have the bikes warmed up when you get back," he said as Lazarus scooped her up in his arms and unfurled his wings.

Scarlet grinned and waved as Lazarus took flight, not looking away from Tobias until he was out of sight.

~

Lazarus strode across the kitchen, locking eyes with the demi-demon they'd come for.

The guy stumbled back a step. "Stay away from me."

Scarlet instantly reached for the guy, but he reared back out of her reach.

"Don't touch me, you crazy bitch."

It was obvious no amount of talking would get through to this guy, and they didn't have time to wait for Scarlet to do her thing, so Lazarus went for him before he threw himself through the window to get away.

Scarlet cursed. "Give me a few more minutes, Laz."

"There's no time."

The demi swung, his fist barely missing Scarlet. Little shit didn't know what was good for him. Lazarus took him down to the kitchen floor, immobilizing him.

Scarlet yanked on the back of Lazarus's shirt. "This isn't helping."

The guy bucked and kicked then spat in Lazarus's face. "Get the fuck off me," he shrieked.

Lazarus's temper flared and before he realized what he was doing, he'd pinned the demi to the ground by his throat. "We're trying to help you," he gritted out.

Scarlet growled and yanked harder on his shirt. "Jesus, calm the hell down and get up off the—" Her words were cut off with a startled hiss.

Lazarus spun around. Her hold on his biceps was so tight her fingernails cut into his skin.

Her eyes were wide. "Laz..."

Crimson bloomed in the center of her chest, like petals unfurling in a sickening rush.

Her legs gave out and she crumpled to the floor. He dove for her, dragged her into his arms, and did his best to staunch the blood pumping from the gaping wound.

The Orthon demon responsible didn't hesitate. It went straight for its target, the demi cowering on the floor behind them, and dragged him screaming from the room.

Lazarus let them go.

All that mattered was Scarlet.

He brushed her wild red curls away from her precious face. "You're all right, Scar. You're going to be all right." He'd never lied to her before, but he knew he was then.

The striking gold flecks in her soft brown eyes dimmed, muted by pain.

"Don't leave me, sweet girl. I need you here with me. Tobias needs you." Her mouth opened and blood bubbled up between her lips, cutting off whatever she was trying to say. He held her to him. "No. Please, God, no."

She rattled out her last breath—and then she was gone.

Lazarus scooped her up. He was taking her home. He needed to take her home.

He landed on the balcony a short time later with Scarlet's lifeless body clutched in his arms, and pushed through the doors into the control room.

Tobias stood on the other side, pale and shaking so hard his teeth chattered. He'd felt it, her loss, like all mates did. God, Tobias felt it. T stumbled forward and took her from Lazarus.

His friend's knees gave out then and Lazarus stood, tears streaming down his face, feeling fucking broken, helpless, as T rocked his mate in his arms, a sound coming from the male that shook Lazarus to his core.

Tobias looked up at him, the desolation in his eyes hard to

look at. "This is your fault," he said. "You were supposed to look after her. You promised me you'd keep her safe."

Lazarus stumbled back a step, but he knew it was true. Scarlet was dead because of him, because of his loss of control.

The agony in Tobias's eyes turned to hatred. "I'll never forgive you for this." He stood, still holding Scarlet, and shifted to his demon form, his clothes falling in tatters at his feet.

Then he strode from the room, diving off the balcony and taking flight.

CHAPTER 1

LAZARUS SENSED the demon before he saw it, could smell the toxic shit coming off it, could feel it prickling over his skin like a chemical spill.

The wind picked up speed, whipping at his hair and face and pulling at his wings. He rode it, gliding above the busy Roxburgh streets, scanning the humans moving below, swarming like ants, in a hurry to get to their next destination. Unaware of what moved among them, of the danger they were in.

There.

The demon had chosen his camouflage well. A human male, small in stature, plain clothing—unthreatening, unassuming. He was anything but, and at that moment the woman it stalked was in serious danger.

Flying lower, he tucked his wings into his back and dropped the last ten feet to an alley floor. His boots crunched on broken glass and other shit littering the ground. His wings vanished when he tucked them into his back, and he grabbed the shirt he'd shoved into the back of his jeans and yanked it on. The acrid scent was more intense at street level. There was definitely more than one.

The thud of two of his brothers dropping down behind him came next and he turned toward Chaos and Gunner as the warriors approached.

Kryos and Rocco were back at the compound and fuck knew where Zenon was. The male preferred to keep his own company. But the three of them were more than capable of putting out the trash.

As Knights of Hell, they'd been created to keep evil off these New York streets. And Chaos was the poor bastard they'd chosen to lead them. The male tucked in his pale gray wings and jerked on his shirt as he strode forward. The streetlights glinted off the tattooed side of his head, and there was a sneer on his lips. "My guess, at least half a dozen."

Gunner rubbed a hand over his buzz cut, the scowl twisting his mouth emphasizing the deep scar through his upper lip. "That shit isn't normal."

It wasn't. The only times demons tended to travel in packs were when they made their escape from Hell. After that they tended to scatter, making them harder to find.

Lazarus led the way out of the alley and onto the street. People rushed past, clearing a path for them like they always did, their flight instincts well and truly kicking in, their subconscious knowing a predator when it sensed one.

Ignoring the stares and gasps of the people around them, they followed the trail, the pungent stench of demon. It took them away from the busy streets, which was not surprising. No one, not even the demons invading Earth, wanted their existence to become public knowledge, not yet anyway. It was an unwritten rule, and the only thing Heaven and Hell agreed on.

The scent grew unbearably strong as they approached a parking garage. A woman's cry echoed off the concrete walls.

They moved in, not wasting another minute, and jumped the stairwell to the lower level.

Standing in a circle were six Sitri demons, laughing as they surrounded the human female. Sitri were known as mischief-makers, lovers of disorder and mayhem. In Hell, they moved in packs; on Earth, they were forced to stay apart, but it looked like these assholes had formed a support group and decided on a night out on the town.

They turned as the knights walked in, instantly baring their teeth and crouching into fighting stances. The woman didn't wait for an invite; as soon as the demons turned their backs she bolted for the exit. Psychos that these particular demons were, they didn't do the same and run for their lives. They grinned...then they ran at them.

Chaos drew his sword and Gunner palmed his Glock. Lazarus let one of his knives fly, the blade burying in a demon's shoulders. Chaos and Gunner were now cutting through the others as Lazarus strode toward the bastard screeching on his knees.

He reached for the knife still buried in the demon—

Fuck.

Lazarus dropped to his knees when what felt like three thousand volts shot up his spine and hammered him in the back of the skull. The demon in front of him took the chance he'd been given, yanked the blade from his shoulder, and buried it in Lazarus's stomach.

Lazarus hissed and fell forward as that same force nailed the base of his spine a second time. He dropped like a sack of rocks, his face making nice with the asphalt. He tried to get up. But nope, moving wasn't an option just yet. His spine torqued as the next wave came, attacking every nerve ending, lighting him up like he'd just taken a seat in an electric chair.

The demon came at him again but was pulled off him by Chaos. Its shriek echoed off the walls a moment before it was cut off by a wet gurgling and the thump of its body hitting the ground.

Lazarus had no choice but to lay there in shock, blinking at the blue Corolla parked beside him while blood leaked from him like a sieve.

Somehow, he knew exactly what had just hit him, the thing that had dropped him to his knees, and he didn't mean the blade that had been buried in his gut.

The powerful instinct couldn't be denied.

He didn't fucking want it. He sucked in a rough breath and tried to sit up. Nope, moving was still a no-go.

This can't be happening.

But it was.

He'd prayed, he'd bargained, he'd wished on a fucking shooting star that this day would never come. Turned out no one gave a fuck what he wanted, and the fates had decided to give him a mate anyway.

And she'd just unknowingly sent him a message.

Now he had no choice but to go get her.

"Let me the hell in!"

Eve peeked around the turquoise and white polka-dot curtain covering the window. Her ex-boyfriend, Eric, was standing there, scowling at her front door. She winced when he kicked it.

Her car was out front. She was obviously home. Hiding wasn't going to work.

She cursed under her breath. "Just leave."

He shouted her name and thumped on the heavy wood for the millionth time. "I'm not going anywhere, not until you talk to me."

He meant it, ignoring him certainly wasn't working. She

hadn't answered any of his calls or texts, and now he was standing at her damn door trying to knock it down.

Their relationship had been toxic from the start. Eric seemed to equally dislike her and want her at the same time. Eve didn't understand it, but she'd had enough, of being treated badly, of this weird love/hate obsession he had with her.

Gritting her teeth and straightening her shoulders, she yanked the door open. This had to stop.

His dark blue eyes flared, latching onto hers as soon as he had her in his sights, then dropped to her breasts, like they always did. "Finally. Jesus Christ, Eve." His tone was one a parent would use on a disobedient child.

Crossing her arms over her chest, she attempted to hide her body. She hated that he could still make her feel worthless. His out-of-control ego had taken a beating when she'd ended their relationship and he was having trouble letting her rejection go.

Eric hadn't started out like this, but over the course of their relationship, he'd changed. At first, she'd brushed off his behavior, coming up with excuses for his hurtful comments, happy that someone actually wanted her. But along the way, he'd turned from a shy, sweet guy into an obsessive, cruel jerk. His treatment of her had gotten progressively worse. He wanted her in his bed, but the rest of the time he was just angry. Everything about her seemed to piss him off. And when he got rough with her in bed as well, she knew it was past time to get out of the relationship.

She looked him in the eyes. "You need to listen to what I'm saying, and you need to hear me..."

Eve gasped and grabbed for the door, squeezing her eyes closed as noise flooded her mind.

Stupid bitch. She should be grateful I put up with her fat ass.

Eve's eyes shot open. "What did you just say?"

11

Eric frowned. "Not a damn thing. You were about to lie to me, and yourself, about ending our relationship." His eyes dropped to her chest again and he licked his lips.

God, I want to bury my face between those massive jugs.

She was hearing him, *his* voice, clear as day, but his mouth was shut. Shit, she really was losing her mind. Over the last four weeks, she'd had...attacks. That's what she'd been calling them. Words whispered in her mind, thoughts that weren't her own, flying through her head.

Maybe I'll get her on a diet. She'd be so much prettier if she lost ten pounds.

She clutched the side of her head, pain pounding through her skull.

"What the hell's is wrong with you?" Eric said, taking a step closer.

Yeah, she's fat, but I don't need to take her out in public, as long as I get to keep fucking her. God, I want to wrap my hands around her throat, choke her while I do it, slap her, watch her cry while I pound into her.

"Stay back," she gasped.

He kept coming. "I don't know why you're resisting this."

Eve shook her head, unable to get her mouth to work. More jumbled thoughts sliced through her mind, words, a voice that wasn't her own.

He ran a hand over his blond hair, gaze raking over her. "God, look at you," he bit out, mouth twisting. "Do you think there'll be guys lining up to ask you out?"

If it wasn't for those magnificent tits, I probably wouldn't bother either. I want to hurt her, want to make her scream. Christ, what's wrong with me? It's not me. It's her. She made me feel like this. I was fine until I met her. God, I want to fuck her.

She jerked back as he reached for her, but she was too late. His hand curled around her wrist and he yanked her

12

forward. She crashed into his chest and his arms came around her, squeezing her tight to him.

His mouth went to her ear. "You want this, Eve, I know you do. No more playing. No more teasing me."

She shoved at him. "Let me the hell go."

He didn't budge, his hold getting tighter as he struggled with his temper for a second then tried to soften his tone when he spoke again. "Come on, baby. You're overreacting, you realize that, right?" He pressed a wet kiss to her temple. "I know you love pushing my buttons, but you need to stop playing me like this. You're seriously starting to piss me off. I want you, and I know you want me. I know you do." His eyes slid back down to her chest.

Damn, look at those big, soft, round...

Eve shook her head trying to make the voice stop. The other times this happened it hadn't been this bad. She was either going mad or, somehow, she was hearing Eric's sick thoughts.

He took advantage of her loss of concentration and pushed her against the doorframe. It dug into her back and she cried out.

"Please go," she whispered.

He shook his head. "I can't...I can't walk away. You're mine..."

A deep sound rolled across her yard, building in volume.

They both stilled, staring into the darkness.

A low, vicious growl came next, so loud it lifted the hair on the back of Eve's neck.

Eric stumbled back a step and Eve took advantage, shoving him away and slamming the door shut. Eric pounded on it again.

She grabbed for her phone, about to call the police when his yelling and knocking was cut off abruptly.

Pulling back the curtain, she peered out into the darkness. Her porch light lit up some of the front yard and she gasped when a huge shadow moved away from the light, melting with the darkened edge of the garden.

Oh God, had Eric been attacked by something? An animal?

The sound of his car starting reached her, followed by it speeding off a few moments later.

Eve released the breath she'd been holding, dropped the curtain, and threw the deadbolt.

CHAPTER 2

LAZARUS SCOWLED. He hated these little towns. True, they made his job easier with fewer witnesses and a hell of a lot less ground to cover. But today he could have been anywhere. It wouldn't have made a difference. He could have located who he'd come for blindfolded.

Despite his distaste for places like this, a day ago the tiny West Coast town might have offered a much-needed change of pace, with its sea breezes and trees and flowers and shit.

But not now. Not today.

The building in front of him was small and sickeningly cheerful. A shock of color beside its more sedate neighbors. He shook his head. Jesus, the place looked like Rainbow Brite threw up all over it. The chill wind picked up, whipping through his hair, stinging his skin, and sent russet-colored leaves tumbling from the trees and spiraling past the shop's sunny yellow door. A door he couldn't seem to go through no matter how long he stood there.

The warring sides of his DNA had never felt more at odds than they did at that moment, which was saying something after everything that had gone down recently. His angel half wanted to protect, do what was expected—do the right thing. But his demon half—well, the demon wanted something else entirely. It screamed louder, fought harder to get free. Jesus, his skin itched with the need to shift into his Kishi demon form.

That scared the shit out of him. He couldn't loosen his stranglehold on the dark fucker writhing inside him, not when he was so close to possessing the key to his salvation and the only way he could win that war.

And she had no idea. No idea who she was or what she was.

Now the only things that stood between him and his mate were wood, glass, and a few cracked feet of pavement.

His gut churned and he clenched his fists against the little zaps of electricity that continued to shoot through him. Shit.

He'd only gotten a glimpse of her last night at her door, and then that human male had put his hands on her, had hurt her, and Lazarus had seen red. The growl that had left him, shit, that had been torn from him, had surprised him more than anyone. But he hadn't been able to hold it back.

He grunted. He hadn't meant to go after the fucker or knock him out. Breaking his nose definitely hadn't been on the night's agenda. Lazarus had been forced to drive the weasel home then wait for him to wake up so he could scrub his memory. The whole thing had messed with his plans, but after the scare that female had, knocking on her door right after all that drama and introducing himself probably wouldn't have been a great idea. Instead, he'd gone back and watched her place until morning. He'd let her enjoy the last night she'd spend in her house.

In her life.

A seabird squawked overhead, jarring him from his thoughts. The breeze increased its efforts, tugging at his shirt. God, he hated this. Hated that he was about to shatter the fantasy this female had been living.

Yeah, she'd pulled the short straw, because he was here to smash that illusion into a thousand tiny pieces.

He caught a brief glimpse of dark hair and bright pink clothing through the window, then she was gone, his view obscured by a large bookshelf. Another wave of volatile energy washed over him and he gritted his teeth. She didn't have the ability to block all that untamed energy she was sending out, and the female's newly acquired power hammered against his defenses. Calling to him. The strength of it still shocked him. Its effects caused pins and needles to lift the hairs on his arms, sending power arcing through his nerve endings and tingling across the surface of his skin.

At least now he could stay upright. He was adjusting to her presence quickly, and thank fuck for that. He may heal quickly, but that knife to the gut still hurt like a bitch.

He couldn't wait any longer. It was time to make a move, but his feet felt rooted to the pavement. He'd stood there like a damned statue for too long already and some of the yokels had stopped to stare. Dammit, he couldn't screw this up. Schooling his features, he ran a hand over his hair, and before he could change his mind, gripped the handle and pushed open the door.

The tinkle of a little bell announced his entrance into The Book Worm. The place was small and warmly lit. Paperbacks covered every available surface. They lined the walls and filled the overflowing bookcases that crowded the limited floor space.

Books were this female's passion and her love for this place was stamped in every corner of the room. From the mismatched bookshelves painted in bright, cheerful colors to the striped overstuffed couch in the corner and the chunky antique counter with its equally ancient, carefully restored cash register perched on top.

Everything about this room screamed soft, feminine... delicate. He glanced down at his worn leather jacket, scuffed boots, and battle-scarred hands. What did he know about soft and feminine? As for delicate, he was more a bull-in-china-shop kind of male. His stomach did another lurch and he wanted to growl his frustration. Shit, if he had any other choice he would turn around and walk back out that door.

There weren't many things he had been certain about in his long life, but when it came to this female, a female who had created her own little piece of heaven—a place of calm, of solace, of joy within these four walls—he knew a few things with one hundred percent unwavering certainty.

He didn't deserve her. He could never give her what she needed. And in the end, he would hurt her.

But despite all that, he would continue on this course regardless.

He had to. There were bigger things at stake than injuring this female's feeling.

Moving farther into the room, he sidestepped the shelf blocking his path. Though he couldn't see her, it wasn't necessary to search for her. He knew exactly where she was. He glanced up, and halfway up a ladder, his demi-demon busily transferred a stack of books from the uppermost step to one of the higher shelves. Her position, slightly bent forward, caused the pink dress she wore to cling to her curves and highlighted a soft, voluptuous figure.

It was rare for the weaker human genes of their mothers to be dominant. More often than not, the hybrids favored the sturdy physical build of their demon sires.

But this female's figure was all human.

"I won't be a minute," she called over her shoulder and started to climb down.

He cursed under his breath when, with each tentative step she took, the fabric pulled taut over her rounded hips and ass.

He couldn't tear his eyes away, and before he realized what he was doing he'd taken several steps in her direction.

Slamming on the brakes, he barely resisted the urge to go up the damn ladder after her. As she got closer, he had to jam his hands in his pockets so he didn't do something stupid like reach for her. He hadn't believed it, but there was no denying it now. The physical connection was as strong as he'd been told it would be.

She stepped onto the floor, straightened her dress, and turned to face him with a welcoming smile curving her full, dark pink lips. "Oh...sorry!" She took a startled step back.

Not surprising considering he was damn near on top of her. Lazarus sucked in a sharp breath, locked his knees, and fought the blow that followed. No fucking way was he falling on his ass in front of this female.

She was attractive—Christ, beautiful—but what had him damn near hypnotized were her startling pale blue eyes. They held him immobile, called to a part of him he never knew existed, a soul-deep connection he never thought he'd find. Had never wanted to find, and would have been more than happy to leave buried.

The drag on his already deteriorating control escalated, and he had to force his lungs to get back to the whole *oxygen in, carbon dioxide out* routine. A meet-cute had never been on the cards, but swooning at her feet wasn't what he'd envisioned either.

The off-balance sensation persisted and he struggled, and failed, to restore his equilibrium. Probably because all the blood had evacuated his head and taken up residence in his now aching groin.

When a demi's powers reached their peak, his kind were

alerted by way of a kind of internal alarm. If it hadn't knocked him on his ass, the fact he was the only one able to sense her would have told him exactly who she was.

Lying on that parking garage floor, he'd only felt dread. And whatever he'd imagined he'd feel coming face-to-face with her for the first time—it wasn't this, this almost violent flood of emotion.

Because he knew her.

It was base and primal and fucked up, but he *knew her.*

He curled his fingers into a fist. He felt torn in two, couldn't decide if he wanted to fall at her feet and worship her like some pathetic, groveling fool, or turn around and run like a pack of hellhounds wanted a chunk out of his ass.

All he knew for sure at that moment was he fucking hated it, this sudden loss of self-possession. He'd rather face an army of Orthon demons than the woman standing in front of him and what she represented.

Like a besotted idiot, he watched, captivated, as her tongue darted out to lick her lower lip then bite down on the plump flesh. He lifted his gaze, and soft pools of blue stared back, round and questioning. Right then, the only thought he could summon was how badly he wanted to taste her.

He took an abrupt step back, man enough to admit that the curvy little demi standing in front of him scared the living shit out of him. Mind sluggish and tongue refusing to work, he stood there, gawking like a damned idiot. The silence had stretched on and her cheeks turned pink.

Her gaze darted toward the closed door then back. "So... was there a specific book you were after? I have a pretty wide selection here."

His stomach clenched at the sound of her sweet, slightly husky voice, and with a great deal of effort, he kept his gaze fixed straight ahead instead of wandering lower. He flexed his fingers, positive he could already feel those lush curves she had in abundance, her soft warmth under his palms. Scowling, he attempted to shake off his messed-up reaction to the female blinking owlishly up at him.

Words would be a great idea about now, dipshit.

"Perhaps if you tell me what type of books you usually read?" She tried again, but this time her smile faltered and she tugged on the front of her dress several times before crossing her arms over her ample breasts.

Great, he was freaking her out.

"I, ah…I don't read much," he forced out.

She jerked back and hugged her arms tighter around her waist. Dammit, he should have kept his mouth shut.

Now he'd startled her, but considering he'd just growled the words at her, he wasn't surprised by her reaction. What the fuck was up with his voice? He sounded like he was gargling nails.

Afraid the skittish female was about to run, he attempted what he hoped was a reassuring smile. It felt awkward and wooden on his face and going by the way her eyes widened in alarm, the pearly white routine wasn't conveying *trust me I'm one of the good guys* but instead *all the better to eat you with, my dear.*

He needed her to trust him, but it wasn't hard to figure out the mute pervert approach wasn't the way to go.

With no other option, and before she bolted for the door, he sent a gentle rush of power to her. It was designed to create calm, to wash away the fear in her eyes, and make this whole shit show a lot easier on both of them. It also gave off a pleasant scent, because good things smelled nice, and bad things smelled like shit, right? He guessed that was the theory behind it.

But before he had a chance to recite the speech he'd memorized, the bell jingled above the door and an elderly woman walked in. She glanced at them briefly before making her way to one of the shelves in the autobiographies section.

His demi released a relieved breath, happy she was no longer alone with him. "Good morning, Mrs. Jensen," she called to the other woman.

Tongue-tied, confused, and without doubt fucking up badly, he forced his brain back into gear. His kind searched their entire lives for what stood within his grasp. Yeah, he wanted it like a bullet to the back of the head. But there was no alternative for him, for either of them. So, clearing his throat several times in an attempt to loosen his damn vocal cords, he tried again. "I need to speak to—"

"Excuse me?"

Dammit.

She turned to face the old woman. Lazarus scowled. He hadn't even heard her approach, so fixed on the female in front of him.

"How can I help you today, Mrs. Jensen?"

The woman didn't reply, and his demi's smile faded as she rubbed at the goose bumps that broke out across her arms. A chill blasted Lazarus, its bite enough to break him free of the hold she had on him. The hair at his nape prickled right before the unmistakable odor of sulfur surrounded him, heavy and cloying like toxic gas. The old woman's eyes flashed to a colorless milky white, and hissing, she lunged, grabbing for the female at his side.

Wrenching her out of the way, he planted his boot in the creature's chest and sent the Orthon sprawling. The savage breed of demon was relentless and wouldn't stop until it had captured or killed its target.

The demon staggered to its feet, gaze darting between him and his female. Before it had time to make its next move, Lazarus ran at it. The form it had taken was heavyset and slow, and instead of trying to escape, it struck out. Lazarus dodged the blow and returned it with a strike to the creature's throat then swept the fucker's feet out from underneath it. Before it could get vertical, he pulled his blade free, grabbed a handful of its soft gray hair, and removed the demon's head with one brutal slice.

Breathing heavily, he looked down at the lifeless creature, at the thick black sludge that oozed from its neck onto the floral carpet.

That had been close, too damn close.

It didn't matter who this demi was to him, or the circumstances. He'd been careless. He'd allowed the intensity of his reaction to cripple his powers. It wasn't the first time he'd lost sight of his duty, had allowed his emotions to rule. Only last time the consequences of his carelessness had been devastating.

He cursed and straightened.

A new demi's powers reached a peak exactly one month after they developed, when all that unstable energy could no longer be contained and escaped in a rush. That energy acted like a kind of beacon for them and helped pinpoint their location. But he and his brothers weren't the only ones able to sense it, and that made the hybrids one hell of an easy target.

Demi-demons were a valuable commodity in the demon world, bought and sold, kept to exploit their unique abilities. If Lazarus hadn't got to her first...

He needed to pull his head out of his ass, and fast.

Still, as adrenaline pumped through his system, heating his blood like it always did after a kill, he couldn't stop himself from turning to her. As soon as he set eyes on her, he was hit by an all-consuming hunger. So fierce he had to lock his knees again or risk falling to them.

Anticipation tingled across his scalp and slid down his spine, but he gritted his teeth and tried to ignore it, tried to shake it off. Whether Lazarus liked it or not, he needed her. If he let her slip through his fingers now, he wouldn't be the only one to suffer the consequences.

Disgusted at himself, he ignored the roar of his body, and that's when he registered the horror on her face. She was watching the Orthon as its headless body convulsed in violent, jerky movements on the floor. It had transformed, shifting back to its natural state. The thing was large in size, its leathery skin grayish in color, and jagged spikes protruded from its spine like some kind of giant reptile.

Its head had rolled to a stop at their feet, lips pulled back in a snarl revealing sharp yellow teeth, and its cloudy eyes were still open, staring blindly up at her.

That's when the screaming started.

CHAPTER 3

ONE OF THE behemoth's giant hands curled around Eve's arm, and he hauled her up against his body, causing hers to collide with the solid wall of his chest. *Oh God*. He was huge. She tilted her head back, taking in his hard features, and her gaze slid higher, locking with startling green eyes.

Her jaw dropped, mouth opening and about to let loose another scream, when his other hand came down over her mouth, cutting it off before she could get it out.

Panic surged through her veins, and she reached up to clutch her attacker's thick wrist, yanking and scratching like a wild cat in an attempt to loosen his grasp. The giant didn't budge. Instead, his grip tightened, holding her immobile in his massive arms.

He decapitated Mrs. Jensen.

His hand still over her mouth, he tilted her head back, forcing her to look at him again.

"Be still," he rumbled. "Think about what you just saw." His voice was deep and rough, more a growl than anything else.

Her mind tried to register what had just happened, what

was happening. And an image of white, colorless eyes flashed through her mind. She squeezed her eyes shut, tried to make sense of what she'd seen.

She dragged a panicked breath in through her nose. Whatever the hell that thing was, it hadn't been the sweet old woman who'd been coming to her shop for the last few years.

Her eyelids snapped open, her gaze shooting back up to his. This guy, this huge, terrifying mountain of a man, had shoved her out of the way, had protected her, hadn't he?

Eve tested his hold, tried to pull free, but still he wouldn't let go. She glanced back up at him. He was watching her, a fierce expression on his face, and those extremely green eyes felt like lasers trying to get inside her head.

She was going to die.

This was how it was going to happen. Some insane, knife-wielding lunatic was going to cut off her head and there was nothing she could do to stop him.

An eerie calm washed through her, taking all her fight with it.

Maybe she was going into shock. She guessed that was a good thing.

Several long seconds crept by, but he made no move to grab that wicked-looking knife. The heavy thud of his heart seemed to pound right through her, like a ticking time bomb counting down—to what she had no idea—while he held her to him, his body unnaturally still.

That feeling of time moving in slow motion, of being submerged, began to lift. She pushed through the haze, struggled to the surface, and her mind began to clear. A muffled sound filled her head and she realized the strangled, frantic sounds were coming from her. His rough, hot palm still covered her mouth, smothering her screams. Her throat burned from the effort, and tears tracked a heated path down her cheeks.

Maybe she was suffering some kind of psychotic episode and all this was some terrible nightmare? But it only took one glance to the floor to know what she'd seen had been no dream.

The creature's remains were still there, right in her line of vision. The corpse was smoldering, flesh bubbling, releasing thick tendrils of acrid smoke. She'd never seen a dead body before, but she was pretty damn sure dissolving wasn't normal. The pungent odor invaded her nostrils and burned a path to her lungs as she attempted to suck down much needed oxygen.

She felt claustrophobic with this giant's oversized paw covering her mouth, and she tugged harder on his fingers. Warm lips pressed against her ear and she stilled.

"I can feel your heart pounding like a frightened rabbit. You need to calm yourself, demi, before I can release you." God, that voice. It was pure gravel.

Calm herself? She wriggled, managing to jerk her head to the side and let out a muffled scream.

"Be still," he hissed.

Like hell. She fought harder, and his grip on her tightened to the point of pain. She couldn't hold back her whimper.

He cursed. "I don't want to hurt you."

Her gaze automatically traveled to the remains on her floor, now nothing but a sooty ash-like residue, the clothes still lying in the shape of a body that had moments ago filled them.

Eve jumped as his mouth brushed against her ear again. "When I remove my hand, you will not scream," the guy growled. "Do you understand?" His warm breath skittered across her cheek, and the deep, raspy timbre of his voice worked its way down her spine, causing her to shiver in response. She nodded, with little choice but to obey.

"Good, that's good, demi," he murmured and eased his hand from her mouth.

She stumbled back a step and stared up at him, getting a better look at his hard futures. His green eyes were unnaturally bright and deep-set, his nose long and straight, and his square jaw in need of a shave. The muscle there jumped as her gaze dropped to his full lips.

The size of the man would intimidate anyone, but coupled with his harsh, almost cruel features, he looked like the brutal killer he was. Panic and confusion caused her pulse to race double time.

Her gaze darted back to the floor. "W-what was that...thing?"

"There's a lot you need to know, but we don't have time for long explanations." He scanned the quiet street beyond her shop's window. "There'll be more trackers coming for us soon. We have to leave."

Her stomach lurched. "Leave?"

"We can't stay here, it's too dangerous," he said.

Eve shook her head. "I don't know who you are, or...or what you want, but there's been some kind of mistake. My name's not Demi. I'm not...I'm not who you're looking for."

His beautiful yet terrifying eyes locked with hers. "There is no mistake."

She shook her head. "I don't understand."

"You will." His brow creased, gaze moving over her, doing a quick scan from head to toe and back. "You're cold."

She blinked up at him. "What?"

"You're shivering. I can hear your teeth chattering."

Eve stared up at him as if he were speaking in tongues. And he stared back, she guessed waiting for a response. She couldn't form one. His fingers flexed lightly around her arm before he released her and slipped off his jacket, revealing a brightly colored tattoo that covered his entire right arm, or what she could see of it at least. She flinched when he reached around her and draped it over her shoulders.

He made a low growling sound. "Put your arms in the sleeves."

She did as he asked, because...well, what else could she do? He zipped the warm leather up to her chin. The gentle action was so completely at odds with what she'd witnessed moments ago, all she could do was stare. God, that weird sense of calm washed over her again, and alarmingly, she felt herself sway closer to him.

The jacket was far too big but, damn, it smelled fantastic. The wonderful scent rose up to surround her, and she couldn't help taking several deep breaths. Heat seeped into her skin from the worn rawhide and managed to ease the bone-deep chill that had gripped her.

Cocking his head to the side, he gave her another once-over and, obviously happy with what he saw, he took hold of her wrist and started toward the door.

His earlier words shot through her head again. "No, stop. I'm not going anywhere with you." As she struggled against his grasp, her gaze landed again on the mess scattered on the floor, and a hit of pure fear spiked through her. She needed to run, to get away from this man, from what the existence of that creature meant.

Without a word, he stopped in his tracks and spun to face her. Grabbing her chin, his lethal gaze collided with hers. "I'm not going to hurt you, but we have to leave." Tilting his head in the direction of the ashy remains, he added, "We sure as hell don't have time for this."

He started dragging her toward the rear exit again.

Never let your attacker take you to a second location— she'd read that somewhere. But the panic swamping her made it impossible to think, let alone come up with some clever way to escape. She tried to pull her hand free from the fingers clamped around her wrist, but it made no difference. He was too strong. Eve tried a different tactic and went completely limp. She was no lightweight, and dragging her feet should definitely have slowed him down…

He didn't even break stride, simply slipped an arm around her waist and carried on.

In a last-ditch effort to save herself, Eve grabbed onto one of the bookshelves and kicked out as hard as she could. He grunted when her foot connected with hard flesh, but still he didn't let go.

Eve clung to the wood for dear life, her nails scratching off flakes of bright yellow paint as he tried to yank her free. When that didn't work, he reached back and tried to pry her fingers loose. His free arm still circling her waist, holding her in place as he worked. The tug of war caused the shelf to topple over with a loud crash and her precious books tumbled all over the floor. Before she could find something else to grab on to, he hauled her toward him and lifted her off the ground as if she weighed nothing.

"No. Let me go."

He jerked her higher, and her face smooched against his shoulder. He held her up with one powerful arm under her butt, manhandling her like she was nothing but a rag doll. As she kicked and struggled, another lungful of that unique scent of his assaulted her, but this time stronger. It filled her senses, spicy and potent, almost drugging. Stilling, and without conscious thought, she inhaled deeply, desperate to take in more.

What the hell am I doing? She couldn't believe she was actually *smelling* her attacker.

Fight, her mind screamed, but her arms were useless, trapped against her sides in his viselike grip. With no other weapon at her disposal, Eve lifted her head and sank her teeth into the exposed flesh between his neck and shoulder. Hard. A snarl rumbled through his chest, and he dropped her back to her feet, his fingers an unbreakable band around her upper arm.

"Stop fighting." He swiped at the wound she'd caused and looked down at the blood on his fingers. "You need to calm the fuck down. We don't have time for this. You're only making it harder on yourself."

Was he serious? "Oh, well, sorry about that," she fired at him. This guy was nuts if he thought she was going anywhere with him. "I wasn't sure about the correct etiquette for a kidnapping." She motioned to the door. "Please, Mr. Giant-Homicidal-Maniac, lead the way."

His eyes narrowed and he cursed under his breath, that death grip he had on her arm loosening a little. "Look, I don't—"

Pressing her palms against his chest, she took advantage and shoved as hard as she could. It was like trying to shift a brick wall. The guy was on her before she'd taken two steps toward the door. One of his huge arms wrapped around her, pulling her in close to his hard body.

"Fucking hell, female. Don't you understand? I'm trying to help you."

"What I understand is that some lunatic, hopped up on steroids, decapitated...well, I have no idea what that thing was, and is now trying to abduct me."

Eve clutched the forearm that surrounded her waist, the muscle bunched hard as stone beneath her palm. She was no match for this man. He could kill her with one flick of his thick wrist and there was nothing she could do to stop him. His warm hands slid from around her middle and drifted up her sides, leaving a hot trail of gooseflesh in their wake. Gripping her shoulders, he turned her to face him.

He looked down at her, brows drawn, determined eyes boring into her.

Suddenly she was a deer caught in headlights—right before impact. And any hope of escape she'd stupidly had sprouted wings and flew out the window with its tail tucked between its legs.

When he spoke, his voice was low, cold, filling her with dread, "Right now, I am the only thing standing between you and life as some sick fuck's slave. So unless you want to wait here for the next Orthon demon to track you down, then, after he's used you in ways that will leave you begging for death, deliver you to your new master, I suggest you come with me quietly."

Demon?

As much as she wanted to reject what this man was saying, close her eyes and convince herself this was all some crazy nightmare, she couldn't.

"Why would it want me?"

"Because you're...special," he said, voice raspy.

The hair on the back of her neck lifted. "What does that even mean?"

His expression softened a little. "I think you have an idea. Something recently happened to you? Something you don't understand, something that scares you?"

"Yes." *Oh God.* "Does this...does this have something to do with me hearing people's thoughts?"

It was the first time she'd said it out loud, and yeah, it sounded even more ridiculous than when she said it in her head. He stared back at her for a moment, opened his mouth like he was about to say something, but then he nodded again.

She swallowed hard. "You're telling the truth, aren't you?"

The muscle in his clenched jaw jumped again and he dipped his chin.

Her limbs went weak, and if it hadn't been for the guy's quick reflexes, she would have ended up in a pile on the floor. His arms came around her, strong and sure, holding her gently against his side. This time she didn't fight him off; she didn't have the energy to. Her mind swam, trying to sort through what was happening, what this all meant. Weirdly, the thought that came through the loudest was how nice it felt to be held.

The last person to touch her had been Eric, and going by his chaotic thoughts, he'd hated himself for wanting her. Had hated her even while he wanted her in some sick and twisted way.

"You good? Or do I need to carry you?" His voice was kind of terrifying, and so damn deep she felt it all the way down to her toes. Shaking her head, she stepped out of his arms.

The adrenaline racing through her blood had burned itself out, and with its departure came a kind of clarity, highlighting the enormity of her situation.

Her choices were limited. And as terrified as she was of this guy, and right now he was up there with the bogeyman, she didn't think she had any other option but to go with him.

Maybe he knew what was going on and what had caused the changes in her. She needed answers, and at that moment he seemed the lesser of two evils. That creature had tried to hurt her, and if it hadn't been for the behemoth standing in front of her, it would have succeeded. That had to count for something.

If more were on the way, she didn't want to be here when they showed up.

Still, it didn't mean he wasn't capable of removing her head the minute her back was turned, but considering the alternative? She swallowed hard, looked into his direct gaze, and searched those harsh features. Yeah, he scared the crap out of her, but he was a better prospect than the thing that dissolved into ash on her shop floor.

Swallowing down the fear still threatening to choke her, she lifted her chin. "Okay...let's go."

CHAPTER 4

"WISE DECISION." Then he was on the move again.

Eve tugged on his arm. "Hang on. First you have to promise you're not going to hurt me."

He arched a brow. "You want me to…promise?"

"Yes." Okay, she guessed that did sound kind of stupid. Like a killer's promise would mean anything in the first place.

"Jesus." He shook his head, looking frustrated. "I promise I will never physically hurt you."

"Right…well, that's good, then."

"Can we go now?"

"I don't really have a choice, do I?"

"No." The bolt on the front door slid into place as if by an invisible hand behind her.

"What the hell are you?" she whispered.

He grabbed her bag off the back of the chair, gave it to her, then took hold of her hand again and led her to the back door. "I'm a demon hunter, a warrior."

She swallowed, her mouth suddenly dry. "A demon hunter?"

He nodded and tilted his head to the side, taking her in. The movement reminded her of something she'd watched on Animal Planet, and left an invisible trail tingling across her skin. She sucked in a sharp breath, and his gaze darted up to hers. It was intense, probing, and—God—hot. Warmth enveloped her, and to her complete horror, her body responded to the heat in those eerie green eyes. The sensation heightened further by her acute awareness of his rough, dry palm against hers.

His eyes seemed to darken oddly.

Jesus, he was big, and there was something about him so, so damn wild and terrifying like there was a monster lurking underneath, and yet as scared as she was, she had this weird compulsion to trust this…this *demon hunter*, this warrior.

He cleared his throat and motioned to the parked cars. "Which is yours?"

She pointed out her red Honda Integra. "Where are we going?"

"Give me the keys."

Digging around in her purse, she found the keys and handed them over. He led her around to the passenger side and she climbed in. He jogged around, adjusted the seat back as far as it would go, and squeezed in behind the steering wheel. It didn't make much difference; his impossibly long legs were still scrunched up in her small car.

"Where are you taking me?" she asked again.

His long fingers flexed around the steering wheel several times, and his fierce expression seemed to soften a fraction. "I'm taking you somewhere you'll be protected, until you're capable of cloaking and controlling your powers. Somewhere safe." He started the car and pulled out into the quiet street.

Powers?

"There must be another way. This whole thing is crazy. I

can't just disappear. What about my business? My home?" How could he expect her to leave everything she'd worked so hard to build?

"I know it's hard, but it's not safe for you here anymore." His voice was hard as granite, leaving no room for argument.

Was this really happening? The coastal landscape tilted and warped through the windscreen. "So you just expect me to...to leave and never come back?" she whispered.

"You don't have a choice. Do you have family, friends here?"

There he went, randomly changing the subject again, catching her off guard.

"Do you?" he asked.

She shook her head. "Um, no, not really. No one close anyway."

"Good. That's good. No one to miss you, not for a while at least."

No, she didn't have anyone. Her parents were gone, and the few friends she had throughout her life—well, acquaintances really—had never stuck around.

It wasn't much, but it was her life, and she didn't want to just walk away.

The reality of her situation hit with sudden and frightening force. Her head swam and her throat constricted like invisible hands were trying to squeeze the life out of her. Gripping the door handle, she struggled for oxygen. Black spots dotted her vision. She was in the grip of a full-on panic attack and moments away from passing out.

"I—I can't..." Her lungs felt bound. She tried to take a breath, but a tight band gripped her chest. The car jerked to an abrupt stop, her shoulders taken roughly. Hands moved up to cup her face, forcing her to look up.

"Christ, you need to calm down. You're doing yourself harm, demi." His thumb gently brushed back and forth across her jaw, and she focused on the contact. One big hand moved down to clutch hers, enveloping her fingers. Warmth radiated from him, making her skin tingle.

"Take slow, deep breaths. That's it. In and out. Good girl." His tone was gentle, and after a few minutes of listening to the deep, raspy timbre of his voice, her heart rate slowed. That intoxicating, spicy scent hit, and she gasped down a much-needed deep breath. It overrode the fear and somehow broke through the terror.

His expression was still hard, but his jaw wasn't clamped shut and his eyes had softened slightly.

She pulled her hand from his, needing space. The way he affected her was almost as terrifying as the man himself. "My name's Eve. Not Demi."

"Okay," he said, watching her carefully.

The hand that had been holding hers dropped to one of his jean-clad monster thighs, and he rubbed it against the denim like he was trying to rub her touch away.

"Why do you keep calling me that? Why are you here and what's happening to me? Please, I don't understand any of this."

He searched her features for several long seconds, unnerving her. "There is a reason you can hear people's thoughts. You are more...you are...different." He shifted in his seat. "Demi is not a name. It's what you are. A demi-demon. Half-human and half-demon."

What?

She shook her head in denial.

No.

How can that be?

Yes, she'd always known there was something different about her, in the last few months more than ever. But a demon? No.

She shook her head. "Demons aren't real. They don't

exist." The logical side of her brain tried to argue, but she'd seen one with her own two eyes, hadn't she? Right there in her shop.

The memory of that disgusting creature caused her to shudder. He was telling the truth. There was no denying it, no matter how badly she wanted to.

She hadn't let herself believe she was truly hearing people's thoughts, but the voices, the words that flew through her mind, they hadn't been hers. And after last night with Eric, she knew it was the truth.

"Mrs. Jensen was a demon?"

"No. Orthon have the ability to take on other forms."

This new bit of information threatened to throw her back into full panic mode. "Orthon? I'm one of those awful monsters?"

He took her hand awkwardly, again like he didn't really want to touch her. "They're a special breed, born trackers. They're lower level demons, the vermin of the demon world. You're not one of them."

"What am I?" she forced out, not even sure she wanted to know.

"I can only guess. But your sire was most likely a Pathos demon. They sense and are drawn to high emotion, usually suffering."

"Oh God." Her stomach churned. "Will I...will that happen to me?"

"No, Eve." Her name rumbled from his chest in that deep, coarse voice, and she shivered. "Demon DNA mutates when mixed with human. In your case, you developed telepathy." He trapped her with his stare. "Your power makes you very rare in the demon world. No full-blooded demons possess your ability. And only a handful of demi have ever been born with your gift."

"That's why I'm being hunted?"

"Yes."

"This isn't a gift. It's a curse."

"You'll learn to embrace it," he said with certainty.

The idea of living with this thing without going insane—she wasn't convinced. "And you're here to…what? Protect me?"

"Yes. And I promise I won't let anything hurt you. But you have to do as I say."

She didn't have much choice but to trust him. "Are you a demon, too?"

"I'm half demon."

"So you're half-human, like me?"

"No."

Okay, by the cold don't-even-go-there look on his face, he wasn't about to share. That was fine with her. The fact that there were demons running around in the first place, and she was one of them, was more than enough to take in for now.

"Your name? You haven't told me your name." A sudden need to know in whose hands she'd placed her life seemed extremely important.

His throat worked before he spoke, Adam's apple sliding up and down his thick throat. "Lazarus."

Tingles danced across her scalp at the way he said it, the sound of that voice. And she felt breathless again for some unknown reason. She cleared her throat. "Lazarus," she repeated, letting it roll off her tongue, liking the feel of it. "I suppose I should thank you, then, for helping me."

"That's not necessary." He looked more than a little uncomfortable.

Why should her thanks make him uncomfortable? The urge to reach out and touch him, to soothe the frown lines creasing his brow was almost too hard to resist.

Eve ignored the crazy impulse. Despite his having saved

her life and calming her during her panic attack, she couldn't let her guard down. Lazarus continued to watch her closely, silently. No doubt afraid she'd flip out again. The silence pressed in around her. The only sounds were coming from the street, muffled inside the enclosed space of her car.

That's all.

Her mind was utterly silent.

"I can't hear you," she whispered.

A dark brow lifted in question.

"Your thoughts, I mean."

"I'm immune. My job is to find your kind when they come into their powers, get them to safety, make sure they're not captured. I couldn't do my job if, for example, you could hear what was going on in my head right now."

The look he aimed at her was so different from the fierce expression he'd had plastered on his face since walking into her shop, and what she saw in his eyes should have terrified her. But alarmingly, what she felt was quite the opposite.

"I can see how that could be a problem." The tightness in her shoulders eased despite all the unguarded intensity he was throwing her way. "I have to admit, the silence is nice."

Although just then it would have been useful to know what he was thinking. Her mind had been crowded for the last month, full of things she could have happily gone the rest of her life never knowing. She'd been positive she was losing her mind.

"Until you're able to control your power, and as long you're beside me, I can block it for you."

"You can do that?"

"Yes."

That kind of freaked her out. What else could he do? "So you're pretty powerful, huh?"

A small nod.

She glanced out the window, took in the familiar scenery,

and pain sliced through her. "What will happen to my store, my house?"

"Eventually we'll set you up with everything you need to start a new life." His gaze skittered away. "Maybe once you've mastered your power you can have another bookstore somewhere," he said as if that would fix everything.

"But not here." Her heart squeezed. Leaving her store and never coming back to this place, a place where she'd created a happy, if lonely existence, physically hurt. Once again her life was out of her hands and she was at the mercy of someone else. "Can I get some of my things?"

"It's too dangerous."

Eve turned back to him, desperate for him to understand, and reached out, resting her hand on his forearm. She sucked in a breath as little tingles shot up her arm. Lazarus's eyes flared and the muscles under her fingers bunched hard.

His gaze dropped, zeroing on where she touched him.

She quickly pulled her hand back, curling her fingers into a fist. "Y-you can't expect me to just leave everything, to just walk away without a backward glance." His gaze lifted back to hers, intense, his mouth a hard line. He was about to refuse her again. "Please, Lazarus."

He continued to stare at her, and his knuckles turned white as he gripped the steering wheel. Finally, he muttered under his breath, "Shit." He started the car again and pulled into the street. "We have to be quick."

Her shoulders sagged in relief. "Thank you."

They pulled into her driveway a short time later.

"Wait here." Lazarus took the keys from the ignition and opened the door, but paused, turning back. "And, Eve, don't try to run. You'd be putting yourself at risk, and I'd have to chase after you. That would piss me off. You don't want to do that."

No. She most certainly did not want to do that. He didn't

move, continuing to watch her, she guessed waiting for some kind of confirmation from her. Unable to do anything else, she gave a jerky nod. With that, he climbed out, jogged up to the house, and went inside. He was gone less than a minute before he reappeared and motioned her in. She got out and hurried up the path. As soon as she stepped inside, he ushered her toward the bedroom.

"Be quick." Somehow he managed to make his rough voice sound almost gentle.

Sadness overwhelmed her as she entered her room. But she swallowed it down ruthlessly. She couldn't indulge in her misery just yet because once the pain broke free, she wasn't sure she'd be able to rein it back in.

Slipping off Lazarus's jacket, she laid it on the bed, grabbed a bag from the top shelf of her closet, and got to work stuffing in as many of her clothes as she could.

She was coming out of the bathroom when she spotted the thick stack of photos on her dresser. Among them was her favorite, taken two weeks before her parents died in a house fire. Whoever had taken it had captured so much joy, so much love between them it was still hard to look at all these years later.

God, she missed them.

From the doorway, Lazarus cleared his throat. She glanced up. Tension lined his brow and creased the corners of his eyes and mouth, conveying the need for haste without saying a word.

"Right, sorry," she murmured. "I was just...my parents." She held up the photos.

He moved closer and looked at the pictures over her shoulder. "I thought you didn't have a family?"

"They died when I was a kid."

He frowned, those creases between his eyes coming back. "Who took over your care?"

SHERILEE GRAY

"My aunt took me in for a little while, but they passed me on to someone else pretty quickly. I spent my childhood being passed from one foster family to the next." She turned to look up at him. "It was the demon thing, wasn't it?"

He shoved his hands in his pockets. "It happens some-times, humans sensing it in children, that there's something different about them, something that keeps them at a distance. Usually in children who end up with powers like yours."

"Like mine?"

"All powers are different, some are just more potent." His expression softened slightly. "They wouldn't have under-stood their…aversion to you."

Eve smiled at his attempt to sugarcoat the fact that her aunt and her family had hated to be around her, the same for the foster families she lived with. It had been hard—God, it had never gotten any easier—and once or twice throughout her life, in her darkest moments, she'd even contemplated ending it. "I always thought it was because I was adopted, because I wasn't their blood that they sent me away. I guess I can't blame them for their reaction to me now. They had a demon in their home."

It explained the changes in Eric, why he'd acted the way he had around her. As a kid, she hadn't understood why nobody liked her. She'd spent all her time trying to please people. If she was a good girl, if she did as she was told and never made waves that maybe they would love her, that they'd keep her. It never happened. She'd spent those lonely years sitting at the edge of the room, watching from the outside while everyone else had fun—usually with a bag of cookies in her hand. Food became her comfort. Eating some-thing delicious made her feel good, filled the emotional void in her life. Still did to a certain extent.

When she looked back up, the tenderness softening Lazarus's expression startled her.

"They were assholes," he said. "Whatever way you look at it, they shouldn't have treated you that way. I don't give a fuck how they felt."

Oh god, she'd blurted everything out loud, about her loneliness, her issues with food. Her face heated. "It's okay... I..." She swallowed whatever she'd been about to say, then a thought occurred to her. "Why didn't my parents have the same aversion to me? They loved me, Lazarus, I know they did."

He watched her carefully. "My guess? At least one of your adoptive parents must have had demon blood. They would have easily sensed it in you as an infant."

"They were like me?" Stunned, she stared at the picture in her hand.

"That's my guess."

Would they have told her who she was? Helped her through this transition? God, how different her life would have been.

Carefully, she placed the photos in her bag. "I know this sounds crazy, but knowing that, somehow it...helps." She smiled at the big male standing in front of her. "Thank you."

He stilled, unnaturally so. His gaze dropped to her mouth for several long seconds then darted back to her eyes. He looked conflicted, God, tormented.

Her hand lifted, was moving to him before she knew what she was doing. She wanted—no, needed—to touch him, had the insane compulsion to try and ease the torment rolling off him in waves, to make some kind of connection.

Impossibly, he stilled further when she pressed her hand to his biceps. He was hard as steel beneath her palm, like he'd been honed from marble. And like last time, something happened between them. Tiny zaps of electricity seemed to flow from his body to hers, lifting goose bumps all over her skin.

His eyes looked different, had somehow changed. She felt…God, trapped, unable to look away from the luminous, swirling pools of emerald. The color flickered dark then light, like a flashlight being switched on and off behind his irises.

She moved closer.

He shook his head, silently telling her to stay back. "We have to go," he ground out.

Captivated, almost mesmerized by the unearthly green staring down at her, Eve jumped and cried out in alarm when her phone started ringing. Lazarus's big frame went still. The vibrant emerald depths holding her frozen darkened, slowly eclipsed by midnight, causing the whites of his eyes to stand out in stark relief.

"Ignore it."

His quietly spoken words had the same effect as a gunshot, breaking her from her trance. Tension radiated from him, and the way his jaw had hardened, it was like he was fighting for control. He was back to being the warrior, and it was terrifying.

And as much as she wanted to turn and run as far and fast she could, she ignored the urge, no matter how tempting it was. Because she believed him. He was the only one who could keep her safe.

At the moment, this man, demon, whatever he was, appeared to be her only hope.

And the longer they stayed, the more danger they were in.

CHAPTER 5

Eve's little pink tongue darted out again, moistening her lower lip. He inwardly groaned.

Jesus. All she'd done was touch his arm and he'd been close to jumping her. The curvy little demi in front of him called to his demon, like she'd tuned into the fucker's frequency and was calling him home to the mother ship.

His need to mark her, to claim her, had reared up, taken him by the balls, and he'd been damn close to giving in to it, to throwing her on that bed and taking what was his. Just her touch had lit up every molecule in his body. Christ, it had turned his limbs to mush.

His craving for this female was illogical in its intensity, but then from what little he'd seen of the mating process, logic wasn't a factor when a warrior found his female.

Lazarus willed his heated body to cool, more than a little unsettled by his reaction to Eve. Going by the expression on her face, he wasn't the only one.

Her lips were kind of puffy from her biting at them, and he licked his own, imagining her taste, the warmth and feel of them against his.

He gritted his teeth, stifling another groan.

The urge to claim her came from a primal place deep inside. A part of him that recognized her as his, and it was screwing with his head, not to mention his body.

Hell, maybe he should just fuck her and get it over with?

Taking her now would solve a lot of his troubles. His cock definitely had no problem getting behind the idea and strained painfully against the stiff denim of his jeans.

Eyes bright, cheeks flushed, Eve gazed up at him. Her lips slightly parted, begged to be sucked and nibbled. Hair like silken ebony waves tumbled over her shoulders, and he barely resisted the urge to reach out and touch it.

Was this how she'd look in his bed after he'd fucked her? Images flooded his mind, and this time a groan did slip past his lips.

Her eyes widened and she stepped away from him. "Lazarus?"

Good work, asshole. Now she's back to being frightened of you.

One touch from her and he'd lost focus again.

This wasn't how this was supposed to happen. He'd been with her for less than an hour and already he was struggling to keep his shit together and had put her in danger. As tempting as she was, he had to remain fixed on his original path. He couldn't allow this force between them to win. Because this wasn't for him. He couldn't keep her.

"We have to leave," he said before putting even more space between them. Keeping his head straight was getting more and more difficult around Eve. He needed to conduct the rest of this mission as he always did—with cold efficiency.

She nodded and went back to biting her damn bottom lip.

He tore his eyes from her, not sure how to handle this, any of it. How was he going to explain what she was to him? How did you tell someone they were the key to your salvation, your only hope? That your future and that of the free world depended on her leaving everything she'd ever known and accepting him as her mate.

A mate who would leave as soon as he'd taken what he wanted.

A mate who could never love her.

Eve would not be another sacrifice to this war. And that's what would happen if he kept her. If he allowed her to get close.

People who got close to him suffered for it. They got hurt.

He'd do whatever it took to prevent that from happening again.

He glanced over at her. Keeping his shit tight wasn't going to be easy. Besides having to deal with his over-whelming physical attraction to her, he feared his possession was moving at a faster rate. Time was almost up, and he had to find a way to explain the reason he'd come for her without sending her running.

What if she refuses you?

He couldn't think about that now. Getting her to safety had to be his number one priority. The shadows had crept in earlier, the darkness trying to take another piece of his soul. Eve had seen it, the difference in his eyes as he fought to restrain his demon. He just had to hold off for a bit longer.

And hope like hell she'd accept him.

Ignoring her questioning gaze, he collected her bags and headed for the door. She looked around her home for the last time, faltering as they passed a large bookshelf, gazing up at the tattered, well-read books.

"Some of them belonged to my mother," she whispered, like she could hear his unspoken question.

Lazarus didn't bother with false platitudes. Nothing he could say would soften the blow. As much as it hurt now, she'd get over it. She had to.

Swallowing down guilt, an emotion he knew all too well, he steered her back out the front door. Eve climbed into the car and stared out the window as they drove away. He guessed she was attempting to absorb every detail of the small coastal town she'd called home. But eventually, no matter how hard she tried, most of the memories would fade. Over time they would lose their sharp lines, become fuzzy and distant. They always did.

An image of Scarlet entered Lazarus's mind. Small and scared. A mass of wild red curls around her grubby face. She'd stared up at him in awe, and instantly stolen his heart. He'd vowed to protect her from that moment on. Even after she'd grown into a strong, independent female—even after she found her own mate—he'd still seen her as his little girl. She might not have been his blood, but she was his, his child in every way that mattered.

She always would be.

He was wrong, some memories never faded, and he was grateful for the cutting reminder. He couldn't afford to make the same mistakes twice.

Any rogue demon could have sensed Eve's powers and come after her. Lazarus should have expected the attack from that Orthon. He should have damn well been prepared.

Tobias would be keeping tabs on him; he had no doubt about that. The male wouldn't back off, not until he had his revenge. He'd once been their brother. In Lazarus's heart, he still was, even though he was lost to them, lost in his own darkness.

Lazarus ignored the inevitable slice of pain that rode shotgun with memories of Tobias and Scarlet; let it settle, cut deeper. It was his price to pay.

He deserved to suffer for what he'd done. For failing them.

Eve didn't, though, not for his sins.

He gripped the steering wheel tighter. What if Tobias had gotten close? He could have figured out who Eve was to Lazarus. So far, the other male had been messing with him, biding his time. This was all some sick game to him. But if he had the tiniest notion that Eve was his mate, his fallen brother wouldn't hesitate to use her to get to him.

Tobias had turned his back on them long before Lazarus or his brothers knew what he planned to do. After Scarlet's death, after Tobias lost her, his mate, their brother had willingly embraced the demon half of his DNA, letting go of that part of himself that held compassion, a sense of right from wrong—the ability to care for another being. He chose darkness, walked away from his family, and in doing so declared war.

After Tobias left, Laz and his brothers had done their best to block the connection that still tied them together, but that connection worked both ways, and the evil shit he was sending back was seriously fucking with all of them, was tipping the scale toward darkness. The only way to sever it permanently was death, and since they couldn't find him, blocking it, or trying to at least, was their only option.

What they'd managed to do had hindered his ability, but it wasn't enough. He was using their connection to help him source the demi he could no longer track on his own. If he found out who Eve was, she'd be that much more desirable to him. Shit, the Orthon back at her shop could have belonged to him.

He glanced at Eve. She had no clue just how important she was.

She sat rigid in her seat, eyes wide as they passed a sign asking them to *visit again soon.* And dammit, he wished he knew what to say to make this easier for her. But anything he said would be a lie, because as bad as it was now, it was only going to get a whole lot worse.

51

She took a shaky breath and turned to him. "So where to now?"

The female was strong, a quality she'd need to draw on more and more over the coming weeks. "We have a plane to catch."

She shifted in her seat. "Where are you taking me?"

"Roxburgh, New York."

Her fingers tightened on the armrest, her only outward sign of distress. "Why are you taking me there?"

"We have a compound. It's secluded, outside the city." He glanced over at her. "Away from prying eyes."

"We?"

"My brothers and I."

The color in her cheeks drained, some of that fire he'd seen in her along with it. Defeat, and though she tried to hide it, fear, was now clear in her eyes. "What will you do to me there?"

Yeah, he'd more than earned her distrust and she'd be wise to remain wary of him.

But as she stared up at him, lost and frightened, he heard himself say, "Have I hurt you? In any way?"

She flinched at his harsh tone and shook her head.

"And I don't plan to."

Her eyes hit his. "You're right. I'm sorry."

He wanted to kick his own ass. She was afraid of him. Just because he felt the pull of this screwed-up connection didn't mean she did. And, boy, did he feel it. Deep down he knew guilt fueled his words, because hurting her was exactly what he'd have to do.

Moderating his tone, he tried to reassure her. "I can help you, Eve."

She sent him a look so full of hope and fragile trust that he wanted to take his own eyes out. It hurt to look at her when she stared at him like that, and before he could stop himself, words were tumbling from his mouth without thought. "I promise I will never do anything that you don't want me to." His voice had turned harsh as images of exactly what he did want to do flashed through his mind.

He dragged a hand through his hair.

Why had he said that? Made her a promise he might not be able to keep.

She remained quiet for a few seconds, eyes downcast, staring at her fingers as she twisted them in her lap. "I'm glad I have you here to help me through this." Her cheeks turned a pretty shade of pink. Then she smiled at him, tentative and sweet.

An erratic thumping sensation stuttered to life in the middle of his chest. The feeling was so foreign it took a moment to work out what had caused it. Any minute now Frankenstein would jump up from the back seat and start yelling, "It's alive! It's alive!"

He clenched his teeth. *Unacceptable.*

The useless damn organ had shriveled to nothing long ago, and that's the way he liked it. The way he intended to keep it. Dead.

Unable to look at her another second, he concentrated on driving.

She remained quiet the rest of the way, besides the odd question about the compound and what to expect when they arrived. He couldn't help but be impressed with the way she was handling the situation, a situation that most took a hell of a lot harder than the feisty, intelligent female sitting beside him.

He was so fucked.

CHAPTER 6

NUMB. There was no other way to describe how Eve felt.

Though, one good thing had come from this nightmare. For the first time in a long time, her mind was utterly silent.

Since Lazarus had come for her, she'd enjoyed relief from all that noise, the multitude of thoughts stomping across her battered psyche, and it gave her hope there might be another way. That she might actually be able to gain control over this thing.

The busy Roxburgh traffic thinned as they moved out of the city. A guy named James, also a demi-demon, had been at the airport waiting for them with a car when they'd landed. Lazarus had barely greeted the guy before he'd taken the keys and gotten behind the wheel. He hadn't said a word since. The plane ride had been much the same. He'd not said more than two words, and scowled the entire flight.

"I'm one of the trainers," James was saying. "Once I mastered my powers the hunters were so heartbroken at the idea of me leaving, they offered me a job." He turned to face the back seat and grinned at her. "Grown men crying…never a pretty sight. What choice did I have? I stayed."

Lazarus growled.

Eve smiled back. James seemed nice, not terrifying at all. Maybe this wouldn't be so terrible.

She'd given up wishing this was nothing but a nightmare. What she'd seen of Lazarus's powers so far—along with her close encounter of the hideous, freaky-eyed monster kind—pointed away from a psychotic episode and made all the crazy stuff that had happened to her impossible to deny.

So she'd made a decision during their flight. She would handle this like any other move she'd had in her life, which had been numerous while growing up. She would accept her new circumstances. Fighting or crying wouldn't help, it never did. She could do this. She had to do this. She would adapt, like she always did. No problem.

Being forced from her home, taken to a new city by a man she didn't know anything about—while on the run from demons—which it turns out would like nothing more than to make her their slave.

Yep, cakewalk.

Information overload didn't cover it, and surprisingly, it was Lazarus's strong, silent presence that had kept her mind from short-circuiting. It was crazy, and she had no idea why exactly, but she trusted him to keep her safe.

They drove for another twenty minutes before the scenery changed and they entered some kind of industrial area. They passed old warehouses and empty lots. The whole area looked postapocalyptic, or at least what she imagined it would look like. No signs of life, everything abandoned and run-down.

At the end of the block, the car turned into a short road and they carried on until Lazarus pulled to a stop in front of a set of steel gates. They were at least ten feet tall, and there was a security camera mounted to the side aimed at them. He slid down the window and pressed his thumb to a small pad.

The gates jolted loudly then groaned into action.

As they slid open, Eve strained to see what was hidden behind the monstrosities.

Oh...wow.

And not a good *wow*; a where-the-hell-have-you-brought-me *wow*. A turn-me-around-and-take-me-anywhere-else *wow*.

The building on the other side was like something from a horror movie, where the serial killer took his victim to torture them before he finished them off. Besides varying shades of gray, the only other colors she could see were streaks of rust bleeding from large steel framework and washed-out green from the dust-covered weeds struggling up between the cracked concrete that surrounded the place.

Eve shivered. The huge, multistory building loomed ahead, casting an ominous shadow that seemed to stretch toward them like a monster about to devour its prey. Eve actually sucked in a breath when they moved from the light and into the darkness.

She tilted her head back, looking all the way up. The windows had been boarded, and some of the iron cladding hung loose, swinging drunkenly in the breeze, squeaking loudly then clattering against the building.

"What is this place?" she whispered.

"Home," Lazarus said without looking back.

Her stomach flipped, and the nerves already tying her belly in knots tightened. Doors slid open in the wall ahead of them and the car tilted forward down a steep ramp into the bowels of the place.

Sensor lights flickered on moments later. They were in a parking garage. Several SUVs like the one they were in were parked there, and a couple of large dangerous-looking bikes were against the far wall.

Lazarus climbed out, came around, and pulled her door open. When he motioned her to follow, she realized she'd just been sitting there, too afraid to move.

Eve scrambled out and had to power walk to keep up with his long strides. He stopped in front of an ancient elevator she guessed wouldn't meet any type of safety code, and she and James walked in after him. He pushed a button, for what floor she had no idea since all the numbers had worn off, and the elevator jarred into action. She stumbled, grabbing for the wall. Lazarus's hand shot out, catching her arm to steady her so fast the movement was almost blur.

There went those weird little zaps again, right where his hand touched her.

She ignored them and focused on the numbers above the doors as they lit up. It ground to a halt on the fifth. Lazarus stepped closer, his hand moving to the small of her back. God, the immense heat radiating off his palm seemed to sear an imprint of that big paw right into her skin through her dress.

"Home sweet home," James muttered as the doors slid open.

It took her brain several seconds to register what she was seeing. The interior was nothing like the shabby exterior. It was clean and modern with a lot of chrome and glass. The floors were a shiny black, and a subtle hint of lemon floor cleaner scented the air. It had an institutional feel and made her nervous all over again.

Several computers were set up around the room, and there was an entire wall covered with monitors. She recognized some of the images from the outside of the building and the underground parking garage.

The three of them stepped out of the elevator. "What is all this?" She turned toward the silent male beside her.

"Our main control area. Besides security for the compound, we also have a visual link to most of Roxburgh and the surrounding areas."

"Why do you need cameras?" He'd told her how his kind tracked the demi-demons they saved. He'd called it a sort of built-in alarm. All this seemed...well, she didn't know what to make of any of it.

"Bringing in demi isn't all we do." He motioned to the cameras. "Sometimes we need modern technology like everyone else."

That cryptic answer told her nothing, but Lazarus seemed tense and she got the feeling it wasn't the time to push for more.

"Are there other demi-demons here like me?"

"The second and third floors house our demi. First, we have a training area, gym. Above the control room, there's a common area and cafeteria of sorts for those who wish to socialize. The fourth floor is apartments, mine and my brothers." He turned to her then, finally looking at her again. "You can find me there if you need me."

His voice had deepened when he said the last, and the gravel in it had her shivering again.

She nodded, unable to make her mouth work all of a sudden.

That intense gaze moved over her. "Are you cold again?"

Eve swallowed and forced herself to answer. "No, I'm not cold."

His head tilted to the side in that animalistic way, gaze boring into hers, and whatever he saw caused it to darken.

She quickly looked away. The fierceness in his eyes made her heart race and her head swim in a way she did not understand.

"Your room," he said suddenly. "I'll get someone to show you to your room."

~

Lazarus led Eve out of the control room, trying to keep his reaction to that little shiver, the way she'd been looking at him, on the down-low. Maybe what he'd been feeling wasn't totally one-sided? Maybe not. Whatever that was, no way she'd understand it, and no way would he take advantage of it.

No matter how much of a game-changer it would be in the war with Tobias. Mating her when she was confused and without all the facts wasn't something he was comfortable with. Not one fucking bit.

He ignored the throb of his groin and steered her out into the hall, more than a little pleased that all his brothers hadn't been there for a meet and greet when they arrived. They were intimidating individually; confronted with more than one of them at a time would have freaked Eve out.

And, shit, if Chaos had seen that little shiver, the way Eve had looked at Lazarus, the prick would have locked them in a room together, mated by morning, and have Lazarus out hunting Tobias by nightfall.

The sound of boots hitting the stairs as they approached them echoed up the stairwell, and he gritted his teeth, sensing his brother before the doors opened. Thankfully, it was Kryos and not Zenon. With his angelic blond curls, warm brown eyes, and handsome face, Kryos was by far the least threatening of them all, at least in looks. Being mated helped. Not only did mating mean he had control of his demon, he at least knew how to talk to a woman without scaring the hell out of her.

He smiled. "Laz." His gaze slid to Eve. "And this is?"

"Eve," Lazarus said.

Kryos's smile turned to a grin and he held out his hand.

"Nice to meet you." His gaze slid back to Laz. "I hope my surly bro here is making you feel welcome."

Eve chuckled.

Laz scowled at the bastard. "Is Meredith here? I thought she might she show Eve around." His brother's mate would do a better job of making Eve feel welcome than he could.

Kryos frowned a little. "I thought you might…"

"Can she or not?"

"Yeah, sure. I'll get her to meet Eve downstairs in a few." Kryos met his gaze. "Have you told her everything she needs to know…about how we do things here?"

Laz stared back, not missing what his brother was asking. "No, there'll be time for that later. I think she's had enough information for one day."

Kryos lifted his chin. *Message received.*

At least he'd keep his trap shut. And as soon as Eve was safe in her room, he'd be sending out a mass text to the others to keep their mouths shut as well. He needed to do this his own way, and he sure as hell didn't need a reminder that time wasn't something he had a lot of.

Kryos left to get his mate, and Lazarus led Eve to the stairs.

An hour later, Eve was in her room, Meredith still with her, and Laz was in his apartment, wearing out a strip in his carpet. What the hell did he do now? What was the best way to approach this: take her somewhere, like a date? Try and win her over?

Christ.

He clenched his fists. Winning her over wasn't the goal here. He didn't want to trick her into this, make her believe they were something that they weren't. Make her think he could give her something he knew he never could. Honesty was his only option. He needed to just lay that shit out and hope for the best.

"Hey, Eve, you're my mate. That means you'll be tied to me for eternity, but I don't actually want you for more than one night. So yeah, wanna come back to my room and fuck?"

Who wouldn't fall at someone's feet after that declaration?

The knock at his door was not unexpected. The only surprise was it hadn't come sooner.

He yanked the door open and Chaos, their unofficial leader, walked through and prowled across the room.

Chaos stopped in front of Lazarus. "Does she know?"

"Not yet."

"So you're not mated?"

Lazarus stiffened and barely resisted the urge to decorate the guy's face with a matching pair of black eyes. "Can I have more than a goddamned day? I'd like Eve to get used to me before I fucking jump her."

The persistent hum he'd woken up with vibrating in the back of his skull, plus the uncontrollable craving for the female now in this building, made him aware of how naive he'd been.

He thought he could take her, make her his mate, then leave. But it wouldn't be that easy, not any of it. His life was not his own. The greater good, it always came first. He'd been created to fight, to protect mankind. His *feelings* never came into it. It had always been that way.

Which meant he hadn't even factored Eve's feelings into any of this, how this fucking nightmare would affect her.

Chaos visibly tensed. "We don't have time to fuck around, and until you finish this, we're all at risk. Diemos and his brethren are just waiting for their chance."

By finishing this, Chaos meant making Eve his mate. His

brother was even blinder than Lazarus when it came to duty. The male was made of stone.

As for Diemos—the most powerful male in Hell—Lazarus would do whatever was necessary to keep his brothers away from that sadistic bastard. The guy had once been Lucifer's most trusted confidant, his right-hand demon, his favorite. Until Diemos betrayed him and cast Lucifer out. Word had it Lucifer refused to kill him, fuck knew why, and instead decided if Diemos wanted the throne so badly he could have it.

The king of Hell was currently MIA.

Lazarus knew it was hopeless, but he had to ask. "There's no other way?"

"You know there isn't." Chaos's gaze held an unyielding determination and a grain of pity that set Lazarus's teeth on edge. "Diemos already has Tobias on the payroll. And the way our brother wants you hurting, you know he's coming for you next. We can't let that happen."

Yeah, T wanted him next, and Lazarus deserved that and more. Shame he couldn't let Tobias have at it. But that wasn't an option. He wasn't the only one that would suffer if he didn't do this.

Chaos's gaze locked on his. "I know how tight you and T were, and I know this is gonna fuck with your head, but we need to sever the bond Tobias has with us before he takes the rest of us down with him. I don't know about you, but I don't get off on the idea of being Diemos's new plaything."

Lazarus rested his hands on his hips and stared at the ground. It had to be done, there was no other choice. But the idea of breaking that bond with their brother fucking killed him. T would still be with them if it wasn't for him. Scarlet would have walked through those doors to greet Lazarus's mate with open arms and a wide smile on her face.

Eve could have been his.

Instead, his brother was lost forever. Scarlet was dead. And Eve's welcome was a ticking time bomb of a mate who she'd end up hating when all this was over.

"Suck it up," his brother said. "How bad can it be? Kryos seems happy enough. That bastard's always mooning after Meredith."

Kryos was the only mated male among them. His demon was leashed, which meant Tobias's deflection didn't pose a risk to him. He'd found Meredith close to fifty years ago, and the pair had been loved up ever since.

Lazarus shook his head. Chaos had no idea he planned to leave after he and Eve were mated. Lazarus didn't need to live there at the compound to do his job, but his brother wouldn't see it that way. "Right."

Chaos shrugged, actually grinning. "I've never heard him complain."

"You'll wanna be next then?" Laz said, knowing the answer before Chaos spoke.

The guy's grin disappeared.

"Yeah, that's what I thought."

"Look, if that female can help keep your shit under control, your head straight, long enough to take out T?" He shrugged again, but Laz didn't miss the pain that flashed across his features with those words. "I figure it's a small price to pay."

Lazarus didn't comment. It felt like a fucking mammoth price to pay to him. He truly didn't give a shit what happened to him. Not anymore. But Eve, whose life he was about to destroy, that was another matter.

Chaos clapped him on the shoulder. "You have no choice, brother."

"I know," he gritted out.

"Good. Don't fuck it up."

"You'll be the first to know."

If he screwed this up, they'd all be a pack of mindless, bloodthirsty demons and Diemos's new playthings within a few weeks.

So, yeah, fucking this up wasn't an option.

CHAPTER 7

LAZARUS GROANED and rolled to his back. Fuck, his eyes felt gritty and dry, his body on fire, limbs achy. He hadn't slept more than a few minutes at a time—how could he when he felt Eve just a floor below him? His demon had mentally paced all night, roaring and whimpering, trying to take the driver's seat and go to her.

He rubbed his hands over his face and jerked back the covers. And then there was this...

He looked down his body and winced. His dick lay against his stomach and was so pumped full of blood it was fucking purple. He didn't think he'd ever been this hard in his life. Christ, his balls throbbed as well. He couldn't leave his room like this.

Fuuuuck.

The ache intensified, and he groaned again.

Eve had just woken up.

He knew it. Somehow, he just knew it.

The surge of power that came from her had him undulating on the bed, teeth gritted, his damn eyes rolling back in his head. He dropped his hand to his cock, hissing when he wrapped his fingers around it. He felt like molten steel under his fingers. He squeezed tighter as another wave reached him. He spread his legs wider, kicking the covers away. They felt like sandpaper against his skin. One foot hit the floor with a thump, the other dug into the mattress as he stroked his dick hard and fast, desperate for release.

The waves of power kept coming and it kept him right there, hovering between pleasure and pain, grunting and straining, sweating all over his sheets, close to losing his damn mind.

Then another surge came, so damn powerful his spine torqued and a roar tore from his throat. He came in powerful spurts of scalding hot come, splashing his stomach and chest and seemed to go on and on until he was shaking so hard his fucking teeth were chattering.

When he was spent, he collapsed back, gasping for breath. What the fuck?

Christ, something had caused her power to do that, those intense surges. Was Eve all right?

His mind instantly conjured up all kinds of scenarios, most of them bad. Lazarus quickly cleaned himself off with the sheet and stumbled out of bed on shaky legs, shoving on his clothes.

He was out the door and in the elevator a few minutes later, and banged on her door as soon as he reached it. Her powers had calmed now. Had died down from a raging storm to gentle waves, and the feeling of biting down on exposed electrical wires had dropped to pleasant tingles over his skin.

He reached down and adjusted his dick when he heard her moving toward the door. Not surprising he was hard again. He'd been hard since she came onto his radar.

The click of the lock came next and he stood straighter when the door opened.

Eve stood there looking flushed and disheveled, her eyes wide and glassy, lower lip red and swollen.

"What the fuck just happened?" Lazarus said, pushing his way into her smaller one-room apartment. He strode to the bathroom and shoved the door open. "Has someone been in here? Did they hurt you? Frighten you?"

She didn't answer and he spun back to her, finally taking in the rest of her. She was wearing a robe, the belt tied tight, enhancing her bountiful curves. His gaze moved back up to her face, the color on her cheeks, the way her lower lip was darker, puffy from biting it, the way her black hair was down and a little wild.

She looked recently fucked.

A growl tore up his throat as he spun to the bed, to its rumpled covers, the pillow knocked to the floor. She'd been with someone? There was no room for anyone under the bed. He strode over and checked the small closet. Empty.

His demon snarled, hating the thought just as much, and reared up, scenting the air. Only one. Eve. Then it hit him, a scent so fucking tantalizing, so intoxicating it almost knocked him on his ass.

Sexual desire.

He spun back to her still by the door, face pink with embarrassment, and he knew.

She'd just come, hard. Just like he had.

Those delicate fingers, currently gripping her robe closed, had been between her thighs, had moved over her slick, hot flesh, bringing her to orgasm at the same time as he had one floor above her. And he'd felt it. Christ, had he felt it.

She cleared her throat. "I..." She swallowed. "I don't know...there's nothing...nothing wrong."

Lazarus's demon fought harder, so hard he felt the stretch and pull under his skin, with the desire to shift. He needed to get the hell out of there.

"I just, I thought I heard something. I'll go." He strode to the door, moving toward her, and another wave of her scent hit him, stronger. She was still turned on. What he wouldn't give to lay her on that bed and bury his face between her thighs, to taste her, to make her come against his tongue over and over before he finally sank inside her.

"Lazarus?" He jolted and looked down at her. He was right in front of her now, hand poised about to touch her, and he barely remembered taking the final steps to reach her.

"Are you okay?" she asked, a slight rasp to her voice that didn't help one fucking bit.

His hand shot out and he grabbed the handle, yanking the door open. "Yeah, fine." *Leave before you do something you shouldn't, before you take her on this floor right damn now.*

Before you shift into your demon form and scare the hell out of both of you.

Lazarus strode out of the room, took the elevator to the control room, and yanked off his shirt as soon as he reached the balcony. The equinox was fast approaching—that had to be it, the reason his control was slipping. He needed to get away from here. Now. His wings sprouted from his back, allowing himself to partially shift, and he dove off the side, taking to the skies.

He flew for hours, but no matter how far he went he could still feel her.

What the fuck was he going to do?

"You're doing great, Eve," James said, smile encouraging. "Now let's try again, okay?"

Eve wasn't so sure. She felt like she sucked at this. They'd been there all afternoon and still she couldn't block him.

"Close your eyes," he said. "That's it. Can you see the door?"

"Yes." She envisioned a solid wooden door with heavy iron bolts and hinges, one she could close and lock, as his thoughts filtered into her mind. He was reciting the alphabet. Listening to him was so different than when she'd had Eric in her head. She didn't know if it was a human/demon thing, but James's thoughts were crisp, focused, not jumbled and scattered. They didn't make her want to scream, so that was a plus.

"Okay, now I want you to start closing it. I want you to block that doorway and lock it shut. Lock me out, Eve."

He finished the alphabet and started on something else; she had no idea what it was. She opened her eyes. He had a book open in front of him, and he grinned and flashed her the cover. Science fiction by the looks.

Eve closed her eyes again and shoved the door closed as hard as she could, but something stopped it. She curled her fingers into fists and mentally pushed against it harder. James's voice continued to fill her head, it dipped in volume several times, cut off for a few seconds, and then she had to let go.

Pain sliced through her head and she gasped.

"Eve, are you all right?"

James got out of his seat and came around, crouching beside her. She nodded, but that made her head hurt more.

"Shit, nosebleed," James said and rushed to a cupboard across the room.

Blood dripped onto the table where she sat. "I'm sorry."

He grabbed a box of tissues and put them on the table beside her. "Here, use these, and you have nothing to be sorry for. I pushed you too hard for your first try—"

The door across the room banged shut and she glanced

up. Lazarus was striding across the room, a scowl on his face, eyes furious.

"Yeah, you pushed her too hard. She's fucking bleeding," he said.

James planted his hands on his hips. "This isn't unusual, Laz. You've seen it yourself—"

"Leave us."

Eve stood. "Lazarus—"

"I said go," he said to James.

James muttered something under his breath, offered her a reassuring smile, and strode from the room.

Eve shook her head. "He wasn't wrong."

Lazarus was in front of her, staring at her like he expected her to fall to pieces in front of him. "About what?" he grunted.

"You really are surly."

One of his brows lifted. "You haven't seen surly, female."

The look in his eyes, the way the bright green had darkened, made her belly warm. Then she remembered earlier that morning, and what he'd almost walked in on. Her face heated and his eyes flared like he was the one who could read minds.

She quickly looked away and the sudden movement had her clutching her head.

He cursed and scooped her up, lifting her off her feet like she was weightless, which she was *not*.

"What are you doing?" she said, feeling even more embarrassed.

"Taking you somewhere you can rest."

"I don't need to be carried."

He ignored her and strode out the door and down the hall. Eve didn't know what to do with her hands and in the end, rested one on his shoulder. The heat of his skin seeped through his shirt. God, he was hot. And his heart pounded against her, faster than what was normal. But then, maybe that was a demon thing as well?

She was so focused on every move, every shift of his muscles, the places their bodies touched, she hadn't noticed when the elevator opened that it wasn't on her floor, not until he shoved a door open and strode into what was obviously his apartment.

He put her on the couch and stepped back as if she'd shocked him then paced away and shook out his hands, like he had in the car the day before right after he'd touched her.

He stopped suddenly and turned to her, looking edgy as hell. "Drink?"

The question threw her. "Um...sure."

He strode to the small kitchen off to the side, grabbed a bottle of water from the fridge and a couple of kitchen towels he'd dampened under the tap, and came back.

"Here."

"Thanks." She took the water from him and used the towels to clean up while he watched her, again from a distance.

"I'm fine, if you'd rather I leave," she said.

"I don't want you to leave."

The way he said that was so low she was surprised the ground didn't shake. "Is there a reason—"

"Are you still in pain?" he asked, talking right over her.

"It's almost completely gone."

"Good, that's...good." He stood, solid thighs braced apart, hands at his sides, fingers curled into fists. He was anything but relaxed. Everything he said was at odds with his body language. "Hungry?"

"No," she said at the same time as her stomach rumbled so loudly there was no way he'd missed it. Cue more blushing. She'd been so nervous about her first training session she'd skipped lunch.

He frowned. "You're hungry. Why did you lie?"

Eve's mouth opened, but she didn't know what to say.

"I frighten you," he said. "You want to leave."

Yes, she wanted to leave, but not because Lazarus frightened her. He overwhelmed her, though, in a whole lot of different ways. "I'm not afraid of you."

"Right," he muttered and walked to the phone, punching in a couple of numbers. She listened while he asked for food to be brought up. When he turned back, she didn't miss the change in his posture, the way he rolled his shoulders and unclenched his jaw as if forcing himself to relax.

He watched her for several long seconds, then said, "Will you eat with me?" He rubbed the back of his neck and his huge biceps bulged. "I know we got off to a rocky start, and the way I've been acting…" He cleared his throat. "Will you eat with me?" he asked again.

Eve had no idea what was going on, or what this was about, but he was making an effort, for whatever reason, and she couldn't bring herself to say no when self-preservation told her to do just that.

For some reason, she couldn't bring herself to leave. There was this draw, this pull to him she didn't understand, and it was messing with her, big time.

Like the way you got yourself off thinking about him this morning.

Yes, thank God it wasn't Lazarus who could read minds.

CHAPTER 8

SHE WAS LOOKING at him again, in that *way*, cheeks pink, lids heavy.

Every muscle in his body locked up. So much for trying to relax. He thought if he brought her here, ate with her, had a conversation, he could explain what she was to him. He could make it as pain free as possible.

She'd been in his room all of ten minutes and already he was losing it. With Tobias doing his damnedest to corrupt them, as well as the equinox almost there, he was struggling. His demon knew the portal would be opening in a matter of days and it felt the call.

If you were mated to Eve that wouldn't be a problem anymore.

And he could finish Tobias and help his brothers regain full control as well.

She was watching him. He strode toward her, taking the seat opposite. Looming over her wouldn't help his cause, even if sitting still made him want to jump out of his damned skin, especially around her.

She watched him, looking slightly alarmed like she knew something was coming, something she wouldn't like.

Her fingers dug into the couch cushions. "What is it? What's wrong?"

Again, he found himself wanting to soothe her. Searching his mind for a gentle way to tell her how important she was to him, that she was literally his very own needle in a haystack. "I need to tell you some things, about me, about your place here. I just don't know where the hell to start."

She pulled one of the cushions into her lap, her eyes so wide, so full of fear he fucking wanted to roar. The female was stuck with him, a broken male who had no clue how to make this okay for her. Because it wasn't okay. None of this was okay.

"You know I'm half-demon?"

She nodded.

"My other half is angel."

She blinked over at him. "Angel?"

"Yes."

She stared at him for several seconds, then choked out, "Of course you are." She looked panicked. "I guess that makes sense. If demons are real then angels only seem logical. Next, you'll tell me vampires and witches and werewolves exist as well."

He just stared at her.

Her eyes widened, her throat working. "That's...yeah, that's..." She shook her head, at a loss for words. "Just great. Not terrifying at all."

He pushed on before they got sidetracked and he fucking chickened out. "You know what we do, what our job is. But being what we are, that mix of dark and light, good and evil...there's this, this constant struggle inside us. This push and pull. Usually, maintaining control, maintaining balance isn't a problem, but something happened to mess with that balance, and we're...struggling."

"That's...wow, a lot to take in. I can't imagine what you're going through, how hard that must be." She shook her head, her dark waves moving around her lovely face. "So something happened and now you're what? Getting pulled to your...um, dark side?"

"Yeah, that's exactly what's happening."

She was frowning, and he shouldn't be thinking how much that made him want to kiss her.

"What will happen to you? Is there something you can do?"

Eve looked genuinely worried, and there was good reason for her to be. Time to finish this. "There is something I can do, but I can't do it alone."

She sat forward, those beautiful eyes so intent on him his demon was damn near mesmerized by her. "What? What is it—"

Someone pounded on the door, startling Eve and she broke eye contact, twisting to look at it.

"Laz," Rocco called through the door. "You there?"

Lazarus cursed and strode to the door, wrenching it open. "What?"

His bother stood there, dressed to fight, his short sword —the weapon gifted to them by the angels and used by all the knights—strapped to his thigh. "Why aren't you answering your damned phone?" He stuck his head in the door. "Ahhh, right. Yeah, sorry, but we need you. All hands on deck."

"What's going on?"

"A bunch of rogues tearing shit up in the city."

"Rogues?" Eve was standing, her gaze on Rocco.

Like all the knights, his brother was tall and built, but he chose to decorate his face with a lot of metal and wore a short blue mohawk. The guy stood out in a crowd.

"Give me five to weapon up," Laz said. Roc gave him a chin lift and left.

"You're going to fight?" Eve said as he strode across the living room.

He stopped at his bedroom door, hand on the frame, fingers digging into the drywall, pissed the hell off. He had been so damn close, so close to telling her.

"Is it dangerous?" she asked, gorgeous blue eyes full of fear.

Was that fear for him? Did she actually give a shit what happened to him? Christ, he hoped not. "It's what we do. We fight demons and we send them back to hell." He walked away, unable to look at her any longer, and quickly strapped on his weapons.

When he walked back out, she was standing in the middle of the room, looking unsure. "Stay here if you want, until you're feeling better. I'll be gone awhile." It was crazy how much he wanted her in his place, to know that while he was out fighting she was here, safe in his room. His demon liked that idea as well, the bastard close to purring at the image that flashed through Lazarus's mind, of Eve...naked, asleep in his bed.

Ready for him when he returned.

He gritted his teeth and headed for the door, every step feeling weighted, everything in him not wanting to leave her. Shit. He yanked the door open and turned back to her. She was chewing on her bottom lip and he wanted to lick it, suck that full, abused lip so bad his gut ached.

"We'll talk tomorrow," he forced out, voice wrecked. Then he left before she could answer, closing the door tight behind him.

The knights weren't the only ones affected by the equinox drawing closer.

The demons that'd made Earth their home could be equally affected, though Lazarus had never seen anything like this.

The back of the sandwich shop was coated in blood, human remains hanging around the room like twisted decorations—a hand here, a foot there, intestines dangling from the light above—while three naked Leathren demons, coated in blood, fucked on the shop floor, completely oblivious to the company they now had.

Leathren usually kept to themselves, preferred their own company, and were known for their shy natures. They didn't eat human flesh or any other for that matter. The demons fed off other people's pain and suffering, but they never caused it. They were scavengers. In Hell, they hung around torture chambers, absorbing screams and cries. On Earth, they were usually found near the sick or stalked human killers and abusers to get their fix.

This was not in their natures, none of it.

Rocco turned to him, brows raised, just as confused as Laz. Gunner stood on the other side of the ménage looking no less confused.

"What the fuck is this?" Roc said.

"I don't even think they know what they're doing," Gunner said.

He was right. Their eyes were glassy as hell, oblivious to the knights standing just a few feet from them.

Gunner twirled one of his blades. "We can't let them live. They've killed humans."

Laz agreed. "We'll take out two of them and bring one in for questioning. Something is way off here."

They were about to move in when all three demons stopped what they were doing, lifted their heads, and turned to them, eyes still glazed and teeth bared.

"Creepy fuckers," Rocco muttered.

He was not wrong. He and his brothers pulled their weapons, about to move in, when all three demons jumped up, ran to one of the work stations, and in unison each picked up a knife. Instead of coming at them, though, they lifted them to the base of their throats.

"Fuck." Rocco ran for them.

He didn't make it.

The three demons were ashing out moments later.

"Christ," Rocco said. "What the hell was the point of that?"

Laz shook his head. "Fucked if I know."

Gunner pulled out his phone. "I'll take pictures of this place, show the others. Zenon might know something."

Zenon was their resident expert on Hell and the only one of their brothers who had been there, though he never spoke of it. If this was some kind of ritual, he'd know.

They left a short time later, leaving the place for the human police to find. Their forensics couldn't pick up demon or angel DNA so they were safe.

"You think Diemos was behind whatever that was back there?" Roc said.

"Fuck knows." The ruler of Hell somehow had the ability to communicate with the demons he sent out, but that wasn't a group of demons following an order. That was something else completely.

"I need a drink," Rocco said.

He wasn't the only one.

They ended up at a bar in the center of the city. It was owned by a demi they knew well, and the clientele was varied, in other words not just human, or demon for that matter. But the difference was the demons that came there followed the rules, had been given sanctuary, and knew how lucky they were to be allowed here on Earth. The other beings here were of no concern to the knights and they left each other alone.

78

Gunner came back from the bar with a bottle of whiskey and three glasses and put it in the middle of the table. Rocco poured.

"So, you mated yet?" he asked, sliding a glass over to Laz.

"What do you think?" He downed the drink and motioned for another.

Rocco sat forward, expression serious. "I *think* you're overthinking this when you know there's no other option. Get it over with. Plus, she's hot. What more do you need?"

"Jesus, you have no fucking clue," Laz said then looked at Gunner. "What about you? Nothing to add?"

His brother shook his head, running his hand over his buzz cut, the scar through his lips twisting his mouth when he smiled. "It's your life not mine, brother. I don't have to worry about that yet, and until I do, I'll take my pleasure where I can find it."

Something moved through Gun's eyes, something he couldn't name. Laz had seen it before, but Gunner didn't like to talk at the best of times. There was no chance of getting the guy to open up.

Gunner stood then and headed toward the group of hellhounds across the bar. The New Jersey pack was lethal and only came to Roxburgh for business. Gunner had struck up a friendship with a couple of them and because of it, they helped the knights out from time to time. One of their males and his bitch had been watching Gun since he came in. Gunner leaned in, said something in the guy's ear, and then they all headed to the back of the club and the exit to the alley.

"The guy needs to talk instead of fucking away his feelings," Rocco said beside him.

Laz snorted. "Besides Zen, I'd say that pretty much describes every one of us." Though as appealing as the idea of fucking away his feelings was tonight, there was only one woman he wanted, one woman he would ever want now he knew she existed. That's just the way it worked.

And he couldn't have her, not tonight, maybe not ever depending on what she said when he finally explained what he wanted, what he needed from her.

"Yeah, you're right," Roc said. "Best I get on that." He stood and melted into the crowd as well, making a beeline to a group of human females.

Laz stayed where he was. He had a bottle of whiskey to finish.

It was three in the morning when they landed on the balcony to the control room and walked inside. Alcohol didn't affect them like humans—they had to drink a hell of a lot more to get wasted—but Laz had managed a nice buzz. Maybe that would help him sleep.

James was behind a desk, working on one of the laptops, and lifted his head when they strode in.

As they neared, the guy frowned. "What the hell's that smell?"

"Gunner," Rocco said.

James's gaze slid to Gunner. "What is it?"

"Hellhound," Rocco filled in helpfully.

Gunner scowled.

"You were fighting hellhounds?" James looked worried.

"Nope," Rocco said, grinning. "Well, maybe. Fuck knows what they get up to between the sheets." He mock shuddered. "Do they stay in human form?" he asked Gunner. "Or does shit get kinky?"

Gunner growled and ran at Rocco, taking him to the floor.

Lazarus ignored them both, their grunts and James's cry

of alarm, because this was nothing unusual. Idiots. He shook his head and left them to it, hitting the hall and jogging down the stairs to his floor. She wouldn't still be there, of course she wouldn't, but the urgency riding him, making him almost run to his door, didn't give a fuck.

Then he felt her, the hum of her so strong he wondered why the door wasn't rattling off its hinges.

She was still there.

He unlocked the door and strode in.

Fuck.

Eve was asleep on the couch. Her body curled in a ball, knees tucked up, hands by her face. Her dark hair was splayed over the cushion under her head and it looked so damn soft he took a step closer, desperate to touch it. Her lashes were thick, the same intense black as her hair, and they rested against her pale skin.

And her lips…

Fuck.

They were cherry-colored and full, and Lazarus wanted to know what they would feel like against his, how they would taste, more than anything in his whole life.

He stood there, unable to make himself move. His demon was right there with him. Eve was in their domain, she was under his roof and under his protection, and both angel and demon couldn't be happier about that.

There was no leaving this spot. He was stuck. If he took another step closer, he'd touch her and he couldn't—not yet, not when he hadn't talked to her and not when he might lose control. But leaving the room, even going to his bedroom, wasn't an option. He needed to be where he could see her.

So he stayed right where the hell he was.

CHAPTER 9

EVE YAWNED and worked at opening her eyes.

Her body felt a little stiff, but her head felt fine, like the debilitating pain she'd felt the day before hadn't ever been there. She stretched and that's when she felt the couch at her back. She was still in Lazarus's apartment. Her eyes flew open as she pushed herself to a sitting position.

And gasped.

"Lazarus?"

He didn't answer her, was just standing across from her, features tight, pained. His jaw was set like granite, the vein in his throat pulsing. He was wearing the same T-shirt and jeans from the night before and the muscles in his arms looked carved from stone.

"Are you okay?"

He still didn't answer but nodded jerkily. It was a complete lie. She only had to look at him to see he was in some kind of pain. She stood slowly. She wasn't sure why, but the way he was looking at her, the unwavering stare, like a hawk about to go after a mouse, combined with the way the green in his eyes seemed to move and swirl—she felt approaching him cautiously was for the best.

His nostrils flared as she got closer, and impossibly, those carved-from-stone-muscles hardened further.

She reached out, placing her hand on his arm. Her gaze dropped to where she touched him. His skin felt a million degrees. He was like scorching rock beneath her hand.

A rhythmic vibrating sound started up.

God, it was coming from Lazarus.

Her gaze shot back up to his, and she gasped when the green of his irises was swallowed by midnight for a moment.

Lazarus hissed.

What the hell was going on? Something was happening, something Lazarus hadn't told her. He'd been about to last night, and she got the feeling the way he was with her, this pain or whatever he seemed to be in all the time, involved her.

"What can I do?" She slid her hand up his forearm to his monster biceps, trying to soothe him. God, pet him. Something. Anything. "Tell me, please."

His nostrils flared and he dipped his head, his movements jerky. Then he dropped his face to the crook of her neck and she froze as he breathed in deeply, dragging his nose up the side of her throat, over her jaw, until his lips were at her cheek, so close to her own.

The rhythmic sounds got louder. God, he was purring. There was no other way to describe it.

"Just one taste," he said. "Please…just one."

Eve swayed toward him, her entire body coming alive from the sound of his rough voice, the plea she heard in it. She didn't know what she was doing, but at that moment she didn't care; she'd give him anything he wanted.

She turned her head, and the outer corners of their mouths brushed. Her heart pounded harder. Lazarus growled and turned to her as well, dragging his lips over hers.

Eve opened for him instantly, her fingers digging into hard muscle, trying to pull him closer, wanting more. His big hand moved up to the side of her face, thick fingers sliding into her hair, and he tilted her head. His tongue licked into her mouth, sliding against hers in a way that was frenzied, hungry. More than meeting her own desperate need for him.

The purring grew louder, the vibrations from his chest going right through her. She squirmed. God, she felt it, right between her legs.

His other hand slid around her waist and he tugged her closer so she was plastered against his rock-solid body.

Someone knocked at the door.

Lazarus stilled, panting, chest pumping.

"You there?" Chaos called.

Lazarus was staring down at her, his eyes bright green now. He cleared his throat. "I need to answer that."

Eve nodded, unable to put together any kind of sentence.

His hands slid from her body and she felt their absence immediately. He stepped back, and again his movements were jerky, stiff.

They'd kissed.

Eve lifted her fingers to her tingling lips, trying to comprehend what she was feeling, what it was about him that drew her so strongly.

Lazarus's hand twitched at his side like he was going to reach for her again. But then Chaos pounded on the door and called out again.

He turned away from her, but not before she saw the muscle in his jaw jump. He yanked the door open. "What is it?"

Chaos took them both in, and if he suspected something

had just happened between them, he didn't let on. "We need you out on patrol."

Lazarus frowned. "You could have just texted."

"I did, and called as well."

Shoving his hand in his back pocket, Lazarus pulled out his phone and cursed. "It's dead." He thrust his fingers through his hair. "I'm right behind you." He turned back to her when Chaos left. "I have to go."

It was unexplainable, but she wanted to prolong their time together. "I'll walk out with you then I can swing by the kitchens and grab something to eat."

He nodded and she followed him upstairs. There was a new tension between them now, even stronger than before, and it lifted goose bumps all over her skin.

"The cafeteria's on the top floor," he said.

"Okay."

His gaze lingered on her for several seconds, like he wanted to say something more, but changed his mind, and finally headed off in the opposite direction. She watched him walk away. *Would* she see him later? Something was going on, something he wasn't telling her. She needed answers. Maybe they could have a meal together when he got back and talk.

Decision made, she ran after him to ask. Lazarus was already at the balcony doors when she walked into the control room.

He tore off his shirt and shoved as much as he could into his back pocket—

Massive charcoal wings sprung from his back.

She gasped and he spun to face her. His wings moved gently, and as they did, light shimmered across them, catching on flecks of silver.

"They're...beautiful," she whispered.

"Eve..."

Her gaze moved over his ripped chest and ridged abs... and the large bulge at the front of his jeans.

He cursed and took a step toward her, his wings folding in as he did. They vanished a second later like they hadn't been there. "Eve, I need you to—"

A low, vicious sound came from behind her, lifting the hairs on her arms. She spun around. Two of the others had joined them. Rocco and another male she hadn't met yet. They stood on the other side of the room, on opposite corners.

Both were huge, chests pumping with their rapid breaths, lips curled back, teeth clenched.

And at that moment they were focused on one thing—her.

Lazarus was suddenly beside her, sliding an arm around her waist, pulling her in close to his side. "What the fuck, Zenon?"

The guy she assumed was Zenon was breathing rapidly and his big body seemed to grow with every inhalation. He wore a black T-shirt that clung to his thick biceps and chest. The skin she could see was completely covered in tattoos. His hair was long and pure black and hung forward, obscuring most of his face.

He didn't take his eyes off her and growled. The sound began so quiet she could barely hear it, but as his chest heaved with every breath, it grew in volume until it was almost deafening.

She tried to scramble back, but Lazarus held her in his firm, unyielding grip, stopping her escape. The terrifying male took a threatening step toward them.

"Do not take another step," Lazarus said, voice deadly.

What the hell was going on? Wasn't this supposed to be some kind of safe haven?

"I don't want to," Zenon gritted out. His nostrils flared

and the look he sent Lazarus was one of pure hatred. "I can't help it. What the fuck is she?"

"What is wrong with you?" Lazarus seemed genuinely confused by the other male's reaction.

Zenon didn't, or couldn't, answer and continued to pant in harsh, ragged breaths.

A hiss came from the opposite side of the room and Lazarus spun to face Rocco. He shook his head like an angry beast, light glinting off his facial piercings. He looked in pain.

"Something's wrong," Rocco said as his eyes lost all color, like Lazarus's had in her bedroom and became a hollow, black nothingness. "You need to get her away from me...or I'm—" He snarled suddenly and flung his head back. His body torqued violently, every vein and tendon strained, bulging through the exposed skin of his throat and down his heavy arms. After a few seconds suspended like that, whatever had held him let go. He hissed and lowered his head.

Then ran at her.

Lazarus shoved her back so hard her body slammed into the wall behind her. Zenon roared and came at them from the other side, his growls loud enough to rattle glass.

Her heart pounding out of her chest, Eve pressed into the unyielding steel at her back, scrambling to stay upright when her foot slipped, desperate to get the hell away. *Oh God.*

Zenon moved faster than Rocco and as he drew near, Lazarus planted his feet, legs apart, blocking her with his body. She curled her fingers around the waistband of his jeans, pressing herself into his back, clinging to him. His muscles bunched hard as he tensed, bracing for impact. But instead of coming at them, Zenon dove and tackled Rocco to the ground.

The sound of their bodies colliding was horrific. Neither one held anything back as they went at each other like wild animals.

The door crashed open again and Gunner and Kryos stormed in.

Their sharp gazes landed on the pair fighting. "What the fuck's going on?" Gunner growled, taking in the men bleeding and grunting on the floor. He had a buzz cut and a deep scar through his top lip. It puckered when he aimed his stare at her and hissed in a sharp breath.

Kryos moved in, dragging Rocco off the floor, tearing him from Zenon. Panting, Rocco dragged the back of his hand across his bleeding lip then pointed at her. "It's her...if Zen hadn't stopped me..." He didn't finish, didn't need to.

Four sets of eyes slid toward Eve. Three of them were nothing but dark, fathomless pools. Only Kryos's remained warm brown and conveyed only concern and curiosity.

"What is she?" Zenon growled again. His long hair no longer obscured his face, and a scar or burn marred his right cheek. Tattoos covered his entire neck, finishing at his jawline. In fact, besides his face, there wasn't a piece of exposed skin that wasn't inked. Intense hatred oozed from him, and when his gaze landed on her, his lips curled in distaste.

"Do not fucking look at her," Lazarus barked across the room.

None of them moved. Their gazes lingered, intense and terrifying.

"Kryos, get them the hell out of here," Lazarus roared.

Kryos, the only one besides Lazarus who seemed to have control, shoved at the males closest to him, but they didn't budge. Their massive bodies remained unnaturally still, heads cocked with identical expressions she couldn't decipher but turned the blood in her veins to ice. Finally, after another shove, they tore their gazes from her and stormed out.

Lazarus released a shaky breath and shoved his fingers in his hair. "Fuck."

Eve turned to him, confused and barely holding it together. "What just happened?" Her voice shook.

He blew out a harsh breath. "Fucked if I know."

When the door slammed open again, Lazarus crowded Eve, keeping her behind him. Her fingers still gripped his waistband, her body pressed close. She was trembling. It took all his self-control not to go after Zen and Rocco and do something he had never entertained once in his long life. Zenon was wild, some might even say unstable. You never knew where you stood with the guy or what he might do next, but Roc? He'd never seen the other male like that. Eve had triggered their demons' violent reaction somehow. He had no idea how, but his little demi had made herself a target.

Chaos stepped through the door and prowled across the room, teeth gritted. He looked more than a little pissed. In only a pair of faded jeans, there was no missing the Kishi demon he housed rippling and moving restlessly below his skin, desperate for release. Chaos's brown eyes flashed midnight as he stopped in front of him then slid briefly to the female huddled at his back. "I think we need to talk."

James walked in and Lazarus waved him over. "Take Eve out onto the balcony for some fresh air, would you?" Her grip tightened and she shifted around behind him, her fists pressing into his lower back. He reached around and gently eased her forward to stand at his side. She was scared as hell, the pulse in her throat fluttering madly as her gaze darted between him and Chaos. "It's okay, Eve. They're gone, and Chaos won't hurt you."

She gazed up at him, offering him a tantalizing flash of

trust. The look in her eyes was so damn innocent it made him yearn for something he couldn't have. He clenched his fists against the guilt that slammed him in the solar plexus with the force of a battering ram, because it was only a matter of time before she discovered the kind of male he truly was.

Their leader flashed a wide, white, somewhat pained grin, and Eve jumped.

"I just need a private word with Laz."

"Right, of course," she whispered.

Chaos's skin twisted and rolled across his shoulders and down his heavy biceps before his eyes flickered to midnight and back to brown again.

"Oh God." Eve plastered her body against Lazarus again. She hadn't let go of him, her fingers now hooked onto the belt loops of his jeans.

"Jesus. Can you put a goddamned shirt on?" Lazarus growled at the other male.

"No." Chaos shrugged, causing another roll. "It's uncomfortable."

Loosening her death grip, he held onto her frozen fingers and turned to face her, using his body to block Chaos from her view. He couldn't help himself and lightly cupped the side of her face. Her skin was smooth and warm, her cheeks flushed. "James is going to take you out on the balcony. I'll make sure no one else goes out there, okay?"

She nodded.

Shit. There it was again, that burgeoning look of trust. His stomach knotted and he turned away, feeling like a bastard. Chaos cocked a brow in question. He ignored him, and with surprising reluctance, handed her over to James, watching as he steered her across the room and out the double doors.

"What the hell just happened here?" Lazarus hissed as soon as she was out of earshot.

Chaos ran a hand over the tattoo covering one side of his shaved head. "Fucked if I know. The autumnal equinox is approaching, making shit a lot worse when we're already struggling."

The equinox was a catalyst, and with a little sacrificial blood to help it along, opened the portal between Hell and Earth. Leading up to it always messed with each of them, but the whole Tobias situation had made it a whole lot worse.

Chaos put his hands on his hips. "Maybe there's something with her power we haven't unlocked yet? Something that's magnifying the effect? Maybe it's something else, something that calls to our demons. Fucked if I know, but, brother, whatever it is, it's strong."

"You feel it?" Laz asked him.

Chaos's jaw ticked. "Yeah, I feel it."

Going by the roll of his flesh and the color of his eyes, Eve's being at the compound affected Chaos just as much as the others. It was only the sheer strength of his will that prevented him from behaving like Zen and Roc, and the reason they had appointed him their leader.

Chaos cursed, sucking in a breath, and grabbed for the desk beside him.

Lazarus winced as the points of his friend's wings stretched below his skin, rising above his shoulders before disappearing again. With the ongoing struggle to keep their demon halves under control since Tobias's defection to the "dark side" the knights had only allowed themselves partial shifts. Wings only. Chances were good they wouldn't be able to change back from their Kishi forms if they did, and that would suck big time.

"In our weakened state, our demons will continue to try to overthrow us. And I'm thinking the only way to protect her, and us is to make her your mate." He gritted the words out as if nothing had happened, as if his demon wasn't writhing just below the surface, desperate to explode out of his skin.

Lazarus scrubbed his hands over his face. That demon side desperate for escape in each of his brothers had sensed something in Eve, something unknown, something extremely powerful.

Which meant Chaos was right.

"The gateway is thinning as the equinox approaches. Without knowing what it is about her that's affecting our demons, we can't control it, and having her here around your brothers while you're unmated, it's too damn dangerous."

Lazarus's stomach knotted. He'd really gone and fucked everything up. He was the reason his world had shattered into a million shards of utter hell. *His* weakness had kicked off the mess they all found themselves in now, and his brothers were still paying the price for it.

Chaos must have read the look on his face, and thankfully, didn't push. "Take her to your room, put up a shield, and keep her the fuck there until you've claimed her. She's too dangerous to move around the compound."

Chaos took off, and Laz collected Eve and led her into the elevator, hitting the next floor down. She was going to be stuck in his apartment, with him, until they figured this out or they mated, and he didn't know how he was going to keep it together having her that close 24/7.

Eve stayed close by his side as he hustled her toward his quarters. Once inside he could use his powers to veil the erratic energy she was throwing out, and hopefully give his brothers a break. She must have a million questions and he knew she was waiting until she was in the safety of his rooms to ask them. And shit, somehow, after witnessing Roc and Zenon losing it back there, and Eve knowing that Lazarus and his brothers were made the same, that they had the same kind of vicious demon inside them—he had to convince her to mate with him.

Fuck.

A crash sounded behind them followed by Kryos's voice echoing down the hall. "Run!"

He didn't bother to turn around. The sound of growling, of pounding boots sprinting after them, said it all. Scooping Eve in his arms, he ran for the end of the hall and threw the door open to his apartment. It slammed behind him and he threw up a field of energy that should keep his brothers out. The other male didn't make it that far. Another crash came as they hit the floor. Kryos had taken him down before he got there. As the only mated male among them, Kryos was the most stable. Eve didn't seem to be affecting him at all. Proving Chaos right. Mating would solve this, whatever it was. Rocco's hissed protests echoed through the door seconds later as he was dragged away.

At that moment, Lazarus became aware of the warm female bundled in his arms. She'd buried her face against his neck and her rapid breaths tickled his skin, sending tingles across his scalp. "You all right, Eve?"

"No," she said, voice muffled.

Her lips lightly grazed his throat when she spoke, and he fought not to shiver in response. Jesus. He couldn't take much more of this. Now he'd tasted her, he wanted to kiss her again in a way that went beyond desperate. Lowering her to the ground, he took a step back. "I'm sorry if they scared you."

"Scared me? I'm terrified. Why did you even bring me here? You said I'd be safe."

That knot in his gut twisted. "You will be, I promise. I will keep you safe."

93

She wrapped her arms around herself. "What was that? What's going on, Lazarus?"

"I know you have a lot of questions, and I will answer them."

"When?"

"Soon." Yeah, he was a fucking coward, but he wasn't ready to have that discussion with her, not yet. It was pathetic, and he didn't know why he was torturing himself, but he wanted one more day. One more fucking day of *what if*, of what might have been, before that look of budding trust on her face disappeared for good and turned to fear and disgust.

He craved that look like a starving animal.

Her eyes narrowed. "Lazarus—"

A quiet knock at the door thankfully interrupted whatever Eve was about to say. "Yeah?"

"It's Meredith. Can I come in?"

He pulled the door open and motioned for Kryos's mate to enter. "How's Roc?"

"Ashamed of himself. He sent me to apologize to Eve."

Eve took in the woman in front of her. Meredith was beautiful, tall and slim, and the stunning smile she directed at Eve was kind. "He really is sorry. If it wasn't for—"

Lazarus cleared his throat, stopping the other woman mid-sentence. Frowning, Eve shot him a look. But he'd moved to the small kitchen off the living room and started messing with his coffee machine.

"Anyway." She tucked her hair behind her ear. "You're safe with Kryos and me. Since we're mated, he has all of that"—she aimed her thumb back toward the door—"under control."

Eve frowned. "Mate?"

Meredith's smile widened and her eyes softened. "Yeah, he stormed into my life and swept me off my feet." She chuckled. "I've been waiting a long time for another—"

"Coffee?" Lazarus barked from the kitchen.

They both jumped and spun to face him.

"No. Thanks," Meredith answered, her gaze moving back and forth between her and Lazarus. He wasn't subtle in the least. He was stopping Meredith from telling her something, and Eve wanted to growl in frustration.

"Okay. I better head out. If you need anything, anything at all, I'm just down the hall." She glanced back at Lazarus as she spoke. "I'll come back in…a couple of days?"

He nodded and crossed his arms.

"If you need to talk before then, just ask Laz for my number."

"Thanks, I—" A sudden wave of nausea took Eve by surprise, causing her stomach to roll. Oh God, she was about to throw up. Her vision swam and she reached for the back of the couch.

"Lazarus." Meredith's voice sounded panicked.

"Eve?" Lazarus called.

His voice grew distant, his footfalls muffled. Her vision dimmed, shrouded in darkness like a shadow moving over her, right before she crumpled to the floor.

The last thing she saw was Meredith's worried expression and Lazarus stalking toward her.

CHAPTER 10

SHE WAS SO STILL.

Lazarus wished Eve would fucking move, make a sound, something. But she just lay there pale and motionless. The two times she'd opened her eyes in the last day and a half, she'd stared blindly up at him, not really there. Not back with him.

When she'd collapsed and he'd pulled her into his arms…

A knot lodged behind his rib cage as unwanted memories and emotions flooded his mind. He squeezed his eyes against them, but this time he didn't have the strength to force them back.

"Don't leave me, sweet girl. I need you here with me. Tobias needs you." Scarlet's *mouth opened and blood bubbled up between her lips, cutting off whatever she was trying to say. He rocked her in his arms. "No. Please, God, no."*

"Lazarus?" Chaos's insistent voice pulled him from the past. The male stood at the door, Kryos at his side. "Are you all right?"

"Yeah." A complete lie. He was nowhere near *all right.*

Chaos narrowed his eyes, seeing it for himself. "Look, Lazarus—"

"What do you want, Chaos?" He was in no mood for a deep-and-meaningful or a fucking lecture.

The big male crossed his arms over his chest, watching him closely then tilted his head toward the bed, toward Eve's still form. "Any change?"

"Not yet."

Laz hoped he'd drop it, whatever was on his mind, but then the guy frowned and ran a hand over his tattooed skull. "We don't have time for this."

Kryos's brows hiked to his hairline. "I'm sure Eve feels terrible that her loss of consciousness is inconveniencing you, brother. You can tell her off when she wakes up."

Chaos scowled. "That's not what I meant and you know it."

Lazarus wasn't interested in listening to their bickering. The two males were polar opposites and butted heads like angry bulls on the regular. Chaos had tunnel vision, always focused on the greater good—more often than not at the expense of everything else, including his own happiness. Kryos sometimes forgot that being a heartless bastard was what made Chaos an excellent leader.

"Enough." Laz stood, reluctantly leaving his post at Eve's bedside.

"We need to talk." Chaos motioned to the living room.

"I'm not leaving her alone. We can talk in here."

That pleased the other male. Chaos didn't even attempt to hide the satisfaction written all over his face, and no doubt assumed Lazarus's unwillingness to leave Eve meant they were close to mating.

Lazarus decided now wasn't the time to correct him.

～

Eve's eyes felt weighted down. Had she ever felt this tired in her life? She tried to move but stopped quickly when pain sliced through her left arm.

Low voices reached her then, penetrating her foggy brain. More than one person was in the room with her. She tried to open her eyes again, but they wouldn't cooperate.

"Is Meredith all right?"

Eve barely suppressed a shiver at the sound of Lazarus's unmistakable deep voice.

"She's worried," someone else said.

This voice held a quiet intensity. It was soothing, nice. She was pretty sure it was Kryos.

"Tobias has left the city, has put distance between us. We can all feel it. He hasn't covered his tracks, at least not his general location. When you get there I'm sure he'll fuck with you. But he wants you to follow."

"He's trying to get Lazarus on his own," Kryos said. "Let me go with him. I'm the only one of us who's stable. Let me go after T."

"Yeah, and Laz has no choice but to follow him. He's not going to reveal himself to any of us. It's Laz he wants. If I send you with him, we'll lose our chance to take him down."

There was a grumbling sound.

"I fucking hate sending you on your own, but it's the only way we're going to get him out of hiding. And with the way your brothers are right now, they're too unstable to be around her. Brent's wards are rock solid. She'll be safe there." This new voice was hard, determined.

"She can't travel, not yet," Lazarus said, low and just as determined.

"As soon as she's well enough to be moved, get her the hell out of here." There was a pause. "Give her this."

"What is it?"

"Silas has decided to insinuate his superior, holier-than-thou ass in our business. We're on the verge of war and *this* he decides requires his fucking attention. I don't like it."

A light jingling sound, then Laz growled. "What the hell do I do with it?"

"You know how mysterious that angel can be. All I know is she has to wear it. He said it's for her protection and will give you the time you need."

Angel?

They talked some more about whatever *it* was, which made no sense whatsoever to Eve. Then Laz said, "She's been in and out of consciousness, but hasn't woken fully. As soon as she does, I'll make the arrangements."

"Good." A pause. "Just remember that Silas's gift, it's not a cure, it's a Band-Aid. You can't fuck around with this."

"You don't think I know that?" Lazarus's deep, rumbling voice carried a note of torment that hit her behind the ribs.

"Once she's out of the compound, things around here will settle back to the usual semi-violent hum. Isn't that right, mighty leader?"

"God, you're a dick," the pissed voice cut in.

"If you say so, oh wise one."

"So help me, Kryos…if you fucking bow to me one more time…"

There was a snort. "Listen, Laz, I know you don't want this, but claiming Meredith was the best thing that ever happened to me."

The room was silent for several seconds then Lazarus said in a low voice, "You're right. I don't want this."

"Shit." There was another pause. "Looks like you got your reprieve. But remember"—there was more jingling—"this isn't a permanent fix."

"You can't claim her yet anyway," someone else said. "Not until she's recovered. The surge of power you send her during the mating could hurt her or worse."

She stiffened. *Claim? The mating?*

"Eve?"

She jumped.

"Are you awake?" Lazarus asked, followed by the sound of someone moving closer.

She blinked heavily, forcing her eyes to open. Her vision was kind of blurred, but she could still make out Laz and Kryos standing a few feet away. Chaos stood behind them, scowling.

"How are you feeling?" Lazarus asked, voice gruff.

She felt weird, fuzzy. But mainly she felt confused.

"Eve…" He took another step closer.

God, she couldn't think when he was near. Her mind spun with everything she'd just overheard. They'd been talking about her. She didn't understand it—or maybe she did, at least some of it—and that scared her all the more. She lifted her hands, panic taking over. "Stay back…I want you to stay the hell back."

The other two males exchanged heavy stares.

"Goddammit, just tell me. Tell me what's going on?" Fear, and she was ashamed to admit, betrayal laced her words. She tried to wiggle back but winced when pain again shot through her arm.

He took a small step back and shoved his fingers through his hair. "You're injured. You need to be still or you'll tear open your stitches."

"Stitches?" She lifted her arm. A thick white bandage was wrapped around it and angry purple bruising peeking out from the edges. "How?"

Lazarus's jaw hardened and the other two exchanged more looks. "You fell when you blacked out. You knocked a glass bowl off the cabinet. It smashed when you landed on it."

Her head throbbed. "I don't understand."

He turned to the other males in the room. "Leave us."

They did as he asked after several more intense looks were exchanged, leaving her and Lazarus all on their own.

Lazarus frowned. "It could've been a lot worse. Do you remember what happened?"

"I felt sick…dizzy. That's all I can remember."

"This ever happen before?"

"No."

His gaze darted away from hers. "Right. Must have been all the excitement. You need to rest. We have a flight to catch in the morning."

Excitement wasn't the word she'd use. And he was still avoiding her question. "Where are we going?"

"Chicago. We'll be staying with a friend of mine there for a while."

"Why?" That wonderful scent of his hit her, surrounded her. He didn't answer, instead watched her closely, and she forgot what was so important that she would rather talk than sleep.

"Rest, Eve." His voice turned velvety smooth and brushed across her skin like a caress. She could do nothing but obey. The sheets were soft and smelled like Lazarus, and she snuggled down, letting her lids drop.

When Eve woke again it was to the smell of food. Her stomach rumbled. When had she eaten last? She couldn't remember.

She flexed the fingers on her left hand and winced. *Ouch.*

The bed dipped and a hot dry palm gentled across her forehead, brushing back her hair.

"Eve, wake up, sweetheart."

For the first time, Lazarus's voice held no anger, no pain,

or urgency. He spoke low and soft, and the natural rasp to it made his words a sensual caress.

He'd called her *sweetheart*.

Her belly fluttered and a zing of pleasure shot between her thighs. The feeling didn't let up, quickly becoming a low, insistent throb.

What the hell is happening to me?

His warm, rough fingers brushed her forehead again. "Eve?"

Goose bumps rose across her skin when he said her name. She didn't like the way her body reacted to the barest touch from him. When she opened her eyes, he sat beside her, watching her. His hair was damp. He wore jeans and a black T-shirt, and the heady mix of the soap he'd used mingled with his own unique scent invaded her senses.

"Hey," he said.

She shivered at the sound of his voice, and her reaction annoyed her. She brushed his hand away then struggled to sit. When she couldn't, she sighed and gave up. Her whole body felt weak for some reason.

"How are you feeling? How's the arm?"

"Okay, I guess. It stings a little."

He checked the tape holding her bandage. "It'll only sting another day or so. Can you sit up?"

"I don't think so."

"Let me help." He slid his arm around her shoulders and gently lifted her forward then tucked another couple of pillows behind her back. His fingers grazed her hip as he withdrew his arm and the skin beneath tingled.

She took a moment to take in her surroundings. She'd been in his apartment but not his bedroom. The bed was huge, the headboard dark wood, and carved into it was an intricate design that she couldn't fully see in her current position. It looked like some kind of battle scene. The duvet cover was deep blue and the pillows were blue and gray. Besides a chunky dark wooden dresser and a pair of bedside tables, there wasn't anything else in the large bedroom.

His features were soft, and she couldn't hold his gaze with him looking at her like that. She felt safe in this room, and the idea of leaving was a frightening prospect. "When we leave tomorrow, what happens if another Orthon comes after me?"

"I'll kill it."

The quiet danger in those three words made her pulse pick up speed. He'd kill for her again, would try to protect her like he'd promised. "What if there's more than one, what if—"

His jaw clenched, and all softness dissolved. "You don't need to worry, Eve. I won't let anything happen to you."

She'd made him angry. Again. And unless they had a handbook on how not to piss off giant scary demon hunters, she guessed this was going to happen a lot.

"So what do you have on the tray?" she asked to change the subject. As much as she wanted answers, she got the feeling she wasn't going to get them from him. Not yet anyway. And honestly, she wasn't sure she was ready to hear them.

His big body relaxed. "Chicken, salad, and a baked potato with sour cream, I believe."

"Sounds good."

He lifted the tray from the bedside table and placed it on her lap. He unscrewed the lid from a bottle of water and handed it to her then sat back against the headboard and watched her. Intently.

"Um, have you eaten?" she asked.

"Yes."

His voice was back to velvet. Okay, no more talking. That voice was doing things to her, things she did not want it to do. If he wanted to watch her eat, so be it. After several tries, it was obvious her injury made it impossible to use her left hand, not until the stinging pain stopped shooting up her arm every time she tried to grip her knife.

Lazarus obviously noticed as well, because he scooted forward, and without a word, took the cutlery from her hands. He cut a piece of chicken then topped it with a little potato and salad, and lifted it to her lips.

Her cheeks heated. "No. I can do it."

"Eat," he ordered.

She stared at him, stunned, though she shouldn't have been. She'd already worked out the guy was a control freak. He stared back until she could no longer bear it.

"Bossy," she mumbled.

His lips quirked on one side, not quite a grin, but close. He didn't say anymore, simply held the fork to her mouth, and waited. She was hungry and the chicken looked good, so she ignored her ire at the order and opened her mouth. He fed her like that, his gaze getting darker and hungrier with every bite she took, and she didn't think it was for the food.

By the time the plate was empty her heart was pounding hard and she was light-headed. He lifted the plate from her lap and placed it on the table.

Covered in blankets, she was utterly decent, but as his gaze moved over her face and traveled the length of her body, she swore she felt the path of his stare heating her skin.

He stood suddenly. "Try to stay awake and I'll run you a bath."

That sounded wonderful. The bathroom was off to the right, and Lazarus went and got the water running, then he walked back out, came around to her side of the bed, and without warning, threw back the covers.

Eve squeaked in surprise.

Lazarus paused, eyes fixed on the parts of her he'd just exposed. The shirt she wore had ridden up past her hips, and she grabbed for the blankets, but his big hand shot out, stopping her.

"What are you doing?" she said, voice shaky.

She hated her thighs and ass and right then it was all hanging out for Lazarus to see. Plus, the way he was looking at her was freaking her the hell out.

He didn't respond. His gaze locked on the birthmark on her hip, half concealed by the edge of her panties. A thick finger grazed her waist then slipped under the elastic, easing down the side of her underwear to reveal the strawberry mark.

"You always had this?"

"Yes." Her heart skipped a beat.

He didn't say any more, but slid an arm under her knees and one behind her back and scooped her up, carrying her *again*. Mortified, she tried to protest. "Please put me down. I can walk. I'm too heavy."

He snorted and completely ignored her. She had no option but to hold on and let him carry her. He strode into the bathroom, lowered her to her feet, then bent over the bath. He turned off the water and tested the temperature. When he turned back he reached for the hem of the T-shirt she wore and started to lift it.

She grabbed his wrists. "What are you doing?"

"You can't take a bath in your clothes, right?" He lifted the faded gray tee past her hips.

She stopped him again. "I'm not getting naked in front of you."

He grinned. A full-on wolfish grin that flashed straight white teeth and a sexy dimple in his right cheek. She felt it in her lower belly, and that throb between her thighs increased alarmingly. His harsh features softened when he smiled.

"You're injured, Eve. I promise I won't look if it makes you uncomfortable."

Dammit. She needed help; there was no way she could lift it over her head on her own. "You can help with the shirt, but you have to close your eyes."

His grin widened, but he did as she asked. And she got mad at herself because all she could think about was how long and dark his eyelashes were resting on his tanned skin.

It took a couple of tries, but after some careful maneuvering, he got her injured arm free. A warm hand moved to her bare back as he lifted the shirt the rest of the way over her head, causing her to stumble forward. Her chest collided with his, crushing her breasts against his body. Her nipples hardened from the contact. She blushed, mortified.

Lazarus sucked in a sharp breath, which meant, yep, he felt it.

Thank God his eyes were still closed.

"You good from here?" he rasped, taking an abrupt step back.

"Yes…thank you."

"I'll be in the other room if you"—he cleared his throat—"if you need anything." He spun around, almost crashing into the wall. He quickly sidestepped, strode out, and shut the door behind him.

Eve didn't linger in the bath long. She managed to dry herself and, with some contorting, put on the clean shirt he'd left for her by herself. Another one of his shirts. It was oversized, like the man himself, and soft. She could smell him on it.

God, that scent of his, it did things to her.

When she walked out, he was sitting on the bed, his bare feet crossed at the ankle, his back against the headboard. He was working on a laptop.

He glanced up from what he was doing when she shut the

bathroom door behind her. His gaze slid down to the shirt she wore, and his eyes flared. She wanted to yank it down to cover her fat thighs, but her arms were crossed over her chest, covering her nipples.

Where the heck were her clothes?

"Get into bed, Eve."

She swallowed hard, unable to make her feet move. "Hmm?"

"You need to rest. We have to be up early in the morning." He flicked back the sheet on the other side of the bed and turned back to what he was doing on the computer.

Now she was more alert, not so drowsy, it felt extremely weird getting into his bed, especially when he was sitting on it. They'd shared that one kiss. Maybe it was nothing. Lazarus hadn't mentioned it again. But it was all she could think about, especially now she was about to crawl back into his bed.

Still, she did as he said, because what choice did she have?

How the hell was she going to sleep with him right beside her?

He sat on top of the quilt, wasn't even touching her, but his presence sat heavy in the room and again made her body react in ways she didn't want it to.

She climbed in, pulling the covers over her. He didn't say anything for the longest time. Maybe he thought she'd gone to sleep.

Finally, the bed shifted when he got up, followed by the sound of the laptop being placed on the bedside table. There was a rustle of clothing and she stiffened.

Was he going to get in and sleep under the covers with her?

"Ah, Lazarus..." She turned to face him. He stood by the bed, and the drawer in the side table was open. He had his shirt off and was wearing some kind of leather holster strapped across his chest. He pulled out one knife after another, strapping them to his ripped chest and thighs.

"I have to go out for a while."

His words registered, and she lurched into a sitting position, gasping when she put weight on her arm.

He quickly tugged on a shirt, and came around to her side of the bed, sitting down beside her. He reached for her, taking her wrist, moving his thumb idly back and forth across the pulse there. She couldn't take her eyes off the wicked-looking blades strapped to his large body.

"Eve…"

"You're leaving?" God, she hated the desperate, needy note to her voice.

"I'll be back before you wake, and James is just through that door if you need anything." He pointed to the door that led to the living room. "As long as you stay in my quarters you're in no danger. Do you understand?"

She didn't want him to leave, she wanted to go with him, but instead, she nodded.

He watched her for several silent seconds. "Good, that's good." He didn't take his hand from her wrist, kept on brushing his thumb over her skin, and whispered, "Sleep, Eve."

The last thing she remembered thinking was how good he smelled.

CHAPTER 11

THE TINY SHOP was painted black, with cursive script painted on a sign above the door. The Cauldron. Not very original, but that wasn't what Willow had been going for. The witch sold harmless love potions and other concoctions to humans to make a living, but what they didn't know was she was the real deal and the most powerful witch in New York. It was one of her spells that warded their compound. She'd helped them out, which meant she was under their protection, not that she needed it. The woman had her shop warded just as strongly.

"She say what this was about?" Lazarus asked Chaos.

The fighter shook his head. "She didn't go into details."

Willow had no room for a man in her life—her words—but she did take lovers, Chaos being one of them on occasion. Which suited him just fine, saved him from actually having to go out and be civil to another being, and God forbid he was forced to have a conversation with a woman. The male was efficient in all things. Even finding partners to bed.

He knocked and the door opened a few seconds later.

Willow looked pissed off, her red hair wild around her face, eyes flashing, and she tilted her head for them to follow. "The back room."

"What happened?" Chaos asked as they strode after her, their shoulders too wide for the tiny hall, forcing them to turn side-on.

"This." She gripped the door handle to her storage room and shoved it open.

"Jesus," Chaos muttered.

Lazarus took in the scene. A demon of unknown breed lay motionless on the floor. Well, its body was at one end and its head was on the opposite side.

"How did it get in here?" Laz asked.

Willow kicked the lifeless demon. "That's what I'd like to know." She turned to them and he was sure he could see flames in her eyes. "Somehow this piece of shit got in. Now I'm going to be up all night strengthening my wards. Do you have any idea how long that takes?"

"What did it want?" Chaos asked.

"There were two." She motioned to a broken window. "The other one got out through there when I was dealing with this one." She pointed to an empty spot on her shelf. "It took something of mine."

Chaos stiffened. "What the hell did it take?"

Her back straightened. "The finger bone of Golath."

"His what?" Chaos growled.

"Finger bone," Willow bit out.

"You had part of fucking Golath and never thought to tell us?"

The ancient demon was the first ever created by Lucifer, and it was his blood Lucifer used to create his handmaids, before the demon betrayed his master and escaped to Earth thousands of years ago.

The story goes that weeks after he escaped, overwhelmed

with hunger, the demon killed a group of children, gorging himself on them, then found a cave to rest. The townspeople tracked him with the help of a witch, and she slaughtered him while he slept. She cut him into pieces and fed him to her pigs so he couldn't be brought back to life.

It was said, but had never been proven, that those bones and where they lay were the location and the catalyst that caused the creation of the portal, the gate to Hell that opened on the equinox and solstice, that the knights protected.

"How much power does that thing have?" Chaos gritted out.

Willow paced away and back. "A lot. More than your average lowly demon would know what to do with...more than most witches could handle." She thrust her fingers in her hair. "Shit!"

"You didn't think to put the fucking bone somewhere more secure?" Chaos growled.

Her back straightened and her eyes flashed. "No one has ever gotten through my wards before."

Lazarus rubbed his temples, his damn head pounding. "Golath was a demon. Why didn't he ash out when he died?"

Willow tapped the demon corpse at her feet with the tip of her boot. "Same reason this fucker is still messing up my floor: a binding spell. He won't be going back to Hell the old-fashioned way. I'll harvest every part of this asshole. There are plenty of things he'll be useful for."

"So they're true, the stories?"

She nodded.

"And this witch, she kept Golath's finger?"

Willow drew in a shuddery breath. "I'm a descendant from her line. It was passed down to me by my mother. It's been in this family for thousands of years...and now I've... I've lost it."

"What would a demon want with it now?" Lazarus asked.

Willow stared at the empty space on her shelf, pain etched on her features, then she turned to them and shook her head. "Nothing good."

Fuck.

They left Willow's shop and walked out onto the street. And a familiar tingle crawled up Lazarus's spine instantly. *Demon.*

"Duck!" someone called from across the street.

A second later an arrow whistled past Chaos, narrowly missing him.

A cry rang out and they spun in time to see a demon drop to the ground behind them.

Lazarus stared down at the flailing demon. "What the fuck?"

The dark figure who had called out the warning, crossbow still in hand, spun and ran off.

Chaos tore off his shirt and extended his wings. "I'll try and catch up with them."

"I'm right behind you," Lazarus said. He quickly removed the demon's head so it would ash out, and then took flight.

Lazarus didn't go to his apartment when they returned to the compound. They were unsuccessful in their search for the owner of that arrow, which had pissed them both off. Something fucked up was going on and they needed to work out what. Or at least his brothers did. He had his own mission.

Tobias.

Head swimming after their search, he'd gone to the gym and trained until he could barely stand then collapsed on one of the couches in the common room. He barely slept because, like every night since Eve got there, since she came into her powers and he discovered her existence, he felt her like a throbbing beat in the center of his chest, beating through his veins, pounding in his head and his gut. And yeah, he knew the only way to stop it was to go to her, to make her his.

"Fuck." He shoved up from the couch and went back to the workout room. The equinox was here. They'd go out tonight, and he planned on avoiding Eve for as long as possible. If he went back to his rooms, Eve in his bed, those big blue eyes on him full of questions, he'd crack, he'd fucking shatter. He'd fall on her like a starving man.

After the fight was over later tonight, after he'd worked off all the volatile energy pounding through him, he'd do it. He'd go to her and tell her the truth.

~

The distant wailing of sirens and the low, steady thump of bass from the surrounding bars and clubs echoed off the walls around them.

The alley was free of the homeless, and no drunken couples were stumbling down there in search of privacy. No, evil permeated this place. Its sickly malevolence coated everything like toxic sludge, ensuring every living thing gave it a wide berth. Even the rats had scattered.

Humans continued to move about their lives, ignorant of what was about to invade their world.

Lazarus stood silently with his brothers, each male focused on the red brick wall ahead of them—but all he could see was a sleeping Eve. He'd caved and gone to check on her before they headed out. She'd been curled up in his bed, in one of his shirts.

Shit. She wasn't even there in the alley with him and she affected him, weakened him, caused him to lose focus.

The males at his side were subdued, feeling Gunner's absence as strongly as he was. Gunner had been too unstable

113

to join them. No one knew why it was hitting him as hard as it was, and it made an already shitty situation worse. To his left, Rocco bounced on the balls of his feet, twirling his blades, twitchy, spoiling for a fight. Chaos stood a little in front, legs braced apart, unmoving, alert. His short sword hung loose at his side. Kryos stood to Laz's right, throwing knives strapped to his bare chest and a Glock fitted with a silencer rested in his hand.

And as always, Zenon stood apart. Concealed by shadow, his wide shoulders hunched, ready to charge ahead at any moment. His hair hung forward, concealing the brand on his face, his Li Kweis, the twin axes he preferred to fight with, were strapped to his back on either side of his leathery wings, and his short sword was strapped to his thigh, like the rest of them.

He was one of them, their brother, but Zenon had chosen to keep that distance between them. Lazarus knew it was because, unlike the rest of them who had been raised on Earth, sired by Kishi males and birthed by fallen females, Zenon was Hell born, sired by an unknown fallen male to a Kishi female. He hadn't trained with them, and no one had known of his existence until he'd stepped through the portal. He was a genetic fluke, but he was as much a knight as the rest of them.

If only he realized that.

Lazarus gripped his own blade tighter—several more strapped to his chest and thighs—and waited.

Their powers were useless this close to the hell's gate, the gateway to Hell that popped up during the solstice and equinox, spewing out its inhabitants. As far as they knew this was the only portal. And the knights had been providing a welcome party for the demons that came through for centuries.

Some demons left out of curiosity, some to wreak havoc.

Others escaped to beg for sanctuary, but most were sent by Diemos, the sick, twisted head asshole of Hell, in his never-ending attempt to grow an army here on Earth. Preparing for the day that he found a way to open the portals for good.

Roc's boots crunched on the loose asphalt as he moved restlessly. "I wish they'd hurry the fuck up. I wanna slice into someone already." He faced the rest of them. "What do you think the chances are of T showing up?"

"He knows how bad we want him. He won't risk facing us all together," Chaos said without looking back. "He'll stay where he is. He knows Laz is coming for him which is exactly what he wants."

Kryos shook his head. "It still feels weird, y'know? T not standing with us."

"He made his choice," Roc snarled.

"We haven't suffered the loss of a mate. We don't know how we'd react." They all shut up at Kryos's quiet reply.

Then Zenon's eerie soft voice drifted from the shadows. "I don't plan on finding out."

Lazarus turned to him. "That's not a choice you get to make, brother."

Zenon reached back and drew his axes, shrugging his big shoulders. "I'm not like you."

Laz didn't get the chance to ask what he meant by that, because the wall ahead shimmered, a ripple of golden light moving across the surface like the brick was liquefying before their eyes. He tensed as five demons of varying breeds stepped through the activated hell's gate. Their hungry gazes darted around, searching for an opening.

"You know, it never ceases to amaze me just how butt ugly some of you fuckers are," Rocco said in a casual tone. "Or how stupid."

Kryos snorted beside him. Rocco wasn't wrong. Even in human form, this bunch made Freddy Krueger look like male-model material. Despite Rocco's casual words, he almost vibrated with rage and a need to fight. This group was nothing but a sacrifice, sent out first to distract them. More would be waiting to take their chances, and as soon as Laz and his brothers were busy fighting, would make a break for it before the gate sealed again.

Two of them were clever enough to realize Roc had just insulted them and growled.

Dropping all pretense of cool, calm, and collected, Rocco's patience evaporated and he lurched forward, his demon writhing restlessly beneath his skin. "Come on, you ugly fuckers. Let's go."

They fanned out, pulling their own weapons. The big one from the back stepped forward, a manic grin splitting its face. They learned why it was so pleased with itself when the mammoth dragged a human female from behind its back. Blood trailed down her neck and other wounds on her battered body. She looked like a walking corpse, her skin bruised and pallid, scarred emotionally and physically from months held below.

She'd been in the hands of absolute evil, her body used mercilessly, and in ways that would turn your stomach.

"Motherfucker," Kryos growled.

For the hell's gate to activate the demons needed to draw blood. Human blood was not necessary, but it was the most powerful. Which meant the gate would stay open longer.

Chaos cursed.

The female's eyes were blank, and she didn't make a sound nor did she struggle. Laz had seen that look before. Her mind had shut down, desperate to escape the unimaginable horrors she'd repeatedly suffered.

The demon fisted her hair and wrenched her head back, dragging its tongue up the trail of blood dripping down her throat. It grinned. "Let us past, Knight, or I'll remove her head."

Before anyone had the chance to answer, a whistling sound echoed above Lazarus's head.

The demons looked up.

Thud.

One of Zenon's axes landed dead center, almost cleaving the fucker's head in two.

"Jesus, Zen," Chaos muttered.

His fugly companions stared, stunned, for several seconds before all holy hell broke loose. The remaining four, knowing their options were limited, rushed them. They weren't particularly skilled and were dispatched with little effort. But more leaped through the portal and kept coming.

Two came at Laz. He took one out on the fly while the other circled him, trying to find an opening. Lazarus's demon rippled beneath his skin, desperate for release. It was a struggle, but he somehow managed to maintain his human form.

The demon struck out with its blade, but Laz deflected it with a kick to the sternum. The demon staggered back just as Chaos spun and swung, removing its head with his sword.

Kryos had closed in on the injured human female and shielded her as he fought. There were more demons than usual, the reason for that he had no idea, but it couldn't be anything good. Lazarus took out as many as he could, but more replaced them as soon as they were down.

He hissed in pain as a blade glanced off his ribs, and swung around to face his attacker. The coward had already taken off, running for the mouth of the alley. The next came at him before he could go after it. While they continued to fight, more were able to slip through and escape.

"There are too many," Chaos roared.

Laz couldn't move from his position as two more came at

him. He looked across at Zenon. He wielded both axes at once and was cutting through the demons surrounding him to get to those making a break for it. Zenon managed to create a gap and took off, his heavy boots ricocheting off the brick walls.

They were bloody and pissed off by the time they'd cleared out the alley, crawling out of their skins, vibrating with the need to take their Kishi forms. Zenon hadn't yet returned, so they partially shifted, unfurling their wings and took to the skies in search of him and any escapees. Kryos flew in front of Laz, the injured human cradled in his arms, then veered off, heading for a human hospital. Her memories of her time in Hell would be blessedly wiped by the time she got there.

Laz let the wind lift him higher, the brittle night air ruffling his hair and whipping through his clothes, cooling his overheated skin. He spotted an Ibwa demon, a monster that feasted on the bodies of the dead, running through an empty parking lot. He dipped his right shoulder and made a tight turn, determined to stop it. But before he could get there, Zenon swooped out of nowhere, his leathery batlike wings catching the moonlight before he scooped the flailing, screaming demon off the ground and took it high into the skies.

Its lifeless body hit the asphalt with a sickening thud moments later, then turned to ash, the breeze scattering it into nothingness.

Lazarus sucked in a sharp breath as Eve's call grew in strength. She didn't even know she was doing it. But it coiled around him, holding fast, making his head spin. He was powerless against it and for once didn't fight it.

He let it lead him home.

CHAPTER 12

LAZARUS WOKE with Eve pressed against him, and a raging hard-on. Not exactly conducive to the serious conversation he had to have with her this morning. First, he had to explain the heavy gold amulet he'd slipped over her head after she'd fallen asleep.

The piece of jewelry Silas gave them was supposed to help him somehow. Fucked if he knew what it did, but the angel had said "it was for her protection and would give him the time he needed"—whatever the fuck that meant. But they were leaving the compound today and he'd take any help offered to keep her safe.

He probably should have given it to her as soon as Chaos had given it to him, but, yeah, that would have meant questions he hadn't been ready to answer, still wasn't ready to answer.

He just hoped the angel's cryptic words meant what he thought they did, that they could slow things down, could take things at their own pace, but with the way he was feeling, he was having his doubts.

When he'd walked in last night, fresh from the hunt,

desperate to calm the demon within, he hadn't been able to resist climbing in with her, seeking her warmth. The connection between them was getting stronger by the day.

Christ. He felt like he was losing his mind.

With a little mewing sound, she wriggled closer, causing her shirt to ride up. Her soft warm belly pressed against his abs, scalding his skin, driving him insane. It took everything he had not to reach down and squeeze her delectable ass, spread her lush thighs, and bury himself deep inside her. His cock swelled and his hips surged forward of their own volition.

Fuck, he had to get out of this bed now.

But before he could move, she threw a leg over his hip, pressed her cheek against his chest, and burrowed a hand between their bodies, accidentally brushing the head of his achingly hard dick. He hissed and jerked back. "Fuck."

Her eyes blinked open, and she stared up at him in surprised confusion, looking way too damned adorable. *Fuck. No.* Shoving back, he scrambled out of bed and bolted for the bathroom before she got an eyeful of the tentpole in his boxers, and slammed the door.

"Motherfucker." Stripping off, he climbed straight into the shower and turned the temperature to cold. The water hit his skin like icy pinpricks, but did fuck all to cool his heated blood. Fisting his dick, he squeezed the turgid flesh, trying to kill his erection. *Dammit.* No matter how hard he tried to ignore it, he could still feel Eve's body pressed against his, her softness imprinted into his flesh, her scent branded into his senses.

His dick twitched against his palm, and he growled in frustration. He didn't want her in his head. She was fucking with his mind, not to mention his traitorous body.

Lazarus cursed himself for a fool, even as he rested a hand against the wall, gripped his heavy cock, and proceeded to jerk himself off with fast, brutal strokes. Sliding his palm from thick base to swollen head fast and hard. And all the while he thought about Eve's lips on his, the way she tasted, the way she felt pressed up against him. How those soft full lips would feel around his cock. That was all it took.

He gasped, coming in violent spurts, so hard his knees felt weak from it.

Resting his forehead against the cool tile, he took a minute to slow the beating of his heart before shutting off the water. On trembling thighs, he climbed out and tried not to think about the fact that in his mind it had been Eve's eyes watching him, Eve's hand working his dick, and Eve's name hissing through his lips as he'd emptied his balls.

Grabbing a pair of jeans from the laundry hamper, he shoved them on, opened the door, and walked into his bedroom.

Eve was sitting up, still under the covers, and she stared over at him warily. The heavy gold amulet he'd put around her neck last night was in her hands.

"What is this?" She traced the detailed angel's wings engraved on its otherwise smooth surface. "It's beautiful."

He doubted the delicate image was necessary for the amulet to be effective. Angels were just that damned arrogant.

When she looked up, she sucked in a breath. Her gaze locked on his chest, his brand. "Is that a burn?"

"Yes."

"That must have been incredibly painful."

"I barely remember. I've had it a long time."

Her eyes widened as she took in the rest of him. "My God, what happened to you?"

He glanced down at himself. He looked a lot better than last night. The bruising had all but gone, and the deeper slice he'd taken to the ribs was nothing more than an angry red line. He shrugged. "It's nothing."

"You've been hurt."

"I'm fine." He shoved his hands in his pockets. "I think it's time I told you a few things."

She released a shaky breath, but her voice didn't waver when she spoke. "I'd like that. I hate feeling so helpless."

Her inner strength truly amazed him. "That," he said, pointing to the necklace, "you must wear at all times."

"What is it?" He moved to her side and took it from her fingers. It was warm to the touch, heated from her skin. Lifting it, he slid it over her head, resting it between the swell of her breasts. It looked lovely around her neck.

Dammit, focus.

"The amulet is imbued with angelic power. I wish I could tell you exactly what it does. Angels like to be cryptic as fuck, but if they want you to wear this, there's a reason for it."

She tilted her head to the side. "Silas?"

Shit. "You heard us talking? What else did you hear?" The words came out harsher than he'd intended.

She shook her head. "Nothing really. I was pretty out of it. Silas is an angel?"

He released a relieved breath. "Yes." He was their own personal guardian angel, one who spoke in riddles and got his kicks out of confusing the shit out of his charges.

She nodded, and again amazed him with her strength. Her fingers brushed across the shiny golden chain. "Will it help with your brothers and how they reacted to me?"

"I don't know." Fucking Silas. Why couldn't he just say exactly what it did? Why all the damn secrets? "But it provides protection, wards against evil."

"Demons?"

He nodded.

She bit her lower lip. "What about…ah, what about you?"

Is that what she wanted? Something to protect her from him? He wished the amulet worked that way, for both their sakes. But when he woke up this morning, he realized it wasn't going to be that easy. Yes, her power was now masked from him, and the part of her that had made it possible for him to track her like he had when she first came into her power was blocked. And yeah, that was a really fucking good thing. No demon would be able to sense her while she wore it. But that weird tight feeling in his chest, the buzz in the back of his skull, that awareness of her, was still there just as intense as before, which meant, he was shit out of luck. Whatever Silas meant when he said it would "give him the time he needed" had nothing to do with dimming his desire for Eve, or the call to mate with her, like he'd hoped it would.

The amulet was designed for something else entirely. And he guessed for something more than what he'd discovered this morning. He just wished he knew what exactly.

"It doesn't affect me in that way," he said.

She tilted her head to the side. "Okay."

He couldn't read her expression, didn't know if she was pleased, disappointed, or indifferent. He shoved his fingers through his hair, at a loss for words, no damn clue how to proceed with her sitting there staring at him. "Christ, Eve, I'm sorry. I'm so fucking sorry."

"For what?" she said, voice a soft rasp that skittered across his skull.

"For throwing your life into chaos, for dragging you into my fucked-up world," he choked out.

Her fingers unconsciously toyed with the golden disk at her throat. "You had no choice. You saved me, Lazarus."

He cursed and stood, pacing away.

"What is it?"

He cleared his throat. "Just...don't take off the necklace."

She blinked up at him. "I won't."

"Look, I know you're frightened. My brothers, they scared you." Mother of all understatements. "But that wasn't them. I've talked to them, and they feel like shit for the way they acted. There's a lot going on at the moment. Shit that's fucking with us in a big way. Just know that I'll do whatever I have to. I'll make sure you're safe. No matter where I am." Once he and Eve were mated and everything had died down, this would be her home. These were her people. He needed her to trust them or he'd never be able to leave her.

She didn't speak, but watched him with those big innocent eyes. She was so damn sweet.

"Eve? Do you trust me to do that for you?" he asked, needing to hear the words from her.

She gave him an unconvincing jerk of her chin. It shouldn't, but her unconvincing response gutted him. He didn't deserve her trust, but he wanted it all the same.

"Take a shower and pack your stuff. We leave in half an hour." She flinched at his sudden abrupt tone. Jesus. He fucking hated that he frightened her so damn easily. But most of all, he hated that he cared.

Eve sat perched on the edge of a bed in the hotel room they'd checked into earlier while Lazarus stalked about restlessly. The guy really was huge, well over six feet. His hair was rumpled from him shoving his fingers into it repeatedly. The disheveled look didn't help soften him any.

The size of him, coupled with those hard features and lately a permanent scowl, ensured the guy had the same effect as an escaped grizzly when he entered a room.

As he moved, she couldn't help but admire the strength of his body, not to mention his lean hips and fine butt. What would it be like to be with a man like him? The thought had plagued her since waking pressed against his hard chest, his hand resting on her hip, his heavy legs tangled with hers.

She almost snorted out loud at the ridiculous notion. She'd certainly never find out. It was like their kiss had never happened. When she'd woken, he'd shoved her back like she had cooties then stormed to the bathroom and shut himself in.

Now they were stuck in an airport hotel due to a mess-up with their tickets, waiting for the next available flight. Lazarus wasn't handling this news well.

His jeans hung low, molded to his powerful legs as they ate up the carpeted floor. Heavy black boots carried him to a small table and chairs in front of the sliding glass doors, and he shrugged off his leather jacket, slinging it over the table.

He scowled deeper, crossing his arms, and glared out the window. The plain black T-shirt he wore strained around his biceps, and she couldn't help admire the intricate tattoo that completely covered his right arm. It snaked its way up the corded muscle, disappeared under the sleeve, and reappeared halfway up the side of his neck.

He was like no other man she had ever met, utterly masculine. She shivered at all that barely restrained power. He was so different from Eric it was laughable.

Would he stay with her when they reached their destination, or would he drop her off and go? Anxiety accompanied the thought along with an unreasonable feeling of loss. God, she was confused. Why couldn't she think when he was near? The desire that stirred inside her when she was with him was intense, completely out of her control, and made absolutely no frickin' sense.

That delicious scent of his filled the small room, demanding a response she didn't understand. Her body reacted once again, but no matter how nice he'd been, how well he'd taken care of her after she'd blacked out, how he'd made her feel when he kissed her, she couldn't allow herself to get attached. She didn't know him, not really. She wasn't anything special. This was his job.

"That's an impressive tattoo you have there. Did it hurt when you had it done?" she asked, needing to get out of her own head. Her reaction to being separated from him was ridiculous.

"I was born with it." He rubbed his hand over the large colorful symbols, each linked to the next. "It tells a story. What we are, where we come from. Each knight has one."

She wanted to ask what the beautiful symbols meant, but his closed-off expression made it clear the subject was not up for conversation. He confirmed it when he turned away, staring out the window again, shoulders tense.

"Are we safe here?" she asked.

"I don't think we've been followed. I can't sense any Orthon nearby, but I can't be sure," he said.

"That isn't very reassuring," she muttered.

He spun around, and his gaze pinned her to the spot. "I won't let anything happen to you," he said with a fierceness that made it impossible to doubt. "I promise you that."

She could only nod in answer, once again caught in the emerald depths of his eyes. Her body heated and her cheeks flushed at the reaction.

He turned back to the window. "I used a protection spell to ward the room. If they manage to track us, they can't get to you without doing serious, even fatal damage to themselves. Can you feel it?"

Ever since she'd stepped into their room, she'd been aware of a kind of faint electric current, a slight tingling across her skin. "I think I can, yes."

Without looking back, he said, "Tell me about your power, Eve."

Not a request. They hadn't really talked about her powers

since her collapse. Her training sessions had been cut short as well, and now she'd left the compound she wasn't sure how she was going to master them. The sudden change of subject was obviously a way to distract her, to stop her from worrying, but now she just had another thing to worry about.

They had the night to kill before the next available flight out. She'd rather watch a movie than talk about how afraid she was of the demon side of herself, but Lazarus wasn't the kind of man you argued with.

"When it first started, I could only hear a person when they were in my immediate vicinity, but lately it seems to have grown stronger. Sometimes I even get the odd image flashing through my mind," she admitted.

"It's developing. It'll only become more intense over time."

He delivered it in that same emotionless, matter-of-fact way. No biggie. Like the other bombs he'd dropped since he'd stormed into her life.

Because of this thing, because of what she was, she'd already been torn from her life. She couldn't see anything positive in her future if she couldn't master her power. How could she ever have any type of relationship with all that noise vibrating through her skull? Suffering through every one of their negative thoughts, streaming directly into her head, smacking her around the cranium until she was emotionally bruised and battered.

All she could see ahead of her was more loneliness.

At that moment, the fragile walls she'd built since Lazarus stormed into her life crumbled. It was too much. Eve tried to hide her face, horrified when the first sob tore from her throat.

"Eve?"

"Why me?" She shook her head in her hands. "I don't

want this. I don't want any of this. I wish you'd just…I wish you'd…" She was unable to say the words.

Footsteps moved toward her. Lazarus knelt and took her frozen hands in his, rubbing them between his large rough ones. He'd seen something in her, had heard it in her voice. "You wish I'd what?" he said, voice low, hard, terrifying.

She didn't want to talk about it. Not now, not ever. "Nothing. Forget I said anything."

"Answer me, Eve. You will finish that sentence." He placed a finger under her chin and made her look at him.

Humiliation colored her cheeks, and her gaze darted away, focusing on anything but the male in front of her. How could she admit to what had been going through her mind? What had gone through her mind more times than she wanted to admit, even to herself?

"Look at me," he growled.

Disappearing sounded like a fantastic idea about now, but he wasn't giving up anytime soon, and last time she checked, vanishing wasn't part of her skill set.

"Eve, look at me. Now."

No. Anything but this. Don't make me say it. As fascinating as the purple flowers on the curtains were, she couldn't stare at them all night. So she lifted her gaze, zeroing in on his chin, and after several seconds trailed up to his lips, lips that made her want things, so many impossible things.

Swallowing down the lump in her throat, she ignored the nerves flapping in her belly and locked stares with him. "I wish…I wish you'd ended all this for me the moment you'd walked into my store," she whispered.

His nostrils flared and his jaw clenched so tight she winced. "You want me to end your life?" he said so quietly she barely heard him.

She cringed. Hearing her own words out loud for the first

time made what had only ever been a thought in the back of her mind during her darkest moments, real.

He shook his head and those lips she'd been admiring curled. "I thought you were stronger than that. You're not the only person in the world to have a shitty life, Eve. And believe me, you're not the only person to want to check out and leave it all behind. But I will tell you this right now. You don't get to bail on me. Do you understand? I won't let you."

Anger welled up inside her. "Why the hell do you care?" she yelled. "You don't know anything about me or my life."

His nostrils flared as he dragged in a rough breath. "I want to…on both counts."

She shook her head, didn't want to hear this, didn't want to risk believing in him, or his empty words.

He cupped her jaw. "This new world, it's your world. Where you belong. It won't be a walk in the park, but things will settle down. You'll meet people like you. You will find acceptance…a life worth living. I promise you that."

Hope bloomed, no matter how much she wanted to deny it or try to squash it and protect herself from any more pain.

"I can help you, Eve. It may take time, but you will eventually be capable of blocking your power when you want to. Until then, I'll continue to do it for you."

She searched his eyes. "Really?"

"Of course." He smiled, a small curve of his lips, not like the one he'd given her in his bathroom back at the compound, but his face transformed. His callused hands worked hers, thawing the chill from her fingers like nothing else could, and sent little tingles up her arms as his skin grazed lightly across hers.

Her gaze moved over his features, hard, fierce, then down to his mouth. He would have looked brutal if not for that sensual mouth. He reached up and, using the pad of his thumb, brushed her cheek with tender care. It came away wet.

"I'm sorry, it's just…this is just…"

"Shhh, it's all right. It's going to be all right." He leaned forward and kissed her next tear away, followed by the next. Featherlight presses of those firm lips moved along her cheek, then worked their way to her jaw and across to her mouth.

Their lips met, the heat of his searing hers. Lazarus's big body tensed against hers for a split second, but then he repeated the touch, tentative at first. His tongue eased out, tasting the seam of her lips in a sensual slide that had her opening for him without thought or hesitation, and he swept inside.

Totally lost to the exquisite, drugging sensation of his kiss, the world dissolved around her. He growled low, pulling her in closer, gripping her tighter. She leaned in as well, needing to feel his body pressed against hers, and clutched at his shoulders. A whimper filled the silence, and she realized the needy sound had come from her. Reaching up, she threaded her fingers in his hair and tried to tug him closer, like that was even possible.

What started as sweet and gentle erupted into almost painful hunger. Her body went up in flames. This wasn't a slow exploration anymore; this was hard, urgent, all-consuming. This was madness, but she couldn't stop, didn't want to stop. Something happened when he touched her, and all sanity flew out the window.

She fisted his shirt and moaned into his mouth as he moved forward, looming over her, forcing her back on the bed. His hard body came down on hers while rough fingers tugged at the buttons down the front of her dress.

When there was enough room, he slipped his large hand inside, groaning as he cupped and squeezed her breast, pinching the hard nipple through the silk fabric of her bra. She whimpered as he continued to ravage her mouth. His tongue moved against hers with a sensual onslaught that left her head swimming and her body hot and desperate for more.

Her legs parted and his large body instantly filled the vacant space. The massive proof of his arousal brushed the most aching part of her and he growled again. One of his hands moved down to cup her rear, holding her tight against him, and he rolled his hips.

Eve cried out, both relieved and tortured by the pressure she'd been desperate for. His mouth trailed down her neck, sucking and nibbling, sending her into sensation overload as he ground against her again, the intense contact only heightened further by the lace of her panties moving against her sensitive flesh. She was wet and hot, and his repeated thrusts quickly brought her to the edge.

She shifted beneath him, tilting her hips to gain closer contact. She needed more, wanted everything. "Please, Lazarus," she whimpered. "Please, I need you."

He stilled abruptly, his powerful biceps locking under her palms. His big body shook and sweat beaded on his forehead.

"What is it?" Midnight flashed across his irises. "Lazarus…your eyes."

He flinched.

She reached up, touching his temple. "What's wrong?"

He shuddered and shook his head. "Nothing."

Her mouth fell open when he rolled his hips again.

"Don't stop," she gasped.

He thrust again, his teeth gritted.

Eve cried out, body trembling beneath him. Then she was coming, waves of heat, of pleasure, washing over her so strong all she could do was cling to him.

Lazarus's face went to the side of her neck, puffs of his

hot breath tickling her skin. They stayed like that for several minutes. He was still hard.

"Lazarus…"

He moved then, sliding off her but staying close. She tried to keep her eyes open.

"Rest," he said.

She didn't have much choice. She was exhausted all of a sudden, boneless.

Eve woke several times during the night, and each time Lazarus was there beside her. When she finally woke to the morning sun streaming under the curtains she was alone in bed. Lazarus stood by the window, looking out at the streets below.

"You're awake," she said, lifting to her elbows.

He turned to her, a tight, pained smile curving his lips. "Yeah. I wanted to make sure we're safe to leave. I can't sense anything close by."

She held the sheet close to her chest. "That's good."

His gaze slid over her. "It's time to get ready. We need to leave soon."

He turned away, giving her what privacy he could in the small room as she climbed out of bed.

"I'll just go freshen up." She rushed to the bathroom and closed herself in.

Some kind of force was pushing her toward him. She felt it, and it was so incredibly strong. She certainly wasn't acting like herself. She wasn't overly experienced, had only slept with two guys, and now she was throwing herself at a man, a demon, she hardly knew.

He'd gotten her off, but hadn't done the same.

She swallowed, a lump forming in her throat. Did he not want her like that? He'd kissed her twice, but last night he hadn't…

Eve shut down the direction her thoughts were going.

She stared at herself in the mirror, her still puffy lips from kissing him, her wild hair, and cringed. God, the guy had only been trying to make her feel better, and she'd jumped him.

Get it together, Eve.

This was a job for him. Nothing more.

She couldn't afford to forget that again.

CHAPTER 13

Lazarus led Eve to their seats on board the Boeing 737. Christ, he hated traveling this way, but they didn't have much choice. They usually used their own plane for times like this when they needed to travel with their demi, but since Gunner was their pilot, that option was out. Gunner had gotten worse, had locked himself in one of the holding cells below their compound, afraid he'd hurt someone.

Lazarus glanced at Eve. She hadn't met his eyes since this morning, had kept them hidden from him since they did what they had last night.

After the way he'd acted, her silence didn't surprise him. He'd come so damn close to taking her, to sinking inside her and losing his head completely. He should have pulled away, but there was no way he could have left her wanting. Every part of him had rejected the idea.

So he'd fucking rubbed up on her until she got off then he'd forced himself to stop before his control snapped completely and he'd taken more. Fuck, it had left him hurting.

That persistent hum, his constant awareness of Eve had

only gotten more intense. It felt like she was plugged directly into his nervous system and sent a continual electrical current straight to his dick.

Shit, having her soft, pliant body beside him had tormented him through the long night, but he couldn't make himself get up and sleep in the chair. She'd wriggled and squirmed in her sleep, had made these breathy little sounds, driving him crazy. He'd barely resisted finishing where they'd left off. Taking what he wanted. What he needed.

The situation was a huge mess, and after her confession last night—that she would rather die, than face this new life —he had to tread very carefully from now on. But the pain radiating from her had damn near killed him.

He scrubbed his hands over his face. His mind whirled, full of contradictions.

What the hell was he going to do? What if he couldn't convince her that mating with him was the best decision for both of them?

And then there was the effect Eve's presence had on his demon, something he hadn't anticipated. Especially since they hadn't mated yet. When he'd touched her, kissed her, his demon had actually calmed. Shit, the bastard had purred. Oh, it still reared and bucked, but only because that dark side of him craved the light it recognized in Eve.

He found he was capable of a level of control over his demon that he hadn't had since Tobias's desertion. Since he found Eve, he'd twice prevented his demon from breaking free and wreaking the havoc it continually screamed for, and both times that had been because of her.

What if they didn't have to mate?

Could sex be enough?

If that was the answer, she'd be able to move on with her life once he'd taken down Tobias. He and his brothers would regain control and she wouldn't be tied to him, not in any way. His desire for her wouldn't lessen, but then he'd already planned to walk away, to face a future craving her and never being satisfied. A price he was willing to pay. Whatever it took to protect her from him.

It would mean deceiving her, but it would be for the best. In the long run, it would be for the best.

He squeezed his eyes shut.

How could he ask that of her? How could he ask her to let him use her body like that? Besides, he wasn't even sure it would work. Was he willing to risk his brothers to find out?

Jesus, he'd lost his goddamned mind.

Until recently, they'd all been tracking Tobias. The situation hadn't been ideal. They still had to retrieve the newly changed demi-demons, like Eve, while hunting rogue demons that escaped into the city. Now they were all unstable, and in Gunner's case, caged like a wild animal. Things couldn't get much worse. His only option was holding off his own demon long enough to find Tobias.

And there was only one way that he knew how to do that with certainty.

Mating with Eve.

Their brother's death was the only thing that could restore the delicate balance between good and evil warring inside each of them. If he failed, the knights would be lost forever, and mankind would become easy prey to Diemos and his demons.

A child's cry brought him from his thoughts and back to the now full plane. Eve was settled back in her seat, still avoiding his gaze, and she continued to do so after they'd taken flight a short time later.

He could feel her fear and had the uncharacteristic urge to provide comfort. He'd never been good with words, or people for that matter, and had no idea how to go about it. But at this point, anything he said would be insufficient.

So he stayed quiet.

He glanced over at Eve again, unable to help himself. She was dressed in jeans and a blue shirt with the words *Read Books Not T-shirts* stretched across her large breasts. The female looked good, too damn good. Her thick, dark hair sat piled on top of her head in a loose ponytail, and some of it had broken free to frame her pale face as she looked around the plane with wide eyes, biting her lower lip nervously.

Don't look at her mouth.

He quickly turned away.

Time dragged, then halfway through the movie they were watching, Eve asked, "You said demi-demons are trained and released?"

"Yes."

"So how long will I be staying with you? When will I be...released?"

Never, if I have my way. But he didn't say that. Hell, he didn't know where the possessive words filling his head had come from. Instead, he said, "Each demi is different. Once they're trained to shield and control their powers, and we're convinced they've mastered those skills and will be safe in the outside world, we allow them to leave and start their new lives."

She nodded.

"It'll be all right, Eve. You can do this." He shrugged. "You have to do this. Failure isn't an option." He was pushing, trying to bring back the feisty woman who fought him in her store. He hated seeing her this way.

She frowned. "You keep saying that, but it doesn't feel all right." She turned and faced him fully, fire flashing behind her eyes. "I can tell you, from where I'm sitting, none of this nightmare feels *all fucking right.*"

There it was: that spirited side of her nature that would get her through this ordeal. She'd been quiet, withdrawn since last night, and it was entirely his fault. He'd acted like an animal in that room.

He couldn't help it; he grinned at her.

Her brows shot up. "What are you smiling about? You think this is *funny?*"

"No. I'd just rather you yell at me than not speak at all."

The corners of her mouth tipped up a little. "It's a lot to take in."

He reached over and grabbed her hand, not just to provide comfort, but because he couldn't help himself. "I know, but it's that strength of yours that will get you through this, Eve. Don't ever forget that."

What the hell? Suddenly I'm a fucking shrink.

She studied his face. "I hope you're right."

"I know I am." He kept hold of her hand. Disturbingly, he was unable to let her go. Her fingers wrapped in his felt good...right.

She dropped her gaze. "I'm glad I've got you here to help me through this."

"I'm not going anywhere." He tightened his grip on her fingers as if to prove the point. "Eve, look...last night, what happened between us..." He ran a hand through his hair. "Shit, what I'm trying to say is..., I acted like an asshole," he stammered out. Christ, he sounded like a spotty teenager.

"After you...after we..." She stopped mid-sentence, apparently having the same trouble.

"Talk to me, Eve."

She looked everywhere but at him. "Something's going on, something I can't explain. I don't usually, you know, dive on guys like that."

Now wasn't an ideal time to explain what she was to him, but then he wasn't sure there ever would be. And so far, all his other attempts had failed. At least this way she couldn't get up and run the fuck away. "There's something I need to tell you."

She looked down. "No, it's fine, really. I understand why you didn't take things further. I just wanted you to know that's not how I usually behave. I know I put you in an awkward position."

She put *him* in an awkward position? "What are you talking about?"

She glanced up at him, puzzled.

"Why do you think I stopped?" he added.

Her cheeks darkened, and she cleared her throat. "You're not attracted to me. You were just being kind."

How could she think that? Words spilled from his mouth like someone else had taken control of his vocal cords. "Jesus, you couldn't be more wrong." He sounded needy as hell, but was past caring. "You cause such a hunger inside me, Eve. As it is, I can barely control myself around you. I want you so bad I can barely think of anything else. And just so you know, right now I'm so fucking hard for you it hurts."

He'd yakked up the contents of his frustrated and confused mind without restraint, and instantly wished he could take it back. But going by the intoxicating, purely feminine scent that drifted up to wrap around his senses, Eve was right there with him.

Her nipples hardened, the peaks straining against her T-shirt. He licked his lips, mouth watering for a taste of her. He might not have wanted to rush her, but being half angel sure as hell didn't make him a saint.

The hard length of his cock burned hot against his stomach. Thank God his shirt was covering all that was going on down there, because the thing had popped past the waistband of his jeans—like it was trying for a look-see at what he wanted so damn bad.

Her cheeks flushed, making him want her even more. She bit her lip, and the innocence that had captivated him the minute he'd laid eyes on her returned in her wide-eyed stare.

"There's more," he said.

She sucked in a breath. "More?"

"Yeah, I just…" Where the hell should he start?

"You're starting to freak me out, Lazarus."

Fuck it. "You're not just a demi-demon, Eve, you are…" He stared into her beautiful eyes. "You are *my* demi-demon."

She blinked several times then blurted, "What do you mean, *yours?*"

Inwardly, he winced at the look of horror covering her face. "You're my mate."

"What? You mean like…" She paled. "You mean like Kryos and Meredith?"

Okay, this was harder than he thought. "Yes. Each knight has a female somewhere in the world." She stared at him, and he shifted in his seat. "She is everything he needs—will ever need. Once they mate, the warrior's strength increases and the demon half of him stabilizes." He reached out, unable to stop himself from brushing a loose strand of hair behind her ear. "And for a demi, mating means immortality…and the protection and devotion of her warrior for eternity."

"Immortality?"

"Yes." The disbelief quickly disappeared from her face.

No, sweetheart, I'm not making any of this shit up.

"And you're my…my warrior?"

Hearing her say those words nearly had him undone. The cabin lights were low for the night flight and high-lighted the shadows beneath Eve's eyes. She looked fragile. He wanted nothing more than to pull her into his lap and convince her everything would be all right. But he couldn't, because it wouldn't. "Yes, and you are my female." He barely recognized his voice, the words rasping past his lips. "But nothing is set in stone. In the end, the decision must be yours, Eve."

Her eyes widened. "I...I..."

"You don't need to decide now." He'd have a better chance of her accepting him if she believed she had a choice in this. He just hoped she made the right one.

She blinked up at him. He wanted to say more, to reassure her, but his reply caught in his throat when unease wrapped around him like a dark shadow, so damn suffocating.

"What's going on?" Eve said, picking up on his sudden change of mood.

Lazarus stood, unable to respond, and stepped into the aisle. He pretended to get something from the overhead storage compartment and glanced across the rows of passengers in the front and behind them, searching. Most appeared asleep or watching a movie. He did another pass.

Fuck.

"What are you doing?" Eve tried again, voice shaky.

Pins and needles tap-danced down his spine, right before milky eyes opened and the fucker returned his stare, smiling.

They were still an hour from Chicago, but the Orthon wouldn't attempt anything until they were free of witnesses. He sat back down without a word.

"What is it?" The concern in Eve's voice and etched into her features caused rage to course through his veins. He wouldn't let anything happen to her. "It's nothing."

Uncertainty shifted through her gaze, and she opened her mouth to say more.

"We'll talk more later." Lazarus surrounded her with the compulsion to sleep. He'd used it a lot on her lately and he felt a little guilty, but it was better than letting her freak out for the next hour. She visibly relaxed and made a *hmm* sound.

In a matter of minutes, she'd drifted off to sleep beside him.

The flight seemed to take forever, but finally, their plane touched down. He reached up and collected Eve's carry-on.

"Are we here?" she asked groggily.

"Yeah."

She stood, and he led her toward the exit. First, he had to get her out of the airport. After that, Brent, another demi, would put them up at a secure location.

He glanced behind them, spotting the Orthon. It was in the guise of a middle-aged male, following and gaining on them quickly.

"What's going on, Lazarus?"

As usual, Eve didn't miss a thing. "We have company," he said with a sharp glance over his shoulder.

Clever girl that she was, no further explanations were necessary. She grabbed his hand and picked up the pace beside him.

CHAPTER 14

LAZARUS STEERED Eve toward a large group of people milling about and pushed his way through the center of the crowd. He turned abruptly, and Eve hung on tight as he pulled her down a short corridor, completely ignoring the *Staff only* sign.

Pausing, he forced her behind his body, pressing her against the wall. Eve peered around one of his thick biceps. A man turned into the hall, colorless eyes trained on her.

Laz swore under his breath.

"Lazarus?" Those weird creamy eyes never wavered from her, and her stomach lurched. This was actually happening. It wasn't a nightmare, and that *thing* was coming for her.

"It won't get anywhere near you."

He pulled her farther down the corridor, following a narrow passage that turned to the left. Lazarus opened the first door they came to.

"In here." He pushed her inside and shut her in.

The *click* of the lock engaging followed.

He'd done that trick using his powers to lock it from the

143

outside, and she instantly felt that electric buzz over her skin, which meant he'd somehow warded the room.

Silence engulfed the small space.

She was frozen to the spot, adrenaline racing through her veins with no outlet. The silence was filled by her pulse echoing through her skull and blood rushing in her ears.

She couldn't hear what was happening beyond the flimsy door—

A deep growl ripped through the room, followed by a thump that rattled the door on its hinges.

Then nothing.

Time seemed to tick by at a snail's pace, and Eve held her breath, waiting.

When it finally came, the lock releasing was barely audible over her thumping heart. She scrambled back until her heels collided with the wall behind her. Frantically, she searched for a weapon, anything. Standard-issue airport one-ply lined the walls, but she didn't think hurling toilet rolls at a crazed demon would cut it.

The handle turned and the door eased open.

Eve's breath caught in her throat—

Then released on a *whoosh*, when Lazarus poked his head in, eyes downcast. "Wait here. I need to make sure he was alone." Then he was gone again.

He seemed calm, like fighting killer demons in busy airports was an everyday occurrence. How could she do this, live this life? Where monsters were real and didn't just go bump in the night. No, they came out in broad freaking daylight. Thinking about that wasn't a good idea, not while she was stuck in here. She concentrated on slowing her heart rate, which wasn't working since she couldn't stop pacing around the tiny floor space.

A few minutes later, Lazarus stepped back into the room. She looked out into the hall, where the Orthon's ashy remains lay on the ground in a pile behind him. Lazarus closed and locked the door.

"He was alone?"

He didn't answer her.

Eve took him in more closely. His chest was pumping at a rapid pace, and the veins and tendons in his neck and hands stood out on his tanned skin. Sweat beaded on his forehead and he was gritting his teeth as the muscles in his shoulders moved unnaturally beneath his jacket.

He wouldn't look at her.

Oh God. "Lazarus?" She took a step forward.

"Don't." His voice rumbled darkly and lifted goose bumps across her skin. "Stay back."

"What's wrong? Are you injured?"

His head shot up. Eyes black and unblinking stared back. Not even a flicker of green remained.

"Lazarus?"

He shook his head, teeth gritted. God, he looked in such terrible pain.

He wanted her to stay back, but how could she? She couldn't bear to see him like that. He said he'd never hurt her, and she believed him. So she took a step closer, approaching him slowly, like you would a wild animal.

He watched her, or she thought he did; it was hard to tell with his eyes washed in black like that.

When she was standing in front of him, she reached for him. She didn't know what she could do, but she wanted to help with whatever had caused this transformation. She lifted her hand and gently cupped the side of his face.

He hissed, his chest pumping rapidly. The light show started in his irises again, like it had back at her house and at the compound. He moaned and turned in to her palm, pushing into her touch like a contented house cat.

"Lazarus? What's happening?" she choked out.

He lifted his gaze, and with the color trying to break back through, they were easier to read. Need, dark and hungry, stared back at her, freezing her to the spot. He looked almost feral. She wasn't afraid, though. No, instead her body heated, responding to the raw lust burning into her.

Despite all she'd gone through in such a short time, her only thought at that moment was what Lazarus had said to her on the plane earlier.

"You cause such a hunger inside me, Eve. As it is, I can barely control myself around you. I want you so bad I can barely think of anything else."

The enclosed space caused his delicious scent to fill the tiny room. His massive body crowded her, surrounded her. She didn't know what was happening to her, to both of them, and right then she didn't care.

"Don't," he rasped, even as he moved closer, as he rubbed his cheek against her palm.

"I can't help it," she replied, more than a little shocked by her actions.

Demons were hunting her. Who knew what would happen when they walked out that door? If she didn't act now, she might never know what it was like to be with him. Could she live with that? No. She was surprised to realize she couldn't.

Eve had played by everyone else's rules all her life. Time after time her family had rejected her then dumped her like garbage. She'd spent most of her life ignored and unwanted —until now. It didn't matter if it was only a day, an hour, hell, a minute—she would take it. It felt too good not to.

His eyes flared. "Don't do this." He drew in a deep, shuddering breath.

"I can't stop myself. I don't want to." She ran her hands up the ridged planes of his abs and across the solid wall of his chest to push the heavy leather jacket from his shoulders. The thump as it hit the floor sounded loud in the quiet room.

"We can't do this," he croaked. "You deserve better than to be fucked against the wall in a goddamned supply cupboard."

She clamped her thighs together in an attempt to ease the ache. "Please." She pressed closer, desperate to have his hands on her.

His eyes bore into hers. "This force between us...it's too strong. I won't be able to stop this time...do you understand?" He shook his head. "Fuck. I need you," his voice caught on the last word.

"I'm here." She'd die if he didn't touch her soon.

"I won't be gentle, Eve. I can't. If you want to change your mind, do it now," he warned, voice ragged.

She shook her head, liquid heat flooding her sex at his needy words. "I won't change my mind."

His eyes did that thing where they flashed between emerald and ebony. "Then touch me, Eve. Just...I need you to touch me."

The desperate plea kicked her into action. She slid her hands under his shirt, marveling at the smooth hot skin beneath before lifting it up and over his head. His body was magnificent, all corded, sinewy strength.

He thrust his fingers into her hair, and the loose hair tie fell away, releasing the heavy mass. His eyes seemed to stabilize then, but remained a darker shade than before.

He reached down and yanked up her shirt, shoving it over her head, tracking every move like the massive predator he was. The pure unrestrained hunger in his eyes successfully eliminated any lingering apprehension she had about the way her body looked. Instead, she felt bold and sexy for the first time in her life.

Large, rough hands cupped her breasts through the white

cotton cups of her bra before he pinched the hardened buds between his fingers. Eve whimpered—she wanted his hands on her bare flesh—and reached for the center clasp. He let out a low moan of appreciation as she undid it, letting her full breasts bounce free.

"Jesus, you're killing me. I have to—" His voice surrounded her, wild and barely in control. Dipping his head, he caught one aching peak between his teeth and sucked hard. She moaned from the sensation of his hot wet mouth on her sensitive flesh and held his head against her. He looked up. His eyes had changed again, were paler. Then rational thought scattered as he moved to her other breast, drawing her hard nipple deep, devouring her. She bit her lip to keep from crying out.

With deft fingers, he undid her jeans then thrust a hand down the front of her panties, sliding through her slick folds, grazing her clit repeatedly. She whimpered and clutched at his heavy arms to stay upright.

Without warning, two thick fingers entered her. She cried out as he pushed inside, driving her higher. Her body moved of its own volition, her hips rolling against his hand.

He rested his forehead against hers. "Jesus, you're so damn hot, so tight and wet around my fingers. I need to feel you wrapped around my cock," he said against her mouth before he kissed her hard and demanding. His tongue moved against hers in an imitation of what was coming.

His other hand slid between their bodies, and he fumbled with his jeans. He shifted back, and his heavy cock sprang free, pre-come already glistened at the head.

He was long and thick, and beautiful.

"I can't wait any longer...need inside you. Need to feel you squeezing me tight, sweetheart."

"Yes." That was all she could manage.

He removed his hand from her panties, but instead of

moving his massive body between her thighs, he looked at his fingers, glistening, covered in her, and brought them to his mouth, sucking each finger clean.

His eyes drifted shut and he groaned. "Fuck, Eve. You taste better than I imagined." The next time I have you, I'm going to take my time feasting on you. I'm going to do all the things I've wanted to do since the minute I saw you." He opened his eyes and the uninhibited desire staring back caused another rush of liquid heat between her thighs. "Do you want that, too?" he asked hoarsely.

She managed a shaky nod.

In seconds, he had removed her jeans and panties completely and pressed her into the wall.

"Now, please," she said, not ashamed to beg.

He lifted her like she weighed nothing, and had her wrap her legs around his waist. He fisted his thick shaft, positioning himself.

Holy hell, the guy was huge everywhere. Apprehension must have shown on her face because he gripped her chin and made her look at him.

"I'm big, but you can take all of me. You were made for me. This body was made for me. I'll make this good for you." He slid the head of his cock through her folds, covering himself in her arousal before working his thick shaft inside her. He drew back a little to allow her body a chance to accommodate his size before feeding her another inch.

"Christ, you're so tight...feels so good," he gasped.

"Lazarus...I need..." She stopped talking as he drew out slow then slid back home, fully seating himself. Her eyes drifted closed.

He groaned long and low.

She loved how out of control he seemed and forced her eyes open to watch him. She gasped when their stares collided, his steady gaze already locked on her as he drew back then slammed home. Too much, those eyes of his were too damn much. She tried to look away, but he gripped her jaw, stopping her.

"Don't hide from me. I want to see your face when you come," he said.

With each thrust he ground against her swollen clit, filling her deeper. She was half out of her mind by the time he leaned in and took her mouth in a brutal kiss.

Hungry for more, she nipped his lower lip. When he hissed, she ran her tongue over the abused flesh and sucked, soothing the sting, and Lazarus seemed to snap. His hips slammed forward, going so deep she gasped. His pace increased, taking her hard and fast. His chest pumped, and his breath came in fast pants.

"*Oh God.*" It was too much. Pleasure sent her reeling when he slammed into her next. She stiffened as her orgasm hit, and sunk her teeth into the muscle of his shoulder to stop the scream about to tear from her throat.

One of his big hands slapped against the wall by her head, and he growled.

Her inner muscles tightened, squeezing repeatedly around him. Lazarus shook, his big body almost vibrating as he moved his hands to her ass. He angled his hips, hitting her deeper as he thrust into her. Then he was coming, and so was she. Again.

He snarled—a wild, untamed sound that was anything but human, and dropped his head to her shoulder, shudders still rolling through him.

His skin felt hot and slick against hers, and goose bumps prickled her flesh as he panted, his warm breath tickling her neck.

After a few seconds, he lifted his head. "You okay?"

Was he joking? She'd never experienced anything like that before. She couldn't help it—she grinned. "Ah, you were in this…um"—she looked around—"cupboard with me, weren't you?"

His lips tilted up, offering her the smallest of grins. As he brushed her hair back behind her ear, his expression turned serious. "Is your arm all right?"

"It's fine."

He frowned.

Was he second-guessing himself and what they'd done? Did he regret it? "Lazarus—"

"It's time for us to go." He glanced down at her nakedness and need once again darkened his gaze.

Her skin flushed with heat. "Okay."

He stared at her for a long second like he was going to say more, but then let Eve slide to the ground and stepped back.

The moment was over.

CHAPTER 15

Oh yeah, what they'd done had complicated the hell out of things. He rubbed a hand over his forearm. Jesus, he had goose bumps, his skin still tingling, fucking alive.

Being buried inside Eve—nothing had ever felt so good. It'd taken everything he had not to yell *mine* when he'd come. The power of his release had almost knocked him on his ass. He could still feel her, tight and hot around him, gripping him—could still smell her sweet scent.

He shifted, trying to accommodate the hard-on that wouldn't quit, his body aching for more of her already. He needed to get his shit back under control, but damn, it was a struggle. Especially with his demon hovering just below the surface, just as hungry for Eve as Lazarus.

The bastard was just waiting for another chance to break free.

He stared out the window of the cab, trying to keep it together. Not fucking likely when he could hear the way Eve kept shifting in her seat, when the scent of her arousal was reaching out to him, coiling around him. He took slow, even breaths, and did his damnedest to ignore the way she was affecting him. *Like that'll help.*

Lazarus knew better. There was no help for it. Because standing outside that door in the airport, protecting his female and waiting to engage his enemy, had sent his demon rocketing to the surface. He'd become consumed by the darkness, more than ever before.

After he'd dispatched the Orthon and made sure there weren't any others, he'd been desperate to get back to her. And by the time he'd reached that supply room door, he'd no longer been in the driver's seat. It was like hovering above himself, watching from a distance. He'd watched his hand rise to release that lock with no control over his actions.

The demon and not the demon hunter had gone back into that room. With serious effort, he'd warned her, told her to stay back. But instead of keeping her distance, Eve had approached him, touched him, and pulled him from the dark, bathing him in her light and warmth.

Thank God he hadn't lost his head completely.

Kryos had warned him, had told him what would happen when he took Eve for the first time. Still, when that silvery thread had appeared in his mind's eye moments after sinking deep inside her, he'd been stunned—not only by its beauty, but by the undeniable truth that Eve was meant to be his. It had called to him, enticed him. All he had to do was reach out and take hold, and Eve would be his, his mate.

She hadn't even been aware of it. Only a male had the ability to complete the mating. He could have made her his that easily.

Without her consent.

He'd resisted. He couldn't bring himself to do that to her.

He curled his fingers into a fist so tight the skin over his knuckles felt close to splitting. He'd fucked up. Badly. He should have been protecting her, not fucking her. He'd left her open to attack.

Eve didn't know what she was doing. How could she? After all she had been through in such a short time, how could she resist the pull of their connection?

He'd taken advantage of that, of her.

Like a goddamned animal.

But in that dark place in the back of his mind, he knew there hadn't been any other option. He was fast becoming a slave to this constant craving for her. He hated to think what might have happened if he hadn't accepted the gift she'd offered him, if she hadn't been there to pull him from the brink. His demon had all but taken him.

Had there been another choice? Not that he could see.

Like he thought, had hoped, Eve had the power to force back his demon with her body. He knew that without a doubt.

Taking her as his mate wasn't necessary.

The realization twisted something deep inside, and he clamped a lid on it, forced it deep down. He knew the sick feeling—the sense of wrongness he felt at that moment would never leave him. But he could live with that; better that than the alternative. This was how it should be, how it had to be.

Bad things happened to the people he cared about, and he wouldn't allow Eve to be the next victim of his weakness. Part of his heart had died with Scarlet, and what remained had iced over when Tobias gave up the fight and succumbed to his demon.

Tobias was lost, and that was on Lazarus.

"Where are we going?" Eve asked beside him.

Her voice caused another stab of guilt, and he had to force down the bitter pill before he could speak. Dragging his eyes from the city lights blurring past the cab's window, he faced her. He wasn't ready to look at her again, and sure enough, as soon as he got another eyeful of those full lips still swollen from his kiss, her large pale eyes, not to mention her soft curvy body, his own hardened to painful proportions. It was as if she'd reached out and touched him.

"My friend owns a club," he finally answered. "There's accommodation. It's well warded, safe."

As if on cue, the cab pulled over and Lazarus handed the driver some cash before he grabbed their bags and climbed out. He waited while Eve scooted over and stepped out beside him. The place looked normal enough from the outside, like any other club, loud music, half-dressed females, and rowdy males looking for a good night. But this place had a unique difference.

Lazarus grabbed her hand and walked to the front of the queue. The bouncer let him past with a wordless nod.

Eve's body pressed in close to his as they squeezed through the tightly packed humans, driving him fucking insane. He ground his teeth, trying to concentrate on retaining his slipping control. Just the warmth of her hand in his was too much. His nerve endings came alive at the slightest touch of her skin. He hurried toward the bar, pushing his way through the crowd.

"Where's Brent?" he barked, too on edge to moderate his tone.

"Out back," the guy, a shifter, shouted over the music. His eyes trailed over Eve, his appreciation blatant. The growl that ripped from Lazarus was unexpected and loud enough for the guy to hear over all the noise. His eyes went wide before stuttering, "S-sorry, man. No offense, yeah?"

"Don't look at her again."

Eve shot him a sharp glance. Apparently, he no longer had control over what the hell came out of his mouth either. The word *mine* was stuck on repeat in his mind. God, he wanted to smash something.

Without another word, he turned from the bar. He didn't need to push through the crowd behind him this time because people parted like the Red Sea, stumbling over themselves to get out of his way.

Once they were away from the bar, he led Eve toward the back, weaving through the sweaty patrons dancing to shitty music. They finally reached the back of the building and a large male opened a nondescript door. Lazarus led Eve into the small hallway, turning a corner and stopping in front of another stocky male, this one a demi-demon, guarding a second plain metal door.

"Tom," he greeted the guy in charge of security.

"Good to see you again, Laz." He grinned.

The guy looked at Eve, winking at her as they passed. This time Laz managed to contain the growl before it escaped. They entered another hall, this one long and dark. Lights edged the floor, lighting their way. The farther they went the louder the thumping bass grew in volume.

"What is this place?" Eve tightened her grip on his hand and moved in closer. He ground his teeth at the contact, positive he felt a tight, beaded nipple graze his biceps.

"It's a club inside a club." They approached another door, and another security guy opened it for them.

"Welcome to the Jungle" by Guns 'n' Roses blasted from the speakers. Yeah, the song couldn't be more apt. He felt rather than heard Eve's gasp as they stepped through the door.

The dimly lit club was fairly full for this time of night. Barely covered males and females sat at tables or on the strategically placed couches around the room. Some talked, some danced, and though it was early still, some fucked.

Brent had opened the sex club more out of necessity than

anything else. The place catered to nonhumans, a place they could come together, where they could have whatever needs they had met. Being the type of demi-demon Brent was, this place was more than just a business, it kept him safe, kept him breathing. Many that came here did so for the same reason.

"Jesus Christ, Lazarus. Where have you brought me?" Eve's hand moved up to clutch his forearm.

He bent down to speak close to her ear and had the sudden urge to dart his tongue out and trace the delicate lobe. "This place is owned by a demi named Brent. His demon side is different from yours. This place provides the cocktail of sex and volatile emotion he needs to keep from losing it." He didn't add that most of the employees and patrons here were *other*. She had enough to take in for now.

"Oh." Her eyes widened as she took in her surroundings.

A Dom passed by them. A leash dangled from his fingers, the strip of leather attached to a collar around another guy's neck. The sub crawled on his hands and knees, cheeks flushed, his excitement obvious as he followed his master to one of the private rooms.

"Is he going to...what do they..." She stopped abruptly, frowning. He guessed she was unsure how to finish her sentence.

"They give each other what they need."

Her cheeks darkened.

"Come on." He approached a waitress, a young demi named Chaya. Brent gave her a job after her release from the compound a few months back. Like Eve, she favored her human DNA and had a curvy build.

A wide smile lit up her delicate elfin features when she turned and spotted him. "Hey, Lazarus, I didn't know you were coming."

"Something came up."

She smirked. "You lot missing me already, huh?"

Yeah, he wasn't touching that one. The female had given them all hell while at the compound, and she'd enjoyed every damn minute of it. "How do you like it here?"

Her low chuckle said she knew exactly why he'd changed the subject. "A girl's gotta pay the rent somehow, right?"

He introduced Eve then asked after his friend's whereabouts.

"He's with someone right now, but he shouldn't be much longer." She glanced over to where the private rooms were located and scowled. "You can wait over there." She pointed to a table.

"Thanks."

"Sure." She spun on her skyscraper heels and disappeared into the crowd.

"So Brent's a…is he a…" Eve started.

Lazarus took pity on her. "His sire was a sex demon."

He led her to the table and Eve sat across from him studying her hands, pretending not to notice what was going on around her. Strobe lights flashed incessantly, irritating the shit out of his eyes, pulsing with the loud music. Each flash revealed a glimpse of writhing, naked limbs tangled in the darkened corners. The smell of sex was thick in the air and heightened his already out-of-control need for Eve. How Brent spent every night in this place, he didn't know.

The music made it hard to talk, and Lazarus was relieved when a door across the club opened and Brent strode out. He was dressed in gray trousers and a black silk shirt, looking sharp as always.

His friend tugged the female who followed him from the room closer, kissed her temple, and sent her on her way. He shrugged into his jacket and took a moment to survey his club.

Brent never let it show, but Lazarus knew the guy still

struggled with the demon side of himself and what it demanded of him. But it was either this or...well, it wasn't worth thinking about the condition Lazarus had found his friend in many years ago.

Brent glanced up at that moment and spotted him, his frown replaced by a wide grin. He made his way over to them, straightening his jacket and running a hand over his slightly mussed hair. "You should've said you were coming. I would've towed out the welcome wagon."

"Sure, you would have."

"You doubt me?"

"Always."

Brent chuckled, his gaze sliding to Eve standing at his side. "You need a place to stay?" he said without looking at Lazarus.

"Yeah, we do."

His dark gaze continued to trail over her and Lazarus wanted to snarl a warning.

The guy smiled when she looked up at him, all charm and model good looks, and extended a hand. "I'm Brent. Nice to meet you. I hope Lazarus hasn't given you too much of a hard time."

Eve giggled. Fucking grinned up at the asshole, and *giggled*. An urge to reach out, grab him by the throat, and wipe that smile off his face nearly won out.

"I'm Eve." She took his hand. "Interesting place you have here." That beautiful open smile covered her lovely face, and Brent sucked in an appreciative breath.

"Would you like the grand tour? The private rooms are... cozy." His friend's voice had dropped an octave, and the charming grin now held an edge of hunger.

Eve blinked up at him. "Oh, I...no. Thank you."

Lazarus decided that perhaps a warning was in order.

He smiled at her when she glanced his way and leaned

closer to Brent, like he was trying to talk over the music. "If you take one step with her toward those rooms, I'll make it so you never walk again. Do you understand?" he said in a low voice.

A dark chuckle rumbled from his friend. "I'm beginning to."

Brent was like family to him, but if he so much as touched Eve, he'd rip the guy's hands off at the wrists.

Brent leaned back. "Can you stop with the crazy-assed smile now? I'm trying to run a business here. You're scaring my customers."

The guy was obviously in the mood to mess with him, or had a death wish, because he turned back to Eve, relaxed and still grinning like Lazarus hadn't just threatened to cripple him. "Would you like a drink, Eve?"

She smiled back, and like always he felt it like a sucker punch to his gut. "Sure, sounds good."

Brent turned to him then and the bastard winked. "Get the female a drink, Laz."

A growl built in his chest before he could stop it. Brent's brows rose, and he said in his own low tone, "You would leave your female wanting?"

Brent was fishing, but it didn't take a genius to work out Eve meant something to him. Not with the possessive way he'd been behaving. The other male's eyes widened when, scowling in silent warning, he turned and stalked to the bar. His need to provide for Eve, to give his would-be mate whatever she needed was a compulsion he couldn't ignore.

After ordering their drinks, he turned back to Eve, unable to keep his eyes off the female for more than a few seconds at a time. Brent looked to be chatting amiably, but then Eve flinched and clutched her forehead.

Shit.

With the way her power was growing in strength, the

short distance between them must have been far enough for the block he had over her telepathy to drop. By the way her mouth was hanging open she'd gotten a head full of his perverted friend's thoughts, not to mention the rest of the room.

Grabbing the drinks, he stalked back to the pair, and after strengthening the block, he put down the drinks and pulled her into his side. "All right?"

She smiled, the strain washing from her face. "I am now."

He let his fingers drift across her shoulder and into her hair so he could massage the back of her head and neck where she would feel the most discomfort. She leaned into his touch and made a little moaning sound that hit him right in the balls. More of his waning self-control slipped. It took effort, but he dropped his hand and stepped back.

"Anything you want to tell me, brother?" Brent said.

He had a stupid look on his face, one Lazarus had never seen on the other male before, and didn't much like. Lazarus glared at him. "Yes. In future, keep your thoughts R13."

Brent shrugged. "Impossible."

"She's telepathic."

The guy didn't look worried in the slightest. In fact, he looked amused. He turned to Eve. "I apologize if I embarrassed you, Eve, but you really are an attractive female."

Lazarus growled through clenched teeth. "In future, don't think about her."

"I'll do my best, but I'm not blind."

"Then don't look at her, or I'll make it so you don't have a choice."

Laughter lit his eyes. "For fuck's sake, if you have your way I'll be in a wheelchair with glass eyeballs."

"And no fucking hands," Lazarus added.

Brent laughed harder.

"Not another damn word," he gritted out.

"It's okay," Eve said beside him. "I'm all right now you're back. Anyway, I'm used to it…well, I thought I was." She looked confused, her cheeks flushed.

"Just take us to the room, you sick shit."

Two apartments were located upstairs: one Brent's, the other kept empty for the knights if they should need it.

Brent took them up, and once inside, Lazarus carried Eve's bag into the bedroom. Eve's quiet laughter drifted in from the living room.

When he walked back in, he raised an eyebrow at Brent who was grinning as well. "What are you talking about?" He didn't like that the other male had caused her happiness when he seemed to only cause her pain.

"I didn't say a word." His friend smirked. Shit, as soon as he'd left the room Eve had gotten another dose of Brent's thoughts.

"What the hell were you thinking about?" he demanded.

"A few images of you I thought Eve might find entertaining." Brent shook his head. "Man, the seventies really weren't kind to anyone, were they? Orange bell-bottoms, Laz, really?"

"I never wore orange bell-bottoms, dipshit."

"No, but I have an excellent imagination."

Lazarus shook his head at the guy's warped sense of humor. "Leave."

Brent ignored his rudeness. "It was nice to meet you, Eve. Call down to the bar if you need anything." Then he left them very much alone.

"This is nice," Eve said after a few minutes of silence looking around the small apartment.

"It's okay."

"Is it all right if I grab a shower?"

"Of course. Everything you need should be in the bathroom." An image flashed through his mind of her naked, water sluicing over her pale skin, hands moving over her voluptuous body, nipples dark and peaked and begging for his mouth.

She didn't move right away, but stood there watching him, waiting for something, something he couldn't give her. Her color was high and she bit her lower lip. "Well, okay. I'll just…" She motioned to the bathroom.

He gave her a sharp nod then watched her walk away.

He didn't go in after her, and it almost killed him. If he was honest, his fear of this growing hold she had over him was the only thing keeping him from joining her in the shower and fucking her hard against the cool tile. But after the way he'd reacted downstairs, he didn't trust himself to have her again without forcing a mating.

His stomach churned. Did she believe he was capable of tender feelings, of love?

Why hadn't he told her the truth?

Maybe because I selfishly want her even though I can never love her.

He didn't want to see that trusting look on her face turn to betrayal, the heat in her eyes turn to dread. He shook off the thought and sat his ass on the couch.

He was incapable of giving her what she deserved, what he'd seen between Meredith and Kryos, and—before everything went to hell—Tobias and Scarlet. Love wasn't something he could offer. Not anymore.

The bathroom door opened a short time later, and he couldn't stop himself from looking at her when she walked out. She wore a pair of red boxers with little white hearts all over them and a white tank top. The outfit should have been innocent enough, but on Eve it was the opposite. The top clung to her out-of-control curves and her beaded nipples were visible through the thin fabric. His mouth went dry.

"I'm going to head to bed," she said.

When she walked through the living room, Lazarus stood. He felt like a puppet and Eve controlled the strings. Without thought or control over his actions, he stepped forward, blocking her path.

"Is everything all right?" She lifted her arm and cradled it to her chest.

Shit. What was he doing?

Her bandage stood out against all that smooth, creamy skin. "I, ah, I need to take a look at your arm."

"It's fine, really."

"Bathroom, Eve." He didn't really need to look at it now, though, did he?

She swallowed hard. "It's not sore. I can check it in the morning."

Her resistance just made him more determined. He couldn't be in the same room as her, but he also didn't want her hiding from him. Where Eve was concerned, he was a mass of contradicting thoughts and feelings. Completely fucked in the head over her. "Go to the bathroom, Eve," he heard himself say.

Her shoulders stiffened, but she turned and walked back toward the tiny room.

He followed and tried to ignore the sway of her heart-shaped ass the whole damn way.

She turned to face him and he gripped her hips, lifting her and sitting her on the bathroom counter. She squeaked in surprise, and the soft heat of her curves branded his palms. After gathering supplies from the cabinet, he removed her bandage and began cleaning her injury with methodical efficiency. All the while trying not to take in her scent and the subtle way her breath hitched when he touched her skin. Taking her wrist, he inspected her wounds. Warmth radiated from her body as he leaned in to get a better look. Her breath coasted across his neck and goose bumps broke out across his skin.

"It's healing well."

"That's good," she said in a hushed tone that only made it worse.

He quickly redressed it. "There, all done. We can change them again tomorrow." How the hell would he get through this again tomorrow? Stepping back, he inspected the new bandage.

Her gaze heated.

Nostrils flaring, he drew in a deep breath. God, he could smell how turned on she was.

She confirmed it when her skin flushed pink. Her cheeks, her chest, the tops of her breasts.

So fucking beautiful.

It took everything he had, but instead of moving back in and taking what he wanted, he started for the door. Her body soothed him, tamed his demon, but he couldn't take her just because his dick was hard, just because he wanted her. That wasn't what this was, not now. It never was.

He had to stay focused, he needed to maintain an emotional and physical distance for both their sakes. "I'll let you get to bed."

"Good night," she called after him.

He paused at the door, struggling, desperate to go back to her.

She made the decision for him when she climbed off the counter and slipped passed him.

He tracked her across the room, unable to look away, until she shut the door, closing herself in the bedroom.

CHAPTER 16

MUSIC DRIFTED up from the clubs and bars as the city moved at a rapid pace below. Lazarus looked down from the top of the building he stood on, the wind ruffling his hair, coasting across his fevered skin. It did little to cool his blood. Shit, he was on fire, burning from the inside out, and had been since he laid eyes on Eve.

He needed it to stop.

An image of Scarlet invaded his mind, a memory that succeeded in shooting ice through his veins and putting another crack though his heart.

"What did you get her?" Tobias asked Lazarus five seconds after walking into his apartment.

"A gun."

Tobias grunted and looked down at the jewel-handled blade in his hand. "Well, I'm giving mine to her first."

Lazarus shook his head and scowled at his brother. It was Scarlet's twentieth birthday and there was no way Tobias was going to give his baby girl a present first. The guy had been acting weird lately, overprotective of her, especially since they'd started taking her along to retrievals. They all loved her, but T's behavior seemed extreme.

"What the fuck is up with you?" Lazarus said, starting to get pissed off.

Tobias rubbed the back of his neck and actually winced. "Okay, so there's something I need to talk to you about." The guy stalled out, looking fidgety as hell.

Lazarus straightened. "What?"

Scarlet walked in, a small smile on her lips. "I guess I'll tell you, since Tobias is obviously going to chicken out."

Both Tobias and Lazarus turned to her, and he noted Tobias looked shocked.

"Tobias is my mate," she said, stopping beside the male.

Lazarus went rigid and Tobias stared down at her with his mouth hanging open. "You know?" he said to her.

She smiled up at T, beautiful and open. "Yeah, of course. I've felt something...I don't know...a connection between us since Laz brought me home. It's changed, though, grown stronger the last few months. It's become something different...um...more." She blushed. "Was that the same for you?"

Tobias made a choking, growling sound and nodded.

She chuckled at the male's continued slack-jawed expression. "So are you gonna kiss me now or what?"

"Like hell," Lazarus barked out.

Tobias touched Scarlet's face, with an expression on his own that Laz had never seen before. Awe. There was no other way to describe it. "Yeah, I'm gonna kiss you, sweetheart, a lot," he said. "But first I have to let Laz kick my ass. It's only right."

Scarlet nodded sagely, her lips kicking up in a grin. "Agreed." She motioned to the door. "I'll be down in your room when you're done."

Tobias sucked in a sharp breath, eyes darkening, and Lazarus took advantage of his momentary distraction and tackled him. Yeah, he knew this was out of the male's control, but it didn't change the fact that his friend was about to mate a female he considered his daughter, and Lazarus was going to kick the fucker's ass before he worked at accepting it.

"I'll be down shortly," Tobias called back, then grunted when Laz punched him in the gut.

"Don't damage any of the important parts!" Scarlet called as she walked out the door.

Tobias groaned. "You're totally gonna go for the important parts now, aren't you?"

"Fuck yes," Laz said.

They'd made their peace and Tobias had made Scarlet his mate. The knight had loved and cherished her, protected and respected her, had been the kind of male any father would wish for his child.

Pain sliced through him. And then Lazarus had destroyed them both.

Lazarus felt the angel's presence at his back before the guy made his arrival known.

"You called?" Silas drawled.

Arrogant asshole.

"Ouch," he said, amusement in his deep voice.

Lazarus turned to face him. "Get the fuck out of my head, angel."

Silas stared at him, silver eyes missing nothing, head tilted to the side. Under the moon, his hair looked like strands of spun gold, the black streaks through it such a contrast it was hard to look at. "You have so much anger and pain, Lazarus. Getting in your head isn't exactly a barrel of laughs for me either."

He looked at the angel who'd trained him many lifetimes ago, the male who had branded him as one of Heaven's warriors, and shook his head. "Then stay the fuck out."

He ran a hand through that unusual hair. "I don't like being taken by surprise, Laz. You know that."

He wore his usual uniform—black jeans and tee. The battle scenes tattooed on his arms in black ink were on full display. His gold wings shifted then settled again, arching high over his shoulders. When they were still they looked like they were made of solid gold, like he carried the intense weight of them on his back.

Lazarus held his gaze. "Since you know why I called you here, let's not waste any more time." When Silas said nothing, he knew there was something the fucker was hiding, something Lazarus wasn't going to like. "What is she?" The wind whipped away his words, but the angel heard him. He heard every fucking thing. "Tell me," he roared. Because he knew Eve was no ordinary demi, not after the way his brothers had reacted to her.

"She has the mark," Silas said.

Lazarus clenched his fists. He fucking knew what the guy was going to say, but goddammit, he'd hoped he was wrong. "What mark?"

Sympathy lit the angel's eerie silver eyes. "She has the Beast's mark. She's a descendant of Lucifer's handmaidens." Silas took a step closer to him. "Lazarus, she's a hell's gate."

Lazarus strode away as fear and anger pumped hotly through his veins. Lucifer's handmaids had served only him. Whatever he wanted, they got, which meant they had the ability to move between realms at will. Eve being a descendant, having the mark, meant she also carried the ability to open a gate.

Making her Diemos's number one target.

Fuck.

The demon needed her. When Lucifer left and took his handmaids with him, he'd trapped the other male in Hell.

If Diemos left during the equinox, before he had an army here on Earth, and 24/7 access to the hell's gate, he risked

169

being locked out and losing the throne he'd worked so hard to take.

He wanted control over the portal above all else.

Lazarus shoved his hands through his hair. He wanted to plow his fist into the angel's face, but it was pointless. Silas would see it coming. "That's why she collapsed back at the compound? The equinox affected her as well?"

"Yes."

"Why didn't you tell me?" he rasped.

"She's safe," Silas said. "The amulet, it has the power to mask what she is, block it."

Lazarus turned to him. "It can protect her if she remains unmated?"

Silas shook his head. "I didn't make the amulet for that purpose."

"You didn't answer my question, angel."

Silas sighed and shoved his hands in his pockets. "Yes. Theoretically, it could protect her throughout her mortal life. Render the gate undetectable by demons...until the time of her death."

A wave of grief washed over him so powerful he barely managed to hold his ground and not stagger back. Without mating, her life would be longer than a mortal, but it *would* end.

But then a full mortal life, one full of love and laughter, would be better than an eternity tied to him.

Lazarus fought to control his conflicting emotions. "The amulet, it would protect her, though? She'd be safe?"

Silas's square jaw clenched. "Yes, as long as she keeps it on."

How could he even contemplate this now? Now he knew what she was and what she could unwittingly unleash onto the world. Still, he had to ask. "I'm not certain," he started carefully, "but the way things are progressing, I don't think it will be necessary for us to mate." The roughness of his voice was humiliating. He hated showing weakness, especially in front of this male.

"You can't hide from me," Silas said softly.

"No shit," he muttered.

"Are you sure about this, Laz?"

"No." What was the point of lying? He'd see right through his bullshit.

"I guess the decision is yours. If you can dispatch Tobias before you're taken by your demon, you may have a chance." He shrugged. "If you're successful, and you then choose not to take Eve as your mate, you'll return to the way you were before Tobias's betrayal."

His gut clenched. No Eve. The idea wasn't as appealing as it would have been a short time ago.

"And Eve?"

"The amulet will keep her safe, and once she is trained and released, she can carry on with her life the way she sees fit."

"Right."

"But your connection to her would still be there. You'd feel her. But harder still, you'd have to allow that connection to strengthen. You'd have to embrace it to make sure she was safe, to ensure she never removed the amulet. Lazarus, you'd know when she was happy and when she wasn't. Could you live with that every day? Feeling her living her life, living it with her in that way? Maybe even knowing she was with someone else...someone that wasn't you?"

His demon, who was usually subdued around Silas, shrieked, the sound vibrating through his skull. Its claws pushed at the tips of his fingers, trying to break free. Lazarus hated the idea as much as his demon, but it would be for the best for Eve. As long as she was happy.

And safe, away from him.

"I would think long and hard before you choose this route," Silas said. "Mating with you is the only way to destroy the gate she carries permanently. Also, there's only one amulet in existence, and Eve will have it." He shrugged his wide shoulders again. "Who knows what trials you and your brothers will face in the future?"

His eyes glittered through the darkness. Yeah, the angel knew. He knew exactly what trials they would face.

Fuck.

"Then tell me, what should I do, Silas?" He hated the desperation in his voice, but fucking hell, he *was* desperate.

Silas shook his head, his wings extending, ruffling in the breeze. "It is not for me to say."

In two steps, Lazarus was in front of him. He grabbed the front of the angel's shirt and shoved. Silas staggered back a step. Lazarus knew he'd only managed it because Silas had allowed it.

"Tell me," he roared. "For once, would you just fucking tell me what to do?"

The angel's eyes gentled then he repeated, "It is not for me to say."

Lazarus shoved away from him and walked to the edge of the building, trying to regain his composure.

"You need to forgive yourself, Lazarus," Silas said close behind him. "Scarlet has."

When Lazarus spun back around, the angel was gone.

Brent's thoughts streamed into her mind, and Eve laughed.

Lazarus shot Brent a dirty look.

Brent smirked, his sensual mouth tilting up on one side. "What? I'm keeping it clean."

Laz turned to her, brow raised.

"He's singing the *Teenage Mutant Ninja Turtle* theme song," she said.

"Jesus," Lazarus muttered.

Lazarus was fresh from the shower, his dark hair still damp and a little rumpled from him thrusting his fingers through it. The jeans he wore molded to his powerful thighs, and his faded T-shirt clung to his wide chest and thick biceps. He looked amazing.

A zing fired through her belly when he trained those pale eyes back on her.

Nope. She couldn't look away.

His tongue darted out, swiping across his full lower lip, and she swayed, fighting the urge to lift up on her tiptoes and taste that plump, firm flesh again for herself.

His Adam's apple bobbed and he cleared his throat. "Let's get started."

Eve stood in the middle of the living room in their temporary home. Lazarus announced that morning that they needed to get back to her training. Since this was her first training session with Brent, she wasn't sure what to expect. But Lazarus had promised to teach her to block her telepathy, and because of her lack of any kind of breakthrough at the compound, she was afraid to believe that it was possible, that she might be able to live a normal—well, normal-ish—life after all.

Lazarus moved closer and her pulse sped up instantly. How on earth was she supposed to concentrate with him standing so close?

"Just relax, Eve," he murmured.

Easy for him to say. He didn't go into cardiac arrest whenever she came close.

He moved around and stood at her back. Heat poured off him in waves, radiating from his chest and searing her back through the thin fabric of her dress. Her skin tingled in a pleasant way and made her want to lean back, take more of his warmth. His hands came down on her shoulders and he leaned in closer. Her knees wobbled.

Fingers tightening, he massaged lightly. "Where do you feel it, Eve?"

She squirmed. Where did she feel it? Oh no, she wasn't going there. "I, ah…"

Brent chucked like he was the one that could read minds, and her face heated.

"Just keep singing, asshole." Lazarus's lips brushed her hair when he spoke next. "When you're listening to him where do you feel it?"

Brent's singing continued.

Eve glanced over at him. "I can't believe you know every word of that song."

He shrugged. "I liked cartoons."

Laz gave her another squeeze. "Focus."

"Right. In my head, I guess."

"No, Eve. Where do you *feel* it?"

Eve tried to zone Brent out and focus on the source of her ability, which she'd never done before, and immediately zeroed in on the low buzz at the back of her skull. She reached back and showed him. "Here."

"Different abilities manifest differently. If your ability had been a physical one, for example, you would have felt it here." He reached around and placed his hand against her chest, his palm skimming the tops of her breasts. Her heart hammered faster. He didn't comment, but there was no way he couldn't feel her reaction to his touch. His hand moved to the base of her skull, massaging gently. "This is the point where all psychic powers are felt, and the point you need to visualize when you want to block it. Understand?"

"I think so."

"Up until your first lesson, you would have tried to block your ears to escape others' thoughts, yes?"

She nodded. "It never worked."

"That's because your hearing has nothing to do with the way your ability works. So from now on, I want you to picture this point right here."

More massaging. Firm, but gentle. Goose bumps were breaking out all over her body from his touch. "Okay."

"Now, as much as I'm sure you love hearing Brent sing, imagine this is a life-and-death situation. Your options are block Brent, or I kill him for you to shut out the terrible sound of his voice."

Eve laughed and Brent's eyes narrowed. Lazarus could be funny when he wanted to be. She liked it.

"I want you to close your eyes and visualize a small black hole, no bigger than the tip of your pinkie. That's where your power flows, allowing all that noise, all those thoughts and images to reach your mind. Now I want you to imagine blocking it."

She did as he said, picturing the tiny black hole. "Okay, I see it. What do I block it with?"

"Gum," Brent said. "When I was training, I used to pretend to stuff a big piece of chewed-up gum over mine. Grape Hubba Bubba worked best."

"Good choice," she said, smiling. "Grape's my favorite, too. I can do that."

She was sure she heard Lazarus grind his teeth behind her. "Whatever works," he said, still close behind her. "Now can you hear Brent singing?"

"Yes."

"Excellent. Now you have ten seconds to block him out, or I'll slit his throat."

Eve tried to spin to face him. "What?"

"Ten...nine...eight..."

175

"No. You wouldn't, would you?"

"Six…five…"

"I'd rather you didn't test him on that, Eve," Brent said.

His singing, still loud and clear, echoed through her mind.

Eve tried to visualize the pinkie-sized hole then imagined stuffing it with gum. All the while Lazarus counted down.

It wasn't working.

"Three…two…" Lazarus's deep voice filled the room.

"Anytime now would be good, Eve," Brent called.

Eve shut everything else out and concentrated on blocking Brent—

Silence.

The kind of silence she'd only experienced since Lazarus stormed into her life.

"One…"

She uncurled her fingers so her nails quit biting into her palms, and released the breath she'd been holding. "Are you doing that?" she asked Lazarus, because how could it be her?

"It's all you, Eve." She could hear the smile in his voice.

"I did it? Oh my God. *I did it.*" She spun around and threw her arms around Lazarus's neck.

Lazarus rested his hands on Eve's waist. She pulled back, arms wrapped around him, and smiled. No, she fucking beamed like he'd just brought her a new puppy. He blew out a breath, the wind knocked clean from his lungs with that one look.

"You did really good," he managed. What else could he say? Hell, he could hardly think, let alone form a coherent sentence with her staring at him like that.

"I did, right?" she said.

Shit, she needed to stop smiling at him like that. She tilted

176

her head to the side. "You really had me going there for a minute."

"Did I?" He wanted to smile back, but fought the impulse into submission.

"Come on, I know you'd never actually kill Brent. Though your rather drastic plan worked."

He reluctantly released her and pushed his hands into his pockets. As soon as she stepped back, he wanted her hands right back where they'd been. "Slitting Brent's throat wouldn't kill him, not the way I'd do it. Besides, he's a fast healer."

"Oh my God, you're terrible." She slapped his arm playfully.

He liked seeing her like this, relaxed, kinda goofy—happy.

She turned to Brent. "Poor Brent. Don't worry, I'll protect you."

Brent pushed away from the wall, that predatory smirk back on his handsome face. "Would you really, sweetheart?"

"You can leave now. You've served your purpose," Lazarus said to him.

Brent sent him a look that was far too knowing and winked at Eve before he left the apartment.

Eve stared at him. "Well, that was rude."

Her defense of the other male did not sit well with him, not at all. In fact, it made him insanely and irrationally pissed. "Was it?"

"Yes."

"And you care why exactly?"

Her eyes widened at his harsh tone. "What's wrong with you?"

He shoved his fingers through his hair. "Nothing."

She went quiet and the silence stretched out.

When he made himself look at her again, her arms were crossed over her chest and she was studying him like she wanted to crawl inside his head, discover all his secrets. It freaked him the hell out that she might be able to see the truth, see the kind of male he truly was.

One thing he couldn't hide anymore was what Silas had told him the night before. She had a right to know what she was. Thinking about how this new bit of information would affect her, terrify her, made him sick to his stomach. He'd do anything to protect her from that.

But he couldn't. It was too important to keep from her. Too damn dangerous to keep from her.

"Thanks for this, for helping me," she said carefully.

"You'll need to practice. The more you do, the longer you'll be able to hold the block. After a while, it won't be any effort."

The worry disappeared and her smile returned, but this time with the wattage cranked way up. "Can we try again tomorrow?"

"Sure." His voice was back to gravel.

The look on her face, all that gratitude, and hope was making it hard to breathe. He didn't deserve it.

She reached out, put her hand on his chest, and the brand burned into his skin there heated, causing the flesh beneath to tingle.

"Lazarus…" Her voice was soft, sweet, a lover's caress. No one had ever said his name like that before, and dammit, he liked it. Wanted to hear her say it again.

He stepped back. "I have to head out."

The smile faded and she crossed her arms again. "Oh…okay."

She looked down hiding her eyes from him. He hated that, hated that he kept on hurting her, but what he hated most of all was that he wasn't even close to being finished.

And then he felt it.

It was unconscious on her part, he was sure, but Eve was

178

reaching out to him, calling to him, and his body responded to the volatile energy she was throwing his way in pulsing waves.

His dick, already hard, stiffened further. Jesus, he wanted her, needed to be inside her again. But he didn't reach for her, even when it was all he wanted, all he could think about.

"I'll see you tomorrow, then?" she said in a quiet voice.

He shrugged on his jacket. "Yeah."

His boots felt heavy as he walked to the door. His body, his demon, was at odds with his mind, screaming at him to stay and take her, make her his once and for all.

No. His only option was to find Tobias and put him out of commission. Then he could let Eve go.

He'd made his decision.

CHAPTER 17

EVE TOOK the stairs down to the club. She needed a drink. Well, that was her excuse, but in reality, she was desperate for company. Even if that company was of the leather-clad and extremely kinky variety.

Besides her training sessions with Lazarus, or as she'd come to think of them, her daily dose of sexual frustration and torture, she barely saw him. He left right after running through her blocking techniques and didn't come back until after she was asleep.

She didn't know what was going on in his head. The male was completely unreadable. He'd told her she was his mate, told her how much he wanted her, but then proceeded to avoid her like the plague. She didn't get it, didn't get him.

Which left her feeling lonely, confused, and kind of pissed off.

Brent had been great. He spent a lot of time with her, helping her with her training. It wasn't easy, but he was a good teacher. Now she could block out the noise on her own, not all day, but for extended periods.

Brent had been hanging out with her a little, taking pity

on her. They'd watched a few movies and sometimes ate together before he headed down to the club, but he wasn't Lazarus, and she felt his absence like a physical ache.

She shook her head. Insane.

The club was quiet when she hit the door, the only sound the low murmur of Brent's voice. He was behind the bar, his staff gathered around him.

The club was empty since it wasn't quite opening time. She'd only come down during the day since they got there, while it was closed, and was surprised at the rush of excitement and flutter of nerves at the prospect of hanging around, maybe staying for a while once it opened.

Being among people who didn't have any hang-ups, who made no apologies for who they were, was exhilarating. They took what they wanted, when they wanted it. Eve envied that.

"We're a dancer down," Brent said.

"I'll do it," Chaya, the curvy waitress she'd met when she arrived, spoke up.

Brent visibly stiffened. "No. You won't."

Chaya narrowed her eyes. "I can dance, Brent."

"I want my customers coming back, and that means having someone who knows what the fuck they're doing. You're working the bar." Chaya flinched and her cheeks heated.

Eve winced. She'd seen another side to Brent over the last week, not so much softer, but more relaxed, a side he obviously didn't share with his staff. Brent didn't seem to notice or care that he'd hurt Chaya's feelings and had already asked another waitress to dance. She glanced between him and Chaya, at the way they were purposely *not* looking at each other.

Eve leaned against the bar and tapped him on the arm. "Hey, um…I can waitress if you're short. I've done it before."

Brent turned and so did everyone else. That slow smile lifted his sensual lips. "You think Lazarus would be happy about that?"

"I doubt it, but it's not really his decision. I don't answer to him."

Brent raised a brow. "I don't think he sees it that way, sweetheart." He turned back to his gathered staff and waved them away. "You know what to do." He turned back to her.

"Come on. Give me something to do," she pleaded.

He crossed his arms. "It's not a good idea."

"He's not here. He's never here. And if you don't let me help, and I'm stuck in that room another night all by myself, I'll go mad."

"You think you have enough control to sustain your block for a few hours?"

She really hoped so. "Yes. And if I start to struggle, I'll go back upstairs."

He rested a hip against the bar. He looked powerful in his dark suit, his height, and good looks no doubt intimidating to most. "If I let you do this, you have to stick to delivering drinks and clearing tables. If anyone worries you, bothers you, you come to me or one of the guys on the floor."

"Guys?"

"George"—he pointed to a huge man standing by the door —"or Mark." Mark stood against the wall on the other side of the room, his gaze taking in his surroundings, not missing a thing. They were both frightening as hell. "They look out for the staff. You need help, you grab me or one of the guys, yeah?"

Excitement bubbled up inside her. "Is that a yes?"

He still didn't look convinced, but finally said, "I guess it is."

"Thank you! You won't regret it."

A wicked glint lit his dark gaze. "We have a certain image

here, and it needs to be maintained at all times. So, if you're doing this, you need to do it right. You need to dress the part. Go get changed."

Did he think that would dissuade her? Eve looked around. Okay, it might. She didn't have anything in her bag that would fit in down here. Who the hell would? "Ah...I'd love to, but rubber gives me a rash."

Brent snorted. "It's not negotiable."

She grinned. "Just when I thought my dreams of wearing a studded collar would never be fulfilled…"

He shook his head at her sarcasm. "If you're determined to do this, go talk to Chaya. You're a similar build. She'll have something you can wear." He was enjoying her discomfort way too much.

"You're loving this, aren't you?"

"I'm looking forward to seeing how you'll look in Chaya's clothes." He chuckled, rough and low. "And what Lazarus will do when he sees you."

Her heart sped up. "I doubt he'll care either way."

His smile turned wicked. "We open soon. Get changed and get your ass back out here."

"Yes, boss."

He walked off, headed to his office, and Eve spotted Chaya on her way back to the bar. "Chaya?"

The other woman stopped in front of her, a wary expression on her face. "Yeah?"

"Um, Brent said you might have something for me to wear. I'm waitressing."

Her eyes slid to the door Brent had just disappeared behind then back to Eve. "Right, come with me."

Chaya wore a short pleated black leather skirt and spike-heeled boots. Her top was red and slashed in strategic places, showing a lot of skin and cleavage, and her long dark hair hung loose, swaying around her waist. Chaya looked gorgeous. No way could Eve pull off an outfit like that.

They entered a room with lockers lining the walls. There were still a few people milling about, talking, and getting ready. "Out," Chaya barked. Surprisingly, everyone scattered without argument.

Chaya flung open her locker and pulled clothes and shoes out. Everything was short and way too revealing, but after some not-so-gentle coaxing, Eve ended up in a short A-line red tartan skirt, black fishnets, and a black sheer tank that showed off the red bra she wore underneath. Eve had never been able to wear heels for any length of time, so Chaya gave her a pair of knee-high lace-up boots with a chunky sole that Eve loved and never wanted to give back.

Chaya stood back and gave her a head to toe. "You look awesome."

Eve looked down at herself. "My fat thighs are out for the world to see."

"We have pretty much the same build. Are you saying my thighs look fat?" Those catlike eyes stared up at her, unblinking.

"No, *you* look amazing. And I…"

"Look hot."

Did she? She didn't know. Dressing like this wasn't really her thing, but she could handle it for a night. It was kind of like playing dress-up, like being someone else. A welcome prospect after everything that had happened.

"What goes on out there? How do you handle being around it every night?" Eve asked while Chaya sat her down to apply a thick coat of charcoal liner around her eyes and fluffed her hair.

She shrugged and planted a hand on her hip. "You get used to it after a while, though I've definitely worn out a few vibrators. I'm on a first-name basis with the woman who owns the adults-only store around the corner."

They both burst out laughing. It felt good to laugh. That hard exterior Chaya had dropped while they'd played dress-up, and Eve started to think that maybe they could be friends. A little thrill ran through her. She could have friends. There were people like her that understood, that wouldn't be scared off by what she was inadvertently sending out.

People she wouldn't have to hide who she was from. Chaya knew, she understood.

A noise came from the door and they both spun around. Brent stood there, expression dark, controlled. The same way he'd looked that first night when she'd seen him across the club, before he'd seen her and Lazarus. This wasn't the Brent who laughed at cheesy movies with her and ate pizza from the box. No, this Brent was the businessman, the sex demon who knew how to wield his power. A force to be reckoned with.

He took her in. "You look good."

"Thanks, I guess. Not too much?"

He shook his head and the corner of his mouth lifted. "No, you'll fit right in." His gaze slid to Chaya and the barely-there grin slid from his face. "I need you behind the bar now. The place is filling up."

Chaya's shoulders stiffened before she turned to Eve. "I'll see you out there." She stormed out.

Eve stared up at Brent. "What's up with you two?"

He crossed his arms over his wide chest. "Nothing."

Yeah, right.

"You ready?" he asked.

"Yep. All set."

"You remember what I told you?"

"Yes."

"Humor me."

SHERILEE GRAY

"If I feel worried or if someone creeps me out, find you or one of the guys then go to the apartment."

"The wards are stronger up there. It's the safest place for you if you feel your block dropping." He shook his head. "I don't like this, Eve. And Laz will have my balls if anything happens to you."

"I doubt that very much." She tugged at her skirt, which kept creeping higher. "I'm just clearing tables and delivering drinks, right? What could go wrong? Plus, you're saving my sanity. That has to count for something."

He didn't look convinced. "Just stay alert."

"Will do." She rubbed her hands together. "Time I got to work." She started toward to door.

"And, Eve?"

"Yeah?"

"Chaya was right. You look hot." He winked then led her out to the club.

A couple of hours into her shift, and she well and truly had the swing of things.

The music thumped so low she felt it in her belly, and the lights pulsed along with the bass. It confused the senses, enticed. The surreal sensation made her feel like she was someone else, free to do whatever she wanted.

It wasn't hard to see why this place was so full.

The club had been busy since she walked onto the floor. The heady atmosphere was electric and led its occupants to sin. Made you crave it.

Lazarus had walked into the club an hour ago and Eve was doing her best to ignore him. He hadn't approached her, but Eve had felt his presence the minute he arrived. She didn't know how, but she knew his gaze had never once left her, followed her wherever she went. She felt it burning a path across her skin.

186

She felt greedy after being starved of his attention for so long. Alive, sexy. Turned on.

Chaya placed two more drinks on her tray. "Over there. The corner," she shouted over the music.

"Okay." Eve weaved her way through the crowd, not shying away from the hands that brushed her skin as she moved by or the offers whispered into her ear. She took a hedonistic kind of pleasure from it, all of it. For some reason, knowing Lazarus was watching, and saw how others reacted to her, desired her, tried to touch her, turned her on even more.

The lights were dim, but with every flash of muted red light, she got a glimpse of glistening skin and tangled limbs. She stopped by the table and unloaded the drinks for the couple sitting there. Beside them a woman lay on the padded vinyl bench seat, legs spread wide, her skirt shoved up around her hips. The guy she was with had his head between her thighs. He feasted on her, worshiped her body with long sensuous strokes. The sheer carnality of the act caused the ache between her thighs to intensify. God, she wanted that.

She couldn't look away. How would it feel to do something like that with everyone watching? Heat washed over her. She was so turned on by the sight a moan broke past her lips.

The woman turned to Eve, a smile spread across her glossy red lips. "Join us?"

For a split second, she imagined what it would be like to say yes. To let go and just feel.

What am I thinking?

She stumbled back a step. "No...I, ah, sorry." Spinning around, she shoved through the crowd blocking her path and headed to the back of the building and the glowing fire exit sign. She needed fresh air. All the raging hormones in this place were getting to her. She grabbed the handle and shoved the door open. Cool night air hit her skin, and she sucked down a lungful.

But before she could take a step outside, someone grabbed her arm and yanked her back.

Eve squealed and spun around.

Lazarus stared down at her, eyes flashing fire. "Where the fuck do you think you're going?"

"I—I just needed some air."

He cursed and dragged her back into the club. "Have you forgotten what could be waiting for you out there?"

Oh God. "I'm sorry. I didn't think." In this place, she couldn't think straight.

Lazarus pulled her through the club and didn't stop until they reached Brent's office. He threw the door open without knocking and strode inside.

Brent was sitting on the couch in the corner, a woman crouched in front of him, his fingers fisting her hair while she worked his cock with eager, hungry sucks.

"I take it Eve's finished for the night?" he said without looking at her.

Okay, that was way more than she'd wanted to see of her new friend, and didn't resist when Lazarus growled and shoved her behind him, blocking her view. "Put your fucking dick away."

Brent laughed, dark and rough. "Can you kick my ass later? I'm a little busy at the moment."

"Count on it." Lazarus led her back out, slammed the door, and dragged her toward the stairs.

When they reached their apartment, he pushed her inside, pulling her through the living room and into the bathroom. The light flicked on and he slammed the door shut, throwing out a hand, using his powers to lock it. The shower came on next.

"What are you doing?"

His expression was dark, intent. "Washing the stench of that place off you. This"—he motioned to her clothes, her face—"isn't you."

She tried to unlock the door. It wouldn't budge. "How the hell would you know?"

"Get in the shower," he growled.

She took a step back. "No."

His eyes narrowed. "Get in the fucking shower, Eve."

Her palms grew sweaty and her pulse sped up. "Make me." She didn't know why, but she wanted to push him, to see him lose control. She wanted him to want her again, to stop ignoring her.

His nostrils flared and he took a step toward her. "Is that what you want?"

"Yes."

What on earth am I doing?

Lazarus didn't hesitate. He toed off his boots, yanked his shirt over his head, revealing all that beautiful smooth skin and thick slabs of muscle, then closed the gap between them and started stripping her. She didn't fight it—why would she?

"I've been watching you," he said against her ear. "Watching you strut around in that little skirt, showing off these perfect tits." He cupped her breast, squeezing the sensitive flesh, making her gasp.

Oh God, she wanted him.

"Did you like it?" he growled.

"W-what?" She couldn't think straight.

His other hand came up under her skirt, and without warning, he pushed her panties aside and slid two fingers through her drenched pussy. She cried out and he cursed. "Watching people fuck, Eve. Did you like it?"

She moaned and gripped his biceps, her head dropping forward against his chest.

SHERILEE GRAY

"Tell me," he said.

More. She needed more.

And like she'd said it out loud, he pushed a finger inside her, going deep, hitting the sensitive bundle of nerves there. She sobbed. "Y-yes."

"I saw them touch you, putting their filthy fucking hands on you when you walked by. You like that, too?"

"Yes." *What is wrong with me?*

He took hold of her chin, tilting her head back, making her look at him. Fury lined his hard features, held his big body rigid, and though it was all kinds of screwed up, she loved that he might actually be jealous, that on some messed-up level he might actually care.

He didn't let up, just continued to fuck her with his fingers in a controlled way that made her want to scream. "Did you want to join that couple? Did you want that male between your thighs, tongue buried in this tight, hot little pussy?"

"No," she gasped, his crude words heightening her already out-of-control desire.

"I can feel how turned on it made you, how wet you got from watching that male fuck his female with his tongue. He did this to you. You want him. Fucking admit it."

"No...I don't. I..."

"Say it." His tone was low and harsh and he tightened his grip on her.

"Yes, I liked it," she cried.

He hissed, lips peeling back from his teeth, eyes flickering to ebony.

"But it wasn't him I wanted," she said, close, so close to coming apart.

He ground his erection against her hip. "Who? Who do you want?" he asked, voice guttural.

190

Gripping his shoulders, she rode his hand. "You. I want you." Then she was coming.

He didn't stop. His fingers continued to move inside her, ringing every last tremor from her body before Lazarus stripped her out of her remaining clothes and carried her to the shower. He climbed in with her, shoved her against the wall, and dropped to his knees. She gasped when he buried his face between her thighs.

Her fingers thrust into his hair, holding on, pulling him closer as he lapped at her, devoured her with deep, hungry strokes of his tongue. He pressed her into the wall, lifting one of her legs over his shoulder, opening her wide for him. Water sluiced over his bare back and drenched his dark hair. Eve couldn't help but fist the glossy strands tighter, close to losing control all over again.

He looked up at her, eyes flashing dark then light, glazed with lust. She loved it, loved that she'd done that to him. That she'd made him so out of control, so crazy for her.

He fucked her with his tongue until she was a writhing, sobbing mess then he wrapped his firm lips around her clit and sucked, sending her over the edge. She didn't hold back —couldn't—and held him to her, grinding against his mouth, lost in sensation. He growled against her, not stopping until she sagged against the wall.

When he pulled back suddenly a few seconds later, she opened her eyes.

Lazarus stood against the tile wall, still in his jeans, the denim drenched and clinging to his hips and thighs. His chest pumped and he gasped out harsh breaths.

Eve took a step toward him.

"Don't." He shook his head. "You can't touch me. Not now. I'm barely hanging on. I'll take what I want. To hell with the consequences."

"Take it," she whispered. "I don't care what the conse-quences are." She wanted it, whatever it was.

"You don't understand." He pressed back into the wall, his face a mask of pain and longing.

Every muscle strained, every vein and tendon stood out on his tanned skin. She couldn't take her eyes off him. He was magnificent, beautiful. A groan slipped past his lips and he reached down to grip his straining cock, squeezing his hard flesh through the wet denim.

She licked her lips. "Lazarus." His name came out as a plea. She had to see him, all of him.

His hands shook as he popped the button and slid down the zip. His heavy cock sprang free, thick and swollen. A constant stream of pre-come leaked from the tiny slit, running down the shaft, and her mouth watered to taste him. She wanted to drop to her knees and take him into her mouth. "Let me—"

He shook his head, eyes wild, slightly unfocused. "Stay back, Eve. I mean it."

He fisted himself and began to stroke, eyes never leaving her. He leaned heavily on the wall, didn't speak, didn't look away. "*Ah, fuck.*" His fist tightened and his strokes increased in pace.

Eve had never seen anything like it, never seen a more beautiful sight in her life. She slid her hand down her body and slipped her fingers between her folds, massaging her clit, too turned on not to. Lazarus watched her every move, and the sound that left him was full of anguish and need and spurred her on. She cupped her breast with the other hand and squeezed like he had earlier. He moaned low then hissed through his clenched teeth. He was wild, untamed. The solid slabs of muscle in his massive thighs locked up tight.

"What have you done to me?" He groaned and grew impossibly long and thick before he finally cried out her name and came hard. Thick creamy ropes spurted from him, washing down the drain.

Eve leaned against the wall and followed him, coming for the third time against her own fingers.

Lazarus was there before her legs gave out, supporting her weight. He turned off the shower, wrapped her in a towel, and carried her to her room. His hands were rough and economical as he dried her off and squeezed the water from her hair.

He pulled back the covers and put her into bed.

Moments later, Eve drifted into a restless sleep.

CHAPTER 18

Eve woke to sounds coming from the small kitchen and the smell of bacon cooking.

Her stomach rumbled.

Shoving back the covers, she tugged on a pair of shorts and a tank and left her room. Things had gotten crazy the night before. Intense. The way Lazarus had been, the things he'd said.

"You can't touch me. Not now. I'm barely hanging on. I'll take what I want. To hell with the consequences."

What did that mean? She was done waiting for answers.

Her belly flipped when she saw him. He was standing at the counter in only a pair of jeans, a mountain of bacon and eggs piled on plates in front of him.

"Morning," she said, voice still husky from having to yell over loud music last night.

He spun around, his gaze moving over her before coming back to her eyes. His chest expanded sharply.

He licked his lips and cleared his throat. "I made breakfast. You hungry?"

"Ravenous."

Lazarus handed her a plate, and they ate for a while in silence.

"Thanks for doing this."

"I thought that maybe we could talk this morning."

"I was thinking the same thing," she said, suddenly not hungry anymore.

Somehow she finished her breakfast and carried her plate to the kitchen. Lazarus followed her in, putting his plate in the sink.

Eve turned to him, looking up at his strong face, down to that wide chest. She lifted her hand and placed it on the burn there. It had a pattern to it, almost like someone had branded him. She'd been wondering what it was since she first saw it.

"How did you get this?" she asked, tracing it gently.

His nostrils flared. "We were given them when our training was complete. The brand is supposed to prevent us from entering Hell, from being corrupted."

"Corrupted?" Eve stared up at Lazarus, trying and failing to control the pounding of her heart.

Lazarus lifted his hand to hers, covering it, curling his fingers around hers. "Let's sit down."

Her belly flipped at his serious tone. He led her into the small living room and Eve moved to the couch and sat...and waited.

Lazarus paced around in front of her for a few minutes, making her even more nervous.

Finally, he stopped and faced her. "There are things you need to know, about me, about us...about you."

"Okay," she said, clutching her hands together.

His jaw tightened. "It has...it's become obvious that *being* with you...it balances me. It gives me the strength to keep control over my demon, control I've been losing over the last few weeks."

"Being with me? You mean like last night?"

He dipped his chin.

"The mate thing?" she said, pulse picking up speed.

He swallowed, throat working. "Yes."

She wished she knew how to wipe away the anguish lining his face. "Why are you losing control?"

He sat on the couch beside her, rubbing his palms on his jean-covered thighs. "A very long time ago, demons discovered a way to leave their realm and began moving among mankind. The angels were clueless, only learning about it after a demi-demon, new to his powers, accidentally wiped out his entire village. The demons were using human females to carry and raise their offspring, and when they were old enough to be of use, they would reclaim them to use as weapons to gain control and power on Earth."

She could barely believe the horror of what he was telling her. But she knew looking into his eyes that it was all true.

"The heavens couldn't allow such atrocities to occur, so six angels chose to fall for the good of mankind."

Eve rubbed her temples, a slow throb building behind her eyes. "Why did they need to fall?"

"To breed with the very demons they despised, to create a race of warriors. The knights of Hell, they called us. The angels had tried and failed to track the demi-demons on their own, to control the demon hordes escaping hell. But with the addition of demon DNA, it would be possible. They had to prevent the demon offspring from being used as weapons. They couldn't allow such evil to corrupt the Earth. Balance must always be maintained."

"And you're one of the knights?"

"Yes. I have no idea which fallen birthed me; none of us do. We weren't raised like human children, Eve. We were raised to be warriors, weapons in the war between Heaven and Hell."

What he described turned her stomach, made her ache

for the little boy he had once been. Yes, she'd suffered repeated rejection by her extended family, but she'd also had many years of nurturing by her mother and father, of feeling loved.

"What happened to disturb the balance?" He kept using that word. It wasn't hard to figure out something had tipped the scale.

"Tobias, one of our bothers, surrendered to his demon after the death of his mate. He chose a life without the memory of her love." He swallowed hard. "Because living without her was just too painful."

She wrapped her arms around herself when a cold, hollow feeling settled in the center of her chest. "How he must have suffered to make such a choice. He's the one you've been searching for?"

"Yes. And because he surrendered to his demon willingly, the possession was gradual. They became one, which enables him to maintain a measure of control, unlike the rest of us. Now he answers to Diemos."

He stood, his back to her. "You see, all knights are connected, a bond that was formed when we were born. It's an added safeguard created by the angels to keep us tied together so we won't be tempted to abandon our purpose, a bond so strong it can only be broken by death. While Tobias lives, he can send his toxic poison to us through that bond. We're absorbing his dark, demonic nature, which is throwing off that delicate balance." He turned to face her. "He's taking the rest of us with him."

The horror of his words and the cold way he spoke them caused her to flinch. "Lazarus, I'm so sorry—"

"No." His deep voice cut her off, startling her. A muscle in his jaw jumped. "Don't be sorry for me."

Anguish transformed his gaze. And whatever had caused the pain and self-loathing she saw there had left a mark on his soul and caused a torment so deep she could see the invisible wound bleeding from his chest. She tamped down the urge to go to him, to comfort him. At that moment he wouldn't welcome it. "What happens now?"

"The angels have taken his actions as a declaration of war. He chose his side, and it wasn't ours. Now you understand the urgency, the reason I need to find Tobias."

She stood and took a step toward him. When he didn't retreat, she moved in close enough to rest a hand on his biceps. The muscle flexed under her palm, hard as stone. "I'll do whatever I can to help."

"You will?" he choked.

"Yes." If being with him helped save him and his brothers, of course, she'd help. How could she not?

"I hate that you have to do this. I hate that you are in danger because of me. But, Eve, I'm also thankful. You don't know how many people you're saving by allowing me to"—he sucked in a sharp breath—"by giving yourself to me in that way." His throat worked several times before he carried on. "Sex seems to provide enough of a calming effect on me that…" He ran a hand over his head before he glanced back at her. "There shouldn't be any need for us to mate fully. I felt it when we were in the storeroom at the airport. And just touching me seems to help a little."

It took effort, but she managed to school her features. Dammit, why did it hurt so much? His words confirmed what she'd already guessed. The idea of being tied to her for the rest of his life was not a welcome prospect. Lazarus would use her body, and when he no longer needed her, he would leave.

She should be used to this by now. Really, she should be as pleased as he obviously was. Even though she knew this was how it must be, it stung. She had grown to care far more than she should for the dangerous warrior.

Realization struck, and her mouth went dry. "That's why you're keeping me close?"

"No." He shook his head. "My main priority has always been keeping you safe."

"You sure about that? Or was it so I could help you control your demon, so you could track Tobias?"

His lips compressed into a thin line. "I had no idea you'd have that effect on me. I promise you that."

The man in front of her was going through hell, doing what he had to for a greater good. But hanging on for dear life while he dragged her through the fiery aftermath wasn't much fun either. Neither was having your life ripped out from under you and treated as nothing more than a means to an end.

The way he was looking at her, she knew that wasn't it, though. There was more. "What aren't you telling me?"

He closed the distance between them and his hand went to her hip, finger sliding into the elastic of her shorts, tugging down the side a little.

Eve watched, confused as he ran his fingers over the crimson birthmark she had there. Her heart rate had picked up speed when she looked back at him.

"This"—another brush of his finger over the mark—"is called the Beast's touch." Eve's whole body jerked and she tried to pull away. Lazarus wouldn't let her, his big hand gripping her hip, holding her there. "As far as we know, only demi who carry this mark can do what you can."

She clenched her fists so tight her knuckles ached. "And what's that?"

"You can open the gates of Hell."

Oh God. She tried to pull away again, but Lazarus wouldn't let her retreat. "How?" she whispered.

"When Lucifer still ruled Hell—"

"He doesn't rule Hell anymore?"

Lazarus's brows lowered. "He was overthrown by Diemos and cast out. No one knows how, or where he is, if he's even still alive."

Eve's head began to pound. "And what does that have to do with me?"

"He had a group of warriors, demons, he called his hand-maidens. They were loyal to only him, guarded him, took care of him, and they also had the ability to open and close the gates of Hell." He squeezed her hip. "You are a descendant of one of his handmaids, and as a result, you have inherited the same ability. You're a hell's gate, Eve."

She started to shake. "I'm a what?"

"Demons can only cross from Hell to Earth four times a year—during the summer and winter solstice, and the spring and autumn equinox. That's when the barrier between realms is at its thinnest."

She wanted to block her ears, didn't want to believe what she was hearing.

"And if Diemos captured you—"

"Diemos?"

"He controls Hell now, and his main goal is to take Earth as well, to rule it. Because of his limited access to Earth, Diemos can only send a small number of his soldiers through at a time. He doesn't like that. The gate opens, he sends demons through, the gate closes, and we get time to whittle down the army he's trying to build. It's a never-ending cycle, and the only way to gain unlimited access is to possess a hell's gate demi. With you, he could activate the hell's gate at will."

Eve was suddenly struggling to breathe.

He rubbed her back. "Eve?" He cursed. "Calm down. I need you to calm down."

She shook her head and pushed at his arms with more

force. He let her go this time, let her stumble back several steps. "Calm down? Are you serious?"

Lazarus stayed where he was as she paced around.

"Eve…"

She shook her head, trying to take it in. All of it. Her stomach roiled. "I think I'm going to be sick."

"Eve, look at me."

She forced herself to look up, to meet his green gaze.

"I won't let that happen. Do you hear me? Now we have you, they can't use you. No one can get to you here. And while you're wearing the amulet, they can't track you either. Your power to activate the gate won't work."

"Is there a way to get this…this gate out of me, to stop it?" She wanted to claw at her skin, tear it out of her body.

His jaw clenched again. "Mating will render the power useless." He pointed to the heavy gold necklace she wore. "But it's not necessary. As long as you wear that, you'll be safe."

She squeezed her eyes closed. God, what she wouldn't give to be in her little bookstore right at that moment, back to living her quiet, solitary existence. She'd spent her life giving to others, trying to please, only to have it thrown back in her face. No more. She was sick of life happening to her, of being overlooked, of being the girl people walked all over.

She let her anger rise to the surface, anger she had kept bottled up for far too long. A bitter laugh escaped, and she didn't recognize her voice when she spoke. "Lucky you, huh?" She curled her fingers around the amulet and held it up. "I can only imagine your relief that this chunk of metal exists. I mean, I'd hate to put you through the alternative."

"Eve—"

"No, it's fine, really. If jumping your bones on a regular basis is what you need from me…" She smiled, though it was more just a baring of teeth. "Well, that's a sacrifice I'm willing to make."

He stiffened and crimson slashed his sharp cheekbones. "Eve." He took a step toward her, reached for her.

She took a step back. "No, you're right, this is extremely good news. So how does this whole thing work? You start to lose control of your demon, and I—what? Jump on your dick and make it better?"

He flinched. "I promise I won't bother you unless it's absolutely necessary."

Ouch. The blows were coming thick and fast, and she felt emotionally battered and bruised as a result. She didn't want to look too deeply at how strong her feelings had grown in such a short span of time. Since he wouldn't be coming to her unless he absolutely had to, she might get a reprieve from his overpowering presence, maybe get a chance to gain some perspective over her jumbled emotions.

"I'd appreciate that," she said.

He stiffened.

"And once you kill Tobias, I'm free to go? I just have to make sure I wear this amulet…you know, so a horde of demons doesn't come after me, yes?"

"Eve, please—"

"What about pregnancy, sexually transmitted diseases? I'd prefer not to be left raising a child on my own." Obviously, this was something she should have considered *before* they'd had sex, but at the time they'd been in a seriously stressful situation and it hadn't exactly been the first thing that had popped into her head right afterward. She curled her fingers into a tight fist. She'd always wanted kids, someone to love and be loved unconditionally in return. It had been something she'd craved almost all her life. A real family.

"I can't carry diseases of any kind. And pregnancy can

only occur between mated couples." His voice was so low she barely heard him.

She shrugged carelessly, despite another verbal slap. "I guess I'm stuck here for a while longer, then. You know, since I'm the go-to girl when you need to get off." Accusation was clear in her voice, but she couldn't stop it, didn't want to. She should have known better than to trust so easily. Would she ever learn? How many times would she extend her hand only to have her fingers bitten?

He stood ramrod straight, his fists clenching and unclenching at his sides. "It's not like that—"

She ignored him and talked right over him. "All my life I've wanted to be special, to be important. Well, look at me now." She threw up her hands. "I got my wish. Turns out I've got a magic vagina." She turned her back on him and headed for the bedroom, needing to get the hell away from him.

He swore under his breath. "Eve, for fuck's sake. Stop."

She paused at the bedroom door but didn't turn around. She hated herself for thinking it, but she wanted him to tell her that wasn't all there was between them, that he cared for her. Even just a little.

The silence dragged out and finally, he said, "I have to go out for a while. Will you be all right on your own?"

Trying but no doubt failing to hide the conflicting emotions stirring inside her, she glanced back at him over her shoulder and shrugged "It's what I prefer. What I'm used to."

His mouth compressed into a thin line, and he ran a hand through his hair before he turned and strode from the room.

He'd been gone less than a minute when her mind headed to a place she didn't want it to go. The constant ache between her thighs made it near impossible to ignore. The question shot through her mind then proceeded to pierce her heart with a force that belied the short time she'd known him.

How long before he came for her?

Eve hated herself for still wanting him.

It shouldn't, but the thought of possessing Lazarus, of being wholly possessed in return, felt right. Unfortunately, she was the only one who felt it.

Still staring at the door after him, she made herself turn, and rubbing the gooseflesh from her arms, walked to the bathroom.

She didn't have a claim over him, never would, and he sure as hell didn't own her. How could he?

He didn't even want her.

She needed a shower, needed to wash off his scent, his touch…his kiss.

The reminders of what they'd done the night before lingered. A tangible thing, crowding the room, almost like he was seared into her skin and, God help her, her soul.

CHAPTER 19

LAZARUS SHUT the door behind him and sucked in a ragged breath.

He'd circled the pits of Hell, had barely resisted the darkness calling him home, and had never believed it possible to sink lower than he had when he lost Scarlet. But at that moment, he despised himself with a fierceness of emotion he thought impossible.

He'd made his decision, but nothing had changed. He still wanted Eve, and he had to get away before he took her, for no other reason than he wanted to feel her body wrapped around his. He didn't need to make her his mate, didn't need to tie her to him for eternity. He should be pleased.

Instead, Eve's reaction to being set free from the life sentence stirred unwanted emotion and a feeling of such overwhelming possessiveness he was surprised his molars hadn't disintegrated to dust attempting to conceal the strength of his reaction.

He never expected to feel anything for her, and relinquishing his claim to her, shit, felt beyond wrong. It felt unnatural.

He mentally flinched, remembering the disgust covering her face and lacing her words. *"No, you're right, this is extremely good news. So how does this whole thing work? You start to lose control of your demon, and I—what? Jump on your dick and make it better?"*

The fact she didn't want him touching her, and because of the situation she found herself in, that she might be forced to have sex with him anyway, made his stomach roil.

Oh, physically she responded to his touch, but their connection removed a certain amount of control over her body's reaction to him.

Acid burned the back of his throat. Fuck, he was going to be sick.

Lazarus pounded down the stairs and out through the club's fire exit. If he was about to empty the contents of his stomach, he didn't want an audience. Palms pressed against the cool, rough brick, he sucked back oxygen trying to fight the nausea, but the stench in the alley only made it worse.

Staying away from her would help. The more time they spent together, the stronger their bond would become, and he couldn't risk growing any more attached to her than he already was. His demon clawed at his mind as soon as the notion crossed it. Silas had made it clear that bond was necessary to protect her, but he couldn't do it, not until this was all over. Not until Tobias was dealt with. And not until he was stable again.

Finding your mate should be a joyous occasion, ending a long and lonely life. Finally gaining the balance his kind fought to maintain their entire lives—the missing half of their soul returned, complete.

It was a rare thing, something he should have cherished and nurtured, not disrespected, and avoided. With the shitty way he'd handled this whole thing, he'd singlehandedly destroyed their one shot at happiness. He would never know the feeling of completing their bond. The exhilaration of fusing their life forces for eternity, or the euphoric surge as their powers increased and grew.

No, he would never know her the way he longed to.

After Scarlet's death, he'd been determined to avoid such a union. He'd barely survived the crippling grief of her loss, but after seeing the suffering of her mate followed by his slow descent into darkness, his own pain paled in comparison.

What if I fail Eve as well?

If something happened to her because of him...fuck, he couldn't think about that. As hard as it was to fight his instincts to claim her, it was for the best.

How could he force Eve to tie herself to someone like him? He didn't deserve her. Not after what he'd done.

Scarlet wrapped her arms around his waist and smiled up at him. That amazing knock-the-wind-from-your-lungs smile he knew so well. The one that reminded him of the little girl he'd found all those years ago.

"Thank you," she said.

"Why are you thanking me, sweet girl?"

She squeezed him tighter and glanced over at Tobias standing across the room. "I found my mate because of you. I have a family because you found me." She went up onto her tiptoes and kissed his cheek. "Lazarus, I owe you everything."

He groaned, the memory hitting hard, the pain accompanying it a knife to the heart.

As soon as this was over, he would deliver Eve to the compound, then he'd leave. He'd watch over her from a distance. His pain was nothing he didn't deserve. All that mattered was her happiness. And if that meant watching her move on, watching her...fall in love with someone else, that's the way it had to be. All that mattered was keeping her safe. Safe from Diemos. Safe from his demons.

And safe from Lazarus himself.

～

Lazarus punched the cushions again and propped his arm behind his head, unfolding his big body on the too-short couch. He'd had another shitty night with absolutely no sleep whatsoever.

Another week had passed, a week of searching for Tobias and of lying scrunched up on this fucking couch.

A week of Eve avoiding him.

He fucking hated it. Last night had been no different from the previous torturous ones. He'd spent every second trying not to go into that damn bedroom. He wanted to go in there and beg her forgiveness. Spend hours with his face buried between those soft, creamy thighs, apologizing for the pain he'd caused her. He wanted to slide into that sweet pussy and take his time fucking her like he'd promised in that airport storage room.

Christ, it had only been a matter of weeks, but it felt so long ago now.

He rubbed his hands over his face.

Now she could barely look at him.

Still, when he'd gotten back from searching the city last night, another night spent looking for Tobias, he'd done what he did every night. He opened her door and watched the subtle rise and fall of her chest as she slept.

And like every night, his desperate need for her freaked him out so much he'd kicked his own ass back to the couch.

The woman's taste still lingered in his memory, branded into his senses. The more time he spent with her, the more he felt. He didn't like it, didn't want to deal with the tender feelings that stirred inside him. He didn't know how to handle them. This was completely beyond his scope of knowledge.

Thankfully, things had settled down some at the compound now the autumnal equinox had come and gone, and with the amulet in Eve's possession, she was at least safe from those who would hunt her.

Now he just needed to find Tobias. He was close, Lazarus could feel it. Then Eve would be free to do as she chose, without him.

He growled. Even the thought twisted him in knots. It was illogical, but during their short time together his feelings for her had become powerful, all-consuming. It scared him. If he let her, the voluptuous female would not only claim his body but make him believe he had a heart worth salvaging.

Weak.

Flawed.

He shook off the direction his thoughts were heading. He'd spent the last few hours twisting himself in knots already.

The stack of books sitting on the coffee table caught his eye again. All of them Eve's favorites, he knew because she'd shared her love of books with him back at the compound, and had told him the ones she reread all the time.

Many were copies of the books she'd been forced to leave behind. Brent brought them for her as a gift. The warm smile she'd given the other male when he'd presented them to her had turned Lazarus inside out with jealousy.

He'd seen the way she'd gazed at the large collection in her home as he'd ushered her out the front door for the last time, or the words she'd quietly spoken. *Some of them belonged to my mother.* He'd known how important they were to her.

He couldn't help but be annoyed that he hadn't thought of getting them for her first. Brent and Eve were sharing mealtimes, and it had become part of their routine to watch a movie before he went down to his club for the night. Lazarus didn't like it.

He hated that he was jealous. He had no right to be, not anymore.

He was lucky Brent was there for her. He'd grown up around humans and better understood human emotions.

His Scarlet, on the other hand, had been more demon than human. He'd recognized that from the moment he'd found her. Eve was a different creature entirely. Lazarus didn't have the first clue how to ease her pain and worry, and right then he wished he did.

The rustle of bedding drifted in from the other room, and he could imagine Eve shifting under the covers, stretching out across the white cotton sheets, all warm and rumpled and sleepy. The T-shirt she had on would cling to her, outlining her curves.

He groaned and squeezed his eyes shut, trying to force the images from his mind. He needed to get a hold of this yearning, this clawing, unending ache for her. But deep down he knew it would only get worse.

Reaching down, he shifted his massive erection, grunting at the contact. He'd go and take care of it himself, but it wouldn't do any good. Only one person could ease this unrelenting need, and she lay in the other room.

Fucking her wasn't all he wanted, though. No, he wanted so much more. He wanted her eyes on him, bright with happiness. He wanted her smiles, and goddammit, he wanted to be the one who had put them on her face. He wanted to talk to her for hours and learn every little thing about her.

He just wanted her. All of her.

You don't deserve her.

He curled his fingers into tight fists. Somehow, he'd managed to control his demon this long without the need to take her again, but it was getting tougher by the day. Harder to resist and harder to keep his demon riding shotgun and not shoving him out of the driver's seat.

But how could he ask her to let him taint her beautiful body after all the pain he'd caused her? To let him have her when the idea disgusted her?

Throwing off the covers, he sat up, groaning as he stood.

His cell rang.

Snatching it from the coffee table, he checked it. *Unknown number*. Not unusual. It could be James calling from the compound with an update. Most of their phones had blocked caller ID.

He put the phone to his ear. "Yeah?"

Silence.

"James?"

When more silence greeted him, he curled his fingers into a tight fist. It didn't take a genius to work out who the mystery caller was. "Tobias."

"Laz," he said, voice cold, brittle.

Pain twisted in his chest, hearing his brother's voice, so sharp he felt like he'd taken a knife to the chest. "Tell me where you are," Lazarus said. "I promise I'll end it quick, brother. That has to better than the slow torture Diemos will take pleasure in handing out."

"Hey, I'm all for torture. Maybe I'll find out if that curvy little demi you have stashed enjoys being on the receiving end." Lazarus barely contained a growl at the mention of Eve. "I'm surprised you left her unprotected. Out in the open like that, anyone could have taken advantage."

He'd had spies here the night Eve worked in the club. Jesus, he could have lost her. She could have been taken from him. If she'd gone outside...

"Tobias—"

"Anyway, as tempting as your offer of a quick death is, I

think I'll wait for you to find me," Tobias said, changing the subject back.

"Brother," Lazarus choked out. "You can't want this."

"I'm not your fucking brother."

Another slice of pain. No, he wasn't. He didn't know this male, didn't recognize the cruelty, the hate in his deep voice.

"We both know it's only a matter of time before you succumb," Tobias said, and there was no missing how much he was looking forward to that day.

"I won't let that happen."

An arctic chuckle traveled down the line. "Yeah? I'm not so sure. As it is, your screwed-up sense of honor makes you weak. Instead of spending every waking hour searching for me, you return to that little demi you're guarding. I can see why you'd want her around, of course. Her power is... impressive, and she is kind of hot. Tell me, have you fucked her yet, Laz?"

Red rage clouded his vision. His demon stirred then roared, clawing to be free, to destroy any threat to his female. "You do not touch her. You don't even think about her. Do you understand?"

Tobias's silence said more than words ever could. With his loss of control, he'd gifted his weakness to his enemy on a silver platter and thrown down a challenge all at the same time. But then, despite Tobias's casual mention of Eve and her power, Lazarus had no doubt he already wanted her for Diemos's army. Her ability to read minds would be a unique prize. And that was without knowing she had the power to open the portal. If he found out...

Yeah, that would be the whipped cream and cherry on top.

"Ah, she's that good?" Tobias said finally. "Will she please me, do you think?"

Lazarus remained silent, refusing to bite, but all the while he was roaring inside.

"You never could control your emotions, could you, Lazarus?" He laughed, the sound causing the hairs on the back of his neck to lift. "That was always your weakness. It seems you've developed tender feelings for your *mate*. How sweet." His voice dropped to a harsh whisper, full of promise and pure hatred. "You have no idea how much I'm going to enjoy taking her from you, asshole, like you took Scarlet from me."

"I loved Scarlet. I'd do anything to bring her back." Lazarus would never forgive himself for her death, and was powerless to stop his reaction. His demon reared inside him, pushed for release with a greater force than ever before.

"You took my mate from me and I'm going to make sure you know exactly what that feels like."

Lazarus gritted his teeth, fighting for control.

Tobias's voice was quiet and controlled when he spoke next. "Did you know as the connection strengthens between the two of you, your senses mesh? You will have the ability to feel what she's feeling."

Lazarus was barely hanging on to his sanity. He didn't want to hear any more.

"No matter where you are, you will feel her take her last breath. Hear her scream your name, knowing there is nothing you can do to save her as her life's blood drains from her used and broken body." Tobias took a shuddering breath. "That sound will haunt you every day for the rest of your life. Best you watch her closely, *brother*." Then the phone disconnected.

Lazarus stood there, in the middle of the room, fighting for control. When that failed, he roared and kicked the wooden coffee table in front of him across the room. It crashed into the wall and splintered into kindling. His demon continued to fight for release and he didn't know how much longer he could keep it at bay.

"Who's Scarlet?"

He turned sharply toward the bedroom door. He hadn't heard Eve come out. She stood in a pink T-shirt and boxers, her hair tousled. He wanted to bury his hands in her hair, shove her against the wall, and fuck her so hard the building shook around them.

He jerked his head to the side, unable to answer.

"What happened to her?" She took a step closer.

"Stay…stay back, Eve. I'm not…I'm not myself." When he looked up, her sharply indrawn breath said it all. His demon had risen to the surface and was looking at her through its soulless black eyes. It twisted and coiled around his mind. It wanted Eve, and this time there was no stopping it.

The restraint he'd been hanging on to by a thread snapped. His demon took control and forced his body to move toward her. Lazarus tried to regain control, but it was no use.

When he got to her, he would take her, and his demon wouldn't let him be gentle.

Nausea churned in his gut and his heated skin broke out in a cold sweat. This couldn't happen, he couldn't allow this to happen, wouldn't be able to live with himself if he hurt her.

Drawing on the last ounce of his strength, he forced his body to turn. His demon's control weakened momentarily with Eve out of sight, but only for a moment. Lazarus gained enough momentum to flee the room, and pounded down the stairs to the now-empty club.

A clinking sound drew his attention as he pushed into the bar. Brent was busy putting away glasses. "What's up?"

"Take me to a room," Lazarus choked.

Brent frowned. "What?"

"You need to restrain me. Now."

The guy didn't need to be told twice. Leaping over the bar, Brent rushed to one of the private rooms with Lazarus hot on his heels.

"Get on here. It's more than strong enough to hold you."

Every muscle strained as he fought to lie down on the rough wooden bench. Brent yanked Lazarus's arms over his head and secured heavy metal shackles around his wrists. Pulling the thick chains taut so he couldn't move them, he quickly and efficiently shackled down his legs as well, pinning him to the sturdy surface.

Now all he had to do was wait and hope like hell that this wasn't the end.

CHAPTER 20

EVE STARED AFTER LAZARUS, stunned. *What just happened?*

His face had been contorted in agony, filled with rage. She'd seen him struggling with his demon before, but nothing like this. Something was terribly wrong.

Eve ran out of the apartment after him.

At the bottom of the stairs, she pushed open the door and entered the club. The room was dimly lit, empty. No leather, no half-naked bodies writhing on the dance floor. No Lazarus.

A moan had her whipping around to the left toward the private rooms. Before she could think better of it, she started toward the anguished sound.

She stopped in front of a glossy red door just as a low rumble vibrated from behind it, through it. That sound, God, it hit every nerve ending in her body, lifting goose bumps all over her skin. Her step faltered.

You can do this, Eve.

Taking a deep breath, she ignored her apprehension and pushed on, an unexplainable need to find Lazarus propelling her forward.

He needed her. Somehow, she knew he needed her.

The low rumble was constant now and deep enough to shake the heavy wood. It sounded like growling, like some kind of wild animal prowled on the other side, desperate to get out.

The logical part of her brain told her to turn around, to get the hell out of there, but Lazarus was on the other side of that door and the longer she stood out here the more he suffered.

Not knowing what she might walk in on, but desperate to get to Lazarus, she ignored her anxiety, gripped the handle, and opened the door.

A roar rent the air and froze her to the spot before she'd barely taken a step. The room was small. Several wooden and iron structures filled the limited space, but the largest piece was a heavy wooden table.

That's where she found Lazarus, or what had been Lazarus, stretched out on its hard surface.

His wrists and ankles were chained down by some kind of metal cuffs, and a thick leather strap circled his middle, restraining him further. Teeth gritted, he thrashed and snarled, fighting against his bonds.

The shredded remains of his clothes lay scattered on the floor, half covered by his large charcoal wings that had sprouted from under his back. They draped over the sides of the bench, taking up most of the floor space. The wall-mounted lights caught the tiny flecks of silver that appeared to be threaded through each of one of his dark feathers. But most shocking of all was his body's complete transformation. His skin was leathery and deep crimson. Horns protruded from his head, just above his hairline, and his lips were curled back, revealing large fangs that extended halfway down his chin. He looked like a gargoyle from the top of one of those gothic-style buildings.

A movement had her gaze slicing to the other side of the room. Brent stood there, his eyes locked on Lazarus.

"How? What...what's wrong with him?" she choked out.

Lazarus stilled, his head turning on his thick neck toward her. Eve took a startled step back. His irises were huge, the whites of his eyes barely visible. Every bit of the emerald green color had been swallowed by midnight. He stared at her, eyes wide and unblinking as air hissed through his teeth in harsh, rapid exhales.

Brent grabbed her arm. "You need to leave."

An inhuman roar tore from Lazarus's throat. "Do not touch her." His voice echoed around the room in an eerie way that sent shivers across her entire body. His gaze tracked Brent and did not waver until he removed his hand and moved away from her.

"I won't touch her again." Brent lifted his hands in the air. "See, I'm not touching her."

Those midnight irises slid back to her and continued to stare with an intensity that was terrifying and made her feel as though he could see deep inside her. "What happened to him?"

"It's his demon. Lazarus has succumbed." Brent scrubbed his hands over his face. "This is all kinds of fucked up."

Oh God. This was her fault. He'd told her what he needed from her. But she'd been so busy nursing her own wounds, working hard to punish him for hurting her, she hadn't considered what could happen.

He hadn't come to her when he'd needed her help, trying to protect her from any more pain, and now his demon had taken him.

Brent slid his hands into his pockets. "If we can't bring him back"—he motioned to Lazarus's writhing form—"*this* will be permanent."

"We have to do something." Again, when she spoke, Lazarus's thrashing ceased. She turned back as a wave of his intoxicating scent hit her, and sucked in a breath when light flickered behind his eyes, like a light bulb about to blow. Emerald sparks trying to break through the inky black of his irises.

"Say something else," Brent demanded.

She was frightened out of her mind, but this was Lazarus and he was suffering, so she forced herself to take a tentative step closer. "Lazarus, it's me. I'm here," she whispered.

This time the green held for a few seconds before being engulfed once more, sucked beneath those inky pools.

She took in his straining body, all of it, unable to miss the massive erection that lay against his defined, currently crimson stomach. His hips jerked at her scrutiny. Well, as much as they could against the thick leather band around his ribs. He groaned as if her gaze had caressed him, eased his hurt.

"I think it's helping," she said, glancing up at Brent.

Brent's eyebrows rose to meet his hairline. "So, it's true. You're Lazarus's mate?"

She nodded.

"Your voice is forcing back his demon." He waved her forward while keeping a safe distance himself. "Touching him might help. Just be careful."

If there was a small chance she could help him, she'd do whatever it took. Taking another step closer, careful not to step on his beautiful wings, she moved to the head of the table. Brent remained silent when she lifted a shaky hand to gently stroke his cheek.

The color of his eyes continued to flicker while he grunted and growled incoherently. Then it started, the purring sound she'd heard him make back at the compound, a deep rumble that vibrated from his chest. He pressed back as much as he could, rubbing his face against her hand.

She carried on stroking him and the sound got louder.

His horns were shiny black and she couldn't resist touching them as well, running her fingers over a glossy tip. His entire body jerked.

"Don't stop what you're doing," Brent whispered from his spot on the other side of the room.

She continued to speak to him, keeping her voice low and soothing. Then the black washed from his irises for several seconds, and though they were darker than their usual pale green, they were Lazarus's eyes, and the fear staring back at her broke her heart. Without thinking, she leaned down and kissed his forehead. His skin felt as leathery as it looked and cool against her lips.

"I'm here, Lazarus," she whispered.

A roar tore from his throat at her words and she staggered back. His body shook then torqued violently on the table. The tendons strained in his neck and across his chest and he jerked several times. Just like that, his body shifted back, besides the wings which still sprouted from his back and lay limp across the floor.

"Lazarus?"

"Don't stop now, he needs more," Brent said carefully.

"What should I do?"

Brent's gaze moved over Lazarus then lifted to hers. "I think you know what he needs, Eve." His eyes softened. "Will you give it to him?"

Still stroking his heated skin, she took in Lazarus's magnificent body, hard and straining. Yes, she knew what she had to do. Without looking up, she nodded. She'd do anything to help him, and deep in her heart, she knew he'd do the same for her.

"Don't stop." Lazarus's voice was a mixture of pleasure and pain. He'd responded to her touch, and her body heated, moisture rushing to her sex in reply.

"It's okay, Brent. I can take it from here." She couldn't bring herself to meet his gaze.

"Are you sure?" He sounded reluctant to leave. "I can stay. I'll turn my back."

Nothing but concern filled his voice. For him, being in a room with others having sex was no big deal.

"Thank you, but I'll be okay. He won't hurt me." Lazarus would never purposely harm her, she knew that much.

"Don't untie him. The table's strong and can hold several people at once..." His gaze moved back to Lazarus's trussed-up form. "Just...be careful."

She nodded. "I will."

"I'll be right outside the door if you need me." Then he turned and left the room.

Running gentle fingers over his damp skin, Eve looked down at the pained expression on Lazarus's face. "What should I do?"

He was panting, eyes wild. "Eve...please...I need you." His body surged up again.

She didn't know if she really was Lazarus's mate, but she couldn't stand to see him this way, and if she could ease his pain she would. She wanted to be the one to help him.

She just wanted him.

The desperate, sounds coming from him sealed her fate. She left the head of the table and moved down his body.

"Don't leave me." The agony in his voice shredded her.

"I'm not going anywhere. I promise I won't leave you." She reached over and stroked his thigh, trying to comfort him.

His body went completely still, and she looked up. He

watched her with those midnight eyes, now shot with sparks of emerald.

The knowledge of what caused that dark gaze sent a shiver down her spine. She pushed the fear to the back of her mind and refused to think about the demonic side of his nature, the side that wanted to dominate the man inside. Lazarus was fighting to regain control of his body and mind, and she would do whatever it took to help the male she cared about far more than she had a right to.

His cock was thick, veins lining his heavy shaft, and she had the sudden urge to bend down and run her tongue along each one, tracing them to the glistening tip.

He writhed under her heated gaze. "Touch me," he pleaded.

She wrapped her fingers around him, fisted the silky length, and began to stroke him slow and easy, not entirely sure how to proceed. Their gazes locked and the midnight turned to deep green again. He hissed and bucked.

Gasping, he panted out, "Take off your shorts."

She nodded, unable to speak, and slid them down her legs. His nostrils flared as the cotton pooled at her feet. Then his gaze traveled up her bare legs and zeroed in on her panties. "Take those off as well."

Her sex clenched, slick from the blatant lust on his face, the undisguised hunger altering his deep voice. It was pure gravel. Doing as he asked, she hooked her finger in the sides and slid the flimsy fabric down her legs.

The metal chains smacked into the wooden table as his big body jerked hard against his restraints. Without conscious thought, Eve took several startled steps back until she hit the wall, rattling the various chains, cuffs, and whips that hung there. His face contorted, but this time it wasn't physical. He looked tormented by her panicked reaction. He hated what he was doing to her, and the need to reassure him brought her back to his side, bolstering her courage.

"It's all right. I'm all right." She didn't know who she was trying to convince more.

He cursed repeatedly between panted breaths. "Climb up." The mix of pain and longing in his voice evaporated the last of her fear and replaced it with raw desire.

The table was wide enough for her to climb up beside him, and she straddled his hips. His breathing grew ragged as she moved up to position his engorged flesh. The head brushed her sex, and he hissed, rearing beneath her.

His heavy arms strained against the chains, the corded muscles bunching as he fought against his restraints.

Teeth gritted, chest pumping rapidly, he sucked back oxygen. "Fuck me, Eve. Please."

She didn't hesitate at his frantic plea and lowered her body, taking him inside her all the way. Her body stretched to accommodate his large size, the sensation almost too much. Lazarus moaned as her body gripped him tight.

"That's it. Take all of me, sweetheart." His foot thumped against the table. "Ah, fuck."

She bent down and brushed her lips against his, unable to stop herself, and he opened his mouth instantly, hungrily sliding his tongue against hers, deepening the kiss. It was desperate and needy. She felt it, too, and she gave him back what he needed.

Clutching his shoulders, she lifted her upper body slightly and began to move, up and back, trying to keep the pace measured. He went so deep with every stroke she could already feel her inner muscles beginning to ripple around him.

He tried to thrust up and growled in frustration. "Undo the band around my waist."

She reached down and unlatched the thick leather and it

clattered to the floor. She wasn't afraid of him, not anymore. How could she be after the way he'd reacted to her touch? The chains attached to the manacles around his wrists and ankles appeared to be one length that ran below the table, and as he kicked out with his feet, his wrists slammed down hard against the top of the bench, pulling them down tight, causing the veins in his arms to bulge under the strain.

He kicked against the chains around his legs until he could dig his heels in against the wood beneath and thrust his hips up powerfully to meet hers. She cried out as he repeatedly hit her right where she needed him, slammed their bodies together over and over in a desperate frenzy, racing toward release.

His massive charcoal wings, which up until now had lain unmoving against the floor, lifted. A cool breeze tickled her bare legs and stirred the loose strands of her hair as they moved, beating gently.

Lazarus snarled, the animalistic sound filling the small room before he thrust up, hitting her at an angle that sent stars exploding behind her lids and caused her inner muscles to clamp down hard, kicking off a powerful climax. She screamed his name while her body gripped him tight, clenching repeatedly around his thick length.

When the waves of pleasure receded, she collapsed against his chest, linked her arms beneath his powerful shoulders, and held on tight as he thrust up. A guttural sound tore from his throat when he found his own release, then those magnificent wings lifted, curling around them both, surrounding them in a dark, silken cocoon.

When she regained some of her composure, she took in his rugged face. He looked like the fierce warrior she knew him to be, despite the chains restraining him. It was hard to believe that she'd somehow helped him tame the demon fighting for dominance inside him.

His eyes were closed tight, and though she thought she knew, she couldn't be sure who had won this battle. Who it was that lay beneath her. Cautiously, she reached up and ran gentle fingers across his brow and down his cheek. "Lazarus?"

His lids fluttered open.

She gasped at the stunning beauty of his bright emerald gaze staring back at her.

"Thank you," he croaked.

She smiled. "I'm glad you're back."

"Is everything all right in there?" Brent's voice sounded muffled from the other side of the door.

"We're fine," she called, sitting up as Lazarus's beautiful wings unfurled from around their bodies. "Let me get you out of these shackles."

When he slipped from her body, she felt the loss instantly. She shook off the feeling and climbed to the floor to study his chains. "How the heck do I undo these things?"

"There's a key over there." He pointed to a hook on the wall.

The door opened a crack and a pair of jeans landed on the floor. "Thought you might need these," Brent said through the gap then shut the door again.

Retrieving the heavy key, Eve undid his wrists, followed by his ankles, and stepped back. Lazarus sat up and swung his legs over the side of the table. He stretched his limbs and flexed his stiff muscles. She stared in awe as those beautiful black shimmery wings folded in. He tagged the jeans from the floor and, without taking his eyes off her, pulled them on, not bothering to do them up. "As much as I want to keep you naked, you should probably get dressed."

"Oh...oh, right." She bent down and grabbed her shorts, but before she could pull them back on, he moved in behind her, pulled her up against his body, and wrapped his arms around her middle. He was shaking.

"I already want you again. I don't think I could ever get enough of you." He ground his already hardening length against her rear, even as his body continued to tremble in the aftermath of what he'd been through.

Her body flared to life, responding instantly.

"I'm sorry you've been dragged into all this. You have no idea how sorry I am," he said.

"It's okay. I'm glad I could...that I could help." She smiled, trying to reassure him as she turned in his arms and rested her hands on his chest. She traced the swirling design of his brand with her finger. The scar tissue was rough and slightly raised. "Let's get you upstairs."

He dropped his hands when she stepped back to pull on her underwear and shorts.

If it hadn't been for Lazarus, God only knew what would have happened to her. He'd saved her life, and she owed him the same in return. Being thrust into this new world was scary as hell, but she knew now she would give him whatever he needed, for as long as he needed it. She owed him that. Whatever was going on with him was bigger than her and her petty emotions.

When she lifted her head, she searched his body for any sign of the demon she'd seen moments ago, and sucked in a breath when he looked down at her again. His eyes were so bright, so startling a green they made it hard to focus on anything else when he was looking at her. His wings were gone now, his smooth back showing no trace of them ever being there, and his skin was once again tan and supple, not the leathery armor of his demon. There was also no sign of the horns that had protruded from his head, not a mark or a scar. Nothing. He was back to his former self. Powerful and raw. Terrifyingly beautiful.

Brent was waiting outside when she took Lazarus's hand and led him from the room. Concern lined his face. "You good?"

Lazarus nodded. "I owe you."

"You owe me nothing, brother," Brent said before he strode off.

Lazarus tightened his fingers around hers, and she led him back upstairs.

CHAPTER 21

IT TOOK everything Lazarus had not to fall on his ass. The shakes racking his entire body wouldn't let up. He'd never been that close to losing himself, had never stared through the eyes of his demon like that, feeling the darkness taking hold and knowing there was nothing he could do to stop it.

Eve continued to hold his hand, and somehow, despite how small and soft and so obviously weaker than his it was, it was that connection, her tight grip, that was holding him up. The only thing.

"You're burning up," she said and wrapped her arm around his waist.

She led him to the bedroom and he followed, struggling, trying desperately to find the words to tell her how he felt. How grateful he was. Christ, that she'd saved his life.

Eve pulled back the covers and turned back to him. She looked worried.

"I'm okay," he managed. "I'll be fine."

Her eyes were wide as she gently ushered him to the bed, making him lie down. "You need to rest."

She started to move away, but he grabbed her wrist, stopping her. "Will you stay with me?" Fuck, she was beautiful. And not just on the outside. Her inner beauty shone through so damn bright he felt the warmth of it soaking in deep, right down to his bones.

"I'm just getting you a drink. I'll be right back."

He tracked her as she left, couldn't bring himself to look away from the door until she was back. She handed him a glass of water and he drank it, then he held his hand out, asking her without words to climb in with him.

She didn't hesitate and slid in beside him, wrapping her arm around his waist. The heat of her skin soaking through her clothes, the weight of her body against him, was comforting. If he had the strength he'd pull her closer.

She tilted her head back looking at him. "I'm so sorry," she said. "This was my fault. You needed me. You needed me and didn't feel you could come to me. You almost lost yourself trying to protect me."

Lazarus stilled. *What?* "No, Eve. God, no. None of this was your fault. None of it. I fucked up. In every damn way I could have. Yeah, I was trying to protect you, because I'd hurt you and I was ashamed of myself."

She pressed a kiss to his shoulder. "I think we need to work on our communication skills. This, what's happening here, is new territory for both of us. I think that allows for mistakes."

He shook his head in awe of her. "I've never met anyone like you. Christ, you...you make me feel things that scare the shit out of me. Have me questioning everything...doubting things, things I thought I would never falter on." He felt her heart beating faster against his side as he buried his nose in her hair and breathed her in. The action, her scent, her warmth, soothed him instantly.

A vision of Tobias doing the same to Scarlet flashed through his mind, along with a large dose of pain. Because, fuck, he got it. If he hadn't before, he did now. The woman in his arms was the most important thing in his world and he'd do anything to protect her.

"What happens now?" she said softly.

"I don't know," he rasped.

Her finger traced one of his tattoos. "I don't either, and I think that's okay."

They were quiet again for several seconds.

"Eve?" he said into the silence.

"Hmm?"

He didn't know what happened next, how to get there, but he did know what he wanted. He also knew what taking it, keeping that happiness would cost him. He didn't deserve it, but right then, lying with Eve, he didn't think he had any other choice but to reach for it. "Hold me tighter, sweetheart," he said into her hair.

She didn't hesitate.

He'd never felt anything like it in his life. No one had ever taken care of him like Eve had, like she was now. He was a warrior. His brothers were warriors. All they knew was fighting and blood and pain.

The angels had screwed them over in so many ways. Except in this.

This was a reward. A gift.

And, God, he realized at that moment just how much he wanted to keep her.

"I want to show you something," Lazarus said as he led Eve up the stairs to the rooftop the next evening. They'd spent the day together and he wasn't ready for it to end. He'd have to go out and continue his search for Tobias soon, but first, he wanted to give Eve something in return for everything she'd given him.

He used his senses to feel for demons, for anything that could cause Eve harm. The coast was clear. She was laughing by the time he pushed through the door to the roof, the sound high and breathy and one of the most beautiful things he'd ever heard.

"Wow, the view up here is…it's gorgeous," she said, beaming up at him when he pulled her to a stop. "Thank you for showing me."

"This isn't it," he said, a smile teasing his lips.

She searched the rooftop. "Where is it, then?"

He shook his head. "It's not down here. It's up there." He pointed to the sky above them.

Her eyes widened. "You mean…"

"You in the mood for some night flying?"

She bit her lip. "So you're going to…" She motioned to his back. "And we'll…"

"Yes," he said, chuckling. "You game?"

Her face lit up. "Um…*yes*, I'd love that."

Lazarus grinned, couldn't help himself. The look on her face was sheer delight. He tugged off his shirt, tucked it in his back pocket, and unfurled his wings.

Eve stepped toward him, her gaze moving over his charcoal wings. "Can I touch them?"

He had to swallow, his mouth suddenly dry. "Yeah, of course."

She moved around him slowly and the feel of her eyes on him had his skin feeling too tight for his body, had tingles sliding over his scalp.

And then he felt it, her hand moving over the inner arch of one of his wings. No one had ever touched him there, not once in his whole life, and he shuddered at the sheer pleasure the sensation shot through him. How it only intensified the more she touched them, petted them.

"The feathers, they're so soft," she said.

He shivered at the sound of her voice. It was like everything grew more sensitive while she touched them. Just her voice lifted goose bumps across his skin.

His cock pulsed hard against the zipper of his jeans.

"No one's ever…" He had to clear his throat. "No one's ever done that to me before," he said.

"Do you like it?" The little rasp to her voice said she already knew the answer to that question.

"Yeah, I like it." He reached back and tugged her around to his front before he disgraced himself, and kissed her, hard and deep, then he lifted her in his arms, spread his wings, and took flight.

Eve gasped, her arms tightening around his neck as he shot higher, carrying her over streets and rooftops until they were high enough to take in the whole of the city. Her arms were still tight around him and she'd pressed her cheek against his.

He wanted to see her face. "Do you like it?"

"Like it?" she whispered. "This is…it's…" She laughed, the sound so full of joy and happiness Lazarus's heart pounded harder. "There are no words. Thank you." She pressed a kiss to his cheek. "Thank you so much for this."

"Any time, sweetheart," he heard himself say.

They were up there for a while. He was reluctant to take her back. He loved the feel of her in his arms, the way her breathing quickened, her soft gasps, her laughter, as he flew through the sky at speed.

He wanted more of this. More nights like this. More nights with Eve…

Lazarus gasped, squeezing his eyes shut as a sharp pain sliced through his skull.

"*Fuck.*"

"What is it?" Eve asked, sounding panicked.

He kept hold of her and headed back to the club as fast as he could.

"It's Tobias," he said. "I can feel him." He'd sensed his brother in this city many times since he'd been here, but he'd always covered his trail.

Tobias wasn't hiding now. He wanted Lazarus to find him.

It had to be a trap. Of course, it was. There was no other reason Tobias would open himself up like this. It didn't matter. This could be Lazarus's only chance.

They landed back on the roof and Lazarus rushed Eve to the safety of their apartment.

"What are you going to do?" she asked, watching him as he strapped on his weapons.

He met her blue eyes with his own. "End it."

Before he walked out the door she called his name. He turned back to her.

"Please. Be careful."

For the first time in a long time, there was someone he wanted to come home to. Someone who made all of it, his long life of nonstop fighting, of struggling, bearable. He rushed down to the club and found Brent, instructed him to watch Eve, but left out his destination. The guy would want to come, and right then it would be more helpful knowing Eve was safe. There was no way he could focus if he thought she was at risk.

He left Brent and headed out to the alley. The narrow space didn't allow much room, but managed to lift off without effort, taking to the skies.

Lazarus followed the invisible trail his brother was showing him. He felt it like a rope attached to his chest, reeling him in. He let it; didn't bother resisting its pull. He hovered above a building below, taking a few minutes to send out his senses, to gather his control.

Tobias was alone.

Not what he'd expected.

He tucked in his wings and dropped, gravel crunching under the soles of his boots when he landed a little way back from the building.

He kept to the shadows and scanned the area. There had been several lights outside, but all were broken. The place was a rundown apartment complex, abandoned, unused, and according to the big sign nailed to one of the boarded-up windows, scheduled for demolition.

The front doors were boarded as well, so he made his way around the perimeter, searching for another way in. Several loud bangs came from the rear of the building, and on silent feet, he moved toward it. An open door swung on rusty hinges. A strong gust sent it crashing into the frame before swinging back once more.

Pulling the door wide, he entered the pitch-black interior. His eyes strained, trying to adjust to the inky darkness. Most demons had advanced sight. Laz was the only one among his brothers who hadn't inherited the ability from his demon father, though his other senses made up for the lack. Both facts Tobias knew.

What he assumed was broken glass crunched underfoot, and the only other sound was his own shallow breaths.

He followed the sense of dread prickling the back of his neck, a dark malevolence that turned his stomach and excited him all at once. A door to one of the ground floor apartments hung open, an obvious invitation to enter.

He stepped inside and tensed as a wave of hatred slammed into him, covering him like a thick shroud.

"Nice of you to pull your dick out of that demi long enough to stop by." Tobias's voice echoed through the gloom.

Lazarus swung around, trying to follow his brother's voice. It seemed to come from all directions and he couldn't pinpoint his location.

"You wanted me to find you," Lazarus said. "So let's get this over with."

Tobias's mirthless chuckle lifted the hair on the back of his neck. "You'll wish you hadn't."

He strained to see, trying to make out shapes in the darkness. "We were your family once, T. Doesn't that mean anything to you?" he called into nothingness, purposely using the nickname. Tobias's hiss and bellow of rage made it clear he'd hit his mark.

"My family is dead. You killed her," he roared back, his hatred echoing off the walls.

"Then hurt me, not the others. Why are you doing this, T?"

"Stop calling me that," he roared, his panted breaths harsh and raw. "And you know exactly why I'm doing this. I want you to suffer like I have suffered. I want you to watch everything that is important to you destroyed."

The pain in the other man's voice shook Lazarus to the core. With his demon in the driver's seat, he shouldn't be capable of feeling any emotion that didn't go hand in hand with hatred. "They were important to you once, too. Your brothers would have done anything for you. You loved them, T. Don't do this."

Images of Scarlet and her mate flooded his mind. The way they'd looked at each other, loved each other. Was that male truly gone?

This was his fault. Lazarus was the reason Tobias had chosen to succumb rather than continue to fight. His reason for living was gone. He got that now, more than ever. Lazarus had taken her from him.

"Shut up," Tobias seethed. "You're wrong. I only cared

about Scarlet. She was my mate, my strength, and you couldn't fucking stand that. You couldn't handle that with us mated, I was stronger than you, my powers greater. So you took her from me."

"I was happy for you, and for Scarlet." Arms outstretched, he began feeling his way along the wall, following Tobias's voice. His eyes had adjusted slightly, but it was still too dark to see much more than faint outlines.

"Bullshit."

Lights flashed on, blinding him for a few seconds. He blinked against the harsh brightness before he spotted Tobias a few yards from him. He wore jeans and a plain white T-shirt. His long blond hair was neatly tied back. His handsome face was smooth, showing no outward sign of emotion.

The only way he could tell this was no longer the male he'd once called brother was the large unwavering black irises staring back at him and the deep jagged scar on his forearm where he'd cut out his angel's brand.

Then he spotted the woman a short distance from Tobias. Tied to one of the building's exposed support beams, a young demi stood motionless. Her head was slumped forward. Rust-colored streaks of drying blood stained her clothing and smeared the length of her bare calves and feet.

The evil inside the male before him, a male he had once loved, still managed to rock him to his soul. "What have you done? Why would you do this?" He barely recognized his own agonized voice.

Tobias slid his fingers under the female's chin, lifted her head, and brushed back her blond hair to reveal her face. His nostrils flared and for a moment he looked as surprised as Lazarus by her features. She was so like Scarlet that her name whispered past Lazarus's lips.

Tobias's black eyes turned back to Lazarus, an expression on his brother's face he had no hope of reading.

236

Finally, he made a mirthless rusty sound that didn't hold a trace of humor. "Apparently, I've been searching for a replacement. Unfortunately, it looks like this one didn't make the cut." He paused, taking in the deep slices marring the petite female's pale skin. "Or maybe she did. Just not in the way either of us hoped."

Lazarus couldn't believe what he was hearing. "Scarlet wouldn't want this. She would despise what you've become."

"Do not speak her name. You know fuck all about that female and what she would want."

Lazarus took in Tobias's cold expression, the blood of an innocent demi drying on his hands, and fought to stay upright. He was so close to falling to his knees under the crushing weight of pain and regret pressing down on him. He'd grieved the loss of this male, a male who had once been his brother. Deep down, he'd held the smallest grain of hope that maybe he wasn't completely lost to them.

That hope shattered the minute the lights came on. Tobias had succumbed to his demon long ago, and though Laz wished otherwise, was beyond help.

Lazarus fought to maintain control as his demon howled for release. He held on with everything he had, and keeping Eve at the forefront of his mind helped. He had to keep her safe.

"Maybe I want my power fully restored," Tobias said. "The kind I can only get from another mate. The kind you..." His gaze bored into Lazarus then his head tilted to the side as if he were focusing on something. He barked a harsh laugh. "You haven't taken her as your mate yet. Still a fucking coward, then?"

And just like that, calm settled over Tobias. The easy grin he flashed Lazarus offered a painful glimpse of the male he'd once been.

"I have to go now, Laz, but we will catch up again soon,

yeah? I promise you that." He motioned to the lifeless female at his side. "I'm kinda busy at the moment. I hope you don't mind cleaning up."

The lights went out again, followed by Tobias's retreating footsteps. Lazarus tried to follow, but he was too late. Tobias had vanished into the night, once again covering his trail.

With his demon clawing at his psyche, Lazarus used what was left of his dwindling power to incinerate the demi's limp, lifeless body, unable to summon the strength to do anything else for her.

His control had all but disintegrated, and there was no stopping it at this point.

He needed Eve.

Wanted her.

God help anyone who tried to get in his way.

He sprinted from the building and took flight.

By the time he reached the club, he was barely hanging on by a thread. He rushed in, snarling and growling, shoving people aside to get to her.

His knees went weak as a rush of energy hit him. *Fuck*, he could feel her.

Close.

She was under his skin. Pumping through his veins.

So close.

Lazarus pounded up the stairs. He just had to hang on a little longer.

He used his powers to unlock the door, and it swung open with a bang. The small living room was dark. The only light was flickering from the television, casting a colorful wash over a surprised Eve.

She sat on the couch dressed in an oversized T-shirt, her smooth legs bare, and Christ, he got a tantalizing glimpse of pale blue panties.

She shot to her feet. "Thank God you're okay. I was worried out of my mind."

He couldn't answer.

She stared at him wide-eyed, her pupils enlarged as she strained to see him clearly through the dim light, trying to see the condition he was in.

"Lazarus?" she whispered. "Are you...is everything all right?"

"Come here," he choked.

"What's going on?"

"Now," he ordered.

Her breath hitched and she took a step closer.

That was when he got a trace of something, something that tightened his already hard cock to painful proportions. Even in the dim light he could see her face darken with desire—there was no mistaking it. He just hoped like fuck there wasn't fear there as well.

His demon senses came alive. He could hear her heart racing behind her ribs, the way each exhale rushed from between her parted lips. Smell the intoxicating scent of her arousal. Her body seemed to be responding to his need.

Thank fuck.

He stalked over to her, chest pumping with every labored breath, and gripped the hem of her shirt, pulling it over her head.

She gasped.

"I can't stop," he choked.

Her tongue darted out, licking her plump lower lip. "It's all right. I'm here." She pressed a soft hand to his chest. "Take it, Lazarus. Take what you need."

He growled at her shakily spoken words, the unmistakable need in her voice, and fisting a handful of her sexy, tousled curls, he hauled her up against him and took her mouth in a hard kiss. He nipped and sucked the tender plump flesh, demanding entrance, and she opened for him without resistance or hesitation. Her heart thudded against his chest, and he moaned at the sweet taste of her, the exquisite sensation of her mouth under his.

He wanted more, so much more.

Lazarus pulled back and spun her around, holding her back flush against his chest, her ass nestled against his hard cock. He walked her forward until they reached the small dining table in front of the windows overlooking the busy city below.

He wrapped his fingers around the back of her neck and bent her forward over the wooden surface then ran his palms down the smooth expanse of her bare back. The feel of her warm skin soothed his demon somewhat, but not enough.

The urge to taste her was overpowering, and he dropped to his knees, unwilling to deny himself any longer. Gripping the sides of her underwear, he tore through the fabric. Her startled cry drew his gaze to hers, had him freezing in place, terrified that he'd frightened her. She watched him over her shoulder, but there was no fear there, only need, hot and intoxicating. Sexy as fuck.

She wanted this just as much as him.

"Open for me," he forced out past the lump in his throat.

She didn't hesitate and spread her legs farther apart. Her scent hit him hard, and he groaned. He'd been craving her, desperate to taste her again.

He parted her tender flesh, and the sight of her glistening and ready nearly unmanned him. He leaned in to taste her fully, lapped at her arousal greedily, drinking her down. She tasted fucking amazing.

Eve gasped and pushed her ass back in an attempt to get closer. Uninhibited, needy. And her sexy little moans had him growling his approval.

He worked her clit with his fingers, fucking her with his

tongue, and he didn't let up until her body spasmed and she cried out. She came hard against his mouth, but he wasn't finished. Not slowing, Lazarus continued to lick her and didn't stop until he'd wrung every last bit of pleasure from her trembling body.

When she collapsed on the table, he stood and ripped open the front of his jeans, freeing his cock. "Hang onto the edge," he said, voice raw with lust.

He fisted his shaft, and skimming past the full cheeks of her lovely ass, plunged into her hot, wet pussy.

She cried out, and for a split second he worried that he might have hurt her, but then she pushed back, trying to take him deeper, and any worry disintegrated under a red haze of lust.

He gripped her hip and pulled out inch by painstaking inch, tormenting them both. Loving the way his cock glistened with her juices, proof of her desire for him.

The tiny thread of control he'd been hanging on to for all he was worth snapped, and he thrust home, taking her like a man possessed. Which wasn't far from the truth at that point.

The table scraped against the tiled floor as his brutal thrusts drove it forward. Eve arched her back and cried out when her second climax took hold, squeezing repeatedly around his cock, driving him damn near insane.

"Shit." He panted hard. He didn't want to come yet, wanted to take her over the edge once more. He *needed* to make this good for her. He'd fucked everything else up. He wanted to at least do this right.

The silvery thread was right there, calling to him, crying out for him to make Eve his mate, but he forced himself to ignore it.

Sweat slicked his skin from the effort of resisting, from holding off his own release. God, he wanted to fill the female writhing beneath him with his seed, mark her with his scent. Reaching around her body, he began to circle her clit with firm, even strokes.

"Oh God. I…I can't," she whimpered.

"You can," he growled, his voice desperate even to his own ears.

Then the first ripples of her orgasm began teasing his cock. He gritted his teeth and held onto her hips tight, thrusting hard, fucking her with short, deep strokes. Eve screamed as she went over moments later, and he exploded, going with her, gripped by the most powerful release of his long life.

When he was wrung dry, he collapsed, resting his forehead against her back. "I'm sorry, Eve," he panted over and over.

After a few minutes, she whispered, "Please, don't be."

He barely registered her words, but didn't miss the hurt in her tone. His cock was still achingly hard, his hunger for her not even close to being sated. He reluctantly pulled out of her warmth and standing her up, eased her around to face him.

He brushed the hair back from her face and cupped her chin, lifting it so her gaze met his. He leaned in and captured her mouth with his own.

The kiss was slow, claiming, and when he finally pulled back, she looked up at him, flushed and sexy as all hell.

He ran his thumb across her swollen bottom lip. "I'm going to carry you to that room and I'm going to have you again, not because I need you to quiet my demon, but because I want you again so bad I can't think straight. Because every part of me craves every part of you."

It was all he could manage before he lifted her off the ground and strode to the bedroom.

CHAPTER 22

MORNING LIGHT STREAMED in from the edge of the curtains and blanketed the room in a muted gold. It made the small space feel cozy.

Eve's soft, warm body still lay pressed tightly against Lazarus, her scent all over his skin. He'd slept well past morning, but at that moment couldn't bring himself to care. His cock was nestled against her round ass, and the temptation to slide into her from behind was driving him fucking crazy.

Nuzzling the back of her neck, he drew in more of her sweet, heady scent. This felt right, more than right. She belonged right where she was.

The woman in his arms had managed something he never thought possible: she'd broken down his carefully constructed walls. Last night she had given herself to him without reservation; not once did she hold back any part of herself. She'd smashed down his defenses, again and again, uncovering feelings he'd tried to keep on lockdown.

He still felt raw, exposed.

He'd taken Eve repeatedly through the night, and he'd

told her the truth—it hadn't been about pacifying his demon, it had been about a male and his unquenchable need for his female. An undeniable, soul-deep yearning he felt even now.

It hadn't been enough.

He would never get enough of her.

Eve stirred, her body moving against his in a maddening way as she stretched and rolled to her back in his arms. The thick sweep of her dark lashes quivered then fluttered open, and his stomach clenched when heavy-lidded sapphire pools stared up at him drowsily.

She was so damn beautiful. She took his breath away.

He bent down and took her mouth in a soft kiss. When he pulled back, her cheeks turned a pretty shade of pink. Damn, he loved the way she blushed so easily.

"Morning," he said, voice still rough from sleep.

"Morning." Her gaze searched his. "Are you okay?"

"Yeah. Thanks to you."

Her hand slid up his biceps. "What happened with Tobias?"

"He got away." Seeing Tobias like that, seeing what he'd done to that demi, it cut to the bone.

"I'm sorry," she said.

"Me, too." Despite the conversation, he loved this, just the two of them, lying there, talking. His stomach rumbled.

Her mouth curled up on one side. "How about I make us breakfast?" She tried to roll away.

No way was he ready to let her go. He hadn't finished savoring the snug way her body fit perfectly against his. "Wait." He grabbed her hip, and she gasped in pain. He let go like her skin was molten beneath his hand. "What's wrong?"

"Nothing."

He tried to pull back the sheet, but she clung to the covers.

"Let me see." He loosened her fingers to reveal her waist,

then farther until her hip and ass were on full display. A dark bruise marred her pale skin. A perfect handprint. "I did this to you?"

"You didn't mean to, and it didn't hurt at the time. Please, don't worry about it."

Even now she was trying to reassure him. *Protect him.*

"I fucking hurt you?" He looked down at his hands in disgust.

"I'm fine, really." She touched his arm to get his attention.

"Hurting you is the last thing I ever wanted."

She brushed light fingers across his jaw and the action warmed the center of his chest. "I know this isn't easy on you. I can't imagine what it's like having your body force you to do something you don't want."

He assumed she was talking about his demon's constant fight for dominance. She'd have an up-close and personal understanding of that kind of loss of control. "Yeah, but you'd know exactly what that feels like," he said carefully.

Her brow scrunched. "What do you mean?"

"Every time I come for you, your body is forced to respond to me because of our connection," he tried to explain.

Last night had been a prime example of what their connection could do. Her body had readied for him as soon as he'd walked through the door.

A blush crept down her neck to the tops of her full breasts. "That's not what's happening, not now anyway. I think I'd know the difference."

"What are you saying?"

She toyed with the sheet. "I know I could lose a few pounds, that I'm not the kind of woman a lot of men usually find attractive. And I know you only want me...*that way* because of the mate thing. But that's not what's happening to me. That's not why I...respond to you." Her gaze darted away. "I'm attracted to you. And I, I…care about you."

She cared?

He never hoped…he never imagined she could care for him in return. When he'd learned of her existence, that was the last thing he'd wanted. But now…

Before he could get too worked up about that astonishing admission, the rest of what she'd said, the way she'd put herself down, sunk in. A growl ripped from his throat before he could hold it back. "I don't want to hear you talk about yourself that way, not ever again. Do you understand?"

"It's okay. You don't need to—"

"You're beautiful, inside and out. You're the most caring person I've ever met." He threaded his fingers in her hair and held her wide gaze. "And you drive me fucking wild. I've never craved another being the way I crave you, and not just because of the mate thing," he said using the same words she had. Her breath quickened and his pulse skipped a beat in response. "I told you, Eve, you make me…want things…"

She licked her lips. "What do you want?"

He shook his head.

"Tell me," she said. "Please."

He held her gaze. "I'm not good for you."

"I don't believe that. I've never met anyone like you. I've never felt the way I do when I'm with you." Those words cost her, and it made him want her all the more.

"You don't know me, Eve. You don't know what I've done," he forced out.

She reached up and ran her thumb over his brow. "Then tell me."

For some reason, he wanted to. Perhaps once she learned the truth she'd leave on her own, saving him all this torment. She'd understand why he would never be good enough to be her mate.

The words spilled from his lips in one ragged exhale. "I failed her. She trusted me and I fucking failed her."

Eve frowned. "Who?"

He sucked in a shallow breath, struggling to take in oxygen. "Scarlet." Her name felt wrenched from his chest. "She's dead because of me. I may as well have buried the knife in her heart myself."

She stared at him for a moment then shook her head and moved to cup his face in her small, soft hands. No scorn or disgust twisted her beautiful face, only concern. "Tell me about her. Tell me what happened," she said.

Removing her hands, he sat up and swung his legs over the side of the bed, resting his elbows on his knees. He couldn't get through this with her looking at him like that.

"It was close to fifty years ago now. That's when I first sensed her, a demi new to her powers. I went to retrieve her, tracked her to an abandoned warehouse. She was homeless, living on the streets. She was only fourteen years old. The youngest demi to ever come into their powers. She was all alone and scared as hell. I took her with me. She became important to me, and I to her. She looked up to me, thought of me as her savior, I guess. I loved her like a father loves his child, and she loved me in return. As she grew older, grew into her powers, we discovered she possessed an amazing physical and mental strength. She was a warrior, had a way with people, too. They were drawn to her, trusted her. We also learned that she was Tobias's mate.

"We decided to use her in the field. Chaos didn't think Tobias working with her was a good idea so she worked with me." He held her gaze. "T trusted me to take care of her. He *trusted* me."

He sucked in an agonized breath. Eve gently glided her hand over his back, reassuring him, like she sensed his pain. He didn't deserve her comfort.

"We were on retrieval together. She'd usually go in first, do the talking." He glanced back at her. "In case you hadn't noticed, tact isn't one of my strong qualities."

Eve actually smiled at that, and his heart thumped in response. Now she'd brought the once dead organ back to life, the thing was liable to put him into cardiac arrest with all the jumping around it was doing.

The tender way she stared at him twisted him inside. He was about to shatter that soft look on her lovely face. He carried on before he could change his mind. "After she'd done her thing, I went in. The guy wasn't taking the news well. I was busy trying to get him out of the house, while Scarlet tried to talk sense into him. I told her to just let me get him out. I didn't care if he kicked and screamed the whole way."

He shook his head. "We always had each other's backs." He rubbed a hand over his face and shook his head. "I failed her that day, failed both of them. I'm ruled by my emotions, usually anger. When that happens, my senses dim, which means I can't pick up on the enemy as easily. She'd tell me to cut the shit, pull my head out of my ass, and get on with it."

Eve remained quiet beside him.

Weak.

Flawed.

"I was getting pissed, totally focused on the male fighting me, stopping us from getting him to safety. I let emotion take over...like I did when I met you." Eve's features changed, showing her surprise. "I didn't notice or even sense the Orthon that had followed us. It killed her before I'd even worked out it was in the house."

CHAPTER 23

Eve ached for the male sitting beside her, not the one who literally carried the weight of the world on his shoulders, but a father who had lost his daughter.

Throat tightening, she struggled for breath as the truth of her feelings hit like a battering ram to the chest. She loved him. Loved him with her entire heart and soul.

As much as it hurt to keep her feelings locked inside, she would. Lazarus didn't need or want to hear it, not now, maybe not ever. He had more pressing matters to worry about. His feelings for her weren't the same, and telling him would only add to his guilt when it was time for them to part.

Not knowing what else to do, she pushed her sadness and anger aside and reached for him. "I'm sorry, Lazarus." It was all she could say. No amount of words would help at this point. So, climbing to her knees, she wrapped her arms around his shoulders and pressed her lips to the tattoo snaking up the side of his neck.

He froze, his large body going statue still. "What are you doing?"

"Kissing you."

"I thought…I thought you wouldn't…"

"What? You thought I'd get up and leave? That I'd think less of you? You loved her." She gripped his chin and turned his head. Their eyes met. "It was a terrible thing that happened, but it was an accident."

He shook his head, but she kept hold of him. "An accident," she repeated, and before he could say anything more, she leaned in and brushed her lips across his.

He pulled away, breathing heavily. "Eve…I'm not—"

"Don't," she whispered, and leaned in, pushed for more. Her lips were an inch from his when he turned away and stood abruptly.

Rejection, cold and sharp, hit her between the ribs, knocking the wind from her lungs. She scooted back on the bed and dipped her chin so her hair fell forward, covering the humiliation heating her face. *Stupid, stupid, stupid.* She should have known better by now.

Before she could scramble off the other side and escape, he gripped her upper arms and hauled her to her feet. With her standing on the bed in front of him they were nearly eye level.

Lazarus brushed her hair away from her face and cupped her cheek. His thumb stroked her jaw then he tilted her head back and stared into her eyes. "Don't ever hide from me. I can't bear it." His hand moved down to the side of her throat in a grip that was firm yet gentle. His thumb continued to stroke her skin and she wanted to lean in, seek more of his touch. The possessiveness of it was undeniable. "I've never known anyone like you, Eve, as good as you."

Before she could reply to that, he nuzzled her throat with a tenderness that should have been impossible for the massive demon warrior. The vulnerability and desperation in that one action tore her heart in two. The soft silk of his hair slid across her palm as she held him to her, as he kissed a path to her mouth, taking her lips in an achingly gentle kiss. The intensity of his mouth and his tongue against hers began a slow burn that turned her insides molten. The sound he made against her mouth was one of longing, of anguish, of hunger.

Eve wanted to love him like he deserved, and suspected he desperately needed. She wanted to show him how wonderful he was. This wasn't about the demon fighting for freedom inside him. It was about Lazarus and nothing more.

"Lie down," she whispered against his mouth.

"Eve..."

She shook her head. "Let me take care of you. Just this once."

He squeezed his eyes shut, going through some kind of internal struggle, but he needed this, needed to let go.

His eyes fluttered open when she took his hand. The vulnerability that stared back at her caused her chest to tighten. He came to her then, his body still deliciously naked and magnificently aroused. Doing as she asked, he lay back on the bed and Eve took a minute to admire his powerful body, hard and defined. Magnificent.

The beautiful symbols that marked his arm and the side of his neck fascinated her. She wanted to trace them with her tongue, and she would because right then, at that moment, he was hers and hers alone.

He was built like a weapon of mass destruction. It was all there, lethal power, unbelievable strength, all at her mercy. She drank him in, his powerful thighs, the hard length of his straining erection against cut abs. Those impressive pecs, then up to his face, a face that would be harsh if it wasn't for those sensual lips. His tongue darted out and he licked the full lower one. She couldn't help mimic the action, hungry for a taste of him. Their eyes met and the primal need there stole her breath.

She crawled over and straddled his hips, and his gaze traveled over her curves as she did. She forced herself to leave her body bared to him, resisting the urge to cover herself. Lazarus liked the way she looked. How could she doubt it with the way he was looking at her?

His big hands gripped her thighs, smoothing up to her hips to softly massage and caress the bruised skin there.

"I hate that I hurt you."

"You didn't." She leaned forward and kissed his whiskered jaw. "I enjoyed every minute of it." She kissed him slowly, licking and nipping his lips like he had hers earlier.

When he reached up to hold her in place, attempting to deepen the kiss, she gripped his wrists and pushed them back against the mattress. He let her. Lazarus could overpower her easily if he chose to, but he let her have her way.

His breathing quickened as she pressed a trail of hot, wet kisses over his jaw then moved down to nibble and suck his throat, following the ink over his shoulder. She continued her exploration and moved to his hard chest. Her breasts grazed his abs while she dragged her tongue over a flat nipple before catching it between her teeth and biting down gently.

He panted and bucked beneath her. "You're killing me, sweetheart."

Encouraged, she tormented the other nipple for a while before carrying on down to trace the deep ridges of his abs. As she moved lower, he threaded his fingers through her hair. She glanced up, holding his dark, hungry gaze then leaned in, licking away the salty bead gathered at the tip of his cock.

He groaned. "*Fuck*."

Desperate for more, she kissed him where she'd just licked, an open-mouthed sucking kiss that had his hips lifting off the mattress. Still, she didn't take him fully into her mouth, and instead took her time to slowly lick and nibble every inch of his thick shaft.

His fingers flexed in her hair, forcing her to look up at him. "Eve." Her name rumbled from his chest in a growling purr that intensified the throb between her thighs. "Take me into your mouth, sweetheart. Please, suck me."

She grinned and gripped him tighter, running her tongue around the ridge one more time, lapping at the tiny slit.

He hissed in a breath through his teeth then growled again. His chest heaving, every muscle straining, locked up tight. "Please, baby."

His plea melted her, and right then she wanted nothing more than to tell him how much she loved him, how amazing he was. Instead, she said, "Since you asked so nicely."

Cupping his balls, she closed her lips over the head of his cock and took in as much of him as she could, moving up and down the velvety shaft with sucking pulls.

He lifted his hips like he had no control, thrusting into her mouth, and all the while he groaned out hot, tender, filthy things that had her squeezing her legs together to relieve the deep ache inside.

The musky, dark scent of him was driving her wild and then he fisted her hair tighter, his groans increasing. She moaned around him, loving how out of control he was.

He stilled suddenly, his spine torqued, muscles bunching. His massive body shook then he released a shout, her name groaning past his lips over and over. She didn't let go when he tried to pull away and swallowed down everything he had.

Finally, she released his cock and looked up at him with a grin. His large body was trembling, and when his gaze captured hers, burned into her, her grin disappeared. She still held him in her hand, and he hadn't softened at all. Her inner muscles clenched.

"Come here," he rasped.

Eve crawled up his body, beyond desperate to have him inside her, and straddled his hips. He reached down, brushing his thumb over her clit. "Ride me, Eve."

Her gaze darted up to meet his. Clear, pale green stared back and her heart soared. She rose up, unable to wait another second, and sank down, taking him to the hilt. God, he made her so full. She moaned, her head falling back.

"Eve...*fuck*."

His big body shook beneath her while his thumb continued to work between her thighs as she rode him slow and easy.

Eve was lost to sensation, the feel of him deep inside, the sound of skin meeting skin, the harsh sounds of their panted breaths. He thrust up, silently demanding she increase the pace, and, whimpering, Eve gave him what he needed, what they both needed.

The tension inside her built in delicious waves, and she slammed down hard, taking him as deep as he could go. He hissed and held her to him, grinding up.

Light exploded behind her eyes, and she held on tight. Lazarus's fingers dug into her ass, holding on to her, and he thrust up harder. "That's it, come for me." His voice was nothing but a growl.

Pleasure lit up every nerve ending in her body and she threw her head back and screamed, vaguely aware of Lazarus stiffening beneath her.

The last thing she remembered after collapsing on top of him, and before sleep dragged her under, was of Lazarus wrapping his big, warm body around hers and holding her close.

~

Eve woke feeling warm and snug, and a little groggy.

The warmth was radiating from the big male pressed to her side. His features were smooth and relaxed in sleep, lacking the tortured expression he often wore like a fierce mask. A state that would disappear as soon as he woke and headed back out in search of Tobias.

He was wrapped around her, cocooning her in his arms. A large palm rested against her belly, his face buried in her hair at her neck, his legs tangled with hers. He'd pulled her in tighter during sleep, and the entire length of his body was pressed against her.

An ache started in the center of her chest. Being with him like this felt good, too good. How would she move on without him when the time came?

Her stomach growled so loud she was surprised she didn't wake him. Lazarus didn't stir. Her empty belly was no doubt the reason she'd woken, and as much as she wanted to ignore it and stay under the covers surrounded by Lazarus, he'd would no doubt need to refuel as well when he woke.

Lifting his hand carefully from around her waist, she slipped from beneath the covers and quickly dressed.

She headed to the kitchen, and after making enough sandwiches for the two of them, she headed downstairs to the bar to grab a couple of Cokes for a much-needed sugar hit.

A *buzz* came from the delivery door, stopping her in her tracks. She waited, not sure what to do. Then Brent, muttering to himself, pounded down the stairs. The buzzer went off again and he cursed.

SHERILEE GRAY

"Hang on, I'm coming," he called, followed by the sound of numerous locks disengaging.

Eve didn't hang around and headed toward the stairs. She hit the first landing when a sharp cry rang out, followed by a heavy thump. Putting the drinks on the ground, she raced back down the steps.

Brent lay prone on the ground, his motionless body propping the delivery door open. There was a deep gash across his temple, leaking blood onto the mat. "Brent!"

She rushed over and crouched down beside him, feeling for his pulse. Still alive. He wasn't moving, was barely conscious, but she could hear his thoughts loud and clear.

Demon. Demon. Demon.

Oh God. She had to get him away from the open door.

In a panic, she grabbed Brent's arm and tried to drag him in enough so she could shut it. This place was warded, Lazarus and Brent had both told her that. She just needed to get Brent out of striking distance and he'd be safe.

A man stepped into view and Eve scrambled back, terror tightening her vocal cords, making it impossible to scream. His gaze lifted to hers and he smiled. Dread slithered up her spine and she stumbled back farther when he shoved the door wider and thrust his hand inside.

The screech he let loose lifted goose bumps all over her skin when he broke through the protective ward surrounding the building then yanked the hand back out quickly.

Demon.

It couldn't get through the wards, not without injuring, maybe even killing itself. But Brent was at an odd angle, and he'd slipped down the wall, God, so close to falling outside. The demon would kill him if he got the chance, she had no doubt about that.

There was no time to get Lazarus, so ignoring her terror,

she grabbed Brent's arm and tried to drag him away from the door again.

The demon hissed with rage. Brent was heavy and she tugged harder on his arm. As he finally fell toward her, one of his legs straightened and his foot slid outside. The demon dove for it. Eve fell forward, grabbed hold of his leg, and jerked it out of reach.

The demon's eyes were milky white, locked on her. Eve scrambled back, but it shoved its hand inside again, over Brent's unconscious body, shrieking in pain but not pulling back this time.

The skin peeled from its arm like it'd dipped it in acid, exposing raw flesh.

Eve froze in horror. Everything around her seemed to move in slow motion. She realized too late that she was in striking distance and there was no way she could get back out of its reach in time. The demon grabbed her by the hair and yanked her hard. She fell onto Brent's legs, and the impact knocked the wind from her lungs. Right then, she was struggling to take in a breath, let alone scream for help.

She reached up and tried to loosen its grip, but her fingers slipped against blood and gore. It hissed in pain but didn't let go, and dragged her through the door, hauling her to her feet. She sucked in a breath to scream, but the demon slapped its uninjured hand over her mouth, stifling the scream she was about to let loose.

Still holding her tight, it began to vibrate. Its body shuddered and began to change, taking its Orthon form.

No. Oh God, no.

A gray claw was clasped around her wrist like a manacle, and it hauled her toward the mouth of the alleyway.

She turned back to the open door of the club a few short feet away. Brent was struggling to stand, but he'd taken a serious blow and collapsed to the ground again. She glanced up to the second-story windows. Lazarus was up there, but he might as well have been on the other side of the world.

Eve tore at its gray flesh with her fingernails, fighting with everything she had. But no matter how hard she fought, she couldn't break loose, couldn't make a sound.

The creature's cold fingers pressed against her lips and she shook her head trying to free her mouth, but it held tight. She bit down as hard as she could, and the demon hissed, striking her across the face.

Pain exploded through her head, her skin stinging from the long claws that had cut into her flesh. She ignored the pain and tried to pull free, to run.

It caught her back up and kept moving, dragging her with it.

A long silver car pulled to a stop in front of her. The creature beside her shifted forms again and was back to looking like a human male.

It yanked the door open, forced her inside, and closed her in. She grabbed for the handle and tugged at it, but it wouldn't open no matter how hard she tried. The car began to ease from the curb.

She cried out and pounded on the window as the club, and Lazarus, got farther and farther away.

"You must be Eve," a rough voice said.

Eve spun around. She hadn't even noticed anyone else in the car with her, too desperate to escape. A man sat beside her, and as he leaned forward, the sunlight streaming through the window highlighted his features. He was striking, chiseled, almost too good looking. Not as hard as Lazarus, but there was an unmistakable cruelty behind his unearthly coal-black eyes.

Definitely not human.

"What do you want with me?" she said, panic clear in her voice.

"I'm Tobias," he said. "You may have heard of me?" He grinned. "Nice to finally meet you."

He searched her face, for what she didn't know, before he said, "I look forward to getting to know you a lot better."

She opened her mouth to tell him to go to hell...but everything went black.

CHAPTER 24

LAZARUS CAME AWAKE with a start and automatically reached out, searching for Eve, only to find the sheet still warm from her body but the space beside him empty. He tensed then shook his head at his behavior, forcing his muscles to relax.

She couldn't even go to the bathroom without him worrying…missing her.

Shit, Lazarus had lain himself bare before her last night, and instead of turning her back on him, she'd embraced him, kissed him…loved him.

Eve had opened herself to him while they'd made love, had given herself over so sweetly. Fighting the link that would bind them together forever had been so damn hard, but he had, because he wanted Eve to know exactly what was happening when they took it there. He wanted her to experience it with him, every moment.

Now he just had to figure out how to ask her. Did he go the human route: romantic dinner? Eve had believed herself to be human for most of her life. Is that what she'd want? Should he get down on one knee and give her a piece of jewelry? Fucked if he knew, but he wanted it to be special.

He rubbed his hands over his face and let out a shaky breath. He'd get down on his goddamn knees and beg her to accept him if he had to. After losing Scarlet, he'd believed he didn't deserve happiness, that he deserved the pain of losing his own mate just like Tobias, and maybe that was still true, but in punishing himself he was hurting Eve as well.

He couldn't do that. He wouldn't. She was all that mattered.

She was everything.

Screw romantic dinners and human traditions. As soon as she returned he'd ask her to be his. He would make her his.

He lay there for several minutes more, getting impatient. His hearing was exceptional and he closed her eyes and used his senses to search her out. Nothing. Silence.

Heavy, empty silence.

Ripping the covers back, he practically flew out of bed.

Something was wrong. He knew it, felt it.

After yanking on his jeans, he pounded down the stairs to the bar, and nearly tripped over a couple of drinks sitting on one of the lower steps. He picked up one of the cans. Ice cold.

She'd been down here, and something had disturbed her before she made it back to him.

Brent stumbled into view, clutching his bleeding head. "I'm sorry, Laz. Jesus, I'm so sorry," he gasped.

"Eve," he barked out.

"Gone," Brent choked.

"No." He grabbed the other male. "Where is she? Where the fuck is she?"

"They took her. They fucking took her."

The delivery entrance door hung open and Lazarus ran out into the alley. This couldn't be happening. He instantly picked up the familiar lingering scent, the unmistakable stench of Orthon, foul and evil.

A roar ripped from his throat, and he clung to the wall. It was either that or fall to his knees. He had failed her. She was in the hands of his enemy, at the mercy of beings that didn't know the meaning of the word.

Forcing oxygen back into his lungs, he tried to calm himself enough to think. He pushed through the door, pounded back up the stairs to their room, and strapped on his blades.

He had to believe she would be okay; that he would get to her in time. Anything else was unacceptable. Tobias had taken Eve, an innocent in all this. The bastard wouldn't care, too far gone for rational thought. Revenge was all Tobias cared about. He wanted to take Eve from him permanently.

Rising panic took over. His demon wanted blood, screamed out for Eve, fought to take over Lazarus, but his rage helped fight his demon back. The bond, now stronger than ever, between him and Eve helped him keep control, the male desperate to find his mate.

Brent was waiting for him when he came back down. "I've called the others." He was leaning heavily on the doorframe.

Laz didn't answer, couldn't even if he wanted to. He nodded and headed down to the alleyway. Cool air and the stench of garbage mixed with the lingering scent of Orthon hit him. With her still wearing the amulet, he couldn't track her, couldn't sense her power. He had no fucking clue where to start.

Not knowing what the fuck to do, he called for Silas. He called the fucker until his voice was raw. The angel never came.

In the end, not knowing what else to do, Lazarus took to the skies, circling, desperate for anything, any sign of Eve or Tobias.

He was standing on top of an apartment building, with no

idea how much time had passed, when the *thud* of boots hitting concrete had Lazarus looking up from the streets below.

Gunner, Rocco, Zenon, and Chaos stood there, wings tucked into their backs, crowding the rooftop.

"Fuck, Laz," Rocco said, strain clear in his voice.

Lazarus didn't want sympathy. He wanted to find Eve.

"You sure it was Tobias?" Gunner asked.

Chaos stepped forward. "It had to be."

Lazarus shoved his fingers through his hair. "Where the fuck would he take her?"

That's when it sunk in: the real reason Silas chose not to fill him in on what Eve was, why he kept it a secret. He'd used her as bait. Diemos had felt her, too, when she came into her powers. Of course he did. The daughter of a handmaid, a way to release all the horrors of Hell on Earth, and a true escape for the demon after being unable to leave for centuries.

The angel knew Diemos would send Tobias after Eve.

Bringing him right to Lazarus. Making it easier for him to kill his brother.

Well, Silas's plan had fucking backfired, and Lazarus was going to end the fucker when he saw him next.

"Do you have something with her scent on it?" Gunner said. "We can take it to Warrick."

Warrick was a friend of Gunner's and a ranking hellhound in his pack. He was also one of the best trackers the hounds had.

Lazarus went back to the club, to their room. The entire apartment was filled with her scent, sweet and delicate. He picked up her shirt, the one she'd been wearing last night, and he held it to his nose, breathing in deeply. His demon cried out, wanted to maim, to kill.

For once they were in full accord.

～

The hounds had set up in Linville, New Jersey, population 3007. Now they ran the place. People here thought they were just another motorcycle club. They had no clue about the monsters they had on their doorstep. The hounds owned the local bar and ran a garage out of the old factory they'd moved into when they liberated themselves from Hell.

They hired themselves out as mercenaries. Loyal to no one. Lazarus didn't blame them, not after the way they were treated by Diemos and his brethren.

It took two hours to reach the clubhouse. Flying made the trip shorter, but coming here still meant losing time they didn't have.

The place was huge. On the surface, it looked like what it was: a run-down factory, and with their patch painted on one of the outside walls, a motorcycle club. But inside, underground, there was a whole lot more.

The pack was big, and that was made more obvious by the number of bikes lined up outside the main doors.

Lazarus landed first, his brothers close behind. Gunner moved ahead, leading them toward the entrance of the clubhouse. A snarl came from behind them, so loud and deep it seemed to vibrate through their feet. Then another from the side.

In moments, they were surrounded by the hounds. They were in their human forms, no claws or massive jaws on display, but that didn't make the large males and several females any less dangerous.

"We're here to see Warrick," Gunner said.

One of the males broke away and moved closer. "You know better than to come here like this, Gunner," he growled. "You use wings to breach our clubhouse without an invite, you get them torn off."

Zenon growled as well, his yellow eyes near glowing, fury radiating off him. "Fucking try it," he rumbled.

"Rein it in," Chaos said to Zenon.

"You know I have respect for the pack," Gunner said. "But we need Warrick's help and we're running out of time." He motioned to Lazarus. "His mate was taken by Diemos. We need to track her before it's too late."

More growls and vicious curses rang out around them. They hated Diemos almost as much as the knights did. After Lucifer was overthrown, leaving Diemos in charge, he had treated the hounds like shit, had used them, forced them to do a lot of things they sure as hell didn't like, which was why they'd finally left as soon as they got the chance.

The knights had agreed to their terms, had given them sanctuary, and they'd agreed not to harm humans, and to help them out on occasion. An understanding had formed between them, a truce. If tentative.

"I need something to scent."

Warrick's voice echoed across the lots as he strode toward them. Lower-ranking pack members backed up, getting out of his way as the huge male joined them.

Lazarus pulled Eve's shirt from the waistband of his jeans where he'd tucked it during the flight, and handed it to Warrick.

The other male put it to his nose and sniffed, drawing her scent in deep, eyes closing. Hellhounds weren't like other canines; they were created in Hell by Lucifer himself, which meant they had their own powers. Warrick was an alpha, would more than likely run the pack one day, and his powers were stronger than most. He didn't need to physically follow Eve's sent. He saw it in his mind, would be able to pinpoint her location from that shirt in moments.

His eyes snapped open, and they were glowing red for several moments before changing back to normal. He pulled his phone from his back pocket, clicked open an app with *maps* written under it, tapped something out, and zoomed in on a location before holding it up to Lazarus.

"She's here."

Every one of Lazarus's muscles was tensed, ready to take flight. "I owe you."

With no time to waste, he stood back, making room for the massive span of his unfurling wings. Charcoal and silver-flecked feathers glittered in the light, and with each lift and pull he caught the air and lifted off with all the power and speed he could muster, his brothers close behind.

Moving at speed, Lazarus rose above the cloud bank.

Urgency, along with guilt reached up and gripped him by the throat. Now he understood what it would mean to lose her, to lose the person that you loved absolutely.

The emotion defied definition.

I love her.

The realization settled over him like a gentle caress, and for once he didn't try to fight it. He loved her. How could he not? If he was honest, he'd been hers from the moment he spotted her up that ladder in her little store, despite how hard he tried to deny his feelings.

Tobias had suffered the overwhelming sorrow of losing his mate, and it had changed him, had destroyed a once fierce and loyal warrior. He was lost forever, and though it pained Laz, he had to end this today. His brother didn't exist anymore. Eve was all that mattered. It was too late for Tobias.

God, Heaven, the fucking uppity angels that resided there, he'd never asked them for anything, not a damn thing, but he prayed now. He prayed for Eve to still be alive. He begged the Fates to keep her safe until he could reach her.

Twenty minutes later he had passed over buildings and

skyscrapers and kept going until he flew over large yards and even larger houses. She was close.

"There," he growled to Chaos who flew at his side.

The house was huge, like the others in the area, with a silver car parked in the driveway. There wasn't much in the way of security from what he could see, but then Tobias wouldn't be expecting him. His brother thought he was untouchable.

As much as he wanted to swoop in, kill anything that moved, and take Eve home, he had to play it safe. One wrong move and Tobias would kill her, or worse—because Eve would suffer a million painful deaths at his hands—deliver her to Diemos. If he knew what she was, what she was capable of...

Fuck.

Lazarus circled the outer perimeter several times, pinpointing entry points and guard positions. His best option would be one of the unguarded doors on a second-floor balcony.

"I'm going in," Laz said to Chaos. "It's too dangerous for all of us to go in at once. If Tobias knows we're here, he'll kill her before I can get to her. Give me time to find her and assess the situation before you follow."

Chaos's jaw tightened, but he didn't try to convince him otherwise because he'd be wasting his breath. "Be careful," he said.

Laz dipped his chin, and letting his powerful wings do the work, slowed his momentum and landed effortlessly on the closest balcony.

The room beyond was silent, empty, and he easily broke the lock. A thick layer of dust covered the furniture and the room smelled musty. The décor was not Tobias's usual taste —lace and ruffles adorned the feminine room.

Eve was in the house, suddenly he could feel her, which

meant Tobias had more than likely found the amulet and removed it.

He gritted his teeth.

Fuck. Stay focused.

Yeah, he could sense her power loud and clear now.

The buzzing awareness of her grew stronger, spiking. It turned his veins to ice, abrading his nerves like coarse sandpaper.

Something was wrong.

He had to get to her. Now.

He listened for movement beyond the wooden door that led from the room into the main house. Silence greeted him.

Easing it open, he moved into the hall, the plush carpet muting his footfalls. As he passed the next room, the smell of death, stale and sickly sweet, wafted from under the closed door. A human. More than likely the owner or owners of the house. Another victim in Tobias's quest for revenge.

The blood on Lazarus's hands grew thicker by the day in the fallout from his carelessness.

He had to stop this now. Eve would not be the next victim. He shook his head, stopping the thought before it sent rage and fear pulsing through his veins and weakened him.

He cursed under his breath at the sound and smell of more than one demon pounding up the stairs, heading in his direction. Stepping back into the room, he waited for them to get closer.

As soon as they were in striking distance, Lazarus stepped out, removing the head of the first with his short sword, then spun, nailing the second in the heart. Quickly dragging the bodies out of the hall, he removed the second demons head then shut them in the room, concealing them before they could ash out and draw unwanted attention.

Making sure the way was clear, Lazarus headed to the

lower level via a rear staircase. The buzz of Eve's power grew even stronger, drawing him deeper. She was in the basement.

He came to a small landing that turned abruptly. Bingo. Golden light ghosted from the deep recesses.

Lazarus's every muscle strained to breaking point with the tension it took to make himself move at a slow pace.

Red rage almost blinded him, but he called on every bit of self-control. All that mattered was getting to Eve.

But before he could make it to the basement, more demons, Orthon, were approaching in front and behind him. This time he had nowhere to go.

He pulled his sword free and prepared to fight.

CHAPTER 25

Eve wanted to scream, the agony pounding through her skull so severe it felt like her head would explode.

The demon stood too close, his rancid breath skittering across her cheek.

"Well, demi?" Tobias asked from his position a short distance from her, the amulet she'd worn around her neck dangling from his fingers.

He wanted her to read the creature's mind, like some screwed-up lie detector for his own entertainment, to confirm yet another loyal servant. For the most part, she had lied. All but a few hated his guts. She'd told him his minions loved him, were devoted to only him.

When, in actual fact, they wanted to rip his head off and…well, eat him.

She shuddered at the disgusting thoughts coming from the Orthon standing beside her. His face was only an inch from hers, staring down at her with cold, soulless eyes, all but daring her to tell the truth.

She panted through the pain. "He is loyal to you."

Once Tobias took the amulet, she'd only been able to maintain her block for a short time; there were just too many of them. Now the strain of having every thought and disgusting image in the room bang around in her brain had become too much and she cried out in agony and frustration.

The demon sneered. Lifting its gray hand, it ran a yellow nail down the side of her face. Not hard enough to break the skin, but enough to leave a mark beside the bloody scratches she already had. It whispered something to her in a language she didn't, or at least shouldn't, understand. But a translator wasn't necessary because the words filtered into her mind in perfect English.

She would be dessert.

"Don't touch her." Tobias kicked the creature, sending him sprawling. "She's more important than you know. Isn't that right, Eve?"

The Orthon hissed.

Tobias laughed. "Leave us," he barked at the demons surrounding them from above. He'd chained her to the wall of a concrete pit in the basement. The creature eyed her as it scrambled from the floor and climbed out. The rest followed in its wake.

Tobias would soon find himself with a full-blown revolt on his hands, and after they'd feasted on him, she would be next, but not before they had used her in other disgusting ways.

Tobias moved toward her, a sneer distorting his beautiful face into something cruel and evil. And like Lazarus, she couldn't hear his thoughts.

"I can see why Lazarus wanted to keep you around. You're a very tempting female. How many times did he fuck you, demi?"

Keeping her eyes locked on his, she refused to give him

what he wanted and rise to the bait. Instead, she pressed her lips together, refusing to answer.

"It doesn't really matter," his deep voice echoed in the confined space. "He didn't mate with you, and that's all that matters. I kind of wish he had. I would have loved for him to feel your pain, your fear the moment you give up and stop fighting. If I'd had my way, I would have delivered your used and broken body to him and taken pleasure in watching him succumb to his demon." He rubbed a lock of her hair between his fingers. "But fate has other plans for you. You know what you are, don't you, Eve?"

Terror made her limbs weak and her heart pound, but she tried to keep her expression blank.

"I may not be able to kill you, but I see I'll have a lot of fun breaking you." He cupped her cheek, letting his fingers trail down her face until he gripped her throat.

She had nowhere to go. Her back was hard against the wall of the deep pit. Leaning forward, he caught her mouth in a hard, bruising kiss. He pressed his fingers into her jaw and forced it open, trying to thrust his tongue into her mouth.

Wrenching her head to the side, she loosened his grip and took advantage by biting down hard on his lip.

"Bitch," he hissed and backhanded her so hard her vision blinked in and out. Her head rang for a few minutes, the force of the blow nearly rendering her unconscious. When Tobias's face came back into focus, the bastard was grinning. The metallic tang of blood filled her mouth and she blinked back the tears she refused to let fall.

His eyes flashed. "Oh yeah, we're going to have some fun." He turned away from her, moved to a small table set up on the other side of the pit, and picked something up.

"What is that? What are you going to do?" she said, terror almost choking her.

He turned to her. In his hands was what looked like a small leather package, brown and worn. He peeled back one side then the other, his black eyes focused on what he was uncovering.

"It's going to help you do what you were born to," he said without looking up at her.

Finally, he took something from the center, something yellowing, long and thin and pointed, and dropped the leather to the table.

"What the hell is that?" she choked.

"It's a bone. A very old and very powerful bone." He placed it in a crude wooden bowl and walked toward her. "As long as you're alive and your blood covers this bone, Diemos will have control over the hell's gate. He will be able to open and close it at will." He was breathing heavily. "Can you imagine, sweet Eve, what your Earth will be like then? With demons free to do what they like, more than the knights will ever be able to contain."

She shook her head. "No...no, please...you can't..."

Tobias ignored her, placed the bowl on the stone floor, and grabbed her wrist. "Time to take you to your new home. Diemos is eager to meet you."

He took the short sword, one that looked almost identical to Lazarus's, from the sheath strapped to his thigh and drew it across her skin without warning or hesitation.

She gasped in pain and watched in horror as Tobias held her arm above the wooden bowl, catching her blood, covering the bone he'd placed inside it.

Crying out, she kicked at it, trying to knock it over, but the chains around her ankles restricted her movements.

Tobias gripped a fistful of hair painfully, holding her still. The bone was soon covered and Tobias leaned in, lapping at her blood, at the open wound in her flesh. She tried to pull away, but he held her too tight.

"You want to stop bleeding, don't you? It won't do for you to bleed out and die. That would ruin all our plans," he said.

Her mind started to shut down, her psyche throwing up walls to protect her sanity.

This can't be happening. It can't be real.

She would never see Lazarus again.

One voice, an Orthon's, rose, cutting through her own thoughts. Its distress penetrated the chaos of her mind and broke past the other voices in the room. Nothing she could put together, though, because its thoughts were far too jumbled.

Then it cut off abruptly, its mind suddenly silent.

More followed.

Their minds screaming, then nothing.

Tobias stood back, and beside her something flashed. A bright light. It was working. *Oh God*, the gate was opening.

She tried to fight her restraints, but it was no good. Her limbs felt weak from loss of blood and she was close to collapsing.

"They're coming," Tobias said, voice filled with excitement.

Her vision dimmed, the colors darkening. Eve blinked several times, positive she was about to pass out. A large shadow had descended over Tobias, half his face eclipsed by darkness. Her eyes were playing tricks on her.

She blinked again, looking up.

Her breath seized in her lungs.

Lazarus stood there, towering over them.

His face was in shadow. She couldn't see his expression, but the glow from the wall-mounted lights illuminated him from behind like a golden halo.

Tobias came forward, grabbing hold of her biceps, his grip painfully tight.

"Get your hands off her," Lazarus said, his voice echoing

around the confined space, full of fury and promising death and suffering to the male beside her.

Tobias's black eyes widened briefly before he chuckled darkly. "You found us, then?" He made a tutting sound. "Pity you're too late. You really should have mated her, Laz, and all this could have been prevented."

Lazarus hissed.

Tobias leaned in and breathed deeply. "She reeks of you." He grinned. "I'm glad she's yours. You have no idea how glad. That I'll be depriving you of your mate...fuck yeah, it made this so much sweeter."

"Don't fucking touch her," Lazarus said, his disembodied voice bouncing off the brick walls.

The portal beside them that had started as a small spark, a flash of light, was swirling, growing in size.

Tobias laughed then gripped her jaw and lifted a knife, placing it against her face. "You're too late. It's done. You've lost, and you've lost her."

Eve struggled, and the tears she'd fought blazed a heated trail down her cheeks. Her reaction seemed to excite Tobias more, and he drew the blade slowly across her flesh. She screamed and felt her blood bubble to the surface of her skin. Its warmth ran down her neck and the inside of her shirt.

"Stop," Lazarus roared.

Tobias leaned in and licked the rivulet from her neck. "Mmm, the taste of power. One of the handmaids' blood runs through her veins. Diemos has been looking for someone like her for centuries, and it'll be me who delivers her to him."

"Do you think he'll reward you? He's using you, Tobias," Lazarus said. "You think he'll pat you on the back, welcome you into Hell with open arms? You spent as many centuries stopping him from reaching his ultimate goal. Once you deliver her, he will turn on you."

The hell's gate pulsed, still growing.

Tobias had stilled at her side. "You're wrong," he roared.

"You know I'm not," Laz said back. "You know it."

Snarling echoed off the stone walls and filled the basement. Tobias pulled Eve in closer to him. "They're coming to welcome us home. Do you hear them?"

Light flashed so bright it blinded her for several seconds. Eve blinked, tears streaming down her face, and when she could see again she cried out in horror. Demons were crawling out of the portal.

Lazarus stepped closer.

"Take another step and I'll take a piece out of her," Tobias said.

Lazarus growled as demons edged toward him from all directions. He drew his sword a moment before they launched at him.

Eve screamed as he roared and tried to fight them off, but more poured out of the hell's gate, coming at him, taking their place instantly.

No matter how many he killed, more came.

"Lazarus!" she cried.

Something was wrong.

Tobias leaned in. "You see, a male's physical strength is irrelevant if he is weak of mind. As I suspected, seeing you bleed has caused his loss of control."

Please, God, no.

Tobias worked on her chains and had her free in moments, then started pulling her toward the hell's gate.

"No." She tried to fight but it was useless.

She cried out, trying to get Lazarus's attention, and hoped like hell she didn't distract him from his fight and get him injured even more. But she needed to do something.

His body stiffened, just a fraction. He'd heard her. She

called his name again and he turned to her. Their gazes collided and held. His body went rigid.

Tobias hissed and clapped a hand over her mouth.

Lazarus snarled, the sound inhuman. He roared, his body seeming to grow and contort. He shook his head from side to side like an angry bull.

He called her name—

And exploded into his demon form, throwing off the demons that had covered him. His chest heaved, light glinting off his crimson skin and glossy black horns. His huge charcoal wings were spread wide, the silver flecks shimmering and dancing across each individual feather as they moved—causing a delicious spicy breeze to surround her, ruffling her hair.

The demons only stayed back a moment then dove at him, attaching themselves to his big body. Their teeth flashed as they bit and tore at his skin and wings with their claws. He peeled them off, but he was bleeding, his beautiful wings damaged.

He didn't seem to notice, and continued to fight in a mindless rage. The audible crunch of bone made her stomach lurch as he dispatched them one after another.

Tobias stilled beside her, releasing a shuddering breath. "His demon has taken him. It's done. It's over."

She shook her head. *Oh God. I can't lose him now.*

The demons still covered Lazarus, tearing at his flesh, and more tears broke free, tracking down her face.

They're going to kill him.

Lazarus was in there. He had to be. He wasn't gone. She refused to believe it. She'd brought him back the last time he lost control of his demon, and she could do it again. She twisted her head, and Tobias was distracted enough by what was going on in front of them that she managed to get her mouth free of his hand. At least long enough for her to call Lazarus one more time.

Lazarus stilled completely and looked down at them. "Let her go," he roared at Tobias. He didn't take his eyes off them as he again methodically peeled demons from his body, until he was free of them and holding back the horde with his sword.

Blood dripped from his wounded body and pooled at his feet. His nostrils flared and his chest heaved as he took a threatening step toward the edge of the pit.

He didn't seem to be struggling against his demon. The two of them seemed to be working together to protect her.

Tobias cursed and lifted his blade to her again. Lazarus froze. This was it. She was about to die without ever telling him she loved him.

Lazarus roared, the animalistic sound ripped from his throat.

She wasn't letting Tobias take her to Hell, no matter the cost. She wouldn't be the cause of these creatures invading her world, or what that would mean for Lazarus.

The bowl filled with her blood was still on the floor, just out of reach. Eve found enough strength to jerk to the side and kick out. She braced for the pain that was coming, as the knife that Tobias held was forced into her flesh with the movement, sinking deep into her shoulder.

The bowl toppled over, her blood splashed out onto the stone floor, and the gate flickered and closed, faster than it came.

Agony burned through her and knocked her legs out from underneath her. Tobias's hold on her vanished…then Lazarus was there.

A battle cry echoed around the brick walls, filled with so much hatred it lifted the hair on the back of Eve's neck. Lazarus's brothers were there. The massive males were fighting the demons that had escaped with brutal and lethal grace.

"I've got you," Lazarus said, chest heaving.

He cupped her face in his large, leathery, crimson hand. He was in his demon form, but his eyes weren't black; they were bright green. He was savagely beautiful.

His gaze dropped, zeroed in on the blood covering the front of her shirt, and he stilled. Fear, stark and violent, twisted his hard features and his eyes turned wild. "Oh, fuck." He made an agonized sound. "Where is it? Where were you cut? Don't leave me, sweetheart. You can't leave me."

Eve gripped his wide wrist. "I'm all right. I'm not going anywhere," she choked. She didn't think he heard her. His gaze focused solely on the growing patch of blood staining her shirt.

"Lazarus? Look at me." Agony lined his face. "I won't leave you. I promise I'll never leave you."

He shuddered, seemed to collect himself, and covered her wound with his big hand, applying pressure.

She hissed.

"You're okay. You're going to be okay," he said.

She got the impression he needed to convince himself as much as her. Eve cupped his face, fighting unconsciousness. "Yes, I am, because of you. You found me." Her voice sounded croaky, barely audible.

"I'm sorry I took so long," he choked. She didn't think he was aware of the tears running down his fierce and beautiful face.

"I knew you'd come for me."

Lazarus gently kissed her lips. "Let's get you out of here."

"He's getting away," Chaos yelled.

They looked up in time to see Tobias heading for the stairs. The other knights were engaged in battle, unable to fight their way to him.

Tobias paused at the foot of the stairs and gripped his head, his gaze sliding to Lazarus. His eyes changed, the black giving way to cool pale blue.

Lazarus sucked in a sharp breath, stiffening, and an anguished sound escaped his throat that broke Eve's heart. Tobias spun away, stumbling as he ran up the stairs.

Eve clung to Lazarus as he lifted them from the pit. Demons surrounded them, watching them with eager, hungry eyes.

But then Lazarus's brothers were there, cutting them back, creating a clear path.

Lazarus didn't turn back, trusting his brothers had his back, and carried her toward the stairs as well. They moved through the house and out onto the yard. Tobias was long gone, and Lazarus took flight, still managing to fly even with his wings as damaged as they were.

Eve clung to him and she was never letting go.

CHAPTER 26

WHEN EVE WOKE, it took several minutes for the fog of sleep to lift. She was in Lazarus's bed, in his room at the compound.

Warm.

Safe.

Home.

She lay cocooned by a mountain of pillows. The big room felt cozy with the lights dimmed. She tried to sit up, but could barely move her arms with the duvet pulled up high and tucked around her securely.

It took a moment for the confusion to clear and her memories to come flooding back. She struggled to get free of the covers again, and pain shot through her shoulder.

Lazarus?

The familiar scent of her mate surrounded her, enveloped her in warmth, and the panic subsided. He was safe.

The door cracked open and his wide shoulders filled the narrow space. With his feet bare and wearing only a pair of black jeans that sat low on his hips, she took the opportunity to search the hard planes of his bare chest, looking for any sign of injury. All that remained of the vicious wounds he'd received from the demon attack were fading pink marks, now barely visible on his smooth skin.

He carried a tray laden with food, and when he glanced up, he offered her a wide smile. "You're awake." He sat on the bed beside her. "You've been asleep so long I was getting worried. How are you feeling? Are you hungry?"

All she wanted to do was touch him, convince herself that he was unhurt, that he was really here with her, that this wasn't just some beautiful dream. "I think so."

"I wasn't sure what you'd feel like. So, I, ah"—he glanced down at the overflowing tray—"yeah, I got some of every-thing." He seemed unsure of himself, nervous.

"A drink would be good to start with." She gave in and rested a hand on his thigh. The heat and hard muscle beneath her palm reassured her like nothing else could.

He handed her a glass of juice and studied her face, searching her gaze for what she didn't know, but his uncer-tainty shone through. Her chest squeezed.

She lifted her hand to her throat. The weight of the gold disk she'd worn around her neck for weeks was noticeable in its absence. "The amulet?"

"Chaos found it where Tobias...where he had you... chained." His voice had grown deeper, rougher.

"What will happen to Tobias?" she asked.

"We can't feel him anymore. For the first time in centuries." His jaw bunched. "Diemos wouldn't have been happy with his failure." His eyes met hers.

"You think he's dead?"

Lazarus nodded.

Even after everything, it still hurt him. "I'm sorry."

He squeezed her hand still resting on his thigh and cleared his throat. His eyes searched hers. "When...when I first came for you, the idea of making you mine, shit, it scared the fuck out of me. I didn't want it, what you represented, what it meant for both of us." The muscle in his jaw bunched. "I didn't feel worthy of you."

Eve shook her head. "Laz—"

"I never planned to stay once I'd made you mine. I was going to leave, Eve."

Her pulse stuttered, raced faster. "You were?" she whispered.

Pain distorted his features. "I don't deserve you, Eve. And truthfully, I never will. I should give you back the amulet. I should leave. Let you find someone worthy of you." His voice was nothing but a broken growl.

She shook her head, unable to speak. She wanted to tell him she couldn't live without him, but her throat constricted, choking off her words.

He leaned forward and stopped her distress with a hard kiss, claiming and possessive. Finally, he pulled back. "But I can't. I won't. I'm too selfish. I want you to be mine, Eve. My mate. Will you?"

She swallowed the lump in her throat. "Yes. There's nowhere else I'd rather be than here with you."

He released a rough breath. "Really? You will?"

"Yes. I want that more than anything."

He cupped her face in his large hands. "I'm never letting you out of my sight, not ever again." He ran his knuckles down the uninjured side of her face. "When I saw you… Tobias's hands on you, bleeding…" His voice broke.

She reached up and grabbed his fingers, threading them with hers. "I'm all right now."

The pain remained, and seeing Tobias like that had to have hurt him greatly. She wanted to ease his pain and she wanted…she just wanted him. She untucked the covers and pulled them back.

Lazarus frowned. "What are you doing?"

"Climb in with me."

"Eve…"

She shook her head, stopping whatever protest he was going to make. "I don't want to wait, Lazarus. Please, make me yours."

His nostrils flared and the green of his eyes flickered dark then light. "Are you sure?"

"I've never been so sure about anything in my whole life."

He stood abruptly, his hands dropping to the front of his jeans and he quickly undid them and shoved them off.

Eve sucked in a breath at the sight of him standing there naked. "You're so beautiful."

He climbed in beside her, that big body shaking with need. "And you take my goddamn breath way, female."

Lazarus stared into Eve's eyes. His mate. *His*. He could barely believe this was happening. That he could feel this happy. That he could trust another being so fully. She held his heart and soul in her hands. This female, so beautiful inside and out, gave his existence meaning. She gave him a reason to keep fighting.

No, he never believed he deserved this, not after losing Scarlet and Tobias, but turning his back on her now was an impossibility. Leaving her was not something he could even contemplate.

One of her arms, the one not injured, curled around his neck and her fingers threaded in his hair at his nape. "I love you, Lazarus."

His heart squeezed and burst into a rapid-fire beat at her softly spoken words. He trembled harder. "And I love you."

He gently pressed his lips to hers and kissed her slow and deep. He was already hard and aching for her, his body demanding he take her, but he had to be gentle. Not easy with the way her thighs had spread wider, hugging his hips, her bare pussy hot and slick against his cock.

He groaned. "You're ready for me now, aren't you, sweetheart?"

Her hips lifted and she rubbed herself against him. "Yes. Now, Lazarus. Please."

A growl crawled up his throat, his demon twisting and snarling, as desperate for the connection as Lazarus was. "I'm gonna take this slow, okay? You're still recovering." He pressed the head of his cock to her opening. "Ready?" he choked out.

She bit her lip and nodded.

Lazarus kissed her then lifted to his elbows, needing to see her face when he slid home. He pressed forward, and they both moaned as he filled her. He made love to her then, both of them shaking from the beauty of it, the desperate need for one another, a need that would never wane or falter. The kind of love and connection flowing between them he'd never even dared to dream about.

It was hard, but he kept the pace slow, thrusting deep.

Oh fuck. There it was. He could see it. The thread that would bind them.

Eve gasped and her entire body bowed as a surge of power moved through her, turning her entire body into a live wire. He knew because he felt it, too. What looked like a full-body orgasm hit her and she cried out, trembling uncontrollably.

Lazarus watched in awe, clenching his fists, gripping the sheet as the link intensified.

He reached for it and grabbed on. His hips snapped forward, staying deep inside Eve. And like a tree sending out tender new roots, the connection thickened and grew, burying deep. Something wrenched deep inside him, the exquisite pleasure drawing out their bliss.

She was his, now and forever. Nothing but death could ever rip them apart, and he'd spend eternity making sure that never happened. He felt it in his heart and soul, and he embraced the euphoric sensation with open arms.

Eve was his mate.

They lay there for the longest time, just holding each other.

Finally, he lifted his head and stared into her glistening blue eyes. "Thank you."

She touched his face, her thumb brushing over his whiskered jaw. "You don't need to thank me."

"You don't realize what you've done, sweetheart. I've fought an internal battle for centuries." He grinned. "I don't... I don't need to fight it anymore. My demon is finally leashed," he whispered then swallowed hard. "Because of you, because you gave yourself to me."

She smiled so wide his stomach clenched.

"I'd fight it again, no matter how many centuries it took, as long as I knew you were waiting for me at the other end," he choked out.

Her eyes grew brighter. "We make a pretty good team, huh?"

"Yeah, sweetheart, we do," he said.

She looked over his shoulder and he knew the moment she spotted it. The large bookshelf full of books, her mother's books, worn and well-read, and precious to her. Her gaze moved around the room, spotting other bits and pieces scattered about, little things. Her things.

She blinked up at him. "You got my books?"

"This is your home now. I want you to be happy here."

She looked around, flabbergasted. "How did you get them here so fast?"

Christ, she was cute. "Wing power, baby. Fastest way to fly." He chuckled at the way her eyes grew wider.

"Really? You did that...for me?" she said, voice raspy with emotion.

Lazarus brushed back a strand hair from her face. "I'd do anything for you. Anything."

A tear streaked down her face and he brushed that away as well.

"Though, in this instance, I can't take all the credit. I sent the others as well, got them to collect as much as they could carry. I'll have the bigger stuff shipped."

More tears slid down her cheeks. "This is...you have no idea how much this means to me."

"I did it for purely selfish reasons. I want you to love it here. I want you to feel at home, to never regret—"

She pressed a finger to his lips, stopping him mid-sentence. "I can live without my things, Lazarus. At the end of the day, it's all just stuff. God, because of you, I've finally found my home, the place I belong. A place I know I will always be loved and cherished. I don't want to live without you. I can't. I love you," she said simply.

Something tickled his cheek and when he swiped at it, his fingers came away wet. This female, what she did to him. "I'm yours, Eve, now and forever." His face darkened with hunger before he bent forward and kissed her again. "God, I love you so much," he whispered against her lips.

It was her turn to wipe his tears away, and then she wrapped her arms around him.

Lazarus buried his face against her neck, breathing in his female.

His mate.

She smelled like home.

EPILOGUE

Three months later

EVE WALKED DOWN THE HALL, arm linked with Meredith's, both ready to do battle.

Meredith squeezed her hand. "I can't believe Chaos went for it. You know, since the guy's completely allergic to fun."

Wasn't that the truth. But Eve had been determined, and in the end, he'd relented. The guys had been fighting a lot, especially with the way the demons in the city had been behaving. They all knew something was seriously off and Eve knew how worried they were. She just wanted a night where they could relax, laugh. "You know we have to beat Chaos now, right? At everything, or we'll never hear the end of it."

Meredith laughed as Eve pushed open the door to the control room. "We'll have to join forces…"

"Go long!" Kryos called and tossed a ball across the room and out the balcony doors. Rocco sprinted after it, jumped to the railing, and dove off the side, shifting into his demon form midair. His clothes disintegrated, falling from his body then he disappeared from view.

Lazarus strode over to her and tugged her into his side. Eve looked up at her grinning mate. "Um…this wasn't the kind of games night we had in mind."

He smirked. "No?"

A heavy *thud* against the balcony floor had them all turning back to the open doors. Rocco, ball in hand, and completely naked, strode back in.

Kryos growled and put his hands over Meredith's eyes, and Lazarus curled his hand around the back of Eve's head and smooshed her face against his chest.

"Put it away, asshole," Lazarus growled.

"Bother, seriously. No one wants to see that," Kryos added.

Rocco chuckled. "Feeling threatened are we, boys?"

Kryos snorted. "As if."

Eve tried to move, but Lazarus wouldn't let her lift her head. "Really?" she bit out.

"I'm sorry, sweetheart," Lazarus said. "But it's just not done. A male does not flash his jewels at another male's mate."

"And if he does, he gets his ass kicked," Kryos said. He sounded like he was gritting his teeth.

"Can I lift my head now?" Eve asked.

"No."

"Okay, let's all calm down," Rocco said. "Instead of kicking my ass, how about you Kryos and Gunner, play me, Chaos and Zen…out there. First to miss a pass loses."

"Loses what?" Chaos said, obviously now joining the ridiculous conversation.

"Their dignity," Rocco said.

Meredith cursed. "You males are so juvenile."

"This *really* isn't what we had in mind for tonight," Eve added.

"You're on," Lazarus said, ignoring her completely.

"Whatever," Meredith muttered. "I just want my eyesight back."

Lazarus tipped Eve's head back and she blinked up at him. "You want to watch me play?"

His hopeful expression made her giggle. "Sure."

"Teams are going to be uneven. Gunner's AWOL," Chaos said.

Lazarus frowned and Eve knew the guys were worried about him. He'd told her Gunner hadn't been himself for weeks.

"I'm out," Zenon said.

Eve hadn't even realized he was in the room.

The male was so closed off, spent so much time alone, she hated that he was leaving. She reached out to touch his arms as he walked by, about to try and convince him to stay, but he jerked back like she'd stabbed him.

"I'm…I'm sorry, I didn't mean to…" What? She wasn't sure how to finish her sentence.

Zenon dropped his chin, letting his hair fall forward, covering his face, and strode from the room.

Lazarus curled his fingers around the side of her neck, drawing her attention back to him. "It's not you," he said. "He just…Zenon doesn't like to be touched."

What had happened to him to make him react like that? She hated to think. Out of all the knights, Zenon was the most distant, the one she wished she could figure out. But she got the feeling there was no getting through to him and that made her heart hurt.

"You ready?" Rocco called.

"I was born ready," Kryos said as he stripped off, shifted, and dove off the side of the balcony.

"Nice work, Eve," Rocco said. "Games night rocks." He winked at her and shifted as well, joining Kryos and Chaos who were already passing the ball to each other high in the air, their massive wings working to hold them at the same height, five floors above the ground.

"Will you be here when I'm done?" Lazarus said, grinning down at her. "When I return victorious and ready to claim my spoils."

Eve grinned back. "I told you, I'm not going anywhere. Not ever."

His eyes softened and he tugged her close, kissing her slow and deep.

"Enough with the sucking face," Rocco called out. "Your stalling tactics won't save you."

Lazarus lifted his head. "Oh, it's on."

Eve watched her mate shift into his demon form and join the others, the thunder of heavy bodies colliding and the ball being thrown hard, following soon after.

Meredith sighed and plonked down on a seat beside her. "Maybe we can get them to play Monopoly next week?"

A window smashed somewhere followed by hoots and cheers.

They both burst out laughing.

Eve wiped her eyes. "Yeah, I'm not liking our chances."

Zenon was torn from his sleep as a wave of...fuck, he didn't know what it was, sliced through him. He gritted his teeth, frozen in place as it smashed through him a second time.

Something he couldn't name pumped through his veins, Christ, sank into his bones. His spine torqued and his eyes rolled back as the feeling grew and grew...then finally, released him.

He collapsed back on the bed, covered in sweat, heart pounding, mind racing.

Zenon knew pain, it was his constant companion, what he'd just experienced couldn't be described as pain, though, it had almost felt, fuck, it had almost felt…*good.*

He shoved his long hair away from his face and stared up at the ceiling as it slipped away, leaving his limbs loose and warm, and a sense of…*knowing* filled him, like there was this thing, this big, important fucking thing, in the back of his mind, just out of reach. Something he needed to remember or know, but couldn't get to.

Another wave moved through him, softer this time, like an aftershock after a colossal earthquake.

A demi.

He could feel one, new to their powers.

What the fuck? He'd never reacted like that before.

With a growl, he shoved the covers back and climbed out of bed, and as he dressed, as he headed to the control room, that feeling inside him pushed forward again causing tingles to dance along his spine, making his head tingle and fucking goosebumps to lift all over his skin.

It was that feeling that had him walking straight up to Chaos and insisting that he send Zenon on the retrieval—something he never did. Ever.

Chaos finally, reluctantly, agreed, then Zenon forced himself to stay calm while he waited for Roc and Gunner so they could leave.

Standing back from everyone, he ignored the worried glances his brothers sent his way.

"You'll let Roc do the talking?" Chaos said again.

Zenon didn't even bother replying. Of course, he would, because when he got close, when he tried to talk to people, they got uncomfortable. Another reason he shouldn't go.

Chaos sighed and walked away. Yeah, he thought Zenon

would fuck this up, and he was probably right. But Zen couldn't make himself stay behind, not when that *thing* he'd woken with was pushing him on, when this sense of urgency was driving him forward.

Laz was about to head off on patrol, and Zenon tried not to watch as his brother leaned in and kissed his mate good-bye, but he couldn't make himself turn away. It was a soft kiss. They kissed a lot. Sometimes hard and urgent, sometimes soft like now. So did Kryos and Meredith.

The affection they had for each other flowed from them, so visceral it had those tingles moving up and down Zenon's spine up their efforts. Eve's arms wrapped around her mate, her dainty hands against Laz's broad back, her hold gentle, light brushes, soothing rubs.

That weird feeling gripped Zen's gut tighter.

What would that be like? To be touched that way? Gentle. Not to cause pain or to humiliate. Not to control.

A growl tried to crawl up his throat.

"Yo, Zen, you ready?" Rocco called.

Zenon jolted, humiliation heating his face at being caught acting like a fucking creeper. He quickly dipped his head lower and nodded.

Yeah, he was more than ready to go.

Whoever this demi was, they were affecting him in a way he didn't understand, a way he didn't fucking like or want.

And he was going to find out why.

KNIGHT'S SALVATION

Knights of Hell, Book 2

CHAPTER 1

"Looks like we're taking the stairs," Rocco said and scowled at the *out of order* sign taped to the elevator.

Zenon looked at the other knight and shrugged, trying to appear unaffected when he was anything but. He still didn't know why he'd come, why he'd forced the issue when Chaos had tried to discourage him.

Zenon never went on retrievals. Ever.

But this morning something had hit him—Christ, immobilized him—and then he'd felt…something. He was used to pain, but this, the feeling that had him crying out, tearing him from sleep, was different. Nothing like he'd felt before.

Fuck. This was a mistake. He should have stayed behind.

Rocco kept with the jaw flapping as they took the stairs, grinning, treating him like he was just another male, like he could be Lazarus or Gunner or Kryos.

Any one of his brothers.

Yeah, they were all knights of Hell, demon hunters, made up of the same basic DNA, but that's where it ended. Because other than that, Zenon was nothing like them. Never had been and never would be.

Even now, after all this time, he expected the males he lived and fought beside to suddenly cry uncle, to realize the mistake they'd made, and kick his worthless ass to the curb. Or worse, back to Hell.

It hadn't happened yet, and until it did, he'd fight beside them, with them, in a world that still felt foreign, a world touched by warmth and light instead of unrelenting darkness and pain.

He was a knight, not by choice but by birth—the fucked-up result of an unholy union between fallen angels and Kishi demons.

"Shit, this place is a dump." Rocco stopped in front of a scarred wooden door, a frown on his handsome face.

Zenon couldn't say one way or the other. His entire focus was centered on the weird vibes coming out of the apartment in front of him.

Something wasn't right; something more than the usual shit anyway. But with every step he'd taken toward that door, the tingly, prickly sensation at the base of his spine had intensified.

Rocco released an exaggerated breath. "Can you unclench your jaw or something? Jesus, you look like someone's giving you a wedgie."

Zenon would have told him to go get fucked, but for Rocco that was a given. And since speaking wasn't an option right then, he pinned the other knight with a stare that said everything he couldn't.

"Just a thought. But if you're okay with the whole nuts-in-vise look you've got going on, then so am I." Rocco gave him another head to toe, shook his head then knocked.

Zenon held his breath.

At the sound of several locks releasing, he reached back, wrapped his fingers around the hilt of the blade he had concealed under his jacket, and braced for what might be on the other side.

The door opened a crack, then wider, and the female demi-demon they'd come for poked her head out. A pair of big blue eyes lifted to meet theirs and her pretty pink mouth dropped open, followed by a kind of strangled sound in the back of her throat.

Zenon released his knife and took a startled step back. Like a champagne cork popping, the weird sensation he'd woken with shot up his spinal cord and nailed him in the back of the skull with the force of a fucking two-by-four.

Whatever this female's power was, it was seriously messing with him.

His fight or flight instincts fired to life, and zeroed in on the defenseless female in front of them. She was no threat to him—he knew this—but right then he wanted to turn around and get as far away from her as fast as he could.

It took all his strength not to turn around and leave a Zenon-sized hole in the wall in his rush to get the hell away.

Which was screwed up and made no sense whatsoever.

Rocco stepped forward and introduced himself. The guy plastered a smile on his pretty face and some of the tension left her shoulders. Rocco had a way with females. They liked him. A lot. This one was no different.

Her bright blue gaze darted to Zenon then back to Roc, and she opened the door wider. "I'm Mia. You, ah, got here fast."

"I would never leave a damsel in distress," Roc drawled, and the female blushed.

For some reason, seeing her respond to the other knight's easy charm had Zenon fighting the urge to introduce Rocco's forehead to the wall.

She invited them in, and ducking so they didn't brain themselves on the doorframe, they followed.

Her place was sparsely furnished, and what she did have was worn out and old. She didn't have any of that knick-knacky crap Kryos's and Lazarus's mates had scattered all over their apartments either.

She stood in front of them, waiting expectantly. Zenon retreated a few steps. Better Rocco did the talking. Communication of any kind, dealing with humans—or any species for that matter—was not where his skills lay. If he tried, he'd just mess it up.

"We have a room all ready for you at our compound, and the plane to take us home will be touching down in an hour or so," Rocco said.

He and Roc had flown the old-fashioned way. Wing power was still the quickest way to fly, but when they transported new demi-demons they used a plane. Not just because carrying someone while flying was an extremely intimate act, but because most new demi were freaking the fuck out, and holding onto someone fighting and screaming was just too dangerous. Something the knights used to do for a lot of years before humans got it together and came up with alternative options for transportation.

Demi-demons like Mia—half human, half demon hybrids —were a hot commodity among full-blooded demons, and were bought and sold as slaves for their unique abilities. A new demi's powers reached a peak exactly one month after they developed, when all that unstable energy could no longer be contained and escaped in a rush. An inbuilt sense, kind of like an alarm going off, alerted the knights when that happened. It was their job to get there first before they could be captured by rogue demons or, worse, taken to Hell where suffering took on a whole new meaning.

But this morning Mia had called them, asking to be picked up, which had surprised the hell out of all of them. And for some fucked up reason, he stepped forward. Unsurprisingly, he'd received more than a few worried glances from his brothers.

Zenon kept all contact with the demi-demons they rescued to a minimum. He fought, he hunted…and he killed. He wasn't good at putting people at ease, wasn't good at small talk. Not like Rocco.

Rocco's gaze softened, waiting for the meltdown that would come next. Not many handled leaving everything they knew behind and never looking back well. But Mia just nodded with a small lift of her lips. "I'm all packed and ready to go."

Zenon didn't usually pay much attention to the females he encountered, but this one was, well, she was different. He couldn't work out how, there was just…something. She was short—five-six, maybe five-seven, but then most people seemed short to him. Being well over six feet that was a given. Her body was rounded, soft, and her skin—her skin looked pale and smooth. His fingers twitched at his side. What would it feel like?

He frowned at the uncharacteristic thought.

She wore jeans and a pale green sweater that highlighted a narrow waist. And her long red hair—shit, it glowed. Yeah, she was—lovely. There was no other way to describe her.

He couldn't sense what type of demon had sired her, but whatever it was had resulted in delicate facial features and a pink heart-shaped mouth that Zenon thought might taste sweet, like cotton candy.

He tore his gaze from her.

What the hell? Cotton candy?

He studied the tiny apartment, looking anywhere but at the pixie-featured female smiling openly at Rocco. People didn't like it when he looked at them, especially females, so he fought the unfamiliar impulse to do just that.

"I've heard so much about all of you from Chaya," she said.

Rocco smiled back, charming as always. "Your sister did a good job teaching you to block that initial rush of power, Mia. None of us sensed you this morning."

Zenon shot a glance at the other knight. What was he talking about? He'd woken up, gut in knots, skin tingling, more than aware of the new demi-demon throwing out enough energy to light up every apartment in Roxburgh. Whatever she was, he'd never felt anything like it before.

"I thought I'd be okay on my own. Chaya was going to see me through the transition, but I, well...I think I'm going to need more help than she can give me." She lifted her hand, and Zenon sucked in a breath as delicate flames licked across the tips of her slender fingers. Her waist-length red hair lifted and flew around her face and shoulders like she was surrounded by a mini tornado.

"Jesus." Rocco looked back at him. "You seen anything like that before?"

He shook his head, making sure to keep his gaze on Roc and not Mia. She'd been darting glances at him since they'd arrived, but he knew it was more morbid curiosity than genuine interest.

"Your and Chaya's father, do you know what breed of demon he was?" Rocco asked.

The fact that this female had a sister was an oddity, one they'd never encountered before. Demi-demons were usually conceived through the most despicable act of violence, but from what Mia had told Chaos over the phone that morning, their mother had loved the male who'd sired them.

She dropped her hands, and the wind stopped. Her straight glossy hair drifted back into place, settling at her waist. "No, and our mother never told us."

"Do you know where we can find him?"

She shook her head. "Sorry. He disappeared when I was a baby."

Her phone started up, the ringtone "Sisters Are Doin' It For Themselves."

Roc snorted, a grin spreading across his face.

She raced to the tatty old couch in the corner and rummaged through her bag. Face flushed, she answered. "Chay?"

There was a pause as she listened. "Yes, they're here now." Another pause. "It's Rocco and…um." She glanced up at him, brow scrunched, and he realized he hadn't told her his name.

He remembered Chaya at the compound a year ago. Their features were similar, elfin, delicate. Their figures, too —voluptuous, rounded…soft. But where Chaya was dark, her sister had fair skin and vibrant red hair.

Rocco cleared his throat. "You gonna tell her your name or glower at her all morning, Zen?"

The phone at her ear creaked, like she'd tightened her fingers around the thing. Mia bit her lip and blinked up at him. Afraid.

"Zenon." It came out a growl, and she flinched. He quickly averted his gaze so she wouldn't have to look at him.

"Jesus Christ," Rocco muttered.

He tried to shrug it off. Her reaction to him shouldn't matter. It sure as hell wasn't anything new. He had that effect on most everyone. But for some reason, her fear pissed him off. He could smell it, bitter and dark. Fear usually fueled him, but he didn't like it coming from that female. He didn't know why he gave two fucks, but he did, and that just made him angrier.

He turned his back on her and stared out the window in an attempt to pull his shit together. And as he suspected, with his ugly mug facing the other direction, the bitter smell faded, replaced by her own wholly unique scent.

She repeated his name to her sister, and his stomach clenched at the sound of it coming from her lips.

The feeling was foreign, odd. He couldn't name it or place its source, but it moved up, squeezing behind his ribs in the center of his chest.

Maybe he'd burned his energy stores already? He thought he'd be okay for another couple of weeks. Yeah, the pain was there, but it was always there. He knew from experience it would only be a matter of time before it became too much, until he could barely walk, his skin burning like acid, like his flesh was being flayed from his bones. Then and only then would he go groveling for what he needed.

A crawling sensation traveled across his skin at the memory of the last time. Cold, grasping hands tearing at his skin...pain, humiliation.

Relief.

Hatred.

He sucked in a breath and forced the memory from his mind, allowing his senses to return to the female at his back. She'd been quiet for a long time. But he didn't need to hear the conversation to know Chaya was warning her sister about him. The demi they rescued and took back to their compound were trained to block and control their new powers so when they were released back into the world they would remain safe, undetectable to the demons that would hunt them.

Zenon wasn't on the training schedule. In fact, he barely interacted with the demi there unless he had to. It was coun-terproductive. They took one look at him, or heard his voice, and lost their shit.

A demi with untrained powers could wipe out an entire town if left to their own devices, and after several *incidents* he'd been encouraged by Chaos, their leader, to take a step back. He'd only relented and allowed Zenon to come today because they had another retrieval elsewhere and were short a man.

He didn't give a fuck what Chaya thought about him, but for some reason her warning Mia to stay away from him pushed him close to the edge, drew his demon to the surface, and sent another lance of anger tearing through his gut. He gritted his teeth.

Keep it the fuck together.

"Okay, Chay. I will...yes...I promise...love you, too." There was a rustling sound then silence.

"You ready to head out?" Rocco asked. "Gunner should be landing shortly."

He tried to fight it, but he couldn't stop himself from turning to look at her. She smiled, but it was forced. "Absolutely."

Rocco walked up and draped his arm around her shoulders, giving her a friendly squeeze. "You're gonna be all right, Mia. I promise."

The unreasonable anger he'd been fighting to keep under wraps ripped from his chest by way of an unexpected growl. It tore through the silence and both Roc and Mia spun to face him. Roc looked pissed and Mia more terrified than she'd been moments ago.

Rocco scowled. "What the fuck is your problem?"

He didn't know what to say, couldn't explain what had caused his reaction if he tried. But then, he never explained himself to any of the males he fought alongside. Instead, he grabbed her bags and headed for the door. "I'll meet you downstairs," he muttered.

The silence left in his wake was deafening.

Mia stared out the window. The sky was clear blue above the cloud bank. Beautiful. And though she was looking, it wasn't the view that had her focus. How could it when her mind was in such a whirl? Her belly fluttered madly with both excitement and stomach-twisting nerves. Her life would never be the same again. Finally, she could start living.

Plus, it was kind of hard to relax when she was trapped twenty thousand feet in the air with two huge males—well, three if you included the pilot, another knight, named Gunner.

She glanced away from the window to the seats across from her, and her nerves shot higher. Okay, Zenon was still looking at her, and he was still scowling. She couldn't see those yellow eyes with his chin dipped, hiding behind his hair, but she could *feel* that cold stare like ice sliding across her skin.

What was his problem?

Dammit, for some reason she couldn't stop her gaze from drifting back to him every few minutes, and every time she did, he caught her and scowled harder.

The big male was intimidating, and the fact that he hardly spoke put her on edge. But that unease got a hell of a lot worse when he did force himself to talk. One-word, snapped out answers that sounded like rusted steel grated against concrete.

And after Chaya warned her to keep away from him, that he was known to be unpredictable and unstable, well, it didn't help settle her nerves any.

Rocco was trying a little harder, and grinned her way every so often. But he also kept sending her puzzled looks, like he was trying to figure her out and failing miserably. She got the curiosity. Her situation was different than other demi-demons'. But she was starting to feel like the bearded lady at a circus.

So much for finding a place where she would finally be accepted.

Rocco twitched and shifted in his seat like he was having trouble sitting still. "So what are your plans after your training's complete?"

"I'll join Chaya. Brent said he'd give me a job in his club." Her sister's boss was a demi-demon as well and had given her sister a job when she left the compound.

Rocco raised a brow. "You know what kind of club it is, right?"

Inwardly she rolled her eyes. "I don't plan on donning a leather corset and whip. I've worked a bar before."

That handsome grin turned wicked. "I don't know, I kinda like the corset and whip idea." He held her stare for several seconds too long and she felt her face burn. With the blue-tipped mohawk and tattoos and facial piercings, he had the whole sexy bad-boy-rocker thing going on, and he knew it, too.

"Not really my style," she muttered.

He shrugged his big shoulders. "Shame." Then he opened a small bag of peanuts and started tossing them in his mouth.

Zenon, who hadn't said a word for the last half hour and didn't appear to be in the mood to change that anytime soon, turned sharply toward Rocco. His chest expanded and a low, rough sound rumbled from him.

Oh God. Was that another growl?

"What?" Rocco asked, looking completely unaffected by Mr. Unpredictable. Zenon stared back with those cold eyes. He wasn't even looking at her, but Mia couldn't help squirming in her seat.

"Someone's cranky." Rocco shook his head then tossed another peanut into his mouth.

"Get fucked," Zenon fired back.

Well, at least now she knew he could string two words

together if need be. The tension in the room shot through the roof. Mia needed a break from all the testosterone humming through the cabin before she broke out in a nervous rash.

The speaker crackled above her head and Gunner's deep voice spoke to them. "Down in twenty." There was another crackle then it was quiet.

Obviously another male who was economical with words. Mia rose and both Zenon and Rocco turned to her. Her face heated. Again. "I just need to use the, um"—she pointed to the rear of the plane—"the bathroom." Zenon quickly looked down, and Rocco just continued to grin. Jesus. Scooting out of her seat, she hustled to the tiny room and shut herself in.

She took a moment to calm her frayed nerves and splashed cold water on her face. She could do this. Her sister managed it, and so could she. She just had to get through her training then she could start her new life. A life she'd had on hold for far too long.

That's what she needed to focus on. Her plans had changed, but she could work with it. It turned out her powers weren't anything like Chaya's. They'd been wrong, which meant her sister couldn't train her like they'd hoped. So there'd been a small bump in the road. Did it really matter? The end result would be the same. It would just take a bit longer to get there. Big deal, right?

She was doing the right thing. This would all be a bad memory in a matter of weeks. Then she could be with her sister again. Chaya might be a hell-raiser, constantly dragging her into her drama, but Mia missed her terribly. They hadn't seen each other since she came into her powers and relocated to Chicago.

She splashed some water on her face, dried off, and pulled her hair back in a ponytail. She stared at herself in the mirror

SHERILEE GRAY

and hated how pale and frightened she looked. "Pull it together, Mia. You just have to get past this last hurdle."

When she walked back out, Zenon was alone, and after the dire warnings from her sister, Mia felt her fear spike.

Her step faltered. "Where's Rocco?"

Zenon didn't look at her but tilted his head toward the cockpit.

The silence stretched out until it became unbearable. She told herself to keep her mouth shut, but words started tumbling out to break the silence before she could stop herself. "So how long does it usually take for a demi to master their powers? I mean, I knew this whole demon power thing was coming and all, and would take some getting used to, but I'm guessing everyone's different? Time-wise, I mean. You know, it's weird, but when you guys were close, I actually felt you coming. Well, not Rocco. Totally freaky, right? Is that normal?"

Oh God, she was babbling, but the guy made her so nervous. His head shot up and his glare had morphed into a frown. When she raised her brows in question, he looked back down. His entire body had gone rigid and his hair hung forward to cover most of his face. "Depends," he finally said.

"What's the compound like?"

"Big."

Okay, they were back to one-word answers. Now would probably be a good time to shut up. Thankfully, Rocco chose that moment to come back in and didn't stop talking until they'd landed. But Mia couldn't help sneaking glances at the big male across from her. He sat so still, so quiet, and had barely lifted his head the entire flight.

Despite Chaya's warnings about him being unstable and dangerous, not to mention her own unease toward him, Mia had the weirdest urge to get close to him. To try and make him talk to her—look at her.

308

She shook off the feeling. She was being stupid. He'd made it more than clear that he had no interest in doing any of those things. In fact, he'd made it clear he didn't like her at all.

She needed to get over her desire to have everybody she encountered like her. This was about her training.

So she could join her sister and finally start living.

The drive to the compound was uneventful. Chaya had tried to describe it to her, but it hadn't prepared her for the sight she faced when the massive gates shuddered open. The large, ominous gray building was cold and uninviting. All the concrete surrounding it made the place seem desolate, like they were the only living things left on Earth.

They drove down a ramp into an underground garage. The temperature dropped, and she hugged herself. But it wasn't the cold lifting the hairs on her arms. *Maybe there's another way? I shouldn't have come here.*

But even as the thought crossed her mind, she knew there was no other option. Until she learned to shield her powers, this hell on earth was the safest place for her to be.

The car stopped and they climbed out. The big males stuck close to her as they walked toward then stepped into a rusted-out elevator. Her stomach lurched as it started its ascent.

The sheer power emanating from the giants surrounding her made her struggle for breath, but it was the ice sliding across her back that demanded her attention. Zenon.

He was always alert, even with his long black hair hanging over his face, hiding that strange scar on his right cheek, and she knew he missed nothing.

Everything about him was designed to intimidate: the tats that covered his arms, the heavy design that covered every inch of his throat, right up to his jawline. And when he trained those cold, freaky yellow eyes on her, she felt his gaze like a physical thing, like he could see right through her.

It worked, because one look from him and she wanted to run in the other direction.

But something kept her rooted to the spot, no matter how wild and untamed he seemed. It was weird, but it was that part of him, the terrifying part, that drew her, to the point where curiosity overpowered her fear. She'd been the same as a little kid, had hungered to touch something savage and uncontrollable, and that thing inside her—that thing she'd never understood about herself—made her want to reach out to Zenon now, to touch him, to…to what?

Inwardly she shook her head. *What the hell is wrong with me?*

When Zenon looked at her, it was with distaste—maybe even hate. Had she done something to make him angry? She couldn't think of anything, but he stared at her like she offended him by breathing. If she ever decided to follow through with the bizarre impulse, he'd more than likely bite her hand off.

The doors slid open and she shook off her crazy thoughts.

"Come on. I'll show you your room," Rocco said and strode ahead.

She started to follow, but stopped when she realized the others weren't coming. She turned and watched as the elevator doors began to slide shut.

Gunner gave her a chin lift. "Later, Mia."

She smiled and waved, waited for Zenon to look up, to acknowledge her in some small way, but he kept his head down. Then the doors were closed and he was gone.

Yep, the guy hated her guts. Whatever. His bad attitude was his problem. But even as she thought it, she had to fight the urge to go after him and ask why.

Rocco showed her to her room, told her where she could find him if she had any questions, and left her on her own to settle in.

The place was nice. Really nice. Better than any of the apartments she'd lived in with Chaya after their mother passed away. Heck, this was a five-star penthouse compared to the usual one-star hovels they'd lived in.

It took a total of ten minutes to unpack her meager possessions and slide her suitcase under the bed.

Now what?

Her first training session wasn't until tomorrow and she still had several hours to kill before bedtime. Her floor housed the demi-demons, and Rocco had said something about a common room on the top floor.

May as well meet the other freaks.

CHAPTER 2

THE COMMON ROOM was what you'd expect: big comfy couches and a huge plasma TV. The room was painted in cool, soothing blue—no doubt in an effort to keep the halfling demon spawn from flipping their wigs and destroying the place—and there was also a pool table over to the right, and a large table and chairs on the opposite side.

A whimper came from the other side of the room. Mia turned to find a young woman, maybe in her early twenties, sitting on one of the overstuffed couches on the far side of the room. Her knees were drawn up to her chest, arms wrapped protectively around herself. An attractive dark-haired woman sat close to her, speaking in soothing tones. Another guy stood against the wall, hands shoved in his pockets, a small frown turning down his full lips as he watched on.

Not wanting to intrude, Mia took a step back, preparing to make a hasty exit. The guy glanced up and his lips lifted on one side. "Hey."

"Ah, hi. Sorry to interrupt. I can come back…"

"No, it's fine. Don't leave." He beckoned her over and

when she reached them, held out his hand. "I'm James and this is Kate. Like you, she arrived here at the compound today." He motioned toward the other woman. "And this is Eve. She's a permanent fixture here, like me."

Eve looked up and smiled. She had a wicked scar on her cheek, causing her smile to be lopsided. It seemed wrong, so out of place on her soft features. "Nice to meet you. Mia, right?"

Mia returned her smile. "Yeah, that's me. Nice to meet you, too."

"I heard you'd arrived. I was coming to you next, but thought perhaps Kate needed me first."

"Sure, no problem. And nice to meet you, too, Kate."

Kate looked up, eyes watery and confused. "This is your first day?"

"Yep." She felt her cheeks heat.

"Why aren't you a mess?" The girl looked dumbfounded and a little annoyed.

"I've known what I am since I was eleven."

Her face crumpled. "Oh."

"It will get better, Kate." Eve's gaze slid to the door, and no joke, the woman's entire face lit up. Mia turned to see what had caused the transformation. A large male stood propped against the doorframe, his arms crossed over his massive chest. The faded black T-shirt he wore clung to his pecs and biceps, and his piercing green eyes were locked on Eve.

"How we doing?" he asked.

Eve squeezed Kate's hand. "She'll be fine. Isn't that right, Kate?"

Kate sniffed and nodded.

Those bright green eyes slid to her.

"Mia," she said, because the male demanded a response with just one look.

313

"This is my mate, Lazarus," Eve said.

Mate? She liked the sound of that.

He pushed away from the door and strode over. "I know your sister, Chaya."

"Please, don't hold it against me," she said, only half joking. She loved her sister more than anything, but she could be a handful at times...well, most of the time.

He smiled kindly. "Would have been helpful if she'd mentioned you."

Mia's face got hot again. "She's protective of me. She thought she had it covered."

He chuckled. "The female doesn't lack confidence, I'll give her that. Last I heard she was keeping Brent well and truly on his toes."

"She talks about him all the time. He sounds like a good boss."

He quirked a brow. "Does she now? All the time, you say?"

Eve snorted. "Okay, stop digging. And anyway, Brent needs someone to throw him off balance every now and then." She looked back at Mia. "Chay's a good friend of mine, actually. I got to know her when Lazarus and I were staying with Brent. I can't believe she kept you a secret." She pursed her lips.

Crap. Had she gotten Chaya in trouble? "Like I said, she's protective of me."

Eve didn't look appeased in the slightest. "Hmm, wait till I talk to her later." She threaded her fingers with her mate's. "Walk me and Kate to her room? We're going to get her settled in." She turned back to Mia. "I'm sorry to leave you on your own. We don't usually get two new arrivals at once. Will you be okay?"

James stepped closer. "I'll keep an eye on her. Make sure she doesn't get lost."

"Excellent. I'll be by in the morning to welcome you properly."

Mia couldn't take her eyes off the couple as they left. Lazarus wrapped the fingers of one of his big hands around the back of Eve's neck and leaned in to kiss her temple. The way he touched her was possessive. Sure. Their eyes met and something passed between them, something only they knew, and Mia felt an irrational tug of jealousy watching them together. She'd never had that. Nothing even close. Had never allowed herself to.

"So what's your power?" James asked.

Caught openly staring at the couple, Mia jumped and, dammit, she flushed for the third time in less than twenty minutes. That had to be some kind of new record for her. "It seems to center around heat and fire."

James's brows lifted. "Cool. Mine isn't half as exciting."

"At the moment it's a little volatile. I hope the trainers here can help me get a better handle on it."

He grinned and dimples creased his cheeks. His dark eyes were warm. Nice. "All demi-demon powers, no matter what the ability, manifest in a similar way. We just have to learn the best way to harness it in each individual. You'll have full control in no time."

"You make it sound so easy."

He grinned at her sarcasm. "It won't be a cakewalk, but it won't be reaching the summit of Everest either."

"Okay, got it. So what are we talking? Stairs to the top of the Eiffel Tower, drunk and in six-inch heels?"

He laughed. "Sounds about right."

She liked James. There was nothing terrifying or intimidating about him. It was the first time since she'd made the decision to come here that she'd felt at ease. "How long have you been here?"

"Close to two years now. I chose to stay after my training.

Now I help with the new demi when they're brought in. I'll be one of your trainers."

She relaxed, not even realizing until that moment how tense she'd been. James's confidence in her gaining full control morphed that restless kind of sadness she'd been carrying around into a thrill of excitement. "How long is no time? I'm kind of keen to get on with my life, or, you know… start one."

"It can't have been easy knowing what you were all this time, waiting for that ticking time bomb inside you to detonate."

That's exactly what it'd been like. "Yeah, you could say that. Sometimes ignorance really is bliss."

His warm gaze held hers and softened further. There was interest there. She didn't know why it surprised her, but it did. And not in a bad way.

He slid his hands into his pockets. "So it's nearly dinner-time. You wanna eat together?"

He was a good looking guy, tall, kind—and he knew exactly what she was. Perhaps she didn't need to wait to leave this place to start her new life after all. "Sure, lead the way."

His grin upped in wattage, and he settled his hand on her lower back in an intimate way that felt very nice and led her back out into the hall.

The large dining room was filled with people when they walked in. Knights, trainers, and demi like her. Most were already seated, and everyone seemed to stop what they were doing and look up as soon as they'd crossed the threshold, all eyes coming to her. The head freak. A pretty impressive title in this room of people.

Great.

She'd hoped coming here, among people like her, would make her feel less of a mutant. Apparently not. She focused on the only other familiar face in the room. Rocco lifted his chin by way of greeting, a big, goofy grin on his handsome face. She waved back.

James touched her arm. "Sorry, you're a bit of a novelty. As far as we know, there have never been full-blooded demi-demon siblings before, and the fact your parents were in a loving relationship is, well…unheard of."

Now she felt crappy for feeling sorry for herself. Most of the demi in this room would have had tougher child-hoods than she could even imagine. At least she'd known what was coming. She'd also had a sister and mother who loved her.

"Sure. I get it." Still, it sucked just a tiny bit.

"Don't worry. They'll get over their curiosity soon enough. Come on, grub's this way."

James led her to a large banquet-style table loaded with food. Her stomach growled. She hadn't eaten since that morning and was too nervous to touch a bite when lunchtime rolled around. She was a curvy girl, had never pretended she didn't love food, and took advantage of the wonderful spread. They filled their plates while James joked and teased, managing to put her at ease despite the gazes she felt burning into the back of her head.

He placed a buttered roll on his plate then handed her one. "So what did you do before you came here?"

She laughed. "Um, yesterday?"

He smiled. "Ah, yeah, I guess so."

"Well, I did temp work mostly. I knew I'd have to move on eventually, pull up roots and leave everything behind once I gained my power. So I never bothered with anything permanent. Besides my sister, I avoided getting involved too deeply with anyone, kept my possessions to a minimum… you know, that type of thing."

He shook his head. "That must've been hard, Mia. Never allowing yourself to get close to anyone or anything." He moved toward some vacant chairs near the end of a table and motioned for her to sit.

"I guess. Though I imagine my situation is easier than those of you ripped from your old lives without warning."

He shrugged. "I don't know. I mean, yeah, it sucks, but at least we've lived…you know, without fear of what was coming, experienced stuff. Sounds like you kept yourself closed off. That's gotta be lonely."

An ache started up in the center of her chest. He was right; of course he was. Yeah, it'd been lonely, especially when Chaya left, but what else could she have done? Instead she said, "It wasn't so bad."

Keeping her head down, she focused on cutting through the chicken on her plate because she didn't want him to see the truth in her eyes.

His hand covered hers, his palm warm, skin a little rough.

"I'm sorry, Mia, that was insensitive of me."

"No. It's fine, really. I'm tougher than I…"

Clunk.

A plate groaning with food crashed onto the table beside her. Zenon dragged out a chair, and his leather jacket creaked when he folded his big body into it. His spicy scent invaded her space and her belly flipped. But he didn't look at her. Those cold unblinking eyes were focused on James.

The warmth of James's hand disappeared and he cleared his throat while looking between her and Zenon. His eyes widened slightly then he dropped his gaze and started eating. It was several seconds before Zenon did the same, and she could tell James was trying not to squirm with all that intensity directed at him. Then as if nothing had happened, Zenon picked up his fork and started shoving food into his mouth. Mia stared at him, shocked by his sudden appearance and unwarranted aggressiveness toward James.

But he didn't glance her way. Not once.

She wanted to ask him what the hell his problem was, but maybe this was her chance to try and figure him out. Maybe rectify his low opinion of her. It kind of pissed her off, actually. He didn't know her, yet for some reason he'd decided to hate her on the spot.

She lightly touched his arm to get his attention. "So, Zenon, do you help with the training?"

He jolted like she'd shocked him then stilled, unnaturally so. The fork on its way to his mouth, suspended halfway to its destination, lowered. It seemed like forever before he turned. He looked down at her hand resting on his forearm then his strange eyes lifted and caught hers. She couldn't help it—she yanked her hand back in surprise. He blinked several times, his thick dark lashes such a stark contrast to the amazing color of his eyes.

"I'm sorry...I..." The savage mask fell back into place and he turned away, dipping his head and letting his hair fall forward to cover his face. Oh God, she'd made it worse. "Zenon..."

He shoved away from the table suddenly, so hard his chair crashed to the ground behind him. The whole room came to a screeching standstill, and again all eyes turned to her. Stunned, she tried to think of what to say. Should she try to apologize again? But she didn't know what she was apologizing for.

Before she could get her brain in gear, he stormed out.

"Jesus. What the hell crawled up his ass?" James muttered. "I mean, apart from the usual."

The guy sitting to his left shook his head. "Beats me."

Mia swallowed the lump in her throat. "It's my fault. I don't think he likes me very much."

"Don't let him get to you. He doesn't like anyone. I'm surprised he even sat down at the table. He never eats with the rest of us. Prefers his own company."

It was crazy, beyond crazy actually, but she had the sudden urge to go after him. To try and pet the beast. But she didn't; she stayed in her seat. He wouldn't welcome her company, and she got the feeling she'd just end up losing a limb.

Zenon ignored the startled glances as he pushed through the doors. What the fuck had he been thinking? That he could talk to her. That she wouldn't take one look at him and recoil in disgust.

That despite who and what he was, they could be...*friends*.

He curled his lip. He hadn't been thinking. All he'd known before he'd lost his mind and walked into the dining room was that Mia fascinated him. And for some fucked up reason, he'd gone with his instincts and sought her out.

He'd tried to put her out of his mind all afternoon and when that didn't work he'd convinced himself that one glimpse wouldn't hurt. He'd stood back, watched her like a damn stalker, but then James had put his hand on her, and he'd reacted like a...like a...he didn't know what that was back there.

She'd flinched. Taken one look into his eyes, seen the monster he truly was, and freaked. And in that moment he'd known how foolish he'd been.

He knew better.

The sound of boots pounding after him pulled him out of his own head. He ignored whoever it was and slammed into the control room.

"Zenon, hold up," Chaos barked.

Zenon stopped, but didn't look at the other knight. Didn't speak. He knew what was coming, and he deserved it.

"What happened back there?"

Chaos's wary tone pissed him off further. "I like to frighten helpless women and children."

"Cut the attitude. I told you to leave the demi to the rest of us. You're not good with that shit, you know that. I shouldn't have to tell you."

Yeah, he knew it. He made himself look at the other male. "Won't happen again. We done?"

Chaos ran a hand over the inked side of his skull. He looked bewildered, as confused as Zenon by his out-of-character behavior. "Yeah."

Kryos was in the control room as well and stuck his head up from behind a computer screen. "Perfect timing. There's a rogue having fun at Havoc downtown. Someone needs to get down there."

"I'll go." Zenon started toward the doors.

"Hang on, Zen."

"What? I'm the motherfucking bogeyman, Chaos. This is what I do." Yeah, he sounded bitter as hell but right then didn't give a crap.

Chaos released a breath then turned to Kryos. "Text Roc. He can tag along."

Zenon didn't wait. He headed for the double doors that led to a balcony off the fifth-floor control room. After yanking off his jacket, he tossed it on the ground, tugged off his shirt, shoved it in the waistband of his jeans to put back on once he landed, and with a partial shift—wings only—he took flight. He needed to get out of that place before he fucking suffocated.

It was still early but the city pulsed with life. The bars and clubs wouldn't be packed for another few hours, but the after-work crowd was giving it a decent shot. He landed behind Havoc, tucked in his wings, and when they vanished from sight, pulled his shirt on and made his way around to the front.

No one manned the door, and people were drifting in off the street like they were in some kind of daze.

The place was dark, with the only light coming from behind the bar and a few downlights edging the room, but it was easy to see the place was near to full. Music pumped from the speakers, a low throbbing bass that seemed to pulse through the room. The scent of sex, dark and exotic, hung heavy in the air.

He looked around. People were grinding on the dance floor, and from where he stood he could see at least five couples fucking in plain sight. It wasn't hard to work out the type of demon capable of transforming the place into an all-out orgy.

"Jesus Christ," Rocco muttered as he moved up beside him. "This shit's out of control. You see him?"

Zen tilted his head to the far side of the club. The sex demon sat on one of the couches that were scattered around the room, holding court, surrounded by panting, grinding, moaning humans. Zenon wished he could say he'd never seen anything like it before, but that would be an outright lie.

Roc reached down and adjusted his dick. "Let's get Casanova under control before I start dry humping a chair."

Zenon shook his head.

"What? You gotta feel it? Tell me you don't have a raging boner right now."

Shame knotted Zenon's gut. His dick hadn't so much as twitched.

As they made their way over to the demon, people bumped into him, touched his hair. It took all his control not to shove them away with brutal force. One female grabbed his ass and pressed up against him. He growled and bared his teeth, sending them all scattering.

He didn't like to be touched. Ever.

He heard Rocco's low moan when they stopped in front of the demon. This close even Zenon could feel the change in the air. It was alive with energy, and going by the Ron Jeremy sized bulge in the front of Roc's jeans, it was definitely having an effect on the guy. Zenon felt nothing but a light tingling across his scalp. That was it.

The demon was relaxed back against the cushions, a human on her knees between his thighs, sucking him hungrily. Another female pressed into his side, her skirt up around her hips, his fingers buried inside her.

Zenon remembered him. He'd come through the hell's gate last solstice, begging for sanctuary.

"I don't usually do dudes," Roc muttered beside him. "But right now I'm having a hard time deciding whether to kill him or fuck him."

The demon's eyes flew open at Rocco's words. "I'd prefer the latter if it's all the same to you. I'm a lover not a fighter." He smiled up at them, his fingers still pumping languidly between the female's legs. The head bobbing in his lap had increased in pace and was just plain distracting.

Roc shuffled forward a little, so his groin made contact with the edge of the table, and groaned. Jesus. This demon wasn't holding anything back. Zenon slammed a hand against Rocco's chest and forced him back a step.

"Right, sorry." Roc had the decency to look embarrassed and shoved his hands in his pockets. "I need out of here, Zen."

Out of patience and not in the mood for small talk—which was good, because the job he did for the knights didn't require him to speak at all—he stepped over the bodies on the floor, grabbed the perverted little fucker by the front of his shirt, then shaking off the humans attached to him, started for the door.

Rocco followed, and when they hit the street, he smacked the demon in the back of the head. "Put your dick away, asshole. Nobody wants to see that."

The demon turned his smug smile toward Roc. "That wasn't what you said two minutes ago." But he did as he was told and tucked himself back in his jeans. His smile vanished when Rocco shoved him against the alley wall.

The demon blinked repeatedly. "Wait. What's going on?"

"You break the rules, you pay the price."

"But…I've been given sanctuary."

"Yeah, dipshit, you were. But we still get to kill you if you breach the conditions set down by Chaos and Silas."

His panicked gaze darted over Rocco's shoulder to Zenon. Zen shook his head. If he was looking for sympathy, he was looking at the wrong knight.

"But…" He floundered and stuttered for several seconds. "But I just went in for a drink. What did I do wrong?"

Rocco shoved him harder into the unforgiving brick. "Are you serious? The entire club was one mass orgy. You used your sex hormone juju on those humans to get off. Not okay."

"I didn't think…"

"What part of *don't use your powers on humans* did you not understand?"

His eyes widened. "I'm sorry. I…" Then his forehead scrunched as Rocco's words registered. "Never?"

Rocco shook his head. "Not even while you jack off, asshole."

"Okay, all right. It won't happen again. I swear."

The guy looked stricken. Zenon almost believed him. Rocco stepped back and looked over his shoulder. "Let me call Chaos, see what he wants us to do with this guy."

Zenon would rather kill him and be done with it. He needed to kill *something*. And sex demons were nothing but filthy pieces of shit that preyed on the weak and vulnerable. He'd left his Li Kweis, the twin fighting axes he usually fought with, at the compound since they tended to attract attention, but he always carried a knife. He slipped the blade from the side of his boot in anticipation of Chaos's order.

Rocco murmured into his phone for a few seconds then slid it back in his pocket. He glanced up at Zen and shook his head. "He wants us to bring him in."

The demon sagged against the wall, and Zenon growled in frustration. "What for?"

The other male shrugged. "Guess we'll find out when we get there."

CHAPTER 3

ZENON CIRCLED THE COMPOUND. From above it looked abandoned, rundown, like it should. The windows were boarded so no light could escape. He couldn't see what went on inside the multistory building, but he could sense those within. Right then, one presence rose above the rest. It called to him like the sweetest song from the heavens. He'd heard it once while training under Silas, the angel who had trained and watched over them. Zenon was sure he'd never again hear anything as sweet. That was until now—until he heard Mia say his name.

The direction of his thoughts sent dread lancing through him. He had to stop thinking about that female. For her good as well as his own.

Tucking his wings in close to his back, he let himself drop from the sky. He plummeted toward the cracked concrete below, feeding off the adrenaline racing through his veins. The rush was the only way he knew to feel alive. To make sure this wasn't all a dream and that at any moment he'd wake, still in hell, chained in his cell like a dog waiting for his next beating.

At the last minute he spread his leathery wings, halting his descent to land softly on his feet. Not long after Silas came for him he'd done the same thing, only from the top of a cliff, but that time he hadn't pulled up at the last minute and discovered hitting the ground wouldn't end his waking nightmare—no, it just hurt like a motherfucker. And waiting weeks for his body to repair itself had nearly driven him insane.

That was how Silas found out about Helena…

He shoved the bitch out of his head.

The compound was quiet as he entered through the parking garage. Chaos had sent a car so they could transport their prisoner, but Zenon hated traveling in cars, hated any type of confined space, and had told Rocco he'd meet him back here. Zenon had taken his time.

The door off the garage was open and he descended the flight of stairs into the basement. His boots echoed off the concrete floor as he headed down the hall to where the interrogation room and cells were located. If this guy needed to be executed, he wanted to be the one to do it. Sex demons were disgusting vermin that needed to be wiped out as far as he was concerned.

What if Mia hadn't called them this morning? What if she'd been in that club? He knew his train of thought wasn't logical, but logic had a way of scattering when he thought about that female.

Rage, wild and barely controllable, reared up inside him. His demon wanted the driver's seat, but he maintained control easily. It wouldn't have been so easy six months ago. When Tobias, a knight and one of their brothers, devastated after the death of his mate, had purposely succumbed to his inner demon, he had nearly dragged them all back to Hell with him.

Being half angel, half demon meant one side was always

fighting for dominance. It was a delicate balance they all had to maintain. And because of the connection between them— a connection they'd shared since birth, a safeguard created by the angels to keep them in line and unable to abandon their mission or each other—when Tobias had succumbed, that balance had been disturbed, not just within Tobias but all the knights.

If it hadn't been for Lazarus and his mate, Eve, they'd all be Diemos's bitches. The head asshole of Hell wanted Earth and the humans who inhabited it. The knights were the only thing stopping him from getting what he wanted. He didn't like being denied.

Zenon had firsthand experience with that as well. Something else he didn't want to think about.

Slipping the key card from his back pocket, he disengaged the lock and pushed inside the interrogation room. When he entered, Chaos and Lazarus were in full-on good cop, bad cop mode. And going by the way Laz had the demon pinned against the wall by his throat, it wasn't hard to work out which role he'd taken.

Chaos stood back, hip resting against the only piece of furniture in the room, a small table, and offered the red-faced sex demon a smile full of mock sympathy. "You sure you've nothing to add to that, Amen?"

The windpipe-crushing hold Laz had on the demon didn't really help with the whole talking thing, but he managed to shake his head vigorously. Chaos turned to him, and Zen lifted his chin toward Laz. "Where's Roc?"

Chaos's jaw hardened. "Amen here thought it would be fun to mess with him. By the time he got here he could barely walk. Blue balls is an understatement. I sent him to the city to relieve the, ah…pressure."

Zenon grunted. No surprises there, then.

Laz released the demon but stood close, crowding the

guy, and Chaos took a step closer. "Lazarus here is kinda… well, crazy. No offense, Laz."

Lazarus grinned. "None taken."

"Cutting off limbs and other…anatomy is one of his favorite pastimes. I have somewhere else I have to be, and I'd hate to have to leave you all alone with him. But I'm not gonna have much choice if you don't start talking."

The guy had sanctuary. His behavior made no sense. And like Zenon, Chaos didn't buy the whole *I didn't understand the rules* bullshit either. The guy was either up to something or he was one of a growing number of creepy-ass fuckers that got a boner over getting close to a knight. Rocco had his own little fan club.

The demon, Amen, hid his fear well, but Zenon could hear his heart pounding from across the room, could smell the acrid scent of it. Amen turned to him then, his blue long-lashed eyes fixed on Zenon's. His gaze sharpened. "I know you." His stare moved over Zenon's body and back to his face. "Not from here, though. Zenon, right?" he rasped past his abused throat.

Bile churned in his stomach and burned a path to the back of his throat.

Please no.

The bastard grinned. "I thought I recognized you earlier. You servicing the knights now, drudge?"

The name was given to the lowest of the low, the scum of the hell realm, and it slithered down his spine and settled like a rock in the pit of his stomach. Only one person called him that, and she only got away with it because she had the power to end his life. Shame darkened his cheeks. He never wanted the males in this room to know what he was, and this asshole had just blown his shit all over the walls for everyone to see.

An all-consuming rage sliced through him. And before he

knew what he was doing, his blade was in his hand and flying across the room. Amen's high-pitched scream as the knife hit its mark gave Zenon little satisfaction. This demon had seen him at his lowest, knew all his dirty, shameful secrets.

His disgrace.

"Jesus, Zen."

Zenon ignored Lazarus.

Chaos moved forward. "What's he talking about?"

Amen whimpered, pinned to the wall by his wrist. Blood poured out of him, pooling on the concrete floor. It wouldn't kill him—removing his head was the only way to accomplish that—but the blood loss would weaken him for several days, and right now would hurt like hell.

"Zen, man. Do you know this guy?" Laz asked, concern in his voice.

He answered honestly and shook his head. He hadn't been permitted to look anyone in the eye. He'd kept his gaze lowered. Plus, during those times when he'd been *on loan* or sent to acquire information, his mistress had usually drugged him to make him more cooperative.

"Helena didn't let him out much, but when she did, he was definitely a favorite. Everyone wanted a piece of him. That angel blood made him a bit of a novelty," Amen gasped out.

He felt both Chaos and Lazarus's gazes burning into him, but he ignored them, couldn't meet their eyes even if he tried, and instead walked over to the demon pinned to the wall. He held his gaze, and Amen flinched, shrank back. For once, Zenon didn't curse the way he looked or the effect he had on others. He wanted this demon scared for his life.

Without a word, he gripped the blade buried in the wall and wrenched it up so the guy's hand was cleaved almost in two and left hanging useless at the wrist. Chaos cursed, while

Laz watched him, concern covering his face. Like he saw too damn much.

They weren't stupid. It wouldn't take a genius to work out what this slimy fucker was insinuating.

Still, when the screaming stopped, Zen leaned in close. "I think you've got me mixed up with someone else, Amen."

The demon flailed and gasped then nodded manically. "Yeah...yes...you're right. I...I've never seen you before."

Without another word, Zenon used the guy's shirt to clean his blade, and ignoring the stunned silence of the other knights in the room, walked out of the basement, through the garage, and back into the yard.

Without bothering to remove his clothes, he shifted, taking his full Kishi demon form, leaving the shredded remains on the ground.

And flew into the night sky.

There was a light knock on the door. Mia put down her book and walked over to open it. Eve stood on the other side, a small smile curving her lips.

"I hope I'm not disturbing you?"

"No. I was just reading."

Eve glanced at the book on the small table by the couch and her smile got bigger. "If you're ever short of something to read, just ask. I'm a bit of a romance junkie. I used to own a book store before I came here, and the romance section took up over half the place."

She couldn't help but smile back. "Thanks."

"I'm at a loose end, actually. Laz is busy, and I know I said I'd stop by in the morning, but I could do with the company. If I can tear you away from your reading."

Mia would be lying to herself if she said she didn't have a few questions. "Would you like to come in?"

"I thought you might feel like some fresh air. The windows have to be covered, and I know it can take a bit of getting used to."

No kidding. "That would be wonderful."

Eve led her out into the hall and to the elevator. When they got in she hit the button for the fifth floor. That floor was the control room. Mia had found it again when she'd been exploring earlier. Another huge male sat behind the desk when they walked in. He looked so out of place behind the desk, dressed all in black, weapons strapped to his chest —it was laughable.

"Hey, Kryos," Eve called.

He smiled. "What's up?"

"Just need some fresh air."

"Go for it." He went back to whatever he'd been doing.

Eve carried on through the room, past the wall of monitors, and toward a set of steel doors. She pushed them open and they walked out onto a largish balcony at the rear of the building.

"As long as someone knows you're out here, you can come as often as you like." Eve rested her forearms on the railing.

The view wasn't exactly inspiring, but it was good to go outside. They were far enough from the city that you could actually see stars. "Wow, the moon looks huge."

Eve was quiet for a few seconds then looked over at her. "So how are you settling in?"

Mia didn't miss the underlying curiosity in the other woman's voice. "You were there during dinner?"

A small smile curved her lips. "No, but I heard about it. Zenon doesn't usually eat with the rest of us." Her gaze turned assessing. "Something must have brought him out of hiding."

Mia shrugged. "All I know is the guy doesn't seem to like me very much."

"Hmm." Eve watched her for a few seconds more, like she was trying to figure something out. "You know how the knights came about, their history?"

Mia nodded. She knew how the knights were created. Her sister had told her after her stay there. The heavens discovered demons here on Earth, which was how demi-demons came to be. The angels couldn't track the demons on their own, so six angels fell for the good of mankind and bred with the monsters they were trying to stop. The resulting offspring were the knights. With demon DNA the knights were able to track and rescue the demi and control the demon hordes invading Earth.

She thought it sounded like some kind of horror movie.

"There's something you should know about Zenon. Unlike the rest of the knights, born to fallen females here on Earth, he was Hell born. His mother was a demon, his father an unknown fallen male."

"Hell born?"

"Zenon is kind of an anomaly—a fluke, I guess. No one knew of his existence until he came through the portal."

The portals that opened during the times of the solstice and equinox and allowed demons to pass from Hell to Earth. After her sister had told her that little tidbit, she'd barely slept for a month.

"So he just showed up?"

"From what Laz told me, Zenon was as surprised as they were. He doesn't talk about his life before he became a knight, and we don't ask. But it's not hard to figure out it was bad. You can't be as closed off and defensive as Zenon is and not have suffered a great deal."

Mia didn't like to think of the horrors he must have lived through. "Why are you telling me this?"

That small smile returned. "No reason. Just that some-times I think he acts a certain way to keep others at bay." She shrugged. "But what would I know?"

Mia got the feeling a hell of a lot more than she was letting on.

"Anyway, enough of that. Do you have any questions about how we do things here, what to expect?"

"Well, I was just wondering…you and Lazarus? You're mated?"

Her smile widened. "Yes."

It was probably rude to ask, but she'd been wondering since she'd first seen the pair together. "How does that work?"

She chuckled. "It's not really something you have any control over. It's sort of a predestined kind of deal. Lazarus knew who I was to him before he even met me. He fought it at first, thought he was doing the right thing for me." She rolled her eyes. "These males are stubborn, all of them, but when they decide you're theirs, well, there's nothing else like it, you know?"

Mia nodded, though she had no idea what having someone love her like that would feel like.

"Did you leave someone special?" Eve asked.

Mia felt her face heat. "Ah, no. I haven't had much luck with men."

"Yeah, I know where you're coming from. Before I met Laz the only boyfriend I'd had was a creep with a boob fetish."

Mia choked a laugh. "At least you've had one. Men have always given me a wide berth."

"It was the same for me. It's that demon DNA we carry

around. Most full humans sense it and without knowing why are scared away."

Great.

"What about after the training? I don't really want to be a virgin for the rest of my life." No, she wanted a life—a real one.

Eve's eyes softened. "You've never been with anyone?"

She shook her head. "I never wanted to risk falling for someone and then having to leave them, or coming into my power and accidentally hurting them. What if they were disgusted by what I am, afraid?" She shook her head "No, I couldn't do that to someone else, or to myself."

Eve's expression turned sympathetic. "Once you've mastered your powers, things will be different. Blocking what you are becomes so easy you don't have to think about it. You'll leave this place, and you'll start your new life, Mia. I promise it's all good from here on out."

God, she hoped so.

"Sweetheart." A deep, rough voice cut through the night and they both turned. Lazarus leaned against the doorframe.

"You're finished for the night?" Eve asked.

"Not even close." A wicked grin lifted his lips, and Mia heard Eve suck in a breath. *Oh my.* He glanced over at her and lifted his chin. "Hey, Mia."

"Um, hi."

His gaze slid back to Eve then traveled the length of his mate. "Ready for bed?"

"I'm keeping Mia company." Even as Eve said the words, she moved toward him. When she reached his side, Lazarus looked down at her, eyes softening before he ran the back of his fingers over the scar on her cheek.

Mia's face heated just watching them. Add in the husky tone to Lazarus's voice, and she felt like she was intruding on an incredibly intimate moment.

"No, I'm fine. You go ahead," she said.

Eve frowned. "You're sure?"

"Yeah, you've been great. Can I stay out here a little longer, though?"

"Of course. You're sure you'll be okay?"

"I'm fine. Really." Surprisingly, she was. Thanks to Eve and James, she had hope. Something she hadn't allowed herself to have much of since she found out what she was.

Lazarus only had eyes for his mate, and Mia felt a familiar longing as they walked away together. What would it feel like to have someone look at her like that?

When she turned back, she looked up into the night. The stars were bright, the sky clear. It was hard to believe she was in the city and not lying in a field somewhere in the country. It was like this place didn't just scare off humans but the smog and clouds as well.

Some of the stars twinkled rapidly, flickering in and out. She looked harder and realized something was up there. And whatever it was…had a massive wingspan.

It shot through the sky then changed direction, heading toward her. Fear had her rooted to the spot. It got closer and she could see moonlight glinting off what appeared to be leathery batlike wings.

Oh God.

It got even closer. Still, she couldn't move, and watched in horror as a gargoyle-like creature arched down toward her. Its skin was deep crimson, and in the dark looked almost black. Horns protruded from its head, black and shiny, and long ivory fangs reached halfway down its chin. Its massive wings pulled at the air on a slow downward sweep and it landed effortlessly in front of her.

Mia stumbled back, grabbing at the railing for support. It didn't move, just stood there staring at her. She met its gaze, and shivered when she recognized the bright yellow irises staring back. Zenon.

She didn't look away, couldn't. His tongue darted out and trailed down a long fang to the sharp point, and his head tilted to the side in a weird animistic way. Like *she* was the oddity.

Before she could change her mind, and with blood rushing through her ears, she took a step forward.

He didn't move.

She lifted her hand and took another step. "Zenon?"

It was his turn to stumble back. He hissed, and without a word, sprang up onto the railing and jumped over the side. Mia raced to the edge and watched in terror as he plunged toward the unforgiving concrete below. She cried out. But just yards before impact, he pulled up, and at the same time his body transformed before her eyes. Zenon landed gracefully. He stood gloriously naked in the middle of the compound grounds. He tilted his head back and met her gaze, a sneer on his face.

Oh my God.

Then he looked down at the ground and strode away, disappearing under the building.

If that display was meant to frighten her, he'd done a good job. But after what Eve had told her, she knew there was a lot more to that male.

If he'd wanted to hurt her, he could have, but that wasn't what that had been about. She pushed her fear aside and what remained was curiosity and a need to learn more about him.

But more surprising, or alarming, was a desperate need to touch his shiny horns and leathery wings, to learn the texture of his beautiful crimson skin.

To pet the beast.

CHAPTER 4

THE NEXT MORNING, Mia stood in the hall outside the training room and stared at the metal door in front of her. It looked solid, and the small window was embedded with wire mesh. She didn't want to think about the reasons for all that reinforced steel.

The nerves she'd woken up with increased their efforts, and she took several slow, deep breaths to calm herself. She didn't know what to expect at this first training session. But after what she'd seen last night, she was glad it was James in charge of her training and not one of the knights. They were good guys. She knew that. Her sister had made a point of telling her many times just how awesome they were. Still, they were overwhelming.

She'd tossed and turned all night, trying to get that cold yellow stare out of her mind. God, Zenon was terrifying. But for some reason, that fear didn't stop her from being incredibly drawn to him. It made no sense. Perhaps avoiding him for the rest of her stay would be for the best, for both of them. His dislike of her was blatant to the point of out-and-out hostility but didn't stop her curiosity where he was concerned.

"You going in?"

Mia spun around and looked up, all the way up. Chaos looked down at her, brow raised.

"Ah, yes...I was just..."

He reached around her and pushed the door open. "Everything will be fine." Then he motioned for her to go in ahead of him.

The room was small, windowless, and the walls—she reached out and pushed on the one closest to her—were padded. Alarm bells fired through her and her gaze shot to James who was already in the room. "Why the hell am I in a padded cell?"

The door clicked shut behind her and she spun around. Chaos stood, arms crossed, blocking the exit with his massive body. "Sometimes during training, things go...where we least expect. It's for your own protection."

"I don't mean to be rude, but what are you doing here? I thought James was in charge of my training?"

He grinned. She guessed in an effort to put her at ease, but it looked more feral than comforting. "Until we learn what our demi can do, I like to be in here as well. Things have on occasion gone wrong. I hear your power source is fire?"

"Yes."

He shrugged his big shoulders. "I'm here so you don't barbecue James."

Oh God.

"Oh." She felt her face heat to scalding proportions. "I'll try not to, ah...do that."

"I'd appreciate it," James drawled then clapped his hands. "Okay, enough talk. Let's get started. Mia, come to the center of the room."

Mia did as he asked, and he moved up behind her. Chaos started to circle around her, she guessed preparing for the worst. She swallowed hard. James's hands came down on her shoulders and he squeezed gently. It felt nice, reassuring. "Roc told me you could call up your power pretty easily."

"Yes." The heat from James's palms had seeped through the thin fabric of her T-shirt and she calmed further.

"Can you do that for me now?"

She nodded and let that tight, volatile energy build in her chest. It always felt so much bigger than the delicate-looking flames she called forth, which was another reason she'd decided to come to the compound.

She felt her power slither across her shoulders and travel down her arms. Warmth tingled through her veins to the tips of her fingers. Heated wind began to swirl around her, sending her hair flying, and she looked down at the small flames that licked from the tips of her fingers.

"Jesus, that wind's hot." But James didn't leave her. He stayed right where he was. "That's good, Mia. The pressure in your chest, is it gone?"

She turned to face him. "How did you…"

"I told you. No matter how different our powers are, all manifest in a similar way."

"Oh, okay."

"Well, has it gone?"

"No. It's hard to describe, but the pressure keeps building and I can't—" Mia gasped, unable to keep it up much longer. James exchanged a look with Chaos. The pressure tightened further behind her ribs, stealing her breath.

"It's okay, Mia. Just let it go."

"I can't… I…"

"Close your eyes," James said against her ear. "Envision that ball of energy in your chest. Imagine it being released, the relief. Let it fly, Mia."

She squeezed her eyes shut and tears of pain and frustration burned behind her lids, sliding down her cheeks. "No. No, I can't. It's too hard. It hurts too much."

James tightened his hold on her. "It's okay. Ease up now. Call it back."

She sagged back against him as the pressure dissipated, and gave him all her weight, too exhausted to be embarrassed about it. The only thing stopping her from falling to the floor was the arm he slid around her waist to hold her up. She felt drained, like all her energy had burned up with it. She'd never pushed herself that hard where her power was concerned—had been too afraid to. Now her chest throbbed from the effort.

When she opened her eyes, she sucked in a sharp breath. The bright yellow gaze that had haunted her through her mostly sleepless night blazed through the window in the door across the room. Zenon's gaze was fixed on the arm around her ribs, holding her upright, and when James leaned in closer and asked if she was all right, the long fangs she'd glimpsed the night before slowly extended to almost halfway down his chin.

She couldn't speak, couldn't form a coherent sentence right then if her life depended on it. His gaze moved up, caught hers. He flinched and reared back like she'd slapped him. Then he was gone.

"Mia? You okay?"

"I...I think so." She straightened and tried to pull herself together then turned to face the males in the room. "So what do you think?"

James gave her a half smile. "I think we have some work to do, but we'll get there."

"Does this happen very often?"

He exchanged another one of those *looks* with Chaos. "Sometimes."

SHERILEE GRAY

What was that supposed to mean? And why didn't any of this make her feel the slightest bit better? Chaya had promised these guys could help her. Now she just felt more confused and unsure than before.

"We'll try again in the morning," Chaos said as he walked to the door. "Don't worry, we'll figure it out." Then he left, shutting the door behind him.

Telling her not to worry made her worry even more. She looked back at James. "What does this all mean?"

"That your power is stronger than we first thought, and that you made the right decision coming here." He must have seen the concern on her face because his eyes softened and he placed his hands on her shoulders and squeezed lightly. "We will get your power to its full potential. We just have to work out what triggers it."

"Are you sure that's a good idea?"

"If we don't find out what you're capable of, we can't train you to control it either. And until we do that, you're pretty much a ticking time bomb."

"Great." Her sister had told her some of the horror stories. Untrained demi accidentally killing innocent people, and of course the story of how demi-demons were first discovered by the angels thousands of years ago, when a single demi-demon, new to his powers, wiped out his entire village.

A small smile tugged at James's lips, and Mia couldn't help notice again what a good-looking guy he was. "Better here than the grocery store or the mall, or some other place full of people, yeah?"

"Point taken."

His gaze lingered, dropped to her lips then moved back up. Was he going to kiss her? This was what she wanted, wasn't it? To start her life. A life that was never going to be normal but could be good if she'd only let go and try. James was a great guy, and he already knew what she was, knew all the crazy baggage that spending time with her would bring. It wasn't crazy to him.

A pair of intense yellow eyes flittered through her mind, and she pushed them back out. That line of thought was pointless and frightening.

"Can I...can I kiss you?" he finally said.

She nodded.

When James leaned in, she stayed where she was and ignored her instincts to pull back when his lips came down on hers. They were soft, warm. He deepened the kiss, and again she let him.

It was brief, and it was—all wrong. So wrong her entire body jarred at the intrusion. Everything in her rebelled against it. She couldn't help it; as soon as he lifted his head she stumbled back several steps.

He looked at her and frowned. "I'm sorry. I just thought that maybe..."

She shook her head. "No. I'm sorry. It's not you, it's—"

"Don't finish that sentence. I don't think my ego could take it." He winced. "Look, I like you, a lot. But if you need more time, I get that. I don't want to rush you."

She released the breath she'd been holding. It came out shaky. He smiled at her and she offered up a weak one in response. Given the way her body seized up at his touch, she didn't think it was time she needed, but she didn't have the heart to tell him. Something was wrong with her. Yes, she was a virgin, but she'd been kissed before, and by guys not nearly as hot as James. He was perfectly lovely, handsome, and she'd reacted like he was a hideous monster.

Another thing to ask Chaya when she called her later. Perhaps it had to do with gaining her power? Those kinds of questions should be directed at your trainers, but she didn't think it was a good idea to ask the guy in question why kissing him had made her want to gag.

So instead she said her goodbyes and headed back to her room.

And on the way, she ignored the urge to seek out the owner of a pair of terrifying yellow eyes.

Zenon had spent an entire day and night trying to scrub the image of James and Mia from his mind. Nothing was working.

Why did he care?

The music pounded through the large workout room, but it wasn't loud enough. He jumped off the treadmill and turned it up. He could still think, and he didn't want to think. He wanted to sweat, to work Mia—a female he had no business thinking about—from his mind.

After toweling the sweat from his bare chest, he yanked his hair back, tied it away from his face, and went to the free weights. He grabbed some dumbbells and started a set of lateral raises. Halfway through his second set the volume was turned way down. Already pissed, he spun around snarling, in no mood for company.

Mia stood wide-eyed by the stereo. "S-sorry. I didn't see you there."

His gut tightened at the sight of her. Her lush, curvy body was highlighted by her workout clothes. He could easily see how round her hips were, how her waist cinched in. Her glossy red hair was pulled back high on her head, enhancing her wide blue eyes and full pink lips.

Another image of James, his arms across her belly, hand resting on her hip, forced its way into his mind, and another snarl slipped past his lips.

Mia jumped. "I-I can come back later. I'm, ah—"

"I'm just about finished," he lied.

He could sense her fear, could see the mad flutter of her pulse at the base of her throat. So why wasn't she running in the other direction?

Instead, she hovered by the door, blocking his exit. *Shit.* It was pathetic, but he didn't want to get too close to her. He didn't like the feelings she stirred in him. The test on his control. It made him confused, and being confused made him angry. She made him long for something he couldn't name, didn't understand.

Trapped, he turned his back on her and carried on with his set, waiting for her to move so he could get the hell out of there.

He could see her reflection in the wall mirrors. She'd moved to one of the machines and started a set of lat pull-downs. She was doing it all wrong and if she carried on that way she'd injure herself. He scowled at her reflection. Why should he care if she hurt herself?

He tried to ignore her.

But it was damn near impossible, especially when her scent filled the room. He clenched his jaw, grinding his molars when she started pulling the bar down behind her head.

He couldn't stand by and say nothing.

Fuck.

He replaced his dumbbells on the stand and said without looking back, "You need to keep your forearms vertical."

"Oh." She bit her lip. "Like this?"

He shook his head. "Bar to the front, not behind your head."

"Could you...could you show me?"

No. I'm too much of a fucking pussy to come anywhere near you.

345

But he couldn't say that without her thinking he was crazier than she already did. Reluctantly, he moved closer. Still, he refused to touch her and kept a good distance between them. "Your grip should be wider than your shoulders. Lean back slightly so the middle of your chest is directly under the cable pulley. Keep your back straight then breathe in and pull the bar toward the middle of your chest."

He gritted his teeth. He didn't want to look at her chest, but he couldn't avoid it.

She tried again. "Like this?"

She wasn't getting it. "Hop up."

Mia climbed off the machine and stood to the side. Zenon straddled the seat and adjusted the kneepads to accommodate his far larger thighs. When he looked up, the tight feeling in his guts knotted into a rock-hard ball. Her expressive eyes were trained on his chest then traveled over his shoulders and arms.

What did she think when she looked at him? Was she disgusted by all the tattoos, the scars?

Why the fuck do I care?

Her gaze moved up, skimmed his throat that was completely inked, right up to his jaw then over to the brand on his right cheek, and lingered there. He realized his hair was still back and he had to resist the urge to pull the tie out and cover his face. Anger rose so suddenly he had to grit his teeth against it. He knew that a lot of people were offended by the way he looked, but he didn't appreciate being stared at like a fucking sideshow freak.

"You get a good enough look?"

Her gaze darted up to his. "I'm sorry. I didn't mean to stare. It's just…" He rose and took a step back, needing the distance between them. "You look so much younger than the others."

What the hell? That's why she was staring at him? He

didn't know what to say to that and dropped his gaze to the floor. He knew this close, looking into his eyes would frighten her, and though that had been his goal, right then it didn't sit well with him.

Pussy.

"And your body." He heard her swallow. "You're a work of art. All those tattoos. They're beautiful."

He kept his head down, couldn't bring himself to look up. And fuck, he felt his face heat. She thought something about him was beautiful?

"Yeah?" His voice sounded raw to his own ears.

"Yes," she whispered.

He'd seen her and Eve on the control room balcony the night before and had purposely gone to her after Eve left. He'd wanted to scare her, to let her see what he was. A monster. Because from the moment he'd laid eyes on her, he'd been drawn to her. So he'd landed on that balcony to wash away the ridiculous fantasies that had filled his mind, fantasies he hadn't allowed himself to have since he was young and full of hope that someday he'd be free. That someday someone might actually give a shit about him.

That day had never come, would never come.

He would never be like Kryos and Lazarus, or any of the others. He couldn't go after what he wanted, when he wanted. So he'd scared her to confirm what he already knew. She wasn't for him. Could never be. He'd foolishly thought that would make it easy to stop thinking about her, to stay away from her.

He was wrong.

Instead of running, she'd recognized him almost straight away, even in his Kishi demon form, and after her initial shock, instead of backing off she'd approached him. He'd been shocked, so shocked he'd fled like a fucking coward.

"The ones on your forearms, what are they?"

He looked at them, anywhere but her. "All knights are born with them. They say what we are. Where we come from."

He felt rather than saw her take a step closer and he fought not to retreat, barely managing to hold his ground.

"What about the tattoos on your neck? Were you born with those, too?"

He shook his head. "Got them when I was fourteen." The words slipped from him without thought. He'd never told anyone that before. What he hadn't told her was that up until then he'd worn a collar. When it was removed, he'd been permanently scarred from it cutting repeatedly into his skin, from years of being dragged around by a chain. He'd hated looking at the scars and had gotten another one of the slaves, known for his talent with the needle, to cover them.

"Fourteen? You were so young. That must've been painful."

He shrugged then braced for the questions he knew were coming next. The ink didn't completely cover the scars, and this close she would see the marks in his skin beneath the design.

But she didn't push, and instead asked, "And what about the design on your chest? The colors are beautiful. It must've taken hours."

He nodded, his throat too tight to speak. She took another step closer and this time he did take a step back. His back connected with the wall, stopping him from retreating farther. *Shit.*

"But I think the one covering your back is my favorite," she said, getting closer still.

With her standing so near, he couldn't remember his own name, let alone what was inked on his back. Zenon's demon stirred as his panic at her nearness took hold. He wasn't afraid of Mia. He was terrified. The way she made him feel just being in the same room, he'd never felt anything like it before.

But what terrified him most was what he might do if his control slipped.

Unlike the other knights who fought with the demon side of their DNA battling for control, that part of Zenon, that dark part of himself, had been a place of safety, a place to retreat to when things had gotten bad. It had always been that way.

When Tobias had succumbed to his demon, abandoning them, it screwed with all of them. During that time of unbalance, all their demons had gone crazy, even his. He didn't like being at odds with that part of himself. It felt wrong, unnatural.

And as Mia moved closer, his demon began to struggle, fighting to come to the surface, to stop whatever was making Zenon react this way—to protect him. It was hard, but he maintained control—until Mia moved even closer.

Her gaze dropped to his abs, to the slave markings covering the right side. "And this one?" She raised her hand and he sucked in a breath when her fingers brushed over his heated skin, gentle, cautious. "What does this mean?"

He went into sensation overload, and his momentary loss of concentration allowed his demon to rush forth. He knew the color had bled from his eyes and they were now a dull, black nothingness when hers widened in alarm. He was aware of everything but was unable to stop what happened next. With a snarl born of confusion, of fear, his demon shoved her away. Mia stumbled back then tripped over the machine behind her, glancing the side of her head before falling to the floor.

His demon retreated immediately and in a way he'd never felt before, until Zenon almost couldn't feel its presence anymore. Mia lay clutching her head, looking up at him in a way that took his self-loathing to a whole new level. She was afraid, angry. She swiped at her eyes, and he realized with utter horror that she was crying.

He didn't know what to do, what to say. Couldn't process the flurry of emotions flooding him. So he went with the one he was familiar with. Anger. "People can't...they don't touch me," he growled.

Her lovely features twisted in pain and she swiped at her eyes with the back of her hand again. "Don't worry. I won't do anything so stupid again."

Fuck.

When she brought her other hand down to look at it, blood coated her palm. She gagged and her eyes did an unfocused roll in her head. Without thought, he moved forward and crouched in front of her. "You might be concussed."

"It's not that. I don't handle the sight of blood very well."

"We need to get you to your room." He lifted a hand and hesitated. *Fucking pick her up, asshole. You did this to her.*

"I'm fine. I can walk back on my own. Without you having to suffer the unpleasantness of touching me." She tried to get to her feet and swayed to the side.

He quickly scooped her up before she fell again, sliding an arm under her legs, the other behind her back. "It's just...you surprised me. I wouldn't...I'd never hurt..." Jesus. He never explained himself, not to anyone. He could feel her eyes on him, but he didn't look at her, couldn't. "I don't hurt females."

He'd never carried one before either, but he'd seen Laz carry Eve after Tobias had hurt her, and he'd seen males do it on television. Without letting himself think on it too much, he lifted her higher before she could protest further. Her warmth immediately seared his bare skin, her soft curves pressing in tight against his chest and stomach.

He tried to numb himself to it. It didn't work. He kicked the door open and strode toward the elevators. The sooner he got her to her room, the sooner he could put her down. Mia remained stiff in his arms, and for some reason he couldn't explain, he didn't want that, despite his own fucked-up issues.

Did being this close to him disgust her?

You just pushed her over, dipshit.

"So what was that back there, your evil twin?" she said, not once glancing in his direction.

He inwardly winced. "You could say that."

The elevator doors opened and he stepped inside, punching the number for her floor. She turned to face him. This close he could feel the warmth of each exhale brushing his jaw and throat, and it took all his willpower not to shiver. In the confined space, the foreign feeling of Mia in his arms was too much.

All he could think about was how different she was, she felt, compared to Helena. Mia was all soft warm curves, not hard angles. Her scent wasn't strong and exotic. It was light and sweet.

He had to stop thinking like that. It was too goddamn dangerous.

"Your demon, right? Eve explained how that works."

"People don't, they don't touch me," he said again. Why couldn't he stop yapping? It would be better if she thought he was the kind of male who wouldn't think twice about hurting a female. Better she fear him than come anywhere near him.

"I'm sorry. I didn't mean to make you uncomfortable."

"You did nothing wrong." Someone needed to staple his goddamned lips together. The doors opened and he strode out, in a hurry to get to her room so he could put her down and get the hell away.

They reached her door and she reached back to pull her key card from her back pocket, causing one of her breasts to press into his chest. A shudder moved through him, tingles sliding over his head.

He leaned forward, holding her away from his body as best he could. She swiped the card and the door unlatched. He carried her inside and quickly placed her on the couch then took several steps back.

Now what? He wasn't sure what the right thing to do was, so he just stood there.

Mia winced, then reached up and removed the tie holding her hair. It fell around her shoulders, and he swallowed hard.

That's when his demon stirred again, slithering to the surface.

But not to attack.

No, the fucker purred.

CHAPTER 5

PEOPLE DON'T TOUCH ME.

That was the second time he'd said it.

Mia couldn't get the look on his face out of her head. Before his eyes had lost color, turned a hollow black, and he'd shoved her away. When her fingers had met hard, warm flesh, there'd been the briefest flash of utter vulnerability then she'd seen his fear, and his inner demon had taken over.

Someone had hurt him, and that pain had marked him in a way she couldn't hope to understand. Had he ever been touched with kindness? Going by his reaction, she guessed not.

Her head hurt—throbbed, actually—and she reached back and removed the tie holding her hair up, letting it fall around her shoulders. Zenon stood several steps away, his eyes trained on her. They flickered between yellow and black, and Mia pressed back into the couch cushions. "Zenon, what... what are you...your eyes..."

He dropped his gaze to the floor. "Don't worry. I won't hurt you again." His voice was deep, rough. "May I take a look?"

"Um, yeah. Sure."

He moved closer and her heart rate picked up, but not from fear. He came down on his knees in front of her, and when he lifted his hand, it hovered for several seconds before pushing her hair back over her shoulder.

He lightly brushed the spot where she'd connected with the exercise machine. His fingers were trembling. His touch was gentle, his skin rough and warm.

He cleared his throat. "It's only a small cut. You don't need stitches. Head wounds just bleed like a bitch."

"Right, thanks."

He continued to prod gently around the area and tingles traveled across her scalp. She watched him deep in concentration. His hair was down again, and he let it hang forward. His shield. It had a slight wave to it and this close she could see how soft it was. She had to fight not to reach out and touch, brush it back. Even with it hanging forward, he couldn't conceal his face completely.

And Zenon was beautiful.

She'd noticed how young he looked back in the gym, but even with his hair tied back he'd hidden behind the permascowl and bad attitude.

But now she took the time to study his face. He had full, firm lips and straight white teeth, high pronounced cheekbones, and wide expressive eyes that he hid by looking down at the ground all the time. It was his strong nose and jaw that stopped him from being pretty. The only thing marring the perfection was the large circular mark on his right cheek. It went from just below his cheekbone to the corner of his mouth. The pattern was an intricate swirl and looked as though it had been burned into his flesh, leaving behind pale scar tissue several shades lighter than his golden skin. She inwardly winced.

"How did you get that? Is it a burn?" She raised her hand,

her fingers hovering above his cheek. He flinched, and she dropped her hand back to her lap.

Stupid.

He'd shoved her for touching him less than thirty minutes ago, and she'd nearly done it again. What on earth was wrong with her? "Sorry," she said.

"All knights have them." He surprised her by answering.

"What?"

"The brand."

"Why?"

"It stops us from entering Hell. An angel named Silas gave it to me when I was brought in for training."

If she hadn't grown up knowing who and what she was, the mention of angels and the fact Hell was real would have been hard to take in. "How does it stop you?"

"We die," he said simply, no emotion in his voice whatsoever.

Jesus.

She was pushing it, but still she asked, "Why is it on your face? I mean, I've never seen any of the other knights with a mark like that, so I'm guessing theirs are in a less conspicuous place."

"I fought them. It was the only place they could get to."

Oh my God.

Her stomach twisted, but he didn't want her pity, so she kept her expression neutral. "You didn't want to join the others?"

"I'd never been to Earth before."

"You didn't know them?"

He shook his head.

"Why did you leave Hell? Why come to Earth?"

He rose from the floor suddenly and took several steps back. Dammit, she needed to learn when to shut up.

"I didn't have a choice," he said roughly.

His answer just gave her more questions, but she squashed them. "That must've been hard."

"Better here than Hell." He answered in a flat voice that told her question time was over.

"Right." What else could she say?

The scowl was back. "You finished the interrogation?"

She nodded.

He was still bare chested, wearing only a pair of dark gray nylon shorts and trainers. He was tall, lean, cut to perfection, and covered in all those beautiful tattoos. But the ink didn't cover the multitude of scars covering his body or the horrifying marks ringing his throat. Her stomach tightened. No one feared touch like Zenon did unless they'd suffered repeated physical abuse. And he had suffered; she had no doubt on that front.

Who would do something like that?

"Zenon, look, I'm sorry for prying. You're just...hard to get a gauge on, I guess."

Hands on his hips, head down, hair forward, he cursed several times then looked up at her. "Before when I...shit." He rubbed his eyes with the palms of his hands. "When I hurt you. I meant it when I said it won't happen again. My demon only comes to the surface when it senses a threat."

"And it thought I was a threat...to you?" Zenon towered over her, massive shoulders, built like a tank. How could she be any type of threat to him?

The muscle in his jaw tightened. "You touched me."

It cost him to say that, she could see it in the way he held himself. Always defensive, always prepared for the next blow. She tried to swallow down the lump that formed in her throat. The thought of being touched by someone, by her, had created enough panic that he'd felt the need to lash out, to retreat. "I won't do it again, Zenon. I promise."

His mouth twisted into something she thought might be pain before he hid it. Seeing that look on his face caused such a visceral reaction inside her she almost went to him. But then she watched that fierce mask come back down. She hated it.

"My demon doesn't see you as a threat anymore. If you... if you touched me, it wouldn't...I wouldn't harm you."

Was he saying he *wanted* her to touch him? "Okay." The vulnerability was there again, but he looked down, hiding from her. "Zenon—"

"I should go. I don't have time for this bullshit."

He didn't move.

Mia stood and he tensed as she moved toward him. She moved slowly, giving him plenty of opportunity to back away, to tell her to stop. "Thank you for bringing me back to my room." When she reached him, she made sure to keep her hands at her sides. Still, he didn't step back. He watched her through his lashes, every muscle in his body held rigid.

She didn't know why she was pushing this—perhaps it was the death wish she'd always had, or perhaps it was that flash of pain she'd seen when she said she wouldn't touch him again—but she wanted to show Zenon that touch could be good.

"I know I promised not to touch you, and I won't...not with my hands. And if you want me to stop, I will. Straight away."

Zenon stayed where he was and continued to watch her...waiting.

Mia moved a little closer. "In our family, this is how we thank people for doing something nice for us." She lifted up onto her tiptoes, but he was way too tall to kiss on the cheek, so she pressed a barely there kiss to his heavy biceps. He sucked in a sharp breath, but still didn't move.

"Okay?" she whispered, looking up at him.

He dipped his chin.

She smiled.

Then she heard it, a deep vibrating sound coming from his chest. Was that…was he purring? Her smile died when his eyes met hers. The heat aimed at her blazed so hot it sucked all the oxygen from the room. He lifted his hand, and for a moment she thought he was going to touch her. She held her breath, but then he dropped it back to his side.

"Don't. Don't do that again," he rasped. He looked confused and his voice sounded almost desperate.

"I'm so sorry, Zenon." Her stomach twisted in knots.

He didn't say any more. He stepped back, walked out of her room, and shut the door behind him.

Chaos stood on the roof of the knights' compound and took in the deserted lots surrounding it. He did this every night. His need to ensure the safety of those under this roof was uncompromising, ingrained in everything that he was, would ever be.

He'd stopped trying to be anything other than what he was a long time ago.

The sound of female laughter carried on the wind and Chaos walked to the edge of the building in time to see Kryos flying in to land on the fifth-floor balcony. Meredith was in her mate's arms, and as soon as the male's feet touched solid ground he took her mouth in a hard kiss. She wrapped her legs around his waist and Kryos's growl could be easily heard as he carried her inside.

Chaos knew one day Fate would intervene, would force him to take a mate, whether he liked it or not. He'd seen it happen to Lazarus. But that kind of passion was dangerous.

Chaos couldn't afford to be tied up in knots over a female. His brothers had chosen him to lead, and with that honor came the responsibility to make the right decisions for them and the demi-demons and humans they protected. Having a mate was a distraction he couldn't afford. A weakness.

Movement in the darkened shadows drew his eye. A dark figure dropped from the top of the perimeter fence and hit the ground hard. Chaos dragged his shirt over his head and unfurled his dove-gray feathered wings. Dropping from the edge of the building, he glided on the wind until he was above their visitor. The sound of the breeze moving across his feathers wasn't loud, but the demon should have heard him coming with its advanced hearing. It didn't look up. Chaos tucked in his wings and dropped from the sky, landing in a crouch in front of the guy.

His gaze was unfocused, dazed, and he tried to walk around Chaos like he wasn't even there.

"Hey." Chaos grabbed his arm and gave him a shake.

He came to then, his wide eyes losing their glazed look. He took in Chaos and looked confused as hell. His darted glances made it clear he didn't know where he was or how he'd got there. Either that or the guy deserved an Oscar.

"What the fuck am I—" He looked at Chaos again. "You're a knight?"

"Bingo."

The demon turned green.

Demons and humans alike did not come near this place. It was warded using a powerful witch's spell, making the area surrounding the compound a human repellant—the malevolence that radiated from the land made sure of that. And demons, if they could find the place, weren't usually stupid enough to risk it.

Something seriously fucked up was going on, had been

for months. "Did you decide tonight was a good night to die? Because I can't think of any other reason you'd come here."

He struggled against Chaos's hold and hissed. "I don't..." He looked around again. Chaos didn't think the guy was faking the confusion. "I don't know how I got here."

"I think we should go inside and have a chat, yeah?"

The demon shook his head frantically.

Chaos ignored him and escorted him to one of the interrogation rooms then sent a mass text to the others. They arrived minutes later. Zenon and Laz first. Ten minutes later Rocco and Gunner who'd been patrolling the city. They were all scowling. Kryos stormed in last, hair mussed, shirt on inside out, and not surprisingly looking pissed as hell. "This better be good."

Chaos tilted his head toward the closed door, the demon locked up safe inside. Zenon looked through the small window at the top and snarled. "What the fuck?"

"He scaled the fence and walked in." Low growls filled the hall, followed by cursing that echoed off the concrete walls.

Kryos crossed his arms. "Diemos is sending spies now?"

That started another round of cursing. "Maybe. All I know is the demon was spaced. Didn't even see me standing in front of him."

"You think they're after Eve?" Lazarus gritted out, his big body vibrating with rage. "Diemos won't stop till he gets his hands on a hellsgate demi."

As an unmated hellsgate demi-demon, Eve had held the ability to unleash the horrors of Hell itself. A hellsgate in the wrong hands could be used to open the portal between Hell and Earth at will.

Chaos stepped in front of the big male. "Diemos is many things, but uninformed isn't one of them. He'll know you and Eve are mated, that she's useless to him now. He has no reason to come for your female, not anymore. Still, for now at least, I think we should keep the females confined to the compound. They're not to leave unless they're with one of us."

Tension radiated from Lazarus. He'd nearly lost Eve not so long ago and it had affected the male in ways even his mate wasn't aware of.

"Agreed. We also need to be extra vigilant with any new demi coming into their powers. No delays getting to them and getting them in," Gunner added with a fierceness Chaos didn't understand. His lip curled, and the scar through the top one twisted his mouth, making him look downright evil. None of them wanted to see any of their demi hurt or taken —they were always top priority—but Gunner had become almost single-minded in this.

But Gunner hadn't been himself since the nightmare with Tobias either. He'd been so out of control, so close to being lost to his demon as well that he'd asked his brothers to lock him down here in one of the cells. He hadn't been the same since he came back out.

Laz ran a hand through his hair. "The demon has to be a scout."

Gunner nodded. "Checking if any of our demi are hellsgate?"

During the solstice and equinox—the only times the link between realms thinned enough for the gateways to open— Diemos sent as many demons through the portals as he could. He wanted an army waiting for him here on Earth, positive the day would come when Earth would be his as well. But the only way for him to gain unlimited access to the portals was to possess a hellsgate demi. They were rare, and they had no idea how many were out there waiting to gain their powers. But the knights would do whatever it took to stop Diemos from taking one back to Hell.

Zenon growled, rage and hatred oozing from every pore,

and before Chaos could do a damn thing to stop him, Zenon strode to the steel door and kicked it clean off its hinges.

"Fuck." Chaos went in after him.

Zenon had straddled the flailing demon, pinned him to the ground by his throat, and it looked as though he had every intention of squeezing the life out of him.

"You know, Zen, you could have just used the fucking door handle," Rocco said behind them.

Kryos approached Zenon from the side but didn't touch him. They all knew better than to do that. "Zen, man. Let him go. We need to question him. We can't do that if you crush his windpipe."

Instead of letting him go, Zenon went nose to nose with the guy. His demon had joined the party, and his voice when he spoke had taken on a malevolence Chaos had never heard before. And that was saying a fuck of a lot seeing how unstable he could be at the best of times. "I'm going to send you back to Hell, and not the easy way. When you get there, you tell Diemos he can't have her." Zenon lifted the demon off the floor, using his throat as a handle, and slammed him into the unforgiving concrete. "Do you hear me?"

Rocco shook his head. "I doubt it. It's kind of hard to hear when blood's leaking from your ears."

"Back the fuck up, Zenon," Chaos growled.

Thud!

"Stand down," he roared.

Thud!

The demon's head would be mush if he didn't do something. Chaos moved in and Rocco and Gunner moved with him. Zenon didn't like anyone in his space, unless they were sparring and he was doing his damnedest to take them down. This could go tits up if he went full-on demon massacre on them. "Now."

All three jumped him, tearing Zenon off the now

unconscious demon. Chaos shoved his arm into the other male's throat and pushed. *Fuck.* Nothing happened. He didn't even take a step back; the guy was rock solid. "Zenon, pull your shit together now." Chaos got in Zenon's face, knew he was pushing it with this particular knight, but didn't give a fuck. They needed information and if the demon died they were screwed. But Zenon was focused on the demon's unconscious body, fangs extended like he wanted nothing more than to rip the little fucker's throat out. "I can't deal with your shit. Get the fuck out of my interrogation room."

Zenon's eyes shifted to him and Chaos shoved again. "Get the fuck gone."

With one last look at the demon, Zenon stormed from the room.

∼

Zenon got out of there. Kept going and didn't look back. He was losing his goddamned mind.

If he thought about that demon getting anywhere near Mia, he'd turn around and rip the bastard's throat out. Adrenaline throbbed through his veins, making him twitch. He needed some kind of release but his options were limited. He couldn't fuck. His only option was to fight.

The gym wouldn't cut it. And he didn't want to risk running into Mia again. If he saw her now, he'd do or say shit he could never take back, and that female needed to stay as far from him as she could manage.

So he headed for his room to weapon up. The doors slid open and he strode down the hall, but as he rounded the corner to his apartment he was forced to slam on the brakes.

Sitting on the floor, her back pressed against his door, was Mia, the last person he needed to see right then. Mia glanced up, spotting him before he could turn and walk the other way.

Zenon's heart picked up speed, pounded behind his ribs, and his demon stirred in a restless, unfamiliar way. She'd showered and changed, her long red hair loose and damp, curling at the ends. She wore jeans and a fitted pink T-shirt with some cartoon cat on the front. Her beautiful face lit up when she saw him.

His lower belly tightened and sent tingles shooting to his balls. "What are you doing here?"

She flinched at his harsh tone. "I was lonely. I thought you might keep me company?"

Did she have any idea how much he wanted that? How much he wanted to just spend time with her, listen to her talk, learn everything about her. Take her to his bed, savor her body, touch her skin, her hair—fuck her hard, then take her slow and easy. He'd hold her in his arms and watch her sleep. Feed her. Take care of her.

Jesus fucking Christ. Where had that come from? *What the fuck was wrong with him?*

He dipped his chin, couldn't look at her. "Why the fuck would you think that?"

Silence. "I just thought after this afternoon that…" Her voice shook, and though it killed him, and every instinct he had told him to worship her—protect her—he ignored it. That wasn't an option. And in the end, would only put her in danger.

He was a piece of trash, tainted, filthy, didn't deserve to breathe the same air as her. Why couldn't she see that as well?

What he was about to do was for her own good.

In two strides, he was in front of her. He wrapped a hand loosely around the base of her throat, her soft, warm pulse thudding against his palm, and backed her against the wall.

His heightened awareness of her just pissed him off more, bewildered him. He let his frustration show. He sneered and gave her a slow hateful once-over. "This afternoon you were lucky I didn't do far worse."

Her eyes were wide, but she shook her head. "You wouldn't...you wouldn't hurt me."

Was she serious? He had her pinned to his door. He could crush her delicate throat in less than a second. Mia thought there was good in him, but there was nothing but rage and hate. "One conversation and you think you have me figured out? You know nothing about me. I'm from Hell, Mia. I've done things that would give you nightmares."

"I don't care," she whispered.

His chest squeezed painfully, and the foreign emotion welling up inside him sent a surge of fury through him. He couldn't deal with it, couldn't process it. His heart hammered so hard he was surprised she didn't hear it. Didn't she know how much danger she was in? "Do you have any idea what someone like me needs, demi?"

She shook her head. The pulse in her neck was fluttering wildly. Good. He needed her to fear him. He let his gaze drift over her curves again then up to her wide-eyed gaze. "Exactly. Now leave."

Her entire body stiffened and her face twisted. "Why are you acting like this?"

"Like what?"

"Cruel." She gripped his wrist and tried to pull his hand from around her throat.

He didn't budge, not yet. He had to make sure she left him alone.

This pull, whatever it was he felt toward her, was too strong. He couldn't resist it, couldn't stay away from her, not on his own. He needed her to be the one to do it. She needed to understand that nothing could ever be between them, not friendship…not anything else.

She needed to hate him.

"You don't know what cruel is," he rasped.

She straightened her shoulders. "I know you're trying to protect yourself…but you…you don't have to with me." She drew in a deep breath. "And I thought that perhaps…that we could spend some time together, that we could be—"

He got in her face, cut her off, didn't want to hear what she was about to say. Couldn't. Her scent surrounded him and he realized like a shot to the gut that Mia wanted him, despite the things he'd said, the way he'd treated her. And if he didn't get rid of her soon, he'd lose his fucking mind.

Why did she have to come here? Why was she doing this? Why would she want…him?

Pain began to radiate from the back of his skull, shooting down his spine. He needed to get into his room. In a matter of minutes he'd be paralyzed in agony.

He moved in closer, and goddamn, did it cost him. He didn't like being close to others, but with Mia he realized it was different. So different. Nothing made sense.

Her soft curves pressed into him, but despite the way his pulse raced and his stomach clenched, it wasn't hard to feign indifference. "There is nothing you have that I want," he said and ground his lifeless cock against her. She sucked in a breath, humiliation slashing across her cheeks.

She blinked and tears tracked down her cheeks. "You don't need to say any more. You've made your point."

When she shoved against him this time, he let her go. And without looking at him again, she pushed past and ran down the hall.

Zenon didn't have time to regret his words, and shoved his key card in the door. He stumbled into his apartment and managed to slam it shut after him before his legs gave out and he hit the floor.

No one could ever know his weakness, what he was. Not his brothers and especially not Mia.

But dammit, as he lay there, paralyzed, lost to the agony, the only thing that stopped him from being sucked under completely was Mia.

CHAPTER 6

Zenon rolled to his back and scrubbed his palms over his face. He'd slept like shit.

He'd gone to sleep again thinking of Mia, and he'd dreamed of her through the night. The feel of her hand on his abs, the way her body felt in his arms as he'd carried her to her room—the press of her soft, warm lips against his bicep.

But he'd woken like every other morning, dick soft and useless against his thigh. He couldn't fuck the woman he wanted, couldn't even jack off. Even if he wanted to risk it all, take Mia for himself—which he could admit to himself he did, so damn much it hurt—he couldn't have her. Not ever, and not just because he was a disgusting, tainted waste of space. He couldn't give her what a man should, what he should be able to give his woman.

Mia had been busy with her training the last two weeks, and Zenon had managed to avoid her, besides the odd glance when he couldn't take it another minute without seeing her. His demon was as frustrated as he was. His constant yearning for that female was pushing him over the edge. Made no damn sense.

The others had noticed the difference in him. And not just because he'd tried to make bolognese out of that demon's head in the interrogation room. But shit, just the thought of that sadistic bastard Diemos getting anywhere near Mia, of even knowing of her existence had released something deep inside him. Zenon would have killed him, would have torn his head off with his bare hands if the others hadn't pulled him off.

Then Mia had been waiting for him at his door. She'd wanted him. He'd smelled her desire for him. For *him.*

He'd never wanted to be like Kryos or Lazarus, not until he'd discovered Mia's existence. She had looked at him for a response, a sign he might feel the same for her, and even the scent of her sweet arousal hadn't caused even a twitch from the useless organ hanging between his legs.

His hand rested on his stomach and he let his fingers trail to his flaccid cock, gripped it in his fist, and squeezed. Nothing.

What was he doing?

None of it mattered. He couldn't have her. He'd pushed her away, to protect her, to protect himself.

And he'd hurt her.

Was still hurting her. It was there in the way she held her body, in the humiliation that colored her cheeks when she saw him.

And he'd never hated himself more.

Shoving back the sheet, he got out of bed. As soon as his feet hit carpet, pain shot from the base of his skull and burned a path through his chest and stomach, blazing acid-like needles down his arms to the tips of his fingers, down his thighs and calves. His knees gave out and he crumpled to the ground, hissing in agony.

Not again. Not now. Please not fucking now. He wasn't ready for this. Not yet. He'd been weakening steadily over the last week but thought he had more time. Zenon curled into a ball and tried to stop from crying out as the sensation of flesh being torn from bone washed over him repeatedly.

He didn't know how long he lay there before the pain began to subside. He'd have to go tonight. Bile churned in his gut, burned a path to the back of his throat.

Still on the ground, he reached up for the phone on the bedside table and sent a text to Silas.

Need to make a house call.

As always, the angel would make sure he had an excuse to be away from the compound for a day or two. He replied almost immediately.

I'll make the arrangements.

He tried to stand but his legs felt like Jell-O, and he was forced to drag himself to the bathroom. Using the wall for support, he pulled himself up and turned on the shower as hot as it would go then climbed in. The heat burned his skin, seeped into his flesh, warming him to the bone, softening his seized muscles. He hated being so damn weak.

Stiff and sore, but mobile, Zenon dressed as quickly as he could and headed to the control room. It was either that or go to the holding cells and finish off every last demon they had down there.

They weren't going to talk. A death delivered by any one of the knights would be a hell of a lot better than the slow, sadistic torture Diemos would subject them to for days before finally putting them out of their misery if they talked. He'd experienced Diemos's special brand of attention himself a time or two, and only knew of one person who deserved that kind of punishment...

He slammed the door on those thoughts.

Zenon wanted the demons dead, wanted the threat to

Mia out of this compound, especially since he'd be gone for a couple of days. But he knew Chaos wouldn't allow it, and right then he didn't have the strength to go head to head with the other knight.

When he walked into the control room, Gunner and Rocco were already there. They lifted their chins in welcome. Chaos turned and did the same.

Zenon gritted his teeth. "Give me something to do. I need to kill something."

Chaos raised a brow at his barked order. "You're gonna have to take your aggression out in the gym. Only job for today is delivering Mia to her new place. Gun and Roc get that one."

Chaos's words hammered around his skull. Everything in him rebelled at the idea of her leaving. "Mia's going?"

Rocco grinned. "It's a nice place. One of ours, and close enough we can keep an eye on her."

"And why would you want to do that?" He heard the menace in his voice but had no control over it.

Rocco frowned. "Do we have a problem here, Zenon?"

"I don't know. Do we?"

Chaos moved in between them. "Is there something going on between you and Mia?" And, yeah, the guy looked confused as fuck about that notion, like the idea was so foreign as to be ridiculous.

He clenched his fists and shook his head.

The knight frowned. "Fuck's sake, Zenon. Do you have to start shit all the time? What's crawled up your ass?"

Zen shrugged.

"We're just trying to look out for her. She hasn't reached her full potential yet. She's capable of a lot more. James hasn't been able to work out what her trigger is. I think her leaving is a stupid idea, but he's assured me she's safe. She can block what she's got going on at the moment and she's agreed to come in for regular training sessions. I could force her to stay, which is what I want to do, but James thinks that will only make it worse. She's unhappy here, she wants to leave, so we'll let her, but we'll keep an eye on her."

She wanted to leave. She was unhappy. That knowledge was like a smack to the back of the head. Confirmed what shouldn't be a big surprise. This whacked-out need he had, pulling him toward Mia like a supercharged magnet attached to his chest, was one-sided. He didn't know why it hurt like a motherfucker, but it did. Fuck it, he was used to pain. At least this way he wouldn't have to see her every day.

"Fuck knows how we didn't sense her right off the bat, because despite her sister's help, she had a lot of work to do with her blocking," Chaos added.

No, the training her sister had given her hadn't been enough. He didn't know what the fuck Chaos was talking about. He'd sensed her loud and clear. "I did," Zen said.

Chaos stilled. "You what?"

"Sensed her."

The males in the room went silent, the creak of leather and the shuffle of boots the only sounds as they all turned to face him.

"You sensed her?" Chaos said, breaking the unsettling silence.

"Yeah." Jesus. Now what had he done wrong? Was this another demon thing? Another difference because he was hell born? He dipped his head, sick of seeing the weirded-out expressions on their faces. He hated whenever this kind of shit came up. Like he needed another reminder that he was different.

"Do you know what that means?" Kryos asked, almost gently.

He didn't want to listen to this, have his differences laid out in front of him, have them point out again what a fucking freak of nature he was. "I have somewhere I need to be." He turned to go, but Kryos grabbed his arm. Zenon hissed and spun to face him. "I said I'm done."

He got as far as the door when Kryos stopped him in his tracks with a few simple words. Words that, when strung together, had the potential to tip his warped little world on its ass. The guy sounded as freaked saying them as Zenon did hearing them.

"I think Mia's your mate, Zenon. I think you've found your female."

Just like that his legs were back to Jell-O, and he grabbed onto the nearest desk to stop his ass from hitting the floor. "No. That can't be." He didn't recognize his own voice, pitched high, shaky.

He felt someone move closer, but they didn't touch him. Chaos. "Zen, none of us felt her. You did."

"So?" Could he get out of here before he passed out like a pussy?

"You must know. Kryos, Laz, when they—"

"In case you missed it, I don't sit around shooting the shit, discussing your goddamn love lives." No, Zenon rarely mixed with the others unless he had to, and he sure as hell didn't know the ins and outs of knight/demi-demon courtship. He'd never stuck around long enough to learn. Never thought he'd need to know.

This couldn't be. Mia, his mate? The very idea had his heart beating like a jackhammer, and another wave of—fuck, he didn't know what it was, couldn't name it, but it kept nailing him in the chest until he was close to hyperventilating.

"Zen? You all right, man?"

"What do you think?" he growled.

Kryos moved around him but didn't get in his space. "I've seen the way you look at her. I think this could be a good thing."

The guy was so caught up with his own mate he couldn't see how far from a good thing this was. "You would give a defenseless female to me? What if I hurt her? I can't...this can't happen." Shit, his voice broke on the last. He needed to get the hell out of there.

Chaos and Gunner looked away. Rocco, unable to hide anything, winced, but worst of all was the fucking pity Kryos was throwing his way. Fuck that. They already thought he was unstable and bloodthirsty. None of them would try to convince him to claim her.

"What are you gonna do?" Rocco asked.

He lifted his gaze and met each of theirs. "Not a dammed thing."

"I don't know. Maybe we have it all wrong?" Kryos said into the silence. "Finding your female has another effect on you that can't be hidden, no matter how hard you try. Being constantly hard, accompanied by a severe case of blue balls, goes with the territory." He cleared his throat. "You having that problem?"

Shame and humiliation caused him to dip his head once more, afraid they'd see it written all over his face. He'd never been drawn to another being the way he was Mia, but he couldn't explain to them the reason he felt nothing but a twisted need he couldn't define or control, or the reasons he could never claim her as his mate. He was half a male, and being anywhere near him would be like signing her death warrant.

"You're wrong. I don't want to fuck her." The words felt torn from his throat. He knew it sounded crude, and he also knew if he was another male, and was privileged enough to be with her, that wouldn't describe what they'd do together. No, if he had that honor, he would worship her like she deserved.

Low sounds of disapproval rumbled from all four males. The words hit their mark, ensuring they didn't get any screwed-up ideas and try to push him down a path he could never take. Chaos cleared his throat. "You're probably right, then."

"Sensing her like I did must be a hell-born thing," he said, knowing no one would question him further. His birth and early years were subjects they all knew to avoid.

Zenon didn't stick around.

He had a mate; he knew that now, despite his denials. And if he'd been one of the others, he would have gone to her now and made her his. No hesitation like Lazarus. No fucking around.

When he hit the elevator, he couldn't stop his hands from hitting the button to the floor he knew he should avoid. He should leave the compound until she was gone, but he couldn't do it. Not now he knew who she was to him. He could never claim her for himself, he knew that. She would never be his, and would never know what she was to him. But before she left, he wanted one thing. Shit, he didn't deserve it. But he would take this one thing for himself. Just this once.

Looking through the glass window into the training room a short time later, he found her, like he knew he would. She was alone, head down, concentrating on her blocking. He didn't hesitate. A sense of urgency he couldn't explain and had no intention of fighting had him pushing open the door. Her gaze lifted to his, and she didn't look surprised, like she'd sensed him, too, and didn't that just send his possessive instincts through the damn roof.

~

Mia had felt Zenon as soon as he stopped outside the door. He stared at her now, so much behind that haunted gaze, so many secrets, so much pain. But then he sucked in a breath and all she saw was longing. He didn't speak, and took a measured step toward her.

"What are you doing?" she said, pulse picking up speed.

Another step closer.

"Zenon?"

She watched for a sign that his demon was in control, but his bright yellow gaze told her that wasn't the case. The wild, almost feral expression was all Zenon.

"You're leaving," he said.

Oh God, his voice. So deep, rough. There was no anger, but a note of something else, something that caused her breath to hitch and her mouth to go dry. "Yes."

His heavy thighs were braced apart, fists clenched at his sides. "Why?"

That one word hit her mid chest. "Zenon—"

"You're leaving. Why?"

Because of you, because I can't be in the same building as you and keep my distance another day. "I want to get on with my life." Not a lie.

His head dipped and his hair fell forward, covering his scarred but beautiful face. He heaved in another breath then looked up. *Jesus.* Her sex pulsed at the raw need directed at her. Then he moved toward her, all lethal grace and untamed power. She backed up, but he kept coming. Didn't stop until she felt the padded wall behind her. He didn't touch her, but he was close enough to feel the volcanic heat radiating from his big body. She remembered the smooth heat of his skin under her palm, and another pulse of need hit her between the thighs.

"Zenon. What's going on?" She lifted her hands, but he shook his head, telling her not to touch him.

"I have to do something, Mia." As he spoke, the fierce mask fell away. He looked almost boyish then, shy, uncertain.

Licking her lips, she curled her fingers into the wall, trapping them behind her back. "Okay." She didn't know what was going on, but whatever was about to happen, she knew she wanted it.

"Please, just…you can't touch me," he said.

"I told you I wouldn't," she whispered.

He surprised her by running gentle, barely there fingers down the side of her face and across her jaw. "You're beautiful."

Was he going to kiss her? She didn't move, didn't breathe, wanting to taste him more than anything she'd ever wanted in her entire life.

His hands moved to the wall, either side of her head, and his gaze dropped to her mouth.

Oh my God.

He leaned in.

She forced herself not to squirm as his lips hovered above hers for several seconds, his breath mingling with hers. It took all her strength not to close the gap. But finally, he did, his lips coming down on hers, dry and soft and warm.

His entire body jerked at the contact, and he went completely still, breath puffing in and out of his nose.

Please, don't stop.

But he didn't. Slowly, ever so slowly, he opened his mouth. Mia's heart was pounding when he finally made a rough sound and ran his tongue across her top lip.

She moaned.

His big body shuddered. "Open," he said against her mouth.

She did as he asked, and his tongue slid inside. He kissed her deep and slow, and somehow she managed to keep her hands at her back and not shove them in his hair and hold him to her, or under his shirt to feel the heat of his skin. He savored her, explored, nipped and sucked until she was dizzy and her legs trembled.

When he finally pulled back, she wanted to scream. She didn't know what had caused him to seek her out, didn't care —all she knew was she didn't want him to stop. Maybe she didn't have to leave. Maybe he wanted her as much as she did him. People didn't kiss like that without feeling something, right?

His head was down again and she couldn't see his face. He was breathing heavily and his big body shook. "Zenon?"

"Thank you," he rasped.

She blinked up at him. "For what?"

He shook his head.

He was thanking her with a kiss, like she had him. Only this was a whole hell of a lot more than the peck she'd given him.

Did he know the hold he had over her? He'd ignored her, literally pushed her away, and within a couple of weeks he'd shattered her defenses, had her ready to change all her carefully thought-out plans. Without even trying, and after doing his damnedest to make her hate him, he'd somehow become important to her.

But despite that kiss, she knew he would never let her in. Could already feel him pulling away. Desperation gripped her. "Zenon, I don't have to go. I can stay." *With you.* He sucked in a ragged breath and shook his head. God, she was such a fool. She wished she could tear those words back.

"You need to go, Mia."

"What was this? Some kind of joke? Punishment?"

"I'm a selfish bastard. I just...I needed to know what it was like to kiss you before you left."

His voice held so much pain it hurt to listen to him. "Why?"

He shook his head again. "I have to go."

"Why, Zenon?" Her voice sounded shrill, panicked, and she couldn't do anything to stop it.

He ignored her and stepped back.

Finally, he turned away and left.

And somehow she found the strength to stay where she was.

She would not go after him.

CHAPTER 7

MIA STOOD in the middle of her new apartment. It was huge, modern…cold.

She liked color, not that she'd gone crazy with a paint-brush at any of her other places, but still. Whoever decorated the place really had a thing for the whole minimalist vibe. White walls, big black marble fireplace, white carpet, and an oversized black leather couch. She kind of wished she was back in her tiny apartment—at least there she didn't feel like a guest in her own home. None of the furniture was hers, and yeah, it was the nicest place she'd ever stayed, but it was just another place to sit and wait, wait for her real life to begin.

Her plans to move to Chicago were on hold indefinitely, at least until this power block thing cleared itself up, or was released, or unlocked, or whatever the hell had to happen so she could leave Roxburgh behind her.

After lugging her suitcase into the bedroom, she dumped it on the bed, flipped it open, and emptied it into the black lacquer dresser. Her very un-designer clothes looked about as out of place in the expensive-looking piece as she felt in the apartment.

Did Zenon have a place like this, a place to escape? She'd looked in every open door, down every hall, hoping for a glimpse of him as she'd left, even though she knew she shouldn't, had promised herself she wouldn't.

But that kiss.

She didn't get it, didn't understand how one minute he was shoving her away, telling her he didn't want her, then the next pinning her to the wall, surrounding her, making her feel more desired, more wanted than she had her entire life.

She had to stop thinking about him. Yes, he'd kissed her, but he'd also made it clear that was all they would share. She hadn't glimpsed him on her way out because he'd made sure he wasn't around. That was for the best. It was.

All she knew was that she had to work out how to unlock this block on her powers so the knights would take her off their radar. Then she could put this all behind her—move on.

This thing, this pull she felt toward Zenon made no sense and went way beyond her fascination with the wild and untamed. Maybe it was some kind of hero worship? She'd fantasized about what the knights might be like, long before her sister came into her power, then she'd heard so much about them from Chaya after she had. She could admit to a small—okay, massive—amount of curiosity in regards to the half demon, half angel warriors entrusted with keeping not just her kind safe but humans as well.

But if that was the case, why Zenon? Why not Rocco or Chaos? It wasn't like he was open or even friendly.

She shook her head. Enough turning this over and over in her mind. She had a bed to make and dinner to prepare. Tomorrow she'd start the hunt for a new job. She didn't know how long she'd be stuck there, and living off the knights didn't sit well with her. She paid her own way. Always had.

Dinner consisted of a grilled cheese sandwich and a can of Diet Coke, and after a quick text to Chaya, she showered, pulled on a pair of boxers and an old T-shirt that was worn and soft, and got ready for bed.

Her bedroom felt huge. It really was an amazing apartment, but she felt like a fish out of water in all this luxury. She could appreciate it, but it wasn't her.

When she flicked off the lamp, lights from the city drew her to the small balcony off her room. Slipping on a sweater, she pulled open the doors and stepped out. The air was crisp and she wrapped her arms around herself. The light breeze ruffled her hair, making her shiver. Sounds of a city alive and humming drifted up to surround her.

She'd never felt more alone in her life.

Leaning against the railing, she looked down at people walking along the sidewalk, mice scurrying to their next destination. They had a purpose, a life. She should be with Chaya in Chicago right now. Instead she was stuck. Stuck in a city she didn't know. Stuck in limbo. Again.

Then it all became too much, pressing down on her, a crushing weight she had no hope of escaping.

She didn't hold back, let the emotion of the last few weeks come flooding out, and by the time she finished she was trembling and not just from the cold. Wiping the tears from her eyes with the back of her sleeve, she turned to go back inside. But a feeling of being watched sent tingles across her skin, and she turned back to the railing.

She looked up and sucked in a breath.

Perched on the ledge of the opposite building was Zenon in all his full demon glory. The lights from the city glinted off his dark red skin, leathery black wings, and shiny horns. His white fangs looked almost fluorescent, and his bright yellow eyes glowed through the shadows.

He was magnificent. Terrifying and beautiful all at the same time.

Unmoving, he watched her right back. She stood frozen, couldn't have moved if the building was burning down around her. His wings spread wide, revealing their impressive span, and with two powerful beats he lifted off and disappeared behind the clouds.

Mia ignored the low throb of need that flared in her belly, the urge to call after him. He wouldn't welcome it. The knights had told her they'd keep an eye on her—that was all this was. It was the only reason he'd come.

Going back inside, she closed and locked the door and climbed into bed. She wrapped the heavy comforter around her to chase away the cold, a bone deep chill that she knew had nothing to do with the cool night air and everything to do with the male who had turned his back on her once again. How could he be so indifferent when everything in her screamed out for him?

She couldn't think anymore tonight; it hurt too much. Closing her eyes, she let blissful darkness claim her.

Mia had been crying. No, she'd been sobbing. And he'd felt her pain across the short distance as if it were his own.

His gut twisted as he flew up into the cloud bank. Seeing her like that killed him, made him want to go to her. But even if he could, what would he do? He didn't know the first thing about soothing females.

He'd said his goodbyes, even if she didn't know the significance, would never know what she was to him. None of it mattered. He couldn't keep her for himself. If Helena got even a whiff of Mia, she'd be out for blood—Mia's blood. He didn't care what she did to him, could take her punishments, but he would never put Mia in that kind of danger.

Even with the bitch confined, her powers half what they had been in hell, his mistress was still a serious threat to those around her. He would never allow that, would never let her lay a finger on Mia.

Arching up, he flew skyward, using energy he didn't have to spare, then shot across the night sky to the other side of the city. Tucking in his wings tight to his back, he let himself plummet toward the Earth. The skyscrapers and cars closed in the more altitude he dropped, and he was rewarded with a short reprieve from the knots in his belly when his internal organs smashed against his spine from the velocity of the drop.

Snapping out his wings, he caught the air and with two powerful beats of his wings landed on a large balcony.

The doors into the penthouse were open, and dim light filtered through the gauzy curtains that hung there floating gently in the breeze.

As always, his mistress knew he was coming, had anticipated his visit.

Mia's delicate pixie features flashed through his mind, and he forced them back out. This was no place for her. It was too dangerous, even in his thoughts. She was everything good and right. This place held nothing but humiliation —pain.

As Zenon stumbled through the door, uncaring of his nakedness, his demon snarled and twisted. But when he breached the threshold it was forced back, suppressed. Helena knew better, had learned the hard way that Zenon's demon would kill her if it got the chance. Bile rose in the back of his throat as his dick filled and hardened, jutting from his body like the evil bitch had wrapped her hand around it, leading him to her.

The very idea of touching her made him sick to his stomach, but when he was in her domain he was hers to control. That included his cock. She didn't like anyone else touching him, and used her powers to make sure she had full control over who he did, and more importantly, did not fuck.

The pain had reached a point of no return, his skin burning like it was being peeled from his flesh. He was weak, had pushed himself to the limit. This was the longest he'd gone without coming to her, and he knew she'd make him pay for that as well. She didn't like to be kept waiting.

He entered the room set up for their time together. She stood by the window, gazing out, her long black hair, sleek and glossy, hanging down her back. She wore a pale blue filmy robe that you could see the outline of her body through as clear as if she were standing naked. She turned, and he flinched, her huge black eyes pinning him to the spot.

Her gaze moved over his body, landing on his straining cock, and the scent of her arousal drifted over, surrounded him, making him want to gag. "Where have you been?"

"You know where I've been." Not like he could go far.

She cocked her head to the side and studied him so thoroughly it sent a shudder of unease through his body. "I've been worried. What on earth could have kept you from me?"

Silas was the only one strong enough to control Helena and had her locked up tight in her ivory tower. She had no choice but to cool her heels and wait. She hated that more than anything.

"I've been busy."

Wrong thing to say. Her eyes flared. "What's more important than your life? You could have died."

"I'm hardly going to let that happen, now am I?"

She pulled open the front of her robe, revealing her perfect, unmarred skin. Slender fingers smoothed over her flat stomach and moved between her thighs. "You realize I will have to punish you?"

"But of course, mistress."

She hissed. She hated when he called her that. But he refused to call her by her name. That was an intimacy he would refuse her until the day he died.

"Get on your back, drudge," she snapped. Oh yeah, she was pissed. She only called him that when extremely displeased.

He did as she said, because Helena held all the cards.

When he was just fourteen, she'd bought him from a sadistic bastard who'd kept him locked up. Chained and collared from the age of six, he'd feared everything and everyone. But she'd treated him with kindness, convinced him she cared for him—loved him.

He would have done anything for her, afraid she would cast him aside, back to that hellish existence. But it hadn't taken long to realize it was all a sick game for her, that he was just a valuable commodity. She used him countless times to gain information and power. Yes, she hated to share him, but to beings who hated angels with fierceness verging on insanity Zenon had been a plaything to extract that hatred upon. He'd fetched a high price for his mistress.

More if they wanted to damage him, taking him out of commission for several days while he recovered.

And that was the reason Silas hovered the fuck around him like a bad smell. Guilt over Zenon's treatment, which made no sense, not when the angel had had no clue of his existence until he'd stepped through the portal all those years ago.

The bed was covered in red silk but felt like a million razor blades cutting into his oversensitized flesh when he lay down. She let her robe slither to the floor and moved up beside him. He locked his eyes on the ceiling, and she trailed long red fingernails down his chest, hard enough to break the skin, hard enough that blood bubbled to the surface. The scent of her arousal increased at the sight of his blood and she gripped his erection and squeezed, pumped his flesh several times, knowing how much he hated that she could force a physical reaction from him.

"You really are a magnificent specimen. As soon as I saw you, even as a filthy little runt, I'd known the kind of male you'd become." She trailed her fingers across his cheek. "That fucking angel will pay for messing with your face. He did it to piss me off, trying to stake some claim over you. But you will always be my pet, won't you, drudge?"

After all this time, she still hadn't worked out the brand on his face had nothing to do with her. If she knew what it was, what it did, she'd lose her shit.

Her goal was to return to Hell, overthrow Diemos, and sit her skinny ass on his throne. It hadn't worked the last time, and because of her failed attempt she'd been forced to flee. Of course she'd dragged him along with her.

Her favorite bartering tool.

Straddling his thighs, she bent down, caught a flat nipple between her pointed razor-sharp teeth, and bit down. He refused to flinch. She took him inside her body, that part of her drenched, surrounded him, and slid over his hard flesh. She rode him hard, gouging his skin with her teeth and nails until the room filled with the smell of her musky arousal and the tangy metallic scent of his blood.

Fuck, he hated her. Hated her to the core of his being.

"Look at me," she hissed.

When he complied, she sent a tiny wave of what he needed through the hand on his chest, enough to stop him dying but not enough to stop the pain gripping his body or return him to full strength. Yeah, she'd make him pay over the next couple of days for his absence.

The creature riding him, using him, felt nothing for him and enjoyed dishing out her punishments, and though he knew he would pay for it, he let all the hatred he felt for her show on his face. She hissed then slapped him using all her considerable strength.

His lip split and warmth trickled across his cheek. The sight of more of his blood only increased her excitement, and she came hard, her muscles squeezing around his dick like a vise.

But he didn't come, refused to give her that. It wasn't hard to deny her. All he had to do was look at the bitch. She hated that more than anything else. But in the end, that was all he had left, all he was capable of holding back from her, the only thing he had that was his. She continued to ride him hard, bringing herself to orgasm three more times before she collapsed on top of him.

When she lifted her head, hatred burned bright. "Why do you persist in holding back from me? You know how much that angers me." When he didn't reply and kept his gaze on the ceiling, she climbed off and yanked on her robe.

Mia drifted back into his thoughts then, and it took everything he had to hold back the sob building to the size of a motherfucking boulder in the back of his throat.

"Get on the fucking rack," she screamed.

Zenon pushed that beautiful female back out of his head because, yeah, this nightmare was too ugly for someone as pure and good as her. And in that moment, any hopes he'd secretly harbored that one day things might be different, that one day he could go to her, dissolved.

He would never be free.

Dragging his body off the bed, he stumbled to the steel frame on the other side of the room and got into position for his mistress.

His punishment had only just begun.

CHAPTER 8

JAMES STOOD at Mia's back as they ran through her relaxation and control techniques. They'd tried several different ways to unlock her power, but the result was always the same: her doubled over, gasping and crying out in pain. In her current state, she was no better than a walking, talking cigarette lighter.

"It's all right, Mia. You'll get this."

His tone was gentle, kind. He hadn't tried to kiss her again, and as pleased as she was about that fact, she was equally disappointed that she didn't feel anything for James. A kind, good-natured male was exactly what she needed. Why wasn't it James she couldn't get out of her head? Someone uncomplicated. Well, as uncomplicated as a half human, half demon could be.

"Thanks, James. You've been great. Really."

"We'll get there. I know how much you want to join your sister."

Tears clogged the back of her throat. God, he was so nice. "You're a really great guy, you know that?"

He gave her a bewildered half smile. "You okay?"

"Yeah, I'm fine. Just feeling a little lost, I guess."

"How's the new place?" He gave her shoulder a gentle squeeze.

"Beautiful...lonely." The tears she's tried to swallow overflowed and tracked down her cheeks.

James dragged her against his chest and wrapped his arms around her. "This is a bump in the road, nothing more." He pulled back and wiped her tears away. "If you're lonely, I'm here. No strings." His mouth twisted up on one side and he let a small amount of heat slip past.

"I'm sorry...I can't."

He shook his head. "Look, I won't lie. I'm attracted to you, Mia. But I can control myself when I have to." He smiled, a full, wide smile that made her wish again that she had some control over her stupid emotions. "Seriously, though, I'm here if you need a friend."

She couldn't help but smile back. "I think I'll need one of those."

He gave her another squeeze. "Look, I wish I could stay and keep you company, but I have another session in ten minutes. You gonna be okay?"

No. "Absolutely."

"Good girl." He headed for the door. "I'll see you in a couple of days. And if you need to talk before then, call me, yeah?"

She nodded, and once he was gone, gathered her bag and headed out as well. After pounding the pavement the day before, she'd finally found herself a job waitressing at a bar not far from her apartment. For once something had gone right. This training thing sapped her energy levels, and she wanted to get home and relax for a few hours before her first night tonight.

As she headed down the hall toward the elevator, a loud grunt followed by the unmistakable sound of flesh smacking flesh carried out from the gym. Without thought, she pushed the door open and jerked to a stop.

In the center of the room, on the sparring mats, Gunner and Zenon went at each other. She'd never seen anything like it. Both males were huge, had rippling, straining muscles, and they weren't pulling any of those powerful punches. No, it looked like they were trying to beat the crap out of each other.

Right then, Zenon turned sharply toward her, spotted her standing there, and Gunner was able to land a solid strike to his square jaw.

She cried out, unable to hold it in, and Gunner spun to face her as well. Zenon dragged the back of his hand across his now split lip, but kept his eyes locked on her. Both males were looking at her like she'd lost her mind.

It was Gunner who spoke first. "You okay?"

All she could manage was a nod. The fear she'd felt when Zenon had been struck was extreme and her heart hadn't returned to its normal speed. Zenon looked magnificent, his beautiful inked body glistening with a fine coating of sweat, and his big chest heaving from exertion. So beautiful.

She hadn't seen him since that first night at her new place, watching her from a distance. It felt too long to her, and she couldn't drag her gaze away from his. Which was ridiculous and humiliating. He'd made his feelings for her more than clear.

But then he was in motion, closing the gap between them, a determined look on his face like the day he'd kissed her. A whirlpool of emotions rose as he ate up the floor with those long strides: excitement, fear, need, apprehension. They twisted and turned inside her, building until they had the power to knock her feet out from under her.

He didn't stop until he was a foot in front of her, and she focused on his chest, suddenly afraid. She couldn't handle any more rejection from this male, not now. He continued to heave in those deep breaths, and his big chest rose and fell in a way that was almost mesmerizing.

"Mia?"

The way he said her name, so rough, hit her low in her belly. She had no choice but to look up, and instantly felt trapped under the heat of his volcanic stare. Her heart skipped a beat then stuttered back to life, fluttering behind her ribs.

Gunner cleared his throat and Zenon snapped out of whatever had come over him. He broke eye contact first and took a step back.

"Sorry to interrupt," she said, voice shaking. "I heard someone in here and thought, well, I don't know what I thought…" She was unsure how to finish, couldn't find the words to explain her compulsion to enter the gym moments ago.

He didn't answer, just continued to watch her with those hard yellow eyes.

Gunner watched them closely, gaze bouncing back and forth between them. "Right, well, I'm gonna hit the showers. Catch you later, Mia."

She watched Gunner walk away, and then it was just her and Zenon. When she turned back, she made herself look at him and noticed thin red lines—scratches—gouged into his broad shoulders and chest. "What happened to you?"

Alarm flashed in his eyes, but then he clenched his jaw and something else replaced it. Something that made her sick to her stomach.

A woman.

Oh God.

He'd gotten the marks from a woman. He'd been with someone. And though she tried to hide it, she knew the conclusion she'd come to and exactly how that made her feel was plastered all over her face. She didn't want to care, and was again surprised at the pain the idea caused her.

He got in close, didn't touch her, but got in her space. His mouth went to her ear. "You don't want the truth," he said. "Go back to your apartment." He stepped back, turned, and headed toward a door on the other side of the gym.

Hurting her seemed to give him some kind of sadistic pleasure, and she felt anger flare past the pain. "God, you are such an asshole. I can't believe I ever felt sorry for you," she yelled after him.

He stopped dead in his tracks and turned to face her. His lips were twisted into a sneer and his eyes flashed. "I don't want your fucking pity, female."

Oh God.

She knew only a little about Zenon's past, but she knew what she'd said was the worst thing she could have to such a proud and wounded male. "I didn't mean that. I just meant—"

"I know what you meant." He shoved through the door and disappeared.

Oh fuck.

Oh shit.

He never wanted Mia to see him like that. See the marks on his body, the remnants of his degradation, his humiliation. It was bad enough his brothers saw the marks. He'd refused to offer up an explanation when they first saw them and now they never asked. They thought he was into some kinky shit. Rocco had implied as much.

But it was his shame that covered his body, and now Mia had seen it, too. Going down hard on the bench seat behind him, he dropped his head in his hands and scrubbed his palms across his face. "Fuck."

His skin itched with the need to go after her, to tell her... what? That it wasn't what it looked like? That she was supposed to be his? That they were made for each other?

God how he wanted her, and even though he couldn't be with her, his body screamed out for her. If he didn't do something to get her out of his system, he'd go insane.

The door slammed open, and Zenon shot to his feet. Mia stormed in after him, looking pissed and beautiful. So damn beautiful. She pointed at him. Fucking pointed. "You don't get to walk away this time. Do you hear me?"

Jesus. He opened his mouth, but she cut him off.

"You don't want me? Whatever. But don't you dare tell me I couldn't handle whatever you can dish out. You don't know shit about me. I have no idea why, but for some screwed-up reason I care about you." She shrugged. "You don't return those feelings, and I won't lie, it hurts. So do me a favor. Next time you see me, turn and go the other way."

She cared?

As she spun and headed for the door, he got a shot of her scent, but it was mingled with something else, someone else. Something snapped inside him and he could sooner stop a freight train than he could his own feet from moving after her.

Mine. The thought screamed through his mind, and he grabbed her arm, spinning her to face him.

The anger drained from her face. "Zenon?"

"You let James touch you again."

"What?"

"James had his hands on you. I can smell him all over you."

She frowned. "He was comforting me."

Was she afraid? He couldn't tell. He felt too hot, restless.

He craved Mia like a dying man in the desert craved water. His mind was fuzzy, and all he knew right then was Mia should be his, was his, and if he didn't taste her right then he would fucking die. He reached around her and threw the lock.

Her eyes widened. "What are you doing?"

"No one touches you," he growled then covered her mouth, crushing it under his in a bruising kiss that shot fire through his body. She gripped his biceps but didn't push him away. No, she groaned into his mouth. So sweet, no resistance. But it wasn't enough.

How would he ever get enough?

Lifting her off the ground, he spun and planted her ass on the bench. "Lie back." His voice sounded wrecked, but he couldn't soften his tone, his need to taste her too strong.

To his surprise and fucking delight, she did as he asked. No questions. She wanted him. The reality of that sent him into a tailspin. He didn't deserve her, was tainted and marked by the kind of shame he could never wash off, but he was past turning back at this point. He kneeled on the floor at the foot of the bench, gripped her rounded hips, and dragged her closer.

Her chest rose and fell rapidly, and the smell of her arousal was heady, sweet. Helena's scent turned his stomach. Mia's turned him fucking feral.

He undid her jeans and she held his gaze as he slid them down her shapely thighs, taking her underwear with them. Her body was beautiful, round, soft. Not like his mistress's.

At the sight of her delicate, glistening flesh, Zenon lost his grip on what limited control he'd managed to cling to.

He looked up and held her bright gaze. "Can I...can I taste you?" If her answer was no, he didn't know what he'd do.

"Yes," she whispered.

Spreading her open, he drank in the sight of her. Her soft

gasp brought his gaze back to hers. Her face was flushed, her lips slightly parted. "I'm going to taste you now, Mia."

She bit her lip and nodded then watched as he lowered his mouth. He couldn't believe this was happening, that she would allow him to do this, to give her this.

When the heat of his mouth touched her tender flesh, she cried out. He growled with satisfaction, and his demon was right there with him. The dark side of him was just as happy about what was happening and caused his growls to sound rougher, then—God—turn into a purr of happiness, of joy.

He drank her in, drew his tongue through her center, and a shudder of pure pleasure shot through his veins, lit up his nerve endings.

Oh God.

He lapped at her, moaned at the exquisiteness that was Mia. She was heaven. Perfection.

So good.

He feasted on her, couldn't stop, couldn't get enough.

This, with Mia, felt so different than any other time he'd pleasured a female this way. But then he'd never done this to a female he'd chosen to be with. It had always been at the command of his mistress. At least in this, he knew he could please her, that he was skilled enough to make her feel good.

Mia cried out and jerked beneath his mouth. He gripped her thighs and pinned her down, loving the way she tasted as she came against his tongue. Then he did it again and again until she trembled uncontrollably and begged him to stop. And when he'd wrung one more shudder from her body, he sat back.

Her gaze was heavy, and her bottom lip was dark red, swollen, like she'd been biting the plump flesh. "That was incredible."

Her satisfaction was his. Making her happy, pleasing her, pleased him like nothing ever had. His chest ached just looking at her lying there. He leaned forward, covering her body with his, and took her mouth in a gentle kiss for no other reason than he wanted to. Her legs wrapped around his back, pulling him in tight, and she ground her hips against him like she couldn't get enough. But then she stilled and he inwardly cringed.

"Zenon, you're not...you don't..." He pushed away, and her gaze dropped to the front of his jeans and his soft, useless fucking dick. Heat slashed across her cheeks, and she sat up and began to yank her jeans back on. "Oh my God. I'm such an idiot." She spun to face him. "Was this you teaching me some kind of sick, twisted lesson?"

What the fuck had he done? He shook his head, couldn't speak, didn't know what to say. He couldn't tell her the truth, couldn't admit to what he was, what he had to do to survive.

A sob broke past her kiss-swollen lips and she covered her mouth with the back of her hand. "Jesus. I knew you had a lot of anger inside you. But I didn't think you'd be this cruel, not to me." She shoved past him and ran from the room.

Zenon kept his feet rooted to the floor. Going after her would be pointless. Nothing had changed. He couldn't have her, and he'd made sure of it. He'd hurt her again, and in the worst possible way.

Lifting the bench Mia had lay across only minutes ago, he let loose a cry filled with all the anger, all the hopelessness of his situation, and threw it across the room.

After staggering over to lean against the wall, he slid to the floor.

He had to let her go. It was for the best.

Then why did it feel like she'd torn his heart from his chest when she'd run through that door?

CHAPTER 9

ZENON HEARD Kryos coming through the night sky before he landed.

"What's up?"

Zenon turned as the warrior folded in his pure white wings, so white they glowed under the streetlights.

"I can only sense one. Go home. I don't need your help." Kryos was a good guy, a lethal fighter. But after what happened with Mia, he was in no mood for company.

As usual, though, he struggled to find the right words, and Kryos assumed he was being difficult.

The big male shook his head, hands going to his hips. "Jesus, Zenon. When are you going to get it through that thick skull that we're in this fight together? You don't do shit on your own. I don't give a rat's ass where you were born."

Zenon hated how strongly those words affected him. He didn't let any of it show on his face, though, and shrugged. "Suit yourself."

Kryos muttered something, but thankfully that was the end of it, and he fell into step beside him. "This place gives me the heebs. It's so damn dark out here."

Zenon snorted. The pair of them were the scariest things out there, far as he could tell. "I'll be sure to get you a night-light for your birthday."

"Shut it. You know what I mean. It's creepy as fuck."

The glow from the streetlights did nothing to illuminate the cemetery, and instead caused long shadows to sprout from the headstones dotted all over what would have been prime real estate if it weren't for all the corpses.

They grew silent as they moved deeper into the grounds. He fucking hated Ibwa demons. This whole thing was way off. They were usually a lot more discreet when it came to feeding time, but for some reason this nasty fucker had decided to dine in rather than take out. And it sure as hell wouldn't do for a late-night visitor, or some poor homeless bastard looking for a quiet place to sleep to come across what was sure to be a grisly sight.

The sloppy sounds of something chowing down reached them in the darkness and Kryos pointed to the right, his face screwed up in disgust.

They moved up behind a shiny new headstone, the smooth white marble almost fluorescent in the dim light. Probably belonging to someone important, the monstrosity stood at least four feet tall with an angel perched on top, at least the same height again, its white wings curled into its back. Without a word they split, taking a side each.

"Fuck me," Kryos said, looking down.

The Ibwa was in full-on munch mode, so engrossed in the act of stripping rotting flesh from bone it didn't look up. Not a normal reaction. Totally screwed up.

The guy was half in the hole he'd dug with his bare hands. His fingernails were torn and bleeding, his suit covered in mud and other more unpleasant things. These guys might eat the dead, but they usually did the digging with a shovel, and they sure as hell didn't do the eating in plain sight.

"Hey," Kryos called down.

Nothing.

Zenon shoved its shoulder with his boot, not in a hurry to touch the guy at this point. The demon glanced up, chewing furiously, and Zenon had to fight to keep the last meal he'd had in his stomach. The Ibwa's glazed eyes were unfocused and looked right through them.

"Shit," Kryos muttered. Zen looked across to the other warrior. "He's like the others. No one's home."

The demon didn't try to flee. Instead it looked back down and continued to eat. "We have to get him out of there."

Kryos took a step back. "Reverse dibs."

"Are you shitting me?"

Kryos screwed up his face. "Nope. It's been called. And according to the international rules of reverse dibs, the guy's all yours."

"Jesus." Zenon didn't waste time. He leaned in, gripped the demon by the pits, and hauled his disgusting ass out of the grave.

That set the guy off. He went gonzo, lashing out and trying to take a bite out of his shoulder. Zen shoved him with one hand and reached back with the other. Gripping one of his ax handles, he pulled it free and swung out as the Ibwa came in for a second bite.

The demon's head landed with a dull thud at Kryos's feet, and the knight kicked it back into the hole.

The body ashed out seconds later and they quickly got to work cleaning up the grave site.

"If someone's controlling these demons, what was the point of that? Seeing if we'd lose our lunch?"

Zenon shrugged. He had no damn clue what the hell was going on.

"They're toying with us." Kryos scanned the surrounding area. "Drawing us out."

That's when the rest of the visitors made their presence known. Demons of varying breeds stepped out from the shadowy edge of the graveyard.

Zenon hadn't felt their presence, still didn't, which was seriously fucked up. "Can you feel them?"

"Nope." Kryos palmed his Glock with one hand and drew his sword with the other.

Zenon reached back, pulling his Li Kweis free. The weight of both ax handles gripped in his fingers felt good, a natural extension of his hands.

As the demons closed in, he didn't miss the glazed look in their eyes or the fact that these guys were focused on one thing: him and Kryos.

Demons lucky enough to slip by them during the solstice or equinox tended to lie low unless they'd been granted sanctuary, because doing stupid shit, drawing attention to themselves, resulted in them getting dead real quick.

None of these guys were acting in a way that could be described as typical. They were here to fight. No guns that he could see, thank fuck, but knives glinted in each of their hands.

This was an organized attack. Someone had gotten them together, armed them, and pointed them in Kryos and Zenon's direction.

He just hoped they got this over with quick, because he had somewhere else he needed to be.

Mia glanced over at the table in the corner.

Rocco and Lazarus had been sitting across the room, watching her for the last hour, checking if anything had changed, if her powers had miraculously unlocked. Obviously sensing that hadn't happened, Lazarus had left, and

Rocco had moved his focus from her to Kyler, one of the other waitresses.

It was rude, not going over to say hello, but if she did that, she'd ask about Zenon, and she didn't want to ask about Zenon. He'd made a fool of her, and she'd let him. The place had been packed all night, though, and the big males would have noticed that and seen how run off her feet she was.

God, why was she worrying about this? Pushing all thoughts of the knights from her mind, she got on with her job and collected another drink order from the bar. In an hour her shift would be over and she could go home for a long soak in the tub and a nice hot cup of tea.

The next hour flew by, and when her replacement arrived, she grabbed her coat and bag from the back and made her way through the crowd toward the door. An arm slipped around her waist from behind, and she was pulled in close to someone. "Hey, baby. You wanna dance?" The guy ground his erection against her ass.

Gross. Mia plastered on a fake smile and turned to face him. "Sorry, I'm just leaving."

His grip tightened. "Oh, come on, stay. Let's dance," he yelled in that way drunk people tended to do, showering her in spittle.

She resisted the urge to wipe her face in front of him. Pissing him off would just make the situation worse. "Sorry. I really have to go." She slipped from his grip and pushed through the wall of people that had closed in. The drunk guy grabbed at her jacket, but thankfully the crowd made it impossible for him to hang on.

The street was busy when she stepped outside, so she stood against the building while she did up her coat. Rocco walked out a moment later, Kyler tucked under his arm, her face flushed and laughing at something he'd just said.

Without even a glance in her direction, they headed off down the street.

Mia didn't know the other woman very well, but couldn't help feeling sorry for her. There was no way she could know what she was getting into. Rocco didn't come across as the kind of guy to stick around, and if Kyler woke up in the morning with any romantic notions about the male, she was in for major disappointment.

Tucking her bag under her arm, she lifted the collar on her coat and started toward her temporary home. The streets stayed busy for the first two blocks but thinned closer to her apartment. The breeze picked up and she shivered, but when the gust died down the goose bumps that covered her skin remained. The feeling of being watched slithered down her neck and she picked up her pace.

She was only two blocks away from her apartment. Glancing around, she realized she was all alone. Like that chill wind had taken everyone with it.

Darting glances into the shadowy corners, she walked quickly and quietly. This was ridiculous. She'd walked home the last two nights without any problems.

Pull it together, Mia. You're being paranoid.

A crash rang out a short distance behind her, she guessed from one of the alleys, shattering the silence. She jumped. "Oh God."

At that point, because she wasn't an idiot, she broke into a jog. Her heart pounded in her ears and she couldn't hear a thing over her rapid exhales. Holding her breath, she turned her head and listened. The sound of heavy booted feet hitting the ground behind her ricocheted off the pavement. Her jog became an all-out run.

No. No. No. This wasn't happening.

Her apartment building was just up ahead and she sprinted the last few yards then punched in the security code.

The door didn't open.

She tried to concentrate on keying in the correct numbers as well as fighting to breathe, while her fingers shook, and those footsteps got closer. It was probably just the drunk guy from the bar. She could deal with him. Couldn't she?

She yanked the door again, but it didn't budge. She was half demon, for Christ's sake, but unless the guy needed a light for his cigarette, she was useless—defenseless. A sob tore from her throat and she spun around to face whoever was behind her.

Nothing.

Shit. She searched the street, but it was deserted. She slumped against the door. Now she was hearing things?

The scrape of a boot had her whipping around to face the other direction.

Zenon stood there, looking pissed. His huge leathery wings were extended like he'd just landed and when he tucked them in tight to his back they disappeared completely.

Her hand flew to her chest. "Jesus. Don't do that. You scared the crap out of me."

"What happened?" he barked.

Mia stared at him. She hadn't seen him since she'd run out on him after he'd humiliated her and used her body against her. But did she get an apology or a measly, "Hello, how are you?"

Nope, he barked and scowled at her like she was the biggest pain in the ass for daring to draw breath, and how dare she encroach on his demon-killing time by fearing for her pitiful life? Which was why she wanted to slap herself silly for still being affected by him.

But dammit, she was.

"Mia." He let out a long breath, like dealing with her was

one huge irritation. "Why were you running?"

His voice was low, threatening, and his obvious anger knocked her out of her stunned silence. "I scared myself, that's all. Some guy grabbed onto me when I was leaving work and I thought for a minute he was following me."

"He touched you?"

What the hell was his problem? "I handled it. I've worked in lots of bars, Zenon. I know how to deal with drunks."

He watched her for several painstaking minutes, in which time his jaw clenched so tight she thought she heard his bones groan in protest. "You're okay?"

She looked back down the street. It was completely deserted besides her and Zenon. *No.* "Yes."

He took a step forward. "Mia…"

She turned her back on him and tried to key in the code a third time, but the damn door still wouldn't open. In frustration, she yanked on it, desperate to get the hell away from him and the effect he had on her—on her body. A condition he did not suffer in return.

During her fourth attempt, he moved in behind her. He didn't touch her, of course, but she could feel his heat through her coat.

"Let me." He placed one hand on the glass door in front of them and reached around her with the other, effectively trapping her between his massive arms.

God, she couldn't bear it.

When his breath grazed her temple, she wanted to scream. After the callous way he'd treated her, her body still betrayed her, responding almost violently. The door released with a *whoosh* and she released the breath she'd been holding.

He didn't move.

"Why are you here?" she asked. But what she wanted to say was *"Why are you doing this to me? Why are you torturing me like this?"*

More silence. "I was on my way home. I saw you."

"Right." Why did she keep doing this to herself? What did she want him to say? *I couldn't stay away?*

"I'll make sure someone's here to walk you home from now on."

"I don't need a chaperone. Do other demi get escorts home from work?"

His silence was answer enough. She pushed the door wider and tried to squeeze through, but he surprised the hell out of her by grabbing her arm.

"About the other day, in the gym...I'm sorry." His voice was guttural, hollow.

She didn't want his apology. God, this was humiliating enough. Anger welled up inside her. She just wanted him to leave her alone. "Don't worry about it, Zenon. I'm happy to tell you, you succeeded. You got what you wanted, because I sure as hell won't delude myself where you're concerned again." She shrugged. "And hey, at least I got a few orgasms out of it, right? What do I have to complain about?"

His eyes flashed. "Don't."

There was an unmistakable warning in his tone, but at this point she was too pissed and hurt to stop and couldn't shut herself up if she tried. "You're good with your mouth, I'll give you that."

"Don't," he repeated, so low her toes curled.

She took a dangerous step closer, got in his space. "You should charge by the hour with a skill like that." She opened her purse. "How much do I owe you?"

The rage contorting his face and the sparks of ebony exploding through the yellow of his irises finally managed to cut off her hurt-fueled rant. She flinched and tried to step back, but she had nowhere to go.

"Shut your fucking mouth," he hissed. Then his fist drew back and plowed into—no, through the glass behind her. The entire thing shattered with an earsplitting crash, and tiny shards of demolished security-toughened glass rained down over the foyer carpet like hail.

She stumbled back. "Oh my God. What the hell is wrong with you?"

The rage washed from his face, replaced with unmistakable horror. "Mia, I'm sorry." He fisted his hair. "I'm sorry."

Mia backed away, glass crunching under the soles of her shoes. "Just…just stay the hell away from me." Then she turned and ran for the stairs.

CHAPTER 10

Z ENON STAGGERED BACK. "FUCK. FUCK. FUCK." His repeated curses were punctuated by the smack of his cut, bleeding fist against the side of his head.

He deserved far worse. His stomach tightened. The look on her face. Jesus. She thought he was going to hit her.

He'd lost his goddamned mind.

An alarm started up, and the sound rang out, echoing around the empty street.

Unfurling his wings, he lifted off the ground but didn't go far, taking his spot opposite Mia's apartment. He couldn't leave even if he wanted to. Christ, he was fucked in the head. He'd lost his temper. Had frightened her again. Now that window was shrapnel, and he'd managed to make her more vulnerable than ever.

Laz or Kryos would sooner cut off a limb than hurt or frighten their mate, would never put them in a position where their safety was compromised. He was so screwed up he couldn't even protect her from himself, let alone anything else that might harm her.

Explaining what just went down was not something he wanted to do right then, but the knights owned that building and the sooner someone came to replace the window the better. Grabbing his phone, he keyed a quick text to Chaos, cluing him in on the damage to the building without specifics.

Mia should have been in her apartment by now, but the place was still dark. He needed to know she was all right. With two strong strokes of his wings, he glided across the street and landed on what he knew to be the living room balcony. Yeah, Mia had made it to her apartment all right. Why the hell had he left his position across the street?

She was curled up in a tight ball, fragile and alone, so small on the overstuffed couch in the middle of that huge room. But what tore him up—made him fucking ill—was the way her body shook with the force of her sobs. The sight of those giant tears streaking down her beautiful face, like liquid diamonds, killed him.

He'd done that. He'd caused that pain.

Zenon stood there unmoving for a long time, not able to unglue his boots from the tile, wishing he was a different male, a male who could walk into that room and ease her pain. But he wasn't that male, never would be. Eventually the sobs didn't look like they were being ripped from her chest and became more shuddery hiccups.

Seeing Mia like that did something to him, something that terrified him, made him feel more out of control than ever before, and brought his demon to the surface with a possessive roar.

The sound of a vehicle pulling to a stop traveled up from the street below, followed by the sounds of clean-up getting started, and gave him a small sense of relief. At least Chaos didn't mess around with shit like this, not when more than one demi lived in that building.

Movement from inside the apartment caught his eye. Mia sat up, wiped her eyes with the backs of her hands, and stood, shrugging off her coat.

A low growl shot up his throat. What the hell was she wearing?

The tight black jeans painted onto her round ass and hips were bad enough, but that shirt—no fucking way. The white fabric was thin and clung to her large breasts. It was so damn low cut it revealed a lot of creamy, soft cleavage. Was that her —goddammit, he could see her nipples as clear as if she were standing there naked. The word *Jackson's* was emblazoned across the front, stretched to the limit. That was her uniform?

Brushing her hair back from her face, she walked to her bedroom, and he flew to the next balcony in time to see her go into the en suite bathroom. When she emerged, she was wrapped in a pink fluffy robe. She went to her dresser and brushed her hair before reaching back and pulling the glossy red locks into some kind of knot at the back of her head. She was so beautiful and, with her hair off her face, somehow even more vulnerable all at the same time.

He would love to have pulled her into his lap while she did that—better yet, brush her hair for her. He shook his head. He had to stop thinking like this.

Even though he'd proven himself inept at all things when it came to that female—like keeping away from her—he'd convinced himself she needed him to watch over her while she was in Roxburgh, while they waited for her to gain her full power, and as it turned out, he equally sucked at that as well. But in the end he didn't have a choice. Every instinct he possessed screamed for him to be near her, to ensure her safety. God, he'd screwed everything up.

The fight at the cemetery had held him up.

Kryos had been injured, and Zenon had to help him back

to the compound. So he hadn't been here to make sure she got home safely. He'd arrived in time to see Mia running for her apartment, looking scared as hell. And instead of soothing her fears, like he'd have the first clue how to do that, he'd added to them.

The last few months had been crazy. Demons crawling out of the woodwork, doing shit they didn't usually do. Something or someone had stirred them up, causing them to risk their necks and raise hell all over the city. And until they found out who or what was causing it, he got the feeling things would get a whole lot worse.

Another reason he needed to stick close to Mia.

Mia let her robe slip from her shoulders and all the breath shot from his lungs on a hiss. Yeah, he turned the corner into Sleazeville at that moment, but he couldn't turn away from the sight in front of him no matter how hard he tried. No way.

The flimsy thing she wore underneath was yellow, shimmery, and short. The skinny little straps were the only thing holding it onto her lush body, making sure all those curves were covered. The scrap of fabric clung to her hips and thighs, outlined that sweet place between her thighs, and strained over her generous breasts, highlighting peaked nipples.

He'd never felt so out of control in his life, so conflicted. He licked his lips, the taste of her branded into his senses. Looking down he almost expected to find a hard-on.

Of course there wasn't. Still, it didn't mean he wasn't desperate for her, hungering for another taste. She slipped between the sheets and tucked her legs up, resting her hands under her cheek. She looked so alone—lonely in that big bed.

What he wouldn't give to be able to go in there, climb in beside her, and soothe her. To be a real male for her. Have the freedom to claim her as his mate.

But as long as he needed Helena to survive here on Earth that would never happen. And he sure as fuck wasn't returning to Hell—not now he knew Mia existed in this world.

Backing up, he lifted off and flew to the opposite building. Being that close—just being able to see her was too much, too tempting.

Moments later, he felt a familiar presence at his back. Silas.

"You're in pain."

Straight to it, then. Yeah, he was in pain. But then he always was. This just rated higher on the pain-o-meter than it should after a house call with his mistress.

He turned to face the angel. Silas stood there, dressed all in black, the battle scenes inked on his arms on full display. His black and gold hair was combed back and his gold wings shimmered and shifted in the breeze. "I didn't go to her soon enough. She decided to make sure it doesn't happen again." He owed Silas the truth. If it wasn't for the guy, he would have died soon after his arrival to Earth.

"Bitch," Silas muttered, his hands fisted at his sides. "When will you return?"

"Soon." Too fucking soon.

The angel walked up to stand beside him and looked over to Mia's apartment. "She's yours?"

Had he seen him creeping around her balcony? More than likely. "You know exactly who she is. And you know exactly why she can never be mine."

Silas tilted his head to the side, his pale silver eyes seeing too much, seeing everything. "Do you want her to be?"

The other male could get into his head if he wanted, and right then Zenon wondered if he had, but Silas had vowed a long time ago never to do that. To do it now would destroy a trust between them that had not come easy. Which meant his feelings about Mia were written all over his face. *Great.* "How I feel is irrelevant. You know that," he gritted out.

Silas shrugged his big shoulders, causing his golden feathers to ruffle in the wind. "Perhaps."

"Don't start with the riddles, angel. I'm not in the mood for your shit tonight."

"I only want what's best for you, Zenon. That's all I've ever wanted."

"Yeah?" Zenon turned to face him full on, locking stares. "Then destroy this thing inside me, the thing stopping me from leaving this spot, from leaving her. The thing that's fucking with my head. I don't want this. Take it out of me." His voice rose, pitched high, panic clear to his own ears. But still he kept talking. "Find her another mate, one worthy of her. One who can be a real male for her. One who doesn't frighten and hurt her."

One of Silas's big hands lifted, but realizing what he was about to do, he dropped it back to his side. "Zenon—"

"I'm a slave, Silas. That bitch may be the one locked up, but I'm still hers. I'm nothing, nothing but a whore selling myself to survive."

Silas shook his head, compassion clear in his pale gaze. "You know what you ask is impossible. It's not for me to decide. The die is cast. You must travel this path. Whether you wish it were so or not is irrelevant."

Zenon turned away. There was nothing more to say. He knew how this worked.

A moment later Silas was gone, and Zenon sat his ass down and got comfortable.

"Thanks for lunch. I was going crazy in that apartment all alone."

"We're here if you ever want to talk or just hang. Right now you're doing us a favor. Laz and Kryos have been driving us nuts since that demon broke into the grounds." Eve scowled. "I haven't left the compound in I don't know how long. Laz won't even let me on the balcony without him."

What would it be like to have a mate? Someone to look out for you, love you like that? "I wouldn't mind that problem," Mia muttered. "It must be awful having someone care about you that much." She grinned and rolled her eyes, and the other two females laughed.

Kryos's mate, Meredith, grinned. "Okay, as hardships go, it's not so bad, I guess."

"Uh-huh."

Meredith glanced at Eve. Something past between them, then Eve gave the other woman a subtle nod before they both turned back to her. And wow, they were serious. Deadly. "There's something we thought you should know," Meredith said.

This couldn't be anything good, and she didn't think she could take any more negative crap in her life. She held up her palms, as if the gesture had the power to ward off whatever these women were about to lay on her. Of course it didn't.

Eve's gaze softened. "Zenon's spent the last week watching over you. He's not sleeping and barely eating."

"Yeah, he looks kinda like shit," Meredith added.

"Laz said he sits on the building across from yours. Doesn't move till sun up."

Mia grabbed for the back of the couch, even though she was already sitting down. "What? But why would he do that?"

They looked at each other again, and Meredith shrugged. "We think he's your mate."

She liked both woman a lot, and she had no idea why

Zenon would watch her place all night. Guilt, maybe? But they were wrong, and she was surprised at how much that reality hurt. "Zenon doesn't even like me. He definitely doesn't want me."

More looks were exchanged and Eve moved to sit beside her. "Zenon keeps to himself. There's a lot about him that's a mystery. But I get the feeling he doesn't trust easily, and he doesn't think he deserves to be loved, not even by his brothers. You need to give him time. He needs to come to terms with what's happening between you both, because right now he's fighting it."

God, didn't they see? Zenon didn't feel that way about her and never would. "There's nothing between us." But as she said the words she knew they didn't ring true. *Something* happened when they were together. She couldn't explain it or put it into words. But she'd seen these females with their mates and had heard the stories of the instant heat that flared between them, even if they resisted at first.

That wasn't how it was for her and Zenon. Well, not for him at least.

They weren't mates. It was impossible.

"I appreciate what you're trying to do...but you're wrong." She stood, suddenly desperate to get out of that apartment. "Sorry...I, ah, have to get going."

"Okay," Eve said gently. "But if you need someone to talk to—"

"I won't. Not about this." It was rude, but she couldn't talk about Zenon, not with anyone. It hurt too much.

Meredith gave her arm a gentle squeeze. "Those males are arrogant, stubborn, and more often than not, complete pains in the ass, but once you have their love, their loyalty, you have it for eternity. They're worth whatever crap they drag you through to get there. I promise you that."

That sounded wonderful, too good, and her cue to get the heck out of there before she started crying. Her feelings for Zenon were extreme for the short time she'd known him. They made no sense, considering his constant rejection and violent mood swings. The last thing she needed was false hope.

They said their goodbyes and she left Eve's apartment, heading to the elevator. But a *thud* from the opposite end of the hall stopped her in her tracks. Several dull sounds followed, and she was sure she heard a groan.

She started back the way she'd come, and knew exactly where she was going before she turned to the left where the hall branched off into a T.

Zenon stood—well, *stood* was too generous a word, more like sagged against the wall. His big body shook so bad he was having trouble getting his door open. Mia took a step forward, but before she could reach him, he shoved it open and fell through, landing hard on the floor.

"Oh my God." She rushed over.

Zenon lay there, arms wrapped around himself, shaking and groaning.

"Zenon?" She crouched down beside him. His yellow eyes darted toward her then slid shut. He didn't speak, but his teeth were gritted so hard she didn't know if he was able. "Hang on, I'll go get help." His hand shot out and gripped her wrist like a vise then he shook his head.

"Something's wrong. You need help." His grip tightened and he shook his head again. Pain shot up her arm and she winced. He let her go instantly and groaned like whatever was hurting him just upped the ante. "Has this happened before?"

He gave a jerky nod.

"Will it pass on its own?"

Another nod. Then his gaze moved back to the door. He wanted her to leave. Like hell. He'd just have to get over his problem with her, for now at least, because if he wasn't letting her get help he was stuck with her. "Can you move?"

He shook his head.

His body continued to shake, and she didn't know if it was from pain, or if he was cold, or both. "I'd like to put my hand on your forehead. Is that okay?"

His gaze locked on hers, but he didn't give her a yes or no this time, like he wasn't sure of the answer himself. She lifted her hand slowly so he saw it coming and placed the back of her fingers on his skin. "You're freezing."

He groaned again then stiffened. Agony lined his face and his skin drained of color. She didn't know if painkillers worked on his kind, but she had to do something. "Hang on." She got to her feet and ran to his bedroom.

His spicy scent was stronger in there. His perfectly made bed sat in the middle of the large room, and on the wall above it a pair of wicked looking axes, their handles crossed over one another, were fixed there. The only other pieces of furniture were a dresser and a small bedside table. There were clothes scattered around the floor, and a pair of worn boots sat against the wall, and that was all. She went to the en suite and checked out the medicine cabinet. There was a decent stash of first-aid supplies, but no pain relief. Great.

She couldn't do anything for his pain, but she could at least try to warm him up. Grabbing his pillow and comforter from the bed, she hurried back to the living room. He hadn't moved. His condition seemed worse if anything.

"Let's try and get you warmed up." She kept talking as she laid it over him, babbling like a crazy person. She didn't know what was wrong with him, but whatever it was was bad enough that he couldn't speak or move.

She didn't know what to do to make him better, and that terrified the hell out of her.

"I need to touch you again, okay?" She paused. "I'm just... I'm going to put this pillow under your head." Crouching down, she tentatively lifted his head and slid it in place. At least she could try and make him more comfortable.

He watched her the whole time and she couldn't work out what was behind that stare, but it caused serious flutters in her belly. She lifted her hand again and slowly reached for him, unable to resist brushing his hair back from his face.

After she made sure he was covered, she offered him a drink of water, but he couldn't unhinge his jaw enough to take a sip. So she sat back and waited for it to pass. Twenty minutes ticked by at a snail's pace, but his condition didn't change. He shivered and groaned, and she'd never felt more helpless in her entire life.

"I'm going to touch your forehead again," she said and placed her hand against his skin, sliding down to his cheek. He watched her, but he didn't pull away. "I've never felt anyone this cold. We have to get you warmed up. If you were human you'd have hypothermia by now."

The best way to warm someone up was body heat. Not something he'd welcome, but at this point she didn't know what else to do. She pulled off her sweater and stripped off her jeans. "I'm sorry to do this to you, but I'm out of ideas, and we need to get your temperature back up. I'm going to lie against you so you can feel my body heat." He started to shake his head. "I know you don't like me, but you can just get the hell over it. I'm trying to help you out here. It's either this or I go get help."

He held still, those unnerving eyes not leaving hers.

"I'll take that as a yes." She didn't waste time and climbed under the comforter, sliding in behind him. His entire body was rock solid, shaking, freezing. Goose bumps rose on her skin from the shock of it. Luckily, he didn't have his leather jacket on and wore only a worn T-shirt and jeans so he could at least feel the heat coming from her.

Keeping one arm at her side and the other tucked under her head so she didn't freak him out more than she already was, she pressed her front into his back. That feeling during her training started to hum in the center of her chest, but for once it didn't become painful or overwhelming. It was weird, but she could feel warmth radiate through her limbs, like she was sending heat to him.

"Can you feel that?" Her power was still so volatile and her control over it was not great. But this, somehow, felt right, like she needed to embrace it.

He dipped his chin a fraction.

"Is it…am I hurting you?"

He shook his head, again barely a movement, but she didn't miss it.

Zenon remained tense, and she started to babble again in an attempt to keep both of their minds off what she was doing. She told him about her mother, how wonderful she'd been growing up. How she'd passed away several years ago. About her sister, and the mischief they'd gotten up to as kids. That she didn't remember what her father looked like, but that her mother had loved him dearly.

She talked and talked until Zenon's shivers eased and his big body relaxed a little.

To her utter shock a short while later, without a word, he reached back, took her wrist, and pulled her arm around him, holding her hand to his chest. She could feel the strong, steady beat of his heart against her palm.

Mia didn't dare move, didn't speak, afraid she'd destroy the fragile truce between them.

A rush of exhaustion hit her about the same time that feeling of warmth flooding her limbs retreated. In the back of her mind she knew it was important, this breakthrough with her powers, with Zenon. But right then she couldn't think.

Not while she was wrapped around the fierce, broken warrior beside her. A male who let no one in, ever. A male who, right then at least, was trusting her to hold him, to care for him.

CHAPTER 11

ZENON WAS AFRAID TO MOVE, to breathe, in case he woke and this turned out to be nothing but the best damn dream of his entire life.

His right ass cheek was numb, and his hip was aching, but he didn't give a fuck. Mia's warm hand rested on his chest where he'd put it an hour ago, and she hadn't moved since. Her soft body was pressed into his, the entire length of her connected to him—and to his utter shock, he wasn't freaking out. This felt...good. No, it felt fucking amazing.

Every puff of her breath tickled his neck and sent tingles across his scalp, and that felt good, too. The effect of having her close was a revelation, an addiction, a glut of sensation he couldn't get a handle on but never wanted to end.

She'd seen him at his worst, seen him weak and vulnerable, but in that moment he couldn't make himself care. He'd suffered far worse humiliation in his life, and what had happened here with Mia wasn't that, and he refused to dirty it by going to that dark place now.

Still, he knew this was insanity. Why was he doing this to

himself? He should get up, get the hell away. But he couldn't. No way was he moving from this spot. Mia had taken care of him, even after the way he'd treated her. She'd never left his side, had lay down on the hard floor and used her body to warm him. Talked to him to take his mind off the pain. Hearing about her life, listening to her voice—yeah, he'd loved every minute of it, wanted to know more, know everything there was to know about her.

But this was all he could have. It would have to last him a lifetime. So, no, he wasn't leaving this hard fucking spot on the carpet for anything.

She moved then, her arm tightening around him as she pressed in closer. He squeezed his eyes closed, absorbing it all, locking it in his memory. In a few minutes she'd wake and this would all be over.

He knew the minute she did. Her soft, pliant body stiffened moments before her fingers curled against him and her hand slipped away. The place her palm had rested went cold.

Sitting up, she scooted back a fraction. "I'm sorry. I'm not sure what happened." She looked down at him. "Are you okay?"

Zenon sat up, and his muscles protested after being locked up for so long. The blood rushed back to his ass cheek, causing pins and needles. He scrubbed his hands over his face. "I'm good."

Her gaze traveled over him like she was assessing him, making sure he wasn't trying to bullshit her. "Good. That's good. I was worried."

She didn't look away and he knew she was waiting for him to offer some kind of explanation. But there wasn't one, not one he could give her anyway.

"I, ah…" His eyes drifted lower. Holy shit. He cleared his throat and averted his gaze. She wore only a thin top and her panties. It took major effort not to stare. Mia was all lush curves and creamy smooth skin. The feel of those curves against him were now imprinted in his flesh.

She looked down at herself. "Oh." Heat fired up her cheeks.

"I'll just…" Zenon stood and turned his back while she gathered her clothes.

There were rustling sounds behind him then he felt her move closer. "I'm dressed."

Thank fuck for that. When he turned back, he had to fight not to grin like an idiot. Her silky red hair was mussed but seriously sexy, and her sweater was on inside out and around the wrong way. When she tilted her head to the side he could see where the carpet had left an imprint on the left side of her face. She looked cute.

He must have been staring because she looked down at herself. "What?"

He stepped closer and touched the side of her face. Now he'd had a taste of her touch he couldn't get enough. "I must have hogged the pillow." His demon stirred, one hundred percent with him where this female was concerned.

When she lifted her hand, her fingers brushed his. And when she felt the dents in her skin, more heat hit her cheeks. This time he did grin, couldn't help it. So. Fucking. Cute.

Her eyes widened then she ducked her head. "I don't know what happened. I lay down and couldn't keep my eyes open. I totally passed out."

"Mia?" She looked up. "Thank you," he rasped.

She bit her lip, blinked up at him. "It was…I was…" She shook her head. "Truthfully? I was scared to death. You were, God, you were cold, Zenon. So cold."

"You warmed me." Jesus, was that his voice?

Their stares locked and held. "Will you be okay now?"

"Yes."

"Does it happen often?"

His hackles instantly rose. Anger was his usual tool to deflect these kinds of questions, but he didn't feel that now. Mia only had concern for him. There was no ulterior motive behind her question. Still, old habits die hard. "Not really. It's my shit to deal with, I guess." He heard the *don't go there* in his voice, and when she took a small step back, he knew the message was received loud and clear. Don't ask the unstable one too many questions.

He hated himself.

"Right." She released a breath and glanced around his place, her gaze landing on the clock. "Crap. I have to take off or I'll be late for work."

He shouldn't drag this out, but... "I'll give you a ride. It's the least I can do."

She shook her head. "It's fine. James offered earlier. I'll just go find him."

Wrong thing to say. Both he and his demon had a serious problem with that entire sentence. But by some miracle he kept the possessive surge burning in his gut from escaping in an inhuman roar, and instead grabbed the keys to his bike off the side table and pulled his jacket on. Grabbing his spare, he held it out for her. "Put this on."

"Zenon, truly. It's fine. You don't owe me a thing."

"Please, Mia. I need to do this." And if she thought it was out of gratitude that was fine with him. He needed to do it because everything in him was screaming not to let her go, that Mia was his, and it was better than him tearing James's head off for daring to offer her a lift.

When they got to the garage and walked right on past the SUVs lined up and stopped in front of his Harley, her mouth fell open.

"You expect me to get on that thing?"

In that moment there was nothing he wanted more. "Yes. Put the jacket on, Mia."

"But there are perfectly good cars just over there."

"They're needed." It was a complete lie and an asshole move. Turned out he was a glutton for punishment, a fool, but he wanted to feel the press of her body against his one more time.

"Oh. Okay." She bit her lip. "Promise me you'll go slow, though."

He grinned for the second time since she'd woken up beside him, which would make that two times more than he had in his whole worthless life. "Jacket."

She shook her head but yanked it on. It was too big, almost reached her knees, and the sleeves hung past her hands.

A weird vibration rumbled from the back of his throat, accompanied by a deep repetitive sound. Mia looked up from zipping it, eyes wide. "Did you just laugh at me?"

Shit. Is that what he'd done? He guessed he had.

She smiled, full wattage, and it was all for him. He turned away and climbed on the bike, not able to deal with the way that smile made him feel in that moment. The bike roared to life and he motioned for Mia to climb on behind him. She hesitated for a split second, but then straightened her spine, slung her bag across her shoulder, and hopped up.

"I'll need to put my arms around you. I'm sorry. I know you don't like that."

"I know it's you," he said before he knew what was coming out of his mouth. Those words were revealing, but they were the truth. "Do you need me to stop by your place? Get your uniform?"

"No." A pause. "How do you know I have a uniform?"

"Lucky guess."

"The shirt's in my bag. I wasn't sure how long my training session with James would last."

Fucking James. "Hang on tight."

Her hands slid around his waist. And if on the way he took a less direct route after learning she tightened her hold and pressed closer when he went around corners, no one would blame him, right?

This had to last a lifetime after all.

$\sim$

"Night, Grace." Mia waved goodbye to her self-defense instructor and headed out. She'd been coming twice a week for the last two weeks. After the fright she got walking home from work, thinking she was being followed, she decided to learn a few things about protecting herself. Grace was a demi-demon as well and an excellent teacher, totally kick-ass, and already Mia felt stronger and more confident.

The sky was starless, the air heavy, threatening rain. She pulled her coat tight around her. The wind had a bite and the yoga pants and T-shirt she wore underneath didn't provide much in the way of insulation.

As usual the streets were busy, groups of people club hopping, laughing, out for a good night with friends.

God, she missed Chaya.

Talking to her sister over the phone wasn't enough. She needed a day of eating junk food, gabbing, and doing each other's nails, followed by a movie marathon of epic proportions. But that wasn't happening anytime soon.

Chay was getting worried about her and had threatened several times to visit. As much as she wanted to see her sister, she'd never been able to hide anything from her, and she wasn't ready to get into her mixed feelings where Zenon was concerned, especially after the lecture Chaya had already given her.

Chaya didn't trust Zenon, maybe even feared him, and she knew her big sister would go all overprotective mama bear if she thought there was something between them. There was no reason to upset her, not when there was nothing actually going on...not really.

Like the bar, the gym was close to her apartment. Getting a cab was a waste of money and seemed ridiculous when her place was only a few blocks away. She refused to let her overactive imagination keep her locked up like a prisoner.

Being half demon and knowing of their existence made little difference. The demons that made it out of Hell usually lay low, preferring to stay under the knights' radar. As far as she was concerned, she had more to fear from humans than any demon jumping out at her.

With nothing else to do but think, her head went right where she didn't want it to. It had been a week since she'd found Zenon in pain on his apartment floor, his skin like ice. An entire seven days since she'd lain down beside him and he'd pulled her arm around him, placing her hand over his heart.

At the time it had felt monumental, like he'd decided to let her in. Then he'd taken her on the back of his bike, again letting her touch him.

I know it's you.

Those words had floored her. They meant she was getting through, that on some level he trusted her.

But the days had crawled by and she hadn't seen him, not once. Not even at the compound after her training sessions with James. And yeah, she'd looked.

She turned the corner and wasn't surprised that this stretch was all but deserted. It was always like this. Her place was only two blocks away now.

An image flashed through her mind of Zenon, bare-chested and fierce as he backed her against the building, rage twisting his features before punching the glass. Zenon kissing her in the training room. Then in the gym, eyes wild, possessive, his head buried between her thighs.

And last, the way he'd looked lying on the floor, body shaking, the way he softened and warmed at her touch.

She couldn't get him out of her head. He was on her mind almost constantly. She craved him. He ran hot and cold, confused her, and at times frightened her, but she wanted him. There was no point denying it, not to herself.

Anger at her own stupidity warmed her wind-cooled cheeks, making them sting. It didn't matter; her feelings were irrelevant. He didn't want her back. Males couldn't hide that kind of thing, and not once had he had any type of physical reaction to her. Nothing.

Still, she looked up. Had he really been watching her? Was he still? It was pathetic, but she stood out on her balcony every night, hoping to catch a glimpse of him. She hadn't, not once, and didn't want to admit how much she'd wanted Eve and Meredith to be right. Proof that maybe he returned her feelings, even a little.

But she was kidding herself; she knew it deep down. He'd been grateful for her help with whatever had caused him pain that day, that's all.

As soon as he'd dropped her off at work, he'd thrown that wall back up, blocking her out. She'd tried to find the right words, something—anything. He wouldn't even look at her. Head down, hair forward covering his face. She'd started to speak, and he'd looked up, his expression cutting off whatever she'd been about to babble. His gaze had moved over her face, landed on her lips and back to her eyes, and then without a word he'd roared off on his bike. Not once did he look back.

Someone grabbed her arm, wrenching her to a stop. Mia shrieked in surprise and spun to face whoever it was. A crazy-eyed mountain of a man looked down at her and grinned. That look sent a crawling sensation across the surface of her skin.

Without giving herself time to overthink it, she whipped the pepper spray from her pocket and nailed him in the eyes. He howled but didn't let go, so she closed her fist and gave him a forceful jab to the throat. When he roared and loosened his hold, she took off running.

He started after her, but she only heard several heavy thumps of his feet hitting the pavement before he cried out. She wheeled around. Another man was there now. Extremely tall, he was dressed in a suit and long dark coat.

He was fighting the behemoth. His blows were fast and powerful enough that she could hear the sickening sound of flesh meeting flesh. Her attacker went down, and her savior pushed his coat aside and pulled a wicked-looking blade from a sheath strapped to his thigh. He used it quickly and efficiently, removing the male's head. Everything went silent.

He cleaned his knife on the dead guy's clothes, slid it back into place, and stood to his full, impressive height. Expression emotionless, he straightened his coat and started toward her.

Shit.

Rooted to the spot—God, frozen—she watched his long strides eat up the short distance.

The sound of screeching tires pulled her out of her stupor and she spun around. A car flew down the street and Mia stumbled back as it bounced up the curb in front of her. Two males jumped out of the back seat and came straight at her. The tall guy was running and plowed into one of the other males coming toward her. They crashed to the ground while the third moved in. She turned to run, but he grabbed her.

She couldn't fight him off or use the pepper spray, since she'd dropped it on the pavement after using it on the behemoth.

The tall stranger couldn't help her, busy fighting two guys now the driver had joined in. She was on her own. The male holding her pressed her into the wall, restricting her movements. She'd never felt more powerless in her life. He looked down at her, and she didn't miss the excitement behind his almost black eyes.

Demon.

Raw fear hit like a blow to the stomach and if the wall hadn't been at her back would have sent her reeling. That feeling moved up and gathered in her chest, growing stronger until it was almost unbearable. This was how she felt when James pushed, when he attempted to get her to release the full force of her power. And as the demon tugged on her arm, dragging her toward the car, she knew this was no wrong-place-wrong-time situation. They'd come specifically for her.

There was no doubt in her mind that if he got her in that car there would be no coming back. It would destroy her sister. And dammit, she refused to lose her new life, her fresh start before it even started.

In that moment fear and rage so fierce it felt like her blood was boiling in her veins took that pressure in her chest to a whole new level, but this time it didn't stop. It smashed through. It spread out and flew down her arms. The release was so hard and fast she shook violently from it, enough the demon lost his grip.

Her hair whipped around her face, scalding wind stinging her eyes. Instinct told her to put her hand on him. She needed to release what was about to shoot from her fingers, and she wanted to give it to the asshole trying to ruin everything.

So instead of pushing him away, she gripped him tight,

dug her nails in deep, and let all the wild energy and heat that had built inside her free. The demon's mouth fell open and his hold on her fell away. He stumbled back and collapsed to the ground, nearly taking her with him. The smell of burning flesh surrounded her a second later.

She was staring down at the demon's lifeless body when Zenon, closely followed by Rocco, literally fell from the sky. The sound of their boots making contact with the pavement echoed off the surrounding buildings like a thunderclap.

The two remaining demons closed in, moving in front of her. They were bleeding and battered but were still able to stay upright. Her savior in the long coat was nowhere to be seen. He'd vanished into thin air. She hoped he was okay.

Rage contorted Zenon's face, the brand on his cheek making his features twist until he was almost unrecognizable. He did not look at her, his stare locked on the demons in front of him blocking her escape. "You all right, Mia?" he said, his voice reverberating oddly, like he wasn't the only one talking.

"Y-yes."

He reached back and drew two wicked-looking axes from the leather harness that crisscrossed his bare chest, the ones she'd seen in his room, and swung them easily in his loose grip. "Who sent you?" he growled. They didn't respond, stepped back, moving in closer to her. "Do not fucking move," he snarled.

Rocco cursed. Mia had never seen the easygoing male like this before. He was almost as terrifying as Zenon. He had a knife in each hand and he spun them slowly, ready to let them loose any moment.

"Who sent you?" Rocco tried this time. Again they didn't answer, and one of them actually grinned. Rocco shook his head in disgust. "Are you stupid? Start talking or die. Your choice."

Zenon swung one of his axes, and it whistled through the air. "You know what? I'm done talking."

"You and me both."

Everything happened at once. Roc let one of his blades fly, nailing a demon in the chest. The other demon turned and came at her. She tried to send him a jolt, like she had the last one, but she had no idea how she'd managed it the first time, and nothing happened.

Then Zenon was there.

The demon sunk its claw into her arms, and as Zenon ripped it off her, she felt her flesh resist then give. Stinging pain shot from her shoulders and down her upper arms. Zenon threw it against the unforgiving wall with a bloodcurdling roar, and when it rebounded, swung his ax, removing its head with one powerful blow.

She sagged against the building at her back, relief and pain draining the last of her energy.

Zenon didn't take his eyes off her as he reached back, secured his weapons, and walked straight to her.

He didn't speak and swung her up into his arms, cradling her gently against his chest. The *snap* of his wings extending was the only sound before he took several massive pulls, catching the wind, and lifted them off the ground.

Rocco followed. His wings were feathered, white and silver tipped, so different from Zenon's leathery ones, and made his angel DNA more obvious.

Rocco didn't hang around, and, man, was he fast. One minute he was there, the next he wasn't. That was when it sunk in. She was flying through the night sky in Zenon's arms. She looked down—way down—and sucked in a sharp breath.

"I've got you," Zenon said, his voice so low she felt more than heard the words.

It felt so right in his arms—God, safe. This time she didn't

433

ask for permission and slid her arms around his neck. He didn't tense at the contact and instead tightened his own hold on her.

Laying her head against his warm chest, she listened to the steady thump of his heart because once they reached the compound, she knew she'd have to let him go.

CHAPTER 12

THE BALCONY JUTTING off the compound's control room came into view. Mia had her arms around his neck, clinging to him. He felt like an asshole for liking it so much. She was hurt, for fuck's sake, but it felt good to touch her again.

If he hadn't gotten to her in time...

He tightened his grip on her. He should have been there. If he was free, free to claim her, to make her his, she'd be safe. He'd never let her out of his goddamned sight. But he couldn't be that for her. He belonged to Helena, and she would see Mia dead before allowing him to have her.

With one deep stroke of his wings, he slowed their descent. His feet barely touched the ground before he was moving again. He strode into the control room and someone moved in.

"Here, let me take her."

Mia stiffened and clung tighter to him like he was her lifeline, and shit, it felt good to be that for her, to be her anchor.

"Let me take her. She needs those wounds looked at." It was Rocco, arms extended. Zenon growled low, offering the other male a warning. His one and only warning before things got messy. No one was coming anywhere near her.

Rocco lifted his hands in surrender and took in Mia, the way she held him. "She's all yours, brother."

Damn straight.

He was shackled where his female was concerned, but he could do this for her. Without another glance at the other warrior, he pushed into the hall. The metallic smell of her blood mixed with her own unique scent was seriously getting to him. His demon stirred, wanting revenge on who dared to hurt what was theirs. It wanted to bathe in the blood of their enemy, and Zenon was totally on board.

"I'm okay. I think I can walk." Mia looked up at him, her face so close to his all he needed to do was dip his chin a fraction and he could kiss her, taste her.

The elevator doors slid open and he stepped inside and hit the button for the fourth floor. Her gaze darted back to his face, but she didn't comment. She also didn't ask to be put down again. As soon as the door opened he strode down the hall, past several apartments, and turned at the end going straight to his door.

He carried her inside and gently set her down on his couch. After unbuckling the holster across his chest, he removed his Li Kweis, and placed the axes on the small table by the door. When he turned back, she sat looking up at him, eyes round and questioning.

"Let me help you with your coat. I need to check those scratches." Kneeling down in front of her, he slid the buttons free and she sucked in a pained breath when he slipped the heavy fabric down her arms.

He cursed. They were deep and needed a thorough clean. "The T-shirt needs to come off."

And fuck, the blush that moved up her throat was so

damn lovely he almost groaned aloud. She struggled for a moment trying to get it off. "I can't lift my arms."

Zenon slipped the blade from his boot. The pulse in her throat fluttered a little faster, and her cheeks got a little darker, but she didn't flinch, didn't bat a fucking eyelash as he sliced through the fabric.

That got to him more than anything could.

She trusted him.

The shirt fell from her shoulders and pooled around her hips.

"How do they look?" she asked.

"That demon made a bit of a mess, but you won't need stitches. I'll go get the shit I need to dress them."

When he walked back in, it took effort, but he kept his eyes trained on her wounds and not all that beautiful creamy skin.

She didn't cry or make a fuss as he cleaned her cuts, and he knew the stuff he was using stung like hell. Mia was strong, and though he didn't have a right to feel shit, he couldn't stop pride from filling his chest.

When he'd tasted her in the gym he'd stayed below the waist, and now she was nearly all patched up he couldn't stop himself from taking in the rest of her. The tops of her breasts looked soft, pale, encased in the type of thing females wore when they worked out. His balls tightened. Jesus.

"Zenon?"

Great, she'd caught him blatantly ogling her. Nice one, dipshit.

He was about to apologize when the door to his apartment slammed open and Chaos stormed in.

"What the fuck?" Chaos wasn't looking at him, his dark pissed-off gaze trained on Mia.

Oh hell no.

"Did you drop your block, Mia?" he barked at her.

Zenon rose to his full height. "First, you don't talk to her like that. Ever. Second, you come into my place when I say and not before."

She'd pulled the scraps of her shredded T-shirt up trying to cover her breasts, and stared at Chaos, confused, worry lining her brow. "No." She shook her head. "At least I don't think so...I..."

"You don't think so?" Chaos hissed. "I told you leaving was a mistake. Female, your powers are too damn unstable. Do you have any idea what could have happened to you, what they would have done if they'd taken you? That entire building has now been compromised. You weren't the only demi living there. Did you stop to think about that? I've got enough to deal with without having to coordinate the fucking evac of half a dozen demi."

Zenon got in Chaos's face. "You do not come into my fucking apartment and speak to my woman that way. I get you're pissed and I get you need your questions answered. But I decide when and where. Now get the fuck out so I can finish dressing her wounds before we have a serious problem."

Chaos's jaw clenched tight. He was pissed and worried, but Zenon couldn't give a shit. The guy was way the fuck out of line.

Dipping his chin, that steely control the guy lived by slammed down, smoothing his hard features, and his gaze slid back to Mia. "Apologies." Then Chaos stormed back out the door.

"You okay?" he asked her.

"Did I do something to cause this? Is this my fault?"

Fucking Chaos. "No. You did nothing wrong. There's more to this, and I'll talk to Chaos about it, but I promise you, you are not to blame."

Shit. There it was again, that look of trust.

He finished dressing her wounds and got one of his T-shirts for her to wear. "I need to talk to Chaos, but I won't be long. Here." He handed her the remote for the TV. "Help yourself to whatever you want."

"Zenon?"

He turned back. "Yeah?"

"Thanks for taking care of me." She had an odd look on her face. "The things you said to Chaos, besides Chaya, no one's ever..." She shook her head. "Thanks for having my back."

His own words echoed through his head. *You do not come into my fucking apartment and speak to my woman that way.* Had he really said that? "Just returning the favor."

That look of hero worship slipped from her face. "Right, of course."

Fuck.

Zenon found Chaos in the control room. Roc, Laz, Kryos, and Gunner were already there and, going by the look on their leader's face, had been filled in on the fact that it was no random attack. They'd been waiting for her, he was sure. They were organized, which meant they hadn't just sensed her from a momentary lapse of her block. It was something else, something worse, and that scared the shit out of him.

Those demons had come after Mia.

"How is she?" Rocco asked.

"Her wounds are superficial, but she's still freaked." He aimed his sights at Chaos. "Blaming herself."

"I get you're pissed, Zenon. Yeah, I was out of line, but your female shouldn't have been out there in the first place."

That was a direct hit and Zenon felt it, no fucking doubt about it. All eyes swung to him, and he knew it was because Chaos had called her his, but right then he wasn't in the mood to correct him.

439

Zenon shrugged. "She's here now, and she's staying until we sort this shit out."

Laz crossed his arms. "Those demons, someone's pulling their strings. And that someone has to be close. Not even Diemos has the power for something like that, not from Hell."

"You think he's found another way to pass through the portal?" Gunner was slouched against the wall.

Chaos shook his head. "I doubt it. I think we'd feel that kind of power encroaching on our territory."

"It's not Diemos, and if it is, not directly." Zenon didn't elaborate and the other warriors didn't question how he knew that for sure. They trusted that whatever made his wings different from theirs, and the time he'd spent below, made him an expert on the sadistic bastard.

"Whoever it is, they're powerful. They've either been topside for a while or blocking all that power to stay under our radar."

"The ones that came after Mia were different. They knew exactly what they were doing, not like the demons at the cemetery," Roc said.

Laz scrubbed his hands over his face. "You don't think Mia's attack is connected?"

"Fucked if I know."

A crawling sensation moved over Zenon's skin and he leaned back, using the wall for support when his knees wanted to give out, as comprehension sank in. Please, fuck no. Was it possible?

Lazarus smiled, flashing straight white teeth. He looked evil as fuck. "Time to pay another visit to our friends downstairs. See if we can maybe jog a few memories."

"Sounds good. Let me know straight away if you learn something. Rocco, go with him. Make sure he doesn't kill anyone," Chaos said then motioned Gunner over and they headed out as well.

"Kryos," Zenon called.

"What's up?" The other warrior turned, brow raised.

"I have to leave. Not sure how long. I don't want Mia to leave my room, and I don't want her on her own. Do you think you could send Meredith down to keep her company?"

"Sure." Kryos studied him and it took all of Zenon's effort to look casual and not as out of his mind as he felt. "You need someone at your back?"

He shook his head. "I'm good."

"You sure?"

He nodded, now too far gone to speak.

"I'll go talk to Meredith."

Zenon walked out the doors and onto the balcony then shifted, letting his demon free as he took to the skies.

The flight didn't take long, and as soon as he landed in front of the penthouse balcony doors he pushed his demon back before she had a chance to. Ignoring the door handle, he kicked the thing off its hinges. Helena stood in the middle of the room, perfect, nothing out of place. A small smile lifted the corners of her glossy lips.

"This is a nice surprise." She lifted an elegant shoulder. "I wasn't sure you'd come."

Zenon didn't stop, didn't slow. He kept on going even after he wrapped his fingers around her slender throat, backing her up until she slammed into the nearest wall hard enough to leave a bitch-sized dent.

Her eyes widened but she didn't fight. She slid her tongue across her pointed teeth. "Has something upset you, pet?"

"Somehow you're controlling the rogues, getting them to stir shit...going after demi. Why?"

"I'm flattered, but you give me too much credit. I can assure you it's not me."

441

"Don't give me that shit."

"Have you had a chance to talk to Amen yet?" she asked, ignoring him.

"What?"

"How did your knight friends react when they learned what you really are?"

His stomach bottomed out. "You knew he'd recognize me. You set me up?"

"Of course. Why else do you think he sat back and let you take him in? I thought seeing him might remind you of your place."

She'd planted Amen in the compound just to mess with him, to humiliate him in front of his brothers. She was only happy when she was fucking him over. He forced himself not to react. "You need a hobby. Maybe you could take up sewing. Make those little voodoo dolls and spend your days sticking me with pins."

Her gaze narrowed. "It's time to stop playing with your new friends. I've had more than enough of this place."

"What are you talking about?"

Her black gaze hardened. "What do you think, drudge?" Her smile turned feral. "We're going home, you and I." His heart smacked against his ribs. "It's where we belong. It's time I took my rightful place on the throne."

"How?"

She smiled triumphantly. "My powers have grown, and it won't be long until they're even stronger than they were before, stronger than even Diemos. I'm already almost back to the way I was before we were forced to leave our home." Excitement made her breathing quicken. "I was able to reach out to Amen and a few other weak-minded demons. Don't you see? I can turn them against Diemos. There isn't a thing he can do to stop me."

"You said you weren't controlling them."

"I'm not. They do my bidding willingly. They do as they're told because it pleases me and nothing more."

More like she made them promises she wouldn't be able to keep.

If she wasn't controlling them, who was? The demon that climbed the compound wall, the ones that attacked them at the cemetery, they hadn't fought willingly. Their eyes had been glazed, no one home, nothing but mindless puppets. Not like the assholes that attacked Mia. They'd been fully alert and had only one target in mind.

He tightened his grip on her throat. "Why are you going after demi-demons?"

At this point she was humoring him. She could easily overpower him if she chose to. "Is that what has you so angry, pet? Is it because I sent them after that female? Don't tell me you were stupid enough to develop feelings for her?"

"No," he said quickly, too quickly.

She moved fast. Her long fingers wrapped around his wrist, gripping tight. "You are mine, Zenon. Nothing will ever change that. I knew who that female was before you even laid eyes on her. I could feel it the moment you sensed her for the first time, and I know she's the reason you stayed away, why you're here now."

She reached up with her other hand and pressed it against his chest. He knew what was coming and was helpless to stop it. A jolt so strong he felt it in the marrow of his bones blasted him back, knocking him on his ass. His back bowed and he convulsed repeatedly on the floor, like he'd sunk his teeth into a thousand volts and couldn't let go.

It didn't stop, grew more intense, and at this point he was just thankful he didn't shit himself, though he wasn't ruling out puking all over the rug.

When the convulsions subsided, she knelt down beside him, her face a twisted mask. Rage and something else, something that was raw and ugly distorted her perfect features. She leaned in and pressed her lips against his ear. "You can't have her."

Zenon shoved back, pushed himself up, and staggered to his feet. "If you hurt her, I will find a way to kill you."

She sucked in a breath. "I know you don't believe this, Zenon, but I have feelings for you. I care for you a great deal."

Once he'd craved that from her. Had longed for any scrap of affection she might give him. He'd gotten nothing but pain for his misguided feelings. She'd relished the way he'd worshipped her, and used it against him when he would have done anything for her.

He wasn't young and I, hadn't been for a long time. She couldn't manipulate his feelings anymore.

He curled his lip in disgust. "I have feelings for you, too. The first that come to mind are hate and repulsion."

She flinched then reached for him, and when he stepped back her eyes flashed. All sign of emotion wiped clean from her porcelain smooth skin. "Fortunately, your feelings don't come into this. My mark is on you, which means you belong to me. You will go back with me when the time comes and you will do it without making a fuss. If you resist in this, I will kill her, and she will suffer first."

Every nerve ending in his body sparked, shooting inward, nailing him behind the ribs, shredding his pounding heart. He would never allow her to hurt Mia. Which meant his time on Earth was over. He was going back. And not even Silas could stop it.

For the time being, Helena couldn't touch her, not while she was at the compound. Now he knew where the threat lay, she wouldn't be leaving. He was shackled to this monster, but he refused to let this sick, twisted bitch anywhere near Mia. He had no choice, no options.

The only way to ensure Mia's safety permanently was for

Helena to go back to Hell, and the only way she'd go was if he said he'd go with her.

His blood turned to ice and he was close to throwing up at the evil bitch's feet. The idea of going back to that living hell nearly broke him right there. But he'd do it, if that would save Mia.

He'd suffer a million lifetimes of pain and humiliation to make sure Mia was never touched by this kind of evil, to know that she was happy and safe and free. He could handle anything as long as he knew that.

"I need your vow," she said.

A boulder sat in the pit of his stomach. "I'll go." His voice was raw and broken, which was exactly how he felt inside.

She smiled, all cat-that-got-the-cream, and stepped closer. Her smile morphed into a sneer as she reached up and fisted the hair at the base of his skull. "Good boy. Now get on your fucking knees."

Zenon went down without protest. He felt oddly detached as she slid the straps of her dress from her shoulders, letting it pool at her feet. He was a slave. He was born a slave and he would die a slave. That was all he had ever been, all he would ever be.

She sat back on a chair and spread her thighs. He didn't wait to be told and walked on his knees toward her. He felt nothing, was dead inside. He didn't resist as she forced his head down, didn't flinch as she tugged and pulled on his hair. No, he did the only thing he was good for, the only thing he would ever be good for.

He serviced his mistress.

CHAPTER 13

HELENA HAD KEPT him for two hellish days, and when he stepped outside, his naked skin throbbed and stung with every step. This time the cool night air did little to soothe the damage she'd done to him.

He locked his knees, refusing to fall on his ass. His body was hard at work, repairing itself, draining energy he didn't have, energy she'd refused to give him.

It's over. I'm going back to Hell...one way or another.

The view from her penthouse apartment's balcony was spectacular, and if it hadn't been for Mia, he'd take a dive off that balcony and forget he had wings. In his weakened state, it might actually finish him off this time.

He'd only survived the last two days because of his unwavering need to get back to her, to make sure she was okay. At least while his mistress was torturing him she didn't have time to go after Mia.

"Zenon." He turned at the sound of Silas's voice. Pain lined the angel's face. "I didn't know you were coming here."

Zenon shrugged, trying to appear unaffected, which was

a major fail since he stumbled to the right and only stayed on his feet because he clung to the railing.

"Fuck." Silas's muttered curse was low, full of rage.

"She's regaining her powers." The wind picked up, whipped around his face. Maybe if it blew hard enough it could carry away the awful truth of his words. "She's going back. I'm going with her." He knew he sounded hollow—dead—but couldn't bring himself to fake it.

Silas thrust his fingers in his hair while doing a whole lot more cursing. But there was nothing he could do, nothing anyone could do. At full power, even Silas wouldn't be able to keep her contained.

If he stayed on Earth and Helena went on her own, Zenon would die without her power and what it gave him—and so would Mia. Helena would make sure of that. If he tried to go back with her, the angel brand on his face still intact, Zenon would die. If he cut the thing out, he could return to Hell. He'd live—but he'd wish he was dead.

"When?"

Zenon shrugged. "I don't know yet. She's keeping it a surprise. I guess when she's back to full power. Soon." Letting his Kishi demon take over, he extended his wings.

"Zenon, wait."

There was nothing more to be said. Ignoring Silas, he headed home. Back to his female, back to Mia.

Mia held the phone away from her ear and waited until her sister finished her tirade. When she quieted, Mia tried again to calm her and convince her she was okay.

"Why didn't anyone tell me you'd been attacked? Goddammit, you were hurt. I'm your big sister. I have a right to know these things. They're supposed to be looking after you. Shit."

"Chay, I'm okay. I promise you have nothing to worry about."

"No, Mia. It's not good enough. That's it. I'm coming. Someone needs to knock some sense into those males. Might as well be me."

"I don't think that's a good idea." Chaya was shorter than Mia but still saw herself as ten feet tall and bulletproof. Despite being only twelve months older, she'd appointed herself as Mia's protector. After their mother died, her protectiveness got a whole lot worse.

"Brent! I'm taking time off," her sister yelled, nearly deafening her.

Before she could say anything, Mia heard a low male voice in the background. Chaya hissed something back in response.

"Chay?" The voices got louder. "Chay, you there?"

"Put me down!" That was all she heard before the phone made a clunking sound.

"Chaya?"

"Ah, hello?"

"Who is this? Where's my sister?"

A low chuckle traveled down the line. "Brent's taken her to his office. He looked pissed."

Great, she was in trouble again. "Can you get her to call me back later?"

"Sure thing." The phone disconnected.

Her sister wasn't happy unless she was surrounded by drama. Mia just hoped she didn't give poor Brent too much of a hard time and he managed to convince her coming here was a really bad idea. The last thing she needed was her pint-sized sister barging in and raising hell. If Chaya lost her job, it would ruin everything for both of them.

After putting the phone down on the counter, she went back to pulling ingredients from the fridge. Dinner for one again. It had been two days since Zenon walked out the door. No one seemed to know where he was, but no one questioned it either, like he just up and vanished all the time. It felt weird being in his apartment, sleeping in his bed. She'd asked for another room, but Chaos told her she had to stay put.

She found this strange, but again she was given no explanation.

She was chopping vegetables when the apartment door opened and Zenon walked in. He was wearing workout clothes and his head was down.

"You're back." She'd been so worried and had missed him so much she wanted to run to him, but knew he wouldn't welcome it.

He didn't look up. "Yeah, ah, sorry I bailed. Had somewhere to be." He walked to his bedroom and closed the door.

What was she supposed to do? Something was wrong, but he didn't like to be touched, so she couldn't comfort him. He didn't like to talk either, so she ruled that out. In the end, she went back to the kitchen and carried on making the dinner, adding a couple of extra steaks for Zenon. He might not want to talk but the guy had to eat, right?

The steak was cooked and she was dishing up the mashed potatoes and salad when she felt him behind her.

"Smells good."

She turned to face him. His hair was damp and he had on a pair of beaten up looking jeans and a faded Harley Davidson tee that clung to his chest and biceps. He looked good, good enough to eat. He also looked tired. "I'm sorry. I know I'm invading your space. But I was told to stay here…"

His yellow eyes pinned her to the spot and cut off her words. "I want you here."

449

Her belly fluttered. Jesus, he was beautiful. "Okay."

He tilted his head toward their plates. "So we gonna eat?"

"Yeah, sure. I'll just…"

He walked over, grabbed both plates, and headed to the living room. She was glad his back was to her or he would have seen her mouth hanging open. The guy barely talked, had pushed her away time and again, and now he was telling her he wanted her in his apartment. There was no figuring him out, but with a male like him she guessed you had no choice but to go along for the ride and figure out where the hell you were when you got there.

After filling two glasses with juice, she followed. Zenon was already eating when she sat down on the couch beside him. She started to put their drinks on the coffee table, but he reached out and took one before it hit the glass top, downing it in one go. His dinner was gone a few minutes later.

She blinked over at him. "Would you like more?"

"Yeah, that'd be good."

Mia filled his plate and poured more juice. He drank the second glass like the first then went at his second helping like a starving man. He'd finished before she was halfway through hers.

When she put down her plate and sat back, he turned to her. "You're a good cook."

"Thanks."

"Someone teach you to cook like that?"

"My mother. She loved to cook."

He was quiet for a few seconds. "So it was you, your mom, and your sister growing up?"

"Uh-huh." Okay, she was freaking out a little. Who the hell was this Zenon and what had he done with the original?

"You miss having a dad around?"

450

Where was he going with this? "Is there...is there something wrong?"

He scrubbed his hands over his face. "Shit." When he looked up, his face was flushed. Was he embarrassed?

"What's going on, Zenon?"

"I just...fuck." His head dipped forward. He was hiding from her again.

She reached out and touched his arm. "Tell me."

"I just want to get to know you, all right?" He growled the words at her, but she wasn't afraid. It hadn't been hard to work out anger was Zenon's default emotion when he was uncomfortable or uncertain.

Heart beating faster, she moved slowly, lifted her legs onto the couch, crossing them in front of her, and faced him. She was afraid something might shatter this—whatever it was that was going on between them. "Yeah, I missed having a dad. My mom talked about him all the time. She really loved him, yanno? He left just after I was born. Chaya was barely one. She never said why he left, but she never got over him. She died loving him."

She knew better than to question him about his childhood and waited, hoping he'd ask her another question.

He watched her again, making her breath hitch and her body warm. "What'd you wanna be when you grew up?"

Of all the questions he could have asked, she hadn't expected that one. She kept her expression serious. "I wanted to be a fairy princess with a crown and a wand, and ride a purple unicorn."

To her utter shock and delight, Zenon threw back his head and laughed. The sound was deep and husky and she felt it all the way down to her toes. He looked even more beautiful like that. She couldn't take her eyes off him.

When he stopped, a small grin played on his lips. "You would've been an amazing princess." He reached out and

451

wrapped a lock of her hair around one of his thick fingers. "You've got all this beautiful red hair, princess hair."

The compliment stunned her, but again she forced herself not to react. "I always thought so, but to become a princess I needed to find my prince. I haven't had much luck so far."

The grin disappeared and he dropped his hand, looked down. Dammit, she wanted to kick herself.

"There been anyone serious, Mia?" The words sounded torn from him. Was he jealous?

"No. I shied away from anything that might get serious. I knew I was a ticking time bomb; that this would happen eventually. I couldn't do that to someone else, couldn't do it to myself."

When he looked up she couldn't read the expression on his face except to say it was fierce, a little wild. "What about you?"

His eyes widened. "Me?"

"Anyone serious?"

She held her breath, not sure if she wanted to hear the answer or not. He swallowed hard and shook his head. "Never."

"Well, looks like—"

"Can I kiss you?" His words came out in a rush.

He looked nervous, almost vulnerable, and her heart squeezed. "Yes." There was no other answer, not for her.

He scooted closer so her knees pressed into the side of his thigh. He lifted a hand to her face, threaded his fingers through her hair, and then ran his thumb across her cheek.

"You're so beautiful, Mia. Inside and out." His breath ghosted across her lips.

"So are you," she whispered back. He shook his head and started to dip his chin, to hide. Mia reached up and ran her fingers over the brand on his cheek. "I've never been one to play favorites, but I think I love your lips best."

He grinned, and Mia felt like she'd won the lottery. Not much could top that—well, that was until he leaned in and brushed those full, firm lips against hers. She dropped her hand to his side and fisted his shirt, holding on but not touching him, letting him take control. He took his time, kissed her slow and soft. She didn't push, didn't try to deepen it.

He tasted and teased her mouth then ran his tongue across her upper lip, once, twice. He tasted like toothpaste and Heaven, and she opened for him. The kiss went from slow and soft to slow and deep. He reached around her waist, tugging her down, and moved over her, pulling her under him so they were lying on the couch. One hand stayed at her waist and the other cupped the side of her face. The achingly tender way he worshipped her mouth almost broke her heart. This meant something to him, something she didn't understand.

He didn't try to take things further, just continued to kiss her, like they were teenagers, like this was their first kiss. A wonderful revelation they were discovering together.

When he pulled back a while later, he rested his forehead against hers. "You taste like heaven."

And just like that, she was done for. She'd already started to fall for this broken male full of secrets and pain, and with those softly spoken words she let go of the ledge, sailed through the air, and hit the ground with enough force to shatter the walls protecting her heart.

Jesus, she wanted him, wanted him to be hers. "You taste like all my dreams come to life," she whispered against his lips.

He flexed his fingers in her hair and buried his face against her throat. His body trembled slightly and she wrapped her arms around him, holding him tight. "I can't be your prince, Mia."

God, that hurt. She hung on, fought back the tears stinging the backs of her eyes. "I know."

He lifted his head, his gaze moving over her face.

"But I'm not greedy. I'll take whatever you can give me, for as long as you can give it to me," she said.

He squeezed his eyes shut. "I'll only hurt you."

"I know what I'm signing up for. You've told me how it has to be, and I'm telling you I want it anyway."

He didn't answer with words. No, he made a sound that was full of need and hunger and had heat curling low in her belly. Finally, he leaned in slowly, so damn slowly, breath puffing roughly from between his lips, and he took her mouth. The smooth warmth of his firm lips covering hers was perfection

He started kissing her with so much anguish and longing it tore her apart.

His hand moved between them, and he took the hem of her shirt in his trembling fingers. He lifted it, tugging it over her head, and flung it aside. His hands moved to her back next so he could undo and remove her bra. When she was bare, he ran his callused fingers over her sensitive skin. Nothing felt better than having his big hands on her. Nothing.

Until he bent down and took an aching nipple into his mouth. She cried out when he bit down gently then sucked away the sting. Need pulsed through her, rushing through her veins like a wildfire.

Oh God, she needed more. She needed to feel his skin against hers, pressed tightly to her own, the heat of it, the texture, the scent of him filling her head. She just needed more of Zenon.

Reaching down, she tugged at his shirt until he did what she wanted and pulled up, letting her lift it over his head. The sight of all that smooth, cut, inked skin made her mouth go dry. She'd seen it before, but now she took her time. "Can I touch you?"

He nodded.

"You're sure? I won't if it makes you uncomfortable."

"I want you to. Touch me, Mia...please."

He watched as she lifted her hands to press against his pecs. She moved them down, keeping an eye on his reaction to her touch the whole time. She didn't want to do anything that might make him uncomfortable. He sucked in a breath as she trailed them over his abs, loving the silky texture beneath her fingers.

"Okay?"

He moaned. "Yes."

The tattoo covering the right side of his stomach was unusual, and she traced the lines with her fingertip. His big body shuddered above her, but then he took her hands and moved them back to his shoulders. That's when she felt them. Fresh scratches marred his already scarred skin. She stiffened.

Zenon shook his head and wrapped his fingers around the side of her neck, squeezing gently. "It's not what you think," he choked. "I promise you that."

Whatever this was, it caused him pain. She could see it in his eyes. The last thing she wanted was to hurt him as well. He couldn't be her prince. She didn't have the right to ask more of him. And nothing he could tell her would change how much she wanted him, not ever. "Okay."

His eyes drifted closed, and then he was kissing her again. She trailed her hand higher, her fingers drifting to the side of his throat, over the rough scars there. His neck was thick and muscled like the rest of him. Her thumb grazed over his Adam's apple and she reveled in the pure masculinity of him. Her head swam as he kissed her so deeply it tugged low in her belly.

One of those big hands moved down between their bodies to work her jeans open and he slid them along with her underwear down her thighs.

When she lay naked underneath him, he pulled back and took her in, all of her, until she was squirming under his heated gaze. A low growl rumbled from his chest, and then his head was between her thighs, strong hands lifting her ass higher, taking complete control of her body.

Mia's thoughts scattered as Zenon took his time loving her, bringing her to the brink time and time again until she was begging and desperate. "Please…oh God. Zenon, please."

Relief came when he slid two thick fingers inside her, pumping in and out of her body at a slow, steady pace while he continued to suck and tease her clit. Moments later she was coming, her orgasm so powerful she cried out, body trembling uncontrollably. And then it started all over again. He took her there over and over, until she was a sobbing puddle beneath him.

She tried to pull him up, wanting him inside her, but he just shook his head and pushed her spent body until she came again. By the time he stopped, opening her eyes was impossible. *Moving* was impossible.

He shifted and tucked her into his side, surrounding her with his warmth. "Thank you," he whispered.

Why was he thanking her?

Then sleep came and she couldn't resist its pull.

Zenon didn't close his eyes, not once through the night. Couldn't. He didn't want to miss one second of his time with Mia. After she fell asleep in his arms, he carried her to his bedroom and lay her down in his bed. Where she belonged. Her scent was all over his sheets, and the knowledge that she'd slept here while he was gone pleased both him and his demon.

The warmth of her body settled over him, through him, blanketing him in everything that was Mia. He'd never been this warm. The chill that lived inside him was absent when she was by his side. He'd left her naked, wanting to have every inch of her bared to him. He wanted her warm skin against his skin, without barriers, and resented the jeans he kept on, especially with her perfect round ass nestled against his groin.

But he couldn't give that to her, that part of him that should belong solely to her. He could never have that with her, and it killed him to think he would die never knowing what it felt like to sink inside his woman, his mate. To share that with her would get him through any nightmare he would face in the future.

He wanted to be her prince. Her everything.

His stomach clenched, and he pushed the pain aside, instead focusing on the female in his arms. He allowed himself the luxury of running his hands over the satin of her skin. He did close his eyes then and let sensation take over as he skimmed over her thigh, up and over her hip, the dip of her waist, around to her soft belly then up to cup her full, soft breasts. Her breath hitched and she wriggled.

He brushed his lips against her ear. "Morning." She made a little mewing sound and tried to turn in his arms. He held her in place. "Don't move. Keep completely still. Can you do that?"

"Yes." Her voice was husky from sleep and sent shock waves of pleasure through his lower belly and across his balls.

Cupping her knee, he lifted her leg up and over his thigh so she was open for him. Her breathing increased to little panting shallow breaths that lifted the hair on his arms and had his scalp tingling in a really good fucking way.

He never knew it was possible to get so much pleasure from giving it. Mia didn't demand. She didn't *take*.

Her back was plastered against his chest and he slid his arm underneath her to take over working her breasts then trailed the other down over her stomach. Yeah, he loved how soft her belly was, how all those curves felt under his hands. Such a contrast to his own body. Mia was delicate, fragile, precious.

Slipping a finger through her delicate folds, he groaned at the feel of her. So hot, so silky. "You're so wet, Mia. That's all for me, isn't it?"

"Yes." More with the husky voice, and he was gifted with another zap of pleasure through his body. She lifted her hips trying to take more.

"No moving, remember?" he whispered then sucked her delicate lobe into this mouth, biting down softly. She growled, and it sounded so damn cute he actually chuckled.

"I never knew you were such a control freak," she said, sounding breathless.

He didn't either. He was running purely on instinct. Somehow he knew this was what Mia needed, what he needed. "You complaining?" He brushed his thumb over her clit, and she sucked in a breath.

"Are you kidding?"

And what do you know, he chuckled again.

"I like that," she whispered.

"What?"

"Hearing you laugh."

God-motherfucking-damn.

He couldn't speak after that. This moment would sustain him for the rest of his miserable life. However long that might be.

This one peaceful, perfect moment with his female would get him through all the shit to come, and he couldn't even tell her how huge that was. How amazing she was, how important she was to him.

The beautiful female in his arms had given herself over to him fully, without reservation, without fear. He didn't deserve the gift she'd given him, but he would take it. He had to. Would die without this moment with her.

He slid his fingers inside her, loving the way she groaned, the way her muscles gripped him, pulled them deeper. He worked her body, bringing her pleasure over and over. And when she came the last time he buried his face against her throat, taking in her scent, feeling the softness of her hair, and pretended that his heart hadn't just torn in two. That he wasn't moments away from crying like a pussy at the hopelessness of it all.

Her body went pliant in his arms and he knew she'd drifted back to sleep. And as much as it killed him, he slid out from behind her and pulled on his T-shirt.

She didn't wake until he placed a cup of coffee on the bedside table. Those big, soft, sleepy blue eyes blinked up at him.

Fucking beautiful.

"Are you going somewhere?"

"Yeah. I'll be back later, though."

"You won't do another disappearing act on me?"

He realized he couldn't make that promise. "If that happens, I'll get a message to you, yeah?"

She bit her lip and turned pink. "Okay."

"What is it, Mia?"

"I'm sorry. I, ah, fell asleep again before you got to... before you...you know."

Fuck.

He swallowed, mouth suddenly dry. "I got everything I needed watching you, giving it to you. I promise you that."

She frowned, little lines creasing her brow. "But I want to do that for you. I want to make you feel as good as you make me feel."

Yeah, he loved hearing that, knowing that he pleased her, made her feel good—that she wanted to do the same for him. It was better than any orgasm he could have.

But he didn't want her to know the truth, know he could only ever be half a man with her, could never give her all of him. He wanted to smash something in that moment, kill something—someone.

Whatever time they had, he wanted it to be good. He didn't want this hanging over their heads. "I want that, too. But"—he scrubbed his hands over his face—"we can't take this, what we have, there. We can't do more than we did last night and this morning in my bed."

She bit down on her lower lip and pulled the covers higher. "You don't...you don't want me?"

He wanted to punch the flaccid piece of flesh dangling between his legs and scream *work, motherfucker*. Instead be took her face in his hands. "I wish so fucking bad that I could have that with you. I would give anything to be that for you. Don't ever doubt that I want you, because I fucking crave every inch of you. This has nothing to do with you."

She stared up at him, eyes round and confused—hurt. "I don't understand."

"There's shit going on that's bigger than you and me." He ran his hands through his hair in frustration. He needed her to understand. "Please, Mia, just...I need you to accept this."

She took his hand and threaded her fingers with his. He could still see the uncertainty there, but she tried to hide it from him. He hated it, didn't want her hiding anything from him.

"Okay. I don't understand what's going on with you, but I said last night that I'll take whatever you can give me, and I meant it."

He wanted to cry with relief, and at the same time despised himself for what he was doing to her. Selfishly taking what he wanted. But he couldn't lose this little piece of heaven Mia was gifting him. Not yet, not until he had to. "You'll be here when I get back?"

"Yes." She lifted his hand and kissed his palm. "I'll be here."

Jesus, he didn't deserve this—didn't deserve her, not when he would have to leave. "Thank you."

He kissed her goodbye, savoring the taste and feel of her mouth. Who knew kissing could feel so damn good? He would never get enough, and wanted to keep on kissing Mia until the day he died.

And it looked like he was getting his wish.

After one last look at the rumpled female in his bed, he made his way to the control room. He planned on getting through this briefing as soon as possible, because he wasn't going to waste whatever time he had left with Mia, not one fucking second.

CHAPTER 14

MIA WATCHED HIM LEAVE, her beautiful, broken warrior.

But he wasn't hers. He wasn't her mate.

Eve and Meredith were wrong. And though she wished otherwise—had never wanted anything more in her entire life—she'd learned a long time ago that wishing for something out of your reach brought you nothing but disappointment.

He carried so many secrets, so much pain locked inside. The way he'd touched her, looked at her. Zenon had a way of making her feel wanted, cherished, like she was precious—important. The fact he didn't think he deserved the same broke her heart.

Was controlling the intimate side of their relationship another way for him to keep her at arm's length? And if so, why go there with her in the first place? There was more to it, she just didn't know what. Was he injured? Maybe there was a physical reason he couldn't have sex? She believed him when he said he wanted her. You couldn't fake the longing she saw in those intense yellow eyes.

Gah. She had to stop this.

She flopped back on the bed and glanced at the alarm clock.

Wasn't there something she had to do this morning?

"Crap." She'd completely forgotten she had a training session with James. Shoving back the covers, she raced out of bed and quickly showered and dressed in comfortable clothes, a pair of black yoga pants and one of Chaya's old Led Zeppelin tees. It was soft and worn and made her feel closer to her big sister.

James wasn't alone when she got there. Chaos stood against the wall. They watched her walk in, Chaos in that predatory way all the knights seemed to have, head tilted to the side, studying her like he was trying to work something out, while James gnawed on his fingernails like it was his last meal.

Great. Now what?

"How are you feeling, Mia?" Chaos asked.

Nerves assaulted her belly and she shook out her hands, trying to warm her suddenly freezing fingers. "I'm good. Thanks so much for the concern."

He raised a brow at her obvious sarcasm but didn't call her on it. "James tells me you had a breakthrough the night of the attack?"

"I guess you could call it that." She was still uneasy around Chaos. He'd been so angry with her after Zenon brought her in, but he'd pulled it back as quickly as he'd lost it, like he'd flicked a switch and turned off his emotions, just like that. That steely control was what scared her most.

Zenon wasn't the only one who had built up a wall, but when Chaos's walls cracked, she got the feeling all hell would break loose.

He took a step closer. "How did you feel right before it happened?"

"I don't know. Angry, scared."

"Which was it, Mia? This is important."

She gritted her teeth, biting back the smart-ass comment on the tip of her tongue. "Anger?" She tried to put herself back there. "Yeah, more than anything else I was angry."

"You sure about that?"

She rolled her eyes. She couldn't help it, he was so damned arrogant. "Yes, I'm sure."

The door opened and they all turned to see Zenon storm in. His cold stare landed on James. "You weren't there when I got back. You didn't tell me you were seeing James today."

Was he...jealous? "I forgot I had a training session until after you left."

"I don't think you want to be here for this," Chaos said, breaking the stare down Zenon and James had going on.

His wide shoulders stiffened. "Why?"

Chaos gave him a hard stare. "You might not like my methods."

Mia's gaze moved between the two hulking males. "What do you mean?"

They both ignored her. "I'm not going anywhere."

Chaos watched Zenon for several silent seconds. The tension was so thick Mia wanted to squirm. "Suit yourself, but if you interfere, you're out."

Zenon didn't reply, but she got the feeling he wouldn't be easy to remove if that was what it came down to.

"Mia, look at me," Chaos all but barked. She jumped and turned away from Zenon, but could feel the heat of his stare burning into her back. "What were you thinking right before you killed that demon?"

She flinched. She couldn't help it. It was stupid. That thing would have killed her if she hadn't done what she had. Still, it freaked her out that she was capable of destroying another living creature with her bare hands. She heard Zenon shift behind her.

Chaos sneered. "You don't like that you killed that monster?"

"No, it's just that I—"

"They would have tortured you, Mia. Taken turns with you. Mutilated you until you were barely recognizable."

Her stomach lurched. "Stop. I don't need to hear this, I—"

"What were you thinking?"

"Why are you—"

"Tell me now." He was yelling at her, but Mia knew he still had complete control.

Oh God. She didn't want to think about that night anymore.

He stepped forward and got in her face. Mia stumbled back. "Have you lost your mind?"

"Are you a coward, Mia?"

"No...I'm—"

He moved back in, crowding her. A quiet growl came from behind her. Zenon.

Chaos's angry gaze darted behind her then back. "You know what I think? I think you're afraid. You're afraid of gaining your full powers because then you'd have to start all over again, start a whole new life, and that terrifies you."

She shook her head. "No."

"Yes, I think—"

"I was thinking about my sister," she yelled. "Of never seeing her again. The pain losing me would cause her. Missed experiences...never knowing what it was like to be..."

"What?" Chaos shouted.

"Loved, all right? Of never knowing what it was to be loved, the way Lazarus loves Eve, like Kryos loves Meredith." The room went silent, but it was too late. That feeling built inside her chest, and like that night it didn't stay buried there. It flew through her limbs. "Oh God," she moaned. She couldn't see them, could only hear the sound of their boots on the floor, moving toward her. "Stay back," she screamed as energy shot from her fingers.

Once it left her body, she collapsed to the ground.

There was a shout followed by shuffling feet, then it went quiet, deathly so. Mia didn't open her eyes, couldn't. The acrid smell of burning plastic hit her the same time someone grabbed her shoulders. "Mia?"

Zenon.

She forced her eyes open and gasped. A basketball-sized hole was singed into the padded wall behind him. "I did that?"

"Yeah." He brushed the hair back from her face.

"Oh my God. I'm a monster."

He looked down at her, fierce, tender. "No, you're not."

"Mia?" James crouched down beside her and she felt Zenon's grip tighten. "I know that was hard, but you did really good. Trust me, it can only get better from here on out."

"I hope so." She looked up in time to see Chaos's back as he left the room. "That guy has the charm of a python."

"He didn't mean any of that, what he said to you." James shrugged. "I didn't have the heart to do it."

Zenon stood, taking her with him, and she squeaked. "Let's go. You've done enough for today." He strode toward the door. Mia only had time to wave at James over his shoulder before they were moving down the hall.

"I can walk, you know."

He grinned and nuzzled her neck. "I know."

"Yet, there you are, still carrying me."

"I like carrying you."

"I've noticed."

He chuckled and her belly tightened. He didn't take her to

his room, but instead to the fifth floor and out to the balcony, putting her down long enough to pull off his shirt. She gasped when his leathery wings snapped out.

"What are you doing?"

"I thought you might need some fresh air." He smiled. God, she loved that smile. He looked so young, so beautiful.

"You're taking me flying?" She had to stop herself from bouncing with excitement.

"Would you like to?"

"Yes. I would love that." His wings were tucked into his back, the tips sitting high above his shoulders. "But first, would you let me touch your wings?"

To her surprise, he dipped his head. "Zenon? What's wrong? If you don't want me to, I won't."

When he looked up, his cheeks were flushed. He looked embarrassed, shamed. "Why would you want to? They're not...they're not soft like the others'. Most find them...disgusting."

"They're part of you. How could they be disgusting? I think they're beautiful." She stepped closer and reached up, running her palm down the outer edge. He sucked in a breath. "Can you feel that?"

"Yes."

"I'm not hurting you, am I?"

"No." He frowned. "It feels good."

"Really?" He nodded, and she moved behind him, brushing her fingers down the center, along the inner curve. He shuddered and moaned softly. "They feel warm and so smooth." She came back to his front and slid her arms around his waist. "Your wings are amazing, unique. Like you."

His gaze darkened. "Thank you."

"You don't need to thank me. Not for doing something

467

that gives you pleasure. Nothing makes me happier, Zenon. Nothing."

He cupped the side of her face, brushed his thumb across her jaw, and kissed her. And when she was almost dizzy from the way he worshipped her mouth, he scooped her up in his arms and took flight.

She squealed in surprise, and he laughed, a wonderful carefree sound that warmed the center of her chest. "Hold tight," he said against her ear. "I'm about to give you the ride of your life."

Later that night on patrol, Zenon stood on a rooftop in the middle of the city and struggled to stay focused.

Mia had liked his wings.

A shiver moved through him when he remembered the way it felt having her hands on them, when she slid her fingers over their leathery surface. Helena hated his wings. She thought they were ugly. Mia didn't, though—she said they were beautiful. Were they? Fucked if he knew. He'd always hated that they were another thing that made him different. But after today, the way she'd looked at them and touched them, he was glad they were the way they were, that they were different. She wasn't the first to touch them, but she was the first to put her hands on them to give him pleasure not pain.

But then Mia had been giving him nothing but pleasure since she showed up.

He missed her. He'd only been away from her for a matter of hours and already he missed her.

He forced himself to focus back on the demon he'd been watching for the last ten minutes, when the guy turned suddenly and crossed the street, moving in Zenon's direction. The demon ignored the honks, didn't flinch or slow when several cars swerved, narrowly missing him. Nope, he kept coming like he was taking a damn Sunday stroll. When there was nothing but brick wall in front of him he stopped and looked up, right at Zenon, and waved.

What the fuck?

Shifting into his Kishi demon form, Zenon stepped off the side between two buildings, letting his wings catch the wind before he reached the alley floor below. He landed in a crouch, and the demon with a death wish appeared at the mouth of the alley a moment later.

He met the other male's glazed-eyed, vacant stare. "What do you want?"

"I have a message for you, knight," the demon said.

∼

This was way too close to home, too close to the compound and too close to Mia.

Zenon moved in, Rocco at his side. The heavy steel door was closed, but that didn't stop the low, muted beats thumping through the warehouse walls and echoing around the secluded lots.

Zenon turned to Rocco. The knight's face was cast in shadow, making him look sinister as fuck. "What the hell is this?"

"Hope you're wearing your dancing shoes, brother. Looks like we're going to a rave," Rocco said.

He had no idea what a fucking rave was but he didn't like the sound of it. "I don't dance."

"No shit." Rocco scanned the area around them. "You sure this is the place?"

"I guess I could have the address wrong. The fucker was choking on his own blood when I asked him to repeat it."

Rocco snorted.

Zenon hadn't planned on killing the demon, but as soon as he'd delivered his message he'd gone for his blade. The guy had basically committed suicide, forced to try and fight Zenon against his will. Because no demon was stupid enough to take him or one of his brothers on alone.

"I don't sense any demons here."

"Me either."

They both knew this was some kind of setup, and had left Kryos and Lazarus back at the compound in case that had been the ultimate target.

"Gunner and Chaos should've secured the rear exit by now. Let's go."

Pulling their weapons, Zenon opened the door and they stepped inside.

Bright flashing strobe lights blinded him immediately. He lifted his arm to shield his eyes. The room was submerged in darkness then bathed in fluorescent light at a speed that would make anyone dizzy. With each flash, he caught a glimpse of the packed warehouse. Humans filled the huge space, moving to the terrible music pumping through the room so loud he couldn't hear anything else.

Someone knocked into him. A human female grabbed onto his arm, mouth wide in a scream, silenced by the repetitive, blaring music. He grabbed her shoulders to steady her and blood bubbled up her throat, pouring down her chin. The female's knees gave out and she fell to the floor.

That's when he saw the truth of what was happening around him. The humans weren't dancing. They were being massacred. Each flash of light revealed people running, screaming. Blood was everywhere, coating the walls, the floor under his boots.

Rocco grabbed his arm and his mouth moved rapidly, but Zenon couldn't hear a word. They moved in, tried to help, to fight, but it was near impossible. Without the ability to sense the demons in the room, he didn't know who to kill.

Then suddenly it all stopped. The strobe stopped flashing and they were cast in utter darkness. The eerie silence lifted the hair on the back of his neck. Then the lights came on and Zenon got his first proper look at the carnage around him.

Bodies littered the floor, not one human alive, and the demons that had slaughtered them stood motionless, unresponsive, coated in blood.

Rocco cursed repeatedly while he searched in vain for survivors.

Chaos and Gunner moved toward them from the other side of the room, stepping over what remained of the humans lured there, and met them in the middle.

Gunner rubbed his hands over his whiskered jaw. "Message well and truly received."

Yeah, no one could miss it. These guys were powerful, organized…and fucked in the head.

Rage hardened Chaos's face, and ice shot from his intense, dark gaze. "How the fuck do we fight this when something or someone is blocking them? We need to find the source, discover who's controlling them."

Zenon couldn't agree more. "First things first. We need to clean this up."

"Burn it to the ground." Chaos glanced at the still motionless demons dotted around the room. "Leave them inside."

Back at the compound, Rocco motioned Zenon to follow him into his bathroom and started pulling first aid supplies out of the cupboard. He'd taken a knife wound in the warehouse and hadn't even noticed.

"So what's going on between you and Mia?" Rocco asked.

They'd talked in circles after they'd left the warehouse and come up with nada. Everyone was stressed to shit, so he wasn't surprised by Roc's need for another line of conversation right then. But Mia sure as hell wasn't it.

Zenon looked at Rocco and cocked a brow.

The other knight dropped his gaze and threaded a needle with surgical nylon like a pro. "You ever wonder what it's like —the mating, I mean?"

Yes. Far more than he should. He didn't say that, though. Instead he shook his head.

"Laz, Kryos, the way they describe it...the little they've shared, anyway." He lifted his gaze to Zenon. "Fuck, it gives me goose bumps, makes the hair on the back of my neck stand on end. That's just from hearing them talk about it. How can something be that good?"

Zenon shook his head. "I've never heard them talk about it," he admitted.

Rocco's brows shot up. "You know how it goes down, though, yeah?"

Zenon shook his head again. He'd always avoided those conversations.

Rocco started cleaning around the cut with an antiseptic wipe. "They say there's this thread, or spark or a light, or whatever, but that you'll know when you see it. That while you're taking her, it appears. Only we can see it." His voice had grown deeper. "All we have to do is reach for it, take hold. That's what binds you to her and her to you." He cleared his throat. "Laz, shit, not even Kryos could find the words to describe how it feels in that moment." He looked up from what he was doing. "Sounds good, right?"

It sounded better than good. And hearing what he would

miss out on, what he couldn't have, yeah, it hurt more than any damn knife wound.

But he didn't miss the look in Roc's eyes, something he hadn't seen before. And he didn't think this line of conversation was just about him and Mia. "What's going on? Is this about that waitress you can't keep away from?"

Rocco sucked in a breath then surprised Zenon by saying, "Yeah, actually." He grinned. "She's mine. She's my mate."

Damn. That, he was not expecting. "She know?"

"Not yet. Soon, though. She hasn't come into her powers yet. Still, I felt her, felt that connection almost instantly. I didn't know that could happen, but there's no mistaking it."

"You gonna bring her in?"

Rocco shook his head and dropped his gaze back to Zenon's wound. "She's hellsgate."

"Fuck."

"She has the Beast's mark, like Eve did."

Zenon took in Rocco and didn't miss the stress on his face. "What are you going to do?"

Roc shook his head. "She's safe for now. And I'm being careful, making sure none of Diemos's minions are watching us. I just...I can't risk bringing her in before she transitions and we're mated, not after what happened with Eve, with our brothers." He lifted his head, gaze meeting Zenon's. "Right now, there's no way for Diemos or any of his army to sense her, not before she gains her powers. And when that happens, I'll be right there with her. They will not touch her."

Zenon dipped his chin. Eve was hellsgate, and before her and Laz mated things had gotten seriously fucked up. Roc had almost attacked Eve, and Zenon hadn't been far behind him. Until Rocco mated his female there was the risk that could happen again.

"You change your mind about Mia?" Rocco asked him.

"No."

SHERILEE GRAY

His course was set. Nothing could change that. He knew what he was doing with Mia was wrong and unbelievably selfish, but he couldn't stop it, not yet.

The other warriors knew Mia was staying with him, and more than likely assumed he'd changed his mind about making her his mate.

He never wanted them to know the truth about him, what he did to survive. Even if they did know, nothing could be done. Not even Silas, a powerful angel, could save his ass.

"Brace, brother, 'cause this shit's gonna sting." Roc pressed open the knife wound to the front of his shoulder then poured what felt like liquid fire into the four-inch gash.

He jolted, gritted his teeth, dug his fingers into the sink behind him to stay upright, and with serious effort managed not to snarl.

He usually took care of his own injuries, but the awkward position meant he had to ask for help. He hated asking for help. Their bodies healed on their own pretty fast, but a knife wound like his would take longer without a helping hand.

Roc squeezed the sides together and got stitching. By the time he'd finished, Zen's patience had dissolved, and though it wasn't Rocco's fault he got stuck with a knife, he was ready to knock the guy's head off his shoulders.

"You done?" The loss of blood had weakened him, used precious energy he didn't have to spare. It was only a matter of time before the pain would swamp his limbs, before he was a living, breathing ball of agony.

"Yes and you're welcome."

Zenon grunted. "Yeah, thanks."

Roc finished taping him up and handed over his shirt. "You all right, man? You look kinda pale."

Zenon gave him a "well, duh" look then tucked his shirt in the back of his jeans. No way was he getting it back on tonight, and not just because of the five stitches Roc had

474

decorated him with either. His skin burned, throbbed. The familiar sensation never got easier, no matter how many times it happened.

He turned to Rocco before he walked out the door. "Good luck, man."

Rocco held his gaze. "You, too, brother."

By the time he got back to his apartment, it was two in the morning and he thanked God Mia wouldn't be awake to see him like this again.

He kicked off his boots and with shaking hands tugged the denim down his legs, unable to bear the rough fabric against his skin. He needed a shower, but there was no time for that now. He should sleep on the couch, but he needed to see her, to feel her by his side. He didn't want to suffer this alone anymore. Even if she didn't know it was happening.

In the past when he'd pushed the time between his visits to Helena and it got really bad, there was always the thought in the back of his mind that maybe he'd left it too long, that maybe he wouldn't come out of it this time. Sometimes the thought was a welcome one, but not tonight.

The room was dark, but he could see her body silhouetted under the covers, could hear the slow measured sound of her breathing, a sound he'd grown accustomed to. Couldn't fucking sleep without. She'd been with him little over a week, and in that week she'd burrowed so damn deep it was frightening. He knew when the time came he'd feel her absence like a missing limb, like a part of him had been ripped away.

Pulling back the sheet as carefully as his trembling hands would allow, he climbed in beside her.

Moments later, everything came crashing down around him. This time was bad, worse than usual. That bitch hadn't given him jack shit, had held back again so he'd be forced to return to her sooner. That, along with the blood loss he'd suffered, was gonna make for a messy night.

Then it all became too much and he concentrated on closing down his mind, trying to disengage from the rest of his body. He focused on Mia, on the sound of each subtle inhalation. Convinced himself that he could feel the heat from her body pressed against his, even though he knew he lay on the other side of the bed, far enough way so he wouldn't wake her.

He closed down his senses, focusing on one thing: getting through this—just one more time. Because this time Mia waited on the other side. Closing his eyes, he zoned out as best he could, letting wave after wave of agony take him away.

When he was pulled from the darkness the first time, he was aware of the warmth surrounding him. Gentle heat seeped through his skin, crept into his limbs and began to ease the deep ache racking his body. He'd been cold, so very cold. He didn't know how many hours had passed, but finally he felt like he could draw breath.

Then he was sucked back under.

When he came around the second time, it felt like he'd been asleep for years. His lids were heavy, his eyes scratchy. Opening them in that moment seemed impossible. But his muscles ached in a pleasant way, kind of like they did after a serious workout and a long hot shower. And then he heard her—Mia.

Her voice was soft, close. She was talking to him. He couldn't make out most of the words, but the tone was one you'd use on someone you cared about, someone important.

Finally, his other senses followed, easing back to life. And oh God, she was pressed against him, her soft curves molded to his front, her arms wrapped around his waist. Her face was buried against his throat, and she murmured softly, causing her warm lips to brush against his skin. It tickled, making his scalp tingle.

Yeah, it was pretty much the best moment of his entire life.

During his time in Hell, or when he was with his mistress he disconnected, didn't want to feel. Feeling anything was bad. But with Mia—shit, it was like his world had moved from black and white to vibrant color.

Still out of it, he only managed to pick up the odd word she was saying. But what he did hear made his gut tighten and his heart seize. They were words no one had ever said to him before, words he never thought he would ever hear, not directed his way. Emotion swamped him with a strength he struggled to process. Mia was warming him, soothing him—taking care of him.

Like he mattered.

She cared about him. No one had ever cared about him, not like this.

Shit, he was close to crying like a fucking pussy again.

"You back with me?" she whispered against his ear.

He shivered and tried to speak, but his voice came out nothing but a croak.

"Shh, don't try to talk yet." She tightened her hold on him and he sucked in a breath to calm his shit down. Mia had twice seen him at his weakest, but no way would she see him sobbing because someone finally gave a fuck.

He cleared his throat and tried again. "I'm...I'm good." The stuttering probably didn't do much to convince her of that.

"It happened again, didn't it? Like last time?"

"Yeah."

She lifted up, and he rolled to his back so she was looking down at him. She bit her lip when her gaze landed on the dressing covering the front of his shoulder. "You're hurt."

477

"Just a scratch. It'll be gone in a couple of days."

She nodded, trusting him to tell her the truth. That equally pleased him and made him feel like an asshole all at the same time. "Can you tell me why this keeps happening?"

He owed her some kind of explanation, something after all she'd done for him. "I was born in Hell, Mia. Yeah, I'm made up of the same basic DNA as the others, but I'm still different...I'm more demon than angel." He rubbed a hand over his face. "But that's not even it. Something mutated when I was growing in that bitch who birthed me. Earth lacks something I need to survive. Over time the pain steadily grows worse until I'm forced to..." He struggled to find the right word. "...recharge. Then the cycle starts all over again."

"So this happens a lot?"

"It's not as bad as it seems." A lie, but better that than the awful truth.

She didn't look convinced, but didn't call him on it. "How do you recharge? Is there something I can do to help?"

He grinned, tried to lighten the moment, play down the hell that was his truth. "It's top secret angel business. Silas would cut off my allowance if I told you that." She smiled in return, but he didn't miss the concern in her beautiful eyes. He pulled her down and touched his lips to hers for no other reason than he had to. "Having you with me helps more than you'll ever know."

She looked tired, and he realized she'd been up all night looking after him. Pulling her down, he tucked her into his side and wrapped her in his arms, again reveling in the sensation of having her so close. It still amazed him her touch didn't freak him out. He craved it.

"Sleep, Mia."

Moments later, her breathing slowed and he knew she'd drifted off. But Zenon didn't sleep. Instead he relayed every touch, every word she'd whispered to him, over and over in his mind, locking it in tight.

And for once he allowed himself to imagine what things might have been. How his life could have been different if he wasn't a slave, if he'd been born different—if Mia could be his.

~

"Harder this time, Mia. Don't hold back," Zenon growled as he came at her again.

He grabbed her arm as if he were an attacker, this time from a different angle. Swinging out, she attempted a knife hand strike to the side of his neck, the move used to temporarily stun your attacker. He grunted and yanked her forward. Mia threw up her other hand, like she would if she were to use the heel of her palm to strike up and under his nose, but pulled back at the last minute.

Zenon growled again and swept her legs out from underneath her, laying her flat.

She hit the mat hard. "Oomph." Mia gasped, worked at getting oxygen back into her lungs.

He held out a hand. "Up. Come on. Again."

Okay, now he was just pissing her off. "I've had enough for today."

He shook his head. "Up, Mia. Now. We're going again."

She tried to stare him down. "No."

"You think a demon gives a shit you're tired?" He was scowling down at her, but after three weeks of amazing orgasms and tender moments, he didn't scare her anymore. Zenon was gentle, attentive—and filled with so much pain it tore her apart every time she saw that shadow creep across his face. But right then he was being a stubborn ass. She'd told him about the self-defense classes she'd started and how

479

SHERILEE GRAY

disappointed she was to be missing them. He'd had her training every day since, almost obsessively.

She shook her head. "I've had enough." He reached down and grabbed her hand, attempting to yank her up off the floor. "I said no."

"Get the fuck up now. You've had enough when I say so."

Oh, that was it. She kicked out then, nailing him in the knee. It jarred back awkwardly and he sucked in a breath. Copying the move he'd used on her, she swung out and swept his leg out from under him.

His big body hit the mat. Hard.

"Shit." She scrambled over to him. "Zenon? Are you all right? I'm sorry." He was making a weird noise. Oh God, she'd really hurt him. "Should I get help? Are you all right?"

When he looked up at her, he was grinning so wide she was almost blinded by all those straight white teeth. The bastard was laughing.

"You think that's funny?"

He nodded, holding his side while laughing so hard she thought he'd rupture something.

She smacked him on the shoulder. "Jerk."

She spun around to make a pissy departure, but before she could take two steps, she was in the air, spun around then flat on her back. Zenon loomed over her. "You're not going anywhere. I told you I haven't finished with you yet."

"Oh right, how could I forget? I've had enough when you say so." She said the last part in a mock deep, growly voice.

"That's right. Finally she gets it." The grin was still firmly in place, and Mia had to work at not smiling in return.

"Okay, you have me where you want me, so now what?" Heat darkened his gaze. She'd grown to love that look. A lot.

"You need to be punished."

"What do you have in mind?" She sounded breathless, needy, and she didn't give a damn.

Sliding his hand up her shirt, he glided rough fingers over her stomach to the sensitive underside of her breast. "If I tell you, the surprise will be ruined."

God, she loved this. This teasing, playful side. It had come out more and more over the last few days, and every time playful Zenon made an appearance she had the urge to hold her breath, afraid to break the spell. Reaching out a hand, he chuckled evilly as he used his powers to lock the door. The sound of it sliding into place filled the charged silence.

He continued to stroke her skin, making her squirm. "It's a good thing I love surprises, then."

The wicked glint in his eyes almost made her want to take those words back. Almost. "You have trouble with self-control and following instruction. Those things are important. So I'm going to teach you."

That didn't sound good. "What are you—"

He shook his head. "For the purposes of this lesson, you will not speak, Mia, not until I tell you to. You will not move unless I tell you to. Nod if you understand."

Her blood rushed faster, her heart pounded harder. She'd learned fairly quickly that Zenon like to take control when they were in bed. She'd also learned that she loved it. She didn't know why, but Zenon needed this, needed to feel as though he had full control, and she was happy to give it to him. He turned from a male who came across as unsure, almost shy at times, to something else entirely.

He pinched her nipple, not enough to hurt, but enough to make her gasp. She nodded.

"Good girl. Now lift your arms." She did as he asked and he pulled up her shirt, but instead of removing it fully, tangled it around her wrists. "Is that all right, princess?"

She nodded again, and he grinned, a lopsided sexy grin that caused liquid heat to flood her sex. He'd also started calling her *princess*. She loved it. Her bra came off next, torn from her body without apology. He slipped off her sneakers, followed by her underwear and yoga pants. He slid them down her legs slowly, his dark gaze moving across her bare skin.

Now completely naked, she lay sprawled on the mat, waiting for what would come next.

"Bend your knees and open yourself for me." His voice was harsh, rough, and she shivered. She did as he asked, heart pounding, anticipation flowing through her veins. He pulled his shirt over his head, revealing all that beautiful inked skin, all those vicious scars she knew marked him inside and out. "So fucking beautiful," he rasped.

He knelt beside her and ran his index finger from the indent in her throat down between her breasts then across to circle a nipple. The touch was light, barely there, and she arched up, needing more. He took his hand away and she groaned.

"No moving, or I stop." The serious note to his voice wasn't very effective, not with the wicked tilt of those tempting lips.

Oh, he was enjoying this.

The throb between her thighs increased and she wanted desperately to squeeze her legs together to ease the ache. She stilled and he chuckled in that dark way that sent delicious shivers across her skin. He ignored all her naughty bits and instead ran his fingers over her arms, her stomach, across her hip. Finally, he bent down and kissed the smooth skin just below her belly button. "Sometimes I can't believe you're real and not something I dreamed up in my mind."

His quietly spoken words stole her breath. How could he say that when he got nothing in return from her? He still hadn't made love to her. He didn't even take off his jeans when they slept together. His attention was always solely focused on her, what she needed, what she desired. And then he'd say something like that and she knew there was so much more to this male. There were things that she would never know about him, things she wanted to know more than anything else in this whole world.

He leaned in and trailed soft kisses from her belly to the underside of her breast. She held her breath, letting it out on a moan when he closed his lips over her nipple and sucked gently. His hand skimmed her waist and moved down. He shifted, moving his thick, muscled thighs between her legs, holding her open while he ran a finger down her aching center.

"So wet, Mia. So hot."

He kissed her deep and hungry, thrusting two fingers inside her, taking her in a deliciously rough way. When she was gasping and panting, he pressed his thumb against her clit. That was all she needed, and she flew apart beneath him. Her body bowed almost painfully, her hips moving of their own volition, dragging out her release. Her body gripped his fingers tight, holding him inside her.

When she came down and her breathing evened out, she opened her eyes. Zenon was watching her, and that dark heat was still there, as well as a possessive hunger she was growing to crave.

I love you.

The words bounced around her head, and she knew they were shining from her eyes like a beacon. Oh God, she loved him.

His lids fluttered closed, and he pulled from her body then pushed to his feet.

"Zenon?"

He paced back and forth a few times, his breath sawing in and out, then he roared, a sound so filled with rage and agony Mia felt it to her bones. She scrambled away until her back met padding, not sure what to do or what to say.

He pulled back a fist and slammed it into wall repeatedly in a frenzy of emotion that saturated the room.

Mia didn't know what had set him off. Why would her loving him make him so angry? But then his grunts turned to sobs and she couldn't bear it.

Scrambling off the floor, she came at him from the side so he knew it was her and placed her hand on his shoulder. "Stop, Zenon. Stop this." He kept at it until blood smeared the wall in front of him, his knuckles raw and split. What the hell had he been through? Who did this to him? Tears tracked a heated path down her face. She squeezed his shoulder to get his attention. "Stop it, Zenon. Please, stop it."

He spun away from her and thrust his hands in his hair, breathing hard, pacing the room again.

"Look at me. Please."

He shook his head and let his chin drop so his hair fell forward, covering his face. That alone killed her. He hadn't tried to hide from her since they'd been together. She knew what it meant, and the pain of it had the power to knock the wind from her lungs.

"What's going on?"

He shook his head over and over. "I can't...we can't do this anymore. I was wrong to use you like this. It was a mistake. It should never have happened."

"No." She wrapped her arms around herself. "You don't mean that."

He lifted his head, eyes blank, distant. "I told you, I can't be your prince, Mia."

She flinched like he'd slapped her, and stumbled back a step. "Why are you doing this?"

"It's time."

That was all he said, all the explanation she got after three glorious weeks. Jesus, it hurt. But this pain wasn't hers alone. His reaction proved that.

"If you need time…if you—"

"I don't need time. It's over."

"That's it? You're throwing me away, just like that, like I meant nothing to you?"

He looked down again. "You said you'd only take what I could give. I don't have anything left. This is…it's too much."

She hugged herself tighter. She got attached, she fell in love. That was her mistake.

"Did I ask too much of you? Did I do something wrong?" She had never felt more vulnerable in her entire life. She was standing there completely naked, all but begging him not to let her go, and right then she didn't give a damn.

"No," he choked. "You did nothing wrong. This is on me."

"So that's it?" She sounded desperate but she couldn't make herself shut up.

"This had to end sometime." Yeah, he'd seen it in her eyes, and now he was running scared. "I'll have your things moved to another room." There was no emotion in his voice. It was completely flat and chilled her to the bone. Goose bumps covered her skin and she tried to rub them away. She didn't think she'd ever feel warm again.

"I'm sorry, Mia."

Anger welled up inside her and she lashed out. "You want to close yourself off, throw me aside as soon as real emotion is involved, that's your deal." She bent down and gathered her clothes, shoving them on.

Then she unlocked the door and yanked it open. She didn't turn back, couldn't. Seconds later she was walking down the hall on autopilot, pain lancing her soul. She tried to shut it down, block it off, but there was no containing what was happening inside her. It pumped through her blood, ripped through her limbs. It went beyond pain, like something had been torn from her body, a vital part of her that she couldn't live without. She headed straight for the elevators and punched in the floor that housed the demi-demons.

She had to find James. The sooner she got her powers unlocked and mastered, the sooner she could get out of this place and join her sister.

She needed to start that new life.

CHAPTER 15

Zenon flew above the compound, circling the building's perimeter for the tenth time. Going in held no appeal. Every room in his apartment reminded him of Mia. Even the goddamned elevator made him think of her, of holding her in his arms.

It had been a week since he'd hurt her—the last thing he'd ever wanted to do. But seeing that look in her eyes, the way her whole face softened when she looked at him, he'd known in that one perfect moment just how badly he'd screwed this up.

She truly cared about him. What happened to him.

Everything he'd ever wanted had been staring back at him in her beautiful blue eyes.

And he'd lost it. He'd never felt so much rage in his entire life. Because he had to turn away from it, turn away from the female he wanted with every fiber of his being. So yeah, he was angry.

But what choice did he have? If he stayed and carried on with what they were doing, it would only hurt her more when he was gone.

When Zenon landed, he strode from the balcony into the control room, keeping his head down. Avoiding people had worked so far. He'd been giving his brothers a wide berth. The last thing he wanted was to talk. Talking led to questions, and right then he didn't have the answers. None he was willing or able to give.

But as soon as he stepped over the threshold, he knew something was wrong. Low level electricity skittered across his skin, lifting the hair on his arms and the back of his neck. Something was way off. Rocco sat at one of the desks, his booted feet propped up on its surface, tapping away on the keyboard resting in his lap.

"What's going on?"

Rocco looked up. "Well, I'm up to level twenty-seven on *Angry Birds Star Wars*. You?"

Zenon growled. "Can't you feel it?"

Rocco dropped his feet to the floor and stood. "Feel what? What's going on?"

"Where's Mia?" He was already moving toward the door.

"In the training room, far as I know—"

Zenon was out the door and pounding down the hall toward the stairwell before Rocco finished his sentence. Shoving the door open, he jumped the rail to the lower level, then the next, and the next, and the next, until he hit the floor with the training rooms.

A weird kind of static buzzed through the air, its intensity rising with every second. He hissed, pleasure and pain assaulting every molecule in his body.

Shit.

When he reached the training room door, he could feel Mia inside. He didn't hesitate and kicked the fucker in.

The sight that confronted him stole his breath. Mia stood in the middle of the room, her long red hair flying around her face and shoulders. Eyes closed tight, tears streaked down her cheeks. Her hands were held out in front of her, glowing fiery orbs of energy flying from her fingers. They hit the opposite wall, leaving behind singed circles in the padding that smoldered around the edges.

James stood to the side, holding his arms up, looking freaked.

Zenon stepped farther into the room.

"Stay back, Zenon." James's voice sounded distant.

Like hell. His heart pounded as he felt a familiar need crawl up his spine, hitting him in the back of the skull. Stepping to the side, he put himself in the line of fire. The first one that hit knocked him to his knees. He grunted but staggered back to his feet and took another step toward Mia. Her eyes flew open and she tried to turn away, but Zenon called her power to him, and each ball she sent flying changed course midair and came at him, nailing him in the chest.

Oh fuck. So good, so fucking good.

He kept coming at her until he was standing beside her. "Stay back. I…I can't stop," she cried.

Grabbing her wrists, he forced her to face him and pressed her hands against his chest. The intensity of all that power moving through his body had his eyes rolling back in his head. Each hit jarred his body, sending pleasure-pain streaking through his nerve endings. Mia fought him, her screams echoing around the room, but he was too far gone to explain what was happening.

After the last hit he dropped to his knees at her feet. Rough hands grabbed at him, pulling him back up. Voices talked over the top of each other but he couldn't make his jaw unclench enough to tell them he was okay. Finally, the last wave of energy pulsed through his system and he slumped against the big body at his back.

When he opened his eyes, he realized he was surrounded. Every knight stood watching him. Chaos was at his back, holding him up. Mia stood to the side, sobbing silently, her arms wrapped around herself.

Shrugging out of Chaos's hold, he moved toward her on unsteady legs. She backed up like she was afraid of him, and he couldn't blame her after that little show. He didn't stop until his chest brushed hers. Cupping her chin, he forced her to look at him. "I'm okay, Mia."

"But, I…but you…"

He shook his head. "I'm not like the other knights. I'm more demon than angel," he said, repeating what he'd said to her when she'd looked after him, hoping she knew where he was going with this. "You wanted to know if you could help me? You…you just gave me what I need." He could barely believe it. Emotion swamped him. "*You* gave it to me, Mia."

Her eyes searched his. So much there, so damn much. "I did?" she whispered.

"Yeah."

"But how?"

"I don't know." He'd only known Helena to possess such a power. Hope surged through him. Could Mia be the answer to his freedom?

"I was so scared. I thought I'd hurt you." She wrapped her arms around him. Her soft body pressed against his, her curved belly and lush breasts. Christ, her scent…

That's when he felt it.

His dick twitched, lengthened, and filled until it strained painfully against the fly of his jeans.

Holy shit. Holy motherfucking shit.

He was pressed close to her and he saw the minute she felt it, that she felt him, his hard, aching cock against her soft curves.

Her eyes went round as saucers, and she sucked in a breath.

"What the fuck just happened here?" Chaos barked.

Reluctantly, he stepped back and turned to face the males who had had his back more times than he could remember. As much as he didn't want to reveal his shame, he wanted his freedom. And after what just happened, he had hope for the first time in his shitty life.

Zenon explained his need for the energy Mia had just given him. The pain he suffered when he was drained of it. They listened without interruption but he could see the question in their eyes, see the realization flicker across their gazes. Putting the pieces together. His unexplained absences —what Amen had said during questioning.

But it was Mia who asked the question. "How have you survived all this time? Who gives you what you need, Zenon?"

He had imagined this moment in his mind many times, telling his brothers what he had been, still was. But telling Mia? He could never have prepared himself for that. The urge to dip his head, to hide was almost overpowering, but he held her gaze as he spoke. He focused on her, his brothers at his back like they always had been and, he realized in that moment, always would be if they got the chance.

"I'm a slave, Mia." A soft gasp slipped past her lips and her hand flew up to cover her mouth. "I didn't come to Earth alone. My mistress brought me here after she attempted to overthrow Diemos. She failed. Leaving was her only option. Silas has her contained, but I need her to survive. When the pain becomes too much, I have to go to her, and she gives me what you just did, gives me what I need to survive...for a price, until the next time."

Muttered curses and what sounded like a fist to the wall could be heard behind him. "Why didn't you tell us?" Chaos said. "We could have done something, helped you."

Zenon turned to face the other male. "No one can help me. Not even Silas has that power." But now that he didn't

SHERILEE GRAY

need that bitch to survive, maybe… "I have a few things to discuss with you all. Tomorrow night before we head out?"

Chaos looked like he wanted to disagree. Their leader wasn't known for his patience, but his gaze moved to Mia standing silently behind him and he lifted his chin in agreement. Then he moved in and held out his hand. Zenon took it, and Chaos pulled him in, one big mitt going to his back. "We will make that bitch pay. I promise you that, brother." Then he turned and strode from the room.

One by one the others did the same, showing their loyalty, letting him know they would always have his back, no matter what. Zenon didn't know what to do, what to say. Shit, he was too choked up to reply.

When they left, he turned back to Mia.

She bit her lip. "That's why you pushed me away, because of her?" Her voice was soft, shaky.

"Yes."

"Do you have feelings for her?"

He felt his face twist in disgust. "I fucking hate her."

She walked over to him and looked up. Her eyes held nothing back. It was all there to see, all the emotion she'd been hiding from him since he turned his back on her in this very room over a week ago. Jesus, he needed that, craved that look from her. His heart started bouncing around in his chest like a fucking hamster on speed.

And just when he didn't think he could take much more, she said, "Will you make love to me, Zenon?" She licked her top lip, and the sight had his cock on the verge of punching through the front of his jeans.

He didn't know if Mia had the power to set him free, but he wanted the chance to find out. What had happened just then was a goddamned miracle. Somehow Mia had cut through the hold Helena had over him. There was no way he could deny himself this.

"Mia." The single word came out rough, needy as hell. He struggled to draw breath. Was this truly happening? How could this amazing, beautiful female want *him*? He wrapped his fingers around the side of her throat, reassuring himself with the feel of her smooth, warm skin beneath his palm, the way her pulse fluttered madly, beating at the same rapid pace as his own. She was real all right, and right then she was his.

An almost violent tremor moved through his body. His need for the female standing in front of him was something he had never experienced in his entire life. No, he wasn't a virgin, but in every way that counted this would be his first time. "It would be my honor, my privilege..." He shook his head, struggling to find the words. "Being with you, in that way, it's more than I ever allowed myself to dream."

He took her hand and led her from the room.

Zenon had pushed her away, avoided her, turned his back and walked the other way when he'd seen her in the halls, but he hadn't hidden it. Even suffering her own pain, she hadn't missed it in him, the way it flashed across those yellow eyes or twisted his beautiful face. Now she knew why. Her beautiful, strong male had suffered, was still suffering, and she wanted nothing more than to make it better for him. She just wished she knew how.

Zenon didn't speak as he led her down the hall to his room, didn't say a word as he swiped his key card and opened the door. The silence was heavy, filled with anticipation.

They walked in and he turned to her. "This is your last chance to turn around and walk away because I'll never do it again. Do you understand? You're mine, Mia. I don't know what will happen after this, but know I'll protect you with my life." His chest rose and fell rapidly, his fists clenched and unclenched at his sides. "Do you understand?"

The decision wasn't a hard one. She didn't want to be anywhere else, not anymore. "Yes."

He squeezed his eyes closed for several seconds and her chest tightened.

She cupped the brand on his cheek. "Kiss me."

When his mouth came down on hers, she reveled in it, drank him in, and hung on for dear life. She'd missed this, missed him. If she was honest, she hadn't been whole without him. He lifted her off the ground, wrapped her legs around his hips, and strode through the living room into the bedroom.

"I don't think I can go slow," he growled against her ear. "I'm sorry, but I need you too badly. Shit, I don't want to fuck this up, Mia."

"Zenon." He wouldn't meet her gaze. His admission embarrassed him. "It's all right." She slid her hands up to rest on his shoulders. "Look at me. Please don't hide from me, not anymore, not now."

His eyelids slid open, yellow eyes, clear, unique, and beautiful, and she shivered at the dark intensity staring back.

Wrapping her arms around his neck, she pulled him close so their lips were touching. "I want you. And I'll take it any way you give it to me." His big body shuddered then he strode to the bed and lay her on the mattress.

He stripped off his shirt, revealing the hard ridges and sinewy muscle under all that inked skin, toed off his boots, and removed his socks. His head dipped, his hair falling forward when he dropped his hands to the button of his jeans, popping it open.

Finally, he slid down the zipper and shoved them down.

Oh my God.

Zenon stood at the foot of the bed, naked and aroused,

completely exposed—beautiful. She couldn't take her eyes off him. She couldn't speak, her synapses short-circuiting. There wasn't an ounce of excess flesh on his body. He was a honed fighting machine. He moved toward her, coming around to the side of the bed. She was mesmerized by the way he moved, like a big cat about to pounce, the way the heavy slabs of muscle bunched and shifted under his skin.

"Stand up, Mia."

She did as he said and got to her feet. Like this, they were almost the same height. He wrapped the fingers of one hand around the back of her head, thrusting his fingers into her hair, and took her mouth, kissing her deep and growling low. They broke the kiss briefly so he could lift her shirt over her head, followed by her bra. He tossed them aside and growled again right before he bent down and took an aching nipple between his lips and sucked. She clung to his shoulders while his hands moved down to work the front of her jeans, sliding them down her legs, taking her underwear with them. Then he stood back and took all of her in.

"Looking at you like that, shit, makes me forget I need to draw breath." His big callused hands slid down her sides to rest on her hips. "Lie down."

She lay back, and Zenon moved onto the mattress beside her.

"Open for me," he rasped.

Her mouth went dry with need, liquid heat flooding her sex. She did as he asked, and Zenon moved up so he was kneeling between her thighs. His dark gaze traveled over her body and she felt it like a physical touch. Without warning, he slid two thick fingers down her cleft and pressed them inside her.

She gasped and arched into the touch, a moan escaping from between her lips. "Oh God."

"You ready for me?"

She heard the desperate need in his voice.

His thumb moved over her clit with sure stokes and she squirmed, managing only to nod in reply. Zenon knew what she needed, how she like to be touched. He dominated her body like he always did, sending her need skyrocketing, and within minutes she was close.

Zenon removed his fingers, moved up, leaned in, and covered her body with his. Then his cock was prodding her entrance, sliding inside her, stretching her, filling her so thoroughly all she could focus on in that moment was where their bodies joined.

She gasped at the full sensation.

He looked down at her, tension lining his face. "You okay?"

She ran her hands over his shoulders to the side of his neck, fingers gliding over rough scar tissue. "Yes. It's just this is the first time I've done this. I don't want to disappoint you or do something wrong."

His gaze sharpened. "You're a virgin?"

"Yes."

"Fuck, Mia." He buried his face against her throat. A low groan vibrated through his chest then he lifted up again and kissed her with everything he was feeling, all the emotion he kept bottled up inside. And she felt all of it, felt it to the depths of her soul.

He cradled her face in his big hands. "You could never disappoint me, do you understand? Not ever. Shit, I don't deserve you."

Holding her gaze, he thrust forward. They both moaned when he went deep, so damn deep. He buried his face in her neck again and his thrusts became hard, rough, and he ground against her every time he pushed inside. She wrapped her legs around his hips, trailing her hands down his back, feeling the thick ridges of scar tissue crisscrossing his back beneath her fingers, and squeezed her eyes closed, trying not to think of how they got there or the pain and humiliation he must have suffered.

She tightened her hold on him. "Don't stop, please, don't stop," she whispered into his ear, letting sensation take over again. This felt amazing, right—perfect.

He lifted up on his forearms. "Look at me."

Seeing all that heat, all that unrestrained need aimed at her was all she needed. Arching her back, she cried out as her body contracted around him, gripping his repeatedly.

A low growl rumbled from deep in his throat, animistic. "You feel amazing." There was wonder in his voice and her chest tightened. She watched him, the strain on his beautiful face, the way the muscles of his chest and arms tensed and bunched as he drove into her. He was wild, his tightly held control blown all to hell.

This was the part of him he'd been holding back, the part she'd wanted him to trust her enough to reveal. She never wanted him to feel like he needed to hide any part of himself from her again, never again.

"Fuck," he hissed. Zenon didn't slow; he moved faster, drove into her harder. He thrust deep, grunting as he ground against her. Mia felt that amazing pressure building again and tightened her limbs around his big body, afraid she'd fly apart if she didn't hang on for all she was worth. Then she was coming again.

He shoved his face back into her neck. Mia loved the feel of his body pressing into hers, his weight, his harsh, ragged breaths against her skin. She felt him swell, grow bigger inside her, then he jerked his head back and his face twisted. There was a brief flash of almost panic, but then he cupped the side of her face and locked those fierce eyes with hers. "Only you, Mia. Only you." His lips parted and his eyes drifted closed. His harsh breaths turned to groans and he came inside her, his big body shaking with the force of his release.

She clung tighter to him, not wanting him to leave her.

But he didn't try and move away. He stayed where he was, still buried deep inside her. His body covered hers, hot and heavy and perfect, as he kissed and stroked her skin, making his purring sound and letting it vibrate through her.

She had no idea how long they stayed like that, tasting each other, touching, hands smoothing over slick skin— soothing each other as they came down. She wanted to stay like that forever. Running her hands over his back and hips, she held him tighter, reveling in his weight, his scent, the racing beat of his heart against hers.

"Are you all right?" he rumbled low, lips pressed against her temple.

"More than all right. You?"

"Princess." It was all he said, all he needed to say. Her name spoken in that way, in that deep raspy tone, held more meaning and emotion than anything else he could have said in that moment.

He tried to move, but she tightened her legs around him. "Not yet, don't leave me yet." She felt him start to harden inside her again.

He lifted up and started to move again, gliding in and out of her body slowly, reigniting the sparks of pleasure, bring them back to life. He leaned in and kissed her, then whispered, "Thank you."

She didn't miss the emotion on his face, dampening his eyes. Reaching up, she smoothed her fingers over his skin and wiped the moisture away. "I can't imagine what you've been through, Zenon. And I don't know if you'll ever be able to share any of it. I truly hope that one day you'll feel safe enough to share some of that burden with me." He stilled and went to dip his head, but she brushed his hair back, not letting him hide. "What I do know is just being in the same room with you gives me something that has been missing my entire life, something I never knew I needed until you walked into my apartment. Something that I've come to realize I don't want to live without."

He sucked in a harsh breath. Maybe she'd said too much, pushed too hard too soon, but right then she didn't care. She wasn't letting him send her away again. Rubbing her thumb across the vicious scars that ringed his throat, she said, "So you don't need to thank me, because there's nowhere else I would rather be, and there is no one else I will ever want to give myself to. No one else but you."

CHAPTER 16

ZENON SUCKED back oxygen until his lungs were at full capacity, but his body didn't give a shit and tried to gasp down another mouthful. So this was hyperventilating. The hype was true—it sucked.

He went down to his pillow and buried his face in all that soft red hair spread across it, focused on the feel of Mia's slick heat gripping his cock, her limbs surrounding his body —and managed to unclog his throat enough to blow out a pained breath. Her hand smoothed over his back, calming him.

She'd floored him again, like she had time and again since he'd walked into that shabby little apartment of hers all those weeks ago.

His body still hummed from the impact of his release, but it didn't matter how hard he'd come. The sheer impact of having Mia beneath him, the feel of sliding in and out of her body already had the next building.

"You are mine, Mia." The words felt ripped from his chest, a vow that could never be broken, no matter what obstacles lay in their path. It was out of his hands now; could not be denied any longer. He'd felt her reach for him while he'd made love to her, that part that recognized him as hers, the part that would bind them, make her his mate. The need to mate her fully, to take her unequivocally as his had been hard to ignore, but he had to make sure she wanted this first, make sure she understood what it meant.

Could it really be this easy?

He didn't need Helena to survive. When he found Mia, he'd gained his freedom.

He was free.

"I'm yours," she whispered back.

He surged forward and she moaned. "I want it all, Mia. I want to make you my mate." The words slipped past his lips before his brain realized what he was saying. He held his breath. He wanted it more than anything, but it didn't mean she did.

"Yes," she said.

Squeezing his eyes shut, he fought the urge to smack himself in the back of the head to make sure this wasn't all a dream. But when he opened his eyes, his beautiful female was still beneath him, looking at him in a way that nearly had him hyperventilating all over again. "There's no going back after we do this. It will be you and me forever, no one else. Do you understand?"

She arched, exposing the column of her delicate neck as he slid back inside her. Asking her while he made love to her probably wasn't playing fair, but he was locked on this course. Nothing could stop him now. "Yes, do it."

She knew what he was, what he had been, and still she wanted him. He could scarcely believe it. "If you changed your mind, if you left me, I wouldn't survive it."

Her soft warm hands moved up to his face. "I love you, Zenon."

No one had ever said those words to him before. Mia was

the first to love him, every part of him, scars and all. She saw the ones he tried to hide, saw how deep and ugly they marked him, and she loved him anyway.

"I'm never letting you go." He quickened his strokes, emotion welling in his chest as he felt that connection between them present itself. He could see it. This was it. He never thought he was good enough to have this, to have someone like her. Mia gasped and stiffened beneath him, screaming through her climax.

He reached for the connection, so damn close…

Something exploded at the base of his skull and he froze. Body shaking uncontrollably, he reared back as pain lanced through his nerve endings, nailing him from all sides. The room spun and he started to lose sight of the silver thread that would link Mia to him. It faded and shrunk back. Zenon roared and tried to reach for it, but no matter how hard he tried he couldn't catch it.

Then it was gone.

It was over.

How stupid could he be? He would never be free. Helena would always have a piece of him. Always.

Rage burned deep in his gut, ate at him like acid, and he didn't have a hope of extinguishing the inferno building inside.

Lost to it, he was blind to everything around him.

When the worst of it drained away, he became aware of the carnage around him. His room was a mess, clothes scattered everywhere, the dresser nothing but kindling. And Mia, her arms were wrapped around his waist, her chest pressed into his back, trying to restrain him as he tore and scratched at Helena's mark inked on his stomach.

"Stop, Zenon. Please stop hurting yourself." The sob that broke past her lips was what snapped him out of it.

"She won't let me go, Mia. She'll never let me go." Every

muscle on his body had locked up tight. The cold started to creep through his bones, making his teeth chatter. Helena was in this room with them, whether the bitch was aware of it or not didn't matter. She'd always be there. "I—I can't have you, s—she won't let me have you."

Mia led him back to bed, and when he lay down she moved to cover him. He rolled to his back, locking his arms around her, and she burrowed against him. The feel of her bare skin against his was amazing. She radiated warmth and he let it soak through him, soothe him.

"Listen to me." Her palms slid to his chest and she lifted up, looking down at him. "She doesn't have you, not anymore. This mark"—she dropped a hand and ran her fingers over his abs, making him shudder—"stopped us mating, but it won't stop us from being together. Do you understand? That's all that's left. That's the only hold she has over you now. I'm not going anywhere. I can give you what you need, for as long as you need it." She brushed her lips against his, giving more of her warmth, banishing the cold. "I'm yours and you're mine, as long as I live. I don't need to be your mate to know that."

He held onto her tight. He couldn't give her immortality like Kryos and Laz had given their females. He and Mia wouldn't get their eternity together. She would live longer than a human, but eventually there would be an end. Another shudder moved through his body. He didn't want to live on Earth or any other realm if Mia wasn't there with him.

When she went, he would go with her.

He pushed it from his mind, couldn't think about that now. That thought alone had the power to tip him over the edge again. "You can't leave me," he whispered. "I can't think without you here. I can't breathe without you. I don't want to."

"I love you. I'm not going anywhere." She leaned in and

pressed soft kisses against the scar ringing his throat. He buried his fingers in her hair and held her tight. Those words shook him to the core, tearing back his defenses until he felt raw and exposed. "I'll never leave you," she repeated as she moved down his body, kissing every scar, every nightmare that marked him.

Zenon trembled beneath her. His emotions were all over the place, and just the feel of her soft lips moving across his oversensitized skin had him close to coming. When she wrapped her fingers around his cock and drew him into the wet heat of her mouth, he thought he might actually die from the pleasure of it.

She sucked him, cupped him, massaging gently. It didn't take long before he felt his orgasm racing up on him. Lifting up to his forearms, he looked down his body, watching her. She glanced up, locked eyes with him, and that was all it took.

He tried to pull away, but she dug her fingers into his ass, holding him in place, her gaze never leaving his as she swallowed every hot spurt that ripped from his body in sharp, wrenching pulls. He was mindless at this point and thrust his hips up to meet her hungry mouth, crying out her name over and over until the last tremor left him. She licked him clean, sending sparks of pleasure down his shaft, then crawled up beside him and burrowed against him.

"No one's...no one's ever done that for me before," he said into her hair.

She stilled for a split second then dropped a kiss to his shoulder. "That was a first for me, too. And I loved every minute of it. So get used to it, warrior. I plan on worshipping this delectable body every day for the rest of my life."

"I'm so sorry, Mia."

"For what? For letting me in? For letting me love you?" She shook her head. "Don't ever be sorry for those wonderful gifts, because I'm not. You give me everything I need, Zenon. I don't need anything but you."

"I love you so fucking much."

She relaxed into him. "It's all we need. Don't lose sight of that. Don't let her win."

He tucked her into the side of his body, listening to her breathing slow as she drifted off to sleep. He knew the love he had for Mia would never wilt or die; it would sustain him for as long as they had together.

Their chance to mate had passed. The thread was gone, he couldn't feel it any longer, and it fucking killed him.

That bitch had taken everything from him, every goddamned thing, and he wouldn't rest until she was nothing but ash on the wind.

Chaos stood at the front of the room, tall, good looking, and oozing arrogance. Mia shouldn't smile at his discomfort, but the guy looked like he'd been thrown into a pit of snakes.

Word had gotten out about Mia's self-defense training, and with demons crawling out of the woodwork all over the city, the female demi in residence had got together and insisted someone teach them to protect themselves as well. Chaos had thought it was an excellent idea, until he'd been roped into giving a lesson.

Despite the scowl, the don't-fuck-with-me posture, and the off-the-scale attitude he was throwing out, the guy really was gorgeous. More than one female in the room watched him with hungry eyes.

Mia had been here weeks, on and off, and she still couldn't get a handle on him. He was a complete enigma.

He clapped his hands. "Right, let's get started." He called the next victim forward with a crook of his finger, and Mia had to fight not to laugh when two women nearly came to blows, fighting over who he was calling on.

"Oh my God. Did that just happen?" Eve whispered beside her.

Mia giggled. "Well, he is a good-looking guy." It was just a shame about the attitude.

"And totally clueless to the fact," Meredith said from her other side.

Mia turned to Kryos's mate. "I don't think I've ever seen him crack a smile."

"Mia." Chaos's booming voice rang out, making her jump.

"Uh-oh, you're in trouble," Meredith whispered.

She turned to face him. Oh yes, he was pissed. "Yes, sir," Mia called back then stood to attention, imitating his stance. Legs apart, hands clasped behind her back.

Eve and Meredith tried to cover their giggles by coughing and failed miserably. She was being juvenile, pushing it, but he'd been such an asshole to her on more than one occasion she kind of wanted a little payback. He underestimated her, had from the moment he'd laid eyes on her.

His jaw tightened. "You think this is funny? I would have thought you of all people would pay more attention."

Ass. "No, sir. I don't think this is funny. Not at all, sir."

"Oh my God," Eve gasped.

"You think you have this covered?" he asked, challenge clear in his deep voice.

Great. Maybe this wasn't such a fantastic idea. "Well, I—"

"Front of the class. Time to show the rest of us your mad skills."

"You've done it now," Meredith mumbled.

Mia moved to the front of the room and waited to see what Chaos would do next. For some reason he had it in for her. She didn't know what his problem was, but she'd had enough. Zenon had stressed on more than one occasion during their one-on-one sessions that he could take whatever she could dish out, but still she'd held back, afraid she might hurt him. Which was ridiculous. These guys fought demons every day. Seriously hurting Chaos was an impossibility. And right then she kind of wanted to inflict some pain on the guy.

Without warning, he came at her. Taken by surprise, she tried to dodge his strike, but he changed tack, shoved her back then hooked his ankle around hers and swept her feet out from underneath her. The extra momentum had her hitting the mat hard.

While she was still sprawled on the mat, flailing, winded, and gasping for breath, he spoke to the class again like she didn't exist. Like he'd made his point, made her the example of what *not* to do.

"You see Mia here? This is what happens when you don't listen to your instructor." His booted feet moved to her line of vision. "Up," he barked in that clipped way that set her teeth on edge.

He sounded like Zenon when they'd first started training.

Anger welled up inside her. She didn't need his shit. She'd had enough to deal with without this arrogant jerk taking pot shots every chance he got.

Stepping forward, he held out a hand. She went to take it, but then he grinned like he'd won. Like she'd proven whatever unflattering opinion he had of her.

Before she could think about what she was doing, she kicked out, nailing him in the balls. Which was kind of an accident, but whatever. When he doubled over, she slammed her foot into his knee like she had with Zenon then swept his feet out from underneath him. His big body slammed into the mat and she jumped to her feet, stood over him like he had her, and said, "Better?"

He shook his head, still cupping his balls. "You fight like a girl."

Wrong thing to say. Making a fist like Zenon had shown

her, and using the weight and momentum of her body, she dropped to one knee, punching him as hard as she could. Bone crunched—she wasn't sure whose bones for a moment, her hand throbbed so bad—but then he rolled to his side, cursing and growling, blood spurting from his nose all over the blue mat.

"You're damned right I fight like a girl," she said.

The room went utterly silent behind her, and she winced as she turned to face her audience. There was more than one mouth hanging open. The astonished silence was broken by booming laughter.

Zenon must have come in sometime during her little display and now clutched his gut, propped against the wall by the door. Kryos wasn't in any better shape beside him. And Rocco was laughing so hard he'd dropped to the floor and was gasping for breath and wiping his eyes.

Chaos stepped in front of her and she jumped. The guy obviously had a quick recovery time. He lifted the bottom of his shirt and wiped the blood from his nose, then offered her a huge full-on white-toothed smile that transformed his face from extremely good looking to off the charts. "Nice work."

Humiliation heated her face to the point her eyes started to water. "I—I ah…"

"But next time, I'd appreciate it if you went easy on the jewels. I prefer them on the outside of my body."

That statement was punctuated by more of Rocco's howling laughter.

Yeah, she knew what just happened was a major fluke, never to be repeated. Chaos obviously hadn't believed she'd go to those extremes and she'd managed to seriously surprise him, but she'd take it. "I'll certainly take your suggestion on board," she said, letting her own grin loose.

The session ended, since she'd broken their instructor,

and as the room started to clear Zenon walked over and snuggled against her back, wrapping his arms around her waist. "Do you have any idea how hot that was?" he said against the shell of her ear. "I knew you could do it."

She looked at him over her shoulder and arched a brow. "You liked that?"

"Fuck yeah, I liked it." Her body heated like it always did when Zenon was near.

Chaos had moved to the other side of the room to grab his towel, and Mia could see him watching her and Zenon, his head tilted to the side like a curious lion.

He pushed away from the wall and came back over to them. "Look, Mia. I'm sorry if I've come across as a hard-ass, but you need to be strong. There's no room for weakness in our world. With the way things are at the moment..." He left the rest of that sentence hanging.

His sharp gaze slid to Zenon, who tightened his arms around her. When Chaos looked back at her, his dark eyes held a weight that looked far too heavy for one man to carry alone.

"We've already lost one brother because his mate was taken from him. I can't..." He ran a hand over the smooth surface of his shaved and tattooed head. "I just wanted you to know that you did good, Mia."

That one sentence said so much about the hard, controlled male in front of her, and she had to swallow the lump that had formed in her throat. "Thank you. And I'm sorry about the, ah...the..." She motioned to his below-the-belt area.

He grinned and inclined his head, stopping her before she said something really embarrassing, then without another word headed to the door. As he passed her troublemaking friends, they started up with the giggles again. And without breaking his stride, Chaos pinned them to the spot with a dark glare. "Your turn tomorrow. Be ready."

Their giggles stuttered to an abrupt stop, and it was Mia's turn to laugh.

CHAPTER 17

ZENON JERKED his ax to free it from the demon's convulsing body, then swung once more to remove its head. Blood splattered his face and covered the pavement. All around the underground parking lot, bodies littered the ground. It was like every demon in the city had crawled out of their holes and decided to alert the world of their presence.

They still didn't know who was behind the influx. Helena had denied it, and even with her increasing power, this just wasn't in her skill set. No, someone else had to be responsible for this. But so far they were coming up blank. Blinded by a powerful block that made it impossible for them to track the puppet master of this shit show.

He wiped the blade of his axe on the demon's shirt. For the last few days he'd felt Helena trying to reach out to him, calling him to her.

He should have been close to death by now, but thanks to Mia he hadn't suffered an attack in several weeks. The bitch was growing impatient. He wasn't stupid enough to think she'd just let him walk, and that could only mean bad things for all of them if he didn't do something.

"Fuck." Lazarus's low curse sent a thread of unease down his spine. Spinning, he saw what the other knight was focused on. More demons swarmed down the exit ramp toward them. And like the warehouse and cemetery, he hadn't felt them coming.

The odds were now utter shit. And none of them were getting out of this without the need of a Band-Aid or ten.

Chaos swung his sword in a deep arc, the blade making a whistling noise that cut through the sounds of war. The demons leading the attack slowed, fear palpable in their glazed, unfocused eyes. Despite their obvious reluctance, they lifted their weapons and came at them. Zenon used his axes to cut through the demons in front of him, making a beeline to Rocco.

They stood back to back and faced the hordes surrounding them. Gunner and Chaos took a similar stance, as did Laz and Kryos.

"Okay, boys," Rocco called out, his voice echoing off the concrete walls and low ceiling. "I've got somewhere I gotta be in an hour, so can we wrap this up real quick?" He was breathing hard, his heart hammering against Zenon's back, matching his own adrenaline-fueled pulse. He knew as well as the rest of them they were in serious trouble.

"We'll do our best," Chaos called from his position a few yards away.

Lazarus waved a hand at the *Walking Dead* cast circling him and Kryos, sending them scattering. After mating, and the increased power that came from it, he and Kryos had a few extra tricks up their sleeves. But like anything, as they tired and their energy levels dropped, their powers weakened as well.

"Yeah, and if you could try not to fuck up my jacket. Eve's gonna be all kinds of pissed if I destroy another one. She only bought me this one last week."

Demons came at them from all sides. He'd no sooner cut one down before another had taken its place. He didn't know how long it went on, but the more hits he took the more he tired. As did his brothers.

Zenon watched in horror as Chaos went down. Gunner was unable to help him, busy fighting off two demons of his own. No one else was close enough. A demon closed in, lifting its knife to finish Chaos off. An agonized roar tore from Zenon's throat as the blade flashed on a downward arc...

A bolt slammed into the demon's chest, throwing it back. Gunner was on it, removing its head with a battle cry that lifted the hair on the back of Zenon's neck. It ashed out moments later.

A figure dressed in black, like a fucking ninja, stood on the far side of the building, crossbow raised in the air. More of them moved in from behind and proceeded to pick demons off one by one.

Chaos stumbled to his feet and the knights closed in around him, waiting until he was solid. As soon as he was, he waded back in.

With their faces concealed, Zenon had no idea who fought by their sides, and at that point he didn't care. If they could help him and his brothers, and make sure he returned to Mia in one piece that was all he cared about.

In no time the place was cleared, and only the knights and the posse dressed in black remained. They stood on opposite sides of the blood-soaked concrete that would soon be nothing but ash, and stared at each other. Chaos stepped forward, clutching a deep cut to his side. His fist clenched and unclenched as they stood silently waiting for what would happen next. One of theirs stepped forward as well, build petite and obviously female.

"Who are you?" Chaos asked.

She shook her head.

"You know of our world." It wasn't a question.

She shrugged.

Chaos tilted his head to the side and his dark eyes narrowed, studying the female in front of him before he said roughly, "Demi." Zenon sensed it then. They were all demi-demons, every last one of them. Her frame tensed and she took a step back. "Not another step." Chaos's voice was low and full of warning.

"Or what?" the female called back, humor lacing her words.

"I'm not in the mood to play games, female."

"I saved your life, knight. I would've thought you'd be a little more grateful."

Zenon heard him grind his teeth. "You could have gotten yourselves killed. Take off the masks."

She snorted. "The only one I saw close to meeting his maker was you, Chaos."

Chaos's big shoulders stiffened.

Lifting a hand in the air, she did some kind of signal with her fingers and the little army at her back started to move, drifting into the shadows. "I'll see you around, knight."

Then they were gone.

They all stood there stunned for several seconds. Rocco staggered to the front, his body battered and leaking from several injuries. He scrunched his face and rubbed a hand over his short mohawk. "Well, fuck me."

Chaos hadn't taken his gaze off the spot the now absent female had been. "Let's get out of here."

As they headed for the exit, dread raced up behind him, wrapped around him, and pulled him to a stop.

He watched his brothers take to the skies but didn't follow. Sucking in a breath, he turned to face the male now standing behind him.

Dressed in a dark suit, tall and well built, he stood with hands loose at his sides, glossy black hair combed back, making his wide black eyes seem huge. He took Zenon in, a slow perusal from head to toe. There was curiosity in their depths, nothing else.

"It's been a while, Zenon."

"What do you want?"

"I think it's time we had a talk, you and I." That low raspy voice skittered across his skin, making the hair on his arms lift.

"We have nothing to discuss."

He stepped forward and a grin tugged at the corners of his mouth. "Ah, but that's where you're wrong."

Mia woke to inky darkness, and though she couldn't see or hear a thing, she felt his presence. Sitting up, she reached for the lamp. "Zenon?"

Rough hands appeared out of nowhere, stopping her. He made no sound as he climbed into bed, pulling her beneath him. His mouth came down on hers and she whimpered, opening for him without thought of resistance. She would never deny him, couldn't, didn't want to. Her need matched his, always. His tongue delved into her mouth, rubbing against hers, sucking, nipping, kissing her so deeply she felt dizzy with her hunger for him.

"Please, Mia. Please, princess," he groaned as he slid rough, needy hands down over her waist and yanked up the T-shirt she wore. Her naked breasts grazed his chest, causing them to tighten and swell. He was naked, and his skin and hair were still damp from the shower.

"Lift your arms," he rasped then pulled the soft fabric over her head. His warm breath gusted across her bare skin, rushing from between his lips and fanning the tips of her peaked nipples.

She moaned when his mouth came down on hers again and kissed him back greedily. As out of control as he seemed, she knew he was holding back, his body hard as stone, rigid from the effort of fighting back his instincts.

He was always gentle, almost reverent with her body, but this—this was different. There was neediness to his movements, a desperation she didn't understand. Mia gasped when the hard ridge of his cock brushed her sex through her panties. He settled between her thighs, painfully hard and thick, his flesh so hot she felt branded by it.

He flexed his hips, rubbing up against her, and in minutes Mia was mindless with desire for him. Shoving the delicate fabric of her underwear to one side, he spread her open and massaged her aching center with thick, clever fingers, using the slickness of her arousal to slide over her highly sensitive clit repeatedly. "Please, Zenon. I need you."

"So wet, princess. All mine."

"Yes," she groaned.

The sound of fabric tearing broke past their harsh breathing. He tossed aside the tattered remains of her panties then Zenon moved down, taking her aching nipple into his mouth and biting down. She cried out, trying to press her hips into his, needing him inside her. He removed his fingers and stopped her movements by lying heavily on top of her. Spreading her thighs, he used his weigh to keep her that way. His tight abs rested against her swollen sex, stopping her from moving, from reaching for the release she so desperately needed. He continued to torment her, sucking and nipping at her nipples until she was writhing and begging beneath him.

"Gonna fuck you now, Mia." His voice was ragged, and his body shook almost violently. "Open wide for me, princess. I want deep inside you. Fuck you so hard you'll feel branded. You'll never forget you're mine."

That would never happen. He belonged to her as well. She just wished he believed that. Mia knew the fact they could never be mated bothered him, and it killed her to see him so insecure. Did he doubt the way she felt about him?

Whatever had happened tonight had brought this on. He needed this, needed to know she wasn't going anywhere, that she loved him. She threaded her fingers through the damp silk of his hair and pressed her lips against his throat. "Always," she whispered against his skin. "I love you."

"Fuck, Mia." The head of his cock pushed inside her. He was big, and when he shoved her knees higher, she gasped at how deep he went. The sweet agony of it had her sex flooding with liquid heat after every measured stroke.

"You belong to me." His voice was filled with hunger and yearning. He thrust into her hard. "Say it."

"I belong to you."

He growled, the sound wild and untamed, and then he unleashed the full measure of his need. And she realized up until then just how much he'd suppressed it, suppressed that side of himself. The thick head of his cock pounded deep inside her, hitting the exact spot she needed him. Squeezing the hard flesh of his ass, she lifted her hips to meet his thrusts. Her back bowed as her climax hit her, and she screamed with the force of it.

Zenon didn't slow, drawing it out with every deep thrust. His body stiffened and he groaned, making the most erotic sound she'd ever heard as he pumped into her, filling her up.

She'd barely recovered when he rose and flipped her onto her belly, lifting her hips so her ass was in the air. He cupped her sex, massaging her, circling her clit until she was a writhing, whimpering mess. "Oh God." She moved against his hand restlessly as another orgasm built.

"So fucking, hot, so beautiful." He pushed two fingers inside her and her muscles began to quiver. One more brush over her clit and she'd explode. She felt him move in closer and then his fingers were gone, but before she could whimper in protest, he thrust his cock back inside her. Mia cried out as her second climax flowed through her. Zenon fucked her through it, his powerful thrusts going deeper than ever before. Gripping her hips, he came again, milking his body with hers until he'd rung every last tremor from his body.

He gently rolled her onto her back and brushed the hair away from her face. Her eyes had adjusted to the dark, and her belly flipped at the intensity of his gaze.

Leaning down, he kissed her shoulder before climbing out of bed. He returned a moment later with a warm damp washcloth and carefully, almost reverently cleaned her.

After throwing it in the hamper, he crawled onto the bed and trailed hot wet kisses from her ankle to the sensitive skin of her inner thigh, until his lips were mere inches from her sex. And even after all the orgasms he'd already given her, she felt her need rise again, wanting more of him.

Spreading her open, he lifted his gaze to hers. His tongue darted out and he soothed her oversensitive flesh with gentle, warm strokes. "You taste so good, Mia, so sweet. I love that I can taste myself mixed with you." He lapped at her again and moaned in pleasure.

Mia bit down on her lip, his erotic words hitting her low in her belly. His dark head between her parted thighs, his powerful shoulders and chest bunching and straining with every move he made, was a sight she would never tire of, not ever.

His movements became restless, almost desperate. The quietness of the moment dissolved, and he cupped her ass in his big hands, holding her tight to his mouth, eating at her like he was starving for her, like he couldn't get enough. Mia threaded her fingers in his hair and ground her hips against him, needing more. When she came, Zenon pushed his tongue inside her, sucking at her greedily, making her quake beneath him.

Boneless, she felt him press a kiss to her inner thigh before climbing in beside her and pulling the covers over them.

"I love you, Mia," he whispered before tucking her into his side and wrapping her tight in his arms.

Her last thought before drifting off was that she needed to talk to him when she woke and find out what was bothering him.

But when she woke the next morning—he was gone.

CHAPTER 18

MIA'S PHONE beeped and she raced over to check it.

Call you when I can.

Zenon's reply did not ease her worry. Not one damn bit. She hadn't seen him for three days, and if it hadn't been for the delicious way her body ached the day he left without so much as a goodbye, she'd think that night had been nothing but a dream.

The way he'd taken her, the needy, desperate way he'd clung to her.

Something was wrong.

Closing her eyes, she tried to calm the unease churning in her stomach. It had almost been like he was trying to tell her something…

Like he was saying goodbye.

No. She couldn't think that. They'd been in regular contact, texting several times day. He'd replied like he always did, if a bit distant, telling her he missed her but he was busy and wasn't sure when he'd be back. She knew there were demons causing trouble all over the city, but something didn't feel right.

Chaos had even tried to reassure her, but she hadn't missed the covert glances they gave each other when she asked about him. They were hiding something from her, and it was driving her crazy.

She didn't want to believe Zenon would keep secrets from her, but she didn't buy it. She wasn't going to let him run away and hide this time. Keeping something from her that was seriously bothering him wasn't going to fly. Not now.

It'd been weeks since she'd left the compound. And she didn't see that changing anytime soon, especially after one of the demons they had locked up below the compound escaped two days ago. The knights had gone into full-on overprotection mode, and she and the others staying there had been further restricted.

No, her only option was to sneak out. She hated to do it, but she had to see Zenon, make sure he was all right with her own two eyes. Thanks to some snooping on the control room computers—in the guise of online shopping—and the GPS installed in Zenon's phone, she knew the area he was patrolling. She'd just text him when she got to that part of town, tell him where she was, and wait for him to come to her. No leaving the car, no taking any unnecessary risks. Simple.

Of course, Chaos wouldn't see it that way, hence the sneaking.

The lift doors slid open and she pulled the keys for the black SUV closest to the basement door from her pocket. She knew from watching the live feeds in the control room that there was a blind spot and as long as she could get in without anyone seeing who was driving, she might have a chance.

She climbed in, started it up, and drove out of the parking garage. That was the easy part. Now her escape would be broadcast to whoever was on watch tonight. The knights were the only ones who could enter without waiting to be let in manually, if they were travelling by car. Everyone else needed to be cleared by camera. Hopefully, if someone was watching they'd assume it was one of the knights driving the SUV. She'd found Zenon's bike keys in the bedside drawer, and she pulled them out of her bag, used the small remote attached to activate the gates, and held her breath.

The metal giants shuddered then kicked into action, sliding open to reveal the dark deserted road beyond the compound. Surrounded by abandoned warehouses and empty lots, the place the knights called home was private, out of the way, and about as far from homely as you could get.

Glancing in the rearview mirror, she watched the gates slide shut behind her and released an anxious breath.

It took forty minutes to drive into Roxburgh and head to the other side of the city. The well-lit streets appeared to be lined with high-end shops and upscale apartments.

It was raining hard, and she had the wipers on full to navigate the unfamiliar streets. The car's GPS told her she was on Jacobson. This was where the compound's computer tracking software said Zenon was located. Pulling over, she looked out the window but couldn't see much through the sheets of rain pouring down.

Taking a deep breath, she keyed in a quick text telling him where she was and asking if he could come to her. He'd be pissed with her for leaving the compound, but what did he expect when he was doing his best to shut her out again?

"Not this time, buddy," she muttered under her breath.

It seemed to take ages, but finally he answered. *Don't move. Sending someone to bring you up to me.*

Okay. So he wasn't working alone. That thought helped her relax. He had someone at his back. Thank God.

Mia jumped and let out a shriek when, minutes later, a

dark figure banged on the driver's door. She opened the window a crack.

"Mia?"

"Yes."

"I've come to take you to Zenon."

If this this guy was some random nutjob he'd have no way of knowing her name or Zenon's.

She opened the door, and the guy took her arm immediately and rushed her across the street and through the doors to one of the apartment buildings. When they got in the elevator, he glanced down at her and grinned. "So you're Zenon's female."

"Is he all right?"

"He's fine." His grin turned wicked. "Though I'm not sure how happy he'll be when he sees you."

Crap. Perhaps coming here hadn't been such a great idea. She didn't want to add to his worries. Well, it was too late to go back now. He'd just have to get over it. Maybe next time he wouldn't run off without telling her first. "How long have you known Zenon?"

He chuckled, and the raspy sound sent a shiver down her spine. "Oh, I've known Zenon for a very long time. We go way back."

The elevator opened to a large entryway. Her escort led her to a set of double doors and knocked once.

It swung open and a tall woman in a beautifully tailored deep scarlet dress stood looking down at her. Her hair was dark, long, and glossy. Her almost black eyes traveled over Mia from head to toe, and the tight-lipped curiosity turned dark with disdain.

"I, ah...I think I'm at the wrong place." Mia took a step back, but the silent male at her side halted her retreating steps.

"No, you're right where I want you. Please, come in."

Why would Zenon be here with this woman? Everything in her told her to go in the other direction, to get out of there. But Zenon had told her he was sending someone down for her, and these people had been expecting her, so pushing aside her misgivings, she stepped over the threshold. The woman started across the room and without looking back crooked a slender red-tipped finger over her shoulder. "This way."

When they entered what she guessed was the living room, the woman stopped and turned to face her. "You really shouldn't have come, demi. Now you've left me no choice."

"What are you talking about? Where's Zenon?"

The woman's beautiful features twisted into what could only be described as utter loathing as she gave Mia a slow perusal from head to toe. She glanced at the male standing behind Mia. "What can he possibly see in such a frumpy little mouse?"

"Excuse me?" *What a bitch.*

"What you don't understand, little mouse, is that Zenon is mine...and that will never change."

That's when she felt the dark power radiating from other woman. This was her, the woman who kept Zenon as her slave. Fear for him gripped her, making her knees weak and a cold sweat coat her skin. "Where is he? What have you done to him?"

"Nothing he doesn't beg for. I promise you that." The sadistic heat in her eyes made Mia's stomach churn and acid flood the back of her throat.

Oh God. Oh God, no.

Reaching behind her, the woman grabbed the door handle at her back and pushed the door wide. "See for yourself."

Her feet took her forward, while fear at what she was about to see seized the breath in her lungs.

The room was dim, but she had no trouble seeing him. A sob burst from her throat. His lifeless form was strung up on some steel contraption, his arms and feet spread wide and shackled to the framework. He was completely naked, his beautiful skin scratched and bruised.

"No." She ran to him. His head was slumped forward, his long black hair covering his face. He didn't move, didn't answer. His breathing was shallow, labored.

She spun around. "What have you done to him?"

"He defied me. This is the price he paid." She sneered. "You can blame yourself for his condition. He took this punishment to keep you safe. You failed him, made all he's suffered for nothing, because now he will watch you die."

Mia barely managed two steps before she was grabbed and thrown roughly onto the bed in the center of the room. The male she now realized was a demon pulled her arms and legs wide and tied her down. When he stepped back, sick anticipation covered his face.

The sadistic monster who'd spent several lifetimes making Zenon's life a living hell stepped forward, and this time when she smiled, she let her pointed teeth peek past her full lips. "Time for the real fun to begin."

Helena fucking him up more than he already was wasn't Zenon's only problem, because right then his mind was playing tricks on him. He could smell Mia. Smell the woman he craved with every fiber of his being. He sucked in another breath and his gut tightened.

Tilting his head, he listened for movement but couldn't hear a thing. Not when his pulse pounded so hard it felt like someone was playing a fucking drum solo against his eardrums.

Helena wasn't in the room, he knew that much. A low buzz vibrated over his skull, the same feeling he got whenever she used her powers. She was in one of her trances somewhere else in the penthouse. He could feel the difference in her power, like she was on a different frequency. In that state, she could communicate with the demons she hoped would help her overthrow Diemos, could get in their heads. She wasn't aware of much when she was like that, so she'd have herself locked away in one of the rooms, have it well warded.

He tried to lift his head but it was a complete fail. His skull felt like a dead weight hanging from his neck. His limbs screamed in protest at being stretched out too long, and his muscles spasmed and knotted, sending sharp stabbing pain to his joints.

He licked his dry, split lips, and a groan slid up his throat.

Yeah, Helena was pissed. And she'd made sure he was fully clued in. He'd never seen her so full of rage. Not only had he refused to service her, but her power over him had failed. When she'd shoved him down on the bed and pumped him full of her toxic lust, his dick had remained lifeless, hanging between his legs. He'd stayed silent, letting his body show her how much she repulsed him, which had sent her into a tantrum of mass proportions.

Refusing her probably wasn't the best idea considering what he had planned, but there was no way in hell he could touch that bitch, not after Mia.

This had better fucking work.

A faint sound made it past the blood rushing through his head. He concentrated on breathing through the pain, and his head began to clear. He heard it again—a whimper. Locking his knees, he tightened his protesting muscles and forced his head up.

The blurry outline of someone came into view. Someone

was on the bed. Blinking rapidly, he worked at clearing the dried blood from around his eyes. They stung and watered, but cleared enough to see who lay there.

No. His legs collapsed from under him and agony shot through his shoulders. He shook his head. *Please let this be a nightmare, a goddamned hallucination.*

Mia.

The sound that tore from his throat was pure animal, raw and untamed, his demon taking control of his vocal cords in a roar that rattled the windows.

She was tied to the bed, at Helena's mercy. One of her filmy robes covered most of Mia's body, but it had ridden up to about mid-thigh with the way she writhed on the mattress, barely aware of her surroundings.

Zenon could smell her fear as well as the heavy scent of her arousal, could feel the deep pulsing beat of her need hitting him in the groin in heady waves. His dick answered instantly, growing heavy and hard, his balls tightening. She thrashed, trying to press her thighs together, but the restraints stopped her.

"Mia? Princess, talk to me."

She spun to face him. Relief made her sag against the mattress before another sob broke free. Now that he could see her better, he saw the tears running down her face, soaking the hair at her temples. "Zenon. I'm…" She stopped suddenly, a moan gasping past her lips. The helpless look on her face fucking killed him.

"Mia," he roared as he bucked against his restraints.

Panic flared behind her wild eyes, and she shook her head. "No, please, not again. I…I don't want…" Her pale skin flushed pink and she squeezed her eyes shut, her swollen lips parting like she did right before she… "No, please no," she sobbed.

Oh fuck no.

Her body bowed, convulsing almost violently. She cried out as if in pain. The orgasm tore through her strung body, racked her small frame with tremor after tremor. When the last moved through her, she lay there shaking with her silent tears.

He called her name, but she wouldn't open her eyes. "Mia, please, look at me."

"I'm sorry. I don't want to…I…he's making me. Oh God, I think I'm going to be sick." She lifted off the bed as much as she could with her arms and legs tied down, and turned away, heaving repeatedly.

He? Zenon looked around the dim room, and a growl ripped from his chest when he spotted Amen, the sex demon from the club, sitting by the door, his uninjured hand down his pants, stroking his dick while he watched Mia. Zenon had been so focused on her he hadn't even noticed him in the room. He was using his power on Mia. Zenon could feel it this time.

Somehow he'd escaped the compound.

"Stop," he roared.

A grin spread across the demon's face.

"Don't you even fucking look at her."

"Nice to see you're awake, drudge." He didn't stop stroking himself. Having another audience member only seemed to increase his excitement. "See how your female comes for me? See how badly she wants it? I don't think I've ever seen anything more beautiful. But she's suffered long enough." He looked back to Mia. "Shh now. I know how it aches. I'll make it all better."

Zenon fought so hard he felt his shoulder pop out of the socket. "Touch her and I'll cut off your balls and make you fucking eat them before I slit your skinny throat."

Amen stood, jeans undone around his hips, still working the turgid flesh jutting from his body as he moved toward the bed. "Well, you're not really in a position to make threats, now are you? I was waiting for you to wake so you could watch me put her out of her misery."

Zenon tugged harder at his restraints, ignoring the pain screaming through his body, the way his raw flesh tore from his wrists and ankles. Mia was struggling, blood leaking from beneath the ropes tying her to the bed.

This couldn't be happening. Being here was supposed to ensure Mia's safety. He'd come here this one last time, taking the only chance he'd get to gain his freedom—to be with the female he loved.

He watched Amen stand beside the bed and run his fingers down her bare arm. "I feel as though I already know you so well." He pulled Zenon's cell phone out of his pocket and dropped it on the bedside table. "I've enjoyed our little chats back and forth."

Zenon growled and continued to fight, tried to break free, but it was hopeless—he was hopeless. He had failed her in the worst possible way.

The bones in his hand shattered when he pulled against the steel restraining him with every bit of remaining strength. He barely felt it, his entire focus locked on Mia.

She turned her head away from the demon at her side and held his gaze. "I love you," she whispered.

Zenon cried out, his heart shredding into a million pieces. She didn't look away from him as Amen climbed onto the bed beside her, her hollow stare desolate, broken. Zenon's frantic struggles were useless. He couldn't get free. He couldn't save her. And as the demon moved to cover her, his soul screamed, rendering him wide open.

Mia flinched.

She'd heard it, too.

CHAPTER 19

BELOW THE WAIST, she was swollen and hungry—above the waist, her stomach revolted and she was on the verge of throwing up.

Her body had been taken hostage, and Zenon would be forced to watch as that creature used her.

"You ready for me, honey?" The bastard cupped her face, but she refused to look at him and kept her gaze locked on Zenon. As soon as she got the chance, she planned to scratch his eyes out.

He ran a finger down the side of her face. "You'll enjoy what I do to you. I promise you that."

She shuddered and started to retch again.

Anger welled up inside her. Her power stirred, tightening in her chest, but something forced it back, locked it down. She cried out.

The bastard laughed. "Your powers are useless here," he said to her. "Isn't that right, Zenon?"

Zenon roared again, his struggles so violent the steel frame bolted to the ground shook.

She swallowed back her sob and held Zenon's wild gaze.

He howled like a wounded animal, a helpless beast, as his eyes flashed between yellow and black. His face contorted suddenly and his fangs burst from the top of his mouth, extended long and white and sharp down over his chin.

She heard Amen suck in a breath.

Then suddenly, he was gone, and the sound of Amen's body colliding with the wall came next.

Whatever spell he had over her lifted and she sagged back.

Gentle hands moved the flimsy fabric of her robe down to cover her, and Zenon broke eye contact, looking at whoever stood beside her.

A tall male stared down at her, expression filled with concern. "You're all right now," he said to her. His voice was deep, gentle.

In her shocked state, she noticed he was handsome in an odd kind of way. His wide black eyes looked at her with a tenderness that softened what she imagined could be hard features. He wore a beautiful suit and shiny black shoes. She knew this man. He'd helped her the night of her attack. He began to untie her, being careful of her damaged skin.

"No one will hurt you again. I promise you that." The fierce way he said it made her believe it was true.

"I'm sorry. I'm so sorry," Zenon gasped out.

Stumbling to her feet, she tried to go to him, but her legs gave out from under her. Her rescuer scooped her up in his arms and held her protectively to his chest. For some reason, she didn't fear this man. He'd helped her twice now. "Please, untie him."

His brows drew together. "I'm sorry, sweetheart, I can't do that." She started to struggle, tried to push away, get to her feet, and go to Zenon, but he was strong and tightened his hold on her.

His big body stiffened, and seconds later the door was

opened and Helena breezed back into the room, her silky dark hair swinging around her waist. Her sharp gaze took in the scene then narrowed on Mia's rescuer. "Marcus."

"Are you happy to see your brother alive and well, Helena?" Sarcasm dripped from his voice.

"Of course." The sneer on her face said the complete opposite. This was not a happy reunion. "Sneaky as always, I see."

Marcus inclined his head, a humorless smile curving his lips.

"You can't have her," Helena said, waving her hand in Mia's direction.

"You can't stop me, and you know it. We're closely matched, you and I. In fact, I'm pretty sure I have the advantage." Her eyes flared. "But if you want a fight, I will happily oblige."

She stepped forward, and lifting a beautifully manicured hand, picked up a lock of Mia's hair, studying it like the red strands held some kind of answer. "Why?"

"Mia is my daughter."

Her father? Oh my God. Her father was alive.

The bitch sucked in a breath, the hatred that flared sharp enough to cut her to the quick.

Realization moved over her face, and her glare slid to Zenon. "She can sustain you?"

Zenon didn't answer.

Hatred rolled off Helena in waves. "If I let you keep your daughter, you must give me your word that you will not come after Zenon. He is mine and he stays with me."

"No." Mia started to fight again, but he restrained her with no effort.

"I will agree to your terms with one caveat: you will leave anyone with my blood in their veins alone. You go against me on this, and I will find a way to kill you."

Mia gasped for oxygen, agony gripping her chest at the thought of never seeing Zenon again, of leaving him in the hands of that monster. She dug her nails into the arms banded tightly around her, trying to break free. She fought and screamed, hysterical in her need to get to him.

"Mia." The strength in Zenon's voice broke through the haze and she looked over at him. She took in his ravaged face, his swollen lips, the pain in his yellow gaze. "This is how it must be."

"No. You can't mean that." Her words were barely coherent past her sobs.

He looked down. "Take her away."

Without another word, she was carried from the room. She watched over her father's shoulder as the bitch, a woman she now knew was her aunt, smiled coldly. Zenon's head remained down, his hair obscuring his damaged face. His body sagged in the steel frame again, lifeless. She called to him, but he didn't look up.

Another sob tore from her throat as she fought to get free.

Helena closed the door.

Oh God. She'd never see him again.

Mia was bundled, fighting and screaming, into a waiting limo a short time later. The man who claimed to be her father climbed in after her, trying to subdue her.

She grabbed at him and tore at his jacket. "Please, go back for him. We can't leave him there." She was crying, her words almost unintelligible.

He gave her another one of those sympathetic looks. "You must trust him."

"W-what do you mean? What aren't you telling me?" She'd gotten a glimpse of that woman's powers. How could anyone best her?

"Please, Mia. You need to calm yourself."

She gripped his arm tighter. "The man I love is in the hands of pure evil, and you want me to be calm?"

He ran a hand through his black hair. "He knows what he's doing."

Mia looked across at Marcus, her *father*, and forced herself to slow her breathing and her still racing heart. They'd been driving around the city for several hours. He refused to let her out because he didn't trust her not to go after Zenon on her own. Which was perceptive. She knew she couldn't win, but she couldn't just sit by and do nothing either.

He also wouldn't give her the damned answers she wanted.

"Tell me," she tried again. "Please."

"You need to trust that Zenon knows what he's doing," he said again for the millionth time.

Mia threw up her hands. "Jesus, you sound like Chaya, talking in damn riddles. What is he doing?"

A smile spread across his handsome face. "How is she? I've been so busy watching you I've not seen her in several months."

Mia stilled. "She knows about you?"

"Yes. But only after she gained her powers. Like you, I've watched her from a distance."

"I can't believe this." How could Chaya keep their father's existence from her?

Marcus shook his head. "I'm so sorry. I know I failed you, Mia. I thought you were safe within the compound walls."

"How long?" she breathed.

"Have I been watching you?"

She dipped her chin.

"Always." Sadness and longing transformed his handsome face. "Your mother, too, until she passed away."

"Why?" Why did you leave? Why did you stay away all these years? Why did you let my mother die of a broken heart? All the questions she'd carried around her whole life swam through her mind.

"Your mother knew why I had to leave. She knew I loved her, loved you and your sister. But I couldn't risk your safety. When Helena escaped Hell, she was weak for many, many years. She was no threat to me or my family. But I sensed the growth in her power over time. I knew eventually she would be strong enough to escape her prison. And I knew once that happened she would come after me and mine. I couldn't allow that, couldn't allow her to hurt the people I loved most." He paused. "You see, I betrayed her, destroyed her chances to overthrow Diemos. Diemos may be an evil bastard, but Helena is far worse."

It was too much to process, especially when all she could think about was Zenon alone with that evil, heartless monster. He leaned over and squeezed her knee. "You have to trust him."

She shoved him away, shaking her head. "Why didn't you help him?"

"It was too much of a risk."

"Is he...is Zenon going to try and free himself from her?" she said, voice shaky.

He held her gaze. "Yes."

"You planned this together?"

"Well, not the part where you showed up and nearly got yourself killed." Pain and guilt twisted his striking features. "Despite her promise, you will never be safe from your aunt. Zenon knows this. As soon as she knew of your existence, you became her target. We must follow this course. She now knows you are his mate and my daughter. This is Zenon's only chance to break free. She will never allow him to be with you, and she won't let you live if Zenon doesn't go with her."

How could this be happening? She stared over at the male in front of her and saw where Chaya got her dark coloring, the determined tilt to her jaw, and held his gaze. "He could die, couldn't he?"

"Yes," he said, not pulling any punches. "But at least he'd finally be free."

It was the eve of the equinox, and power stirred through Zenon's blood. The excitement vibrating from Helena wrapped around him and crawled over the surface of his skin. Made him want to take an acid shower to scrub it off.

Taking a deep breath, and using her newly regained powers, Helena claimed her freedom. He expected to find Silas waiting for them, but there was no sign of the angel.

That male did nothing without reason, and his absence meant whatever was about to happen—good or bad—was meant to.

"No sign of that bastard Silas," Helena said beside him, like she'd read his thoughts.

Wrapping her hand around his arm like they were taking a fucking stroll in the park, she tugged him into motion. The night before, she'd given him a small boost of power, enough to heal most of his injuries, but not enough that he could attempt an escape. Not that he had any intention of running.

Nine days had passed since Mia had cried out his name and he'd watched her father carry her away from him. Nine excruciating days of wondering if she was all right, of missing her so bad it surpassed any punishment Helena had dished out. Being separated from her was killing him.

They walked into the elevator and Helena stared in confusion at the buttons. Watching her flounder gave him a small measure of enjoyment.

Her grip tightened painfully on his forearm. "Why are we in this box? I don't like it."

"It takes us out of the building." He punched the button for the ground floor and her eyes widened in alarm. Helena had been contained since they escaped Hell many, many years ago, controlled and moved around by Silas. This was her first taste of the outside world.

When they walked out of the building and onto the street, she looked around with something close to fear and not a little wonder. "I can see why Diemos wants to conquer this realm."

The closer they got to the portal, the more alive Zenon's senses became. He felt his brothers nearby. Mia's father would have spoken to them, like they'd agreed. Told them what was going to happen here tonight, what was at stake. That there was no other option.

That Zenon had to do this alone.

Filling them in was the only way to ensure they didn't try to stop what was about to happen.

As they stepped up to the mouth of the alley, Zenon's chest tightened.

His brothers lined the walls on either side. Chaos, Gunner, and Kryos stood to the left, while Laz and Roc stood to the right.

"What is this?" Helena hissed. "I was guaranteed a clear passage."

"Are we standing in your way?" Chaos said. The hatred in his voice was so thick you couldn't miss the fact his demon had come to the surface.

Helena's nails dug into his flesh. "If you take one step toward us, I will kill him."

A muscle in Chaos's jaw jumped, but he didn't make a move. She was too powerful for any of them to kill. He saw the moment his brother realized that, the moment he felt it. Sharp pain dimmed Chaos's dark eyes and a single tear streaked down his rough cheek. Seeing that, fuck, it hurt more than any torture Zenon had suffered in his life.

Yeah, he had no doubt Chaos had planned to try and take Helena down despite what Marcus had told them.

And now his brother knew why he couldn't.

The damage Helena could do here on Earth would be devastating, which was why she needed to go back to Hell. Besides Silas, the only beings strong enough to keep her under control were Lucifer and Diemos, and Chaos understood it now.

His brother stood rock solid. "We won't get in your way. We have a purpose here tonight, like we do every time the portal opens, as you well know."

Zenon felt the stares of each warrior trained on him as he followed in Helena's wake. But he didn't feel shame. No, he felt the strength they were giving him. He felt their respect.

Zenon looked up as he passed Rocco, their gazes locking, and fuck, he felt all the pain and helplessness his brother was feeling.

Gunner was giving off more of the same, his jaw tightening when Zenon met the warrior's eyes. Kryos was next, and the torment, the love he felt when their gazes locked had Zenon choking down the boulder in his throat.

Lazarus thumped his fist against his chest, right over his heart, and let out a battle cry that lifted the hair on the back of Zenon's neck, his anguish and rage ringing out loud and clear.

The others followed his lead, their cries echoing off the brick walls, filling Zenon to overflowing with their love and strength.

In that moment, Zenon knew if he'd only lifted his head instead of dropping his gaze in shame he would have seen the same thing from the very beginning from all his brothers.

Their hands were tied; they couldn't help him, and it was hurting them to see him this way, facing this on his own.

He couldn't fuck this up.

There was too much at stake.

The red brick wall in front of them began to flicker to life, and his brothers stepped out into the center of the alley, taking their positions, ready for whatever came out at them.

"Move to the side if you don't want to get trampled," Zenon said to Helena.

She did what he said without question. Her excitement had faded and the acrid scent of her fear replaced it. Going back was a huge risk for her, and if things went badly, she'd soon wish she was back in her ivory tower. But, like him, she was willing to risk it all, even death to gain her freedom.

Zenon clenched and unclenched his fists. This had to be timed perfectly. He didn't know how long he could survive once he stepped through to the other side.

Chaos lifted his gaze and cursed. Zenon looked up. Above them, lining the alley walls, were about ten demi dressed in black, all concealing their faces. Looked like Chaos had backup whether he wanted it or not.

"Don't move until I tell you," Zenon said.

Helena moved restlessly at his side but had a determined look on her face. She didn't fool him; she was freaking the fuck out. It had been a long time since she'd been home, and she was counting on allies that had more than likely hitched their sorry asses to the next power-hungry asshole.

The wall flashed behind them and the portal opened. Demons instantly scrambled through. Zenon pulled Helena farther to the side, out of the way. The fighting began, his brothers engaging their enemy with single-minded focus. He needed to keep it that way. The sooner he was out of sight the better.

Ropes came down the walls from above, and some of the demi descended, while others picked off demons with crossbows from above.

It was time.

The nerves in his gut weren't fluttering—no, they felt like goddamn boulders smacking into the back of his ribs. He took Helena's hand and stood in front of the portal. Before he stepped through, he turned. Chaos stood in the middle of the alley, fighting going on all around him, blood dripping from a slice to his shoulder. Their eyes met, and Zenon lifted his chin. Chaos did the same then turned away to engage the next demon gunning for him.

"All right. Let's do this," he said.

Helena sucked in a breath and they stepped through.

CHAPTER 20

THE SMELL WAS the first thing that struck him. A smell that brought to life the living nightmares of his past.

But he'd been wrong about one thing. There was no delay. He felt it straight away. The angel brand on his face, the safeguard that prevented a knight from entering Hell, was doing what it was meant to. If they became fully possessed by their demon and tried to return to Hell, they could be used as a weapon against mankind, against their brothers. That was something the angels could not allow.

He was slipping away as he stood there.

Without warning, his knees gave out and he hit the rough stone hard enough to rattle his teeth. Helena dropped to his side. "What are you doing? Stand, damn you."

He pointed to his face, to the brand Silas had given him all those years ago. "This isn't a claim of ownership. This is what will free me from you."

She reared back as if he'd slapped her, shaking her head. "No."

The realization that this was it hit him like a wrecking ball to the chest. Their planning had been for nothing. No

541

way could he get back through the portal. He could barely fucking blink, let alone get to his feet and fight his way back out. His vocal cords protested, but he forced out the words. "Thanks to Mia, I know what it is to be loved. And I would rather die happy, holding onto the memory of that, of her, than live another minute with you."

Pain flashed across her dark eyes in a rare glimpse of vulnerability, but then she fisted his hair and tugged hard. "I can't do this without you. I order you to get up, Zenon. Now."

He chuckled, a mirthless rasp that managed to hold several lifetimes of contempt for the female kneeling in front of him. "I hope you suffer before you die."

"Oh, she will." Diemos stepped from the shadows. "You've come home, Helena. How nice to see you again."

Helena stumbled to her feet. Zenon could see she was trying to use her powers, but each attempt was met with failure. She scrambled back. "No, this can't be."

"You're not the only one who's grown stronger." Diemos lifted his hand and Helena moved toward him like a puppet on a string. She tried to fight as several Orthon demons moved toward her, but her powers were no match for Diemos.

"Zenon!" she screamed as the demons took hold of her.

Zenon ignored her, refused to look at her as they carried her away to her new prison.

The light show that started up around them meant the portal was moments from closing. He squeezed his eyes closed and pictured Mia, love shining in her pale blue eyes. This place would not be the last thing he saw before he died.

His organs began to shut down one by one, his limbs growing heavy, like a great weight had been draped over his body.

"Do you enjoy soaring through the clouds, my son?" Zenon forced his eyes open at the sound of Diemos's voice.

Crouched in front of him, the new demon king of Hell watched him closely. Lifting long slender fingers, he slipped them down the buttons of his shirt, opening them one by one, revealing his bare chest. His skin was smooth, so pale Zenon could see the blue veins running beneath. He slipped it off his shoulders and turned. The stubby remains of what would have once been wings protruded from his back. When Diemos turned back to face him, he smiled. "Now you know why I crave the light."

Diemos was a fallen angel.

He crouched down and ran a cold finger down the side of Zenon's face, and for the first time Zenon looked into Diemos's eyes. Yellow, like his.

No.

The way Diemos studied him so intently, like he could see right through him, made his skin crawl, and if it hadn't been for the fact that he couldn't fucking move he'd have pulled away.

"It's why I could never claim you as my child. As a babe you didn't have the ability to conceal that part of you." He shrugged. "No one here can know what I am. The only angel tolerated in Hell was my father. They would have come after me if they knew what I was. You know that, don't you, son?"

"Lucifer's your father?" Zenon choked.

"I concealed you from him like he concealed me from the demons who worshipped him. I was a disappointment, you see. He hated that I had wings when his had been taken. That's why he took mine. He wanted another son, so I knew if he found out about you he'd cast me aside." Hatred transformed Diemos's face. "He'd want you and not me at his side. I waited, bided my time. I told him about you when Helena left with you. Your grandfather went after you. And I took a chance. Warded the portal, took my place on the throne." He slid his fingers down the side of Zenon's face. "I must thank you for that."

Zenon couldn't believe what he was hearing.

Diemos had stood back, watched him be tortured, degraded. More than once he'd dished out the punishments himself, had enjoyed every moment of the pain he'd inflicted, and all the while the bastard had known—known Zenon was his son.

"Flesh of my flesh, blood of my blood." Diemos's dark gaze traveled over him. "We are enemies now, you and I. But I will let you go."

He smiled in a way that made Zenon's skin crawl. "I plan on taking Earth as soon as I can figure out how to kill my father. He is my only real obstacle." His pupils turned midnight. "Who knows? One day I may have use of you again."

A pop and a flash of light filled the cavern, indicating their time was up—the portal was about to close. Diemos stood, taking Zenon's limp body with him, and dragged him the short distance to the opening.

"You were no mistake, my son," Diemos whispered darkly against his ear then shoved him through the hell's gate.

Zenon hit the ground hard. Blinking, he got an eyeful of red brick wall, and the smell of the city burned a path into his lungs. Lungs that were struggling to draw breath. He gasped several times, but it was no good. It was too late.

Darkness descended.

Then there was no more pain.

Mia sat wrapped in a blanket, staring at the television in front of her, but had no idea what was on. All she could see was Zenon, the way he'd looked when she was carried away.

She didn't know if he was alive or dead. All she knew for sure was he had been suffering, could still be suffering. She couldn't help him, and no one would do *anything*. Chaos refused to go in and get him out of there, wouldn't even talk about it with her—none of the knights would.

Eve told her to have faith. In what? No one was doing anything.

To make matters worse, she had a constant guard on her so she couldn't leave the compound. James followed her around like a shadow, casting her sympathetic looks and trying to distract her.

"You want to watch something else?"

She looked away from the television. James sat beside her, holding the TV remote. She shook her head. "I think I'll go to bed." Where she could smell Zenon's scent in the sheets and imagine he'd he home any minute, imagine he was there with her.

"You need to eat."

"I'm not hungry." She shrugged off the blanket and tried to stand, but James grabbed her arm.

"Mia, you haven't eaten in days. You look like shit. You want to be on death's door when your mate comes home?"

She stilled. "Is he?"

He shook his head. "I wish I knew. I hope so, for both your sakes. My guess, there's more going on than you and I know. Those guys never do anything without good reason, and it has to be something huge to stop them going in after one of their brothers."

"I can't take much more of this, James. Knowing he's with that monster. What if she's already taken him back to Hell? What if I never see him again?"

"Tonight's the equinox. If it's happening, it's happening tonight."

Mia started toward the door, but James was in front of her, blocking her escape before she touched the handle. "I have to go to him. Please, let me go."

James pulled her into him and wrapped her in his arms. "I know this is hard, Mia. But you'll only get in the way. You want him to come home safe. Getting in the way and distracting them isn't going to help him."

He was right, she knew he was, but it did little to stop her desire to get to him. She nodded against his chest, her tears soaking into his shirt. "Goddammit."

"Come on, come back and sit down. I'll make you dinner."

After she'd eaten, James pulled her into his side and ordered her to close her eyes. Not only had she not been eating, she'd barely slept.

Somehow she must have managed to drift off to sleep, because she woke to a loud *bang* and a string of curses from James. Mia shot to her feet and nearly fell to the floor with a mixture of relief and abject horror. Chaos and Rocco carried Zenon in. He was limp in their arms.

They lay him on the couch and stepped back.

"What's wrong with him?"

The look in Chaos's eyes was haunted, a mix of pure rage and soul-destroying agony. "He's dying."

Pain sliced through her, and she dropped to her knees beside him. She touched his forehead, his dry lips. He was cold to the touch and his skin was a sickly gray. Resting her hand on his bare chest, she felt the slow, erratic beat of his heart. He didn't move. "No. This can't be happening. You were supposed to save him. Why didn't you save him?"

"I'm so sorry, Mia," Rocco choked beside her. "There was nothing we could do."

The other knights moved in and gathered around them.

They were all grief stricken, straight from a fight, and covered in blood, clothes torn. A couple were wounded badly, but no one moved. They stood there looking as help-less as Mia felt.

The grief that tore through her in that moment was an agony she never knew existed, a weight that was so crushing she could barely breathe, knives so sharp she felt sliced to shreds, and she cried out from the enormity of it.

This couldn't be happening.

They'd just found each other.

Zenon was meant for her and she for him. How would she live without him? How would she go on without her beautiful, broken warrior by her side? Resting her head on his chest, she threaded her fingers with his and laid the other on his stomach. The beats against her cheek slowed further and she whimpered. *No, please no.*

She didn't hear anything else; her sole focus was on that slowing beat.

Then it stopped.

"No. No, no, no." She held his face in her hands. "Zenon. Please come back to me. Don't go." She shook his shoulders. Her sobs made it hard to draw breath and she gasped for air.

Someone pulled her roughly into their arms and held her. "He's gone, Mia. He's gone."

She fought until they let her go, and she crawled onto the couch with his still body, wrapping herself around him protectively. No one was taking him, not yet. Not yet.

"Fuck, this is killing me. What do we do?" It was Lazarus, and she could hear the grief in his voice.

"Leave her with him," Chaos choked out.

The pain in her chest throbbed. Pain over losing the male she loved, and anger over what he had suffered. It filled her until it became unbearable, heating her from the inside out. Unable to contain it, she released it, all of it. All the pent-up

547

rage and grief swirling inside her. There was a sound of scrambling feet and cursing. Furniture being knocked over. But she couldn't stop, was too far gone.

Scalding wind whipped around her, lifting her hair and tugging at her clothes. Still she didn't try to rein it in. She lost herself to it. Let the energy fly from the tips of her fingers, hoping she'd burn into nothingness. Disappear.

She didn't want to be here, not without Zenon.

Someone shouted her name.

She squeezed her eyes closed and poured everything out of her until there was nothing left, until she had drained every last bit of her power. She sagged against Zenon's still form.

"Mia, Christ. Are you all right?" Rocco said from close by.

She shook her head, tears streaming down her face. "I'm still here."

"Zenon wouldn't want this…"

Thump.

Rocco's words drifted into the background.

Thump.

She moved higher and placed her fingers loosely over his cracked lips. Warmth rushed across her skin.

"Mia?" Lazarus said.

"He's breathing," she whispered, scrambling off him to give him space.

Rocco bent down and put his ear to Zenon's chest. "Shit. She's right."

James came up beside them. "You were glowing."

She tore her gaze away from Zenon. "What?"

"Lit up like the freakin' fourth of July. That energy you give him, you just fired a whole hell of a lot into him. I think it…I think you healed him."

Zenon wheezed in a deep breath, and she fell back to her knees beside him. "Zenon?"

His eyelids fluttered open, yellow irises finding and focusing on her, and he smiled. A wide grin that spread across his beautiful face. "Mia," he rasped then he closed his eyes again, this time to sleep.

Mia dropped her head into her hands and cried, but this time they were happy tears.

~

Zenon leaned over the bed and kissed Mia's soft, warm lips. She wiggled and released a breathy sigh, but was still out cold. Healing him had hit her hard, and she'd been out for hours.

Reluctant to leave, he tucked the covers around her and watched her sleep for several more minutes. She'd lost weight, and her thick lashes didn't hide the dark circles under her eyes.

His beautiful female was as fragile as any human. And he planned on spending however many years they had together, taking care of her, making sure she knew how much he loved and cherished her.

Another wave of emotion washed over him.

I'm free.

He still couldn't believe it. And it was all thanks to the precious female in his bed. He owed her everything.

The pull came again. Someone wanted to talk to him and he'd kept him waiting long enough. He reluctantly left his apartment and made his way to the control room then out onto the balcony.

Silas stood looking beyond the barren land behind the compound and into the muted glow of the setting sun. "I didn't know if you'd come," he said.

Zenon moved up beside him. "You knew."

His big shoulders lifted, causing his golden wings to shift, the feathers dancing in the breeze. "Yes."

"When did you find out? Why didn't you tell me?"

He turned, face half concealed in shadow, but still Zenon could see the strain etched into his features. "Your arm." He pointed to the set of markings each knight was born with, telling the story of where they came from, what they were. "That is the mark of Lucifer's bloodline on your skin. When I saw it, I knew. As for why I didn't tell you, you weren't ready. You had enough to deal with without adding to it."

"What happens now?"

"We make sure Diemos stays in Hell."

"That easy, huh?"

A grin tugged at Silas's lips. "Sure."

"What about Lucifer?"

"You have nothing to fear from him. Besides, he has his own problems to deal with," he said cryptically.

You were no mistake. Diemos's words drifted through his mind, and he resisted the shiver that moved through him. "I hope you're right. For everyone's sakes."

"Me, too."

Zenon watched him carefully. "You don't know?"

Silas ran a hand over his face, and for the first time in all the years he'd known him, the other male looked tired, exhausted. Worried. "Things can change. The path isn't set in stone."

"Jesus."

"No. Just an angel."

Silence stretched out. Zenon finally broke it. "Thank you, Silas."

His brows lifted. "For what?"

"For forcing me into this new life, even if I fought you all the way."

Silas smiled. "You were worth it, Zenon."

Ah, shit. A lump formed in the back of his throat. "That part of my life…before, will always be there, yanno, trying to drag me down. The shame." He shook his head when Silas opened his mouth to speak. "Yeah, it'll haunt me for the rest of my life. I know that, but with Mia by my side, I know I can fight back the nightmares."

"That you can, my son." They were the same words Diemos had used, but coming from Silas they meant something, meant so much. The other male took a step back. "Now, go to her. It's time you claimed your mate."

"I can't. We—"

"You're free, Zenon. Go to her." The angel extended his wings and took to the sky.

Was it possible?

Zenon walked back through the control room, and as he entered the hall, broke into a jog. Too impatient to wait for the elevator, he jumped the flight of stairs to the lower level and didn't slow until he reached his apartment. As he opened the door, Mia walked out of the bedroom. A smile lit up her face when she saw him. How did this happen? How did he get so fucking lucky?

"You're back. I missed you." Her smile faltered when she took in his expression, and a small gasp slipped past her lips, not missing the need in his eyes.

"You okay?" he rasped.

"Good as new."

Reaching back, he pulled his shirt over his head and continued toward her. "I need you, Mia." He didn't slow, lifted her off the ground, and carried her back into the bedroom. There was no time for finesse. All he wanted was his female naked, wanted deep inside her.

Standing her on her feet, he pulled the T-shirt she wore over her head then took her mouth, kissing her hard and urgent.

"Is everything all right?" she whispered, clutching his shoulders.

"No. I'm not inside you," he growled against the soft silk of her hair.

Her fingers trailed down his chest, over his abs to unzip his jeans, and her bare breasts brushed his stomach. She rested her forehead against his heart, and they both trembled when she took his cock in her hands and began to work his straining flesh. "I need you, too."

He needed her touch, craved it. "Are you ready for me, princess? I don't think I can wait." He cupped her sex, sliding a finger through her cleft, and groaned when he felt how wet she was for him.

Releasing him, she stepped back and climbed onto the bed, lying back on the rumpled sheets. Zenon stalked her and covered her lush curves. She opened for him, wrapping her legs around his waist. "Please." It was all she said, all she needed to say.

Zenon pushed inside the wet heat of her body, and they both moaned. They'd been apart too long and there was no way he could take this slow. He jerked back his hips and slammed forward. Taking her mouth in an almost brutal kiss, he let sensation take over. Mia thrust a hand in his hair, kissing him just as fiercely. Her other hand gripped his ass, egging him on, asking for more without words. He gave it to her. He was lost to the desperate need he had for her, and she was right there with him.

And then it appeared, that silvery thread he thought had vanished forever, the connection that would link them together for eternity.

"It's there," he gasped out. "It's back. I see it."

A sob broke past Mia's lips. "It's there?"

He looked down at her, choking on the emotions clogging his throat, and nodded. "You ready?" he rasped.

Her arms tightened around him and he stared into her beautiful eyes welling with tears.

"Take it," she said. "Make me yours."

He grabbed on, held on tight. Mia cried out, digging her nails into his skin as she came.

No, there were no words for what he felt in that moment, and there never would be. Nothing existed that could describe something that was this perfect, this pure. Every part of him was alive. It was Mia, she made him feel this way, and when he looked back down at her he knew she felt it, too. That he did that for her as well.

Thrusting into her one last time, burying himself to the hilt, he held her to him and came hard, filling her, claiming her as his mate. The primal sound that left him was raw, untamed, staking his claim over the female beneath him.

He pressed his face against her throat and breathed in her scent while he tried to slow the beating of his heart. "You're mine now, Mia. I'll never let you go. I can't."

She ran her hands up his back, threaded her fingers in the hair at his nape, and massaged gently. "And you are mine." She pressed a kiss to his temple. "If you ever tried to let me go, I'd just follow."

"Jesus. I love you." Lifting up, he kissed her.

"I love you, too."

He pulled out a little and slid back inside her, loving the way her lips parted, her gasp puffing across his skin. He grinned. "I don't plan on letting you out of this bed for a while." He continued to move in slow, measured thrusts, torturing them both.

Her face flushed and she tightened her arms around his shoulders. "If you tried to get out right now, I'd tackle you to the floor."

He laughed, and her eyes turned liquid. "What is it?"

She sniffed and smiled up at him. "I love hearing you laugh. I'll never tire of hearing it."

No words existed that could express what she did to him when she talked like that. So he leaned in and kissed her deep, pouring every bit of emotion he felt into it, swallowing her moans while running his thumbs across her smooth skin, wiping away her tears.

"I love you, too," she whispered against his lips when he finally let her up for air.

"Damn, female, I'm trying to go slow here, but with you talking to me all sweet like that…"

Mia quirked a brow. "And that's a problem?"

Zenon couldn't help it. He threw back his head and laughed again. When he finally pulled his shit together enough to stop, and after taking his time kissing her again, he tortured them both and made love to his mate slowly.

EPILOGUE

MIA LEFT their new guest with Eve and Lazarus. The demi was still pretty shaken up after his retrieval earlier that day. And by the sounds of it, getting to him in time had been a close call. Lazarus and Gunner had more than a few cuts and scrapes to prove it.

There was a lot going on, inside the compound and out, but despite it all, the last few months had been the happiest in Mia's life.

And now it was going to get even better.

Brent was opening a new club in Roxburgh and Chaya had volunteered to move to the new location. Mia would finally be with her sister again. She hated being apart from Chaya. Texts and phone calls just didn't cut it. And with their father here as well, they'd all be in the same place. They'd be like a family again.

She picked up the pace, in a hurry to get to Zenon and tell him her good news. Her mate had been a little cagey this morning, the look on his face one she had trouble working out. He'd been extremely affectionate as well, even more than normal, which meant he'd barely let her out the door, and there'd been this...energy buzzing around him, an excitement that was infectious.

He was up to something. She just had no idea what.

When she walked into their apartment she heard murmured voices coming from the living room, Zenon and someone else. She shut the door, walked in, and pulled up short.

Zenon was laying on a fold out table and a guy she'd never seen before, his entire body covered in tattoos, was bend over, a tattoo gun in his hand, working on her mate's stomach.

Zenon turned to her, a sheepish look in his face. "You're back early."

Mia crossed her arms. "What's going on?"

The guy working on Zenon straightened. "All done."

Mia had become more in sync with her powers lately, with who she was, and as a result the blinders had well and truly come off. She instantly recognized the male in their apartment as a Hell hound. He wiped down Zenon's stomach then quickly packed up.

Mia stayed where she was as the guy gave Zenon a fist bump then after dipping his chin to her, walked out.

She was desperate to go and see what he'd had done, but he was holding his shirt in front of him, right over the spot his slave markings had been.

"Does that surly brother of yours know you had a Hell hound in the compound?" she said instead of asking what she desperately wanted to know.

Zenon gave her a little grin that made her knees weak. She would never get enough of it, of seeing him like this, of seeing him happy.

"Yeah, as a matter of fact. Roman's going to Chaos next," he said.

She bit her lip and motioned to him. "So are you going to show me?"

He stood. "Come here, princess."

When she was close, he curled his big hand around the side of her throat, sliding his thumb under her chin and tilted her head back. Then he leaned in and kissed her, soft and slow. "You made this possible, Mia. *You*," he said against her lips. "I can't even think about a life without you in it and not feel like the grounds collapsing beneath my feet."

He stepped back and Mia's gaze dropped to his stomach, to the right side where his slave tattoos had been, where he'd carried Helena's mark since he was fourteen years old. Mia's hand flew to her mouth and tears immediately filled her eyes.

"I'm free," he said. "Because of you, I'm free from her, free from the hell she made my life. No one owns me, not anymore, Mia. I decide who I give my body and my heart to, and I chose you. I'd choose you a million times over."

Mia dropped her hand, let it hover over the beautiful new ink on his skin. The memory of the first time she saw him, the first time she touched him, flashed through her mind and more tears streamed down her face.

"You put my name on your body," she whispered. "And it's...it's..." She struggled to find the right words. Her name was written in vivid blue, and it was surrounded by light, a stylized sun shining from behind it and there were several red roses in full bloom, making sure every last bit of what lay beneath was covered.

"The blue is for your eyes," Zenon said, voice hoarse. "The sun, for the way you make me feel, for how you pulled me from the dark and bathed me in your light and warmth, and the roses, they're our future, full and rich and bright."

More tears streaked down Mia's face. She couldn't take her eyes off it.

Zenon slid his fingers under her chin, bringing her eyes back to him. "You really like it?"

"Like it?" she whispered. "I love it. It's beautiful. It's...perfect."

He kissed her again then, and she felt him smile against her lips, felt the joy inside him wash through her. She slid her hand up the side of his neck, running her fingers over the rough scars there, over his strong jaw, teasing the corner of his mouth, touching that grin with the tip of her thumb.

Finally, he lifted his head and looked down at her.

"I want one, too," she said. "I want your name on my skin."

He stilled. "Princess," he rasped, with so much feeling in the word it was all he had to say.

"And for the record," she said. "I'd choose you a million times over as well."

Her mate's smile widened, reaching the corners of his eyes, and it was breathtaking.

Two months later

Brent Silva stood by the bar sipping his water and cursed as Chaya strutted across the floor in one of her sexy as hell outfits, every bit of fabric and leather clinging to her petite, curvy figure. Christ, he couldn't tear his gaze away from her.

Get your shit together, asshole.

But no amount of cursing himself out would help. There was no stopping it, this obsession he had with her, no stopping his incubus senses from reaching out to her, from letting them slide and caress, taste and revel in everything that was the maddening, tempting demi now on the other side of the bar.

What was she doing to him?

Fight it. Ignore it.

He didn't.

Instead, he let his eyes drift shut and his senses wrap around her tighter. She sank deeper inside him, into his bones, spiking a longing inside his gut, his chest, his fucking cock, that he needed to resist, but didn't know how.

She wasn't for him.

And every time he allowed this, this surrender, it pushed him closer to the edge.

Shit.

His cock got harder, and he gritted his teeth.

Letting her move to Roxburgh with him, to help start up his new club, was the dumbest thing he'd ever done. But how could he say no? She was good at her job, good with the customers, and her family lived here.

And yeah, the thought of leaving her behind...

His gut gripped tight.

No, he hadn't been able to do that, to be parted from her.

Good thing he was partial to a little pain—okay, more than a little—because this was fucking agony. The female was his own personal brand of torture.

His incubus side was utterly fascinated by her. She made him crave things, so many impossible things. Things he could never have.

Her gaze lifted then and collided with his, and his heart smacked into the back of his ribs.

You can't have her.

No, he sure as hell couldn't be the male she needed. He couldn't give her what she wanted from him, could never fulfill that longing in her gorgeous eyes.

Shoving his drink aside, he tore his gaze from her and headed for his office.

She wasn't for him. She didn't even know who...*what*, he truly was.

And there was nothing he could do to change it.

DEMON'S TEMPTATION

Knights of Hell, Book 3

CHAPTER 1

B<small>RENT</small> S<small>ILVA</small> <small>UNBUTTONED</small> his jacket and sat forward, gripping his phone tight enough to make it groan. "Tell me you got it?"

"The building's yours, sir."

He shot to his feet and paced around to the front of his desk and back. "It's mine?" The second property he'd acquired here in Roxburgh.

"Yes, sir." His lawyer's thin voice continued to echo through the receiver, but Brent didn't hear a word of it, his mind already racing ahead. *Let this be it, the hit that finally draws the bastard out.*

"Mr. Silva?"

He forced himself to concentrate on what the guy was saying. "Yeah, I'm here."

"If you don't mind me asking, what do you plan to do with it?"

"Not a damn thing." The first acquisition, the building he currently occupied and had recently opened for business, was a sex club like the one he'd owned in Chicago. Toxic had made him a lot of money. Demi-demons like him—half demon, half human—were often drawn to this lifestyle, especially those with incubus or some other species of sex demon making up half their DNA, but he didn't really give a shit about money at this point.

It had been time to make the move, to come back. He'd left Roxburgh after Lazarus—one of the knights of Hell, half demon, half angel warriors created to protect Brent's kind —had rescued him over three years ago, and after he'd recovered and finished his training, he left. He never thought he'd come back. But as he'd grown stronger, his hatred and need for revenge had grown with it. If he wanted to take that fucker down, he had to be here, in this city.

And right now, all that mattered was he'd beaten Garrett to another property. It wasn't as satisfying as putting a bullet in the demon's head, but it was another dent in the guy's armor nonetheless.

So far, the male remained a shadow. Brent had never seen his face and his voice had always been disguised. He didn't even know if Garrett was his first name, last name or something else entirely. He'd endured the fucker's breath down the back of his neck, his cold, grasping fingers on his skin, completely under the monster's command—but he wouldn't recognize him if he passed him on the street.

And that's what kept him up at night, had him waking in a cold sweat.

"Are you sure that's wise? It's a prime location. More than one buyer was clambering to get their hands on it. You can't just let it sit there."

"No?" Steel laced Brent's voice, emotion from the direction his thoughts had taken slipping through. He had no desire to explain his actions to anyone, least of all someone who was paid extremely well to do as he was asked and keep his mouth shut.

"Apologies," the guy murmured. "I'll have the paperwork sent over to you right away."

"I'd appreciate it." Disconnecting, he shoved a hand through his hair and paced the room, trying to ease the tension thrumming through his body.

Garrett was the last one. He'd hoped the constant barrage of attacks on his businesses would draw him out. So far, nothing. Not a fucking peep.

It'd been time to up his game, which meant moving back into Garrett's territory and making sure Brent was seen.

When he'd been freed from that hell that, as it turned out, had made him his own jailor, a place he never imagined could exist, not until he'd been lured there, seduced, intoxicated on lust and emotion, betrayed by his new powers to the point he had lost himself completely—he thought he would never recover.

Two months he'd been there, helpless, ruled by the incubus blood he'd inherited from his father. A father he never knew existed.

That was how he learned what he was. How he discovered that demons existed on this Earth. That he wasn't entirely human.

Four years later—with nothing to go on but the name of the monster who had preyed on him, who had used what he was against him—he'd managed to find out the building he'd been found in by Lazarus had been owned by Garrett Industries.

Garrett.

He'd made it his mission to track and target anything with the name attached to it.

But the male himself remained elusive. A goddamned ghost.

Snatching the bottle of water off his desk, he drank deeply, mouth suddenly bone dry. He needed this to be over but at this point wasn't any closer to putting the bastard down than he'd been the day he walked away from that nightmare.

He was still lost. Would remain that way until Garrett was six feet under.

"Fuck!" He sent the bottle flying, the thud of plastic colliding with the opposite wall not nearly satisfying enough.

God, he was close to crawling out of his skin. He needed a drink, a real one, a whole damned bottle, but that wasn't an option. He'd never walk out onto that floor with an ounce of alcohol in his system. The risks were too high, especially in his current frame of mind.

Tonight he needed to release all the tension eating him from the inside out before it completely corroded his self-control. Usually feeding from the emotions pouring off the beings that came to his club, a few one-on-one sessions, were enough to satisfy him. Sex wasn't necessary…wasn't wanted. Tonight, though, he needed more.

The deep, pounding bass of heavy rock thrummed through his office door. He let it move through him, did his best to force the swirl of volatile emotion down, swallowing the memories along with it. Tonight he needed his barriers rock solid. Anything else was too dangerous.

Putting on his game face, he straightened his jacket, and opened the door. Muted red light greeted him, blanketing the entire club. He scanned the room—the place was packed. The new club had done exceptionally well in its first few months of business. Bodies moved on the dance floor, others made use of the darkened corners.

Using the place the way it was designed to be used.

Before he knew his intention, he unconsciously reached out with his senses…for *her*.

There.

His eyes drifted shut, like a heroin addict finally getting a much-needed hit. And like always, Chaya's presence slammed into him, wrapped around him, threatened to tip him over the edge.

Shit.

His cock filled, hardened instantly. With the way he was feeling, he should send her home. He needed to fuck, to release the pressure building to unbearable levels inside him, and as always, that female was like a goddamned Siren.

He should never have agreed to her coming with him. But she'd argued that he needed staff familiar with the business, people with experience. There was also the fact that her sister was in Roxburgh, as was her father, a male Chaya had thought dead until recently. How the hell could he say no?

The incubus inside him wanted her, wanted to taste her lust, wanted to surrender to her, be dominated by her. Wanted to feel the full force of all that attitude and fire turned on him, wanted her to give him what he truly craved. The human part of him needed more, wanted everything.

And that was unacceptable.

It was also impossible.

No one at the club knew what he truly was. He'd been playing the part of Dom for such a long time he'd even fooled himself on occasion. But that longing never went away, no matter what he told himself. It was always there, just below the surface.

He'd felt so betrayed by his own body during those weeks with Garrett, and he'd vowed never to put himself in that position ever again. The way he'd chosen to live his life since, it was self-preservation.

Playing the Dom had felt like the only way to move forward. He was also the owner of two sex clubs frequented by beings, creatures, driven by instinct, many who would see him as weaker, someone to be walked over if they knew his true nature.

Now he was stuck.

God, he'd been fighting it so long.

And tonight the strength of that pull to Chaya was like a force of nature. It lit up every nerve ending, lifted the hair on his arms and the back of his neck. A rough sound escaped his throat. Oh yeah, he needed a fix, but not her.

Chaya was willful, defied him constantly, pushed him daily. But all that attitude, that smart mouth of hers, was a front. She'd made it clear she was a submissive and that she wanted him to be the one to take her in hand. But he couldn't pretend to be someone—something—else, not with her.

Still, everything about her drew him. She shone like a beacon, calling to him at a soul-deep level. Fate's way of fucking with him some more, obviously, like they hadn't fucked him over enough.

It didn't stop him from fantasizing that Chaya could be the one to fulfil the endless ache, the desperate need that throbbed inside him every damn day.

But she wasn't for him. And he couldn't risk her seeing the truth of his nature. He couldn't take that kind of rejection, not from Chaya.

He also knew that once wouldn't be enough, not with her.

And he'd hurt her. In the end, he'd hurt her.

He didn't do permanent. Never more than once with anyone, and only when he'd reached breaking point, like he was close to doing tonight. Sex always made him feel empty somehow, hollow. He preferred to give others what they needed and feed on their emotions. He sure as fuck couldn't deal with his own. The volatile twisted shit swirling inside him was better off ignored.

Scanning the room, he searched for someone to suit his purposes...

The light dimmed for a few moments then a new song began, starting out slow, heavy bass, sensual. Several people

567

had turned, eyes trained toward something or someone on the other side of the club.

Jesus.

Pins and needles danced down his spine.

Chaya.

The energy and emotion she was throwing out hit him in the gut, an unfurling, erotic burn that made his skin itch and sweat slide between his shoulder blades. He took several steps forward, like she'd reached out and touched him, beckoning him closer.

Then he saw her.

In one of the cages, gripping the bars in front of her, she moved—no, fucking writhed—to the music. All that long, dark hair was wild around her face and shoulders, her skin flushed. The bass got heavier, the pace increasing, and she dipped her perfect round ass, swayed those lush hips in a way that sucked all the oxygen from his lungs. He was already hard as iron. The maddening female made him ache.

The leather corset she wore was molded to her out-of-control curves, the lacing up the front barely contained her generous breasts. The front plunged low enough that he could see a delicate chain taut across her chest. The jewelry would be clamped to each nipple, heightening the sensation of the leather moving against her sensitive skin.

What the fuck is she playing at?

He gritted his teeth, gaze traveling down over the rest of her. She wasn't wearing one of the little leather skirts she usually favored, but instead she wore delicate black lace panties and stockings. A stark contrast to the corset, showing a vulnerability and confidence all at once.

Christ, to have her fist his hair and force his face between those lush thighs.

She continued to dance, but what got to him most, what had him close to tipping over the damn edge, were the spiked heels of her boots making her look taller than her petite five-foot-four frame. He wanted to feel them digging into his back, his ass, while he serviced her, while he eagerly gave her everything she demanded of him.

Not going to happen. Keep it the hell together.

He'd warned her, told her repeatedly that she was not to dance, that she could work the bar or waitress but the cages were off limits. He knew what seeing her like that would do to him, what seeing other males looking at her like that would do to him. By human standards that would make him a selfish, controlling asshole, but he wasn't fucking human, not anymore. The same goddamn rules didn't apply. He was a demon with demon instincts and desires.

Instincts he still struggled with. Instincts that had homed in on Chaya the moment he laid eyes on her and screamed for her, were still screaming for her. Desires that would get the better of him, would take him over completely if he let them, if he didn't manage them the only way he knew how.

Desires that ruled him and would ultimately lead to him hurting her if he fully gave into them. That he was terrified would take over completely if he dropped his guard and let someone in.

He didn't even know if he could be with just one person. If the incubus, the sex demon side of himself would be satisfied or if it would eventually drive him to seek out others. It was a risk he refused to take, even if he could keep up the pretense around her, not when Chaya was the one who would be playing guinea pig.

And right at that moment, not only was object of his deepest, darkest desires dancing up there, she had the attention of every person in the damn club.

No, the demon he was now didn't like it. Not one fucking bit.

Her gaze lifted, came right to him and locked on him,

daring him to come to her, to take up her offer. For a moment he allowed himself to imagine she was his Domme, demanding with her eyes that he come to her, that he kneel at her feet.

His knees actually went weak with the desire to drop to them.

His cock pulsed, balls drawing tight. She didn't know what she was doing by tormenting him this way, what this little show might push him to do. What might happen.

She had no way of knowing what she might reduce him to, what she might expose.

Her eyes stayed locked on his, sending him a *what are you waiting for* that everyone in the room could see. Chaya was challenging him, asking him if he had the strength to strip down those hard layers to the soft, tender parts beneath.

He wanted to fucking weep because that's what he wanted from her, more than anything.

After what had happened to him, how he'd lost control four years ago, the truth was he didn't know what he was capable of. And until he got his revenge, until he made Garrett pay, he wouldn't risk trying to find out.

Still, seeing her standing there like that, asking him to be that male for her—yeah, in that moment he'd never wished more that he could change who he was. That he could be the kind of male she needed.

It was hard, but he didn't look away. Not with all these people watching. Even from the distance separating them, he could see the uncertainty shift across her features. Goddammit, she needed to understand, needed to stop this.

Chaya stilled suddenly, her thick black lashes fluttering then lowering as she dropped her gaze. She bowed her head slightly and trained those beautiful dark eyes on the floor.

All eyes moved to him, waiting to see what he'd do. What could he do? He couldn't have her, no matter how much he craved her, hungered for her. But he wouldn't humiliate her either.

Fighting his instincts right then was like trying to fight back a storm with a miniature battery-powered fan. But he had no choice. He did the only thing he could do—he moved through the crowd toward her. She still hadn't looked up, her gaze sweetly downcast. Every muscle in his body was hard as stone as he moved closer.

He stopped in front of the cage. "Out, Chaya." His voice was nothing more than a low rasp. Her gaze shot up, searching his. "Now," he said.

The cage was opened and she climbed down. He didn't touch her, instead tilted his head for her to follow and moved back through the crowded club. He didn't need to turn back to know she was right behind him. He could feel her there. He led her to the opposite side of the room, where it was darker, away from prying eyes.

When he turned to face her, the attitude was back, in her posture, her expression, and it hit him full force. Fuck, his cock filled, hardened instantly. She was a smart girl. He hadn't taken her to one of the playrooms. She knew what that meant.

She stared at him, unblinking, and shrugged. "What?"

Forcing himself to play Dom, he let his gaze move over her, purposely lingering on the delicate chain taut across her chest. He saw rather than heard her soft indrawn breath. He needed her to stop pushing him like this. Reaching out, he gave it a light tug, and she sucked in another breath.

He arched a brow, doing his best to play the role she expected, that everyone expected. *"What?"*

She pulled herself together fast, barely missing a beat. "I'm working. Why the hell did you pull me out of the cage?"

That flash of fire, the defiance in her words—Christ, it

made him so damned hard. He struggled to say what he needed to, to reprimand her.

"Your job description does not include dancing. Get back on the floor and serve drinks like you're paid to." He made sure steel laced his words when he spoke.

Her jaw hardened, lips thinning.

Electricity fired between them. Being this close to her lit him up inside, made him restless, hungry. She crossed her arms, causing her heavy breasts to lift high enough that one of the tiny D-rings attached to her nipple clamps peeked out. "What's your problem? I was only dancing. What the hell's the big deal?"

"After that little display, you're going to play coy?" He shook his head and let his gaze travel back down to that chain glinting between her breasts, tormenting the hell out of him.

She swallowed hard. "I have no idea what you're on about."

"No?" he gritted out.

She bit her lip but shook her head.

Why are you pushing? Let it go. Get the hell away.

"You need to know this isn't some game. You're playing in dangerous waters, Chaya. You dip your toes in again and a monster might latch on and not let you go." He stepped closer, crowding her. "Might drag you under, into the dark waters with him. Are you prepared for that?"

She looked stubbornly up at him, but for once the wild cat was at a loss for words.

He forced his facial features into what he hoped was a bored expression "That's what I thought. I don't have time for amateur hour, sweetheart."

A wave of pain washed over him—and not the kind he liked either, mixed with pleasure. Her emotions were all over the place and he wanted to reach out and touch her, soothe away the damage he'd caused. But he couldn't.

And all the while, his incubus gorged on that emotion pouring off her. He hated himself for it, for the twisted feeling it gave him. The demon side of his nature wanted more. Anything it could have of Chaya, even her pain, and that messed with his head in more ways than he could count.

Which was why he needed to stay the hell away from her.

Being this close to her had become too much. He was close to coming out of his skin, and if he didn't get the hell away from her now, he'd do something he couldn't take back. She was looking up at him, waiting for more, for him to give her something, to acknowledge what was between them. But he fucking couldn't.

"I've got shit to do," he said, gut in knots, and headed across the club, trying to get far enough away that her emotions wouldn't reach him. But he didn't think that was possible, not with her.

The night dragged and his control cracked more and more until his skin was hot and tight and he couldn't get a handle on the amount of emotion he was taking in.

He was leaning against the wall, and when he tried to straighten he actually fucking staggered like a damn drunk. Which wasn't far from the truth at that point.

This was his addiction, something he lived with and fought every day. He glanced up, spotting Chaya delivering drinks over in her section. Emotion was his drug, and somehow every day he had to take enough to survive but not enough to fucking OD.

He glanced at Chaya again. And right there was his downfall—if he ever allowed himself to give in to tempta-tion. Everything about her—her beautiful body, her wild spirit, and her sweet, intoxicating emotion—called to him like a love song. Like the best high he'd ever have.

Giving in to that need would be too dangerous, for both of them.

He needed to regain his control. Now.

A young demi stood a short distance away. Brent had seen him at the club the last few nights, his interest in what Brent could give him written all over his face. He was a beautiful male, but Brent's stomach knotted, fisted, a sense of wrongness washing over him that made his palms sweat.

Before Chaya started working for him, he wouldn't have thought twice about spending time with the male. Male or female, it didn't matter to him. But he wasn't who Brent wanted.

Unfortunately, the demon part of Brent didn't allow him that luxury.

Brent crooked a finger at him.

He moved toward Brent immediately, hands loose at his sides, eyes downcast. The perfect sub.

Perfect for what he needed tonight, anyway. The only kind of partners he dared take into the privacy of the play-rooms lately. He took the utmost care with his subs, always, but with the volatile emotions hammering him, he didn't trust himself with a female. Afraid he might be too rough. He would never forgive himself if that happened.

But that wasn't the only reason he'd been choosing males, he couldn't deny it, not even to himself. There was only one female he wanted, and he couldn't have her.

He couldn't pretend with her.

Brent didn't look back at Chaya as he led the guy to his playroom.

He couldn't bear to, he might not be able to go through with this again if he did, and what that might lead to didn't bear thinking about. God, he could still taste the pain he'd caused her, the humiliation.

He tried to tell himself that Chaya knew the people he

took into those rooms meant nothing to him, that what he did in there fed his demon, nothing more.

Still, it caused her pain.

They were stuck in a fucked-up cycle and he didn't know how to stop it.

What did she want from him?

Why did she stay?

Why couldn't he let her go?

Brent admired Spencer's once-pale skin. The other male's ass was nice and pink from the paddle Brent had just used. Sweat slicked his flesh and his thighs trembled. Smacking the guy's ass again, Brent forced the butt plug deeper, making him writhe and moan, beg.

"Come," Brent said, low. "Now."

Spencer cried out, doing exactly what he was told, humping into the spanking bench he was bent over.

Brent moved around to stand in front of him. The male was naked, strapped down, and helpless, and Brent gorged on the emotions pouring off him. All that hunger and lust, the satisfaction, the relief, the gratitude, not to mention the delicate, delicious wave of pleasure pain each time Brent had used the paddle.

Jealousy spiked through him.

He wanted that.

To be restrained, the sweet sting of a paddle on his ass, forced to come.

But not by some faceless male who used him when he was at his most vulnerable, but the female he craved more than anything else in existence.

Stop.

He sucked in a deep breath. Christ, what Spencer was

sending out was a heady mix and the reason he needed the utmost control. If he didn't keep it together, it would be so easy to get lost in it. To take and take, to gorge until he was lost, and accidentally hurt someone who had put their trust, their pleasure in his hands for the short time he had them in this room. The incubus he'd become was a greedy bastard, was all-consuming, never satisfied.

"I think you've earned a reward, Spencer, for being such a good little sub." He stepped closer to the guy's face, brushing his still-covered erection against his fevered cheek. He brushed his hand through Spencer's damp hair, massaging his scalp, and the guy purred. "I'm going to fuck your mouth, Spencer."

"Y-yes, please, Sir."

He moved away briefly and the guy whimpered, already licking his lips. They were pretty lips, but that wasn't the mouth he wanted. His voice wasn't the one he wanted to hear. He grabbed a blackout blindfold hanging on the wall and moved back, covering Spencer's eyes. Unzipping his pants, he freed his cock, and nudged it against his lips. Spencer opened without hesitation, like he knew he would, and Brent fed him his hard dick.

He didn't want this, didn't want this male…didn't want to be in this room playing at being Dom, but his body, the incubus side of his DNA wouldn't let him walk away, not after Chaya's little show, and not after another failed attempt at drawing Garrett out.

It was either this or lose it completely.

Self-destruction.

The door was shut, he couldn't see her, but Brent could still feel her just beyond it. Taunting him, calling to him.

Hissing a curse, he fisted Spencer's soft curls and slipped deeper, began fucking the guy's mouth like he'd promised. Closing his eyes, he tried to let sensation take over, to get lost in the feel of a hot, moist mouth, but all he could see was Chaya. The seductive way she'd danced in that cage, those spike-heeled boots. How, for a split second, she'd held his stare and he'd fooled himself into seeing something he wanted so desperately. Christ, imagined that she'd walked out of that cage, right up to him, and instead of him having to hurt her, she'd ordered him to his knees.

That she'd made him hers.

And then memories, twisted and vivid, invaded his mind like they always did. The confusion, the disgust, the fear—the desperate, unending craving for more he'd felt when he became a demi-demon in that place four years ago. The guilt and self-loathing over the way he'd begged for more every damn day.

He struggled with that even now, like it was yesterday. The damage it had caused, that *Garrett* had caused, was more than he knew how to deal with.

His balls drew tight, and as good as this guy was at sucking cock, it wasn't enough. It never was. And the reason Spencer wore a mask. This was Brent's shame, and his alone.

Reaching down, he fisted his balls and squeezed hard. Punishing himself was the only way he could get off now. Punishment for what he'd allowed them to do to him, for what he'd *asked* them to do.

The pain nearly buckled his knees. Familiar agony shot through him, nausea hitting him low in the gut.

With an agonized shout, he came.

Finally. Sweet release.

577

CHAPTER 2

CHAYA FINISHED CLEANING off the mascara smeared under her eyes making her look like a deranged panda. What she wouldn't give for the ability to scrub memories right then. The club's dressing room had been empty when she walked in, which was good because she so wasn't ready to face anyone yet.

At least she was in the same city as Mia now, because she needed some sister time stat. The move to Roxburgh and helping open up the new club had kept her busy. She hadn't spent nearly enough time with her sister since moving as she'd have liked. Tomorrow's lunch catch-up with the girls at the compound couldn't come fast enough.

Covering her face with her hands, she groaned. "I'm an idiot."

Humiliation, disappointment, and plain old hurt swamped her. For a second there, she actually thought he might…

She shook her head.

Stop it.

She was through fooling herself. Yeah, there was an

578

attraction between them, but it didn't matter—he wasn't going to act on it. He'd well and truly proven that tonight.

She wasn't a fool. She was a strong, independent, intelligent female. Her mother had made sure she and her sister respected themselves, knew their worth...but for some reason, when it came to Brent Silva, all of it, every damn shred of common sense dissolved into a puddle of stupid. Her feelings for him refused to die, no matter how hard she tried to force them down, no matter how many times he ignored her advances.

Her seduction technique was obviously for shit because if dancing around in front of him in her undies hadn't enticed him enough to make a move, she didn't know what would.

Good thing she hadn't moved to Roxburgh just for Brent. No, there was another reason she was in this city. There was a war going on and she was done sitting on the sideline watching demi-demons, just like her, live in fear. Or worse, be hunted like animals and kept prisoner. And lately, demons who had sought refuge, allowed to stay in this city safely and freely, after agreeing to rules set down by the knights, had been acting out. It was like they were being controlled en masse by something or someone powerful. Demi couldn't just sit by and do nothing. They needed to help themselves. This was their war as well.

But before she could save the world from invading demons, she needed to get through the rest of the night.

After squeezing out another glob of concealer, she dabbed it around her eyes. *Crap.* The deranged panda was gone but there was no way to hide her red eyes.

God, the way he'd looked at her across the room, the heat, the hunger. A shiver moved through her. She'd actually thought *this is it, it's finally going to happen.*

So stupid.

As a demi-demon—half human, half demon—she had a

certain amount of power. Her sister, Mia, had some amazing fire-throwing, energy-giving power that her mate, Zenon, a Knight of Hell—giant demon-killing dudes that were the result of demons and fallen angels getting it on— needed to survive on Earth. It was a big deal, had some serious kick.

This shouldn't have been a surprise. Their father might not have been back in their lives very long, for reasons beyond his control, but they'd learned since he'd returned that he was an extremely powerful demon. But unlike Mia, all that amazing power had not passed on to Chaya. Oh no, her only gift was the ability to sense emotions and draw them into herself. Which sounded cool, but so wasn't. Because once she took it inside herself, she had a hard time getting rid of it. And if she held on to those emotions long enough, they became her own for a while, causing her bouts of depression, rage, lust, with no release from them. And if she got enough, they could be completely debilitating. So, no, not cool.

One of the knights' jobs, besides killing rogue demons, was to watch over her kind when their demon powers developed, usually between their late teens and early twenties. When she'd developed hers, they'd taught her how to block her empathic ability. They'd also taught her how to release the emotions she drew into herself, but it wasn't easy. She needed a willing participant—well, the willing part wasn't necessary—to use as a conduit. But she'd never do that to someone without their consent, and volunteers weren't exactly easy to come by. Having someone else's emotions pumped through you was no barrel of laughs.

So more often than not, she blocked them out. But tonight, for the first time in months, she'd tried to sense what Brent was feeling...and as usual, the male had been locked up tight. She'd never felt anything like it. It was like he'd surrounded himself with ten-inch-thick steel. And there was no crack in his armor, no way in.

"Shit." She threw her lipstick down and sat back in her chair.

The male was so closed off. How the hell could she get through to him? If she wasn't sure he felt something for her, it would be a heck of lot easier to give it up. But the electricity that flowed between them was undeniable. Had been since she moved to Chicago where Brent's other club was located, and where he first gave her a job.

For so long it had just been her and her sister. After their mother died, they hadn't had anyone else. And unlike other demi-demons, they'd known what they were since they were young. Which meant forming long-lasting relationships was a waste of time, because they knew a day would come when the demon half of their DNA would make itself known and they'd have to leave it all behind, start again.

When it did happen, she'd been excited. Finally, she could start living, could allow herself to care about someone else, put down roots.

As soon as she'd seen Brent, she'd known he was that person for her. No other male existed to her after that.

Unfortunately, he didn't see things her way.

The guy was a sex demon, an incubus, and she understood that he needed this place and what he could get here for his survival. She did her best to keep her jealousy at bay when he was with someone. But the guy was a demon, or half one at least, just like her, so she understood that what he did in that room behind that glossy red door was pure instinct, was the nature of the demon side of his DNA. Still, it wasn't easy to watch, to accept.

But she understood. She got it.

What she didn't get was why it couldn't be her.

One of the biggest problems, she was sure, was the stubborn jackass didn't think she could take it, couldn't take what he needed in that playroom, and unless he let her prove herself, how could she ever prove him wrong?

Music started blaring from her phone, making her jump. Picking it up, she checked caller ID. Eve.

"Uh…hey."

"How did it go?"

Chaya cringed. "It didn't."

"Oh, hon…"

"Stop. Don't say another word. I can't talk about it, not yet. Anyway, my humiliation is probably being posted on YouTube as we speak. Just search *dancing dork in cage* and you should find it."

Eve and her mate, another knight named Lazarus, had stayed in one of the apartments above the club back in Chicago when they'd needed a safe place to hide out. She and Eve had quickly become friends, and alarmingly, it hadn't taken long for the other female to work out how gone Chaya was over her boss.

"Come on, Chay, give me something?"

She blew out a breath. "He pulled me out of the cage but didn't take me to the playrooms." She winced. That part was the worst. How pathetic she must have looked trailing after him like some lovesick puppy. "I knew it wasn't going to happen, so instead of pushing for what I wanted, I bottled it and played dumb to the whole thing."

"Jesus…you know I love Brent, but that male is a complete idiot."

"You didn't tell Mia, did you?" The last thing she needed was her sweet, overprotective younger sister concerned about her. Not to mention if she involved her intense, rather terrifying mate, the guy would more than likely fly over and break both Brent's legs for upsetting her, then all holy humiliating hell would break loose.

"No, I'd never do that, though I haven't exactly had much of a chance to talk to Mia lately. That girl's still all loved up. We only see her when Zen's out on patrol."

Not a surprise. Chaya had never seen two people more in love.

She heard Lazarus's voice in the background and Eve chuckled. "Let me finish my call with Chaya." There was more murmuring in the background. "Oh, for God's sake. Sorry, Chay, hang on a sec. Yes, you big oaf, I am also completely loved up. Is that better?"

The next time Laz spoke he was clear as a bell. The guy was obviously right there by Eve and demanding she show him just how loved up she was.

Eve squealed. "Um, I'm sorry, Chay. I have to go."

Her chest squeezed. What would that be like to have someone love you like that? Want you like that? "It's fine. I'm fine."

"Hang in there, hon. We'll talk more when I see you tomorrow." Then the phone disconnected.

Chaya had been hiding out long enough. The club was busy and her break was well and truly over. Grabbing her favorite pleated leather skirt, she slipped it on, covering the flimsy lace panties she'd bought on a whim. A complete waste of money. After another check in the mirror, she fought down her embarrassment and lifted her shields. No one would know Brent had hurt her because she refused to let anyone in to see. And she sure as hell didn't want a dose of the emotions they were feeling when she walked back out either.

As she suspected, the club was packed when she hit the main floor, the bar staff run off their feet. She signaled to Eric behind the bar that she was back from her break, pointed to her section, and got back into it.

The rhythm of taking orders, making small talk, and

delivering drinks made the time move quickly, keeping her mind off a certain infuriating incubus. The music was great and she found herself enjoying it like she usually did. Shaking her ass on the way to the bar, she did a little dance, laughing with some of the other girls. Either no one really noticed what happened earlier or they were too nice to mention it. Whichever it was, she was thankful for it.

On her way back toward her section of the club, she took in all the action going on around her. Unlike a lot of other clubs like this, most came to Toxic for one-night hookups. Still, some found lasting relationships.

One of their regulars, a Dom, sat with his now long-term sub. She kneeled at his side, a collar around her neck. He petted her, fingers running through her long hair. The female kept her eyes downcast, but their devotion to each other was unmistakable.

Could Chaya do that? Be like that female? She tried to imagine it, but for some reason she felt herself identifying more with her Dom.

Christ, what kind of a freak did that make her?

She didn't want to think about it and quickly looked away, taking in the different couples, long-term and casual, and she felt that familiar ache behind her ribs...

Heat hit the back of her neck and coasted down her spine, making her shiver. Just like that she knew he was back on the floor and he was watching her. Did he do it on purpose? Was he trying to screw with her head? Because he'd made it clear tonight, despite the blatant desire he fired her way, nothing was going to happen between them.

She spun around and searched through the crowd. *There.* She met his stare and the bastard didn't look away. She felt frozen to the spot, like she had earlier. Why was he tormenting her like this? She gritted her teeth and refused to look away first. *No more.*

To her surprise, he did, dropping his gaze, then he strode away.

She clenched her fists. She had to beat this craving for a man who refused to give her a chance, give her any damn thing but mixed signals and rejection.

She turned away and took another drink order, doing her *fucking job* like he'd told her to. She was weaving her way through the crowd, heading back toward the bar, when he stepped in front of her.

Goddammit.

"Chay, we need to talk." His jaw was hard, but his eyes had softened, didn't hold that edge she'd seen earlier.

Right then she wanted to do physical harm to the guy. No way did she want to have a damn chat with him. "Jesus, do you have a split personality or something? You told me to work. I'm working."

She tried to step around him, but he grabbed her arms. The smell of sex washed over her. She jolted. She'd heard the talk, that Brent never usually fucked the people he took into that room. She'd definitely never smelled it on him like this before. Pain washed through her.

What was wrong with her that she wanted a man who said in every way but words that he wanted her then turned her away and fucked someone else? Sex demon or not. She had a damn screw loose.

She pulled her arm free. "It'll have to wait. I have orders to fill."

"I don't give a shit about your orders."

He stood in her way and motioned to his office.

Goddammit, was he was going to stand there all night if she didn't do what he wanted? Jesus. She just wanted this over with. Storming past him, she strode to his office. When he followed her in, she spun on him. "What the hell is your problem?"

He shut the door and turned to face her. "I wanted to apologize."

"You dragged me in here for that?"

"Chay—"

"Oh, no you don't." She shook her head and headed for the exit. She didn't want to hear it. He was an expert at screwing with her head, her emotions. Her resolve was finally set. Nothing was going to happen between them, but again here he was confusing her, intentional or not, giving her hope where there was none.

His big hand slammed against the door, stopping her from escape. "Chay...wait." He took her shoulders, turning her to face him. "I don't want there to be this tension between us. You're important to me. You know that." He ran a hand through his hair. "Can we...can we be friends again?"

Yeah, there was tension. Huge, pulsing amounts of sexual tension that he could try to deny all he liked, but it wasn't going away, would never go away if she stayed there.

She stepped closer, crowding him, trying to force him to acknowledge it because, goddammit, she couldn't help herself.

His throat worked. "Please, Chay."

She held his wild stare, waiting for something, anything, but he did nothing. She shook her head. "I'm sick of the bull-shit, Brent. I'm sick of you saying one thing then pulling shit like this. I don't want to be your friend, and I'm...I'm sick of pretending." She somehow found the courage she'd struggled to find earlier and forced the words past her lips. "You know what I want."

He stilled, and her heart started hammering in her chest. His breath rushed through his lips, ruffling her hair, his surprise obvious. He clearly never thought she had the stones to say it, to acknowledge the thing that sparked between them and blazed so hot she felt like she was on fire whenever they were together.

But then the wall came down, his eyes going flat, lifeless. He shook his head. "I can't give you that." His gaze hardened, the muscle in his jaw jumping. "You don't know what you're asking, Chaya, don't have the first clue what being with me entails."

He wasn't even prepared to try to give her a chance to prove herself. "Then let me go," she whispered. They both knew she didn't just mean physically.

"Shit." He jammed his hand through his hair again, making it stick up at odd angles. "Just...just tell me we're good?"

What did you expect, Chaya? A declaration? That he'd admit the way he felt about you?

"I'm not telling you a damn thing. Now get out of my way. You smell like that guy you fucked, and it's turning my stomach."

A low blow, but she was willing to use any weapon at her disposal right then to protect herself against this man. A man who didn't even know the power he held over her.

He hissed, cursed a string of foul words, and shoved away from the wall.

She didn't wait, yanked the door open and did her best to act like her heart wasn't breaking into a million pieces...and went back to work.

She knew the minute he came back out onto the floor, and she made sure to avoid him for the rest of her shift.

Lifting her tray high, she dodged a couple dancing and went to deliver her last drink of the night. She'd seen the guy here a time or two. He had salt and pepper hair and dressed a lot like Brent, wearing his expensive dark suit with confidence. The male was definitely a dominant. He'd taken his jacket off, and his shirt sleeves were still buttoned at the cuff, emphasizing his long, elegant fingers. Several subs had been watching him, but he seemed content to sit back and watch.

She stopped beside him. "Here's your drink, sir."

He glanced at her, a small smile lifting the corner of his mouth. "Thank you." He picked up his drink and took a sip. "Do you have a moment to sit with me?"

If this guy thought she was in the market for a Dom, especially after what had happened tonight, he was sniffing around the wrong fire hydrant. "I'm actually just about to head off."

"I only want a few moments of your time." He held up his hands. "Nothing untoward, I promise."

The guy smiled again, putting her at ease. Her curiosity piqued, she placed her tray on the table. "Um…sure."

She sat across from him, and he aimed his silver eyes at her. She sensed he had demon blood, but how much she had no idea. He was more than likely a demi like her.

He laid a hand on the table and slid it toward her. When he lifted it, a plain white card rested in front of her. *The Dungeon* was embossed in fancy silver lettering. "This is a club I frequent. Membership is exclusive. You can't join without an invitation from a member. This card allows you three visits as a voyeur."

Okay. "Why are you giving me this?"

He sat back in his seat. "May I ask your name?"

She stared at him for several seconds. She was tempted not to answer, but her curiosity got the better of her. "Chaya."

"I saw what happened earlier, Chaya. That male was an idiot to turn down the gift you offered him. If you're ever interested in exploring that side of your nature, I would be more than happy to oblige." He tapped the card. "But first I ask that you come and watch."

She inwardly groaned. He'd seen her humiliation. Jesus.

How many others were pitying her for her stupidity? "I work here, Mr...."

"Victor."

She toyed with the corner of the card. "What do you think you can show me that I haven't already seen?"

"We don't keep all the action behind closed doors, Chaya. You'd be surprised."

He stood, shrugged into his jacket, and smiled down at her. "I hope to see you there sometime." Then he made his way out of the club.

Chaya didn't hang around. The last thing she wanted was to be stuck there after closing with Brent, forced to endure another conversation like the one they'd had earlier. Quickly changing into her street clothes, she grabbed her bag from the dressing room, and, head down, walked out into the street.

As soon as she was out of the club, her mask dropped and the pain returned unbidden. She crossed her arms against it burning in her chest, and something bit into her palm. She looked down at her hand and realized she was clutching that damn card.

Could she?

She'd told Brent she wanted him to let her go. She was full of shit. The pull toward him was as strong as ever. She wasn't ready to give up yet. Whether that made her a glutton for punishment or a complete idiot, she didn't know. The male could pussyfoot around it all he wanted, but he wanted her, too. He was right about one thing, though: she didn't have the first clue what being with someone like him entailed.

Like Victor said, all the good stuff happened behind closed doors at Toxic. Maybe she could just go check it out, a place where no one knew her, where she could be anonymous.

Maybe Brent wouldn't be so quick to turn her away if she wasn't some green newbie.

Brent wanted a sub. She needed to learn to be what he needed. Her mother had been born with that kind of nature, always giving, letting others lead, making sure those people she loved came first in all things. Her sister was that way as well. Chaya had been striving to be like them her whole life, but her need to push limits, to take charge, her stubbornness, had always come forward, had gotten in her way.

The opposite a male like Brent wanted.

If she wanted him, she had to fight for him.

He said he wasn't interested in amateur hour.

What if the next time she went to him she wasn't an amateur?

CHAPTER 3

"So how's the new club going? I was hoping Laz might take me," Eve said, grinning.

Chaya snorted. "Yeah, good luck with that. He handled it so well the last time you were at one of Brent's dens of iniquity."

"Honestly, after what Eve told me about her time in Chicago living above Havoc, I'm more than a little curious myself," Mia added before popping another piece of chocolate in her mouth.

Chaya took Mia's hand and looked her in the eyes. "You, sister dear, are bonkers if you think Zenon would ever, in a million years, let you put even one of your precious pinkie toes over the threshold."

Eve chuckled. "She has a point there."

"As if Lazarus is any better," Mia said.

Eve sat back in her seat, nodding. "You know, mating's only made them worse. I thought it would calm them down...you know, eventually, but boy was I wrong. Laz actually growled at some poor demi the other day for daring to touch my arm. The male was just getting my attention to ask about his training schedule."

"I guess that's what happens when you hitch your wagon to one of those non-human types," Chaya said, trying not to let the jealousy steadily rising inside her show. "They don't act human."

"And thank God for that," Eve said, going for the chocolate herself.

That depended on the male. Setting your sights on a sex demon certainly hadn't been a barrel of laughs.

Painful memories flashed through her mind. Her first and only ill-fated attempt in the bedroom was with a demi she'd met at the compound, not long after her transition. They were fooling around in his room and she'd made a complete idiot of herself.

She'd been too rough, too aggressive, he'd said. Both things males didn't like, apparently. But something had just...come over her. In the end, he'd told her to leave, that he wasn't feeling it anymore. So she left, virginity still intact.

He'd made her feel abnormal, undesirable.

The humiliation of that night still burned.

And like her sister, Chaya had never dated human males, which meant their experience was limited. But knowing what was coming, that they had a demon side just waiting to be unleashed, they'd been cautious, afraid to form attachments or risk getting their hearts involved.

"So, Chay," Mia said. "Has Brent hired anyone nice? Maybe some hot males working the bar? What about the bouncers or security?"

"They're all nice," Chaya said, being evasive.

Her sister rolled her eyes. "You know what I mean...a guy that you can—"

The door opened and Zenon walked in.

His brows dropped, a scowl covering his face. "What guy?"

As usual, his gaze went straight to Mia.

Chaya had noticed a big change in Zenon, but he still felt most comfortable around her sister or his brothers.

Mia stood and walked over to him, her sister instinctively knowing he needed her close. "I was just asking Chaya about the guys she'd met at the new club."

His yellow gaze slid to Chaya and she forced herself not to jolt or look surprised by that direct stare.

"Who are they?" Zenon said, or more growled. "They touch you? Hurt you?" His fingers curled into tight fists. "Names, Chaya."

Chaya knew her mouth had dropped open but she couldn't do anything about it. "Um…"

Mia placed her hand on her mate's chest. "No one's hurt her. I was just asking if she'd met anyone nice, that's all."

His chin dropped, eyes going back to Mia. "And has she?"

"No. Well, I don't think so." Mia turned to her, brows raised in question.

Jesus. If she had met someone, she certainly wouldn't own up to it now. It was like watching Animal Planet, and Mia was doing a good impersonation of David Attenborough. "Nope. Just me, myself, and I."

"See," Mia said. "No one for you to threaten or maim, not yet anyway."

Zenon's lips curled up on the side and Chaya again had to work at not showing her surprise. She'd only seen that small grin once before, and it only came out when he was with Mia, but it damn near knocked her out of her seat. Zenon was a different male to the one she'd met when she came here after her own transition. She'd avoided him, walked the other way if she saw him coming. She'd been afraid of him. Now she knew how badly she'd misjudged him.

SHERILEE GRAY

The pain he'd been living in.

Zenon loved fiercely. He loved Mia more than Chaya thought it was possible to love another human being. He'd been prepared to give up his life to ensure her safety.

For that, Chaya loved him as well.

They were family, and going by his reaction now, he thought of her in the same way.

Chaya stood and lifted her hands in surrender. "Okay, put down the shotgun. I always wondered what it'd be like to have a brother, and it's as annoying as I expected," she said, smirking. "Dude, are you going to inspect every guy I have the hots for?"

Zenon's gaze came back to her and he looked as surprised as she had a moment ago, and then he went and shocked her again. "Yeah, as a matter of fact. And I will feed them their own dicks if they step out of line."

Eve and Mia started chuckling.

"You're not serious?" Chaya said, because she had no damn idea. Did Zenon even make jokes?

He shrugged. "That's what brothers do, right?" He turned away and she was sure she saw him grin. Maybe.

Chaya was both touched and alarmed at the same time. "Ha ha. Good one."

He said nothing more, kissed Mia, and headed for the door.

"You're joking, right?" she called after him. Chaya spun to Mia. "Tell me he's joking?"

Then Zenon was gone.

Chaya stared at her sister. "Mia?"

Mia finally turned to her and winced. "Um...yes?"

"The lack of conviction behind that answer is not exactly filling me with confidence."

Mia gave her a sympathetic look. "He's still a little protective. And you're family so someone to be protected."

How could Chaya be pissed at that? "Best I keep my love life to myself, then," she said.

Mia pointed at her. "Ha! So you have met someone!"

Chaya picked up her bag and slung it over her shoulder. "Well, I'm not likely to tell you now, am I?"

Eve and Mia grinned then couldn't hold in their laughter.

"Seriously?" Chaya said.

Eve wiped her eyes. "I'm sorry, but the look on your face when Zenon threatened to feed whoever you date their own dicks. That was priceless."

"Awesome," Chaya said. "You're both jerks, by the way."

They laughed harder, and then Chaya couldn't help it and ended up laughing as well.

She left not long after that, and after avoiding more questions about Brent from Eve, who had insisted on walking her to the elevators, she headed to the ground floor. But not to leave the compound, not yet.

James, a demi-demon as well, could usually be found down there. He lived there full time and helped train the new demi the knights brought in, freshly transitioned and desperate for help controlling their powers. And she was right. He was coming out of one of the training rooms when she exited the elevator.

"Just the man I'm looking for," she said.

A warm smile lit up his face. "Hey, Chay. Good to see you. I heard you were back."

"You heard right. Will we be seeing you at the club anytime soon?"

He crossed his arms and leaned against the wall. "I had thought about stopping by."

"You totally should."

"So what's up?" he said, seeing through her completely.

Chaya motioned to the small room he sometimes used as an office. "A quick word, if you've got a little time?"

He dipped his chin. "I've got fifteen before my next training session, if that'll work."

"Absolutely."

She followed him in and shut the door behind them.

"What's going on, Chaya?"

She leaned against the door and took a steadying breath. "You're one of them, aren't you?"

He shifted from one foot to the other, but his expression didn't change. "I'm not sure what you mean."

"The demi that have joined the war. You're one of them."

He started to shake his head.

"The knights, they don't know you're involved." That much was obvious.

His jaw tightened.

"Look, I'm not here to blow your cover. I won't tell anyone your secret, not ever. I think what you're doing is amazing."

"So why are you here, Chay?"

She noticed he still hadn't confirmed or denied his involvement. But as soon as she'd heard about the group of renegades, she'd known without a doubt that James would be one of them. The male saw more, knew more about what they faced than most. His position here, his job with the knights made sure of that. And she'd witnessed his frustration over what was happening, over how vulnerable the demi were, at feeling powerless.

"I want to help. I want to join the fight," she said.

He stared at her for the longest time, like he was trying to read her mind, and for all she knew he could. She had no idea what the guy's power was.

When he still hadn't answered her, she said, "Look, my power may not be earth shattering, but I know I can help, I know it. I want to."

"If Zenon found out—"

"He won't, not from me. I promise you that." She hoped he saw the sincerity on her face and could hear it in her voice.

He shoved his fingers through his hair. "I need you to know why I'm involved in this."

"You don't need to explain."

"I see them, Chaya, every damn day," he said, an intensity on his face she'd never seen before. "Battle weary and battered from the fight. Those males, they can't remember a time when they weren't fighting. It's all they know. They're my friends, my family, and I just...I want to help them."

She moved in, touched his arm. "I never thought, not for one moment that you were betraying them, James. And I promise, no one will ever know about your involvement from me."

The muscle in his jaw jumped. "Thank you." He let out a rough breath. "Okay, I can organize for you to talk to someone. But I can't make any promises, yeah?"

Excitement filled her. "That's all I want." She smiled at him. "You won't regret it."

He didn't look convinced. But that was understandable given who she was now related to. She would prove herself, though.

To all of them.

CHAPTER 4

WITH A GROAN, Brent rolled to his back, scrubbing his hands over his face, and glanced at the alarm clock. Early evening. He'd slept the day away…and woken with his dick so hard it felt like molten steel burning against his stomach.

Images of Chaya had tormented him all damn night— shit, the last two nights, and what little sleep he did manage had been plagued with dreams of her. Instead of getting her out of that cage, and the shit show that followed, Chaya had walked across the club in those spike-heeled boots, right up to him, and turned the tables on him. She'd pressed those soft curves against him, those pixie features hardening, hunger bright in her expressive eyes, and she'd led him to his office.

Then she'd ordered him to his knees, and after getting him to pleasure her with his mouth repeatedly, tugging on his hair, taking every damn thing she wanted and then demanding more, she'd freed his aching cock, climbed onto his lap, and rewarded him for being a good sub by taking him deep inside her, fucking him with all the pent-up frustration burning between them.

598

His cock twitched against his abs. "Shit." Who would have thought needing to come several times a day would be such a goddamn burden? But it was, especially when you were as messed up as he was.

Gripping his shaft, he kicked off the blankets. He didn't think he'd ever been so hard. The veins bulged along the thick length, the head an angry purple, glistening from the pre-come leaking from the tiny slit in a constant stream.

He stroked himself, squeezed and tugged on his aching cock until his hips were bucking off the bed, instinct taking over. All he could see was Chaya, her hot little body, those out-of-control curves as she danced in that goddamn cage, tempting him, tormenting him, making him want things he couldn't have. Sweat slid down his chest, across his abs, and he jerked it faster, harder.

He hissed, wanting—needing—to come so bad he hurt, throbbed. His balls drew up tight, ass clenched, every muscle in his body as hard as his dick. So close, he was so close.

He continued to fuck into his fist, his panted breaths turning to gasps. But he couldn't come, not like this, never like this.

He needed others' emotions to survive, but he'd numbed himself so much to his own he had to cause himself pain to come during sex so he could feel something, even if it was pain.

That's what he told himself anyway.

No, you're messed up. Fucked in the head.

He shoved Chaya's image from his mind, spread his legs wide, and brought his hand down hard and sharp against his scrotum. Hissing in pain, back arching off the bed, he finally came, long and violent.

He slumped back against the mattress, gasping, waiting for the nausea to pass, the pain in his groin and lower belly to cease. For the indescribable relief to finish rocking through him. His cock lay flaccid against his stomach, his biceps and thigh muscles spasming, trembling from the strain.

"Fuck this." On shaky legs, he stumbled out of bed, collided with the wall, righted himself, and somehow made it to the bathroom without falling on his face, suddenly desperate to wash off the come and sweat coating his skin. And before he could shut it down, an unwanted memory slammed into him without warning.

"That's it, boy. Clean up the proof of your lack of control." He trailed his hand down Brent's back, along his spine, and squeezed his ass painfully. "You have disappointed me. You need to learn control. Punishing you pains me as much as it pains you."

Brent didn't answer. Answering just got him in more trouble. Those rough hands continued to move over his body. The touch made him want to throw up, to pull away, but to his horror, his cock began to harden again and the word "please" escaped without his say-so.

"Hmm, you are such a rare find, Brent. See how my touch affects you? Your incubus nature knows what you want, what you need even if your human side continues to deny it." He fisted his hair. "You are sex, Brent. Nothing more, nothing less. And you are mine."

"No," he hissed, turning the shower to hot. Garrett would pay for what he did, not just to him but the others he'd held in that building. Brent thought he had a handle on the memories, the nightmare of the past. He needed to regain control. It was all about revenge now, making that bastard pay. Then it would be over, this darkness would finally lift.

When he climbed out of the shower, he took his time dressing, allowed the ritual of putting on his suit, of donning his armor, his guise, to rebuild his defenses. He needed to regain control, to rebuild his walls. He couldn't let anyone see who he truly was underneath the carefully constructed veneer.

But then, he didn't really know who was underneath it all anymore.

Who would surface if he let it all go.

He played the game well, had everyone around him convinced, almost had himself convinced there for a while, but then those memories would rear back up and he'd lose his balance all over again.

Leaving his apartment, he went down to the club and straight to his office. Some of his staff had already arrived, but he wasn't ready to see anyone yet. Taking a seat at his desk, he fired up his laptop. A stack of mail sat beside it and he flicked through. The documentation for his new purchase was there, delivered this morning while he was still asleep. He entered the password on his computer then unlocked the bottom drawer of his desk and shoved the envelope inside with the others. All the other bites he'd taken in the hope that the bastard would eventually bite back. Since that hadn't happened yet, he'd decided to make it easy on the fucker by putting himself right under Garrett's nose.

There was a light knock on his office door. He knew who it was instantly and slammed the drawer shut. "Come in."

The door opened and Chaya stepped inside. She'd called in sick the night before and he knew it was because of him, because of the way he'd hurt her. He waited for the onslaught of emotion to wash over him, but nothing happened. She'd locked herself away, something she'd never done around him before, not like this, and for once he had no sense of what was going on in her head, how she was feeling. He hated it.

Her gaze skimmed over his then focused on something over his shoulder. "You got a minute?"

"Of course."

"Do you mind if I leave early tonight…and tomorrow as

well? I called Jasmine; she'll cover for me so you won't be short."

Chaya never took extra time off, had never asked for it in the eighteen months she'd worked for him. "Why?"

Her gaze shot to his. "I don't really think that's any of your business, do you?"

He shrugged, heart racing a little faster. "I guess that depends on what you're doing."

He was pushing her, pushing for something more than the cool indifference she was giving him. He couldn't have her, but he couldn't bear there to be this wall between them. That's why he'd tried to put things right after he'd hurt her, tried to make her understand. Instead he'd made everything a whole lot worse. Still, here he was again, wishing, hoping, pushing for something that would never, could never happen. *Fool.*

She crossed her arms, drawing attention to the way her top plunged low, giving him a fantastic view down the front, a teasing look at her beautiful body.

"Are you serious? You said the other night you wanted us to be friends. Well, pulling this shit isn't doing you any favors, just FYI."

"Are we? Are we friends, Chaya?" All he could think about was how she'd looked in that cage, how sexy, how badly he still wanted her. His fantasy of what he wished had happened instead.

He stood and moved toward her before he realized what he was doing. The incubus in him was pissed she was hiding from him and wanted a taste of her heady emotions. Wanted to feast, to get closer, to nuzzle into the warmth of her skin and breathe in her scent. The human he'd once been knew how fucked up that was.

She was wearing another little pleated leather skirt, this one deep purple. Her shapely legs were covered in black fishnets and her favorite spike-heeled knee-high boots. His gaze traveled over her and back up to that top, the way it hugged her breasts.

She licked her lips. "You tell me."

He put the brakes on before he reached her, before he did all the things he knew he shouldn't. Moving to the front of his desk, he rested on the edge and crossed his arms. "I'd like nothing more."

She flinched, and he realized how his choice of words might sound to her.

Shit.

"Right. Well, since that's sorted, I should get to work." She turned to leave.

"Chay." She stilled in front of the door but didn't turn to face him. "I care about you. You know that. A great deal. Hurting you is the last thing I want."

Her hand that had been resting on the door handle dropped, and she spun to face him. "What is your problem, Brent? Really?" She moved in then, full of confidence and fire. Came right up until she stood between his splayed thighs, challenging him. The incubus, the sub rejoiced, desperate to accept.

His stomach clenched at the same time his cock hardened. Her gaze dropped, landed on his rapidly growing erection, and her eyes flared before lifting back to his.

"Chaya," he said, trying to project a warning in his tone.

She took another step closer so her hips brushed his inner thighs, and he froze. "Are you going to deny *that* as well?"

Different emotions fought for dominance inside him and he struggled to speak. Finally, he got it together enough to shake his head. "I'm a sex demon, an incubus, Chaya. *I am sex.*" The words flowed easily from his mouth, words that only one person had ever said to him. A person who had used him when he was at his most vulnerable, when he'd had no control over the new demon side of his nature.

She leaned in. "Bullshit."

"Don't." His voice was nothing but a needy rasp, but he didn't have the power to push her away. Her hands landed on his thighs and he hissed.

"So I could be anyone…and you'd react this way?" One of her small warm hands stayed on his thigh, the other trailing up over his abs then continued on to rest at the center of his chest. "Anyone could make your heart pound like this?" She continued her exploration until her palm landed on the frantic pulse at his throat, her fingers brushing the hair at his nape. "Could make your pulse race?"

He didn't touch her, afraid of what might happen if he did. The hand resting on his thigh burned through the thin fabric of his trousers. The other gripping the side of his throat, her thumb smoothing over his skin, brushed his jaw. The hold was confident…possessive.

Fuck. He couldn't move. Groaning inwardly, he fought to keep his expression neutral. "I spend ninety-five percent of every day ready to fuck, Chaya. It's the nature of my demon." His voice was deceptively steady, even though he had to lock every damn muscle in his body so his thighs didn't tremble.

She leaned in so her breasts rested against his folded arms, her lips only an inch from his. "Bullshit," she repeated, then her tongue darted out and slid across his lower lip.

In that moment, with that one touch, common sense deserted him. Adrenaline and hunger pumped through his veins like liquid fire. He was about to beg her to live out the dream that had tormented him the last two nights, when she stepped back suddenly, spun on her heel, and without a backward glance strode out of his office, shutting the door after her.

Chest pumping, he sucked down several deep breaths in

an effort to get oxygen to his scrambled brain. To stop from getting to his feet and going after her. Instead, he kept his ass cemented to the desk and took a few minutes to get his mind and body under control.

He didn't usually drink at work, especially if he planned on taking someone to his playroom, but tonight he needed one, a strong one. It took effort, but when he stood, he forced his feet to take him to his seat instead of the door and sat behind the desk. Slumping in his chair, he grabbed the whiskey from his drawer and took a shot straight out of the bottle.

Fuck.

He took another pull, the smooth burn a welcome relief. Glancing at his computer, he noticed several new emails in his in-box. One in particular caught his attention.

Parting was such sweet sorrow.

Opening it, he frowned when he saw a video was attached. He instantly recognized the room in the still frame. Shit, it felt like his heart had crawled into his throat.

He hit play.

A young male in his early twenties, mask covering his eyes, fucked a woman beneath him while another male fucked him from behind. All around them others stood watching. The male cried out...begged for more.

The young male in the middle was him.

New to his completely out-of-control incubus side, he'd been confused and afraid. Full of so much hunger and need, so much fear and pain, he barely knew which way was up.

This was filmed a week after he'd gone through his transition, a fledgling demi-demon. He'd been ruled by lust, afraid of his body's reactions. Too far gone to fight for himself, to understand what was happening to him. One minute he'd fought, screamed for them to let him go, the next, lost in what he was becoming, he'd begged for it, ached for it.

The pleasure, the pain.

Their dominance.

He'd submitted. Every. Damn. Time.

Had craved it.

And that was what he struggled with most.

A message was typed underneath.

Don't fuck with me or I'll fuck with you.

Brent took another swig of whiskey.

Wrong, asshole.

He was not that same naive, lost kid anymore.

And, finally, he'd drawn the bastard out of hiding. Picking up the phone, he called an old friend, a demi-demon who had helped him search for anything with Garrett Industries attached to it and knew his way around a computer like no one else.

Time to intensify the hunt, track Garrett down, and finish this.

CHAPTER 5

CHAYA STOOD in the doorway of Deluca Gym and checked out the large room. In the middle, padded mats covered the floor, and exercise equipment had been set up on the outer edges. A group of females stood in the middle, moving in unison as another barked out drills, kicking and punching the air in a kind of synchronized dance. She guessed it was some kind of martial art or combat fighting.

Chaya took in the female at the front, the one instructing them. She was lithe and tall, her hair pale blond, almost white, and she had it pulled back in a long ponytail.

This was obviously Grace, her contact.

There was a seat close to the door and Chaya sat to wait. They were amazing to watch, and the longer she sat there, the more she worried that she wouldn't have anything to offer this group of demi. Because that's what they were, she realized. All of them. Females who were strong and skilled, brave and determined.

She'd never been in a fight in her life. Did she really think she could face off against actual demons, ones determined to take over her world?

What the hell was she doing here?

The class ended and Chaya quickly stood. She'd made a mistake. What could she possibly contribute here? She slung her bag over her shoulder and turned to leave.

"Chaya?"

She stopped in her tracks and turned.

The female standing there frowned a little. "Do you have to go?"

Chaya shook her head. "No, I…" She met the other female's direct stare, who Chaya was now positive was Grace going by the description James gave her. "This was a mistake. I can't fight like that…"

Grace took her hand and stopped her from taking another backward step. "Not everyone in this war is fighting it in the physical sense."

"No?"

Grace shook her head. "Why don't we have a chat and go from there?"

This female had a strength that could not be missed, a determination that drew you in. She was also extremely beautiful, and her striking mahogany eyes were almost hypnotic. There were no powers at work here, though, just a female, a leader, who was determined to save her kind.

"I'd like that." Chaya followed her across the room and into a small office.

Grace took a seat and motioned for Chaya to do the same. A smile warmed her perfect features. "I know your sister."

That surprised her. "You know Mia?"

"Oh, she had no idea what we were doing here. She took my self-defense class a while back. I sensed she was power-ful, but there was also a giant demon hunter sniffing around her so I decided she might not be the best candidate to recruit for our cause."

Chaya didn't see any reason to keep secrets. "That giant demon hunter is Zenon and they're now mated. He's family. Also, like all demi, my father was a demon, but unlike most, I know him. We have a relationship. He's a good male, Grace. Which is another reason I want to help in this war. Not all demons are created equal, and I want to make sure demons like my father aren't persecuted. Is that going to be a problem?"

Grace stood and took two bottles of water from a small fridge by her desk. "No." She offered Chaya one. "Not if you keep our identities a secret, at least for now. And I agree, not all demons are bad or evil. We don't go around killing indiscriminately. As for your father, the relationship isn't a problem; may even be helpful in the future."

Chaya took the water. "I would never reveal your identities. And not just because it'd be a dick move. No one would be happy about me joining forces with you, especially not my family. Zenon would lose his shit and Chaos would probably lock me in one of the holding cells."

Grace stilled, her expression flattening. "No, I'm sure Chaos would be pissed that he's being shown up, but maybe if he did his goddamn job we wouldn't be where we are now."

Okay, so no love lost there. Still, she asked, "Have you thought about approaching them, working with them?"

Grace shook her head then took a swig of her water. "Not possible. And besides, it's our lives on the line. We should be able to defend ourselves without asking permission to do so."

Fair enough. And that was kind of how she was feeling, how she'd been feeling for a long time. "So how do you think I can help?"

Grace sat again. "We have eyes and ears all over this city, some demi, some human, some other. The humans don't know what we are, of course, but they don't mind giving information for a fee." She rested her forearms on her knees.

"We're pretty sure the knights suspect a high-level demon is behind the strange activity in the city. Someone powerful." Her gaze leveled on Chaya. "I understand you have a wide and varied clientele at Toxic?"

Chaya straightened. "Well, yes."

"We know there are powerful demons in this city who have grown in strength since they came to Earth but, to anyone watching, appear to be toeing the line, following the rules set out by the knights. We think it's one of them."

"Okay," Chaya said, a nervous twist in her stomach.

"We don't just need fighters, Chaya, we need eyes and ears on the ground floor. Toxic is the kind of place they frequent."

Chaya knew exactly what Grace was asking.

"Being those eyes and ears, is that something you're willing to do?"

"Yes," she said instantly. "I just want to help."

Grace nodded and stood, grabbed her phone off the desk, and came back to Chay. Grace tapped at the screen and showed Chaya three photos. "These are the demons we're most interested in. All I need you to do is look out for them. First and foremost, you need to be safe, but if one of them comes in, watch them, who they're talking to, who they're with."

Chaya reached for the phone. "Can I take another look?"

Grace handed it to her. She'd never seen either of the males in the first or second pictures, but the third— "I know him," she said, holding up the phone to Grace. "His name's Victor."

"That's right," Grace said, moving closer.

Chaya quickly rummaged around in her purse and found the card he'd given her. "I spoke to him a couple of nights ago when he came in. He gave me this." Chaya quickly explained what it was for.

Grace's eyes flashed with excitement. "You game?"

The elevator opened, and Brent walked out and into the control room of the knights' compound. He hadn't been here since he left four years ago. Incubi were one of the rare breeds of demi, for some reason, and the whole process after he'd been found and liberated had been humiliating and time consuming.

So although this was the place where he'd learned to regain his control, it held no happy memories for him.

The door opened and Rocco walked in. The knight grinned. "You're late."

"I'm sure you've been watching the clock in anticipation," Brent drawled.

Rocco walked up, took Brent's outstretched hand, and tugged him in, giving him a rib-rattling back thump. "Brother, good to see you."

"You, too."

"Been meaning to come by the club, check it out, but shit's been…" He paused like he was searching for the right word. He settled on "fucked."

"So I hear." Brent followed him through the doors and into the stairwell. "Anything I can do?"

"As soon as we nail down who's behind it, yeah, possibly. Right now, we're not entirely sure what we're dealing with. But I have a feeling things are only going to get worse. Like all-hands-on-deck kind of worse before this shit show is over."

Brent was surprised to hear this. He'd offered help a lot, but never had one of the knights accepted it, not to that level anyway. He knew things were bad, but he thought they had them somewhat under control.

They reached the landing and Rocco led him to the cafeteria doors. Through them he could hear people talking and the clatter of cutlery.

Rocco turned to him. "Brace, brother. The females got a little excited about this family dinner idea. Eve banned weapons and Meredith went and got one of those cloths for the table."

"A tablecloth," Brent said, biting back a grin.

"Yeah, one of those things, and napkins, the kind you don't throw away," Roc said, looking genuinely bemused.

"The horror. Real napkins. What in God's name is she thinking?" Brent said, chuckling because there was no holding it in now.

Rocco scowled at him. "Dick."

"Just wait until the rest of you find mates. You won't stand a chance."

Instead of scowling harder, the male's face actually lit up. "Yeah, I guess not." He pushed the door open and Brent followed him in.

Fuck knew what that was about.

He took in the room. In the middle, several tables had been pushed together to make one large one, and, yes, it had been covered by a tablecloth. It was beautifully set and everyone—the knights and their mates, James, Mia and Chaya's father, Marcus, and near the end, Chaya herself—was seated.

He'd kept himself busy the last couple of nights, kept to his office, made sure they didn't cross paths. And here she was. Of course she was here. Every part of him homed in on her like he hadn't seen her in weeks not days. He started toward her, his feet taking control and guiding him right where he wanted to be.

"You can sit here," Eve said, her voice cutting through the haze surrounding him, *controlling* him.

Shit.

There wasn't even a seat beside Chaya. What did he think he was going to do? Tug her out of hers and pull her onto his lap?

Kneel on the floor beside her?

He inwardly groaned. That's exactly what he wanted to do. Instead, he took the seat next to his friend and did his best to ignore his hunger for the female a short distance away.

They ate and talked, and as the night wore on people got up and moved about, changed seats. Except Gunner, since the male had already left. Brent couldn't put his finger on it, but the male didn't seem himself, seemed distant, and as soon as the meal was finished he'd excused himself and strode out. His departure was noted by his brothers and Brent hadn't missed the concerned looks.

"We're close," Chaos said, breaking through his thoughts.

Brent was sitting at the end of the table with Laz, Chaos, and Rocco.

"There are demons in this city who've been here a long fucking time, almost as long as us. Okay, yeah, that's a fucking long game, but you can't tell me some of them haven't grown in power, that they couldn't somehow now be in league with Diemos."

Diemos, Lucifer's son and the current head asshole of Hell, since Lucifer was AWOL, wanted Earth and he wouldn't stop until he got it. If anyone was behind the unrest in the city, it had to be him, but there was only so much Diemos could do from Hell. Finding out who's strings he was pulling here in Roxburgh was top priority.

Chaos glanced meaningfully at Brent. "We know there are powerful demons out there."

Brent shifted in his seat, fought the heat rising from under his shirt collar. "You have any leads?"

"Several," Rocco said. "We're watching. But with the block they have covering their tracks, it's a slow fucking process. And while we try to figure this shit out, their army is growing."

"If that's the case, you're going to need help."

Chaos's fingers tightened around his glass. "I've been in talks with the Hell hounds."

"Yeah, and how's that going?" Brent said.

"Could be better."

Rocco snorted. "Now there's an understatement. Our last *talk* ended with more than one black eye and a dislocated shoulder."

"Still better than the meeting before that," Laz said, resting his forearms on the table and smirking at Roc. "I forgot how much noses bleed. At least yours is straight again."

Rocco flipped Lazarus off.

Brent bit back a laugh at the disgruntled look on Rocco's face, then said, "My line of work brings me in contact with a lot of different beings. Some could be very useful. If there's anything I can do. Anything at all, I'm here…"

Chaya's scent hit him a second before she spoke.

"Me, too," she said. "I want to help."

The knights stilled and all eyes shifted to her.

"We won't be needing your help, Chaya," Chaos said. His voice said *don't even think about arguing with me*. But this was Chaya, and she didn't give a shit about warnings.

"Why? Because I'm a female?" she said, arms crossed, expression defiant as hell.

"No," Chaos said. "Because you have no training and no idea what we'll be up against."

"You need more than just fighters," she said. "This has gone far beyond that, hasn't it? You need eyes and ears. You need people all over this city. We're here and we're ready to help. All you have to do is ask. Brent's right, you need us. You have an army already right under your nose, ready and waiting."

Brent stood. "That's not what I said—"

She ignored him. "Diemos is clever enough to know how useful we could be, that our powers could be used to take this city. We're hunted by his demons, targeted from the moment we transition. This is our fight as well. Use us, Chaos."

The whole room had gone quiet, everyone around the table watching the exchange.

Chaos stood as well. "I won't send a group of untrained civilians into a fight to be slaughtered."

Her back straightened. "Hang on a minute—"

"We were created, put on this earth, to protect you," Chaos said, voice hard. "We will not use you as weapons. It can only end badly, Chaya. For all of us."

Chaos was being patient, not something he did often, but if Chaya pushed this, he wouldn't be so kind.

"Use me. Use us. We want you to," she said, voice getting more forceful.

Hearing her say those words—*use me*—every muscle tightened. Christ, it felt like his skin was too small for his body. He wanted her to *use him* in any and every way she could dream up.

"We?" Chaos said, voice deceptively soft. "Who's we?"

Chaya stiffened. "I just mean demi, all of us. We want to help ourselves."

"And you speak for them? All of them?"

Chaya growled. "Of course not, but—"

"That's enough, Chaya," Brent said beside her.

She turned to him, eyes flashing. "You don't tell me when and when not to speak."

"Okay," Rocco said with a clap. "Who's for dessert?"

615

Everyone started talking again and heading for the desserts on the table. Chaya shoved past and headed for the exit. Mia followed.

Brent caught up to Mia at the same time as Zenon did. "Let me go after Chay. I can give her a ride home."

Brent thought he'd come up against protest, but Mia had obviously worked out her sister wasn't in the mood to be around any of the knights, not even Zenon, because her mate would definitely not entertain the notion of either his mate or his mate's sister taking up arms against some unknown demon force.

Mia thanked him and he strode after Chaya.

CHAPTER 6

"CHAYA, WAIT," Brent called after her.

She stilled but ignored him and carried on across the parking garage under the compound and out the door.

He was probably the last person she wanted to see but there was no way he was leaving without her. "Goddammit, Chay. Where the hell are you going?"

There was nowhere to go, she didn't own a car, and she wasn't exactly wearing walking shoes, though she had no trouble striding away from him in her spiked heels. The kind that made his mouth water. Add in the way she looked in her leather pants and the top that was a complete contrast, soft and skimming her lush curves, and he was gone. That was without images of those pointed heels digging into his ass while she ordered him to fuck her. So, yeah, walking was getting kind of difficult.

She reached the large corrugated gates that she needed to get by to escape and was forced to stop. She stared up at them, body rigid.

They both stood there for long seconds in silence. Finally, Brent moved up behind her. "We can stand here all night, you ignoring me, both of us getting cold, or you can get in my car and I'll give you a ride home."

Without a word, she spun on those sexy heels and started back the way they'd come. He followed her to his car and opened the door for her. She mutely climbed in.

Okay, so he'd count that as a small win. But then Chaya was a smart woman. She might let her emotions rule sometimes, but she was also tuned into that part of herself.

Yeah, her understanding of her emotions was spot on and she knew exactly when to let them take the lead.

Unfortunately for Chaya, recently they'd led her to him. And his own emotional state was, well, in the eloquent words of Rocco...fucked.

He climbed in beside her, and as soon as he pulled the door closed he was bathed in her scent. Spicy and rich, almost as intoxicating as the taste of her emotions when she didn't lock him out. God, he hated that. His powers were a burden, but he'd grown used to knowing what people were feeling. It provided him with a level of comfort as well as a way to feed the incubus side of himself.

He hated that Chaya was purposely keeping him out, keeping him at a distance. It was selfish to want that from her, but he wanted it all the same.

"So what was that back there?" he said as he drove toward the gates. They shuddered open and he hit the street.

"I thought I made it pretty clear," she said, eyes aimed forward and purposely not once coming to him.

He hated that as well.

"Jesus. You really want to fight in this war?" he said, and just saying the words sent fear and dread through him so hard and fast he couldn't fucking see straight.

She shrugged. "Not necessarily. But I think demi need to be given a chance to do more, to defend themselves as well."

"You can *defend* yourself. No one is stopping you. Maybe

you should start coming to the self-defense classes they're doing here. It's going on the attack that the knights want to discourage. There's already a group of vigilante demi out there causing trouble. That's more than enough for the knights to deal with."

She turned to him, and even though she was pissed off, he soaked it up, letting the warmth that her gaze gave him lift tingles all over his skin.

Her hands rested on her thighs and she slid them up the soft leather to her knees and back.

He had to hold back a groan.

"The way I hear it, those *vigilantes* saved Chaos's life not so long ago," she said.

Brent frowned. "Who told you that?"

"Mia. And she would know."

He wasn't sure what to say without sounding like a hypocrite. He felt the same as Chaya, mostly anyway, which was why, though he hadn't actually joined the fight, he did know who was behind it and kept it to himself. It put him in a tough position but he felt loyalty to both the knights and the demi making a stand. But he'd sure as fuck prefer that Chaya wasn't involved.

"Chaos is just trying to protect you," he said in the end, because that was the truth. The knights had been fighting for hundreds of years, making sacrifices all for the good of mankind.

"I know," she said. "And I appreciate that, but this might be bigger than them, and if it is, they need to accept help for the same reason."

She was right, but they couldn't solve the troubles in this city right then in this car, and the last thing he wanted to do was fight with her.

So he kept his mouth shut. They drove in silence for the next fifteen minutes. And despite the conversation they'd just had, he couldn't ignore the current zapping between them. It nailed him over and over again and he absorbed it like junkie, taking whatever dregs he could get.

His cock was impossibly hard and his skin felt almost painful it was so sensitive. He wanted to tear his clothes off and just fucking bask in it, in her and what she was sending out. It was like she was so full with emotion it couldn't be contained and lapped over the edges of her psyche like gentle waves washing over him. He'd never experienced anything like it before. Like a tickle below the skin you couldn't pinpoint to scratch and relieve it. Hovering at the breaking point of unimaginable pleasure. And because she was still holding back, the break, the fall, wasn't ever going to come.

Sweat slid down between his shoulder blades and he was close to writhing in his damn seat. He tried to focus on the road, but he realized when he watched Chaya squeeze her lush thighs together that he wasn't the only one affected by the close proximity.

Fuck.

The intensity just kept growing and he didn't know how much more he could take. He was fucking shaking. Could she see it? Could she see the way she affected him? That he was close to begging her to give him more, something—anything—to relieve the state of pleasure and pain she had him suspended in without even trying.

Her apartment came into view and he had to grit his teeth so they didn't chatter in his damn head.

He finally pulled over and watched as her trembling hands fumbled with the seat belt. No, he wasn't the only one affected, not by a long shot. She turned to him, her dark brown eyes clashing with his, and he sucked in a rough breath, which only fed him more of her scent, now tinged with her lust. Fuck, he was this close to begging her to fuck him in his seat.

But then she tore her eyes away. "Thanks for the ride. I'll see you at work tomorrow." She shoved the door open and climbed out.

As she did, she dropped her block. Let it fucking collapse. And every emotion, all the hunger and pain and frustration and affection she was feeling came at him. So much, too much, washed over Brent, giving him the peak, the fall, he'd been hovering above.

He couldn't form a reply and she didn't wait, oblivious to what was happening to him as she shut the door and strode away. He moaned as he watched her, and, yeah, writhed in his seat, hips moving, sweating, skin prickling, cock pulsing. He gripped the steering wheel so tight it groaned. He cursed. He needed release. Now.

With one fumbling hand, he grabbed for the keys and yanked them out of the ignition, flicked open the small switchblade there, and dragged the blade across his forearm.

He started coming.

In his pants.

Like the pathetic asshole he'd become.

He kept his eyes on Chaya until she disappeared into her apartment building.

Thank fuck for tinted windows.

He looked down at himself with disgust. Even if he could have Chaya, he didn't know if he was strong enough for her. Not anymore.

How long could he hide this weakness?

Chaya hit the number that had been programmed into her phone and held her breath. After her run-in with Chaos, she was more determined than ever to join the fight. Yes, she got where he was coming from. But these demi weren't untrained fools. They were organized, skilled. They knew what they were doing.

"Chaya?" Grace answered, voice strong confident.

Chaya tried for the same. "I've made my decision." Nerves fluttered behind her ribs, but she ignored them. "I'm in. I'm going to The Dungeon tonight as a voyeur."

There was music in the background, some movement then it quietened down, like Grace had changed rooms. "The main priority is always your safety. Always. You are there to observe only. Get a lay of the land. See who's there. If Victor's there, who he associates with. I want you to turn on the GPS on your phone so we can keep track of you. If you change location let me know. And I want regular check-in times. Anything happens that you don't like, you get out of there. If for some reason you can't, message me, and we'll come for you. If you can't do that and you miss your check-in, we'll come for you. Understand?"

Her nerves tried to fight their way forward again, and Chaya fought them back. "Yes."

"Excellent. Message me with the details for tonight and I'll make sure someone is keeping track of you."

Chaya straightened her shoulders. "Thanks."

"And Chaya?"

"Yes?"

"Good luck."

Chaya kept her head down as she walked through the grand foyer of The Valencia. The place screamed money—shit, it dripped from the walls. She felt insanely out of place. Stepping into the elevator, she hit the button for the private club located in the penthouse suite.

As she ascended, she fired off a text to Grace that she'd

arrived, and then took a moment to try and calm her out-of-control nerves.

You can do this. You have to do this.

For all the demi yet to go through the transition. For the ones who had lost their lives to the demons constantly stalking them.

And if, while she was there, she learned a thing or two about the way Brent's mind worked, the world he was determined to keep her out of, well, that would be a bonus. Because after that car ride earlier, God, her skin still tingled. She tried to stay pissed off at him, to not want him, but there was this thing between them that was *so* strong. Jesus, she wished she could ignore it but she couldn't.

It had taken an hour for her pulse to slow and the throbbing ache between her thighs to lessen. If her first assignment also taught her a thing or two about the man she wanted, she'd use every bit of that knowledge. Then maybe she could prove to him that she was more than capable of fulfilling his needs, all of them.

The elevator doors slid open, and with trembling hands she showed her pass card to the attendant waiting at the door. He grinned down at her but didn't comment on her obvious nerves. She guessed most were nervous their first time, which definitely worked in her favor.

He took her coat, and she smoothed her hands over the leather covering her hips and straightened her shoulders.

There's nothing to worry about. The place is full of people.

Plus, she could leave anytime she liked. She was there because she chose to be. No one was holding a gun to her head.

He opened the door for her and Chaya walked in.

She took a moment to absorb the large room.

The only similarity this place had to Toxic was the patrons. They were mostly *others*, and not just demons either.

But the biggest difference was that the scenes were taking place on the main floor for everyone to see.

When it came to the more hardcore stuff, Brent insisted it was done in the privacy of the playrooms. She wasn't sure why that was, since voyeurism was a big part of the kink for some. But it was his club and his rules.

Here the entire suite was open, one large room. From what she could see, there were alcoves and sectioned-off areas but nothing was completely blocked off, and by the way people were moving around the room or grouped watching, you could go wherever you wanted, watch whatever you wanted. The walls were covered in red silk, and soft lighting cast a heavy golden wash over the room. Wall sconces were dotted around strategically, ensuring the place not only had dark intimate corners but several places where the light was deliberately brighter.

Chaya moved to one of those corners where a crowd had gathered. A Dom had his sub on display. She was over a spanking bench, her bottom pink. He spanked her and she cried out. Her juices coated her inner thighs and the male with her leaned in, talking to her in low tones, petting her.

Chaya felt a deep pull in her belly, a longing that had her squeezing her thighs together. Several other scenes were being played out around her, and though one or two looked seriously intense, she had learned enough from working at the club, even with the action happening behind closed doors, to know nothing was happening to anyone here that they didn't want.

She forced herself to move on. She wondered around the room for the next hour, watching different scenes, and as she did, the longer she observed, something...something shifted inside her.

Since before working at Havoc in Chicago, she'd had this

feeling inside her, a coil of need in her belly that no amount of time with her vibrator could quench.

But she thought she did now.

And it was not what she'd expected.

She wanted this, what these couples were sharing.

And she wanted it with Brent.

Only…maybe, not in the way she'd thought.

She moved around and watched a Domme flogging a male, her sub's sharp cries turning to moans of ecstasy when she put down the flogger and took her time stroking his reddened skin lovingly, praising him.

Chay swallowed hard, mouth suddenly dry. This scene in particular had her belly tightening and her breath quickening. Chaya studied them both. It was impossible to miss their connection. The male's pleasure was his Domme's, it was there in the way she held herself, in the tender expression on her face as she looked at him.

That.

Oh God, Chaya wanted that.

She shivered and emotion clogged her throat. The truth of her feelings, of what she wanted, what she was, hit her all at once.

All this time she thought…

She bit her lip. Being dominated wasn't what she wanted.

She wanted to be the one in control.

A knot coiled in her belly. What would that mean for her and Brent?

Stop. You can't think about this now. You're here to work.

She forced herself to move on to the next scene, to shove out all the thoughts racing around her mind. She couldn't allow herself to get distracted here, no matter how churned up, how confused she felt in that moment.

Chaya took in the room again as she moved deeper. There was a bar along the back wall. She headed in that direction, needing a drink of water. More seating areas were dotted around back here: sofas, private alcoves piled with cushions.

She ordered her drink and was taking a sip when she felt it, the buzz of power. Chaya glanced over her shoulder. Four males—demons—dressed in suits stood a short distance away. And yeah, there was no mistaking that they were extremely powerful. One of them turned to her and she sucked in a breath.

Victor.

He'd been talking to the male beside him, head in close, but when he saw her a smile spread across his face. He said something to his friends and they all turned to face her.

It took effort not to bolt with four demons, who had most likely been on this Earth a hell of a lot longer than her, staring at her. And if these were the males Grace had been watching, and they had the ability to control lower-level demons, they probably ate demi like her for breakfast.

Victor waved her over.

This was it.

She grabbed her drink and, plastering a smile on her face, made her way over to the intimidating foursome.

"Chaya, you came." Victor took both her hands and held her arms out, taking in her outfit…and the rest of her. Her skin crawled. "You look absolutely stunning."

Her leather skirt hugged her hips and thighs, and her top was white lace, sheer, showing off the white corset she wore underneath. "Thank you. I wasn't sure I'd see you here," she said.

His smile turned to a wicked grin. "A happy coincidence." He turned to the male beside him. "This is my friend, Ian, and these are his brothers, Ezra and Nolan."

Brothers?

All eyes were on her now, and they didn't try and

conceal what they were. Three sets of black soulless eyes were trained on her. Goose bumps lifted all over her body and it took everything in her not to take a startled step back.

"Who is this female, Victor?" Ian's nostrils flared like he was drawing in her scent, which was confirmed when he said, "She smells...exquisite."

His voice sounded like broken glass, and when he tilted his head to the side she saw a jagged scar circling his throat, as if someone had once sliced it.

"This is the little demi I mentioned, the one who has been terribly neglected," Victor said. "Isn't she lovely?"

Ian gave her a head to toe, like a hawk sizing up a rabbit. His brothers were watching her more closely as well, and the dread that moved over her had her frozen to the spot. If these males, demon, were in league with Diemos they'd be trying sense her power, what it was, how strong. Deciding of she was worth keeping for the army Diemos was trying to create here on Earth.

She did her best to keep it blocked from them, but had no idea if she was succeeding.

Yeah, she'd well and truly exposed herself.

"She is a delicious morsel," he said to Victor, then to her, "Are you here looking for a sub, lovely?"

She froze. Was it that obvious? Did they see something in her that gave it away? She'd only just realized it herself and these demons had her figured out before she fully had herself. "No, I...I'm not a Domme." Victor thought she was a sub, God, she'd thought she was a sub, and she needed to stick to her story.

Ian stared at her for several long seconds, an odd expression on his face. Shit. He wasn't buying it. "You're a sub?"

She nodded.

He glanced at his brothers and chuckled. "Did you hear

that, Ezra? She's a *sub*." Ezra's eyes glittered in response. "Do you belong to anyone, demi?" Ian asked.

Victor's gaze sharpened on his friend and the tension became unbearably thick.

Chaya forced a laugh, doing her best to pretend that she didn't feel the pure evil pulsing from them, that she didn't hear the internal alarm bells blaring, telling her to run like hell in the opposite direction. "I was working on that the other night when I met Victor. Unfortunately, my efforts went unnoticed." She lowered her eyes, playing coy, playing the part, not sure if she was pulling it off because she'd never been coy a moment in her damned life. "I'm hoping to learn a thing or two here and change his mind."

The words came easy enough, since there was some truth to it.

"Have you ever belonged to anyone, love?" Ian said, his voice even grittier than before.

She shook her head, finding she was unable to lie, not with all of them watching her so closely.

Ian reached out and it took everything in her to hold her ground when he cupped the side of her face. His touch was cool and sent a feeling of dread through her like nothing she'd ever felt.

"Hmmm, such a rare find. Untried. How delightful." His head tilted to the side again, like the predator he so obviously was. "I find I am...drawn to you, Chaya." He glanced at his brothers, and Victor shifted like he was suddenly uncomfortable. "My brothers and I share, in all things, and we like you a lot." His brothers hadn't said one word. But they also hadn't taken their eyes off her. "This other male, you have your heart set on him?"

Chaya nodded, couldn't make her mouth work if her life depended on it, and right then it very well might.

"That is disappointing. If you find your circumstances

change, ask for me here and they'll make sure I get your message." Then he turned to leave, his brothers following in his wake. He paused and looked back at Victor, who was still beside Chaya. "Are you coming?"

"I'm going to show Chaya around," Victor said.

Ian dipped his chin and walked away.

Victor turned to her, his eyes searching hers. "Did he frighten you?"

Chaya shook her head. Lying was easier with just one of them watching her. "They were definitely intimidating, though."

"Yes. Best we try to avoid them next time. Once Ian sets his sights on someone, he's not easily swayed. Tuesdays and Thursdays are his usual nights here," Victor said before taking a sip of his drink. "You'd be wise to remember that." He placed a hand on her lower back. "Let me see you out."

He was rushing her from the club, which meant she was in danger from Ian and his brothers despite what he said. She let Victor guide her back to the exit. Why was he helping her? Protecting her? Because that's what he seemed to be doing. Would the kind of demon capable of controlling his own kind, of forcing them to do sick and twisted things, care about the well-being of a demi he barely knew?

He walked her right to the elevator.

"Will you come back?" he said when they came to a stop.

"Maybe?" Right then she was just desperate to get the hell gone.

"I'd like to see you again," he said. "I'll be here next Monday. I hope to see you here then."

She gave a noncommittal nod and rushed into the elevator when the doors finally opened.

"It was lovely seeing you again," he said as the doors slid shut.

Chaya collapsed against the wall, her entire body shaking

as adrenaline pumped through her veins. With shaking hands, she sent Grace a message telling her that she'd left and shoved her phone back in her purse.

Grace's reply came when she hit the street.

Grace: I'll be in touch with a time and place for us to meet.

CHAPTER 7

BRENT FROWNED as Chaya came to the bar for the second time, grabbed her order, and headed off to deliver it.

She was ignoring him.

He found he didn't like that, not one bit. She'd come in late for work and now she was pretending he didn't exist. The last time he'd seen her, he'd come in his pants from just sitting close to her, and she had apparently gotten over her feelings for him completely, if her current attitude was anything to go by.

He was well aware the shit floating around in his head might be something a lovesick teen might be thinking. He could no more control his thoughts than he could his dick or his feelings for the sexy demi-demon currently heading back toward the bar.

Christ, he crumbled around this woman, fucking fell apart.

Brent leaned more heavily on the bar, took a skip of his Coke, and tried not to stare at her.

Yeah, right.

Not looking at Chaya when she was near was like starting your day without a hit of caffeine.

She was wearing a tight knee-length skirt tonight, a black, stretchy, silky fabric that clung to her ample hips and thighs and the sweet, soft curve to her belly. He wanted to kiss it.

Kiss every inch of her soft, fragrant skin.

The end of the bar where she'd been getting her orders filled was full, and she was forced to come closer to him, the end he'd been propping up since opening, unable to have her out of his sight.

Which meant she had no choice but to acknowledge him. Her gaze darted in his direction and held for a long second. "Hey," she said.

Hey.

One simple, meaningless word, and his heart started thundering in his chest.

He took another sip of his drink. "Hey," he said back and smirked.

She wanted to slap him when he smirked. It was hard to miss. Maybe that was why he did it. He wanted her to slap him out of this constant state of confusion and hunger for a female he couldn't have.

Unfortunately, that would have the opposite effect.

Her eyes flashed and she lifted her chin stubbornly, responding like he knew she would.

"Did you have a nice night off?" he said, keeping the conversation neutral. He needed her eyes on him, her attention, to hear her voice. "Do anything...fun?"

Her eyes stayed on his and her nostrils flared, a little color hitting her cheeks.

What the fuck was that?

Finally, Chaya shrugged. "It was okay."

She was lying, and she wasn't doing as good a job at

masking her emotions tonight. He drew them in, tasting every perfect morsel. Fear, excitement, lust. That was what she was feeling when she thought about her night off.

She was seeing someone.

An ugly feeling twisted in his gut. "Who is it?" he said, unable to stop himself even though he knew it was none of his damn business.

Her brows lifted. "Who what?"

Brent straightened. "Who are you seeing?"

She jolted. "What?"

Keep your damned mouth shut. Don't say it. "You met with another male last night." The incubus in him wanted to know so he could kill whoever dared to touch what was his. Holding back those words, as fucked up as they were, had been an impossibility.

She straightened her shoulders. "How is that any of your business?"

Her reply, of course, was what he'd expected. "Chaya…"

She slid her tray of drinks off the bar and spun away, disappearing into the crowded club. Brent stayed where he was. He realized in that moment that his demon side had staked some kind of claim over Chaya and he couldn't leave, his feet glued to the spot. The idea of someone else touching her had made him want to commit an act of violence.

One of the reasons he had taken so long during his training to gain a semblance of control was that incubus/human parings were rare. The breed of demon was too strong for a mere human and it usually ended in a horror story. Even worse than Brent's own.

His worked more like the knights'. His demon side constantly fought to overpower his humanity, to make him into a creature of lust and sex, gorging on emotion.

It was hard to resist.

But for once they both wanted the same thing. Chaya.

Only Brent knew why that couldn't happen. The incubus didn't give a fuck.

Denying it, fighting it, was getting harder and harder. The demon side of him was a predator, and predators killed to protect what was theirs.

He was in trouble, there was no doubt about it.

And when she came back to the bar to hand in her next order, he had the strong and sudden urge to bury his face in the crook of her neck and inhale her scent, to rub it on his skin and his on her.

"Hey, beautiful," a male said, coming up beside her.

Chaya smiled but ignored the guy. A shifter of some breed. Canine most likely.

He moved in closer and did what Brent had just been desperate to do. He breathed her in deep, then put his arm around her shoulders, touching her, putting his scent on her. She grabbed her tray and tried to pull away, but he grabbed her wrist, making her let it go.

"Come on now, sexy, I just want to spend some time with you over in one of those dark corners. What do you say?"

"Let go now," she said, the kind of command in her voice that Brent had fantasized about since he met her.

The guy looked taken aback for a split second, but Brent was already moving. Fuck, he'd never felt this ruled by his demon DNA, and that was saying a lot after everything he'd been through.

He grabbed the dog by the scruff off his shirt and wrenched him back. Chaya's tray went flying, drinks and glass covering the floor. Brent didn't give a shit. He slammed his fist into the male's face over and over again. He took a couple of hits from the guy, but he barely noticed through the red rage riding him and rushed the male, taking him down to the ground. Brent hit him and kept on hitting him until the male stopped fighting back. "You touched what's mine, asshole," he growled in his face. "You ever touch her again and I'll kill you."

Someone grabbed him from behind and pulled him back. Two of the bouncers held him off the guy while another carried the unconscious male out of the club.

That's when he realized the place had gone silent. The music had stopped and all eyes were on him.

That was the moment he realized what he'd done, what he'd said in front of all these people.

In front of...

He spun to where Chaya had been standing. She looked frozen to the spot, eyes wide.

Brent wrenched free of the males still holding him and, ignoring all the onlookers, walked toward her. "Chaya—"

"What *the hell* was that?" she bit out.

Adrenaline was pumping through his veins and being this close to her was messing with him, but he needed to try and explain. Not that he fully understood himself. "Can we talk?" he said, voice nothing but a gritty rasp. "Somewhere else?"

She gave him a small nod then he was striding to his office, Chaya following him. He heard her walk in behind him and shut the door. Brent paced to one side of the office and back.

"Jesus, you're bleeding all over the place," she said to him. "Sit down. Let me clean you up."

"It's fine."

"It was my honor you were defending, right?" she said and held his stare. "Sit down."

His gut tightened at her tone, the command he heard in her voice, and he did what she asked instantly. What the fuck was going on here? Not a damned thing. It was wishful thinking. *Your overactive imagination is getting away with you.*

"Just be a sec." She walked back out to the bar. A minute

later she returned with a dish towel and a bottle of water and shut them back in.

She stared down at him. "You've got blood on your shirt."

He glanced down. Jesus. He tugged it out of his pants and yanked it over his head, tossing it on the floor.

She opened the water and poured some on the towel. "So you really lost your shit out there," she said, sitting on the couch beside him, taking his hand, and examining his knuckles.

What the hell could he say? Denying it wasn't an option. She'd seen it for herself. He had lost it. Lost complete control again. He felt more demon than man lately, especially around Chaya.

She cleaned away the blood and looked up at him. "You said you wanted to talk, Brent."

Yeah. Right. Shit.

"I don't know what happened out there," he forced out. "What came over me. I'm not…myself around you." Getting into this with her was the last thing he wanted, but she deserved answers, even if they made zero fucking sense. "It's like the demon in me…"

"Takes over?" she said. "Like our demon sides are calling to each other, like there's this massive energy pulling us together."

He shoved his fingers through his hair. "Yeah." Fuck, that's exactly what it felt like.

She dropped the towel in her hand and her eyes locked on his. "So why are we resisting it?"

His pulse thundered, blood roaring though his ears. "It's not…I can't give you…" He gritted his teeth and shook his head. "This can't work," he forced out.

Her lips curled up on one side. "So what are you going to do—beat the fuck out of every male who touches me?"

"Yes," the demon in him roared. But he didn't say that out loud and kept his mouth shut.

She lifted his hand and pressed her full, soft lips to his abused knuckles. Evidence of his obsession, the claim he'd just staked over her in front of the whole club. His cock throbbed hard when she pressed those lips to his skin again. "You want me," she said.

Not a question. He was slipping over the damn edge. "Yeah, I fucking want you, but you don't know what...the things that..." He bit back the confession on the tip of his tongue.

"Tell me." She moved closer, so close her scent filled his head.

He couldn't fucking move. He should put distance between them, but his limbs refused to take him away from her.

She rested her hand on his chest like she had that day in his office but this time skin on skin, and he knew she could feel the way his heart pounded. "Give in," she whispered, mouth an inch from his.

She closed the gap and her lips were on his. He combusted. His arms came around her and he thrust his tongue between her lips. Her taste, the heat of her mouth, the smell of her skin hit him like a thousand volts. He thrust his fingers in her dark hair and deepened the kiss. Everything about it, about her, felt right, like this was where she was meant to be.

Her hands moved over his bare skin and he groaned, desperate for more contact.

Chaya broke the kiss suddenly and rested her forehead against his.

He tried to move back in to take her mouth once more.

"Stop," she said, again in that tone that had his gut in knots. "No more kissing, not until you tell me."

Confessing the whole twisted truth about what had happened to him, his confusion, his shame, what he was—of what he was afraid of happening in the future—wouldn't change a thing. He'd still be him. "I can't."

She shook her head. "You won't." She pulled away and stood.

"Don't go, Chaya. I want you, fucking need you." It killed him to say it, to make himself vulnerable like that, but he didn't think he could fight it anymore.

"You want to fuck me, but you won't give me more."

He got to his feet and closed the distance. "No, I…I can't give you more. But I can give you what you need, Chaya. I can make that ache deep inside you go away." He knew how to play the Dom, and he realized he'd to that for her, he'd do anything for her, fulfill her needs, if she'd let him. He could at least give her that.

She lifted her hands, telling him to stay back. "It's not enough." She took another step back, putting more distance between them. "I want all of you, not just the dregs you choose to give me."

"Chaya," he growled. Man and demon could feel her pulling away and, fuck, Brent didn't know how to make her stay.

Chaya was strong, willful, perfect. If he took a wrong step with her, if he let his emotions take over, if he got lost in her and lost control, he could hurt her, and he would never forgive himself if that happened.

And until he made Garrett pay, he was no good, not to anyone.

Apart from sex.

"You are sex, Brent. Nothing more, nothing less."

Garrett's voice filled his head, and Brent hated that he was right.

That's all he was good for, all he could give her. The rest of him was fucked up beyond repair.

Chaya blinked over at him, hurt clear in her eyes. "You don't trust me."

"That's not it."

"What else can it be?" she said as she headed for the door.

She sounded disappointed in him, and he fucking hated that. Frustration, desperation had him growling under his breath. "Don't walk out that door. Christ. Please, Chaya."

"You've offered me nothing but an orgasm, Brent. I can do that for myself." Then she walked out, shutting the door behind her.

He stood there, body shaking, nerve endings sparking, gaze still locked on the door she'd just walked through. Emotions he didn't know what to do with hammered him, and then there was that ever-present, all-consuming hunger turning him inside out for her. But there was nothing he could do. Nothing would appease the incubus and what it roared for, not anymore.

Because he only wanted Chaya. He didn't want anyone else, and the idea of taking anyone else into one of the playrooms now, which was what he desperately needed to get his shit back under control, turned his stomach.

A serious problem for a sex demon.

He was well and truly fucked.

CHAPTER 8

GRACE'S JOB, when she wasn't teaching self-defense classes or chasing down demons, was at a burlesque club. And when Chaya walked in, the other female was dancing on one of the raised stages placed around the room. Tall and sleek, she was dressed in a beautiful turquoise vintage bra, corset, and panties set with garter and stockings to match.

This hadn't been what Chaya expected when Grace asked her to meet her at work.

The other female drew attention, her pale blond hair glowing under the lighting. But then maybe that's what she wanted. This place would be just as good to gather intel as Toxic if the clientele were any indication.

Grace sat across from her now, eyes intense after Chaya had shared what had been said and what she'd seen during her trip to The Dungeon. She'd learned more than what she'd set out to, that was for sure, but her realization about herself would stay private.

Grace reached out and took Chaya's hand. "You did fantastic. I've heard of Ian and his brothers. We wrote them off. They seemed to have other...priorities." Grace shuddered. "But maybe they're worth another look," she said more to herself. Her gaze slid back to Chaya. "But Victor we're definitely still interested in. We've struggled to get intel on him." She gave Chaya's hand a gentle squeeze. "Are you comfortable meeting him again?"

Despite her apprehension, there was only one answer. "Yes. And I'm positive there's more to him. Honestly, I think he's hiding something." The truth was Chaya was more determined than ever.

She needed something to fight for that wasn't a lost cause.

Grace gave her hand another squeeze, her eyes bright, determination shining through. "Excellent." She sat back. "Now that's shop talk over with," Grace said. "How about a drink?"

Chaya scanned The Dungeon for Victor. It looked like she'd gotten there first. This was the third time she'd meet with him. The second, they'd spent most of the evening observing other couples.

The more they'd observed, the more she learned about herself. She was a dominant, there was no denying it anymore, and the more she watched, the more she wanted to experience what she'd seen in those scenes herself.

Being with Brent now seemed an impossibility.

Not letting her head go there, she looked around for Victor. They'd talked quite a lot the last time they'd met, and she'd managed to ask him a few questions without him getting suspicious. Well, she hoped like hell she'd pulled off her mini interrogation. He'd seemed relaxed enough while they spoke.

Besides being a demon, Victor was a businessman. A very successful one and she assumed a lot of his associates were demons as well. He'd mentioned an upcoming event, an exhibition, one that could provide them with names, perhaps even info on the demon or demons trying to take over the city. Because that's what they were trying to do. This was war, and she was now one of many soldiers fighting in it.

In any war there were casualties, and she hadn't gone into this blindfolded. If you didn't know the risks, you had no business being there. She knew exactly the kind of danger she'd put herself in.

And she wasn't backing down. She wanted an invite to that exhibition, which meant getting closer to Victor.

Tonight, at his suggestion, she'd agreed to a scene with him.

As his sub.

The price of admittance to his world and a way of proving herself.

She knew it was coming, and accepting had been the only way forward.

A price she was willing to pay for the greater good. For their cause.

She'd spent several hours making her own list of hard and soft limits last night, as requested. And though she was new to this, she knew the sub was really the one with all the power. They dictated what they did and didn't want. She was in control.

Was she afraid? Yes, she was terrified of what was about to happen. She'd thought she'd wanted this. She knew now this was the last thing she wanted, especially with this male.

What she was about to do was a means to an end. That was it.

She didn't trust this demon with her body, and she sure as hell didn't want to be dominated by him, but she needed him to believe the opposite. The club was full, there were witnesses, she had a safe word. Everything would be fine.

She had to admit, the male had a way about him. That smooth melodic tone he used could lull anyone into a false sense of security. She wasn't stupid enough to trust him, though. She'd kept to her story about Brent and their messed-up relationship. She had a feeling he'd see through her if she tried to lie. So she'd stuck with the truth as much as she could. He'd told her he wanted to spend more time with her and then made his offer to train her so she could surprise Brent and show him she knew what she wanted and wasn't afraid to go after it.

If nothing else, Brent had provided her with a great cover story.

But an invite to the exhibition would only come if she did this. If she turned him down now, she had a feeling he'd lose interest in his little project and she'd miss her chance.

A cool hand landed on her shoulder.

She started and spun around.

Victor stood behind her, tall and lean, dark suit impeccable, expensive. His salt-and-pepper hair was cut neatly, his jaw smooth. Nothing out of place.

"Eyes down, Chaya," he admonished.

"Right, sorry." She forced herself to look down. His nearness made her shiver, but it wasn't the good kind. Her reaction was born of unease, not desire.

You can do this.

She thought of her aunt, a powerful demon who had tortured Zenon then had come after her sister, and her resolve strengthened. She wanted these assholes out of her damn city and she'd do anything to make that happen. Even do something that, now she knew what she was, felt so damned unnatural it made her feel ill, to bring them out in the open so the knights and demi like Grace could take them down.

"I think maybe you should try that again, don't you?"

643

Victor's voice was velvety smooth but held an edge she'd never heard before that rasped across the surface of her skin.

Keep it together, Chaya. "Sorry, I forgot myself, Sir."

He made a low sound in the back of his throat then cupped her jaw, lifting her chin slightly. "Are you?" He ran his thumb across her lower lip, stretching the skin awkwardly, not enough to cause pain, but she sure as hell didn't like it. The urge to jerk out of his hold almost won out.

Heat hit her face, her anger getting the better of her. "Yes, Sir." Was he into humiliation? The male probably got off on it. Luckily, she'd made that a hard limit.

"Very good, Chaya. I'd advise you not to forget again." He was silent for a few seconds, his gaze burning down at her. "Do you have the list I asked you to prepare?"

"Yes, Sir." Since she'd left her coat and purse out front, she'd tucked it down the front of her leather corset. She pulled it out and handed it to him.

His low chuckle lifted the hair on the back of her neck. "Hmm, it's still warm from your skin. You have lovely skin, Chaya."

"Thank you, Sir." Her palms grew sweaty as he opened it up and looked over her list.

He made a tsking sound. "This won't do. This won't do at all. Do you not grasp what you're doing here?"

Her stomach turned over. "I'm not sure what you mean… ah, Sir."

"This lifestyle is about sexual freedom, the exchange of power, the surrender of it, trust. If a Dom is lucky, he'll receive total and compete submission from his sub. I can't teach you if I can't touch you sexually." He released a long breath, trying to make her feel like an idiot, letting her know she'd disappointed him greatly. She didn't give a shit if she disappointed him, but she had to make him believe the opposite. "You either amend this list, or you leave and stop wasting my time."

The idea of this male touching her intimately, strapping her down, controlling her, felt wrong in every way possible. She'd wanted to explore this yearning she had, this need for more that had always left her feeling unsatisfied and frustrated, but only with Brent. Only him.

But that wasn't happening.

"No sex, Sir," she bit out.

He was quiet for several seconds and she didn't dare look up. "I think you need to clarify, Chaya. What are we talking here? Fingers, tongue, cock?"

She gritted her teeth, stomach in knots. "Cock...Sir."

He slid a manicured finger under her chin and made her look at him again. "That wasn't too hard, now was it? That's a hard limit for you." He took a pen from the inner pocket of his jacket and made the changes on her list. "Right, are you ready for your first scene?"

Her belly was so full of nerves all she could do was nod jerkily.

He raised a brow.

Shit. "Y-yes, Sir."

What the hell are you doing, Chaya?

"Follow me." He strode through the large room, sure and confident. She ignored her inner self screaming at her to turn and run the other way. Somehow she got her feet moving forward, one in front of the other, until he stopped near the back of the club.

"Since this is your first time, I thought you might appreciate some privacy."

"Thank you, Sir." Though the room was only blocked off by a half wall and anyone could watch if they chose to, it felt more intimate, private.

The small area was set up like a medieval dungeon. The

walls were made to look like stone, the fixtures heavy steel and rough-hewn wood. A small table sat against the partition wall, what lay on its surface concealed by a red cloth.

Victor placed her list on top of the table. "Take off your clothes and stand in front of the St. Andrew's cross."

His deep tone demanded obedience, and she had to force herself to comply. Everything about the situation felt wrong in every way. Was she really going to do this? Stand naked in front of a male she wasn't attracted to in the slightest, let him touch her body, control her, tie her up?

She could still back out if she wanted to.

But how could she look at herself in the mirror again if another demi was slaughtered and there'd been a chance that she could have stopped it? That by doing her part in this war, she could have prevented it.

Taking a deep breath, she loosened the laces of her corset and slid it down her legs. After unzipping her boots, she set them aside and removed her skirt. That left her in her bra, panties, and fishnet stockings.

"The bra, too, Chaya."

Shit. She shook off her rising panic. Reaching back, she undid her bra, letting it slide down her arms. Not allowing herself to think about what she was doing, she walked to the cross in a kind of daze and stood waiting for his next order.

He moved in and walked around her slowly. "You have a beautiful body. Exquisite breasts." He stopped in front of her and trailed a finger across her collarbone then down over the top of her breast, circling her nipple. It puckered under his touch. But it was a purely physical response and left her feeling shallow, empty in a way that made her bite her lip to hold back a whimper.

"Turn around. Lift your arms," he whispered roughly against her ear.

She did as he asked, going against every single one of her

instincts, and tried to fight a wave of panic as he secured coarse rope around each wrist. A sense of wrongness, even stronger than before, overpowered her.

What am I doing?

She tried to convince herself again that she could do this. That it would mean nothing, that this was all about the cause, but she suddenly realized, for her, this did mean something. Nothing about this felt right. Not here in this club that despite all the warm lighting felt cold and clinical, not tied to this cross—and not with this male.

Ice snaked its way through her veins and she tugged, trying to free her hands. "I've changed my mind."

He chuckled, dark and low. "It's just nerves, my sweet. Nothing more." He moved in close and brushed her hair away from her shoulder. "I promise I'll take care of you. You need to trust in that. You need to trust me."

She didn't. Of course she didn't trust him. And she'd just let him tie her up. Her back was to him. She had no idea what was coming. She was utterly vulnerable, completely at his mercy.

Grace had the guy at the door on payroll and had said she'd arrange for someone to be at the club, that they'd be watching and would get her out if she ran into trouble. Chaya looked around desperately. She didn't recognize anyone. Were they watching now?

Ah, shit. She was on the verge of a panic attack. She started sucking in big gulps of oxygen until she felt dizzy. Her brain had turned to mush and she couldn't think. God, she felt like she was drowning. What was the safe word again? She squeezed her eyes shut. "Let me go. I want you to let me go. Now."

"That is not how you speak to your master, now is it?" She could hear the smile in his voice. "Oh dear. Now I'll have to punish you."

647

The lights went out for a split second and the music went up, then a strobe started, disorientating her. She blinked out into the club. It was too dark, and she could only see flashed snapshots of the people there.

Pale faces, people moving, coming closer.

Chaya screamed.

CHAPTER 9

BRENT FLASHED the plain white card at The Dungeon's door attendant. He'd been forced to call in more than one favor to get hold of one of the elusive visitors' passes. They weren't easy to come by, and unless you knew someone who frequented this place, you were shit out of luck.

Coming here hadn't exactly been top of his bucket list, but after a frantic call from James, who was supposed to be here but his contact fell through and he had no way of getting in, Brent had no damn choice. The other male had been sparse on details—there hadn't been time, since Brent had to chase down a pass of his own—but James was going to text once Brent was in and fill him in.

What he did know was one of Grace's demi was here undercover and needed backup or at least help with a quick escape if necessary.

No, Brent hadn't joined their numbers, not with his association to the knights, but he knew Grace, and James had asked for his help as a personal favor. He was a good male, a friend, and Brent would help any way he could. James's call had come as a surprise, though. He'd had no idea the male was part of Grace's band of vigilantes.

Stepping through the door, he was struck instantly by the intensity of emotion swirling around the room. The place smelled of sex and need. The taste was heady. The cries, screams, and moans of pleasure that filled the large space crashed over him. Drawing out the incubus, the predator. He wanted to feast on their lust, their pain. Get drunk on it. Brent couldn't stop himself from sucking in a gasping breath as the heady mix kept coming, hitting him low in the gut. He was in incubus heaven.

But overindulging was dangerous. He knew that all too well. So he locked it down, blocked it out. He needed a clear head, and if he carried on gorging himself like he was, he wouldn't be capable of helping anyone, and worse, would make himself vulnerable.

Something he would never allow himself to be again.

He moved through the room, observing, playing the voyeur, something he did not enjoy one damned bit, while he waited for James's text with further instruction. The male had been extremely vague, apart from get the fuck there as soon as possible.

As he feigned interest in a particular scene, the lights dropped, the music increased in volume, and a strobe started flashing across the room.

Excitement rippled through the place, another delicious hit that sent tingles down his spine.

Rein it the hell in, Silva.

The music was deep, bassy, instrumental, and ebbed and flowed around them, its seductive notes no doubt selected to heighten the erotic atmosphere.

His phone vibrated in his pocket. He pulled it out and quickly read it.

. . .

James: It's Chaya.

Brent stared at it, trying to understand what he was reading. What was Chaya?

His phone buzzed again.

James: The demon she's with is named Victor. Don't get involved unless she's in distress.

The fuck?

Chaya was working with them? She was here, with a motherfucking demon. He spun around, like he'd somehow see her through the darkened room and flashing lights. Panic gripped him behind the ribs, and he was on the verge of roaring her name to find her.

But then emotion hit him, so acute it smashed past his barriers and had him grabbing for the nearest wall as it battered him from all sides. The pain hammering into him was not edged with pleasure—no, it was bound by fear. Shit, it turned his stomach.

This pain he knew all too well. This was the kind of terror he had never wanted to taste again. But even stronger than that was anger, outrage.

Whoever it came from was afraid but also pissed the hell off. He knew who it was instantly.

He rushed forward, colliding with people in the darkness, shoving them out of the way. His feet carried him forward to the very back of the club. A female's cries, sharp and desperate, broke over the loud music.

He rounded a partition.

Through the flashing lights, he saw a female facing away, bound to a St. Andrew's cross.

Oh fuck.

The music changed and the incessant flashing stopped with it. The lights came up.

Chaya.

She was bare to the waist, and the smooth expanse of her golden skin was streaked with pink from just above the flare of her hips to her shoulder blades.

Her physical pain appeared to be minimal, but this sure as fuck wasn't where she wanted to be. It was her emotional pain that had cut him to the quick, had reached out to him. Everything about this felt wrong to her.

"Stop, goddammit. Now," she gasped.

Moving without thought, completely on instinct, he snatched the crop from the male wielding it and threw it aside. "Chaya? *Jesus Christ.*"

The male who had terrified her, hurt her, stepped forward. "I hope you have a good reason for interrupting my scene." His face was a mask of outrage, but as Brent tried to push past his barriers, to learn more, he was locked out. The guy's shields were rock solid, giving away nothing.

Brent didn't try to hide what he was feeling, which was damn near homicidal, and let it wash over the other male. The guy wisely took a startled step back. "Chaya belongs to me. She is mine. Is that a good enough reason for you?" He heard Chaya's sharp indrawn breath but was too far gone at that point to filter what came out of his mouth.

The guy stared at him for several seconds then bowed his head. "I apologize for stepping on anyone's toes. I didn't know."

"You do now," Brent growled.

The guy nodded, turned, and walked away.

Brent went straight to her. She jumped when he rested a

hand on her shoulder. "Shh, it's me." He reached up and quickly undid the knots at her wrists. She slumped back, trembling in his arms. "I've got you."

He turned her around and she went to him without resistance, pressing in close, seeking comfort. He took slow, measured breaths, trying to calm down, to stop himself from going after that irresponsible asshole. The damage he could have done. He pulled back and looked down at her. Her eyes were wide, wild.

He brushed the pad of his thumb over her cheekbone, needing to touch her. He felt desperate, scared out of his mind. "What the hell were you thinking?" he said, voice low, harsh.

"I was fine. I didn't need you to step in. I had everything under control," she said even as her body trembled in his arms.

"Bullshit." He searched her dark eyes. "What the hell are you playing at?"

Her chin lifted. "You wouldn't give me what I wanted, so I found someone else who would."

He tried to control his breathing. She was lying. This wasn't what she wanted, not one bit. He'd felt it, like a living, breathing thing. She was here for Grace, for the cause.

Chaya was one of the strongest females he knew. She had self-confidence in spades and knew her worth. She met him head on, refused to bow down to him, to anyone.

How had he missed it?

Jesus, she'd been as confused and conflicted as he had been. He'd continually pushed her away, then the next minute demanded she stay close. Because of his own issues, he'd messed with her head and her heart repeatedly.

And. He'd. Missed. It.

There was no mistaking it now. It radiated from her.

He stared down at her. "Are you okay?"

653

Her eyes steadily held his. "I told you, I'm fine."

Fuck. So beautiful.

Her body was bared to him. Her soft, large breasts brushed against his chest, her nipples firm and dark, begging to be sucked and licked. To be worshipped. He wanted to smooth his hands over her gently rounded belly, the curve of her hips, up to her waist then follow the path with his mouth, tasting every inch of her golden skin.

That bastard had seen her like this, had put his fucking hands on her. Touched her.

"I know Grace," he said, breaking the silence. "I got a call to provide backup for one of her demi."

Chaya's mouth opened then closed. Her back straightened. "Yes, and now you've messed everything up. You shouldn't have interfered."

"You're a bad liar," he said. It was hard, but he kept the Dom veneer in place. It was essential with so many eyes on them. "You get this little crease right here"—he rubbed his thumb between her brows—"when you lie." He stayed close, silently begging her to touch him, to put him out of his misery. "You weren't just here for Grace, were you? You were seeking something else here, something you didn't think you could get from me."

Her eyes didn't leave his, but she kept her mouth clamped shut.

Fuck.

"Maybe you should get dressed." He said it calmly, but there was no missing the quaver in his voice from the need thrumming through him.

Her eyes narrowed.

"Please, Chaya." *Mistress.*

Her nostrils flared, but she moved, went to where her clothes sat stacked on a chair, and with assertive hands, quickly dressed. When she moved back to him, he took her hand without a word, and led her from the club. Seeing her like that with another male had torn something inside him, shattered his resolve.

A dominant forced to submit was as damaging as a sub like him being forced to do the same without trust or affection.

Because of it, he hadn't recovered from his time with Garrett, but he wouldn't let what happened here tonight with Chaya fester and grow inside her, let that damage become a permanent scar.

If he wasn't the one to sate her desires for dominance, someone else would, someone who didn't know her like he did. Someone who might not take care of her the way she deserved.

They took the elevator down to the parking garage. He opened the passenger side door when they reached his car and she climbed in without comment. Good thing, too, because words were an impossibility just then.

He climbed into the driver's seat and turned to her. "You took a serious risk tonight."

Her eyes flashed. "I knew what I was doing. Demi need people like me in this war and I want to help."

"That's not what I mean, and you know it. Handing your body over to a demon, a powerful one, a male who doesn't know you, who could have hurt you…" He ground his teeth before more of his control slipped. "How do you know that male? Did Grace point you in his direction?"

"No. As a matter of fact, he comes into Toxic." Chaya explained how she'd gone to Grace, and how Victor being a target was a "happy" coincidence.

"Tell me this is the first time you've seen him."

Chaya didn't look pleased by his question, but she answered anyway. "Three times."

He struggled to control the fear burning him up inside.

"You've done this before?" He couldn't stop his next words even though he wasn't sure he wanted to hear the answer. "Did you…have you let him fuck you?"

She stared at him, lips thinned, then finally shook her head. "No, we never had sex."

He had to fight not to fold, to rest his head in her lap and beg her to stroke his hair, to help him control the rage and fear, the relief.

"This was the first time we did a scene," she said. "The other times I just watched. I was safe, Brent. He didn't suspect me. There were people everywhere, and I gave him a list of my limits."

Thank fuck for that. He started the car and headed out. The drive back to the club only took fifteen minutes, but by the time they got there he was jumping out of his skin. Chaya had stayed quiet at his side, and he wished he could climb inside her head and know what she was thinking. What the hell was going through that beautiful head of hers?

He pulled up to the lot behind the club, climbed out, and jogged around to open Chaya's door before she could. Taking her hand, he threaded his fingers through hers and led her inside. He noted she didn't resist.

The place was still fairly busy, but he ignored everyone, barely acknowledging the staff that greeted them, and motioned her toward his office.

She walked in and he closed the door behind them.

Chaya turned to him then, looking exquisite in her tight skirt and corset, those spiked heels. "Now what?" she said. "Are you going to call Chaos? Zenon?"

He shook his head. "May I see it?"

She frowned at him. "See what?"

"Your list." He'd seen her jam it down the front of her corset when she was getting dressed, trying to hide it from him.

"Is that really necessary?"

"Please, Chaya." There was no demand in his voice. He'd dropped the Dom act completely, and yeah, *right there*, she'd seen it, felt it.

Her eyes widened, nostrils flaring, lips parting slightly.

She yanked a piece of paper from the front of her corset, not letting up on the attitude—not yet—still too afraid to believe what he was telling her without words. He didn't expect anything less.

She placed it in his hand, and he read it carefully, noting the changes. She was going to allow that male to put his hands, his mouth on her. She was going to allow another male those privileges.

He focused on the piece of paper in his hands when he spoke. "No fucking?" he rasped, then looked up.

She held his stare, back rigid.

"That's a hard limit?"

"Yes," she said. "I told you I was there for the cause, for Grace. I wasn't going to let him fuck me."

He stared down at the list again for several more painfully long seconds, trying to find the words. Trying to push past the fear that he'd been wrong, that he'd somehow read her wrong. That if he said the next words, she'd reject him, maybe even be disgusted in him.

He cleared his throat, then lifted his eyes to hers. "My limits, they're pretty much the same," he said, voice husky with need. "Only I don't like to be watched, and you...you could fuck me any way you wanted."

Heat flashed in her eyes. "What?"

He didn't know how to convey what he was feeling, what he wanted, so he showed her. He closed the distance between them until he was only a few feet away, and dropped to his knees, bowing his head. Offering the Domme in front of him his submission.

And held his breath.

She remained utterly still in front of him.

It felt like forever before she moved, one step then two, until she was right in front of him. "You really want this?" she whispered.

He tilted his head back and let her see it—the need, the hunger for what only she could give him. "Yes."

"How long?" she asked.

He searched her face, her eyes, for disgust, for the rejection about to come, and saw none. "For as long as I can remember." He shook his head. "What happened tonight, I know you were scared, Chaya. Confused. You were forced to do something against your nature. That can cause damage, could hurt you. I want to make that right," he said. "It's the job of your sub, his fucking privilege, to take care of you, to serve you. I don't want that negative experience to taint what we could share. I don't want you going to bed tonight with the shadow of what happened hanging over you, making you doubt what you want, what you need. I want to wash it away." He clenched his fists at his sides, staring up at her, and hoped like hell she would give them this. "Will you let me do that?"

Her chest expanded with her sharply indrawn breath. "Yes," she said, eyes bright with emotion, with excitement, with a need as wild as his.

God only knew why or what she saw in him, but he refused to fight it anymore. Refused to turn away from her again. And maybe, yeah, he hoped that Chaya could wash it all away, wash away what Garrett had done, what he'd made him feel.

She bent at the knees, lowering herself so they were eye level. "Do you trust me?" she said.

Oh fuck, this was really going to happen. He swallowed the lump in his throat. Trust? He wasn't sure he knew how to trust anymore, but he knew he'd never wanted anything more. So he said, "Yes."

"Yes, what?" she said, no hesitation.

His cock filled, hardened, and he had to clear his throat to speak. "Yes, Mistress."

Fuck yes, that pleased her, and seeing that pleasure in her eyes almost had him undone.

He hadn't done this, not since before Lazarus came for him. He'd suppressed, hidden, denied this part of himself. Not that what was about to happen resembled in any way what he went thought with Garrett.

But it had been a long time for him and would be a first for Chaya.

This would be a learning curve for them both. But, fuck, he wanted it, whatever she gave him.

She stood smoothly and moved to the front of his desk. She'd slipped into the role of Domme like she was born to it. Her shoulders were back, chin high, stare unwavering. "Stand here," she said, pointing to a spot in the middle of the room.

He growled under his breath as he got to his feet. He wanted this, but his instincts told him to resist, listening to the voice in the back of his mind telling him not to lose control completely, to be careful.

He moved to the spot she'd directed him.

"Clothes off," she said, voice firm.

He reached for the buttons of his jacket and slid one free under the weight of her stare.

Please don't let this be a dream.

CHAPTER 10

CHAYA FOUGHT to keep her composure, not to show how damned nervous she was. She thought of the Dommes she'd watched at The Dungeon, how cool and controlled they could be, and channeled them as best she could.

Brent slipped his jacket off his shoulders and flung it to the couch. Her gaze moved over him. This was actually happening. She'd never in her wildest dreams imagined Brent was a sub. He'd hidden it so well, she guessed for such a long time, it had become second nature to him.

She couldn't imagine what that must have been like. How hard that must have been for him.

After what happened tonight, he wanted to take care of her, to take away the memory of what happened with Victor. But she wondered how long Brent had been suffering without this. How long he had been unfulfilled, craving, feeling hollow, alone. She wanted—no, needed—to make this good for him.

Besides the tame scenes she'd watched here and the ones she'd observed at The Dungeon, she'd done a lot of research online since her revelation, searching for answers.

She'd found some, had read as much as she could, but she was far from an expert. She didn't want to make some terrible mistake and, God, hurt him—that was the last thing she wanted—so they needed to start slow.

His shirt came off next and she struggled to remain impassive. His bare chest was perfection. The male was gorgeous, his skin a beautiful deep gold despite barely seeing the sun. He was all cut, lean muscle, and there was a large cross tattoo on his ribs on the right side and numbers, a date, on his forearm. He looked lethal.

And for tonight at least, he was all hers.

"Besides being put on display, is there anything else that's not on my list that you don't like?" she said, mimicking what she'd seen and heard at The Dungeon.

He'd just taken off his socks and shoes. He looked up at her as he undid his pants and shoved them and his underwear down his long legs. "No, Mistress."

There was a growl to his words that had her skin tingling all over. And this time hiding her reaction was definitely not as easy. His muscled body was completely bared to her, long legs, thick thighs dusted with dark hair. His chest was smooth—she dropped her gaze—but there was a trail of dark hair just below his belly button leading to his cock, nestled in more dark hair.

She was already turned on, but the sight of his long, thick cock, hard and heavy, so heavy it was angled down from its own weight, made her pussy contract with need.

Chaya moved in and relished the way he stilled, the way his chest expanded with his sharp, indrawn breath as she drew closer. She moved around him, like she'd seen others do, slowly examining their playthings for the night. Brent wasn't just a plaything, though, not to her. He was so much more.

His back and ass were just as muscled and honed as the

front, and she couldn't wait to run her hands over his body. But not yet.

"You're beautiful," she said as she moved around to the front. His eyes had darkened and were almost black. "What's your safe word?

"Blue, Mistress," he said, fingers clenching and unclenching at his sides.

He was impatient to get started. That knowledge just made her hotter. "We're going to take this nice and slow," she said. "Ease in." She let a small smile curl her lips. "I know what I want to do to you, but I think it best we not rush things."

"What do you want to do?" he growled.

She quirked a brow.

"Mistress," he finished roughly.

She allowed the slip because it was exciting to see him this turned on, so desperate for her that he forgot himself.

"Do you like being restrained, Brent?" she said and again dropped her gaze to his impossibly hard cock.

Somehow he was even harder.

"Yes…Mistress, very much."

She moved to the desk and crooked a finger at him, like she'd seen him do to subs out in the club before. His abs and thigh muscles tightened before he started toward her.

When he reached her, she moved behind him. His ass clenched and she bit back a moan. "You've kept this side of yourself hidden from me for a long time. You've denied us both." No, she hadn't known what she was, what she wanted, not until recently, but she needed an excuse to punish Brent because that's what he wanted—she knew that much. Now she thought about it, looking back, she'd seen the longing in his eyes when others had been spanked in the club. She realized now he'd been longing to be on the receiving end of one of those spankings. So she said, "I think that maybe you should be punished for that, don't you?"

He hissed. "Yes, Mistress."

Oh yes, that's exactly what he wanted. She was so wet now her upper thighs slid together when she walked, slick with her arousal. "Bend over the desk," she said, voice soft but firm.

There was no hesitation this time, oh no, but Brent shook slightly as he did as she asked.

Unable to deny herself any longer, she ran her hands down his back to his firm ass and squeezed before sliding a finger up through the cleft. "Legs apart," she said. "Nice and wide."

His cock and balls hung heavily between his solid thighs, the position chosen to make him feel vulnerable, exposed, and going by the way he trembled, he liked that. A lot.

She forced herself to step back, when all she wanted to do was force him to use that big cock on her, to make her come over and over again.

Instead she walked over to his discarded pants and slid his belt free, then moved around to the front of the desk so he could see her. His face was flushed, eyes bright. She cupped his cheek, heart thudding when he gazed up at her, so hungry. All hers. "Are you ready for your punishment?"

His eyes were already glazed with lust, mouth slightly open. His tongue darted out and dampened his lower lip. "Fuck yes, Mistress."

"I'm going to restrain your hands."

He nodded.

Frustration over her lack of knowledge pumped through her veins. She wanted to push him to the edge and force him over. She wanted to tie him down, helpless to do anything but accept whatever her heart desired. She wanted to make his body sing with pleasure, pain. To never regret giving her this gift.

The muscles in her thighs trembled and she pressed them together seeking relief. She was so hot, so ready for him.

"Offer me your wrists," she said.

He stretched his arms out in front of him, thick sinewy veins and tendons bulging. She secured the worn leather around both then bent down to secure the remaining length to the drawer handle. She glanced up and his eyes were burning into her, moving over her face, her mouth, back up to her eyes. He wanted to kiss her.

She wanted that, too, but not quite yet. She stood and took him in, trussed up and bent over his own desk. "You look exquisite, Brent. I wish you could see yourself."

Moving around behind him again, she ran her hand down his spine, loving the way goose bumps lifted, the way he arched into her touch, seeking more like a greedy house cat. So responsive, so eager.

She swept her fingers lightly over his firm ass then massaged the flesh. "You have a great ass. But it'd look so much better with my handprint on it." Without warning, she brought one down hard.

Slap.

The sound rang out, as did his startled grunt. She'd watched several scenes where spanking was involved. It was one thing allowed out on the floor here at Toxic, so she didn't feel too out of her depth. She followed the first slap with three more in quick succession then massaged his pinkening ass cheek. "Okay?" she rasped.

"Yes...Mistress," he all but groaned as he angled his ass up, asking without words for more.

"I'm not quite finished. You were very bad, remember?" She smoothed her hand down his back to his ass again. "Do you remember your safe word?"

"Yes."

"What is it?"

"Blue."

"Good boy. Are you ready for more?"

"Fuck yes."

She smoothed his ass in a circular motion, then...*slap.*

"Will you ever keep something like this from me again?"

He growled. "No, Mistress."

Slap.

"Who does this fine body belong to?"

"Ahhh...you, Mistress."

Slap.

His back arched again. Beautiful. His cock swayed with every slap, rubbing against the desk. Pre-come dripped from the head in a steady stream. Triumph filled her. God, nothing had ever felt this good.

She was lost to him, totally gone, and right then, with Brent bent over his desk, taking his punishment so beautifully, his grunts of pleasure filling the air—she didn't care. Nothing in her life had ever felt this right, this good. That hollow feeling inside her that she'd always had was filled to overflowing.

"Two more," she rasped, close to coming herself.

Slap.

She was powerless to stop her next words. "Tell me, Brent, who do you belong to?"

Slap.

He groaned, a soft sob breaking free, pulling at her heart. "You. I belong to you!"

She reached down, gripped his cock in her fist, and tugged on it, stroking his thick length hard and fast.

"Fuck...fucking fuck me," he growled.

She stroked him until he was shuddering, teetering on the brink, but still he didn't go over. He gasped and growled but didn't come. She wanted to demand he come but was worried she was doing something wrong.

"Hurt me," he gasped out. "I need you to hurt me."

She didn't miss the shame in his words.

Why would he feel shame? She had no time to contemplate; she just wanted to give him what he needed. Grabbing the metal ruler sitting on his desk, she brought it down hard on his ass while she tugged his cock with the other hand.

His hips started jerking, his throaty moan the sexiest thing she'd ever heard. Then he came, spilling into her hand. She dropped the ruler and reached down, taking his balls with her other hand and squeezing gently. Not so hard to cause him serious pain but enough to cause discomfort, and like she thought, that sent another shudder through him along with the last of his orgasm.

He collapsed on the surface of his desk, breathing hard and fast.

Chaya stood there for a moment, pulling her shit together, because, yeah, what had just happened had been life-altering, the most real and honest thing she'd ever experienced.

When she had it somewhat together, she wiped her hand on Brent's discarded shirt and moved around, crouching down in front of him again, running her fingers through his damp hair. "Did you enjoy yourself?"

He blinked up at her, but there was something behind his eyes, something she had no hope of comprehending. What she did recognize was hunger. Despite how hard he'd just come, he wanted her. Good thing, since she wasn't finished with him, not yet.

"Yes, Mistress." he said huskily.

She untied the belt from the drawer and released the buckle around his wrists then moved around, placing her hand at the small of his back when he stood on unsteady legs.

"You were amazing, Brent. The hottest thing I've ever seen." She let her gaze move over him. "In fact, watching you come like that has made me wetter than I can ever remember being."

His nostrils flared and he swayed toward her, hand lifting like he was going to touch her. "Hands at your sides," she said, voice firm. "You touch when I say you can and not before."

Brent growled.

Chaya loved it, loved how much he wanted her, that he couldn't hide it from her. Her gaze dropped and she bit her lip. He was hard again already. *Fuck.*

As much as she wanted him inside her, she didn't want to rush. She wanted the delayed gratification, the anticipation to build. But until then...

Stepping back, she slid her skirt down her thighs, let it drop to the floor, and kicked it aside, then did the same with her panties. In only her boots and corset, she moved to the couch, sat on the edge, and spread her thighs wide.

Brent made a rough and hungry sound that had her pussy clenching in anticipation. "On your knees, sub," she said, doing her best to keep her voice even.

He dropped to the floor immediately, walking toward her on his knees. When he was close enough, she reached up and fisted his hair then forcefully guided his face between her thighs. Not that he was putting up any resistance.

"I want you to fuck me with that wicked mouth of yours and keep on doing it until I tell you to stop. Understand?"

"Yes, Mistress," he said, voice nothing but gravel before she shoved his head the last inch, pressing his mouth to her wet pussy.

He moaned against her, opening his mouth and sucking, licking at her swollen wet flesh. She leaned back on one hand

and kept the other in his hair, fisting the silky strands, tugging it, guiding as she ground against him.

And going by the way he moaned and growled every time she pulled his hair, he loved it. His hands came up suddenly and he gripped her ass, his big fingers digging into her flesh, holding her to his mouth before shoving his tongue deep in her pussy.

He'd touched her without her say-so, but she couldn't find it in her to give a shit, not when she was so close to coming. He thrust into her, grinding his face into her clit, and she curled her legs around his head, the heels of her boots digging into his back, which only seemed to make him even wilder.

His vicious growl against her was so animalistic and raw she started coming. Unable to hold herself up any longer, she fell back, fisting his hair so hard and grinding up with such force it would be a miracle if he could still breathe.

When the last tremors pulsed though her and she got her shit somewhat under control, she ordered him to do it again. When she collapsed back the second time she must have passed out for a while because when she woke, he was holding her in his arms and the throw blanket that sat on the back of the couch was down and wrapped around her.

They lay there quietly for several minutes after she woke while he pushed her hair over one shoulder and smoothed his fingers over the fading marks Victor had left on her skin.

"Tell me you won't go back to that club, Chaya," he rasped.

She stilled. "I won't stop my involvement in the war."

"That wasn't what I asked," he said.

Instead of reacting, of biting back, she relaxed into him and gave him the truth, "I'm not sure I could now, even if I wanted to."

"Thank fuck. I don't think I could take finding you like

that a second time." He leaned in and kissed the side of her neck.

She sighed.

"Why don't you rest now?" he said.

Boneless and emotionally wrung out, she was helpless to do anything else. They needed to talk, but with him stroking and kissing her hair, soothing his hands over her skin, she couldn't muster the energy.

He didn't say anything more either, just kept playing with her hair, and her lids grew heavy.

Finally, she gave in to it.

When she woke next, she was on the couch alone and had no idea how much time had passed.

She pulled herself into a sitting position and looked around his office. He'd left. Shoving the blanket off her shoulders, she walked on trembling legs to her clothes on the floor and quickly dressed.

After tugging on her boots, she walked out into the now empty club. Brent was behind the bar at the register, cashing up.

He glanced up. "You're awake."

She took him in, trying to gauge his mood. Did he regret what had happened? "Looks that way."

His dark gaze moved over her from head to toe, the muscle in his jaw jumping. He still wanted her, there was no mistaking it, but he was waiting for her to take the lead. She was still struggling to get her head around that.

She started toward the door. That muscle in his jaw jumped again and his throat worked. "I'll see you tonight, then?" he said, hunger making his voice rough and sexy.

"You will, since I'm rostered on." Trying not to wobble in her heels because her legs were still shaky from the orgasms he'd given her, she kept walking, but before she went out she stopped and turned back to him. "And Brent?"

His gaze that hadn't left her lifted to her face. "Yes?"

"As soon as my shift finishes tomorrow, I want you to go up to your apartment, strip off your clothes, and wait for me on your knees at the foot of your bed. I want to find you, head bowed, facing the door, thighs spread."

The need he fired at her after those words had her soaking her panties all over again.

"You want me to…"

"You heard what I said. And make sure you get some rest. You'll need it."

Okay, it wasn't exactly hearts and flowers between them, but that wasn't the kind of girl she was anyway. She wanted Brent, and he was finally offering her a piece of him.

She'd be damned if she wouldn't take it.

His lips quirked up on one side. He was smirking. "Yes, Mistress," he said, a teasing note to his voice.

Chaya dipped her chin, spun on her heels, and strode out.

Once she'd punished him for that smirk, they were both going to get a reward.

CHAPTER 11

BRENT SAT behind his desk while images of Chaya with her thighs spread, leaning back on his couch, offering her pussy to him, flooded his mind. Jesus, she had tasted like heaven. He could still feel her ass in his hands, still taste her juices on his tongue.

She'd been magnificent. He'd come so damn hard he thought he might die from the pleasure of it. And then he'd instantly felt shame for the way he'd begged her to hurt him. The twisted feeling of longing and guilt that he struggled with every time he came, something that had somehow become a part of him.

Christ, he didn't want Garrett in his head anymore. Chaya hadn't seen it, had she? No, he was sure he'd hidden it because she hadn't looked at him like he was fucked up. She'd given him exactly what he needed and then ordered him to service her.

A shiver of pleasure moved through him. Christ, that one perfect moment when he'd first gotten a glimpse of the dominant Chaya had kept buried, when she ordered him to call her mistress. Fuck.

It was magnificent.

And she'd shown it to no one but him.

Still, he'd tried so hard to distance himself afterward. It had killed him to let her go, to get off that couch after having her cradled in his arms. In that moment, he'd been hers. And she'd been nothing but soft, sated female.

The emotional drop after what they'd done could be hard on both sub and Dom, especially someone new to it like Chaya, and he'd found himself loving every minute of her in his arms, like he always knew he would. She'd curled into him, not bothering to hide the emotion, the affection she had for him, and it had humbled him deeply. God, he'd glutted on the emotions pouring from her tender heart.

But it had equally terrified him.

Under all that fire lay a beautiful open soul.

She'd chosen him to be her first sub.

He didn't deserve the honor.

Because he was terrified of what would happen if he let her get too close, if he fully let go with her. If she *saw* him. If he allowed her to believe this could be anything more than a sexual relationship, he'd end up hurting her.

She deserved someone to love her, cherish her. That male wasn't him. The shadows inside would eventually leach out and tarnish that clean, trusting soul, and he couldn't do that to her. Couldn't soil her with that kind of darkness.

All those thoughts had plagued him as he'd held her in his arms, run his fingers through her dark hair, listened to her breathe slow and easy in sleep. He'd made the decision, convinced himself he had to let her go, that putting distance between them was for the best.

He'd even managed to keep it together when she walked out of his office and looked at him with those dark eyes, round and questioning at first, then full of attitude and fire the next. And fuck him, his damn knees had gone weak all over again.

All he'd wanted to do was beg her to punish him again, to make him come like she had earlier, in a way he hadn't in his life. And maybe, eventually, in a way that didn't make him feel worthless and pathetic.

He'd resisted temptation.

Until she'd headed for the door.

He'd almost lost his mind watching her walk away.

And when she'd turned and ordered him to wait for her after her shift he hadn't been able to say no.

He didn't want to.

Chaya was his drug. She was in his blood and he was hooked.

"Shit." He shoved back from his chair and paced around his office. It would kill him if he hurt her. As long as she knew where things stood, everything would be okay. And when she ultimately came to the realization he was messed up and no good for her, they could move on. Things could go back to the way they were before, but without all the pent-up sexual tension between them.

He groaned. She'd felt so good against his mouth, fingers tugging on his hair, demanding, taking—so perfect. He'd had perfection...and still he hadn't been able to come without the guilt he always felt for craving pain with his pleasure. It was nothing unusual in this lifestyle, but every damn time he needed it, he felt Garrett's hands on him, the monster's cold ministrations forcing him to feel pleasure, feeding Brent's demon, pumping him full of emotion until he was totally defenseless.

His brain got all twisted with what he'd felt back then, with the desperate need, the self-loathing, and worse, the relief.

Yeah, he was beyond fucked up.

A *ding* came from his computer, letting him know a new email had landed in his in-box. He shook off his conflicting thoughts and took his seat behind the desk.

Always the slow learner.

The subject line turned every muscle in his body to stone. He knew exactly who it was from before he opened it.

You're looking for me. You don't know how pleased that makes me. But you won't find me, not yet. It's not time. Anticipation is all part of the fun, yes? I remember how much you liked your punishments, and as you know, disobedience cannot be ignored.

You've been very bad, Brent.

Tell your little computer friend to stop searching or the next video won't conceal your face.

There was a link to a public YouTube channel. Sweat coated his skin and an icy trail slid down his spine.

He clicked it open.

Tied down, his arms and legs were spread wide. He watched himself struggle to break free. Face covered by a leather mask, he frantically turned toward the slightest sound, not knowing what would come next. He was hard, hips rolling, even as he strained against his restraints to get free. A shadow moved in the corner, then a figure came into view. A female. She climbed onto the bed and crawled on top of him. Three others moved into the frame, settling in to watch...

He shut the screen. He didn't need to watch it. He'd lived it. Two long months before Lazarus had found him and had taken him to the compound.

Coming to terms with his new power would have been hard enough. The sexual turmoil, the longing, the unquenchable hunger. But having that used against him. The disgust, the pain, the terror, he'd felt it all in those months. And his body had betrayed him time and time again.

For him, the worst had been the helplessness, the loss of control. He'd always had submissive tendencies, even before he transitioned, but he'd only just entered the scene and had still been finding his way. Having it used against him had fucked with him in ways he still hadn't recovered from.

Picking up the phone, he called his friend and told him to stop his search. The last thing he wanted was to put anyone else at risk or make them a target. Brent smiled despite Garrett's threat of posting more video footage.

He'd well and truly got the fucker's attention. It was just a matter of time before he came after him.

And Brent would be ready.

Chaya wrapped her coat tight around her body and hustled down the street toward her favorite coffee shop. She'd woken this morning feeling restless and hungry. She couldn't stop thinking about the punishment she'd given Brent the night before, the way he'd reacted to her orders, her touch.

Just thinking about what they'd done sent a rush of need straight to her core. She'd never expected it to be that way. She'd hoped, but nothing she'd imagined compared to the reality of having a male like Brent bend to her will.

God, she'd gotten off on it so hard, and that was a lot to get her head around.

What did it all mean? What did it mean for them?

Did he want more than just sex? And if he didn't, could she do that? Could her heart take it if he turned her away again?

"Chaya?"

She jumped at the sound of her name, so lost in thought the city had dissolved around her. Chaya turned to the familiar voice and barely stopped herself from stumbling back. "Victor," she said. "I mean...Sir?" Calling him that felt incredibly wrong, but she had to play her role. Needed to play this carefully.

He grinned at her, the lines at the corners of his eyes crinkling. "Just Victor outside The Dungeon, honey."

She tucked a loose strand of hair behind her ear, going for shy, not sure if she was pulling it off. When she glanced up at the attractive older male in front of her she tried to see the truth, who he was really beneath the unthreatening features and the at times kind eyes, but she came up blank.

The male revealed nothing.

Her instincts could have been completely wrong, but she didn't feel as though she was in any danger from him, not right then. And if she'd managed to keep her cover intact, she might be able to salvage her assignment yet.

"Look..." She glanced down, attempting to look coy. Not something she had a lot of experience with. "I'd like to apologize for freaking out on you like I did. And for Brent. I had no idea he'd followed me." She looked up at him under her lashes and hoped like hell he bought the apology.

He held up a hand, cutting her off. All humor fled from his expression, and surprisingly, only worry and concern remained...or at least that's what he wanted her to believe. "No. It's me that should be apologizing. I should have realized you were in trouble. The fault is all mine. I confess it's been a long time since I've played with an inexperienced sub. My expectations were too high. I failed you, Chaya, and for that I'm truly sorry."

His hands were in his pockets and his distinguished salt-and-pepper hair ruffled in the breeze, making him look younger. "It's fine, really. I'm fine."

Yes, he was a demon of interest, but so far Victor had done nothing to make her think he was part of some nefarious plan to take over Roxburgh. Didn't mean he wasn't dangerous—far from it—which was why she needed to see this through.

"You don't know how glad I am to hear that." He tilted his head toward the coffee shop. "Will you let me buy you a coffee and a slice of something sweet perhaps, as a peace offering? I'd like us to still be friends." He smiled again, all ease and charm, and she found herself smiling in return.

Brent's words floated through her mind. She'd promised not to see Victor again, hadn't she? No, she'd only promised not to go to the club. Perhaps a technicality, but he hadn't played fair, asking her while she was still recovering from the orgasms he'd given her.

But the truth was they weren't in a committed relationship, and even if they were, she would never allow any male to dictate what she did. This was her chance to find out one way or another whether Victor was a threat.

"Sure. I'd like that."

His smile brightened and he took her arm and led her inside. He got a table, ordered their drinks as well as a piece of chocolate cake, and settled in the seat across from her.

He tilted his head to the side, eyes fixed on her, a sad smile lifting one side of his mouth. "So...I'll take a wild stab and assume our arrangement is now null and void? You won't require me to train you?"

She tried to look contrite. "I'm sorry for wasting your time."

He shook his head. "You need to stop apologizing, Chaya. The regret is all mine, I assure you." He reached out and took her hand. It was cold and smooth. "Submission is a gift. Not just anyone will have the ability to make your body sing with pleasure. I knew almost right away that wouldn't be me, as much as I wished otherwise. You will make some lucky Dom very, very happy one day."

No, she wouldn't. That would never happen.

But if she wanted to learn more about the demon sitting across from her, she needed to keep up the act and get him talking, which meant opening up a little about herself, making him think she trusted him as a confidant at least. "I'd never really acknowledged that part of myself, what I wanted, not until I met…"

"Ah, this…Brent? That was him, the male who came for you last night?"

"That was him."

"He brought this out in you?"

"Yes."

"He's a very lucky man. And you are a very rare find." He squeezed her hand then released it.

Oddly, his understanding warmed her. "He's a stubborn ass at times. He's refused to acknowledge the connection between us until now, and I'm still not sure he'll ever allow himself to truly let go or to see what's right in front of him."

Victor chuckled. "He and I are cut from a similar cloth, I think."

He held her gaze, full of intensity. She realized she was staring back, staring him down—not the actions of a sub. She quickly glanced down at her hands.

"Sometimes the only option is to push until they fall," he said into the silence.

She looked up, her heart kicking up a notch at the dark note to his voice. But there was nothing dark about his expression. He smiled. "I'm sure you'd provide a soft landing."

"Are you implying I'm on the curvy side?" she said in mock affront.

He winked. "In all the right places." Then he grew serious again. "I understand what it is to love someone, to have them take you for granted."

"Oh, you have someone?"

He shrugged. "Like you, I feel invisible at times. I've loved him for the longest time. I do things to please him that I would never do for anyone else, in some cases things that I regret deeply...still, it's never good enough..." He shook his head. "Sorry, I'm going on."

His pain was acute. He was letting her read him and it was deep and *real*. This was no act. "You're not. It's good to get these things off our chests, to talk about it." She reached out and gave his hand a squeeze. "You won't leave?"

"No, I could never walk away."

"I'm sorry."

He forced a smile. "Don't worry about me, honey. I'm tough as old boots." Sliding a hand into the inner pocket of his jacket, he pulled out a brochure. "I think I told you that one of the galleries I own is hosting an exhibition?"

Chaya fought back her excitement. This was the event she'd wanted to attend. A way to hopefully learn more about Victor.

"I'm showing a few of my own pieces, actually, and thought the subject matter might interest you?" A bit of heat drifted into his gaze.

"You take photos?"

He smiled. "It's a passion of mine."

She flipped through the brochure. The images she saw were striking. The focus of the exhibition was bondage. "These are...amazing."

"I'll leave your name at the door." He leaned over the table and kissed her cheek. "I'm really glad I saw you today, Chaya. Like I said, I'd love us to remain friends." He tapped the brochure. "I hope to see you there." Then he stood and strode from the coffee shop.

She looked back down. She had every intention of going,

even though she was having serious doubts that Victor was any real threat. Maybe if she went to this exhibition she could find out more about him and the people he associated with. Possibly rule him out once and for all.

Brent didn't have to know.

She took out her phone and hit Grace's number.

CHAPTER 12

BRENT STOOD BY THE BAR, keeping a close eye on things. There were a couple of tame scenes playing out, one which involved some spanking and another across from him that was nearly all wrapped up since the male had his female bent over the table and was fucking her ruthlessly and with the obvious goal of blowing his load. His gaze slid back to the spanking scene.

His gut clenched remembering the stings and burn of Chaya's hand connecting with his ass and the deep satisfying throb afterward.

Jesus. Focus.

He glanced around the room again. Everything was the way he liked it.

The rules were simple: You could fuck in the main club, but anything beyond a spanking had to be conducted in one of the playrooms. They were his rules, for his benefit. He didn't like to be watched, and he sure as hell didn't want anyone seeing what he did to get off. Not even the subs he forced himself to take into the playrooms knew how he got off, if he chose to, since he blindfolded them before he came.

Pulling his phone from his pocket, he checked his email. Nothing.

At least no more videos had been posted. But he felt like he'd come up against a brick wall. For now, he had to wait for Garrett's next move. Not a position he enjoyed being in.

He was ready to do something drastic, because he wouldn't be happy until the bastard was bloated and rotting at the bottom of Roxburgh Lake.

The scent of sex hung heavily in the air, and he took a moment to calm his frayed nerves. Closing his eyes, he fed on the euphoric emotions swirling around him. Shit, it felt good.

Tingles moved over his skin as he zeroed in on the female who called to him every minute of every damn day. His body heated as soon as he felt her, his breathing growing heavier, his stomach tightening.

He snapped his eyes open when he felt her move closer. She didn't look his way, and he didn't know if she'd seen him on the other side of the bar or if she was tormenting him on purpose. She was laughing with some of the other staff members, joking and smiling. The female was exquisite and tempted him in every way.

When he went up to his apartment later, like she'd ordered him to, would she follow? Or had she come to her senses?

Could he stand by and let her walk out the door if she had?

One of the other waitresses came up beside her and said something that made Chaya throw her head back and laugh. His cock hardened, pulsing along with his now racing heart. Fuck, he loved that. How she threw everything into all she did. Full of energy and joy and beauty.

No, he realized he couldn't let her walk away. Not now. Not yet.

She turned away to face the dance floor, her long dark hair swaying as she danced by the bar, waiting for her order to be filled. It took all his strength to stay where he was. The urge to walk over to her and beg her to take him up to his room now, this minute, pounded through him with the beat of the music. Eric, one of the guys working the bar, leaned over and touched her shoulder to get her attention. Brent had stepped forward, a growl rumbling from the back of his throat before he could stop himself.

His reaction was extreme since the guy was only handing over the drinks she was waiting on, but he'd learned the other night, when he'd almost beaten another male to death, that he had no control when it came to Chaya.

Except when she ordered him to. That thought made his already hard dick harder.

And it had only gotten worse after seeing her tied to that cross with that fucker standing over her. Every bit of his restraint had crumbled away. He didn't know what that meant or if he could rebuild his defenses. For her sake, he hoped so.

With his control slipping further with every passing second, he turned away, retreated to his office, and shut himself away. He couldn't think clearly when Chaya was near, and he could no longer stand there counting down the hours until her shift finished, wondering if she'd follow him up to his bedroom or not.

He buried himself in paperwork, did his best to keep his mind occupied until there was a knock at the door. It opened and Eric poked his head through. "I'm heading home, boss. John's arrived for the next shift. I'll catch you tomorrow."

"Yeah, thanks." Eric ducked back out and closed the door behind him.

Brent looked up at the clock. Eric and Chaya were

rostered on for the same shift, which meant she was finished as well. Nerves and anticipation throbbed through him.

He stood and left his office. The club was still busy when he walked through, the music following him as he headed out the back, through the door to the small hall, and up the stairs to his apartment. God, please don't let her change her mind.

A short time later, Brent sat as instructed at the foot of his bed, a fine sheen of sweat coating his bare skin.

He'd left the door unlocked for her.

Fifteen minutes had ticked by. And still she hadn't come.

The place was silent, utterly.

His cock throbbed painfully and his gut was in knots.

Fuck, please, let her come.

But then he heard it—the door to his apartment closing, the soft *snick* of the lock being engaged. He sucked in a relieved breath as the faint scent of vanilla hit him.

She was just outside his bedroom door.

What was going through her head? Was she nervous? Turned on? Both?

Several minutes passed before the door was pushed open, and it took everything in him to keep his head down and not drink in the sight of her. He could see her feet. Those boots.

Motherfuck.

He wanted to see what else she was wearing and what was in that bag she held down at her side, nice and low so he got a look at it, so he knew whatever she carried in it was meant for him.

He didn't speak. He waited, let the anticipation of what was to come build. He wasn't sure he could even if he wanted to with how tight his vocal cords felt. There was a clatter and a thunk as she placed the bag on the side table.

The muted sound of her boots on the carpet as she moved

around the bed came next and then she was standing in front of him.

Chaya stood, feet slightly apart, not a twitch or a sound for several long minutes. All he could do was breathe her in —vanilla mixed with the heady aroma of aroused female. Christ, he was positive he could feel the heat radiating off her.

The female made him crazy. Jesus, she'd had him running around in circles from the minute he met her, constantly pushing him, challenging him. He realized now how much she'd needed this, that she'd been seeking it out the only way she knew how, whether she was aware of it or not. They'd been dancing around each other. Silently screaming for what the other could give them.

Because Brent sure as fuck wouldn't drop to his knees for just anyone. Christ, Chaya had come alive when he had that first time.

And the only place he wanted to be right then was exactly where he was.

Her breathing had grown heavier, as had the scent of her arousal.

And finally, finally, she slid a finger under his chin and tilted his face up so he could see her. She was flushed, eyes bright. As hungry for him as he was for her. It was written all over her lovely face.

"You have no idea how much you've pleased me tonight, Brent." She licked her lower lip and he felt it across the head of his cock. "Last night I showed you a little of what I expect from my sub. You misbehaved and you were punished." The pulse at her throat beat steadily. "And tonight you'll be rewarded for your obedience."

The muscles in his thighs tightened and his cock felt impossibly heavy. A growl of need was there, crawling up the back of his throat.

"Are you ready, sub?"

"Yes, Mistress," he murmured.

She took several steps back so he finally had a better view of her. While she stood outside his door she'd obviously changed. She was wearing a garter and panties in electric blue, paired with black stockings and a black corset. She took his breath away.

Her gaze dropped to his dick and there was no mistaking she liked what she saw. Her head tipped to the side a little, then her eyes came back to his. "Have you been thinking about tasting my pussy again?"

The growl did come then. Christ, there was no holding it back. "Yes, Mistress."

Her gaze remained firm. "Good." She reached down and ran her fingers lightly over her lace-covered pussy. "Do you want me to use that big cock of yours, Brent? Do you want me to ride you until you can't take another second?"

He groaned. "I could fuck you right now if you wanted me to. Fuck you so hard you'd come screaming my name in minutes," he said, so turned on he forgot himself completely.

She moved in, slid her fingers in his hair, fisted, and shoved his head back. "Is that the way you speak to your mistress? Did I ask for your opinion?"

He almost came then and there. "No, Mistress," he choked out.

She stared at him narrow eyed. "Looks like you'll need punishing after all." As he swayed forward, she stepped back. "On your hands and knees. Now."

He didn't speak because he hadn't been asked a direct question and quickly did as she said, anticipation buzzing through his veins. She was a fast learner. Chaya had him fucking on the verge of coming and she'd only been in the room fifteen minutes.

He wanted his punishment and his reward. He wanted it all.

She moved around him slowly, but unlike last time, she didn't touch him. "Are you okay with ass play?" she said into the silence.

Brent swallowed the boulder that had formed in his throat, and his ass clenched. "Yes."

She moved away and he heard her at the bag on the bedside table, taking something out, then she came back. "You have such a stunning ass, Brent, I've been thinking about decorating it all day."

She ran her finger through the cleft, and he shivered.

There was a soft noise, and when her finger was back, it was slippery and warm. She massaged his hole with lube, preparing him, making him squirm and push back. Christ, wanting her to push one of those fingers inside him.

Then she did, slow, just a little at first, and he gasped, a moan escaping immediately after.

She hummed her approval and slowly pushed deeper, giving him more until she was leisurely fucking his ass with her finger and he was trembling.

After tormenting him for a while longer, she added a second, stretching him, hitting that spot inside him, bringing him right to the edge. He couldn't help himself and humped back against her hand desperate for more.

"Fuuuuck. Oh fuck. Fuck me. I think I'm going to come, Mistress." It was the closest he'd come to orgasm without pain in four years.

"No, you won't, not until I tell you to."

After a few more leisurely pumps of his ass, she removed her fingers and he actually fucking whimpered. But a second later something hard and slick was at his hole. She pushed it in steadily until the butt plug was all the way in and he was panting, sweating, and shaking.

Chaya smoothed her hands down his back. "You took that so well." She moaned softly. "But that's just the beginning. You've been bad, remember? This fine ass needs to be paddled."

Oh God, oh fuck. He wouldn't survive it.

His arms started to shake.

"Are you ready, Brent?"

No. But somehow "Fuck yes" burst past his lips.

"You were very disrespectful. I'm going to paddle your ass eight times. And you will not come, Brent, not until the last strike. Do you understand?"

"Yes…Mistress," he choked out, not knowing if he could. Because he could feel that plug in his ass, stretching him, pressing against his prostate, and he hadn't even fucking moved yet.

"One," she said.

The leather paddle connected with his ass, low across both his cheeks, and he jolted forward. He groaned as the plug moved inside him.

"Two."

He rocked forward again, gasping for breath.

"Three."

His cock slapped against his stomach, the plug making him insane as he moved back into position, as he fucking tilted his ass, silently begging for the rest.

"Four."

Fuuuuuuck.

She moved around to the other side. "Five."

"Please, oh fuck, I need to…"

"Six."

"Fucking shit. Fuck."

"Seven."

He was shaking so hard his arms gave out.

"Eight," she said, sounding breathless.

The last made contact with his ass and Brent's hips jerked. The sound of the paddle hitting the floor came next then she took his balls in her hand, giving him the pain he still needed to come. She applied pressure while she used the palm of her other hand to press down on the plug in his ass, forcing it a little deeper. He fucking shuddered and started fucking the air as he came so hard he had no idea which way was up. Deep, wrenching pulls that didn't seem to have any intention of stopping.

He vaguely heard Chaya over his own moans and cries.

"That's it, come for me," she said. "Just like that."

God, her huskily spoken words just made him come harder.

Finally, after what felt like forever, the last shudder moved through him.

He lay there helpless, head resting on his forearms, ass still in the air, as she stroked his sweaty skin, as she gently removed the plug from his ass, causing another wave of pleasure to course through his spent body.

Her hand went between his thighs and she wrapped her fingers around his flaccid cock, massaging, stroking. It should be impossible, but he started getting hard again the moment she touched him.

"Get on the bed, Brent," she said softly. "Lie on your back and spread your arms and legs for me."

He'd do any damn thing she wanted. He couldn't get enough of her, wanted only to please her, serve her. He climbed to his feet on shaky legs and crawled onto his bed.

"Very good," she said and went to the bag on the dresser again and pulled out two sets of leather cuffs. Each was attached to a length of chain that could be attached to his bed frame.

She secured the chains to each corner of the thick wooden head and end boards then fastened and buckled each cuff around his wrists and ankles, making sure they weren't tight enough to cut off his blood supply, but that he couldn't get free. "You look good enough to eat like that. Leather suits you."

He'd never brought anyone up to his apartment before. He'd definitely never been tied down to his own bed like this either. Images of the video he'd seen of himself earlier flashed through his mind, but he forced them out. That didn't belong here. What they were doing didn't resemble the ugly shit he'd done in that room.

This felt right. Honest. This was where Chaya belonged. In his bed.

Fucking owning him.

The playrooms weren't for her. Because who he was when he stepped through that shiny red door, cold, emotionless, a fraud…he didn't want Chaya to be part of that.

He watched, damn near drooling as she slowly undid her corset and let it fall to the floor. Her bare breasts bounced free, full and soft, and he grunted and tugged at his restraints, desperate to touch. She was left in her garter, panties, stockings, and boots, and he nearly swallowed his tongue when she crawled up between his spread thighs, skimming her hands over the arch of his foot, up his calves, and across his thighs. The chains clattered against the bed again when he tried to get to her.

"Are you ready for a taste of me, Brent?"

He was trembling now. "Yes. I need you…please."

Jesus. She was killing him.

She slid higher up his body and straddled his face, but up on her knees so he couldn't reach her. Then she reached down, and that was when he saw the slit in her panties. She used her fingers to part the fabric, revealing her pretty pink pussy to him, then she traced her drenched folds, opening herself up, exploring, forcing him to watch and not touch or taste.

"Sit on my face, Mistress." He wasn't even going to pretend that he wasn't begging. "Please."

She grazed her clit, and her thighs and belly quivered beautifully. He couldn't take his eyes off her.

She circled her opening and his hips surged off the damn bed. She played, tormenting him until he was trembling with need.

Her soft whimpers turned to sharp cries.

"Please. Please, Mistress," he begged, shaking harder.

"Please what?" She gasped as she increased the pace of her movements.

Jesus fucking Christ. "Please let me taste you. Come on my face, against my mouth. Please."

A moment later, she gave him what he wanted, removing her own hand and lowering herself onto his mouth. He chased it, lifting his head as best he could, sucking and licking, shoving his tongue inside her. She ground down on his face and, throwing her head back, broke apart for him. Her body bowed hard, her cries filling the room.

The chains rattled as he lifted his head, following her, staying right there, lapping her all up, every delicious taste she gave him.

Her hands were on the headboard and she rocked her hips against his mouth until she'd worked every last tremor from her body and slid off him, collapsing beside him all boneless, sexy female.

He watched, waited for her to open her eyes, and when she finally blinked up at him, he knew he looked feral by the satisfied smile she gave him.

"You're very good at that," she said as her eyes traveled down his body to his painfully hard cock. "I left you hard last

691

time, didn't I?" She grazed her fingernails over his nipple. "I could do that again, or…"

All he could do was shake his damned head.

"You want me to fuck you, don't you, Brent?"

"More than anything, Mistress," he rasped.

"Usually that admission would have me walking out the door, leaving you wanting, anticipating, until next time I had you tied down and hard. But I promised you a reward, didn't I?"

He wanted inside her so bad he would die if she left him like this.

She climbed off the bed and he barked out a protest, but she didn't leave. No, she removed the rest of her clothes until she was completely naked. All creamy, soft curves. The sexiest, most beautiful female he had ever laid eyes on.

Then she climbed back on top of him and slid her hands up his chest.

She sat there on top of him, so damn beautiful he ached.

Chaya leaned in, her luscious mouth hovering an inch above his. He reveled in that first mingling of breath, the way his hitched when the tip of her tongue darted out, moistening the plump crimson flesh of her lower lip.

He realized she hadn't kiss him yet, and he needed her to more than anything in this whole damn world. He hadn't kissed anyone since before becoming a demi-demon. With Chaya, he'd been afraid that if she did, if she offered him that intimacy, he would go to a place he could never return from, and at the end of this she'd take the last of his humanity with her. That she'd take what remained of his heart.

But he would never, could never turn away or deny her what she wanted, what they both wanted.

Cupping his face in her small hands, she closed the gap, brushing her mouth against his. *Oh fuck*. He indulged in the smooth, soft texture of her lips. She moaned and opened her mouth, sliding her tongue against his in an undemanding way while still controlling the kiss, while they explored each other's mouths, their taste.

He knew instantly he'd made a huge mistake. One taste and he was addicted to her more than he already had been. He was dizzy from it. There was no going back. He would never get enough of this. The way she moaned, the way her lips grew even softer, swollen, the more she kissed him. The taste of her desire, the gentle warmth of her mouth against his.

When she finally pulled away, he made a sound of protest, lifting his head, trying to follow. He watched as she sat back, drawing in a shaky breath as she took a condom from her bag.

Jesus. This is happening.

She tore it open and rolled it down his hard length.

Finally—finally—she moved back, and holding his cock in her hands, positioned him between her spread thighs.

She glanced up at him then sank down.

His hips jerked up all on their own and they both moaned when he filled her to the hilt. He couldn't take his eyes off her. There was no warm-up; she was as hungry for him as he was for her. She lifted up almost all the way and came back down. She screamed and he could feel her inner muscles already fluttering around him. Dipping her head, she sucked hard on one of his nipples, grazing it with her teeth and nipping.

Gasping and grunting, he fucked her back, unable to stop from slamming his hips up to meet hers. He pounded into her, getting lost in the feel of her wet pussy clamped tight around him, the heat of her skin burning against his.

Her mouth dropped open in a silent scream.

"Oh fuck, that's it," he gritted out.

Head thrown back, she sucked in a startled breath and

came a second later, crying out, shaking almost violently from her release. She fell forward. Sweat slicked their skin, their bodies sliding together as he continued to pound up into her. His balls were drawn tight, skin prickling, tingles radiating out from his lower spine and the base of his cock.

So close, so damn close, but as always, just out of reach.

He needed pain—oh fuck, he still needed pain. He hated himself, but he thought he might die if he didn't finish inside her.

Like she could read his mind, she slowed the roll of her hips and reached out, freeing his wrists. Before she could lift back up, he buried his face against the side of her throat, drowning in the sweet scent of her hair.

"What do you need?" she said softly against his ear.

"Put your hands on me," he rasped. "Let me feel your nails in my skin."

She rolled them so he was on top of her, and those soft, warm hands were on him in a second, moving over his back as he thrust into her. When he felt her pussy start to spasm around him for the second time, he nipped her earlobe. "I need your nails, your teeth." Then he slammed into her again, brutally. Her nails sunk into his waist, her teeth into the muscle of his shoulder.

The shot of sweet pain was enough, and he roared, shuddering against her as he came hard and deep inside her. But it wasn't pain, it was pleasure that took him over.

Chaya had given him that, and she had no idea how huge that was.

CHAPTER 13

CHAYA WOKE to a tickle on her skin. She glanced down.

Brent had scooted down the bed and was nuzzling, pressing kisses to her hip. His eyes were aimed up at her, raw hunger in their depths shining back.

She threaded her fingers through his hair. "What are you doing down there?" she said, voice still husky from sleep.

"Waiting for you to wake up." He pressed another kiss against her bare skin.

She knew exactly what he wanted, and she was more than happy to oblige. Keeping her fingers buried in his hair, she rolled to her back, spread her thighs, and guided him to her bare pussy.

He opened his mouth over her instantly, lips and tongue working her, and his groan of satisfaction vibrated against her still-sensitive flesh.

Curling her toes, she fisted the sheets with her other hand. "Ahh…so good."

Brent's warm breath drifted across her bare thigh, his dark chuckle sexy as hell.

"I wouldn't get…too…cocky…if I were you. You'll…

ahhh…earn yourself another p-punishment." God, he was good at this.

He sucked on her clit and she arched off the bed, already close.

"You'll get no complaint from me," he said, causing his whiskered jaw to scrape against her bare skin and send her even higher.

He pressed his tongue inside her pussy, swirling then sucking on her, making her buck against his mouth, giving her the hottest, dirtiest kind of kiss. In seconds she was panting, reaching for release. His big hands rested on her inner thighs, holding her open for him, and when the first tremors started, he lifted his gaze and watched her come, lips wrapped around her clit, tongue flicking over her relentlessly. The whole time, those intense eyes never left hers.

It was too much, too good. She cried out, writhed beneath him, rode out the pleasure he was giving her without holding anything back.

When she finally stilled, he bent down and kissed her hip. "Not sure I'll ever get sick of watching you come."

God, she hoped not.

She rolled to her side and held out her hand. "Come here. I want to taste you, too."

His chest expanded sharply, and he bared his teeth in a way that made her body fire back to life. "I wish, but I have a meeting to get to and I'm already late." When he stood, she noticed his hair was damp, and though his chest was bare, he had on pants. He'd showered while she'd slept.

The night was over, and he was donning his armor. She flicked back the covers and grabbed her underwear from the floor, pulling them on as she stood.

Brent came up behind her, his bare chest hot against her back, and he nuzzled the side of her neck. "You don't need to rush off, Chay. Stay a little longer. Rest." He ground his erection against her ass. "Will I see you tonight?"

Tonight was her night off, and she'd thought that it might be a night off for them as well. Was she finally getting through to him?

"I'd like that. I'm going to an exhibition tonight, but I'll come over after that."

He gently sucked her earlobe and she sighed. "Who's the artist?"

"I'm not really sure. A friend invited me, and I thought I'd check it out."

Both hands slid across her belly, so she was effectively cocooned in his arms. She never wanted him to let her go.

"When I get here after the exhibition, I want you in one of the playrooms, and I want to find you like I did last night. When I open the door, the first thing I want to see is you naked and hard and ready for me. Understand?"

His swallow was audible. "The playrooms, they're a hard limit for me."

She turned in his arms. That was where he took the subs he selected those nights he played Dom, something she still didn't understand but wanted to more than anything. Why were they off limits to her? His arms flexed around her, then he released her and stepped back.

Her instant reaction was to push for a reason why, but people had limits for a lot of reasons, and just because they were fucking didn't mean he owed her one.

"Okay, if that's the way you feel."

He dropped his gaze from hers. "Yeah, it is." His voice had changed, now rough, deeper.

The look on his face said he was worried he'd disappointed her. Seeing him hurting hurt her. "Come here," she said softly.

His nostrils flared and then his big body moved toward her, smooth and sexy. He stopped right in front of her.

"You were perfect last night, in every way," she said and cupped his whiskered jaw. He leaned into her hand, seeking more of her touch. She gave it to him freely, smoothing her other hands over his shoulder, his chest. "I couldn't have asked for a better first time."

"But this wasn't…" He frowned. "With a paddle?" he said, looking adorably confused.

"The first time I had sex."

He stilled. "What?"

She smiled.

"I was…your first?" he said, voice pure gravel.

"Yep." He seemed at a loss for words. "Are you okay?"

"But why…"

"Why you?" she finished for him. "You trusted me with your body, Brent. And I trust you with mine. Now kiss me."

He growled in that delicious way of his and leaned in, their lips meeting in a hot kiss that had her toes curling all over again.

When she finally ended it, she said, "We don't need the playroom. I'm a creative girl. I want to find you in this room when I get back tonight, ready and waiting for me. I have all day to plan our evening." A shiver moved through his big frame.

"I look forward to it," he said.

"Oh, you definitely should."

She stared after him when he left. Why wouldn't he let her take him to the playroom? What was he hiding?

Dare she hope it was because she meant something to him? That she meant more to him than the casual hookups he took to those rooms? Her stomach flipped at the thought.

After dressing quickly, she headed down to the bar. The place was empty. It wouldn't open for hours yet.

He wanted her, what she could give him, what they could give each other—that much was undeniable. Now, if only he'd drop his barriers.

If only he'd let her in.

~

Hours later, Chaya climbed out of a cab. She rarely came to this side of the city, tending to stay close to home. To the club.

To Brent.

The gallery was lit up behind massive double glass doors, with people—and more than likely a lot of other creatures as well—moving about inside.

This wasn't her usual scene. She'd never been to an exhibition in her life and had struggled with what to wear. In the end she'd selected the black knee-length pencil skirt her sister had bought her last Christmas, and paired it with her dark green satin corset and a few chunky bracelets.

She needed to look the part.

Grace trusted her to get the job done and wanted details on who was there, who Victor spoke to, and anything else she might be able to find out. Chaya didn't want to let her down.

She plastered a smile on her face, and the woman at the door did the same as Chaya approached. As promised, Victor had left her name there and she was shown straight in. The room was huge, open, all white with cathedral ceilings. People moved around, champagne flutes in hand, admiring the images suspended from thin wire. They'd been placed strategically to make the place feel less cavernous. Well, she guessed that was the artist's aim. Besides Victor, she didn't know who the other artists were. She'd only flipped through the brochure Victor had given her, then lost it somewhere.

She looked around the room and wondered how many people attending were part of the lifestyle. How many were here out of curiosity?

Grabbing a glass of champagne from a passing waitress, she started moving around the room. Victor had to be there somewhere.

Some of the pictures were beautiful, arousing. Some shocking. All were of males and females tied or restrained in some way. She stopped in front of one where a woman was tied with a length of rope. It came around her back, circling each bent leg, forcing her thighs up and open. She was blindfolded, mouth open in a silent scream, but even without seeing her eyes Chaya felt her fear.

She shivered. Something was off about it, something that made her skin crawl. The two times she'd restrained Brent he'd made it clear that he loved every minute of it, but this…

"Chaya, I'm so glad you could come." She turned to find Victor standing there. He'd moved up beside her and was watching her look at the disturbing piece in front of her. "What do you think?"

She didn't know what to say. She didn't want to piss him off, since he clearly knew the artist, or, God, it was one of his. Telling him what she really thought wouldn't help her gather information or get closer to his inner circle. "I'm not…I'm not really sure it's my thing." She tried to give her opinion as diplomatically as possible. Since she couldn't lie for shit, she might as well go for a half truth.

His grinned. "No?"

She took a sip of her champagne, needing a moment to gather her thoughts. "I've never seen anything like this before. I guess they're just so…so confronting."

He chuckled. "Yes. Yes, they are that." He rested his hand on the small of her back. "Come, I have another I'd like you to see."

She let him lead her across the gallery. Now she just had to get him talking like she had in the coffee shop. Let him think they were besties and get him to reveal more of his deepest and darkest secrets.

Easy, right?

∼

Brent walked into his room and stared down at his rumpled sheets. She'd only been there with him one night, but he could still smell her, remember the way she'd looked in his bed. Sitting down, he tagged the pillow and pressed it to his face, groaning when he breathed in her vanilla scent.

Shit.

When she'd sunk her nails and teeth into his skin, when she'd marked him and made him come, without even realizing it, she'd claimed him. He was hers. He was helpless against the hold she had over him.

Throwing the pillow back down, he blew out a frustrated breath and stood. What was the next step? Where did they go from here?

Something caught his eye on the floor. He picked it up. A brochure. The exhibition Chaya was going to. She must have dropped it when she was getting dressed. He flipped it over.

And frowned.

The image on the front told him exactly the subject matter the artist had chosen to photograph. Then he spotted one of the photographers' names. Victor.

He shot to his feet.

She'd promised not to see that bastard again. She'd lied. *Fuck*. He didn't trust that male, not with Chaya. He understood her desire to help Grace and the other demi in this city, but to keep this from him, to put herself at risk like this?

Something ugly curled low in his belly.

Shoving on his jacket, he strode from his apartment, and every step he took, his rage increased along with his fear. His mood hadn't improved by the time he climbed into his car, and it only got worse as he drove from the lot, and ignoring the speed limit, covered the distance in record time.

The gallery came into view, and he parked out front. The valet intercepted him as he climbed out. "I'll be five minutes." He handed over the keys and strode toward the glass-fronted building.

The woman stationed there tried to stop him, but he ignored her and strode through the doors. The place was packed, people getting in his way as he frantically searched the room for Chaya. Pushing through the crowd, he moved toward the back of the room. That's when he saw her staring up at a photograph. It was huge, covering most of the wall.

The male in the picture stood facing out, hands stretched above his head, forced up on his toes. He wore a mask covering his entire head. His skin was flushed, cock hard, jutting from between his thighs. A female stood behind him, riding crop in her hand, frozen high in the air after striking his flesh. His back was arched, and every muscle and tendon in his body stood out, straining beneath his skin.

With the mask on you couldn't see the tears sliding down the male's face, couldn't hear his begging and pleading for her to stop, to make all of it stop. You couldn't hear the shame in his voice when, despite it all, he was begging her to finally let him come.

He knew this because the male was him.

His legs went weak, momentarily threatening to come out from under him. He clenched his fists and fought down the humiliation, the rage pumping through his body. The all-out terror.

Garrett.

The room seemed to close in as he moved forward. Chaya

was focused on his image and jumped when he grabbed her arm.

She spun around, eyes landing on him, wide…guilty for a second then they narrowed. "Brent, what are you doing here?"

"Don't," he growled.

Somehow Garrett had arranged this and was somehow connected to Victor. He'd brought her here to look at this picture. Was more than likely still here, in this room somewhere, watching him right at that moment. The sadistic bastard had him by the balls.

Garrett knew his weakness and he'd successfully used it against him. Now Brent had no choice but to tell Chaya about his past, all of it, or leave her exposed and vulnerable.

He wanted to storm this room, raze it, and kill Garrett with his bare hands, but he needed to get Chaya to safety and as far from that monster as he could.

The fucker had won again.

Rage burned through his veins as he scanned the room.

Anything could have happened to her, and she stood there staring him down, like he was the one who was in the wrong, like he was the one who'd lied.

"I need you to walk out of here with me now," he said through gritted teeth.

Chaya's gaze moved over his face, and yeah, she saw it. She didn't know what he was freaking out about, but whatever it was had pushed him past breaking point.

She sensed it. He knew this because she didn't voice the protest he knew was on the tip of her tongue and started toward the exit of the gallery and out onto the street. That beautiful mouth of hers stayed firmly closed as she watched him in a way that made him feel exposed. He snatched the keys from the valet and opened the passenger door for her to get in.

As they drove away, putting distance between Chaya and the monster who had kept him and used him for months, the fucker who had ruined his life, he struggled and failed to gain control. Instead, one horrific scenario after the other flashed through his mind.

The urge to go back was riding him hard. But the demon wasn't stupid. Brent could tear down that building brick by brick with his bare hands and find no trace of him. Garrett would be found when he chose to be and not before, and that just sent Brent even closer to the edge.

How many times had Chaya been near him? How many times had that fucker had the opportunity to hurt her?

The leather creaked as she turned to face him. "Brent, I…"

"You lied to me." The emotions coming off her were so strong he had to grit his teeth against them. "You said you wouldn't see him. You…Christ, you fucked up tonight, Chaya."

"I'm not a damned child to be scolded. I told you I had no intention to stop what I was doing, that I wasn't going to stop helping Grace."

"You put yourself in danger."

"You know Grace. Do you think she'd let me go in there without safeguards in place?"

"That isn't the damned point," he gritted out.

That unwavering stare of hers hardened and, fuck, his cock did as well.

"No? How about you fill me in?"

If looks could kill, he'd be a corpse. Yeah, that just made his dick strain harder against the zipper of his pants. She thought he was being heavy handed but had no idea he was half out of his mind. And there was no way he was having the conversation he needed to have with her right then, especially not in the car while he was still struggling to keep his emotions in check.

He felt her eyes burning into the side of his head when he focused back on the road.

"I think we've had a serious communication breakdown here. I do not answer to you. I do not answer to anyone, understand?"

"Is that right?" he forced out through clenched teeth.

"If I were you, I'd check my tone." Fire burned in her dark gaze, but her lips had parted and her cheeks were flushed, and then he caught her scent. She was aroused, hot as fuck.

Her voice was hard, unwavering, and his cock throbbed in reply.

Everything in the enclosed space had shifted. Right at that moment he was sitting in the car with his Domme, and he couldn't help but respond to her dominance.

Silence filled the car and Brent thought he'd lose his damn mind waiting for her to speak again. All the while his mind continued to race, coming up with scenarios where he hadn't seen that brochure, where Chaya never made it back to him.

"Communication is key in any kind of relationship," she finally said in a soft but firm voice that lifted the hair on the back of his neck in a fucking good way. Fear still pumped through him, and still his body responded. He craved her constantly. "And so far, we've done our best communicating with our clothes off."

He glanced over at her.

She smirked. "Oh, the plans I have for you and that disrespectful mouth."

In that moment, after what had just happened—the gallery, Garrett, Victor—he was feeling so much, too much. What he and Chaya had done the day before. The way she'd mastered him so effortlessly, the freedom, the joy...the peace she'd given him. It would be so easy—So. Damn. Easy—for him to let go completely. But then what? He'd be back to that male, the one he'd been when Garrett had come for him, all over again. Lost in emotion, addicted to what Chaya gave him. Addicted to her.

Vulnerable.

He didn't think she'd hurt him, but he would end up hurting her and himself when he became that…creature. When he lost sight of who he was and fed, gorged, until he didn't know which way was up. Until he gave himself to anyone who wanted him to get more of that high.

Nausea twisted in his gut.

Chaya didn't speak again until they pulled up outside the club. She turned to him. "Walk inside. Do not speak to anyone. Go straight to your bedroom."

"The playroom," he choked out. "I want to go to the playroom."

Silence filled the space again for several long seconds. "That was a hard limit."

He shook his head. "I want it." He swallowed. "I need it." The place he went when he needed release, where he fed his incubus. Where he could shut down his emotions. And fuck, he needed to shut them down. Now. Before it was too late.

"Are you sure?"

He nodded. It was all he was capable of.

"Go to the end playroom, take off every piece of clothing, and wait for me on your knees," she said without missing a beat.

He didn't wait to be told twice. He shoved the door open and strode inside the club, all the while trying to rein in the fear of seeing Chaya in that room. Seeing her looking up at that picture of him tonight and knowing who was behind it.

Chaya had been in danger this whole time and he'd had no idea.

So, yeah, reining it in wasn't an option.

Loosening his tie and ignoring everything and everyone

around him, he made his way to the end room as instructed. He'd used it many times. One of the rooms where he unleashed the dark desires that resided inside him. A side of him he'd never wanted Chaya to see.

He'd always played the Dom here—not tonight. God, not tonight. But it was all the same. He needed pain—dishing it out and feeding off it or being on the receiving end of it.

Yeah, in here it was all the same.

He just wanted to get lost in it. He was past the point of rational thought. He was fear and desperate hunger.

He was sex.

What he could get in that room, *who he was* in that room called to him, consumed him, drove him forward. And only Chaya could sate his need.

CHAPTER 14

CHAYA MOVED THROUGH THE CLUB, mind racing as fast as the beat of her pounding heart.

She had to get this right. Couldn't fuck this up.

The look on Brent's face when he found her at Victor's gallery. Her first instincts were to tell him to back the hell off, but then she'd looked at him. Really looked at him. And she knew she had to get him out of there.

Because she would never let anyone or anything hurt him, and what she saw deep in his eyes told her he was in pain.

The playroom. I want to go to the playroom.

I want it. I need it.

He needed it.

She'd convinced herself that his reluctance to come here with her was because she meant more to him than one of his casual one-nighters, that this place and what went on in these rooms represented something *less* than what they had, and that in his eyes, if she brought him here, it would send her the wrong message, would somehow diminish what was growing between them.

Now she wasn't so sure.

What he did in these rooms he *needed*. But this was a place where he'd gone against his own nature, against everything that he was, that he cried out for.

He'd hurt himself here. He'd mentally tortured himself every time he brought a sub to one of these rooms, every time he denied what he truly wanted, and he'd hurt himself.

The last door in the lineup of shiny red doors was in front of her. How many times had she seen the torment on his face when he opened these doors and walked out onto the floor after a session? Every damn time.

This room he came to with strangers, he fed his demon without the risk of forming any kind of lasting connection.

What he got was release without attachment.

This was not a safe place for him. A place of peace. Of affection and respect.

But it would be when she was done.

God, the way he'd reacted when he'd walked in and found her at that gallery. She'd never seen him like that. Something had changed, something in him. She didn't understand it, but she wanted to. Desperately.

Straightening her shoulders, she gripped the door handle and walked in.

Her heart squeezed when she saw him. Kneeling on the floor. Stripped bare. Desperate for her to give him what he needed, but too afraid to tell her what that was.

Toys were lined up on shelves. Restraints. Whips, paddles, floggers. This was what he needed, and up until now she hadn't been able to give it to him, not fully. He hadn't let her.

Her boots clicked on the polished hardwood floor as she moved into the room. Placing her purse and jacket on one of the benches, she turned to study him. Silent and still. So still.

Maybe she was overthinking it. Maybe the real reason he hadn't brought her here was that he didn't think she couldn't handle the full force of his desires. That she wasn't capable of taking him where he needed to go to find that peace she knew he longed for.

Fuck that.

Straightening her spine, she moved to the center of the room. Worrying wasn't helping either of them.

No way was she letting him give up on them.

She let several more minutes tick by before she spoke. "Spread your legs wider."

Her voice was gritty, shit—*demonic*. Something she had never experienced before. It was like she had finally, truly tapped into that part of herself that had always been there just waiting for her to set it free.

Brent didn't miss it. His head jerked slightly, and goose bumps lifted all over his naked body. The sight tugged low in her belly deliciously. She didn't lift his face to her like she had the night before. No, she crouched down and, grabbing his knees, pushed them wider so he was completely exposed and vulnerable.

"When I ask you to spread your legs, you spread them as far as you can." She made a tsking sound. "We're not getting off to a very good start tonight, are we? First you charged into that gallery without a proper explanation, risking my assignment, and now I'm forced to correct a basic position, one I've already gone over with you."

He blew out a harsh breath, and it tickled hair at her temple. He was pissed off and turned on. She'd thrown him off balance. Good.

"Are you behaving like a brat on purpose?"

He made a rough sound. "No."

She shook her head and slid her fingers across his jaw, gently tilting his head back so he was forced to look into her eyes, and quirked a brow. "No?"

His nostrils flared. "No...Mistress."

"What is it, then?" she said harshly. "What's your excuse for charging in there like that?"

"You know why," he said growled. "You weren't safe."

This was a side to Brent she had never seen before. His demeanor was different, his voice lower, rougher. He was angry or afraid, maybe both, and he wasn't trying to hide it.

She stared into his eyes. "You're wrong. I had backup. Fighting in this war, it's something I have to do. Something that you will have to get used to if we're going to continue this."

Anger flashed through his eyes. "I still have visions of that male with his filthy hands on you, can still taste the fear he caused you, can still hear your screams. And you want me to just...be okay with you spending time with him? Be okay with him *touching* you for some greater good?"

He'd forgotten himself again. Was pushing. He wanted her to punish him, correct him. And she would. "The assignment was nearly over. He will not be touching me in that way again." She held his intense stare and cupped his stubborn jaw, sliding her thumb back and forth until he let out a shuddery breath, until his eyes drifted shut. "And because the only man I want is you."

His eyes snapped open, and there was a flicker of something in his eyes. He liked what she'd just said. Then it was gone before she could attempt to name it.

Without warning, she dropped her hand between his legs and curled her fingers around his cock, giving him several soft strokes, too soft, but a small reprieve from the ache she knew he must have been feeling.

A reward for showing her, even for a split second, that she'd affected him.

She leaned in. "So hard," she rasped against his ear after stroking him for several seconds longer. He growled when she released him. "Are you looking forward to your punishment, sub?"

"Yes," he whispered roughly.

Before he knew what she was going to do, she slapped his sac, not too hard, but enough to make him jolt and groan. Pre-come started leaking from the head of his cock.

She nearly came watching him right there on the spot. "Is that the correct way to address me?"

"No…Mistress."

"Are you looking forward to your punishment?" she repeated.

"Yes, Mistress."

She chuckled, and his taut stomach clenched. "Better." She stood, taking a step back. "Stand."

He did as she asked and silently waited for what would come next.

Walking to the table behind him, she selected what she wanted and moved back to stand in front of him. "Holding the head of your cock, angle it up for me," she said.

The sight of his long fingers wrapping around his beautiful cock had her desperate to squeeze her thighs together. She opened her hand, showing him the adjustable leather cock ring she had, then wrapped it around the base of his penis, carefully adjusted it to the right size, and snapped it into place. Nice and firm.

Brent grunted.

"Lovely," she said and gazed meaningfully at his broad chest before she trailed the tips of her fingers down from his collarbone to one of his small tight brown nipples and squeezed.

Brent sucked in a startled breath as she leaned over and took it into her mouth, tugging and nipping at it. He bucked, a low groan vibrating through his chest.

Chaya continued to torment him until his nipples were

tight and sensitive, then after one last suck and lick, she released him.

"You know what's next, don't you?" she said and grabbed what she wanted from the table beside them: a pair of bull-nose nipple clamps. "Since you seemed to enjoy looking at mine the other night after I danced for you in that cage, I thought you might like some of your own."

Those sexy abs tightened again, chest expanding.

He gasped when she clamped on the first and adjusted the pressure. "How does that feel?" she said, watching him closely.

"Fucking good, Mistress."

She had to bite back her smile. She moved in closer so his engorged cock was trapped between them, and she felt him press into her, trying to grind his cock against her for some relief.

Chaya gave the chain attached a tug. "You'll get relief when I give it to you and not before." She gave his balls another light tap, and his hips bucked forward.

"Motherfucker," he hissed between his teeth.

She could see he was already desperate to come. She wanted him so hot he begged for it. She gave the other nipple the same treatment. When it was aching and stiff, she secured the second clamp and gave it an experimental tug, watching him closely the whole time.

She lifted to his lips the thin chain connecting the two clamps. "Open." He did as she asked. "Hold this between your teeth and don't under any circumstances let go unless I tell you to. Do you understand?"

"Yes, Mistress." He took the chain between his teeth, which caused the clamps to pull deliciously at his nipples, and his eyes drifted shut for several seconds.

"Go to the St. Andrew's cross, facing me," she said, and moved in close to him again once he did as she asked. She slid her fingers down the side of his face. "What happened to me at The Dungeon caused you distress. I'm okay, I promise you that. But I want us both to experience how good it can be, together."

She got another lovely flash of emotion, bright in his eyes.

He dipped his head, his breathing harsh, every muscle and tendon straining. He was so beautiful her heart ached.

She walked around him in a slow circle, letting him see how hungry she was for him, how beautiful she found his naked body. Goose bumps broke out across his skin again and she wanted to cheer at the way he was reacting to her. The constant ache between her thighs intensified.

She stopped at his side. His cock was huge, swollen and so hard it was obscene. Just looking at him had her struggling to keep her composure. To stop herself from ordering him to fuck her right then.

"Eyes ahead at all times," she said then dropped to her knees. She made sure he felt each puff of breath as she moved up his body. His low growl reached her ears and she had to fight not to jam her legs together or grab that straining cock and taste him. She carried on up his hip, his stomach, slowly higher until she was at his shoulder.

She watched as he bit back a moan when she skimmed her hand up the side of his throat into his hair and tugged lightly.

Before he'd finished sucking in a breath, she released him.

She moved away from him and smiled to herself when he swayed toward her again. Her cool demeanor was getting to him. He was feeling vulnerable, off balance…and desperate to come. Her male was hungry for some kind of reassurance. Desperate for it, for her to look at him in *that way*, a way that she had from the start. She knew it, had felt him watching her when she worked the bar, silently asking her to look at him. He'd even sought her out when he couldn't take it anymore.

He looked at her as if she was everything he wanted and needed, that he wanted to grab hold of the connection she knew they had but wasn't sure how. Giving him that was all she wanted. Was everything.

Somehow she had to get him to let her in, then they could have it all.

Turning back to him, not letting her thoughts show on her face, she said, "Turn around and lift your arms."

He did and she quickly and efficiently shackled him to the cross. There was no missing the anticipation, the need on his face as he watched her over his shoulder move to the wall and take her time looking over the floggers.

He trusted her to look after him, to give him what he needed. To know how much he could take. She'd done her research. She'd also spoken to several of the experienced Dominants at the club, not sharing who her sub would be, of course.

Still, she could admit she was a little nervous.

Breathe, Chay.

She moved in behind him and pressed tight against his back, letting him feel all of her. He made a rough sound. Reaching around, she pulled the chain from his mouth, and he groaned when she gave it a little tug before releasing it.

She leaned in, pressing her lips to his biceps. She couldn't get much higher even in heels. "You are mine," she rasped.

His big body shuddered.

"I don't know who put that hollow look in your eyes, who caused you pain, but I will make sure that never happens again. I promise you that." She trailed one of the floggers over his ass, tickling, teasing his bare skin. "Do you understand?"

Another deep tremor moved through him. "Yes, M-

Mistress." His voice broke on the last word and she wanted to pull him into her arms.

And then Brent dropped his guard—just for a split second, that's all, but it was enough—and what he was feeling suddenly hit her. A wave of fear, his fear, washed over her, along with so much *need* and an emotion so powerful it could only be one thing. It hit with force, making her belly knot and forcing her to bite back a sob. Did he...could he...*love* her?

Show him how much you love him. Give him what he needs.

Sucking in a steadying breath, she picked up the smaller flogger she'd selected and spun it in a downward circular movement striking his upper back, warming him up, making sure to avoid the no-go areas. She then did the same on his ass but in an upward movement, preparing him. His head dropped forward, his breathing growing quicker because he knew what was coming.

When she was sure he was ready, she switched to the heavy leather flogger and tested its weight. "You're getting fifteen strikes," she said and let the flogger fly.

It came down on his ass. Once...twice, and a third time. Brent's rough panted breaths filled the room. She dished out the fourth and fifth, changing positions, striking his ass and his upper back.

With each subsequent strike he groaned and strained, his skin getting pinker.

"Ten more," she said, positioning herself for another backhand strike.

Brent's emotions filled the room, mixing with hers, filling her to overflowing, and made it hard to stay focused.

She hit him with more force this time.

"Harder." Brent groaned. "Fuck, harder, please."

She did, bringing the flogger down on one cheek and then the other. The heavy thud of the leather cords meeting skin filled the room until Brent cried for more, begging for her to hit him harder and harder.

Every strike's impact was far more than physical. Every hit revealed more of Brent, his fear, his need for reassurance —how he felt about her. Every bit of emotion behind each strike he received was deeper than anything she'd ever felt.

Her heart was so full there was no holding back her tears and soon they were running down her face.

She hit him the final time, dropped the flogger and, pressing herself against his back, reached around and released his cock ring with one hand and cupped his balls with the other, stroking and squeezing his cock at the same time.

The desperate sounds he made had her biting her lip. She turned her head and caught sight of the two of them in the wall-mounted mirror.

Jesus. The anguish on Brent's face broke her heart.

He'd gone to a dark place, a place he kept locked deep inside, a place he didn't like anyone to see. His eyes met hers in the mirror and he silently begged her to help him, to bring him back.

And in that moment, she knew why he hadn't brought her in here.

He'd been afraid.

He hadn't wanted her to see this side of him, to see the depth of his pain, of his need.

She couldn't look away, merely watched as his panted breaths turned to gasps. The agony she saw was unmistakable. He tilted his hips, silently begging her for more, for rougher treatment.

"Please," he said. "Please."

She knew what he was asking for. Releasing his balls, she gave one of the nipple clamps a hard tug.

His roar was soul shattering. Trembling and calling her

name, he started coming, fucking into her hand while she held him and stayed close, pressed into that big strong back, supporting him as best she could.

Finally, he went limp, head hanging forward.

It took several minutes before he moved. She'd stayed where she was, pressing her lips and running her hands over his heated skin. When she was sure he had his footing, she reached up and freed him.

He hissed suddenly then groaned, the sound filled with agony. "Ah, fuck. Ah, shit." He stumbled back, hitting the wall, looking lost, destroyed. "I'm so sorry. I'm so sorry," he rasped.

She looked up at him, pale lines creasing his handsome face. "What are you talking about?"

He stayed where he was, keeping distance between them. "I lost control. Oh fuck, I lost control."

She moved closer and reached up to touch his face. She wanted to kiss him, but he was too tall. "You did nothing wrong. Nothing."

He didn't seem to hear her.

She took his hand and led him to the chair in the corner. She needed to get him upstairs. "Hold on. This will hurt a bit." She released one of the nipple clamps and bent down and gently sucked and licked his nipple to ease the pain as the blood rushed back. She repeated the action on the other side.

She nuzzled his throat and kissed him, trying to bring him back, trying to get through to him. "Look at me."

He stared up at her, eyes frantic, lost.

"It's okay," she whispered.

His throat worked as he swallowed hard. He looked ill. He shook his head. "No. It's not. Nothing will ever be okay."

CHAPTER 15

BRENT FOLLOWED Chaya through the club and up to his apartment on shaky legs.

He'd lost control.

He'd lost control, and he'd let emotion take over, had devoured, glutted on it until he was nothing but sex and need. He'd dropped his barriers, leaving him vulnerable. Like he had back then. If Chaya hadn't been able to bring him back...

Chaya's had slipped into his, shaking him from his thoughts as they reached his apartment door. He realized she'd been talking to him the whole time, tone soft, soothing, but he couldn't hear her past the blood pounding through his skull.

What she must think of him.

Shit, he didn't need to hear the words to know she was trying to comfort him. While he'd fucked into her fist, he'd been lost to the lust pounding through his body, controlling his mind.

He'd never let himself lose control like that, not in the

playrooms. He thought he was safe there. But then he'd always played the Dom.

Twisting the door handle to his apartment, she shoved it open, and led him straight to his bedroom. "Lie down," she said.

Numbly, he did what she asked.

His mind swam, overloaded with so many thoughts and feelings. He couldn't remember what he'd done, what he'd said. His mind had been utterly blank, silent, while she worked him. There had been no roar in his mind. All he'd been able to do was feel what she was doing to him, and it had been perfect. She'd been perfect.

The peace he'd felt after he'd come in her arms…

She slid his shirt off his shoulders, inspecting his skin. "Did I hurt you?" she asked softly.

"No, Chaya. God, no."

Tonight he'd let his emotions get the better of him, and the incubus in him had been there, ready and waiting to take the reins. He'd let his fear and anger rule him.

His stomach churned as he gently pushed her long dark hair over one shoulder and ran his fingers over the bare skin of her shoulder. "I don't know what to say, Chay. I don't know how to make this right…"

"Brent." She sat down on the bed beside him. "What is this all about? What do you think you did?"

He swallowed audibly.

She lifted her hand to cup his face. "There's nothing wrong with enjoying pain with your pleasure. Not one damned thing. But you know that already."

He shot to his feet and started pacing around the small room.

"Jesus, would you stop this and talk to me?" she said, dark eyes following him.

"I lost control down there. Fuck, Chaya, I lost control. That can't happen. That can't ever happen."

Standing, she moved to him and slid her arms around his waist, looking up at him. "You didn't. Not once." She gave him a gentle squeeze. "You were right there with me."

He shoved his hands in his hair. "You don't understand…"

"Then tell me. Please, would you just tell me what's going on? Does this have something to do with what happened tonight? With Victor?"

"Don't!" The word exploded from him. He clenched and unclenched his fists against the adrenaline, the emotion pumping through his veins. "Don't say that fucker's name. Not ever again."

Her gaze sharpened and she narrowed her eyes. "You're keeping something from me, something I need to know, and I want you to tell me. Now."

He stared at her, heart racing, gut churning, sweat sliding down his spine. He had to tell her all the details of his sordid past. Garrett had made sure of that. He wanted to be sick.

She stared at him for several seconds, those dark exotic eyes seeing so much more than he ever realized.

Brent swallowed past the lump in his throat, gently set her back from him, and paced to the other side of the room. He turned back to her. "When I was about to go through my transition, right when my incubus side was about to come forward, someone sensed it in me. It'd already been affecting me. I was having these blackouts, waking up with random strangers, not sure how I got there, feeling like I was hungover when I knew I hadn't been drinking. I had no idea what was going on. And a…a demon recognized that in me, and before I could hit the knights' radar, he came for me."

Chaya froze, all color washing from her face. "What?" She took a step closer.

He shook his head, stopping her, asking her without words to stay where she was or he couldn't get through this.

He shoved his fingers through his hair. "He took me to a place…there were demons and demi mainly, occasionally others as well. I was afraid, but he made it impossible to resist. He was sex and seduction, and the budding demon in me wanted what he had to offer in that place. A short time later, I went through my transition and I had no control over any part of it. I gorged on the emotions around me. I was… drunk on it. And I let them…use me. I begged for it, Chaya." He curled his fingers into fists to stop his hands from shaking. "*Begged* for it."

Chaya's eyes filled with pain. "Brent…"

"That's how Lazarus found me. Two months later. Naked and drunk on emotion, fucking…submitting, to anyone and everyone…letting them fuck me. I hadn't been eating, didn't know what day it was, how long I'd been there. I had lost myself completely." He shook his head. "Beating the demon inside me, fighting against what it wanted *all the time,* and regaining my control, was the hardest thing I've ever done. That's why I play the Dom, Chaya. It forces me to maintain that control. And that was why I resisted you. Because I wanted you—want you—like I've wanted nothing else in my life. The taste of your emotions, they're like a fucking ambrosia to me, and the hunger I feel in the pit of my stomach every time I see you, the soul deep ache, the desperate need to sink inside you and stay there, threatens that control. I have to fight it every moment I'm with you. And tonight, it won." He was breathing heavily when he finished.

She stared at him, eyes bright, and shook her head. "No. It didn't win. I saw you. You were right there with me the whole time. Deep inside you know. You know, Brent." Her eyes gentled. "You didn't lose control...baby, you finally let go."

Brent froze. He thought again about the stillness, the peace, the feeling of being...loved. Is that what happened?

She moved to the bed, sat on the side, and lifted her arms. "Come here."

He was helpless to resist and moved toward her. Kicking off his shoes, he climbed onto the bed. They lay down and she wrapped her arms around him.

"I'm so sorry," she said, pressing kisses to his throat, his jaw. "What he did to you. I'm so sorry."

"There's more, Chay," he rasped. "That photo you were looking at when I came for you tonight. That male..."

She stilled in his arms. "That was you?"

"Yes," he said hollowly. "That's why I freaked out. Victor, he has something to do with that time in my life. He targeted you because of me. I've been hunting them, taking down those I recognized, the ones who used us, seduced us. They want me to back off and they're using you to get to me."

Chaya cursed, clinging to him tighter. "They'll pay for what they did to you."

He tilted her head back and pressed his lips to hers. "I just want to keep you safe. I need to know you're safe. Will you let me do that?"

Her chin was stubborn, but her eyes were soft, full of fear for him. "Whatever you need I'll give it to you. You know that, don't you?" she said.

"Yeah, sweetheart, I know," he said.

"Good. Because right now I want to take care of you. Roll onto your belly for me."

He did as she asked, because he knew they both needed it.

She straddled his upper thighs and massaged the back of his neck before leaning in and kissing him there. He should leave her alone, send her away, but he couldn't. Being parted from her was something he wasn't sure he'd ever be able to do again.

Her fingers gently ran over his skin and he moaned in pleasure.

"You're sure I didn't hurt you?"

"You didn't hurt me." He rolled to his back and she came down onto the bed beside him. He lifted up on his elbow and looked down at her. "I've never experienced anything like that in my life. Somehow you smashed through all my barriers and flayed me wide open."

"I just want to bring you out of the darkness. I want you here with me."

Fuck, she destroyed him. All he wanted to do right then was serve her. He lowered his eyes before he spoke next. "May I touch you, Mistress?" he asked, because he needed to more than anything else at that moment. "May I kiss you?"

"Yes," she whispered.

He leaned in and kissed her beautiful mouth. "Let me take care of you. Please, I want to make you come."

"I want that, too," she said.

She was half on her stomach, and he gently maneuvered her onto her belly. After loosening the laces on her corset, he removed it and dropped it to the floor. He kissed his way down her spine, and she wriggled and let out a sigh. He dragged her skirt down next, removed her boots, and sliding his fingers in the sides of her panties, dragged them down her legs.

He couldn't stop from pressing more kisses to her lush ass. "Will you open your legs a little for me, Mistress?"

She complied and he growled at the sight of her, bare and slick.

The scent of her arousal drifted up and surrounded him. His cock hardened instantly, but he ignored it, ignored his desire to take her.

She wriggled. "Brent?" The need in her voice was unmistakable and his chest squeezed in response.

He could do this for her, could pleasure her. He didn't need to take for himself. Making her feel good was all he wanted to do.

He moved one of her legs, bending it at the knee and lifting it up beside her so she was open for him. He kissed her ass again, sliding his tongue along the cleft of her soft cheeks, then moved his hand under her mound, lifting her slightly, using his palm to massage her clit.

She gasped and moved her hips against the hold. He kept her suspended there so he could slide his tongue farther down to the soft folds of her pussy, her tight opening.

She whimpered and moved against his palm more urgently. He'd barely touched her and already she was close to coming apart against his mouth, still worked up after what they'd done downstairs. Both hands were busy holding her where he wanted her, so he penetrated her with his tongue, sucking, kissing her soft damp flesh while she writhed against his hand.

"That's it," she said. "Oh God, that's it." She stilled abruptly, then cried out, contracting against his mouth, letting him taste her orgasm.

He groaned as he watched her body's response to his touch, tasted it, felt it. "So beautiful, Chaya."

When she collapsed against the mattress, he tried to move back, to give her space, but she reached out and grabbed his wrist. "Don't you dare walk away from me. Don't you dare, not after that. Not after tonight."

She wanted him. Needed him. Maybe almost as much as he needed her right then. Even after everything. Everything he'd told her. She still wanted him.

Her grip on him tightened and she rolled to her side. "Come here," she whispered.

He was powerless to fight it. Could do nothing but crawl up beside her. She placed her hand on his shoulder and pushed him to his back. His cock was straining, hard against his stomach. He lay there mesmerized, bewitched.

Leaning forward, the curtain of her silky dark hair fell around them, surrounded them. She brushed her lips across his. "I can't get enough of you."

Her tongue swiped across his lower lip and he kissed her in reply, burying his hand in her hair as she slanted that perfect mouth so she could deepen the kiss. Perfection. Chaya was perfection.

When she pulled away, he had to fight not to drag her lips back to his, to keep tasting that delectable mouth. She straddled his hips. "You're so beautiful," she said. "All of you."

He couldn't speak, could only watch her, the way her mouth moved, parted slightly as she licked her lower lip. He stared in wonder at the exquisite beauty of her dark eyes as they ate him up. He'd hadn't given control in bed to anyone since he had been freed from Garrett, only for Chaya.

But lying beneath this female, desperate for her touch, near panting with the need to have her hands on his bare skin, felt so damn right. Everything they did felt right.

Please stay.

He never wanted this to come to an end. He lifted up seeking her mouth, and she pushed him back down and trailed her hands over his chest, down over his ridged abs.

"You okay?" she asked, sounding breathless and turned on, but he could see in her eyes that, after his admission, she wanted to make sure he was there with her and that the shadows of the past weren't.

"Yeah. More than okay."

Her teeth sank into her bottom lip, and his female—his mind stuttered over the word *his*. But he couldn't deny it, didn't want to fight it, not then. *His* feisty, headstrong, sexy

726

female blew him away. A gentle smile curled her lips. "All you have to do is say stop and I'll back off."

His belly flipped at that smile. "I'd tackle you and drag you back to bed if you tried."

She chuckled. "Trying to earn yourself another punishment, I see?" Her hands moved to the top of his pants and she popped the button then slid the zip down. Taking him in her hand, she stroked him gently.

His hips surged of their own accord. "It's kind of hard to see anything with my eyes rolled to the back of my head."

She scooted back a little more, and without any warning, leaned in and dragged her tongue across the head of his cock then drew it past her lips and sucked hard. He bucked beneath her and she lifted her head, a wicked grin curving her lips. "Like that, did you?" Before he could croak out an answer, she did it again.

She was driving him crazy. Both her hands were wrapped around his shaft, working him while her mouth paid undivided attention to the swollen head of his cock. It was so hard not to thrust up and make her take all of him. Those full lips worked their way around the ridge, licking and sucking the sensitive underside until he was close to begging.

She worshiped his cock with her beautiful mouth. Then her hands were gone and she sucked him in deep, taking him all the way to the back of her throat. A deep groan rumbled from his chest, and her hands went to his balls, massaging his sac while she moved up and down his dick, her tongue swirling around the head on every upswing. His balls drew tight and he knew she felt it when she upped the suction.

Still, it wasn't going to happen, not without pain, not when he was still in his own head.

Fuck.

"Chay…baby," he choked. "Please."

Her eyes lifted to him, and he watched as she slowly drew

those swollen pink lips up his cock, sucking hard on the tip, making him curse and hiss before releasing him with a pop. Crawling up his body, she trailed tiny wet kisses along his jaw around to his ear. "You want inside me?"

"Fuck yes."

She was amazing, still worried about him. He could see it in her eyes. He hated that he had to tell her about his past, but he loved that she knew him better than anyone ever had in his entire life.

He cupped her face, and she came down for a slow, deep kiss. "I want you to ride me so bad I can barely breathe," he said against her lips.

She leaned over him and grabbed a condom from the nightstand, tore it open, and rolled it down his achingly hard cock. Lifting up slightly, she sank down, taking him all the way.

He couldn't take his eyes off her: her soft, curvy body bared to him completely; her full breasts bouncing as she moved; the way her lips parted when she sank down; how every damn time she took him deep her tight pussy grasped his dick; the way her eyes were glazed with desire.

Sliding his hands up her thighs, he massaged her hips then placed one hand around the base of his cock so he could feel her as she came down, feel her taking him inside her. Her hair was wild around her face and shoulders, her color high. Her breathing quickened, and when she sank down again, grinding against him, she placed her hands on his shoulders so she could lean forward to increase the friction. He added his thumb, circling her clit.

She increased the pace, getting herself off, using his body to take what she needed, and he loved every second of it, watching mesmerized as she came apart. Her mouth dropped open, her breasts and throat flushed. Then she screamed, her inner walls clamping down on him so tight for a moment he though he actually might come without pain.

Chaya dropped against his chest, her panted breaths hot against his damp skin. He wrapped his arms around her and held her close as she continued to move against him. Wave after wave of emotion pounded into him, hers and his own, and he was helpless to fight it, fight the depth of his feelings for this female.

She pressed her face against his throat, kissed his jaw, and lifted up, looking down at him. "Give it to me," she whispered, and he felt her take it—*literally*, take it from him. She knew what he needed. *She knew*. It had been impossible to hold it all back, and what had escaped, the twisted confusing emotions that fucked him up, the need to punish himself for what had happened back then, vanished. For that moment, she took it all. And he was free.

"Let go, baby," she gasped out. "I've got you."

Staring up into her eyes, he did exactly what she asked. His cock swelled inside her, and his balls grew unbearably tight.

She ground down against him harder. "I've got you," she said again against his mouth.

And she did. So he let go.

That's when his body took over, hips slamming up into her. Spine torquing as he totally lost it. He shook, mindless, as he bucked jerkily without rhythm beneath her, into her. Ass clenched, toes curled, he gasped as his orgasm hit, shot through his balls, out of his pulsing cock. He pumped his hips, riding it out, roaring through it. Swept up in the euphoria, the sheer joy of what was happening. Of what Chaya had given him.

Collapsing back, trembling, he struggled to pull it together. She wrapped herself around him and spoke softly, kissed him, and ran her hands over his fevered skin. Soothing him…loving him.

Helpless against the emotions bombarding him, the way he felt about Chaya, he gave in and couldn't fight them anymore. And just like that, the walls crumpled down around him, nothing but dust at his feet. He didn't have the strength to rebuild them, not then, not with Chaya so trusting, so beautiful and giving in his arms.

In that moment, he was completely and utterly lost to her.

CHAPTER 16

LEANING AGAINST THE BAR, Brent brooded over the glass of whiskey he'd been nursing. Victor had vanished. The coward had gone to ground right after the exhibition and it didn't look like he was in a hurry to resurface. Brent had people looking, combing the city, and as soon as Victor poked his head out, Brent would be there to remove the fucker from his shoulders.

His phone vibrated in his pocket and despite the direction of his thoughts, when he saw who it was from, he struggled not to grin like an idiot.

Chaya: Whatcha doing?

Chaya's message blew his efforts all to hell, and a grin twitched at the corners of his lips. He fired off a reply.

. . .

Brent: Trying not to think how hot you look wielding a flogger.

It was Chaya's night off, their first night apart since their scene in the playroom a few days ago. And honestly, he was still getting his head around what had happened between them. The female affected him so much he could barely think when she was around. When she was in the room, all his focus homed in and locked on her. The club could be burning down around him and he wouldn't notice, not if Chay was near.

His phone vibrated again and he glanced at the screen.

Chaya: I can give you an up-close demo later if you want.

He growled low.

Brent: I always want where you're concerned.

He took a sip of his drink and ignored his hard dick. He had no intention of playing tonight, not without Chay. So, for once, he allowed himself a drink.

His phone lit up on the bar beside him.

Chaya: Are you wearing panties?

He choked on his drink and barked out a laugh.

. . .

Brent: I'm a guy, Chay. What do you think?

Chaya: Commando, huh? Mr. Silva, you'll turn me on talking like that.

Brent: And are you turned on?

Chaya: I am now.

Jesus, his dick went from hard to iron rod in a matter of seconds, so hard he felt light-headed from the rush of blood evacuating his brain. He fired off his reply.

Brent: I'll be there in thirty minutes.

Chaya: Don't rush over on my account. If you're busy...I have a vibrator.

His fingers flew over the screen.

Brent: Fuck, Chaya. What are you doing to me?

Chaya: If you get over here, you can be doing it to me.

.   .   .

Fuck. Anticipation already started pumping through his veins.

Brent: Is that an order?

Her reply seemed to take forever, then finally it flashed on his screen.

Chaya: Yes.

He groaned, shoved his fingers in his hair, and glanced around the club. The place was busy, but his staff could handle it without him.

He slid his unfinished drink across the bar to Eric. "I have to head out for the rest of the night. Can you close up?"

The guy smirked. "Hot date?"

Getting hotter by the minute, he imagined. "You could say that."

"Nice. And don't sweat it. I have it covered."

"I'll have my phone if anything urgent comes up." He felt it vibrate in his pocket again.

He turned away and checked the screen. But it wasn't a text. It was an email. Opening it up, he froze as picture after picture popped up.

Ah, fuck.

They were from Garrett.

Chaya, most of them. At The Dungeon, walking around the club, watching the scenes, talking to Victor, her eyes downcast while he stood over her. Chaya...tied to a St Andrew's cross, Victor's filthy hands on her beautiful breasts.

Brent kept scrolling.

Chaya at the gallery...gazing up at the picture of him.

More of Brent, fucking, being fucked. Naked. Tied down. Helpless. Hating it.

Loving it.

Nausea swamped him, along with rage so strong, he couldn't think. He felt on the verge of losing his shit completely. And fear, fear that this asshole was going after Chaya, because that's what this was—his way of making sure Brent knew he'd had the chance, that he could have taken her at any time, that Brent had put a spotlight on her the moment he'd showed interest in her.

He quickly scanned what was written at the bottom, and his fears were confirmed.

Do you think Chaya would like to stay with me for a while? Do you think we'll get on as well as you and I did, Brent?

He'd been watching. Garrett had been watching him, probably had been since Laz had come for him.

He headed for the door. He needed to get to Chaya. Now.

Someone bumped into him from behind, a hand went to his back, and a wave of emotion hit him so hard he nearly dropped to his knees. Someone pumped him full of lust and anger so volatile he had to throw a hand out and use the wall for support.

His block, *fuck*, it was already weak after seeing those pictures of Chaya, plus the surge of his own emotions, and with that wave it had dropped completely.

He spun around, feeling like a fucking drunk, trying to see who'd touched him.

Someone came at him from the other side, hands locking around his biceps, and another wave came as they purposely fed him their emotions like it was being pumped into his veins intravenously. It was so strong he stumbled to the side.

Oh fuck.

No.

This can't be happening.

Someone crowded him from behind, laughing close to his ear, and he didn't have the power to fight them off as a third person grabbed his waist and did the same, pushing their emotions into him until he didn't know what were his and what were theirs.

His block was decimated.

He was defenseless as all the lust and excitement in the room came at him like a tsunami, trying to wash his feet out from under him.

Palms to the wall, head bent, he concentrated on his breathing, on trying to pull it together. It wasn't happening. Just like back then, he felt himself slipping away. Being washed away, unable to find an anchor. She wasn't here.

He spun around and the room spun with him. The incubus, the demon half of himself, sprang to the surface. Dark and cold, full of rage, of uncontrollable need. *Hunger.* It took hold, glutting on the creatures in the room, everything they were feeling. Brent's mind swam. He couldn't remember what he'd been about to do.

He squeezed his eyes shut, trying to clear his head, but it was like seeing through fog. Nothing made sense. His cock throbbed and his heart raced.

Names and faces swam through his mind, but he couldn't place them. Couldn't remember his own damn name.

He was need. Sex.

Release.

He groaned.

He needed release.

His skin itched with an uncontrollable need, a volcano simmering deep inside, ready to explode at any moment.

Stomach clenching, skin too tight for his body, he turned to the room, to the people filling it, a growl of hunger tearing at his throat.

"You okay, boss?" a male said from behind him, brows raised in question.

Brent looked at the male's face through the red haze covering his eyes but couldn't remember his name or what either of them were doing there.

Ignoring the guy, he turned away and spotted another male across the room watching him. He was appealing enough. It didn't matter what he looked like, he just needed release. Anyone willing would do.

He crooked a finger at the male, and he stood instantly, eyes downcast, and made his way toward him. He led the younger male to one of the rooms off to the side. He might not remember what the fuck he was doing there, but he knew that was where he wanted to go, where he'd get what he needed.

Opening the door, he motioned for the male to follow, and as the guy slid past, he drank down his emotions, taking another hit.

The haze in his mind thickened and he stumbled, shoulder hitting the doorframe.

More.

He needed more.

∾

Chaya fired off another text to Brent. He said he'd be there in thirty minutes. She'd been waiting an hour.

An uneasy feeling moved through her, but she squashed it. He'd been held up at work, that's all. Then why hadn't he texted? Things were so good between them right now. But what if he was feeling guilty again, beating himself up over something he'd had no control over? What if he was having second thoughts?

Pulling on her jacket, she shoved her keys in her pocket.

No way. I'm not letting you push me away again.

The streets were busy, but her apartment was just around the corner from the club, so this area was always bustling, alive.

Not sure if the alley entrance would be open, she went through the front. She smiled at Brian and the bouncer let her straight in. She pushed through the crowd and went straight to the door off to the side. The closer she got, the more intense her sense of dread became. *If anything's happened to him...*

Everything looked as it always did, business as usual. She glanced around the room but didn't see Brent. Keeping her head down, she made her way to his office and knocked. There was no gruff bark to enter, but she opened it anyway and walked in.

Empty.

Shutting the door again, she turned toward the back, about to head to his apartment, when Eric came up beside her. The guy's eyes were wide, and he looked uneasy as hell. "Hey...I, ah, I thought you were off tonight?"

"I am. I'm just looking for Brent. You seen him?"

He rubbed the back of his neck and swallowed hard. "Ah..." His gaze darted toward the playrooms. "He's, ah... kinda busy at the moment."

Her stomach bottomed out and she took an unconscious step back. "He's...he's with someone?"

Eric's face softened. "Yeah, babe."

She tried to shove past the guy, but he grabbed her arm, stopping her in her tracks.

"Let me go."

He searched her face, and she knew he saw it, the pain, the betrayal. It was impossible to hide. He cursed under his breath. "Look, I'd have to be blind not to know something's going on between you two. But you need to wait until he comes out of that room. You barging in there now won't help anything, yeah?"

"Let. Me. Go, Eric. Now."

"Don't go in there, Chay."

She yanked her arm free, and despite the way her legs trembled, made it to the shiny red door at the end of the lineup, the one they'd used and the only one in use. For safety reasons the rooms were never locked, but a small red light shone beside the door, letting everyone know it was occupied.

Heart in her throat, she gripped the handle.

Why the hell am I doing this to myself? Turn around and get out of here.

But she couldn't do it. She had to see for herself, had to see with her own eyes.

Without giving herself a chance to back out, she turned the handle and shoved the door open.

Brent stood on one side of the room, fully dressed. A thick leather paddle dangled from his fingers. A young male kneeled on floor on the opposite side, back to Brent. It was the same guy Brent had brought in here just before they got together, and the sub was shaking like he'd been in that position a long time.

Brent hadn't even noticed her yet, looking straight ahead,

gaze fixed on the opposite wall, expression made of stone. Sweat coated his brow and his hands trembled.

Finally, he turned to her and blinked, like he'd only just realized someone else had entered the room. She didn't recognize him, didn't recognize the desolate, blank stare. Nothing. There was no recognition.

The guy on the floor whimpered, and Brent flinched, seeming to snap out of whatever held him. He glanced down at the male like he'd forgotten he was there, then back up to her.

"No." He frowned, shook his head, and took a step toward her. "This isn't—"

Chaya held up her hands. "Stop," she said in a hard voice.

"Chay," he rasped.

She shook her head. This wasn't him. What the hell was going on here? She took a step back, and he came after her, pressing his face into the side of her throat. "Don't…go. Shit. I…I lost it. I needed—"

"You lost it?" she repeated, not understanding any of this. "All you had to do was ask, and I would have given you anything."

"I didn't fuck him, Chay," he growled. "I haven't laid a hand on him. They touched me and there was just…just so much darkness that I…" He shook his head. "I got lost, and even then I couldn't do it."

She shoved him back, needing space, so damned hurt and confused she didn't want to listen. "Let me go."

He looked as ill as she felt. "I can't…I fucking won't."

"Now," she said, hard and low.

Brent dropped his eyes and stepped back, chest working hard, fists clenched so tight it must have hurt.

She wasn't stupid enough to think this was about sex. She knew there was so much more to it for him, especially after what he'd told her about his past. Not to mention the emotions she'd taken from him when they'd had sex. She felt the turmoil inside him, had lived with it for several days afterward without a conduit to release them. But she didn't know what to do with this.

Was this what would happen every time something happened to throw him off balance? Would she ever be enough? She wasn't so sure. And that thought hurt more than anything else ever could.

"I can't do this, Brent. Without trust this is pointless. I can't be with you until you address the pain you're carrying around, the anger, or this will happen time and again. I can't watch you self-destruct." She bit her lip to hold in the sob stinging her throat. "And I can't watch you come in here night after night with someone that isn't me, not anymore. It hurts too much. It's killing me."

He dropped to his knees in front of her, in front of the whole club. "I'm sorry, Chaya. Fuck, I'm so sorry."

She reached down and cupped the side of his face. "I know you are, I do. But I don't think...I don't think I can do this..."

"Don't say it. God, please don't say it," he said and wrapped his arms around her legs.

She needed to get away, to clear her head. "You need to let me go."

His face twisted. "No, fuck that."

She met his wild gaze, heart in her mouth. "Can you promise me this won't happen again?" She hated the way her voice shook, the desperation there, but was powerless to stop it.

His grip tightened then he let her go, his head dropping again.

Her heart shattered into a million pieces. "I just...I need time to think." She turned to leave, but something slammed

into the back of her and forced her to grab for the doorframe
to keep her footing.

When she turned back, she realized Brent hadn't moved.
The blow hadn't been a physical one. Emotion flowed from
him in suffocating waves, battering then knocking down her
own block, bombarding her with his pain and turmoil. If she
hadn't been holding the door, she would have fallen to the
floor. What she'd taken from him during sex had been
nothing compared to this. He'd still been holding so much
back.

It was too much, all that he kept locked inside. His stare
collided with hers, and horror covered his handsome face at
the realization of what was happening, that she felt it all, his
pain, fear, humiliation, rage, lust…love.

He truly loved her.

Brent stayed frozen, completely paralyzed as she lurched
from the room, desperate to escape it.

She needed air, needed the emotion hammering her to
stop filling her—shit, being trapped inside her. She couldn't
think, could only feel. Using the wall for support, she headed
for the exit. The room felt suffocating. Struggling to process
Brent's emotion, she stumbled out to the alley. It filled her,
swam through her, until she could scarcely breath and
couldn't think straight. She needed to get away from the
club. Her block had crumbled and there was no slamming
the door again, not with what was going on inside her.

Using the rough brick wall for support, she made it out
onto the street. She'd barely gone half a block when a car
pulled up beside her.

Victor climbed out and raced toward her. "Chaya, Jesus,
what's happened to you?" He wrapped an arm around her
shoulders, and she was too weak to fight him off. "Come on,
let me give you a ride home."

Words wouldn't form. Her mouth wouldn't move, wouldn't voice her refusal.

This male was somehow involved with what Brent had gone through. A monster who preyed on the weak.

And, oh God, he was leading her to his waiting car. She tried again to fight, but nothing happened. She couldn't move. Her body and mind were struggling to process the new emotions swirling inside her. Her legs gave out, and Victor swung her up into his arms.

Then everything went dark.

CHAPTER 17

Brent jolted, like someone had shoved an electrical charge into the base of his spine.

Chaya.

What the hell have I done?

Seeing her had shaken him from the haze and he was slowly regaining control.

Someone had set him up, had targeted him.

Fuck, he needed to find Chaya.

He shoved through the crowed gathering and ran after her. She was in serious danger. He couldn't lose her now, not now. She was *every fucking thing* to him.

He searched the club, but he couldn't see her, couldn't feel her.

His stomach twisted. She was out there on her own.

Heart pounding, he pulled his phone from his pocket and dialed her number. It went straight to voice mail. "Chay, please call me back. I need to know you're okay."

Cursing, he disconnected and ran for the exit. The only other place she could be was her apartment. His phone vibrated and he yanked it from his pocket. Chaya's name flashed on the screen. *Thank God.* But when he answered, he realized it was a video call.

Victor's face filled the screen.

"Sorry, Chaya can't come to the phone right now. She's a little tied up." The camera moved and landed on her. She lay motionless on what looked like the back seat of a car.

"Chaya, sweetheart?" She didn't speak, didn't struggle, eyes lost and glazed. It was more than fear. There was something else causing her to withdraw, to sink inside herself. She whimpered and he called out to her again.

The camera came back to Victor. "There, you see. So far she is unharmed."

"What do you want?" Brent snarled.

All traces of humor slipped from the guy's face. "You have no idea, do you, my boy?"

Brent froze. "Garrett?"

The other male rubbed a hand across his jaw and shook his head, a grin tilting up his lips. "No, afraid not. But if you hand yourself willingly over to me, I'll help you find him and let her go."

Brent stared into the guy's eyes through that little screen and tried to work out what the hell was going on.

"You still don't remember me?" the bastard said before Brent could reply then frowned dramatically. "I'm hurt. We had some good times, you and I."

His stomach bottomed out. That voice? A memory came crashing back, an unwelcome one. He'd never seen his face, but Victor had been there, too, held in that place, and like Brent, he'd been confused and lost. They'd used what he was against him.

"Why are you doing this?" Brent rasped.

Victor's eyes hardened. "Will you do the exchange?"

Brent would endure anything to keep Chaya safe, to get her away from that psycho. "Where are you?"

Victor's nostrils flared and he licked his lips. "You agree to my terms?"

Like hell. "Yeah. Now tell me where you are."

"I'll meet you at her apartment. You have fifteen minutes to get there, alone, before things get unpleasant for her." Victor disconnected.

He contemplated calling for backup anyway, but Victor was clearly unhinged, unstable. Brent didn't know what the guy might do if someone other than him showed up. He couldn't risk Chaya.

He reached her apartment with barely five minutes to spare.

The door was locked when he tried it but then swung open before he could put his fist to it. Like the fucker had been waiting with his eye pressed to the peephole.

Victor stood with a gun in his hand, but it wasn't aimed at Brent. It was aimed at Chay. She lay on the floor, tied up. Arms at her back, her body was bound tight enough to cut off her circulation, to cause pain.

Victor's gaze traveled over Brent, making his skin crawl. "Come in. Make yourself at home."

Brent took a step toward Chaya's still form and reached for her.

Victor shook his head. "I wouldn't go any closer if I were you."

"Can I at least talk to her?"

The male's cold eyes darted down to her then back to him. "You can try." He shrugged. "She wasn't well when I found her stumbling down the street. Made for an easy target, though."

Victor had set him up and had those demons attack him in the club. The bastard knew exactly what would happen when they force-fed him their emotions because he'd witnessed it firsthand four years ago.

746

Brent turned back to Chaya. "Sweetheart? Can you hear me?" She didn't acknowledge him, eyes fixed straight ahead. "What have you done to her?"

"Nothing yet." He motioned him away with the gun. "Over there."

Brent had no choice but to do as he was told and moved to the other side of the room. "I did what you asked. I'm here. Untie her and let her go. She has nothing to do with this. This is between you and me."

"Hands behind your back." Victor pulled a pair of cuffs from his back pocket. "Turn around."

"Let her go first," Brent gritted out.

"I'm not stupid, my boy."

My boy.

Shivers skated down his spine. God, he'd never wanted to hear that again. That's what Garrett had called them, the demi and other demons being used there. *My boy. My girl.* Turning his back, he offered the other male his hands. A cuff clicked into place on his right wrist then Victor threaded it through the old radiator pipe attached to the wall and secured the other. "You have me where you want me. Now let her go."

With Brent immobilized, Victor seemed to relax further and took a seat on the couch, resting the gun on his knee. "I was very angry when your friend came and set us free. The knights should have stayed the hell away." He stared blankly at the wall, deep in his own head. "You were his favorite. Did you know that? The master knew what you liked, what made you scream in pleasure…in pain." His nostrils flared and his face twisted. "I loved him, and you ruined everything. When the knights came, they didn't just take you, they took everything. They destroyed everything."

Brent had to fight not to react. Lazarus had not only rescued him; the knights had freed the others being held.

Garrett and a few others had already made a run for it. Brent had hunted and taken down every one—every one except the male Victor spoke so fondly of.

Victor sat forward and rested his elbows on his knees. "I have nothing left. I'm rich, but money means nothing when you don't have the one you love to share it with. But now I have you, Brent, his favorite. We can go to him together and he'll take us back. He'll take me back."

Love. The bastard was insane. "It was you, wasn't it, who sent the pictures, the video? Not *him*."

Victor smirked. "Yes. The master knew of my skill with a camera and utilized it. I knew where they were kept and went back for them after the knights raided the building. Everyone left so fast. They were locked away and missed."

Brent ground his teeth. "You're Garrett Industries?"

He nodded.

"Is Garrett even his name?"

"Honestly? I don't know. Garrett Industries dissolved after we were released. I created my own business under the same name, a way of sending him a message. To let him know I wanted him to come for me." He tilted his head to the side. "Then you started coming after anything with Garrett Industries attached and you led me straight to you. I knew then how to get the master to come for me—you...his favorite."

"But he hasn't, though, has he, Victor? Not for either of us. He doesn't want you, not anymore."

Victor flushed red with rage. "He will. It's only a matter of time."

Brent stared the male in the eyes, trying to get through. "You're wrong. You know you are. It's been four years."

Victor shook his head furiously. "I'm not and we can help him, you and I, to take this city. It's the master, I can feel him.

He's behind it, the unrest. His power is so much stronger. He needs us."

Jesus. He'd lost it completely. The male was seriously unhinged. He needed to get Chaya away from him.

"I told you I'll go with you. I'll go willingly. I'll even help you find him, but only if you release Chaya."

His eyes narrowed, mouth twisting with displeasure. "Do you love her?"

He shook his head, lying. "She's an employee. I look out for the people in my club, that's all." Behind Victor, he saw Chaya move. *Let her be okay.*

Victor stood and made a tsking sound. "Now you're lying to me. I don't like liars."

He strode across the room, crouched down, and grabbed a hunk of Chay's dark hair, wrenching her head back.

That dead, lost stare caught and locked onto Brent's. He bit his tongue. Any show of distress would only prove him right.

"Chaya told me all about your relationship. She told me she has feelings for you, that she believed you felt the same way. You came for her, you rushed to her side. I think maybe she was right." Victor's grip tightened, and she winced, lucidity creeping back. "I've been watching you for a while, waiting for the right time." He glanced down at Chaya. "The right motivation to get you to see things my way. I've seen the way you look at her, the way you watch her."

Brent yanked on the cuffs, making them clatter in the quiet room. "No. You're wrong."

Victor looked down at her, a sneer covering his face, then back at Brent. "Now I've explained everything, you know, you understand. I know you want this, too. But how can we start our new life with the master with this uncertainty hanging over our heads?" He shook his head. "No, I won't have it. The master won't like it. There's only one way for me to be sure you won't run from us, run back to her, and hurt him again. That's to make sure she won't be a problem." He lifted the gun and pressed it against her temple.

"No." Brent yanked harder on the cuffs, now slick with his blood. "Don't—"

～

Pain shot through Chaya's head as Victor yanked harder on her hair, pulling her from the emotional agony surrounding her. Brent's agony. His humiliation, confusion, pain, and lust had become her own and she struggled to break free. It was suffocating.

But that bite of pain brought her back, pulled her from the darkness.

What Brent lived with daily, Jesus, she couldn't stand it.

That's when she became aware of him. He was here. In her apartment. He was yelling, but she couldn't hear his words because every one of her senses had zeroed in on the cold hard steel pressed against her temple.

A gun.

And if she didn't act, she was going to die. She knew it with one hundred percent certainty. She would not let this asshole take her away from Brent.

Summoning all the strength she could muster, she jerked her head to the side, and Victor immediately wrapped his fingers around her throat to hold her in place.

It was all she needed.

Skin-to-skin contact.

Opening up her senses, she used the powers she was given and pushed out all the emotion trapped inside her, her own and Brent's. She forced it out of her body, pouring it all into Victor, unloading all the agony he'd caused back into him. The gun immediately dropped from his hand and clattered to the floor. The force of that initial rush was enough to have him crumpling to the floor.

There was a groan of metal and a crash as Brent tore the pipe from the old radiator out of the wall, freeing himself. He came straight at her, coming down beside her. "Chay? Speak to me."

She opened her mouth but nothing would come out.

Brent twisted and yanked the key for the cuffs from Victor's pocket and managed to unlock them before he quickly secured them on Victor. Next, he went to work on her ropes. As soon as she was free, he pulled her into his arms, rocking her, kissing her hair. "God, I love you. I'm so sorry. I'm so sorry."

She wrapped her arms around him in return, his distress helping her to find her voice. "I'm all right. I'm okay."

He held her like that until Victor stirred beside them. Brent kissed the top of her head. "I need to deal with him." He released her and palmed the discarded gun.

She shook her head. "Please, leave it to the knights. You don't want his blood on your hands." She climbed to her knees and wrapped her arms around his neck. "He was a victim once, like you. Please. Call Zenon or Lazarus."

His body was hard as stone. She could see he was struggling with his rage, his need to kill the male at his back. "This is important to you?"

"Yes."

"He was going to kill you," he gritted out.

"You've been through enough. Dealt with so much on your own. Let someone else do this, take this burden from you. Please."

Finally, he took his phone from his pocket, and called Lazarus.

When he ended the call, he gagged Victor so they

wouldn't have to listen to him and made good use of the rope that had been used on her.

She didn't know what to say, how to make this better for him. So she just sat with him, comforting him as best she could while they waited for Lazarus to come and take Victor away.

Lazarus arrived with Zenon a short time later. Lazarus's sharp gaze landed on her. "You okay, Chaya?"

She nodded and offered up a wobbly smile. "Yeah."

He nodded in return then pulled Brent aside.

Zenon, her scary as hell brother-in-law, stood in the corner several feet away, and those eerie yellow eyes moved to her. "He hurt you?"

"I'm okay, Zen."

His hard gaze did not falter. "Not what I asked."

Shit. "He, ah, slapped me around a bit, tied me up. Nothing I couldn't handle."

Murder filled the male's eyes, his nostrils flaring, teeth bared. That terrifying gaze moved to Victor and locked on. Victor began struggling, eyes wide, terror evident in his panicked stare.

Lazarus and Brent joined them again but Brent's eyes locked on the male tied and gagged, so much going on behind that troubled stare.

Zenon stepped forward, fists clenching and unclenching at his sides. "Chay's my family. I want to take care of this." His hard stare shifted to Brent, and his next words, simple as they were, hit her behind the ribs hard. "And she's Brent's."

Brent was family, too. The unspoken meaning behind his words was clear.

He looked after family.

She had no idea how he knew about her and Brent, probably never would, but she could see his words affected Brent as much as they had her.

Zenon would right the wrong inflicted on those he considered his family. It was that cut and dried for the knight. The male loved her sister more than anything on this Earth, and because of that, loved her as well. He would kill for those he loved, as would all the knights. Lazarus looked to Brent, and he nodded, giving the okay.

Without another word, Zenon moved in, ignoring Victor's renewed struggles, and lifted him like he weighed nothing. His massive black leathery wings sprung from his back and he strode to the large fire-escape window. One minute they were there, the next they were gone.

She had no idea where Zenon would take Victor or how he planned to end his life, and she had no desire to ever find out.

Laz and Brent talked for a while longer before the knight left the same way Zen had.

Brent turned to her, closing the distance between them. "You okay?"

She nodded. "Now I know you're safe." She pulled him close, and he buried his nose in her hair, breathing in her scent.

"Victor sent demons after me, used his knowledge of my weakness so he could get to you," he said. "But, Chay, even as lost as I'd been, as confused and ruled by instinct, when I closed that door, when I looked at that male waiting for me to fucking do something, I hadn't been able to. I spent an hour frozen on the opposite side of the room. I couldn't even bring myself to touch him."

"It's okay...it's over."

"Can you ever forgive me...for everything?" He shook with emotion. "I love you, Chay. So much. I'll do better. I'll do anything. Anything. Just, fuck...don't leave me," he said, voice low and gritty.

She took his hand and pulled him into her bedroom, not

wanting to be in that room after what had happened. She sat him on the bed, and moving in close between his parted thighs, cupped his face, looking down into his troubled eyes. "I'm not going anywhere."

He sucked in a shaky breath. "No?"

"I know now what you live with every day, everything you're feeling and struggling with. You've kept so much locked up inside you, Brent."

"I stupidly thought being with you would make it harder, would test my control even more." His big hands lifted to her thighs. "But, Chaya, you make it better. Just being with you makes everything better. The demon inside me, it's changed. Its only focus now is you. I think we both needed you."

"That's because you are mine. You were always meant to be mine." She smiled but shook her head. "But as much as I wish I was, I'm not the cure. You have to do this for yourself. You have to want it."

He pressed his forehead to her belly. "I do. Fuck, I don't want to live like this anymore."

She threaded her fingers through his hair. "The knights can help you, but you have to ask for it."

"I know and I will," he said.

She climbed into his lap. "When you're struggling, I want you to tell me. Promise me you won't suffer in silence anymore."

His arms tightened around her. "I promise," he rasped. "I only want you, Chay. I only need you." She could feel his big body trembling.

She smiled, unable to stop herself. "I love you, you know that? I've loved you since we first met. I took one look at you and I was a goner." He wrapped his arms around her tighter. "I'm just glad you finally caught the hell up." She pressed a kiss to his lips.

Brent kissed her back. "I love you so much."

Threading her fingers though his hair again, she tilted his head back and nipped his lower lip. "Good. Now take me home. I need you to make love to me."

He chuckled darkly. "God, I love it when you're bossy." Then he kissed her long and slow and carried her from the apartment.

He took her home.

EPILOGUE

~

Three Months Later

Chaya stood in front of the beautiful, intricately carved double doors of the Conway hotel's grand room and tried to calm the fluttering in her belly.

Mia's hand brushed hers as she came up beside her. "You look amazing, Chay. Just…" She sniffed, eyes welling up for the hundredth time. "Gorgeous."

Her sister's vibrant red hair was piled on top of her head, and the satin green dress she wore made her look like some exotic flower. She gave Mia's hand a squeeze. "You look pretty amazing yourself. I'm surprised Zen let you out of his sight looking like that."

She pursed her lips. "Well, there was talk of cuffing me to the towel rail in our bathroom before we left."

They both giggled, a ridiculous girlie sound she never thought she'd ever make, but right then she was feeling kind of giddy.

"Never have I heard a sweeter sound," their father rasped as he joined them. "My girls. You look stunning." His gaze turned wistful, and some of that light dimmed. "Your mother would have been so proud of you both."

"Thanks, Dad. I wish she was here, too."

He held his arm out for her. "Shall we?"

"Let's do this." Mia gave Chaya a quick hug and, after fixing one of the miniature white roses in her hair, moved behind to straighten the short train of her dove-gray gown. With a nod from her father, the doors were pulled open.

Music started playing, a beautiful piece that Brent had picked out that, even without words, managed to express the way they felt about each other. No one had questioned Brent and Chaya's decision to have a human wedding ceremony. They couldn't mate like Zen and Mia or the other knights, and though it was just a piece of paper, it was something they both wanted.

They'd kept it low key, just the knights—in suits, something she still couldn't believe—and their mates. The people she loved.

She sucked in a breath when she spotted Brent. He looked good enough to eat in his black tux. He'd turned and was watching her as she made her way down the aisle, with so much emotion in his dark eyes that it almost overwhelmed her. When they reached him, her father kissed her cheek and placed her hand in Brent's. Brent slid his other arm around her waist and pulled her tight against him. The intensity in his gaze broke for a moment, and he smiled, warmth and love all there for everyone to see.

Chaya reached up, cupped the side of his jaw, and brought him down for a kiss, slow and easy.

When she pulled back, he grinned down at her. "Hey, I think we're supposed to wait till the end of the ceremony for that."

She grinned back. "Couldn't do it."

There were a few chuckles around the room, then the ceremony started. It was quick, simple, and utterly beautiful, and Brent kissed her again when they were pronounced man and wife—but this time there was nothing slow or easy about it.

Everyone came forward to congratulate them, Mia and Zenon joined them last. Her sister hugged them both, tears shimmering in her eyes. "That was beautiful. I'm so happy for you both."

Zenon looked down at Chaya, expression as fierce as always, but there was something else as well, something softer. "You look beautiful, Chay."

She nearly fell on her ass. Doing her best to hide her surprise, she smiled up at him. "Thanks. You scrub up pretty good yourself." She was trying to keep it light but failed miserably when her voice came out husky with emotion. She'd been blinded by fear when she first met Zenon, fooled by the hard exterior. Now she knew what a truly good male he was. She kind of wished she could hug him in that moment, but he didn't really allow anyone but Mia to touch him.

His expression went from fierce to scary as hell when he turned to Brent. "Do I need to say it?"

Brent looked at his friend, a grin on his handsome face. "What? That you'll disembowel me with a bread knife if I hurt her?" He shook his head. "No need."

Zenon shrugged and the corner of his mouth quirked up. Jesus, was that an actual smile? "I had something more creative in mind, but, yeah, that's the gist of it."

Brent was suddenly serious. "I'd die before I hurt her again, Zen."

The massive knight nodded solemnly. "Sounds good to me."

"Zenon," Mia admonished, and slapped his arm playfully. He grunted, wrapped his arm around her waist, lifted her, and without a word, carried her like a rag doll toward the exit. "Um…I'll be right back," Mia called.

Brent took her hand and led her to a quiet corner, sliding his arms around her waist, pulling her in tight. "Have I told you how beautiful you look, Mrs. Silva?"

"Nope." She wrapped her arms around his hips and squeezed his butt. "And you look hot as hell in your suit."

He growled and leaned in, brushed his lips against hers, and rested his forehead against hers.

"You're mine now," she said. "There's no escape."

His mouth came down on hers again, and he kissed her, giving her everything, conveying all she meant to him as if he'd spoken the words out loud.

"I love you, too," she whispered when he lifted his head.

He pulled her in closer. "I'll never get sick of hearing that."

"Good, 'cause I'll never stop saying it."

"Shit, sweetheart." He sucked in a shaky breath, then a grin turned up those sensual lips. "You keep this up and you're looking good for employee of the month."

"I intend on holding that title for the rest of our lives."

"Sounds pretty good to me," he rasped.

And then her husband kissed her. Again.

One month later

Chaos flew under the cloud bank, scanning the streets below. There was only one reason he was in this part of the city, why he'd been flying in circles for close to an hour, scanning every dark alley, every moving shadow.

Then he saw her.

A small figure ran full speed across the roof of a building, crossbow strung over one shoulder. He sucked in a breath when she didn't pause and instead leaped the two-meter-wide gap to the next roof, body rolling into her landing, then jumped back to her feet and carried on running.

He landed behind her, keeping the drop to the street below between them. The reasons for that he didn't want to think too closely about.

To his surprise, she skidded to a stop and turned, like she sensed him there. She was wearing that goddamned mask concealing her face from him, but as the wind whipped around her, a piece of pale blond hair slipped free from beneath.

He reached out to her with his power, and as usual, she was locked up tight. But something swirled below the surface, something he couldn't name, just out of reach. This female was strong in more ways than one.

She moved forward until she was standing at the very edge of the building across from him. He didn't like seeing her so close to the edge. He also didn't like the fact that he cared that she didn't give a shit about her own safety.

"What are you hiding, demi?" he called across to her.

She lifted her hands to her hips, and he was pretty damn sure he heard her snort as she shook her head. "Jesus, you sound like a goddamned robot. Just how far do you have that stick wedged up your ass?"

He clenched his fists and clamped his teeth together so damn tight his jaw cracked. "This isn't a game you want to play with me, I promise you that."

A quiet chuckle traveled across the distance to him, and he thought he might fucking explode. She had no sense of self-preservation.

"Dude, seriously, don't burst a blood vessel." He could

hear the smile in her voice, which just pissed him off more. "And to answer your question, *knight*...if I wanted you to know what I was hiding, I wouldn't be blocking it from you, now would I?" She said it in a deep voice, imitating him, mocking him.

"Female, you don't know who the fuck you're dealing with."

Her spine straightened. "Oh, I know." There was an edge to her voice when she spoke again. "You're an incompetent, reckless, arrogant, egotistical, misogynistic, control freak...to name but a few. I could go on if you like?"

A flash of her helpless, naked, tied to his bed, at his mercy, flashed through his mind and his cock filled, hardened to painful proportions. "That won't be necessary. And the only one acting recklessly is you and your little gang of renegades. Chaya put herself at risk for your cause and was almost killed. I won't let anything like that happen again."

"Neither will I. There's been enough death," she whispered the last, but he heard her, the words carried to him by the wind. There was pain in her voice.

He ignored his instincts, which screamed at him to fly across the short distance and force her to tell him what had caused that pain. Instead he said, "This is your last warning. Stop what you're doing. Next time I won't ask, I'll shut you down myself."

Her low, husky laughter filtered over to him again, and it hit him in the balls.

"Oh, you can try, big man." She spun on her heel and sprinted away, disappearing into the shadows.

He could follow her. But right then he was afraid of what would happen if he caught her. What he would do if she was close enough to touch.

Knowing where she lived—where she slept.

No. It was best if he didn't know that. Best that he stayed as far from her as he could.

Because at that moment, he wanted nothing more than to punish her for the way she tempted him...punish her until she screamed out his name.

I hope you enjoyed the first three books in the Knights of Hell series!

Chaos and Grace's book is next in
KNIGHT'S DOMINION

Fight. Eat. Sleep. Fight some more. Chaos's world is raw, uncompromising and solitary - just the way he likes it. But when Hell's bid to conquer the earth escalates, the Knights need help. If only their best chance wasn't a beautiful demi-demon warrior who fires insults like arrows...and makes Chaos burn hotter than hellfire.

After she lost everything, Burlesque dancer Grace Paten vowed to rid earth of the demon scum murdering and enslaving her people. But one brutal, arrogant Knight stands in her way...the man who destroyed her world, the man who ignites her temper almost as much as he ignites her lust. The last thing she expects is a request to fight alongside him.

Only working together can win this deadly war. Yet Grace must keep a secret from Chaos that could not only test loyalties, but hearts as well.

ABOUT THE AUTHOR

Sherilee Gray is a kiwi girl and lives in beautiful New Zealand with her husband and their two children. When she isn't writing sexy contemporary and paranormal romance, searching for her next alpha hero on Pinterest, or fueling her voracious book addiction, she can be found dreaming of far off places with a mug of tea in one hand and a bar of chocolate in the other.

Broken Rebel

Beautiful Killer

Ruthless Protector

Glorious Sinner

Merciless King

Boosted Hearts:

Swerve

Spin

Slide

Spark

Axle Alley Vipers:

Crashed

Revved

Wrecked

Black Hills Pack:

Lone Wolf's Captive

A Wolf's Deception

Stand Alone Novels:

Breaking Him